Praise for the stunning Dream trilogy

DARING TO DREAM

"Brains, humor, and sex."

—*Publishers Weekly*

HOLDING THE DREAM

"Witty narrative, sassy dialogue, and the savoir-faire that readers have come to expect from her." —*Publishers Weekly*

FINDING THE DREAM

"Nora Roberts's novels are always an entertaining mix of high romance and high drama, and her Dream trilogy is no exception." —*BookPage*

Praise for the novels of

NORA ROBERTS

"Nora Roberts is at the top of her game." —*People*

"Roberts, a huge name in the romance genre, delivers . . . luscious prose."
—*The Boston Globe*

"You can't bottle wish fulfillment, but Ms. Roberts certainly knows how to put it on the page." —*The New York Times*

"A page-turner." —*The Washington Post Book World*

"[An] amazingly talented and prolific author." —*The Romance Reader*

"Roberts is indeed a word artist, painting her story and her characters with vitality and verve." —*Los Angeles Daily News*

"Roberts is always a crowd pleaser." —*Library Journal*

"Thank you, thank you, thank you, Ms. Roberts."
—*The State* (Columbia, SC)

Turn the page for a complete list of titles by Nora Roberts and J. D. Robb from The Berkley Publishing Group . . .

Titles by Nora Roberts

HOT ICE	TRUE BETRAYALS
SACRED SINS	MONTANA SKY
BRAZEN VIRTUE	SANCTUARY
SWEET REVENGE	HOMEPORT
PUBLIC SECRETS	THE REEF
GENUINE LIES	RIVER'S END
CARNAL INNOCENCE	CAROLINA MOON
DIVINE EVIL	THE VILLA
HONEST ILLUSIONS	MIDNIGHT BAYOU
PRIVATE SCANDALS	THREE FATES
HIDDEN RICHES	BIRTHRIGHT

Anthologies

FROM THE HEART
A LITTLE MAGIC
A LITTLE FATE

MOON SHADOWS
(with Jill Gregory, Ruth Ryan Langan, and Marianne Willman)

The Once Upon Series
(with Jill Gregory, Ruth Ryan Langan, and Marianne Willman)

ONCE UPON A CASTLE	ONCE UPON A ROSE
ONCE UPON A STAR	ONCE UPON A KISS
ONCE UPON A DREAM	ONCE UPON A MIDNIGHT

Series

The In the Garden Trilogy

BLUE DAHLIA

The Key Trilogy	*Three Sisters Island Trilogy*
KEY OF LIGHT	DANCE UPON THE AIR
KEY OF KNOWLEDGE	HEAVEN AND EARTH
KEY OF VALOR	FACE THE FIRE
The Irish Trilogy	*The Born In Trilogy*
JEWELS OF THE SUN	BORN IN FIRE
TEARS OF THE MOON	BORN IN ICE
HEART OF THE SEA	BORN IN SHAME
The Chesapeake Bay Saga	*The Dream Trilogy*
SEA SWEPT	DARING TO DREAM
RISING TIDES	HOLDING THE DREAM
INNER HARBOR	FINDING THE DREAM
CHESAPEAKE BLUE	

NORA ROBERTS

LOVERS & DREAMERS

BERKLEY BOOKS, NEW YORK

THE BERKLEY PUBLISHING GROUP
Published by the Penguin Group
Penguin Group (USA) Inc.
375 Hudson Street, New York, New York 10014, USA
Penguin Group (Canada), 10 Alcorn Avenue, Toronto, Ontario M4V 3B2, Canada
(a division of Pearson Penguin Canada Inc.)
Penguin Books Ltd., 80 Strand, London WC2R 0RL, England
Penguin Group Ireland, 25 St. Stephen's Green, Dublin 2, Ireland (a division of Penguin Books Ltd.)
Penguin Group (Australia), 250 Camberwell Road, Camberwell, Victoria 3124, Australia
(a division of Pearson Australia Group Pty. Ltd.)
Penguin Books India Pvt. Ltd., 11 Community Centre, Panchsheel Park, New Delhi—110 017, India
Penguin Group (NZ), Cnr. Airborne and Rosedale Roads, Albany, Auckland 1310, New Zealand
(a division of Pearson New Zealand Ltd.)
Penguin Books (South Africa) (Pty.) Ltd., 24 Sturdee Avenue, Rosebank, Johannesburg 2196, South Africa

Penguin Books Ltd., Registered Offices: 80 Strand, London WC2R 0RL, England

These are works of fiction. Names, characters, places, and incidents either are products of the author's imagination or are used fictitiously, and any resemblance to actual persons, living or dead, business establishments, events, or locales is entirely coincidental.

PRINTING HISTORY
Berkley trade paperback one-volume edition / January 2005

Library of Congress Cataloging-in-Publication Data

Roberts, Nora.
      Lovers & dreamers / by Nora Roberts.—Berkley trade pbk. one-volume ed.
      p. cm.
      ISBN 0-425-20175-9 (pbk.)
      1. Monterey (Calif.)—Fiction.   2. Social classes—Fiction.   3. Love stories, American.
I. Title: Lovers and dreamers.   II. Title.

PS3568.O243A6 2005
813'.54—dc22
                                                                        2004055091

PRINTED IN THE UNITED STATES OF AMERICA

10   9   8

CONTENTS

DARING TO DREAM

PROLOGUE

HE WAS NEVER coming back. The war had taken him from her. She felt it, felt his death in the emptiness that had spread through her heart. Felipe was gone. The Americans had killed him—or perhaps his own need to prove himself had done so. But as Seraphina stood on the high, rugged cliffs above the churning Pacific, she knew she had lost him.

Mist swirled around her, but she didn't draw her cloak close. The cold she felt was in the blood, in the bone. It could never be vanquished.

Her love was gone, though she had prayed, though she had spent countless hours on her knees begging the Virgin Mother to intercede, to protect her Felipe after he had marched off to fight the Americans who so badly wanted California.

He had fallen in Santa Fe. The message had come for her father to tell him that his young ward was killed in battle, cut down as he fought to keep the town out of American hands. His body had been buried there, so far away. She would never, never look on his face again, hear his voice, share his dreams.

She had not done as Felipe had asked. She had not sailed back to Spain to wait until California was safe again. Instead, she had hidden her dowry, the gold that would have helped to build their life together—the life they had dreamed of on so many bright days here on these cliffs. Her father would have given her to Felipe when he came back a hero. So Felipe had said as he kissed the tears from her cheeks. They would build a beautiful home, have many children, plant a garden. He had promised he would come back to her and they would begin.

Now he was lost.

Perhaps it was because she had been selfish. She had wanted to stay near Monterey and not put an ocean between them. And when the Americans came, she hid her bride gift, afraid they would take it as they had taken so much else.

Now they had taken everything that mattered. And she grieved, afraid it was her sin that took Felipe from her. She had lied to her father to steal those hours with her love. She had given herself before the marriage was sanctified by God and the Church. More damning, she thought, as she bowed her head against the vicious slap of the wind, she could not repent of her sins. Would not repent them.

There were no dreams left to her. No hope. No love. God had taken Felipe from her. And so, defying sixteen years of religious training, against a lifetime of belief, she lifted her head and cursed God.

And jumped.

ONE HUNDRED THIRTY years later, the cliffs were drenched in the golden light of summer. Gulls winged over the sea, turning white breasts to the deep blue water before wheeling off with long, echoing cries. Flowers, sturdy and strong despite their fragile petals, pushed their way through hard ground, struggled toward the sun through thin cracks of rock, and turned the harsh into the fanciful. The wind was as soft as a stroke from a lover's hand. Overhead, the sky was the perfect blue of dreams.

Three young girls sat on the cliffs, pondering the story and the sea. It was a legend they knew well, and each had her own personal image of Seraphina as she had stood in those final despairing moments.

For Laura Templeton, Seraphina was a tragic figure, her face wet with tears, so alone on that windswept height, with a single wildflower clutched in her hand as she fell.

Laura wept for her now, her sad gray eyes looking out to the sea as she wondered what she would have done. For Laura the romance of it was entwined with the tragedy.

To Kate Powell it was all a miserable waste. She frowned into the sunlight, while plucking at stubby wild grass with a narrow hand. The story touched her heart, true, but it was the impulse of it, the mistaken impulse that troubled her. Why end everything when life held so much more?

It had been Margo Sullivan's turn to tell the tale, and she had done so with a rich dramatic flair. As always, she envisioned the night electrified by a storm—raging winds, pelting rain, flashing lightning. The enormous defiance of the gesture both thrilled and troubled her. She would forever see Seraphina with her face lifted high, a curse on her lips as she leapt.

"It was a pretty stupid thing to do for a boy," Kate commented. Her ebony hair was pulled neatly back in a ponytail, leaving her angular face dominated by her large almond-shaped brown eyes.

"She loved him," Laura said simply. Her voice was low, thoughtful. "He was her one true love."

"I don't see why there has to be just one." Margo stretched her long legs. She and Laura were twelve, Kate a year behind them. But already Margo's body had begun to hint at the woman just waking inside. She had breasts and was quite pleased about it. "I'm not going to just have one." Her voice rang with confidence. "I'm going to have hordes."

Kate snorted. She was thin and flat-chested and didn't mind a bit. She had better things to think about than boys. School, baseball, music. "Ever since Billy Leary stuck his tongue down your throat, you've gotten wacky."

"I like boys."

Secure in her femininity, Margo smiled slyly and brushed a hand through her long blond hair. It streamed past her shoulders, thick and wavy and wheat-colored. The minute she'd escaped her mother's eagle eye, she'd tugged it out of the band that Ann Sullivan preferred she tie it back with. Like her body, and her raspy voice, her hair belonged more to a woman than an adolescent girl.

"And they like me." Which was the best part, in Margo's estimation. "But I'll be damned if I'd kill myself over one."

Automatically Laura glanced around to make certain the swear word wasn't overheard. They were alone, of course, and it was blissfully summer. The time of year she loved most. Her gaze lingered on the house crowning the hill behind them. It was her home, her security, and it pleased her just to look at it with its fanciful turrets and high, arching windows, the soft red tiles of the roof baking in the California sun.

Sometimes she thought of it as a castle and herself as a princess. Just lately she had begun to imagine a prince somewhere who would one day ride up and sweep her away into love and marriage and happy-ever-after.

"I only want one," she murmured. "And if something happened to him it would break my heart forever."

"You wouldn't jump off a cliff?" Kate's practical nature couldn't conceive it. You might kick yourself for bobbling a routine fly, or bombing a test, but over a boy? Why, it was ridiculous. "You'd have to wait to see what happened next."

She, too, studied the house. Templeton House, her home now. She thought that of the three of them, she was the one who understood what it was to face the worst, and wait. She'd been eight when she lost her parents, had seen her world rip apart and leave her drowning. But the Templetons had taken her in, had loved her, and though she'd only been a second cousin on the unstable Powell branch of the family tree, had given her family. It was always wise to wait.

"I know what I'd do. I'd scream and curse God," Margo decided. She did so now, slipping as easily as a chameleon into a pose of abject suffering. "Then I'd take the dowry and sail around the world, see everything, do everything. Be everything." She stretched up her arms, loving the way the sun stroked her skin.

She loved Templeton House. It was the only home she remembered. She had been only four when her mother left Ireland and came there to work. Though she had always been treated as one of the family, she never forgot that she was a servant's daughter. Her ambition was to be more. Much more.

She knew what her mother wanted for her. A good education, a good job, a good husband. What, Margo wondered, could be more boring? She wasn't going to be her mother—no way was she going to be dried up and alone before she was thirty.

Her mother was young and beautiful, Margo mused. Even if she played both facts down, they were facts nonetheless. Yet she never dated or socialized. And she was so damn strict. Don't do this, Margo, don't do that, she thought with a pout. You're too young for lipstick and eye powder. Worried, always worried that her daughter was too wild, too headstrong, too anxious to rise above her station. Whatever her station was, Margo thought.

She wondered if her father had been wild. Had he been beautiful? And she'd begun to wonder if her mother had had to marry—the way young girls did. She couldn't have married for love, for if she'd loved him, why didn't she ever speak of him? Why didn't she have pictures and mementos and stories of the man she'd married and lost to a storm at sea?

So Margo looked out to sea and thought of her mother. Ann Sullivan was no Seraphina, she reflected. No grief and despair; just turn the page and forget.

Maybe it wasn't so wrong after all. If you didn't let a man mean too much, you wouldn't be too hurt when he went away. But that didn't mean you had to stop living too. Even if you didn't jump off a cliff there were other ways to end life.

If only Mum understood, she thought, then shook her head fiercely and looked back out to sea. She wasn't going to think about that, about how nothing she did or wanted seemed to meet with her mother's approval. It made her feel all churny inside to think of it. So she just wouldn't.

She would think of the places she would someday visit. Of the people she would meet. She'd had tastes of that grandeur living in Templeton House, being a part of the world that the Templetons moved in so naturally. All those fabulous hotels they owned in all those exciting cities. One day she would be a guest in them, gliding through her own suite—like the one in Templeton Monterey, with its staggering two levels and elegant furnishings and flowers everywhere. It had a bed fit for a queen, with a canopy and thick silk-covered pillows.

When she'd said as much to Mr. T., he'd laughed and hugged her and let her bounce on that bed. She would never forget the way it felt to snuggle against those soft, perfumed pillows. Mrs. T. had told her the bed had come from Spain and was two hundred years old.

One day she would have beautiful, important things like that bed. Not just to tend them, as her mother did, but to have them. Because when you had them, owned them, you were beautiful and important too.

"When we find Seraphina's dowry, we'll be rich," Margo announced, and Kate snorted again.

"Laura's already rich," she pointed out logically. "And if we find it we'll have to put it in the bank until we're old enough."

"I'll buy anything I want." Margo sat up and wrapped her arms around her knees. "Clothes and jewelry and beautiful things. And a car."

"You're not old enough to drive," Kate pointed out. "I'll invest mine, because Uncle Tommy says it takes money to make money."

"That's boring, Kate." Margo gave Kate's shoulder an affectionate jab. "You're boring. I'll tell you what we'll do with it, we'll take a trip around the world. The three of us. We'll go to London and Paris and Rome. We'll only stay at Templeton hotels because they're the best."

"An endless slumber party," Laura said, getting into the swing of the fantasy. She'd been to London and Paris and Rome, and she thought them beautiful. But nothing anywhere was more beautiful than here, than Templeton House. "We'll stay up all night and dance with only the most handsome men. Then we'll come back to Templeton House and always be together."

"Of course we'll always be together." Margo slung an arm around Laura's shoulders, then Kate's. Their friendship simply *was* to her, without question. "We're best friends, aren't we? We'll always be best friends."

When she heard the roar of an engine, she leapt up and quickly feigned disdain. "That's Josh and one of his creepy friends."

"Don't let him see you." Kate tugged hard on Margo's hand. Josh might have been Laura's brother by blood, but emotionally he was every bit Kate's too, which made her disdain very genuine. "He'll just come over and hassle us. He thinks he's such a big shot now that he can drive."

"He's not going to bother with us." Laura rose as well, curious to see who was riding shotgun in the spiffy little convertible. Recognizing the dark, flying hair, she grimaced. "Oh, it's just that hoodlum Michael Fury. I don't know why Josh pals around with him."

"Because he's dangerous." She might have been only twelve, but some females are born able to recognize, and appreciate, a dangerous man. But

Margo's eyes were on Josh. She told herself it was because he irritated her—the heir apparent, the perfect golden prince, who continually treated her like a slightly stupid younger sister, when anyone with eyes could see she was almost a woman.

"Hey, brats." With the studied cool of sixteen years, he leaned back in the driver's seat of the idling car. The Eagles's "Hotel California" blasted out of the radio and rocked the breezy summer air. "Looking for Seraphina's gold again?"

"We're just enjoying the sun, and the solitude." But it was Margo who closed the distance, walking slowly, keeping her shoulders back. Josh's eyes were laughing at her beneath a shock of windblown, sun-bronzed hair. Michael Fury's were hidden behind mirrored sunglasses, and she couldn't tell where they looked. She wasn't overly interested, but she leaned against the car and gave him her best smile. "Hello, Michael."

"Yeah," was his reply.

"They're always hanging out on the cliffs," Josh informed his friend. "Like they're going to trip over a bunch of gold doubloons." He sneered at Margo. It was much easier to sneer than to consider, even for a moment, the way she looked in those teeny little shorts. Shit, she was just a kid, and practically his sister, and he was going to fry in hell for sure if he kept having these weird thoughts about her.

"One day we'll find them."

She leaned closer, and he could smell her. She arched a brow, drawing attention to the little mole flirting with the bottom tip of it. Her eyebrows were shades darker than all that pale blond hair. And her breasts, which seemed to grow fuller every time a guy blinked, were clearly outlined under the snug T-shirt. Because his mouth was painfully dry, his voice was sharp and derisive.

"Keep dreaming, duchess. You little girls go back and play. We've got better things to do." He roared away, keeping one eye trained on the rearview mirror.

Margo's woman's heart pounded with confused longing. She tossed back her hair and watched the little car bullet away. It was easy to laugh at the housekeeper's daughter, she thought with bubbling fury. But when she was rich and famous . . .

"One day he'll be sorry he laughed at me."

"You know he doesn't mean it, Margo," Laura soothed.

"No, he's just a male." Kate shrugged. "The definition of an ass."

That made Margo laugh, and together they crossed the road to start up the hill to Templeton House. One day, she thought again. One day.

CHAPTER 1

WHEN SHE WAS eighteen, Margo knew exactly what she wanted. She had wanted the same at twelve. Everything. But now she had made up her mind how to go about attaining it. She was going to trade on her looks, her best and perhaps only talent as far as she was concerned. She thought she could act, or at least learn how. It had to be easier than algebra, or English lit, or any of those other stuffy classes in school. But one way or another, she was going to be a star. And she was going to make it on her own.

She'd made the decision the night before. The night before Laura's wedding. Was it selfish of her to be so miserable that Laura was about to be married?

She'd been nearly this miserable when Mr. and Mrs. T. had taken Laura and Josh and Kate to Europe the summer before for an entire month. And she had stayed home because her mother had refused the Templetons' offer to take her along. She'd been desperate to go, she remembered, but none of her pleas, nor any of Laura's and Kate's, had budged Ann Sullivan an inch.

"Not your place to traipse off to Europe and stay in fancy hotels," Mum had said. "The Templetons have been generous enough with you without you expecting more."

So she'd stayed home, earning her keep, as her mother called it, by dusting and polishing and learning to keep a proper house. And she'd been miserable. But that didn't make her selfish, she told herself. It hadn't been as if she hadn't wanted Kate and Laura to have a wonderful time. She'd just ached to be with them.

And it wasn't as if she didn't hope that Laura's marriage would be perfectly wonderful. She just couldn't stand to lose her. Did that make her selfish? She hoped it didn't, because it wasn't just for herself that she was unhappy. It was for Laura too. It was the thought of Laura's tying herself to a man and marriage before she had given herself a chance to live.

Oh, God, Margo wanted to live.

So her bags were already packed. Once Laura flew off on her honeymoon, Margo intended to be on her way to Hollywood.

She would miss Templeton House, and Mr. and Mrs. T., and, oh, she would miss Kate and Laura, even Josh. She would miss her mother, though she knew there would be ugliness between them before the door closed. There had already been so many arguments.

College was the bone of contention between them now. College and Margo's unbending refusal to continue her education. She knew she would die if she had to spend another four years with books and class-rooms. And what did she need with college when she'd already decided how she wanted to live her life and make her fortune?

Her mother was too busy for arguments now. As housekeeper, Ann Sullivan had a wedding reception on her mind. The wedding would be held at church, then all the limousines would stream along Highway 1, like great, glinting white boats, and up the hill to Templeton House.

Already the house was perfect, but she imagined her mother was off somewhere battling with the florist over arrangements. It had to be be-yond perfect for Laura's wedding. She knew how much her mother loved Laura, and she didn't resent it. But she did resent that her mother wanted her to be like Laura. And she never could. Didn't want to.

Laura was warm and sweet and perfect. Margo knew she was none of those things. Laura never argued with her mother the way Margo and Ann flew at each other like cats. But then, Laura's life was already so settled and smooth. She never had to worry about her place, or where she would go. She'd already seen Europe, hadn't she? She could live in Templeton House forever if she chose. If she wanted to work, the Templeton hotels were there for her—she could pick her spot.

Margo wasn't like Kate either, so studious and goal-oriented. She wasn't going to dash off to Harvard in a few weeks and work toward a de-gree so that she could keep books and read tax law. God, how tedious! But that was Kate, who'd rather read the *Wall Street Journal* than pore over the glamorous pictures in *Vogue*, who could discuss, happily, interest rates and capital gains with Mr. T. for hours.

No, she didn't want to be Kate or Laura, as much as she loved them. She wanted to be Margo Sullivan. And she intended to revel in being Margo Sullivan. One day she would have a house as fine as this, she told herself as she came slowly down the main stairs, trailing a hand along the glossy ma-hogany banister.

The stairs curved in a long, graceful sweep, and high above, like a sun-burst, hung a sparkling Waterford chandelier. How many times had she seen it shoot glamorous light onto the glossy white and peacock blue mar-ble tiles of the foyer, sparkle elegance onto the already elegant guests who came to the wonderful parties the Templetons were famous for?

The house always rang with laughter and music at Templeton parties, she remembered, whether guests were seated formally at the long, graceful table in the dining room under twin chandeliers or wandered freely through the rooms, chatting as they sipped champagne or cozied up on a love seat.

She would give wonderful parties one day, and she hoped she would be as warm and entertaining a hostess as Mrs. T. Did such things come through the blood, she wondered, or could they be learned? If they could be learned, then she would learn.

Her mother had taught her how to arrange flowers just so—the way those gleaming white roses in a tall crystal vase graced the Pembroke table in the foyer. See the way they reflect in the mirror, she thought. Tall and pure with their fanning greens.

Those were the touches that made home, she reminded herself. Flowers and pretty bowls, candlesticks and lovingly polished wood. The smells, the way the light slanted through the windows, the sounds of grand old clocks ticking. It was all that she would remember when she was far away. Not just the archways that allowed one room to flow into another, or the complex and beautiful patterns of mosaics around the tall, wide front door. She would remember the smell of the library after Mr. T. had lighted one of his cigars and the way the room echoed when he laughed.

She'd remember the winter evenings when she and Laura and Kate would curl up on the rug in front of the parlor fire—the rich gleam of the lapis mantel, the feel of the heat on her cheeks, the way Kate would giggle over a game when she was winning.

She'd imagine the fragrances of Mrs. T.'s sitting room. Powders and perfumes and candlewax. And the way Mrs. T. smiled when Margo came in to talk with her. She could always talk to Mrs. T.

Her own room. How the Templetons had let her pick out the new wallpaper when she turned sixteen. And even her mother had smiled and approved of her choice of pale green background splashed with showy white lilies. The hours she'd spent in that room alone, or with Laura and Kate. Talking, talking, talking. Planning. Dreaming.

Am I doing the right thing? she wondered with a quick jolt of panic. How could she bear to leave everything, everyone she knew and loved?

"Posing again, duchess?" Josh stepped into the foyer. He wasn't dressed for the wedding yet, but wore chinos and a cotton shirt. At twenty-two he'd filled out nicely, and his years at Harvard sat comfortably on him.

Margo thought disgustedly that he would look elegant in cardboard. He was still the golden boy, though his face had lost its innocent boyishness. It was shrewd, with his father's gray eyes and his mother's lovely mouth. His hair had darkened to bronze, and a late growth spurt in his last year of high school had shot him to six two.

She wished he were ugly. She wished looks didn't matter. She wished he would look at her, just once, as if she wasn't simply a nuisance.

"I was thinking," she told him, but stayed where she was, on the stairs, with one hand resting casually on the banister. She knew she'd never looked better. Her bridesmaid's dress was the most glorious creation she'd ever owned. That was why she'd dressed early, to enjoy it as long as she possibly could.

Laura had chosen the summer blue to match Margo's eyes, and the silk was as fragile and fluid as water. The long sweep of it highlighted her frankly lush figure, and the long, sheer sleeves showcased her creamy ivory skin.

"Rushing things, aren't you?" He spoke quickly because whenever he looked at her the punch of lust was like a flaming fist in his gut. It had to be only lust because lust was easy. "The wedding's not for two hours."

"It'll take nearly that long to put Laura together. I left her with Mrs. T. I thought they . . . well, they needed a minute or two alone."

"Crying again?"

"Mothers cry on their daughters' wedding day because they know what they're getting into."

He grinned and held out a hand. "You'd make an interesting bride, duchess."

She took his hand. Their fingers had twined hundreds of times over their years together. This was no different. "Is that a compliment?"

"An observation." He led her into the parlor, where silver candlesticks held slim white tapers and sumptuous arrangements of flowers were decked. Jasmine, roses, gardenias. All white on white and heady with scent in the room where sunlight streamed through high, arched windows.

There were silver-framed photos on the mantel. She was there, Margo thought, accepted as part of the family. On the piano sat the Waterford compote that she had recklessly spent her savings on for the Templetons' twenty-fifth anniversary.

She tried to take it in, every piece of it. The soft colors of the Aubusson carpet, the delicate carving on the legs of the Queen Anne chairs, the intricate marquetry on the music cabinet.

"It's so beautiful," she murmured.

"Hmm?" He was busy tearing the foil off a bottle of champagne he'd snatched from the kitchen.

"The house. It's so beautiful."

"Annie's outdone herself," he said, referring to Margo's mother. "Should be a hell of a wedding."

It was his tone that drew her gaze back to him. She knew him so well, every nuance of expression, every subtle tone of voice. "You don't like Peter."

Josh shrugged, uncorked the bottle with an expert press of thumb. "I'm not marrying Ridgeway, Laura is."

She grinned at him. "I can't stand him. Stuffy, superior snot."

He grinned back at her, at ease again. "We usually agree on people, if little else."

Because he hated it, she patted his cheek. "We'd probably agree on more if you didn't enjoy picking on me so much."

"It's my job to pick on you." He snagged her wrist, annoying her. "You'd feel neglected if I didn't."

"You're even more revolting now that you've got a degree from Harvard." She picked up a glass. "At least pretend you're a gentleman. Pour me some." When he studied her, she rolled her eyes. "For Christ's sake, Josh, I'm eighteen. If Laura's old enough to get married to that jerk, I'm old enough to drink champagne."

"One," he said, the dutiful older brother. "I don't want you weaving down the aisle later." He noted with amused frustration that she looked as though she'd been born with a champagne flute in her hands. And men at her feet.

"I suppose we should drink to the bride and groom." She pursed her lips as she studied the bubbles rising so frothily in her glass. "But I'm afraid I'll choke, and I'd hate to waste this." She winced, lowered the glass. "That's so damn mean. I hate being mean, but I can't seem to help it."

"It's not mean, it's honest." He moved a shoulder. "We might as well be mean and honest together. To Laura, then. I hope to hell she knows what she's doing."

"She loves him." Margo sipped and decided that champagne would be her signature drink. "God knows why, or why she thinks she has to marry him just to sleep with him."

"Nice talk."

"Well, be realistic." She wandered to the garden door, sighed. "Sex is a stupid reason to get married. The fact is, I can't think of a single good one. Of course, Laura isn't marrying Peter just for sex." Impatient, she tapped her fingers against the glass, listened to the ring. "She's too romantic. He's older, more experienced, charming if you like that sort. And of course, he's in the business, so he can slip right into the Templeton empire and reign right here so she can stay at the house, or choose something close by. It's probably perfect for her."

"Don't start crying."

"I'm not, not really." But she was comforted by the hand he laid on her shoulder, and she leaned into him. "I'm just going to miss her so much."

"They'll be back in a month."

"I'm not going to be here." She hadn't meant to say it, not to him, and now she turned quickly. "Don't say anything to anyone. I need to tell everyone myself."

"Tell them what?" He didn't like the clutching feeling in his stomach. "Where the hell are you going?"

"To L.A. Tonight."

Just like her, he mused and shook his head. "What wild hair is this, Margo?"

"It's not a wild hair. I've thought about it a lot." She sipped again, wandered away from him. It was easier to be clear when she couldn't lean on him. "I have to start my life. I can't stay here forever."

"College—"

"That's not for me." Her eyes lit, the cold blue fire at the center of a flame. She was going to take something for herself. And if it was selfish, then by God, so be it. "That's what Mum wants, not what I want. And I can't keep living here, the housekeeper's daughter."

"Don't be ridiculous." He could brush that off like a stray mote of lint. "You're family."

She couldn't dispute that, and yet . . . "I want to start my life," she said stubbornly. "You've started yours. You're going to law school, Kate's going off to Harvard a full year early, thanks to her busy little brain. Laura's getting married."

Now he had it, and sneered at her. "You're feeling sorry for yourself."

"Maybe I am. What's wrong with that?" She poured more champagne into her glass, defying him. "Why is it such a sin to feel a little self-pity when everyone you care about is doing something they want and you're not? Well, I'm going to do something I want."

"Go to L.A. and what?"

"I'm going to get a job." She sipped again, seeing it, seeing herself, perfectly. Centered in the light of excitement. "I'm going to model. My face is going to be on the cover of every important magazine there is."

She had the face for it, he thought. And the body. They were killers. Criminally stunning. "And that's an ambition?" he said, with a half laugh. "Having your picture taken?"

She lifted her chin and seared him with a look. "I'm going to be rich, and famous, and happy. And I'm going to make it on my own. Mommy and Daddy won't be paying for my life. I won't have a cozy trust fund to bounce on."

His eyes narrowed dangerously. "Don't get bitchy with me, Margo. You don't know what it is to work, to take responsibility, to follow through."

"Oh, and you do? You've never had to worry about anything but snapping your fingers so a servant can buff up the silver platter you're served on."

As hurt as he was insulted, he crossed to her. "You've eaten off the same damn platter most of your life."

Her color rose at that, shaming her. "That may be true, but from now on I'm buying my own platters."

"With what?" He cupped her face in tensed fingers. "Your looks? Duchess, beautiful women clog the streets in L.A. They'll gobble you up and spit you out before you know what hit you."

"The hell they will." She jerked her head free. "I'm going to do the gobbling, Joshua Conway Templeton. And no one's going to stop me."

"Why don't you do us all a favor and think for once in your life before you jump into something we'll have to pull you out of? This is a hell of a time to start acting up like this." He set his glass down so he could push his hands into his pockets. "Laura's wedding day, my parents half crazy because they're worried she's too young. Your own mother running around with her eyes all red from crying."

"I'm not going to spoil Laura's wedding day. I'm waiting until after she's left on her honeymoon."

"Oh, that's damn considerate of you." Fuming, he spun around. "Have you thought how Annie's going to feel about this?"

Margo bit hard on her bottom lip. "I can't be what she wants. Why can't anyone understand that?"

"How do you think my parents are going to feel, thinking about you alone in L.A.?"

"You won't make me feel guilty," she murmured, feeling exactly that. "I've made up my mind."

"Goddamn it, Margo." He grabbed her arms, throwing her off-balance so that she toppled against him. In her heels she was eye to eye with him.

Her heart thudded hurtfully against her ribs. She thought—she felt—something was going to happen. Right here. Right now. "Josh." She said it quietly, her voice shaky and hoarse. Her fingers dug into his shoulders, and everything churned inside her, yearning.

The rude clatter on the stairs had them both springing back. When she managed to draw a breath, he was glaring at her. Kate clomped into the room.

"I can't believe I have to wear something like this. I feel like an idiot. Stupid long skirts are impractical and just get in the way." Kate stopped plucking at the elegant silk dress and frowned at Margo and Josh. She thought they looked like two sleek cats about to spring. "Do you two have to fight now? I'm having a crisis. Margo, is this dress supposed to look like this, and if so, why? Is that champagne? Can I have some?"

Josh's gaze remained on Margo's for another humming moment. "I'm taking it up to Laura."

"I just want a sip before— Jeez!" Pouting now, Kate stared as Josh strode out of the room. "What's with him?"

"The same as always. He's an arrogant know-it-all. I just hate him," Margo said between gritted teeth.

"Oh, well, if that's all, let's talk about me. Help." She spread her arms.

"Kate." Margo pressed her fingers to her temples, then sighed. "Kate, you look fabulous. Except for the incredibly bad haircut."

"What are you talking about?" Kate ran her fingers through the ruthlessly short black cap. "The hair's the best thing. I barely have to comb it."

"Obviously. Well, we'll cover it up with the hat anyway."

"I wanted to talk about the hat—"

"You're wearing it." Instinctively, Margo held out her champagne to share. "It makes you look very chic, Audrey Hepburnish."

"I'll do it for Laura," Kate muttered, then dropped with little grace onto a chair and swung her silk-draped legs over the arm. "I gotta tell you, Margo, Peter Ridgeway gives me a pain."

"Join the club."

Her thoughts revolved back to Josh. Had he actually been about to kiss her? No, that was ridiculous. More likely he'd been about to shake her like a frustrated boy whose toy wasn't working to his liking. "Kate, don't sit like that, you'll wrinkle the dress."

"Hell." She rose reluctantly, a pretty, coltish girl with oversized eyes. "I know Uncle Tommy and Aunt Susie aren't happy about all this. They're trying to be because Laura's so happy she's practically sending off radiation. I want to be happy for her, Margo."

"Then we will be." She shook off worries of Josh, of later, of L.A. Now was for Laura. "We have to stand by the people we love, right?"

"Even when they're screwing up." Kate sighed and handed Margo the champagne flute. "I guess we should go up and stand by her then."

They started up the stairs. At the door to Laura's room, they paused, joined hands. "I don't know why I'm so nervous," Kate murmured. "My stomach's jumping."

"Because we're in this together." Margo gave her hand a squeeze. "Just like always."

She opened the door. Laura sat at the vanity, putting the finishing touches on her makeup. In the long white robe she already looked the perfect bride. Her golden hair was swept up, curls falling flirtily around her face. Susan stood behind her, already dressed for the ceremony in a deep-rose gown touched with lace.

"The pearls are old," she said, her voice raw. In the shining mirror framed in carved rosewood, her eyes met her daughter's. "Your grandmother Templeton's." She handed Laura the lovely eardrops. "She gave them to me on my wedding day. Now they're yours."

"Oh, Mom, I'll start crying again."

"None of that now." Ann Sullivan stepped forward. She looked lovely and restrained in her best navy dress, her deep-blond hair in short, quiet waves. "No swollen eyes on our bride today. You need something borrowed, so I thought . . . you could wear my locket under your gown."

"Oh, Annie." Laura sprang up to hug her. "Thank you. Thank you so much. I'm so happy."

"May you stay half so happy for the rest of your life." Feeling her eyes well, Ann cleared her throat, smoothed the already smooth floral coverlet on Laura's four-poster bed. "I'd best go down and see if Mrs. Williamson is dealing with the caterers."

"Mrs. Williamson is fine." Susan took Ann's hand, knowing their longtime cook could handle the most fussy of caterers. "Ah, here are the ladies-in-waiting now, just in time to dress the bride. And how lovely they look."

"That they do." Ann turned to run a critical eye over her daughter and Kate. "Miss Kate, you could use more lipstick, and Margo, you less."

"We'll have a drink first." Susan picked up the champagne. "Since Josh was thoughtful enough to bring up a bottle."

"We brought along a glass," Kate said, shrewdly omitting they'd already had some. "Just in case."

"Well, I suppose it's an occasion. Just half a glass," Ann warned. "They'll be tippling at the reception if I know these girls."

"I already feel drunk." Laura watched the bubbles rise in her glass. "I want to make the toast, please. To the women in my life. My mother, who's shown me that love makes a marriage bloom. My friend," she said, turning to Ann, "who always, always listened. And my sisters, who gave me the best of families. I love you all so much."

"That's done it." Susan sniffed into her wine. "My mascara's shot again."

"Mrs. Templeton, ma'am." A maid came to the door, all eyes as she peeked in at Laura. Later, she would tell the downstairs staff that it had been like a vision, all those lovely women standing in a room with the sun streaming patterns through fluttering lace curtains. "Old Joe the gardener is arguing with the man who's come to set up the tables and chairs in the garden."

"I'll see to it," Ann began.

"We'll both see to it." Susan touched Laura's cheek. "It'll keep me too busy to blubber. Margo and Kate will help you dress, baby. That's how it should be."

"Don't wrinkle those gowns," Ann ordered, then slipped an arm around Susan's shoulders and murmured something quietly as they left the room.

"I don't believe it." Margo's smile spread. "Mum was so distracted she left the bottle. Drink up, ladies."

"Maybe one more," Kate decided. "My stomach's so jittery I'm afraid I'll throw up."

"You do, and I'll kill you." Margo recklessly tossed back the champagne. She liked the exotic sensation of it tickling her throat, bubbling through her brain. She wanted to feel just like this for the rest of her life. "Okay, Laura, let's get you into that incredible dress."

"It's really happening," Laura murmured.

"Right. But if you want to change your mind—"

"Change my mind?" She laughed at Kate as Margo reverently slipped the full-skirted ivory silk gown out of its protective bag. "Are you crazy? This is everything I've ever dreamed of. My wedding day, the beginning of my life with the man I love." Eyes misty, she circled as she slipped off the robe. "He's so sweet, so handsome, so kind and patient."

"She means he didn't pressure her to do the big deed," Margo commented.

"He respected the fact that I wanted to wait until our wedding night." Laura's prim expression collapsed into wild glee. "I can't wait."

"I told you it's not that big a deal."

"It will be when you're in love." She stepped carefully into the dress as Margo held it for her. "You weren't in love with Biff."

"No, but I was wildly in lust, which counts for something. I'm not saying it wasn't nice, it was. But I think it takes practice."

"I'll get lots of practice." Laura's bride's heart fluttered at the thought. "As a married woman. Oh, look at me." Stunned, Laura stared at herself in the chevel glass. Yards of ivory silk were sparkling with tiny seed pearls. Romantic sleeves puffed at the shoulders, then tapered to snugness. When Kate and Margo finished attaching the train, Kate arranged it in an artful spill of embroidered silk.

"The veil." Margo blinked back tears. With her advantage of height, she slid the pearl circlet smoothly around the neat bun, then fluffed the yards of tulle. Her oldest friend, she thought as a tear snuck through. The sister of her heart. At a turning point. "Oh, Laura, you look like a princess in a fairy tale. You really do."

"I feel beautiful. I feel absolutely beautiful."

"I know I kept saying it was too fussy." Kate managed a watery smile. "I was wrong. It's perfect. I'm going to get my camera."

"As if there aren't going to be half a million pictures by the time it's over," Margo said when Kate dashed from the room. "I'll go get Mr. T. Then I guess I'll see you in church."

"Yes. Margo, one day I know you and Kate are going to be as happy as I am now. I can't wait to be a part of that."

"Let's get done with you first." She stopped at the door, turned again, just to look. She was afraid that nothing and no one would ever make her feel whatever it was that put that soft light in Laura's eyes. So, she thought as she quietly closed the door, she would settle for fame and fortune.

She found Mr. T. in his bedroom, muttering curses and fumbling with his formal tie. He looked so dashing in the dove gray morning coat that matched the Templeton eyes. He had broad shoulders a woman could lean on, she thought, and that wonderfully masculine height, which Josh had inherited. He was frowning now as he mumbled to himself, but his face was so perfect, the straight nose and tough chin, the crinkles around his mouth.

A perfect face, she thought as she stepped in. A father's face.

"Mr. T., when are you going to learn how to deal with those ties?"

His frown turned to a grin. "Never, as long as there's a pretty woman around to fuss with it for me."

Obligingly, she moved over to tidy the mess he'd made of it. "You look so handsome."

"Nobody's going to give me or any other man a second glance with my girls around. You look more beautiful than a wish, Margo."

"Wait until you see Laura." She saw the worry flicker into his eyes and kissed his smoothly shaven cheek. "Don't fret, Mr. T."

"My baby's grown up on me. It's hard to let him take her away from me."

"He could never do that. No one could. But I know. It's hard for me, too. I've been feeling sorry for myself all day, when I should be happy for her."

Footsteps sounded in the hall, rushing. Kate with her camera, Margo thought, or a servant hurrying to take care of some last-minute detail.

There were always people in Templeton House, she mused, filling it with sound and light and movement. You never felt alone there.

Her heart hitched again at the thought of leaving, of being alone. Yet mixed with the fear was such dizzy anticipation. Like a first sip of champagne, when the rich fizz of it exploded on the tongue. A first kiss, that soft, sultry meeting of lips.

There were so many firsts she yearned to experience.

"Everything's changing, isn't it, Mr. T.?"

"Nothing stays the same forever, however much you'd like it to. In a few weeks you and Kate will be off to college, Josh will be back at law school. Laura will be a wife. Susie and I will be rattling around this house like a bunch of old bones." Which was one of the reasons he and his wife were thinking of relocating to Europe. "The house won't be the same without you."

"The house will always be the same. That's what's so wonderful about it." How could she tell him she was leaving that very night? Running toward something she could see as clearly as her own face in the mirror. "Old Joe will keep on guarding his rosebushes, and Mrs. Williamson will be lording it over everyone in the kitchen. Mum will go on polishing the silver because she doesn't think anyone else can do it properly. Mrs. T. will drag you out to the tennis court every morning and trounce you. You'll be on the phone scheduling meetings or barking orders."

"I never bark," he said with a gleam in his eye.

"You always bark, that's part of your charm." She wanted to weep, for the childhood that had gone so fast though she had thought it would never end. For the part of her life that was behind her now, though she had strained so hard to pull away. For the coward that lived inside her that shrank from telling him she was leaving. "I love you, Mr. T."

"Margo." Misreading her, he pressed his lips to her brow. "Before too much longer I'll be walking you down the aisle, giving you to some handsome young man who couldn't possibly be good enough for you."

She made herself laugh, because crying would spoil everything. "I'm not getting married to anyone unless he's exactly like you. Laura's waiting for you." She drew back, reminding herself that this was Laura's father. Not hers. This was Laura's day. Not hers. "I'll go see if the cars are ready."

She hurried downstairs. And there was Josh, staggering in his formal wear, frowning at her as she paused breathlessly. "Don't start on me," she ordered. "Laura's coming down in a minute."

"I'm not going to start on you. But we're going to talk later."

"Fine." She had no intention of talking with him. The minute the last grain of rice was thrown, she would make a quick and quiet exit. She carried the hat she'd brought down from her room to the mirror, instinctively arranging the wide blue brim to the most flattering advantage.

There's my fame, she thought, studying her face. And my fortune. By God, she would make it work. Lifting her chin, she met her own eyes and willed it to begin.

CHAPTER 2

Ten years later

O N THE WILD, wild cliffs above the restless Pacific, Margo watched the storm build. Black clouds boiled in a black sky, crushing every hint of starlight with their weight and temper. The wind howled like a feral wolf hunting for blood. Needle-bright spears of lightning slashed and snapped and shot the jagged rocks and spewing surf into sharp relief. The witchy scent of ozone stung the air before thunder exploded.

It seemed that her welcome home, even from nature, was not to be a gentle one.

An omen? she wondered, jamming her hands into her jacket pockets to protect them from the biting wind. She could hardly expect anyone at Templeton House to greet her with open arms and joyous smiles. The fatted calf, she thought with a wry smile, will not be served for this prodigal.

She had no right to expect it.

Wearily, she reached up and pulled the pins out of the smooth twist to let her pale blond hair fly free. It felt good, that small liberation, and she tossed the pins over the edge. She remembered quite suddenly that when she'd been a young girl she and her two best friends had thrown flowers over that same ledge.

Flowers for Seraphina, she thought, and nearly smiled. How romantic it had seemed then, the legend of that young girl hurling herself over the edge in grief and despair.

She remembered that Laura had always cried a little and that Kate would solemnly watch the flowers dance toward the sea. But she herself had always felt the thrill of that final flight, the defiance of the gesture, the bold recklessness of it.

Margo was just low enough, just tired enough to admit that looking for thrills, being defiant and embracing recklessness were what had brought her to this miserable point in her life.

Her eyes, a brilliant cornflower blue that the camera loved, were shad-

owed. She'd retouched her makeup carefully after her plane had landed in
Monterey and had checked it again in the back of the cab she'd taken out
to Big Sur. Christ knew she was skilled in painting on any image required.
Only she would be aware that beneath the expensive cosmetics her cheeks
were pale. They were, perhaps, a bit more hollow than they should be, but
it was those slashing cheekbones that had boosted her onto the cover of so
many magazines.

A good face started with bones, she thought and shivered as the next
flash of lightning bolted across the sky. She was fortunate in her bone
structure, in the smooth, poreless skin of her Irish ancestors. The Kerry
blue eyes, the pale blond hair had undoubtedly been passed on by some ancient Viking conqueror.

Oh, she had a face all right, she mused. It wasn't a matter of vanity to
admit it. After all, it and a body built for sinning had been her meal tickets,
her pathways to fame and fortune. Full, romantic lips, a small, straight
nose, a firm, rounded chin and expressive brows that needed only the
slightest bit of darkening and shaping.

She would still have a good face when she was eighty, if she lived that
long. It didn't matter that she was washed up, used up, embroiled in a
scandal, and bitterly ashamed. She would still turn heads.

A pity she no longer gave a damn.

Turning away from the cliff edge, she peered through the gloom.
Across the road and on the crest of the hill she could see the lights of Templeton House, the house that had held so much of her laughter, and so
many of her tears. There was only one place to go when you were lost,
only one place to run when you had no bridges left to burn.

Margo picked up her flight bag and headed home.

ANN SULLIVAN HAD served at Templeton for twenty-four years. One year
less than she'd been a widow. She had come, her four-year-old daughter in
tow, from Cork to take a position as maid. In those days, Thomas and Susan Templeton had run the house as they ran their hotels. In grand style.
Hardly a week would go by without the rooms overflowing with guests
and music. There had been a staff of eighteen, to ensure that every detail
of the house and grounds was seen to perfectly.

Perfection was a trademark of Templeton, as was luxury, as was
warmth. Ann had been taught, and taught well, that fine accommodations
were nothing without gracious welcome.

The children, Master Joshua and Missy Laura, had had a nanny who in turn had boasted an assistant. Yet they had been raised by their parents. Ann had always admired the devotion, the discipline, and the care with which the Templetons had reared their family. Although she knew it could, wealth had never outdistanced love in this house.

It had been Mrs. Templeton's suggestion that the girls play together. They were, after all, the same age, and Joshua, being a boy and four years their senior, had little time for them.

Ann would forever be grateful for Mrs. Templeton, not only for the position and the simple kindnesses but for the advantages she had offered Ann's daughter. Margo had never been treated like a servant. Instead, she was treated as the cherished friend of the daughter of the house.

In ten years, Ann had become housekeeper. It was a position she knew she had earned and one she took great pride in. There was no corner of the house she hadn't cleaned with her own hands, no scrap of linen she hadn't washed. Her love for Templeton House was deep and abiding. Perhaps deeper and more abiding than for anything else in her life.

She had stayed on after the Templetons moved to Cannes, after Miss Laura married—too quickly and too rashly, to Ann's mind. She'd stayed after her own daughter ran off to Hollywood, and then to Europe, chasing glitter and glory.

She had never remarried, never considered it. Templeton House was her mate. It stood year after year, solid as the rock on which it was built. It never disappointed her, defied her, questioned her. It never hurt her or asked more than she could give.

As a daughter could, she thought.

Now, as the storm raged outside and rain began to lash like whips against the wide, arching windows, she walked into the kitchen. The slate-blue counters were spotless, earning a nod of approval for the new young maid she had hired. The girl had gone home now, and couldn't see it, but Ann would remember to tell her she'd done well.

How much easier it was, she mused, to earn the affection and respect of staff than it was to earn that of your own child. Often she thought she'd lost Margo the day the girl had been born. Been born too beautiful, too restless, too bold.

As worried as she was about Margo, after the news had broken, she went about her duties. There was nothing she could do for the girl. She was bitterly aware that there had never been anything she could do for, or about, Margo.

Love hadn't been enough. Though, Ann thought, perhaps she had held too much love back from Margo. It was only because she'd been afraid to give the girl too much, for to give her too much might have made her reach even further than she had seemed to need to.

And she simply wasn't very demonstrative, Ann told herself with a little shrug. Servants couldn't afford to be, no matter how kind the employer. She understood her place. Why hadn't Margo ever understood hers?

For a moment she leaned on the counter in a rare show of self-indulgence, her eyes squeezed tight against threatening tears. She simply couldn't think of Margo now. The girl was out of her hands, and the house required a final check.

She straightened, breathing deep to balance herself. The floor had been freshly mopped, and the same slate-blue as the counters gleamed in the light. The stove, an aging six-burner, showed no remnants of the dinner it had cooked. And young Jenny had remembered to put fresh water in the daffodils that stood sunnily on the table.

Pleased that her instincts for the new maid had been on target, Ann wandered to the pots of herbs sitting on the windowsill above the sink. A press of her thumb showed her the soil was dry. Watering the window herbs wasn't Jenny's responsibility, she thought, clucking her tongue as she saw to it herself. The cook needed to care for her own. But then, Mrs. Williamson was getting up in years and becoming slightly absentminded with it. Ann often made excuses to remain in the kitchen during meal preparation, just to be certain that Mrs. Williamson didn't chop off anything important, or start a fire.

Anyone but Miss Laura would have pensioned the woman off by now, Ann mused. But Miss Laura understood that the need to be needed didn't diminish with age. Miss Laura understood Templeton House, and tradition.

It was after ten, and the house was quiet. Her duties for the day were done. Giving the kitchen one last scan, she thought of going into her quarters, brewing some tea in her own little kitchen. Perhaps putting her feet up and watching some foolishness on TV.

Something, anything to keep her mind off her worries.

Wind rattled the windows and made her shudder, made her grateful for the warmth and security of the house. Then the back door opened, letting in rain and wind and biting air. Letting in so much more. Ann felt her heart jolt and stutter in her breast.

"Hello, Mum." The bright, sassy smile was second nature, and nearly reached her eyes as Margo combed a hand through the hair that dripped like wet gold to her waist. "I saw the light—literally," she added with a nervous laugh. "And figuratively."

"You're letting in the wet." It wasn't the first thing that came to Ann's mind, but it was the only practical one. "Close the door, Margo, and hang up that wet jacket."

"I didn't quite beat the rain." Keeping her voice light, Margo shut the storm outside. "I'd forgotten how cold and wet March can be on the central coast." She set her flight bag aside, hung her jacket on the hook by the door, then rubbed her chilled hands together to keep them busy. "You look wonderful. You've changed your hair."

Ann didn't lift a hand to fuss with it in a gesture that might have been natural for another woman. She had no vanity and had often wondered where Margo had come by hers. Margo's father had been a humble man.

"Really, it suits you." Margo tried another smile. Her mother had always been an attractive woman. Her light hair had hardly darkened over the years, and there was little sign of gray in the short, neat wave of it. Her face was lined, true, but not deeply. And though her solemn, unsmiling mouth was unpainted, it was as full and lush as her daughter's.

"We weren't expecting you," Ann said and was sorry her voice was so stiff. But her heart was too full of joy and worry to allow for more.

"No. I thought of calling or sending a wire. Then I . . . I didn't." She took a long breath, wondering why neither of them could cross that short space of tile and touch the other. "You'd have heard."

"We heard things." Off-balance, Ann moved to the stove, put the kettle on to boil. "I'll make tea. You'll be chilled."

"I've seen some of the reports in the paper and on the news." Margo lifted a hand, but her mother's back was so rigid, she let it drop again without making contact. "They're not all true, Mum."

Ann reached for the everyday teapot, heated it with hot water. Inside she was shaking with hurt, with shock. With love. "Not all?"

It was only one more humiliation, Margo told herself. But this was her mother, after all. And she so desperately needed someone to stand by her. "I didn't know what Alain was doing, Mum. He'd managed my career for the past four years, and I never, never knew he was dealing drugs. He never used them, at least not around me. When we were arrested . . . when it all came out . . ." She stopped, sighed as her mother continued to measure out tea. "I've been cleared of all charges. It won't stop the press from speculating, but at least Alain had the decency to tell the authorities I was innocent."

Though even that had been humiliating. Proof of innocence had equaled proof of stupidity.

"You slept with a married man."

Margo opened her mouth, shut it again. No excuse, no explanation would matter, not to her mother. "Yes."

"A married man, with children."

"Guilty," Margo said bitterly. "I'll probably go to hell for it, and I'm paying in this life as well. He embezzled a great deal of my money, destroyed my career, made me an object of pity and ridicule in the tabloid press."

Sorrow stirred inside Ann, but she shut it off. Margo had made her choices. "So you've come back here to hide."

To heal, Margo thought, but hiding wasn't so very far from the truth. "I wanted a few days someplace where I wouldn't be hounded. If you'd rather I go, then—"

Before she could finish, the kitchen door swung open. "What a wild night. Annie, you should—" Laura stopped short. Her quiet gray eyes lighted on Margo's face. She didn't hesitate, didn't merely cross that short span of tile. She leaped across it. "Margo! Oh, Margo, you're home!"

And in that one moment, in that welcoming embrace, she was home.

"SHE DOESN'T MEAN to be so hard on you, Margo," Laura soothed. Calming troubled waters was instinctive to her. She had seen the hurt on the faces of mother and daughter that they seemed blind to. At Margo's shrug, Laura poured the tea that Ann had brewed and Laura had carried up to her own sitting room. "She's been so worried."

"Has she?" Smoking in shallow puffs, Margo brooded. Out the window, there was a garden, she remembered, arbors that dripped with wisteria. And beyond the flowers, the lawns, the neat stone walls, were the cliffs. She listened to Laura's voice, the calming balm of it, and remembered how they had peeked into this room as children, when it had been Mrs. Templeton's domain. How they had dreamed of being fine ladies.

Turning, she studied her friend. So quietly lovely, Margo thought. A face meant for drawing rooms, garden parties, and society balls. And that, apparently, had been Laura's destiny.

The curling spill of hair was the color of old gold, styled with studied care to swing at her fragile jaw. The eyes were so clear, so true, everything she felt mirrored in them. Now they were filled with concern, and there was a flush on her cheeks. From excitement, Margo mused, and worry. Emotion always brought either quick color to Laura's cheeks, or drained it.

"Come sit," Laura ordered. "Have some tea. Your hair's damp."

Absently Margo pushed it back so that it cleared her shoulders. "I was down at the cliffs."

Laura glanced toward the windows, where the rain whipped. "In this?"

"I had to build some courage."

But she did sit, took the cup. Margo recognized the everyday Doulton her mother had used. How many times had she nagged Ann into teaching her the names, the patterns, of the china and crystal and silver of Temple-ton House? And how many times had she dreamed about having pretty things of her own?

Now the cup warmed her chilly hands, and that was enough.

"You look wonderful," she told Laura. "I can't believe it's been nearly a year since I saw you in Rome."

They'd had lunch on the terrace of the owner's suite at Templeton Rome, the city spread beneath them lush with spring. And her life, Margo thought, had been as full of promise as the air, as glittery as the sun.

"I've missed you." Laura reached out, gave Margo's hand a quick squeeze. "We all did."

"How are the girls?"

"Wonderful. Growing. Ali loved the dress you sent her for her birthday from Milan."

"I got her thank-you note, and the pictures. They're beautiful children, Laura. They look so much like you. Ali's got your smile, Kayla has your eyes." She drank tea to wash away the lump in her throat. "Sitting here, the way we used to imagine we would, I can't believe it's not all just a dream." She shook her head quickly before Laura could speak, tapped out the ciga-rette. "How's Peter?"

"He's fine." A shadow flickered into Laura's eyes, but she lowered her lashes. "He had work to finish up, so he's still at the office. I imagine he'll just stay in town because of the storm." Or because he preferred another bed to the one he shared with his wife. "Did Josh find you in Athens?"

Margo tilted her head. "Josh? Was he in Greece?"

"No, I tracked him down in Italy after we heard—when the news started coming through. He was going to try to clear his schedule and fly out to help."

Margo smiled thinly. "Sending big brother to the rescue, Laura?"

"He's an excellent attorney. When he wants to be. Didn't he find you?"

"I never saw him." Weary, Margo rested her head against the high back of the chair. That dreamlike state remained. It had been barely a week since her life had tilted and poured out all of her dreams. "It all happened so fast. The Greek authorities boarding Alain's yacht, searching it." She winced as she remembered the shock of being roused out of sleep to find a dozen uniformed Greeks on deck, being ordered to dress, being questioned. "They found all that heroin in the hold."

"The papers said they'd had him under observation for over a year."

"That's one of the facts that saved my idiotic ass. All the surveillance, the evidence they'd gathered, indicated that I was clean." Her nerves still grinding, she tapped another cigarette out of her enameled case, lighted it. "He used me, Laura, finagling a booking here where he could pick up the drugs, another there where he could drop them off. I'd just had a shoot in Turkey. Five miserable days. He was rewarding me with a little cruise of the Greek Isles. A pre-honeymoon. That's what he called it," she added, sending out smoke in a stream. "He was smoothing out all the little hitches on his amicable divorce, and we'd be able to come out in the open with our relationship."

She took a steady breath then as Laura patiently listened. Studying the smoke twisting toward the ceiling, she continued. "Of course, there was never going to be a divorce. His wife was perfectly willing to have him sleep with me as long as I was useful and the money kept coming in."

"I'm sorry, Margo."

"I fell for it, that's the worst of it." She shrugged her shoulders, took one last, deep drag, and crushed the cigarette out. "All the most ridiculous clichés." She couldn't hate Alain for that nearly as much as she hated herself. "We had to keep our affair and our plans out of the press until all the details of his divorce settlement could be worked out. On the outside we would be colleagues, business partners, friends. He would manage my career, use all of his contacts to increase the bookings and my fees. And why not? He'd nailed me some solid commercials in France and Italy. He'd finalized the deal with Bella Donna that shot me to the top of the heap."

"I don't suppose your talent or your looks had anything to do with your being chosen as spokeswoman for the Bella Donna line."

Margo smiled. "I might have gotten it on my own. But I'll never know. I wanted that contract so badly. Not just the money, though I certainly wanted that. But the exposure. Christ, Laura, seeing my own face on billboards, having people stop me on the street for my autograph. Knowing I was doing a really good job for a really good product."

"The Bella Donna Woman," Laura murmured, wanting Margo to smile and mean it. "Beautiful. Confident. Dangerous. I was so thrilled when I saw the ad in *Vogue*. That's Margo, I thought, my Margo, stretched out on that glossy page looking so stunning in white satin."

"Selling face cream."

"Selling beauty," Laura corrected firmly. "And confidence."

"And danger?"

"Dreams. You should be proud of it."

"I was." She let out a long breath. "I was so caught up in it all, so thrilled with myself when we started to hit the American market. And so caught up in Alain, all the promises and plans."

"You believed in him."

"No." At the very least she had that. He had been only one more in the line of men she'd enjoyed, flirted with. And, yes, used. "I wanted to believe everything he told me. Enough that I let him string me along with that shopworn line about his wife holding up his divorce." She smiled thinly. "Of course, that was fine with me. As long as he was married, he was safe. I wouldn't have married him, Laura, and I've begun to realize it wasn't that I was in love with him so much as I was in love with the life I imagined. Gradually he took over everything, because it was easier for me not to have to bother with details. And while I was dreaming of this glorious future where the two of us would bop around Europe like royalty, he was siphoning off my money, using it to finance his drug operation, using my minor celebrity over there to clear the way, lying to me about his wife."

She pressed her fingers against her eyes. "So the upshot is that my reputation is in tatters, my career is a joke, Bella Donna's dropped me as their spokeswoman, and I'm damned near broke."

"Everyone who knows you understands you were a victim, Margo."

"That doesn't make it better, Laura. Being a victim isn't one of the faces I'm comfortable wearing. I just don't have the energy to change it."

"You'll get past this. You just need time. And right now you need a long, hot bath and a good night's sleep. Let's get you settled in the guest room." Laura rose, extended a hand. "Where's your luggage?"

"I'm having it held. I didn't know if I'd be welcome."

For a moment Laura said nothing, merely stared down until Margo's gaze faltered. "I'm going to forget you said that, because you're tired and feeling beat-up." After tucking an arm around Margo's waist, Laura led her from the room. "You haven't asked about Kate."

Margo blew out a breath. "She's just going to be pissed at me."

"At the circumstances," Laura corrected. "Give her some credit. Is your luggage at the airport?"

"Mmm." She was suddenly so tired it was as if she was walking through water.

"I'll take care of it. Get some sleep. We'll talk more tomorrow when you're feeling better."

"Thanks, Laura." She stopped at the threshold of the guest room, leaned against the jamb. "You're always there."

"That's where friends are." Laura kissed her lightly on the cheek. "Always there. Go to bed."

Margo didn't bother with a nightgown. She left her clothes pooled on the floor where she peeled them off. Naked, she crawled into the bed and dragged the cozy comforter up to her chin.

The wind screamed at the windows, the rain beat impatiently against the glass. From a distance, the sound of the surf roared up and snatched her into dreamless sleep.

She never stirred when Ann slipped into the room, smoothed the blankets, touched her hair. Offered up a quiet prayer.

CHAPTER 3

"TYPICAL. LYING AROUND in bed until noon."

Margo heard the voice dimly through sleep, recognized it, and groaned. "Oh, Christ, go away, Kate."

"Nice to see you, too." With apparent glee, Kate Powell gave the drape cord an enthusiastic pull and sent sunlight lasering into Margo's eyes.

"I've always hated you." In defense, Margo pulled a pillow over her face. "Go pick on someone else."

"I took the afternoon off just so I could pick on you." In her efficient way, Kate sat on the edge of the bed and snatched the pillow out of Margo's hands. Concern was masked behind an appraising eye. "You don't look half bad."

"For the waking dead," Margo muttered. She pried open one eye, saw Kate's cool, sneering face, and shut it again. "Go away."

"If I go, the coffee goes." Kate rose to pour from the pot she'd set at the foot of the bed. "And the croissants."

"Croissants." After sniffing the air, Margo warily opened both eyes. She was greeted by the sight of Kate breaking flaky bread in two. The steam that poured out smelled like glory. "I must have died in my sleep if you're bringing me breakfast in bed."

"Lunch," Kate corrected and took a hefty bite. When Kate remembered to eat, she liked to eat well. "Laura made me. She had to run out to some committee meeting she couldn't reschedule." Still, Kate lifted the tray. "Sit up. I promised her I'd see that you ate something."

Margo tugged the sheets over her breasts and reached greedily for the coffee. She drank first, felt some of her jet lag recede. Then, sipping slowly, she studied the woman who was briskly adding strawberry jam to a croissant.

Ebony hair cut gamine short accented a honey-toned triangular face. Margo knew the style wasn't for fashion, but for practicality. It was Kate's good luck, she mused, that it suited so perfectly those large, exotic brown eyes and sassily pointed chin. Men would consider the slight overbite undeniably sexy, and Margo had to admit it softened the entire look.

Not that Kate went in for soft, she thought. The trim navy pinstriped suit was all business. Gold accessories were small and tasteful, the Italian pumps practical. Even the perfume, Margo thought as she caught a whiff, stated clearly that this was a serious, professional woman.

The don't-mess-with-me scent, Margo decided and smiled.

"You even look like a damn CPA."

"You look like a hedonist."

They grinned foolishly at each other. Neither of them was prepared for Margo's eyes to fill.

"Oh, God, don't do that."

"I'm sorry." Sniffling, Margo rubbed her hands over her eyes. "All this stuff inside me just keeps swinging up and down, back and forth. I'm a fucking mess."

With her own eyes watering, Kate pulled out two tissues. She was a sympathetic crier, particularly where her family was concerned. And though there was no blood between them, Margo was family. Had been family since Kate, eight years old and orphaned, had been taken in and loved by the Templetons.

"Here, blow your nose," she ordered briskly. "Take some deep breaths. Drink your coffee. Just don't cry. You know you'll get me started."

"Laura just opened the door and let me in." Margo mopped at the tears and struggled to level her voice. "Just welcome home, get some sleep."

"What did you think she would do, kick you into the street?"

Margo shook her head. "No, not Laura. This whole ugly mess may bleed over onto her. The press is bound to go for that angle soon. Disgraced celebrity's childhood friendship with prominent socialite."

"That's reaching," Kate said dryly. "Nobody in the States really considers you a celebrity."

Torn between insult and amusement, Margo leaned back. "I'm a very hot name in Europe. Was."

"This is America, pal. The media will toss a little fish like you back in no time."

Margo's lips moved into a pout. "Thanks a lot." She tossed the covers aside and rose. Kate scanned the naked body before reaching for the robe Laura had draped over the footboard.

The centerfold body—lush breasts, tiny waist, sleek hips and long, dangerous legs—hadn't been adversely affected by the scandal. If Kate hadn't known better, she would have said the figure her friend boasted was the result of modern technology rather than the good fairy of genes.

"You've lost a little weight. How come you never lose it in your boobs?"

"Satan and I have an understanding. They used to be a part of my job description."

"Used to be?"

Margo shrugged into the robe. It was her own, a long, flowing swirl of ivory silk. Laura had obviously had her luggage delivered. "Most advertisers don't care to have adulterous drug dealers endorsing their products."

Kate's eyes clouded. She wouldn't tolerate anyone talking about Margo that way. Not even Margo. "You were cleared of the drug charges."

"They didn't have any evidence to charge me. That's entirely different." She shrugged, walked to the window to open it to the afternoon breeze. "You've always told me I ask for trouble. I suppose I asked for this."

"That's just bullshit." Incensed, Kate leapt up, began to pace like an angry cat. Her hand automatically dug into her pockets for the always present roll of Tums. Her stomach was already on afterburn. "I can't believe you're taking this lying down. You haven't done anything."

Touched, Margo turned back, started to speak, but Kate was barreling on, popping Tums in her mouth like candy as she stormed the room.

"Sure, you showed poor judgment and an incredible lack of common sense. Obviously you have questionable taste in men, and your lifestyle choices were far from admirable."

"I'm sure I can count on you to testify to that if it should become necessary," Margo muttered.

"But." Kate held up a hand to make her point. "You did nothing illegal, nothing that warrants losing your career. If you want to spend your life posing so people run out and buy some ridiculously overpriced shampoo or skin cream, or in ways that make men lose twenty points of IQ on impact, you can't let this stop you."

"I know there was moral support in there somewhere," Margo said after a moment's thought. "I just have to weed it out from my poor judgment, questionable taste, and foolish career. Then again, I have to remember that your judgment is always good, your taste perfect, and your career brilliant."

"That's true." There was a flush on Margo's cheeks now and fire in her eyes. Relieved, Kate grinned. "You look beautiful when you're angry."

"Oh, shut up." Margo marched to the terrace doors, wrenched them open, and strode out onto the wide stone balcony with its mini garden of impatiens and violas.

The weather was clear and fine, one of those unspeakably beautiful days drenched with gilded sunlight, cupped by blue skies, perfumed with flowers. The Templeton estate, Big Sur, stretched out, tumbling gardens and tidy stone walls, graceful ornamental bushes and stately old trees. The pretty stucco stables that were no longer used resembled a tidy cottage off to the south. She could just catch a glint that was the water of the pool, and the fanciful white gazebo beyond it, decked with pretty four-o'clocks.

She'd done some dreaming in that flower-drenched gazebo, she remembered. Imagining herself a fine lady waiting for a devoted and dashing lover.

"Why did I ever want to leave here?"

"I don't know." Kate came up behind her, draped an arm over Margo's shoulder. In heels she was still an inch shy of Margo's stacked five ten, but she drew Margo against her and supported her.

"I wanted to be someone. Someone dazzling. I wanted to meet dazzling people, be a part of their world. Me, the housekeeper's daughter, flying off to Rome, sunning on the Riviera, decorating the slopes at Saint Moritz."

"You've done all those things."

"And more. Why wasn't it ever enough for me, Kate? Why was there always this part of me that wanted one more thing? Just one more thing I could never get a grip on. I could never figure out what it was. Now that I may have lost all the others, I still haven't figured it out."

"You've got time," Kate said quietly. "Remember Seraphina?"

Margo's lips curved a little as she thought of how she had stood on Seraphina's cliff the night before. And of all the lazy days when she and Kate and Laura had talked about the young Spanish girl, the conclusions they'd come to.

"She didn't wait and see." Margo leaned her head against Kate's. "She didn't stop and see what the rest of her life had to offer."

"Here's your chance to wait and see."

"Well." Margo blew out a breath. "As fascinating as that sounds, I might not be able to wait for some of it. I think I may be in some stormy financial waters." She drew back and tried to put on a sunny smile. "I could use your professional help. I figure a woman with an M.B.A. from Harvard can decipher my poorly kept and disorganized books. Want to take a shot?"

Kate leaned back against the rail. The smile didn't fool her for a minute. And she knew if Margo was worried about something as casual as money, it was a desperate time.

"I've got the rest of the day. Get some clothes on, and we'll get started."

MARGO KNEW IT was bad. She'd expected it to be bad. But from the way Kate was grumbling and hissing, she understood it was going to be a hell of a lot worse.

After the first hour, she stayed out of Kate's way. It did no good to hang over her shoulder and be snapped at, so she occupied herself by unpacking, carefully hanging dresses that had been carelessly packed into the rosewood armoire, meticulously folding sweaters into the scented drawer of the mirrored bureau.

She answered Kate's occasional questions and tolerated the more than occasional abuse. Desperate gratitude flooded through her when Laura opened the door.

"Sorry I was gone so long. I couldn't—"

"Quiet. I'm trying to perform miracles here."

Margo jerked a thumb at the terrace. "She's working on my books," Margo explained when they were outside. "You can't imagine what she pulled out of her briefcase. This little laptop computer, a calculator I'm sure could run equations for the space shuttle, even a fax."

"She's brilliant." With a sigh, Laura sat down on one of the wrought-iron chairs and slipped out of her shoes. "Templeton would hire her in a heartbeat, but she's very stubborn about not working for family. Bittle and Associates is lucky to have her."

"What is this crap about seaweed?" Kate shouted.

"It's a spa treatment," Margo called back. "I think it's deductible because—"

"Just let me do the thinking. How the hell can you owe fifteen thousand dollars to Valentino? How many outfits can you wear?"

Margo sat down. "It probably wouldn't be smart for me to tell her that was for one cocktail dress."

"I'd say not," Laura agreed. "The kids will be home from school in an hour or so. They always put her in a good mood. We'll have a family dinner to celebrate your homecoming."

"Did you tell Peter I was here?"

"Of course. You know, I think I'll make sure we have champagne chilled."

Before Laura could rise, Margo covered her hand. "He's not pleased with the news."

"Don't be silly. Certainly he's pleased." But she began to twist her wedding ring around her finger, a sure sign of agitation. "He's always glad to see you."

"Laura, it isn't nearly twenty-five years of knowing you that lets me see when you're lying. It's that you're so lousy at it. He doesn't want me here."

Excuses trembled on her tongue, but they were useless. It was true, Laura admitted, lying was a skill she'd never mastered. "This is your home. Peter understands that even if he isn't completely comfortable with the situation. I want you here, Annie wants you here, and the kids are thrilled that you're here. Now I'm not only going to go see about that champagne, I'm going to go bring a bottle up here."

"Good idea." She would have to worry about guilt later. "Maybe it'll help Kate keep me in the black."

"This mortgage is fifteen days overdue," Kate called out. "And you're over the limit on your Visa. Jesus, Margo."

"I'll bring two bottles," Laura decided and kept a smile in place until she'd left Margo's room.

She went to her own, wanting a moment to herself. She'd thought she had gotten over her anger, but she hadn't. It was still there, she realized, high and bitter in her throat. She paced the sitting room to work it off. The sitting room that was becoming more of a sanctuary. She could come here, close herself in with the warm colors and scents, and tell herself that she had correspondence to answer, some little piece of needlework to finish.

But more often she came here to work off an emotion that choked her.

Perhaps she should have expected Peter's reaction, been prepared for it. But she hadn't been. She never seemed to be prepared for Peter's reactions anymore. How could it be that after ten years of marriage she didn't seem to know him at all?

She stopped by his office on the way home from her committee meeting on the Summer Ball. She hummed to herself as she took the private elevator up to the penthouse suite of Templeton Monterey. Peter preferred the suite to the executive offices on the hotel's ground level. It was quieter, he said, made it easier to concentrate.

From her days of assisting and learning the business in the nerve center of the sales and reservations offices, she had to agree. Perhaps it separated him from the pulse, from the people, but Peter knew his job.

The sheer beauty of the day, added to the pleasure of having her old friend home again, lifted her mood. With a spring in her step, she crossed the silver-toned carpet to the airy reception area.

"Oh, hello, Mrs. Ridgeway." The receptionist offered a quick smile but continued working and didn't quite meet Laura's eyes. "I think Mr. Ridgeway is in a meeting, but let me just buzz through and let him know you're here."

"I'd appreciate it, Nina. I'll only take a few minutes of his time." She wandered over to the seating area, quietly empty now. The leather seats in navy were new, and as pricey as the antique tables and lamps and the watercolors Peter had commissioned had been. But Laura supposed he'd been right. The offices had needed some sprucing up. Appearances were important in business. Were important to Peter.

But as she gazed through the wide window she wondered how anyone could care about navy leather seats when that awesome view of the coast presented itself.

Just look at how the water rolled, how it stretched to forever. The ice plants were blooming pink, and white gulls veered in, hoping some tourist would offer a treat. See the boats on the bay, bobbing like shiny, expensive toys for men in double-breasted navy blazers and white slacks.

She lost herself in it and nearly forgot to retouch her lipstick and powder before the receptionist told her to go right in.

Peter Ridgeway's office suited the executive director of Templeton Hotels, California. With its carefully selected Louis XIV furnishings, its glorious seascapes and sculptures, it was as erudite and flawlessly executed as the man himself. When he rose from behind the desk, her smile warmed automatically.

He was a beautiful man, bronze and gold and trim in elegant Savile Row. She had fallen in love with that face—its cool blue eyes, firm mouth and jaw—like a princess for a prince in a fairy tale. And, as in a fairy tale, he had swept her off her feet when she'd been barely eighteen. He'd been everything she'd dreamed of.

She lifted her mouth for a kiss and received an absent peck on the cheek. "I don't have much time, Laura. I have meetings all day." He remained standing, tilting his head, the faintest line of annoyance marring his brow. "I've told you it's more convenient if you call first to be certain I can see you. My schedule isn't as flexible as yours is."

Her smile faded. "I'm sorry. I wasn't able to talk to you last night, and when I called this morning, you were out, so—"

"I went by the club for a quick nine holes and a steam. I put in a very long night."

"Yes, I know." How are you, Laura? How are the girls? I missed you. She waited a moment, but he said none of those things. "You'll be home tonight?"

"If I'm able to get back to work, I should be able to make it by seven."

"Good. I was hoping you could. We're having a family dinner. Margo's back."

His mouth tightened briefly, but he did stop looking at his watch. "Back?"

"She got in last night. She's so unhappy, Peter. So tired."

"Unhappy? Tired?" His laugh was quick and unamused. "I'm not surprised, after her latest adventure." He recognized the look in his wife's eyes and banked down on his fury. He wasn't a man who cared for displays of temper, even his own. "For God's sake, Laura, you haven't invited her to stay."

"It wasn't a matter of inviting her. It's her home."

It wasn't anger now so much as weariness. He sat, gave a long sigh. "Laura, Margo is the daughter of our housekeeper. That does not make Templeton her home. You can carry childhood loyalties too far."

"No," Laura said quietly. "I don't think you can. She's in trouble, Peter, and whether or not any of it is of her own making isn't the issue. She needs her friends and her family."

"Her name's all over the papers, the news, every bloody tabloid show on the screen. Sex, drugs, name of God."

"She was cleared of the drug charges, Peter, and she certainly isn't the first woman to fall for a married man."

His voice took on the tedious patience that always put her teeth on edge. "That may be true, but 'discretion' isn't a word she seems to be aware of. I can't have her name linked to ours and risk our standing in the community. I don't want her in my house."

That brought Laura's head up and erased any thought of placating him. "It's my parents' house," she tossed back with fury sizzling in every word. "We're there, Peter, because they wanted it to be lived in and loved. I know my mother and father would welcome Margo, and so do I."

"I see." He folded his hands on the desk. "That's a little dig you haven't tried in some time. I live in Templeton House, work for the Templeton empire, and sleep with the Templeton heiress."

When you bother to come home, Laura thought, but held her tongue.

"Whatever I have is due to the Templeton generosity."

"That's certainly not true, Peter. You're your own man, an experienced and successful hotelier. And there's no reason to turn a discussion of Margo into a fight."

Gauging her, he tried a new tack. "It doesn't bother you, Laura, to have a woman with her reputation around our children? Certainly they'll hear gossip, and Allison, at least, is old enough to understand some of it."

The flush rose to her cheeks, then died away. "Margo is Ali's godmother and she's my oldest friend. She's welcome at Templeton as long as I live there, Peter." She straightened her shoulders, looked him dead in the eye. "To use words you'll understand, those terms are nonnegotiable. Dinner's at seven-thirty if you're able to make it."

She strode out and controlled the urge to slam the door.

Now, alone in her room, she fought back the resurging temper. It never did her any good to lose it, only made her feel foolish and guilty. So she would calm herself, put on that smooth false front she was growing so accustomed to wearing.

It was important to remember that Margo needed her. And it was becoming painfully clear that her husband did not.

"CAN I TRY your perfume, Aunt Margo? The one in the pretty gold bottle. Please?"

Margo looked down at Kayla's hopeful face. If they were casting angels, she mused, this one with her soft gray eyes and winking dimples would win the role hands down.

"Just a couple of drops." Margo took the stopper out and dabbed a whisper behind each of Kayla's ears. "A woman doesn't want to be obvious."

"How come?"

"Because mystery is a spice."

"Like pepper?"

Ali, three years superior to Kayla's six years, snorted. But Margo hauled Kayla up on her lap and nuzzled her. "In a manner of speaking. Want a dab, Ali?"

All but salivating over the fascinating bottles and pots on the vanity, Ali tried her best to sound nonchalant. "Maybe, but I don't want what she has."

"Something different, then. Something . . ." Playing it up, Margo waved her hand over this bottle and that. "Bold and daring."

"But not obvious," Kayla chimed in.

"That's a girl. Here we are." Without a thought, Margo sacrificed a few dabs of a two-hundred-dollar-an-ounce scent. It was Bella Donna's new Tigre. She probably had twenty of the gorgeous handblown bottles in her Milan flat. "You're growing up on me," she accused and tugged the gold curls spilling to Ali's shoulders.

"I'm old enough to have my ears pierced, but Daddy won't let me."

"Men just don't understand these things." Because she did, perfectly, she patted Ali's cheek before shifting Kayla on her knee. "Decorating ourselves is a woman's privilege." Giving Ali a bolstering smile in the mirror, she went back to perfecting her makeup. "Your mom'll talk him into it."

"She can't talk him into anything. He never listens."

"He's very busy," Kayla said solemnly. "He has to work and work so we can stand."

"So we won't lose our standing," Ali corrected and rolled her eyes. Kayla didn't understand anything, she thought. Sometimes Mama did, and

Aunt Kate always listened, but she had hope, great new hope that her glamorous and mysterious aunt Margo would understand everything.

"Aunt Margo, are you going to stay now that those bad things happened to you?"

"I don't know." Margo set down her lipstick with a little click.

"I'm glad you came home." Ali wrapped her arms around Margo's neck.

"So am I." The unstable emotions were stirring again. She rose quickly, grabbing each child by the hand. "Let's go down and see if there's anything fun to eat before dinner."

"We're having hors d'oeuvres in the front parlor," Ali said loftily, then giggled. "We hardly ever get to stay up for dinner with hors d'oeuvres."

"Stick with me, kid." She stopped at the top curve of the stairs. "Let's make an entrance. Chins up, eyes bored, stomachs in, fingers trailing carelessly along the banisters."

She was halfway down behind the girls when she saw her mother at the bottom landing. Ann stood with her hands folded, her face solemn.

"Ah, Lady Allison, Lady Kayla, we're honored that you could join us this evening. Refreshments are being served in the front parlor."

Ali inclined her head regally. "Thank you, Miss Annie," she managed before she bolted after her sister.

It wasn't until Margo had reached the bottom that she caught the twinkle in her mother's eyes. For the first time since her return, they smiled easily at each other.

"I'd forgotten how much fun they are."

"Miss Laura is raising angels."

"I was thinking the same thing myself. She's done everything right—everything I haven't. Mum, I'm sorry—"

"We won't talk about it now." But Ann laid a hand briefly over her daughter's on the newel post. "Later—but they're waiting for you now." She started to walk away, then paused. "Margo, Miss Laura needs a friend just now as much as you do. I hope you'll be a good one."

"If something's wrong, tell me."

Ann shook her head. "It's not my place. Just be a good friend." She walked away, leaving Margo to enter the parlor alone.

Ali was already crossing the room, her tongue caught in her teeth, her hands full of a flute of fizzing champagne. "I poured it for you myself."

"Well, then, I'll have to drink it." She lifted the glass, scanned the room. Laura had Kayla on one hip, and Kate was sampling the finger food arranged on Georgian silver. A sedate fire flickered in the hearth framed by rich lapis. The stunning curved mirror over the mantel tossed back reflections of glossy antiques, delicate porcelain, and rosy light from globe lamps.

"To being home with friends," Margo said and sipped.

"Eat some of this mini quiche," Kate ordered over a full mouth. "It's outrageous."

What the hell, Margo thought, her weight was hardly a burning issue any longer. She took one bite, hummed in pleasure. "Mrs. Williamson's still a wonder. Lord, she must be eighty by now."

"Seventy-three last November," Laura corrected. "And she can still whip up the most incredible chocolate soufflé." She winked at Kayla. "Which, rumor has it, is on for tonight."

"Daddy says Mrs. Williamson should be retired and we should have a French chef like the Barrymores in Carmel." Because Margo had, Ali sampled a quiche.

"French chefs are snooty." To demonstrate, Margo put a finger under her nose to lift it into the air. "And they never make jelly tarts with leftover dough for little girls."

"Did she do that for you, too?" The image delighted Ali. "Did she let you flute the edges?"

"Absolutely. I have to admit, your mother was the best at it. According to Mrs. Williamson, I was too impatient, and Kate worried too much about getting it just right, but your mom had a feel. She was the champ jelly tart maker."

"One of my major accomplishments." Margo heard the edge in Laura's voice and lifted a brow. With a shrug, Laura set Kayla on her feet. "That's a fabulous dress, Margo. Milan or Paris?"

"Milan." If Laura wanted the subject changed, she could oblige. She struck a pose, head tilted, one hand on her hip. The clinging black silk molded itself to her body and stopped daringly short at the thighs. The low square neckline hinted at cleavage, while sheer sleeves journeyed from the curve of her shoulders to wrists where twin diamond bracelets winked. "A little something I picked up from a sassy new designer."

"You'll freeze before the night's over," Kate commented.

"Not when my heart's so warm. Are we waiting for Peter?"

"No," Laura decided on the spot, then buried her annoyance when she caught Ali's worried look. "He was afraid his meetings might run over, so there's no telling when he'll get away. We'll start dinner without him." She took Kayla's hand, then glanced over as Ann came to the doorway.

"I'm sorry, Miss Laura, there's a phone call."

"I'll take it in the library, Annie. Have another glass of champagne," she suggested as she started out. "I won't be long."

Margo and Kate exchanged a look, one that promised they would talk later. Deliberately cheerful, Margo topped off the glasses and launched into a story about gambling in Monte Carlo. When Laura came back, the children were wide-eyed and Kate was shaking her head.

"You're certifiable, Margo. Betting twenty-five thousand on one spin of a little silver ball."

"Hey, I won." She sighed in memory. "That time."

"Was it Daddy?" Ali wanted to know, hurrying over to tug on her mother's hand. "Is he coming?"

"No." Distracted, Laura brushed her fingers over Ali's hair. "It wasn't Daddy, honey." She wasn't so distracted she didn't notice the way her daughter's shoulders drooped. To soothe, she crouched down, smiling. "But it's really good news. Something special."

"What is it? Is it a party?"

"Better." Laura kissed Ali's cheek. "Uncle Josh is coming home."

Margo dropped to the arm of the sofa and found she needed to gulp down the champagne. "Wonderful," she muttered. "Just wonderful."

CHAPTER 4

JOSHUA CONWAY TEMPLETON was a man who did things in his own time, and in his own way. He was driving south from San Francisco because he'd decided not to fly to Monterey from London. He could have excused the detour by pretending that Templeton San Francisco needed a quick study. But his family's landmark hotel ran like a well-wound clock.

The simple fact was that somewhere along the flight he'd decided to buy a car.

And a honey it was, too.

The little Jag roared down Highway 1 like an eager Thoroughbred at the starting gun. It took a wide, sweeping curve at seventy and made him grin.

This was home, this rugged, lonely coast. He had tooled along the spectacular Amalfi Drive in Italy, sped through the fjords of Norway, but not even their heart-stopping beauty could match the sheer drama of Big Sur.

It had more. The glinting beaches and gleaming coves. The cliffs that speared defiantly from savage sea to pristine sky. Brooding forests, the surprise of a stream that cascaded out of a canyon like liquid silver. Then there were miles of tranquillity, broken only by the din of seals, the cold fire of the surf.

Always, the glory of it grabbed at his throat. Wherever he had been, however long he had traveled away, this single spot on the globe pulled at him.

So he was coming home, in his own time and in his own way. Recklessly he tested the Jag on the wild, twisting curves that dropped off to jagged rocks and unforgiving sea. He punched the gas on the straightaway and laughed as the wind rushed over him.

It wasn't hurry that pushed him, but the simple love of speed and chance. He had time, he mused. Plenty of it. And he was going to use it.

He was worried about Laura. There'd been something in his sister's voice on the phone that alerted him. She'd said all the right things. But then, Laura always did. He would do a bit of probing there, he decided.

There was business to see to. He'd been happy enough to leave the California executive offices of Templeton Hotels primarily in Peter's hands. Spreadsheets simply didn't interest Josh. He took an interest in the vineyards, the factories, even in the day-to-day running of a busy five-star hotel, but bottom lines were Peter's concern, not his.

For most of the past decade, he'd enjoyed the freedom of traveling through Europe, spot-checking, overseeing the necessary renovations, revamping policy changes of the family chain. Wineries in France and Italy, olive groves in Greece, orchards in Spain. And, of course, the hotels themselves, which had started it all.

Josh understood and supported the long-held Templeton view that the difference between a hotel and a Templeton was the fact that they served their own wines, used their own oils, their own produce, manufactured their own linens. Templeton products were always offered in Templeton hotels. And part of his job was to see that they were used well.

His title might have been executive vice president, but in essence he was a troubleshooter. Occasionally he handled or supervised the handling of a few of the legal complexities. A man with a Harvard law degree was expected to keep his hand in. Still he preferred people to papers, enjoyed watching a harvest, drinking ouzo with the staff, or closing a new deal over Cristal and beluga at Robuchon in Paris.

It was his charm that was his most valuable asset to Templeton—so his mother said. He did his best not to disappoint her. For despite a careless, somewhat reckless lifestyle, he took his duties to his family and the business seriously. They were one and the same to him.

And as he was thinking of family, even as gravel spit out from under his tires and had the family of four in the sedan he shot past gaping in shock, he thought of Margo.

She would be depressed, he mused. Shattered, penitent, miserable. Not that she didn't deserve to be. His lips curved in something between a smile and a sneer. He'd pulled strings, cashed in markers, and generally executed a wild tap dance to see that she was quickly and completely cleared of any criminal charges in Athens.

After all, Templeton Athens was an old, dignified hotel and, with Templeton Resort Athena, it lured a great deal of money to the country.

There was little he could do about the scandal, or the damage it had done to the career she'd built in Europe. If you could call sending sulky looks into a camera a career.

She'd just have to get over it, he decided, his smile now tinged with arrogance. And he intended to help her. In his own way.

In an old habit he was hardly aware of, he swung over to the side of the road and brought the car to a screeching halt. There, higher still on the rugged hill, surrounded by trees going lush with spring and trailing vines spilling rich blossoms, was home.

Stone and wood, two of the resources Templeton had profited by, rose out of the rugged earth. The original two-story structure had been built by an ancestor as a country home and stood for more than a hundred twenty-five years, surviving storms, floods, quakes, and time.

Wings had been added by subsequent generations, spearing out here, there, tumbling down to follow the shape of the hill. Twin turrets rose up defiantly—an addition of his father's fancy. Wide wooden decks and sturdy stone terraces shot beneath tall, arched windows, wide glass doors to offer dozens of panoramas.

Flowers and trees were blooming, pink and white and yellow. Spring colors, he thought, fresh and inviting. And the grass was the soft, tender green of beginnings. He loved the way it flowed up out of a rocky base, growing more lush and more tended as it met the house.

The land and the sea were as intricate and as intimate a part of the house as its curving trim and glinting stone.

He loved it for what it was, what it had been, and what it had given him. Knowing Laura watched over it, nurtured it, warmed him.

Pleasure at simply being there had him swinging fast across the road, shooting up the snaking lane carved into the rock, then, in shock, slamming on the brakes to avoid crashing into a high iron gate.

He scowled at it for a moment before the intercom beside his car buzzed on.

"Templeton House. May I help you?"

"What the hell is this? Who put this damn thing up?"

"I— Mr. Joshua?"

Recognizing the voice, he struggled to bank down on his irritation. "Annie, open this ridiculous gate, will you? And unless we're under attack, leave the damn thing open."

"Yes, sir. Welcome home."

What the hell was Laura thinking of? he wondered as the gate swung silently back. Templeton had always been a welcoming place. His friends had roared up that curving lane constantly during his youth—on foot, on bikes, then in cars. The idea of its being closed off, even by something as simple as a gate, spoiled his pleasure in the drive from rugged ground to manicured lawns and gardens.

He swung bad-temperedly around the center island, planted magnificently with hardy spring perennials and nodding daffodils. He left both his keys and his luggage in the car and, jamming his hands in his pockets, mounted the lovely old granite steps to the front terrace.

The main entrance door was recessed, ten feet high and arched, framed by intricately placed mosaics that formed a pattern of trailing purple bougainvillea echoed by the trellises of living blooms spilling over the archway. He'd always thought it was like walking through a garden.

Even as he reached for the door it was swinging open. Laura literally leapt into his arms.

"Welcome home," she said, after she'd rained kisses over his face and made him smile again.

"For a minute I thought you were locking me out." The puzzlement in her eyes made him pinch her chin. An old habit. "What's with the gate?"

"Oh." She flushed a little as she backed up and smoothed her hair. "Peter thought we needed some security."

"Security? All you have to do is climb over a few rocks to skirt around it."

"Well, yes, but . . ." She'd said the same herself, and since it was Josh, she gave up. "It looks secure. And important." She cupped his face in her hands. "So do you. Look important, I mean."

Actually, she thought he looked windblown, dangerous, and annoyed. To soothe, she tucked her arm through his and made admiring noises over the car in the driveway. "Where did you get the new toy?"

"In San Francisco. She drives like a bullet."

"Which explains why you're here a full hour before you were expected. Lucky for you Mrs. Williamson has been slaving all morning in the kitchen preparing all that sweet Master Josh's favorite foods."

"Tell me we're having salmon cakes for lunch and all's forgiven."

"Salmon cakes," Laura confirmed. "Allumettes, asparagus, foie gras, and Black Forest cake. Quite a combination. Come in and tell me all about London. You did come from London, right?"

"Just a quick business trip. I'd been taking a few days off in Portofino."

"Oh, that's right." She moved into the parlor to pour him a glass of the sparkling mineral water that Templeton bottled. The curtains were open, as she preferred them, forming frames around window seats made welcoming with colorful pillows. "That's where I hunted you down when I heard about Margo."

"Um-hmm." He'd already been hard at work on Margo's behalf when Laura had called. But he didn't pass that information along. Instead he gave a sprig of freesia tucked with its fellows into a Meissen vase a careless brush. "So how is she?"

"I talked her into sitting by the pool for a while, to get some sun. Josh, this is so terrible for her. She looked so beaten when she came home. Bella Donna is going to drop her as their spokeswoman. Her contract with them was coming up for renewal, and it's pretty much a given that they'll let her go."

"It's rough." He sat in the wide wing chair nearest the hearth, stretched out his legs. "So maybe she can tout someone else's face cream."

"You know it's not that easy, Josh. She'd made a mark in Europe endorsing Bella Donna. It was her main source of income, and now it's cut off. If you've paid any attention to the press, you know that the chances of her being offered anything like it here in the States is slim to none."

"So, she'll get a real job."

Loyalty had her jerking up her chin. "You've always been so hard on her."

"Somebody has to." But he knew that arguing about Margo with his sister was useless. Love always blinded Laura. "Okay, sweetie, I'm sorry for what happened to her. The fact is, she got a raw deal, but life's full of them. She's been raking in the lire and francs for the last few years. All she has to do now is sit on her portfolio, lick her wounds, and figure out what comes next."

"I think she's broke."

That shocked him enough to have him setting his glass aside. "What do you mean broke?"

"I mean she asked Kate to look over the figures. Kate hasn't finished yet, but I have a feeling it's bad. Margo knows it's bad."

He couldn't believe it. He'd taken a good long look at the Bella Donna contract himself, and he knew that the salary and benefits should have set her up comfortably for a decade.

Then he let out a sound of disgust. Why couldn't he believe it? They were talking about Margo, after all.

"For Christ's sake, what has she been doing, heaving her money into the Tiber?"

"Well, her lifestyle . . . after all, she's a celebrity over there, and . . ." Wasn't she worried enough without having to explain? Laura wondered. "Hell, Josh, I'm not sure, but I know she had that slime who got her into this mess managing her for the last few years."

"Pinhead," he muttered. "So she comes crawling home, sniveling."

"She did not snivel. I should have expected you to take this line," she went on. "It must be men. None of you have any loyalty or compassion. Peter wanted to toss her out as if—"

"Let him try," Josh murmured with a dangerous glint in his eye. "It's not his house."

Laura opened her mouth, closed it again. If this emotional roller coaster she was stuck on didn't stop soon, she was going to jump. "Peter didn't grow up with Margo the way we did. He isn't attached to her the way we are. He doesn't understand."

"He doesn't have to," Josh said shortly, and rose. "She's out by the pool?"

"Yes. Josh, you're not going out there and start poking at her. She's unhappy enough."

Josh shot her a look. "I'll just go and rub some salt in her wounds, then I think I'll run out and kick some puppies on my way to foreclosing on my quota of widows and orphans."

Laura's lips curved. "Just try to be supportive. We'll have lunch on the south terrace in about half an hour." It would give her time to have his luggage taken upstairs and properly unpacked.

MARGO KNEW THE moment he stepped off the flagstone path onto the skirt of the pool. She didn't see him, hear him, smell him. Her instincts when it came to Josh went into a sixth sense. When he didn't speak, merely sat on one of the padded lounges on the pool terrace, she continued to swim.

It was too cold to swim, of course. But she'd needed to do something. The water was warm enough. Steam rose from it into the cooler air, and every stroke she took brought her arms into chilly contact with the freshening breeze.

She cut through the water in long, slow strokes and risked a quick glance at him. He was staring off toward the rose garden. Preoccupied, she thought.

He had Laura's eyes, she thought. It always surprised her to see Laura's lovely gray eyes in Josh's face. His were cooler, she thought, more impatient, and often brittlely amused at Margo's expense.

He'd gotten a tan somewhere, she noted as she pivoted and started back across the length of the pool. Just a nice warm hint of color that added another dash of appeal to what was already a sinfully handsome face.

As one who accepted that she'd lucked out in the gene pool, she didn't set much store by simple good looks. It was, after all, just a matter of fate.

Joshua Templeton's fate had been superior.

His hair was shades darker than his sister's. Tawny, Margo imagined was the term. He'd let it grow a bit since the last time they'd run into each other. What was that—three months before in Venice? It flirted with his collar now, the collar of a casual chocolate silk shirt with sleeves rolled up to the elbows.

He had, she recalled, a good, expressive mouth. It could smile charmingly, sneer with infuriating style, and worse, curve in a smile so cold it froze the blood.

The jaw was firm, and thankfully without the beard he'd sported briefly in his twenties. The nose was straight and faintly aristocratic. Over it all was an aura of success, confidence, and arrogance, all shimmering together with a glint of latent danger.

She hated to admit that there had been a time during her adolescence when she'd been both allured by and frightened of that aura.

She was sure of one thing. He was the last person she would allow to see how badly she was now frightened by the present, and the future. Deliberately she stood in the shallow end. Water slid off her body as she slowly walked to the steps. She was freezing now and would have turned into a chunk of bluing ice before she would have admitted it.

As if she'd just become aware she wasn't alone, she lifted a brow and smiled. Her voice was low, throaty, and just shy of hot. "Well, Josh, the world's much too small."

She was wearing a couple of stingy scraps of sapphire spandex. Her curves were lush, sleek, with skin as smooth as polished marble with the sheen of fine silk. Most men, she knew, took one look at what God had given her and shot straight into fantasy mode.

Josh merely tipped down his Wayfarers and studied her over their top. He noted that she'd lost weight, that that glorious skin of hers was prickled with gooseflesh. In a brotherly fashion he tossed her a towel.

"Your teeth are going to chatter in a minute."

Annoyed, she swung the towel around her neck, fisted her hands. "It's invigorating. Where did you drop in from?"

"Portofino, by way of London."

"Portofino. One of my favorite spots, even if the Templetons don't have a hotel there. Did you stay at the Splendido?"

"Where else?" If she was going to be idiotic enough to stand there and freeze, he'd let her. He crossed his ankles, leaned back.

"The corner suite," she said, remembering. "Where you stand on the terrace and see the bay, the hills, the gardens."

That had been his intention. A couple of days to wind down, to do a little sailing. But he'd been too busy negotiating via phone and fax with the police and politicians in Greece to enjoy the view.

"How did you find Athens?"

He was nearly sorry when he noted her eyes flicker, but her recovery was quick. "Oh, not as accommodating as usual. A little misunderstanding. That's all taken care of. It was annoying, though, having my cruise disrupted."

"I'm sure it was," he murmured. "So inconsiderate of the authorities, too. All that inconvenience over a few pesky kilos of heroin."

She smiled easily. "My thoughts exactly." Negligently, she reached out for the robe she'd slung over the back of a chair. Not even pride was going to hold off the shivering much longer. "I can use the time off, though, a little break from the routine. It's been too long since I've been able to squeeze out any real time to visit with Laura and Kate, and the girls." She belted the robe and nearly sighed with relief. "And you, of course, Josh." Knowing it irritated him, she bent down to pat his cheek. "How long are you going to be in the area?"

He took her wrist, knowing it irritated her, and rose. "As long as it takes."

"Well, then." She always seemed to forget he was four inches taller than she. Until she was faced with that long, rangy build. "It'll be just like old times, won't it? I think I'll go in and get into some dry clothes."

She kissed his cheeks briskly, called *"ciao"* over her shoulder, and strolled down the path toward the house.

Josh watched her go, hating himself for being annoyed that she hadn't been teary and wrecked. Hating himself more, much more, for the undeniable fact that he was, and always had been, in love with her.

IT TOOK MARGO six tries before she settled on the proper outfit for lunch. The flowing silk tunic and slacks in fragile pink seemed just casual enough while maintaining a certain elegance and style. She accented the outfit with gold door-knocker earrings, a couple of bangle bracelets, and a long braided chain. Shoes added another ten minutes before she was inspired to go barefoot. That would lend an air of insouciance.

She couldn't explain why she was always compelled to impress Josh, or struggle to outdo him. Sibling rivalry seemed too tame and much too ordinary an explanation.

It was true enough that he had teased her unmercifully as a child from his lofty advantage of four years; had tormented her as a teenager; and had, as their paths crossed in adulthood, made her feel foolish, shallow, and irresponsible in turn.

One of the reasons the Bella Donna contract had meant so much to her was that it was a tangible measure of success that she'd been able to flaunt under his disapproving nose. Now she didn't have that any longer. All she had was image—bolstered by the wardrobe and glitters she'd desperately collected over the years.

She could only thank God that she'd gotten out of the mess in Athens before he'd had to come riding in on his white charger to save her. That would have been a humiliation he'd never have let her forget.

It was Laura's laughter she heard first after descending the stairs and wandering toward the south terrace. It made Margo stop. That's what had been missing the past couple of days, she realized. Laura's laughter. She'd been too tangled in her own miseries to notice. However Josh's presence got on her nerves, she had to be grateful—he'd made Laura laugh again.

She was smiling when she stepped out and joined them.

"What's the joke?"

Josh merely leaned back with his water glass and studied her, but Laura reached for her hand. "Josh is always telling me some horrible secret crime he committed when we were kids. I think he does it to terrify me about what Ali and Kayla are pulling off under my nose."

"The girls are angels," Margo said as she sat down at the round glass table under an arbor of sweetly blooming wisteria. "Josh was the devil's spawn." She spread foie gras on a toast point and bit in. "What's the crime?"

"Do you remember that night when you and I went out to Seraphina's cliffs with Matt Bolton and Biff Milard? It was summer, we were just fifteen. Kate wasn't with us because she was a year younger and couldn't date yet."

Margo cast her mind back. "We double-dated with Matt and Biff a lot that summer. Until Biff tried to unhook your bra and you bloodied his nose."

"What?" Josh immediately came to attention. "What do you mean he tried to unhook your bra?"

"I'm sure you've attempted the maneuver once or twice, Josh," Margo said dryly.

"Shut up, Margo. You never told me he'd tried to . . ." His eyes took on a warrior's glint. "What else did he try?"

Laura sighed and decided she was enjoying the salmon cakes more than she'd anticipated. "Nothing worth you flying to Los Angeles to hunt him down and shoot him like a dog for. In any case, if I'd wanted him to unhook my bra, I wouldn't have punched him in the nose, would I? To get back to the story, that was the night we heard Seraphina's ghost."

"Oh, right, I remember."

Margo helped herself to more pâté. It was the Tiffany porcelain lunch service today, she noted. The Monet pattern with its cheerfully bright blue and yellow. And to set it off, a silver vase filled with yellow frangipani from the greenhouse. Her mother's touch, she thought. She'd used the same china, the same flowers when she allowed Margo to have the tea party she'd so longed for on her thirteenth birthday.

Was it, she wondered, her mother's quiet, unspoken way of welcoming?

With a shake, she brought herself back. "We were sitting on the cliffs necking."

"Define necking," Josh demanded.

She only smiled and stole one of the matchstick potatoes from his plate. "There was a full moon, and all this lovely light on the water. The stars were so huge and bright and the sea went on forever. Then we heard her. She was crying."

"Like her heart would break," Laura added. "It was intense, but very soft, like something carried up into the air. We were terrified and thrilled."

"And the guys were so spooked they forgot all about scoring and kept trying to get us back to the car. But we stayed. We could hear this whispering and moaning and crying. Then we heard her speak." Margo shivered remembering it. "In Spanish."

"I had to translate because you'd been too busy painting your nails in class to pay attention to Mrs. Lupez. She said, 'Find my treasure. It waits for love.'"

Even as Margo sighed, Josh was chuckling. "It took me three days to teach Kate how to say that without fumbling it. The kid never had an ear for languages. We nearly fell off the ledge laughing when the two of you started to squeal."

Margo narrowed her eyes. "You and Kate?"

"We planned it for a week." Since she didn't seem that interested, he forked up her salmon cake and transferred it to his own plate. "She was feeling pretty left out when you two started dating. I got the idea when I came across her sulking on the cliffs. Everybody knew you two hung out there with Dumb and Dumber, and I thought it would cheer Kate up." He swallowed and grinned. "It did."

"If Mom and Dad had known you'd taken Kate scrambling down the cliffs to cling to a ledge at night, they'd have murdered you."

"It would have been worth it. It was all you two talked about for weeks after. Margo wanted to call in a psychic."

She winced. "It was just a suggestion."

"You started looking them up in the phone book," Josh reminded her. "And went down to Monterey and bought tarot cards."

"I was experimenting," she began before a laugh bubbled out. "Damn you, Josh, I blew every penny of my spending money that summer on crystals and palm reading when I'd been saving desperately for sapphire studs. It would have served you right if I'd stumbled on the secret of Seraphina's lost dowry."

"Never existed." He pushed his plate away before he ate more and regretted it. In any case, how could a man eat after that hoarse, sexy laugh of hers had driven a spike of lust into his gut?

"Of course it did. She hid it to keep it out of the hands of the invading Americans, then jumped into the sea rather than live without her lover."

Josh sent Margo an affectionately amused glance. "Aren't you past the fairy-tale stage yet? It's a pretty legend, that's all."

"And legends are persistently based on fact. If you weren't so close-minded—"

"Truce." Laura lifted her hands as she rose. "Try not to take any chunks out of each other while I see about dessert."

"I'm not close-minded," he said before his sister had cleared the doors. "I'm rational."

"You never had any soul. You'd think someone who spent as much time in Europe as you, exposed to Rome and Paris and—"

"Some of us work in Europe," he interrupted and had the satisfaction of seeing her eyes go dark and dangerous. "That's just the look you had for that perfume ad," he said easily. "What was that called? Savage."

"That campaign upped Bella Donna's sales ten percent. That's why what I do is considered work."

"Right." He topped off her water glass. "So, Margo, did Matt ever try to unhook your bra?"

She was calm, she told herself. She was in control. She lifted the glass, looked Josh dead in the eye. "I never wore one." She watched him frown, watched his gaze wander down. "In those days," she added. Laughing, she rose, stretched. "Maybe I'm glad you're home after all. I need someone to fight with."

"Glad to oblige. What's wrong with Laura?"

She looked down. "You're quick, Josh. You always were. She's worried about me. That might be all, but I'm not sure."

He'd find out, he thought and nodded as he rose. "Are you worried about you?"

It surprised her, the gentleness in his voice, the light brush of his knuckles over her jaw. She could lean against him, she realized with a jolt. She could lay her head on that shoulder, close her eyes, and for a moment at least, everything would be all right.

She nearly stepped forward before she decided it would be foolish. "You're not going to be nice to me, are you?"

"Maybe." It might have been the confusion in her eyes, or that sultry scent that wafted from her skin, but he needed to touch. He laid his hands on her shoulders, rubbed while his eyes stayed on hers. "Do you need help?"

"I—" She could taste something on her lips, and was baffled that it was anticipation of him. "I think—"

"Excuse me." With her face carefully blank, Ann stood on the terrace holding a portable phone. Her eyes flickered with something that might have been amusement when Josh dropped his hands as though she'd caught him tearing off her daughter's clothes. "Miss Kate's on the phone for you, Margo."

"Oh." Margo stared down at the phone her mother put in her hand. "Thanks. Um . . . Kate, hi."

"Something wrong? You sound—"

"No, no, nothing at all," Margo interrupted brightly. "And how are you?"

"It's coming on to tax time, pal, how do you think an accountant is? Which is why I just can't get away to come over there. I really want to talk to you, Margo. Can you get over here to my office this afternoon? I can give you some time between three and three-thirty."

"Sure. I suppose. If you—"

"Great. See you."

Margo clicked off the phone. "She's always been one of the champion communicators."

"It's nearly April fifteen. Crunch time."

Margo lifted a brow. He seemed perfectly at ease, she noted. All that tension, all that . . . anticipation must have been her imagination. "That's about what she said. I have to get over to her office. I'd better see if Laura can lend me a car."

"Take mine. It's out front. Keys are in it." He gave her dubious expression a quick, charming smile. "Hell, Margo, who taught you to drive in the first place?"

"You did." Her eyes warmed. "And with uncharacteristic patience."

"That's because I was terrified. Enjoy the drive. And if you put a scratch on her, I'll toss you over Seraphina's cliff."

When she sailed off, he sat down again, calculating that not only would he get her share of cake but he would now have the opportunity to pry out whatever was troubling his sister.

CHAPTER 5

K ATE POWELL WAS consistent, focused, and often inflexible. As Margo strode down the corridor of the second-floor offices of Bittle and Associates with their buzz of activity, ringing phones, and clattering keyboards, she realized this was exactly what Kate had had in mind for herself since childhood. She had, without detour, worked steadily toward it all of her life.

There had been the advanced math courses in high school, which of course she'd aced. Her three terms as class treasurer. The summers and holidays she'd worked in bookkeeping at Templeton Resort to advance her training and on-the-job experience. From there the scholarship to Harvard, her MBA, followed by her refusal, gracious but firm, to take a position in any of the Templeton offices.

No, Margo thought, eyeing the discreet carpet and walls, feeling the jittery tension in the tax-time air. Kate had chosen Bittle, taken an entry-level position. Her salary would have been higher at a firm in Los Angeles or New York. But she wouldn't have been able to stay close to home.

In that, Kate was also consistent.

So, she'd worked her way up in the firm. Margo didn't know a great deal about accountants other than they were always whining about taxes and shelters and projected earnings, but she understood that Kate was now responsible for several important clients in the old, respected, and—in Margo's opinion—musty firm of Bittle and Associates.

At least all those years of effort had earned her a decent office, Margo mused as she peeked into Kate's door. Though how anyone stood being cooped up in four walls, facing away from the window all day was beyond her. Kate, however, looked contented enough.

Her desk was neat, and that was to be expected. No tchotchkes, no fancy paperweights, no frivolous doodads cluttered its surface. To Kate, Margo knew, clutter was one of the Seven Deadly Sins, along with impulse, disloyalty, and a disorganized checkbook.

A few files were arranged in an orderly stack on the edge of the plain, boxy desk. Dozens of lethally sharp pencils stood in a Lucite holder. A jazzy little computer hummed as Kate rattled the keys.

She'd taken off her navy jacket and hung it over the back of her swivel chair. The sleeves of her crisp white shirt were rolled up in businesslike fashion. She was frowning, a concentration line dug between her brows above the studious horn-rim reading glasses. Though her phone rang busily, it didn't earn a blink of response.

Even as Margo stepped in, Kate held up a single finger, continuing to work the keys one-handed. Then with a grunt she nodded and looked up.

"You're on time for a change. Close the door, will you? Do you know how many people wait until April's knocking to hunt up their receipts?"

"No."

"Everybody. Have a seat." As Margo took the dung-brown chair across from the desk, Kate rose. She rolled her shoulders, circled her head, murmuring what sounded like "relax." After slipping off her glasses, she tucked the temple into the breast pocket of her shirt so that the glasses hung there like a medal. Then she turned, chose two plain white mugs from a shelf, and reached for the pot on her coffeemaker. "Annie said Josh was home."

"Yeah, he just got in, looking tanned and terrific."

"When did he ever look anything else?" Noting that she'd neglected to open her blinds again, she did so now and let natural light slant into the room to war with the glow of florescents. "I hope he plans to stay a while. I'm not going to have any free time until after the fifteenth." From her desk drawer she took a bottle of Mylanta, uncapped it, and guzzled like a veteran wino with a bottle of Crackling Rose.

"Christ, Kate, how can you do that? It's hideous."

Kate only lifted a brow. "How many cigarettes have you had today, champ?" she said blandly.

"That's hardly the point." Grimacing, Margo watched Kate tuck the bottle back into the drawer. "At least I know I'm slowly killing myself. You should see a doctor, for God's sake. If you'd just learn to relax, try those yoga exercises I told you about—"

"Save it." Kate cut off the lecture in midsentence and checked her practical Timex. She didn't have the time or the inclination to worry about a nervous stomach, certainly not until she finished calculating the realized capital gain and loss summary currently on her screen. "I've got a client due in twenty minutes, and I don't have time to debate our varying addictions." She handed Margo a mug, slid a hip onto the edge of her desk. "Has Peter shown up?"

"I haven't seen him." Margo struggled for a moment, but lecturing Kate had always been a study in frustration. Better, she decided, to concentrate on one friend's problems at a time. "Laura doesn't have much to say about it. Kate, is he living at the hotel?"

"Not officially." Kate started to bite her nails before she studiously stopped herself. Just a matter of willpower, she remembered, and drank coffee instead. "But from the buzz I get, he spends more time there than he does at home."

She moved her shoulders, still working out kinks. Her head was throbbing nastily. Between tax time and the mess her closest friends were in, she welcomed each day with a tension headache.

"Of course, it's a busy time of year for him, too."

Margo smirked. "You never liked him."

Kate smirked right back. "Neither did you."

"Well, if there's trouble in paradise, maybe I can help Laura through it. But if he's just staying away because I'm there, I should leave. I could stay at the resort."

"He missed plenty of bed checks before you rolled back into town. I don't know what to do about it, Margo." She rubbed tired eyes with unpainted fingertips. "She won't really talk about it, and I'm lousy at giving advice on relationships anyway."

"Still seeing that stud CPA down the hall?"

"No." Kate shut her mouth firmly on that. Closed book, she reminded herself. Even if it did still burn. "I don't have time to date. The fact is, as tied up as I am for the next week or so, I'm really glad you're there, with Laura and the kids."

"I'll stay unless it looks like it's complicating things for her." Absently Margo tapped her fingers on the arm of the chair, lovely shell-pink nails bumping against the chair's dull brown. "She's awfully happy to have Josh back. I don't think I realized she was so unhappy until I saw her with him today. Which reminds me . . ." She set the coffee aside. Kate brewed it strong enough to pump iron. "Weren't you worried about risking a haunting by mocking Seraphina's ghost?"

Kate's face went blank. "What?"

"Huddling on a ledge and moaning in bad Spanish about your dowry. Laura and I weren't fooled for a minute."

"What are you . . . Oh. Oh!" As memory flooded back, Kate roared with laughter. It was not the laugh of a thin, serious-minded woman; it boomed straight from the gut, grew deeper in the throat, and tickled Margo into grinning back. "God, I'd forgotten that. Oh, I was so jealous, so *pissed* that you and Laura were dating and Uncle Tommy and Aunt Susan were making me wait another year. I didn't even want to date, but I hated you getting ahead of me." As she spoke, she got up to top off her coffee. "Christ, Josh always had the best and wildest ideas," she added, as she perched on the desk again.

"You're lucky you didn't slip off the ledge and get to meet Seraphina face-to-face."

"We had ropes." She chuckled into her coffee. "I was scared boneless at first, but I didn't want Josh to think I was lame. You know how he is about a dare."

"Mmm." Margo knew very well. A Templeton never refused a challenge. "Both of you would have been grounded for weeks."

"Yeah, those were the days," Kate said with a wistful smile. "Anyway, I got caught up in the whole thing. Playing Seraphina and listening to the two of you calling out to her was one of the highlights of my life. I can't believe he ratted on me."

"He probably thinks I'm too mature now to pull out your hair." Margo tilted her head and smiled. "I'm not, but you have so little of it to begin with." Then she clasped her hands around her knee. "Well, I know you, and you didn't ask me to come into such professional surroundings to have a giggle over old times. You might as well give it to me."

"All right." It was cowardly, Kate knew, to wish she could postpone the moment. "We can say there's good news and bad news."

"I can use some good."

"You still have your health." At Margo's nervous laugh, Kate set her own mug aside. She wished she had a better way to do this, wished she'd been smart enough or clever enough to find an escape clause for Margo. "Sorry, bad accountant joke. You have to have a pretty good idea that you don't have a hell of a lot else, Margo. Financially, you're fucked."

Margo pressed her lips together, nodded. "Don't soft-pedal it, Kate. I can take it."

Appreciating her, Kate slid off the desk, sat on the arm of Margo's chair, and hugged her. "I put everything in a computer program and printed out a hard copy." And got less than three hours' sleep, thanks to the extra workload. "But I thought you'd get more out of the whole picture if I boiled it down. You've got some choices."

"I don't . . ." She had to pause to level her voice. "I don't want to file bankruptcy. Only as a last resort, Kate. I know it's pride, but—"

Pride Kate understood, enormously well. "I think we can avoid that. But, honey, you're going to have to seriously consider liquidating, and you're going to have to be prepared to take a loss on some of your assets."

"I have assets?" Margo asked hollowly.

"You have the flat in Milan. There isn't a lot of equity, as you only bought it five years ago and your down payment was low. But you can get out what you put in, and with luck, a little more." Because it was personal, Kate didn't need her notes, or the file. She remembered all the details. "You have the Lamborghini, and it's almost paid for. We arrange to sell it, quickly, and you'll save on those exorbitant garage and maintenance fees."

"Okay." She tried not to regret her beautiful flat, lovingly furnished, or the glamorous car she'd adored driving fast in the countryside. There were a great many things she couldn't afford, Margo reminded herself. Top of the list was self-pity. "I'll put them on the market. I suppose I'll have to go over and pack everything up and . . ."

Saying nothing, Kate rose to open a file, not to refresh her memory but to give herself something to do with her hands. She perched her glasses back on her nose. "There's the dead animals."

Sunk in depression, Margo shook her head. "What?"

"Your furs."

"That's such an American attitude," Margo grumbled. "Anyway, I didn't kill those stupid minks."

"Or the sables," Kate said dryly, peering over the tops of her horn-rims. "Sell them and that also saves you cold storage fees. Now your jewelry."

It was an arrow straight to the heart. "Oh, Kate, not my jewelry."

"Toughen up. It's just rocks and minerals." With her free hand she picked up her coffee again, ignoring the faint burning under her breastbone. "The insurance premiums on it are killing you. You can't afford it. And you need the cash to meet your debts. Dressmakers' bills, salon bills. Taxes. Italian taxes are stiff, and you didn't exactly save for a rainy day."

"I had some savings. Alain had been siphoning them off." She realized her fingers were aching and made herself untwist them. "I didn't even know it until last week."

Bastard, Kate thought. But that was then and this was now. "You can prosecute."

"What's the point?" Margo said wearily. "It would just feed the press."

Pride again, she thought. It was useless to ask Kate if she could afford a few miserly spoonfuls of pride. "So, basically I have to give up everything. Everything I have, everything I've worked for, everything I've wanted."

"Okay." Miserable, Kate put the file aside. "I'm not going to tell you they're just things, Margo. I know they're not. But this is a way out. There are others. You could sell your story to the tabloids, pick up some quick, ready cash."

"Why don't I just go down to Hollywood and Vine and sell my body? It would be less humiliating."

"You could go to the Templetons."

Margo shut her eyes. It shamed her that for a moment, just a moment, she was tempted.

"They'd bail you out," Kate said gently. "Float you until you were on your feet again."

"I know. I can't do that. After all they've done for me and been to me. Added to that is how it would make my mother feel. I've upset her enough without going begging."

"I can lend you ten thousand right away. That's what I have liquid," Kate said briskly. "It would put a finger in the dike, and I know that Laura and Josh would plug the other leaks. It wouldn't be begging, and it would be nothing to be ashamed of. Just a loan between friends."

Margo said nothing for a moment. Touched and ashamed, she stared down at the sapphires and diamonds winking on her hands. "So I can keep my pride and my furs and diamonds." Slowly, Margo shook her head. "No, I don't think I'm going to be able to keep any of it. But thanks."

"You'll want to consider this, weigh your options. The offer stays open." Kate took the file, proffered it, wished there was more. "The figures are all there. I calculated the fair market value of the jewelry from the insurance appraisals. I've got the sale value of your car, the flat, and so forth calculated with a ten percent leeway, deducted all the expected fees and taxes. If you decide to liquidate, you'll earn some breathing space. Not a lot, but enough to keep your head above water for a while."

And then what? Margo thought, but she didn't dare ask. "Okay. I appreciate you wading through all the mess."

"That's what I do best." Just at that moment, it seemed pitifully little. "Margo, take a couple of days. Mull it over."

"I will." She rose, then laughed weakly when her knees shivered. "Christ, I'm shaky."

"Sit down. I'll get you some water."

"No." Margo held up a hand. "I really need some air."

"I'll go with you."

"No. Thanks, but I need a minute."

Gently, Kate brushed a hand over Margo's hair. "Want to kill the messenger?"

"Not right now." Instead, she gave Kate a hard, fierce hug. "I'll be in touch," she said and rushed out of the office.

SHE WANTED TO be brave. All of her life Margo had yearned for adventure, the glamour and romance of it. She wanted to be one of those carelessly daring women who don't simply follow trends but create them. She had, most of her life, quite deliberately exploited her sense of style, her looks, her sexuality to gain her own ends. Her education had been no more than a necessary phase, something to get through. Unlike Laura or Kate, she had merely put in time in the classroom. What would she need with algebraic formulas or historical facts in her life? It was much more important what they were wearing this season in New York or who the up-and-coming designers were in Milan.

It was, Margo thought as she stood on the windswept cliffs above the sea, pathetic. Her life was pathetic.

Even a month before, she had thought it perfect. Of course, then everything had been streaming along exactly as she wanted. She had a flat in the right part of the city, was recognized and catered to in the right restaurants and boutiques. She had a circle of friends that included the wealthy, the well known, and the wild. She attended fashionable parties, was thrillingly dogged by the press and pursued by men. And, of course, she feigned weariness and ennui over the articles that speculated about her private life.

She had a career that had put her precisely where she had always wanted to be. In the limelight.

Then there was her lover of the moment. The suave, gorgeous older man, as she preferred. French. Married, of course, but that was merely a technicality. An obstacle, again fashionable, that would eventually be overcome. The very fact that they had been forced to keep their affair secret had added a thrill. A thrill that, she realized now, she had so easily mistaken for passion.

Now it was all over.

She hadn't believed she could be any more shocked or frightened than in those first hours after she had been taken into Athens for questioning. The terror of being so alone, so exposed, had bounced her roughly from a privileged world into a dangerous one. And when no one from that carefully selected circle of friends had come to her aid or her defense, she had been forced to stand on her own and reevaluate Margo Sullivan.

But that didn't seem to be enough.

She sat on a rock, absently tugging a woolly white blossom from its slender stem. Laura would know the name of the wildflower, Margo mused. But then, Laura, despite the privileges of birthright, was the wildflower type, whereas Margo was strictly hothouse.

She was ruined.

Somehow it had been easier to handle the possibility of being broke before Kate had put it all in stark black and white. Possibilities were abstract and changeable. Now it was reality. She was, or soon would be, without a home, without an income. Without a life.

She stared down at the flower in her hand. It was simple, it was stubborn, planting its roots in shallow soil, fighting its way to the sun. Rip off the bloom, another would grow.

She understood now that she'd never had to fight for anything. And she was afraid, deeply afraid, that now that she was uprooted, she would simply wither.

"Waiting for Seraphina?"

Margo continued to study the flower, twirling it as Josh settled on the rock beside her. "No, just waiting."

"Laura took the girls to dance class, so I thought I'd take a walk." Actually, he'd been considering a quick jaunt to the tennis court to work on his serve. But then he saw Margo on the cliffs from his bedroom window. "How's Kate?"

"Busy and efficient. I'd say she's found her Nirvana with Bittle and Associates."

He shuddered. "Scary."

The quick chuckle felt good. Tossing her hair back, she smiled at him. "We're so miserably shallow, Josh. How do we stand ourselves?"

"By never standing still long enough to take a close look. Is that what's got you down, Margo?" He tugged on the hair she'd pulled sleekly back from her face. "Have you been looking too close?"

"That's what happens when you get a mirror shoved in your face."

He slipped her shaded glasses off, narrowed his own eyes. "It's a hell of a face," he said lightly, then tucked the glasses back on her nose. "Do you want to know what I see?"

She pushed off the rock, wandered closer to the edge of the cliff. "I'm not sure I could take another shot today. You've never bothered to sugarcoat what you thought of me."

"Why should I? When a woman looks like you, she collects flattery, tossing the less inventive lines aside like last year's fashions. You're the most beautiful woman I've ever seen." He watched her turn, and though her eyes were hidden, he sensed her surprise. "It's a sinful face, a sinful body. They almost punish a man for wanting them, for wanting you. All that abundant, hot sex with hints of the wild driving it. And you use it without even thinking. A look, a tilt of the head, a gesture. It's a phenomenal, and occasionally cruel, talent you have. But you've heard that before."

"Not exactly," she murmured. She wasn't sure if she was flattered or insulted.

"But most of that's an accident of nature." He rose and walked to stand beside her. "You were born to be a fantasy. Maybe that's all you can manage."

The hurt was so sharp, so sudden she couldn't even gasp. "That's cold, Josh. And just like you."

When she started to whirl away, he took her arm, his grip unexpectedly strong, his voice infuriatingly mild. "I haven't finished."

Bright, bubbling fury spewed inside her. If she could have wrenched away and clawed him, she would have. "Let go of me. I'm sick of you and everyone like you. I'm worth bothering with as long as I fit the mold. The party girl. For a good time, call. But the minute there's trouble it's so easy to say I wasn't anything to begin with. Just a scrabbler, reaching above my station."

He slid his hands down to cuff her wrists, his voice still detestably patient. "Were you?"

"I'm not a damn picture in a magazine. I have feelings and fears and needs. And I don't have to prove anything to anyone but myself."

"Good. Good for you. It's about time you realized that." With an easy strength that both baffled and infuriated her, he simply pulled her back from the cliff and nudged her down on the rock. He kept his grip firm as he crouched in front of her. "You're the one who played with the illusion, Margo, who used it. And you're the one who's going to have to shatter it."

"Don't tell me what I have to do. If you don't take your hands off me—"

"Shut up. Just shut up." He gave her a brisk shake that made her mouth fall open in shock. "You'll have to get used to that, too," he told her. "Being treated like a human being instead of a pampered Barbie doll. Life's finally been tossed in your face, duchess. Deal with it."

"What do you know about life?" Bitterness ached in her throat. "You were born with everything. You never had to struggle for a single thing you wanted, never had to worry if you'd be accepted or loved or wanted back."

He stared at her, grateful for the moment that she couldn't see that he'd spent nearly half of his life worrying that she, the single thing he wanted, would accept him, love him, and want him back. "But we're not talking about me, are we?"

She turned her face, stared hard out to sea. "I don't care what you think of me."

"Fine, but I'm going to tell you anyway. You're a spoiled, careless, and reckless woman who has for a good long time hardly given a thought to anything beyond the moment. Up till now your ambitions have melded nicely with your fantasies. Now you've been given a very rude slap. It'll be interesting to see if you'll be able to draw on your other qualities to pull yourself up again."

"Oh?" she began icily. "I have other qualities?"

He wondered what perverted twist in his makeup caused him to adore that frosty, fuck-you tone of hers. "You come from strong and resilient stock, Margo, a temperament that doesn't take failure lying down." Absently, he lifted her hands and kissed them. "You're loyal and warm and compassionate to those you care for. What you lack in common sense you make up for with humor and charm."

The emotions that swirled inside her threatened to erupt in laughter or tears or screams. She forced them to wither and kept her face as blank and cold as her voice. "That's a fascinating analysis. You'll have to bill me for it. I'm a little short of cash."

"No charge." He drew her to her feet again, brushed at the loose hair that danced wildly around her face. "Listen, if you need something to tide you over until—"

"Don't you dare offer me money," she interrupted with a snap in her voice. "I'm not some destitute family retainer."

It was his turn to be insulted. "I thought you were a friend."

"Well, keep your money in your numbered Swiss account, friend. I'm perfectly capable of taking care of myself."

"As you like." After a shrug, he held out his hand. "How about a lift back to the house?"

Her lips curved coolly. "How about you stick out your well-manicured thumb?" She strode away, picking her way with careless grace over rocks. Moments later he heard the panther roar of his own car and the skid of tires on pavement.

Christ, he thought with a quick laugh. He was crazy about her.

SHE WAS STILL seething with fury when she marched into the house. Temper carried her well down the central hallway before the sound of voices registered. Calm, reasonable voices. Overly calm, Margo realized at once. Coldly reasonable and bitingly formal.

It made her shudder to think that husband and wife would speak to each other in such lifeless tones. However wrenching it had been, she much preferred the passionate exchange she'd just had with Josh to the kind of studied argument going on between Laura and Peter in the library.

The heavy pocket doors were open, allowing her to step up to the threshold and observe the entire scene. Such a civilized room, Margo thought, with its soaring ceiling, its two levels walled with books and diamond-paned windows. The old Bokhara rug and the smell of leather. A civilized room, she thought again, for a civilized argument.

How perfectly horrible.

"I'm very sorry you feel that way, Peter. I simply can't agree with you."

"The business, the running of Templeton hotels, our place in society, and the media are hardly your fortes, Laura. I would not be in the position I'm in, nor have the responsibilities I have, if your parents and the board of directors didn't value and respect my opinion."

"That's true."

Margo stepped quietly to the doorway. She could see Laura standing in front of the window seat, her hands clasped loosely. There was such temper and distress in her eyes that Margo wondered how Peter could remain oblivious to it.

For himself, Peter was in front of the lovely old Adam fireplace, very lord of the manor with one hand on the mantel and the other wrapped around a Waterford lowball glass gleaming with light and unblended Scotch.

"In this case, however," Laura continued in that same quiet, empty voice, "I don't believe the family would share your concern. Josh certainly doesn't."

Peter let out a hard, dismissive laugh. "Josh is hardly one to worry about reputation. He's more at home flitting off to clubs and rubbing elbows with Eurotrash."

"Be careful." Laura only murmured the warning, but there was force behind it. "You and Josh approach things differently, but you're each an important part of Templeton. My point is that Josh fully supports Margo's remaining at Templeton House as long as she chooses. And, foreseeing this altercation, I contacted my parents this morning. They're delighted Margo is home."

His lips went thin and white at that. Margo would have been pleased by the reaction if his temper hadn't been directed at Laura. "You went behind my back. That's typical of you, isn't it? Running to your parents whenever we disagree."

"I don't run to them, Peter." There was weariness now. As if giving in to it, Laura sat down on the padded window seat. Light streamed in through the lovely arched window at her back, causing her to look fragile, pale, and heartbreakingly beautiful. "And I don't discuss our private problems with them. In this case it was, in your words, business."

"And business is for me to handle." His voice was clipped, all reason with an undertone of carefully controlled impatience. "You only have the house to run and the children to see to. Both of which you're putting in second place to some misguided sense of loyalty."

"No one and nothing comes ahead of my children."

"Really?" A small smile curved his lips as he took a sip of his Scotch. "I don't suppose you found time in your busy and demanding day of manicures and luncheons to watch television? One of the tabloid shows dedicated an entire thirty minutes to your old friend. There was a particularly interesting clip of her sunbathing topless on a yacht. Several of her close friends gave interviews detailing her many affairs and her so-called free-spirited lifestyle. Naturally the show didn't fail to report her connection with Templeton, and her long-standing friendship with Laura Templeton Ridgeway."

Pleased that she didn't respond, he inclined his head. "It included a picture of the two of you, and the children. In addition, a waiter at the country club was happy to tell them how the two of you and an unnamed woman had a giddy champagne lunch by the pool two years ago."

Laura waited a beat. "Kate's going to be annoyed they didn't get her name." Out of patience, she waved a hand and rose, and he saw that what he had taken for shame was annoyance. "Really, Peter, it's all nonsense. The last time we were on the Riviera you were irritated with me because I was too shy to go French, yet you're condemning Margo because she did. And if any of those people had been her friends, they wouldn't have been chafing to give interviews, which they were paid for, that gossiped about her. And nearly half the women I know get snockered at the club regularly. If we wanted to have a giddy champagne lunch to celebrate being together, it's no one's business."

"You're not only blind and stubborn, but you're foolish. And this attitude you've developed of late has gone on long enough."

"Attitude?"

He set his glass on the mantel with a snap. "Questioning me, defying my wishes, neglecting your duties in the community. Margo's presence here is merely an excuse for you to go on behaving badly."

"I don't need an excuse."

"Apparently not. I'll put it another way, a clearer way, Laura. As long as that woman lives in this house, I don't."

"An ultimatum, Peter?" Very slowly, she inclined her head. "I think you might be rudely surprised by my answer to that."

On impulse, Margo stepped into the room. "Hello, Peter. Don't worry, I'm every bit as thrilled to see you as you are to see me."

With a brittle smile, she walked over to the decanter. Though she rarely drank anything other than wine, she poured two fingers of Scotch. She wanted something to do with her hands.

"I know I'm interrupting, but I was on my way back to speak to Mum." She took a quick, bracing sip, shuddered it down.

"You seem to be taking your most recent debacle in stride," Peter commented.

"Oh, you know me. Roll with the flow." She gestured widely, rings glittering. "I'm sorry I missed the show you were telling Laura about. I do hope those shots of me sunbathing were flattering. Those long-range lenses can distort, you know." Beaming smiles, she lifted her glass to him. "And you and I understand all about appearances, don't we, Peter?"

He didn't bother to conceal his disdain. She was, as she had always been to him, the housekeeper's inconvenient daughter. "People who eavesdrop on private conversations rarely hear anything flattering."

"Absolutely true." Resolved now, she took a last sip before setting the glass down. "As you'd be aware if you'd ever heard any of my private conversations about you. You can rest easy. I was coming in to tell my mother I have to go back to Milan."

Distress made Laura step forward, step between them. "Margo, there's no need for that."

She took the hand Laura offered, squeezed it. "There is. I left dozens of things hanging. I needed this little breather, but I have to go back and tend to the details."

Ignoring Peter, she gathered Laura close. "I love you, Laura."

"Don't say it like that." Alarmed, Laura drew back, searched Margo's face. "You're coming back."

She gave a careless shrug even as her stomach jittered. "We'll see how the wind blows. But I'll be in touch. I need to talk to Mum before I pack." She gave Laura a last hug before turning toward the door. Not sure if she'd have another chance, she went with impulse again and turned back. She offered Peter her sultriest smile. "One more thing. You're a pompous, egotistical, self-important ass. You weren't good enough for her when she married you, you're still not good enough for her, and you never will be. It must be hell for you knowing that."

As exits went, Margo thought as she glided out, she'd never done better.

* * *

"I'M NOT RUNNING away," Margo insisted as she hurriedly packed.

"Aren't you?" With her hands folded at her waist, Ann watched her daughter. Always in a rush, she thought, to get from one place to the next. Never stopping to think.

"I'd stay if I could. I'd rather stay, but—" She tossed a cashmere sweater into her bag. "I just can't."

Out of habit, Ann took the sweater out, folded it neatly, replaced it. "You should take more care with your possessions. And your friends. You're leaving Miss Laura when she needs you."

"I'm leaving to make things easier for her, damn it." Out of patience, Margo tossed her hair over her shoulder. "Can't you ever give me credit for doing something right? She's downstairs right now arguing with Peter because of me. He threatened to leave her if I stay. He doesn't want me here."

"This is Templeton House," Ann said simply.

"And he lives here. Laura is his wife. I'm just—"

"The housekeeper's daughter. Odd, you only remember that when it suits you. I'm asking you to stay and do what you can for her."

Oh, guilt works so well, she thought as she stalked over to wrench a blouse out of the armoire. Like a bell to Pavlov's dog. "I'm a cause of tension in her marriage, an embarrassment. I will not see her torn between me and the man she's been married to for ten years. You know I love her."

"Yes." Ann sighed a little. "Yes, I know you do. Loyalty isn't one of your failings, Margo. But I'm telling you she needs you here. Her parents are off in Africa someplace. They know little about what's gone on in this house and little, I suspect, of what's happened to you. They would be here otherwise. But you're here, and you should stay. If you would for once listen to what I say, do as I ask."

"I can't." She sent her mother a thin smile. "Some things don't change. Kate and Josh are here for her. And you," she added. "I have to get out of the way so she can work things out with Peter. If that's what she wants. Though God knows why—" She cut herself off, waved a hand in dismissal. "That's her decision. Mine is to go back to Milan. I have to deal with things there. I have to pick up my life."

"Well, you've made the mess of it, you'll have to clean it up. You'll hurt her by going," she said quietly. And me, Ann thought. Can't you see how it hurts me to see you walk away again?

"I hurt her by staying, too. So either way I'm of no use to her. At least in Milan I can try to put some of my own pieces back together. I need money, I need work."

"You need." Eyes cool, Ann studied her daughter. "Well, then, that naturally comes first. I'll arrange for your cab to the airport."

"Mum." Washed with regret, Margo took a step after her. "I'm trying to do what's right. If it's a mistake, then it's a mistake, but I'm trying to do what I think is best. Try to understand that."

"I only see you're going when you've hardly come home." Ann closed the door behind her, the only good-bye Margo would have.

CHAPTER 6

MARGO HAD FALLEN hard for Milan at first sight. She had been dazzled by Paris, awed by Rome, amused by London. But Milan, with its busy streets, impeccable style, and easy panache had won her heart.

Her career had fulfilled her childhood dream of travel, tickled the wanderlust that had always been part of her soul. Yet, in her own way, she had needed roots, a base, a place to call her own.

She had chosen the flat on impulse, because she liked the look of the building, the charming terraces that offered a view of the street and a glimpse of the spearing towers of the Duomo. And because it was a convenient stroll from her door to the elegant shops of the Montenapoliane.

She stood on her terrace now, sipping chilly white wine, watching the late-evening traffic punctuated by the high, double-toned blare of sirens. The sun was setting, gilding the view and making her lonely for someone to share it with.

She had been right to come back. It was perhaps the first selfless thing she'd done in too long to remember. Though Laura had argued until the cab whisked Margo away, and Josh had simply stood eyeing her coolly with an expression that accused her of running, she knew she had done what was best.

Still, doing what was right wasn't always comforting. She was miserably lonely. Fears of the present and the future weren't nearly as difficult to overcome as the isolation.

In the week since her return, she hadn't answered the phone, or returned any of the messages already crowding her machine. Most of them were from reporters or acquaintances hoping for a tidbit of gossip. Mixed among them were a few offers she was afraid she would have to consider.

If she were truly brave and daring, she mused, she'd shimmy into some little black dress and stroll into one of her old haunts to set the room buzzing. Maybe she would before it was done, but for now she had a few more wounds to lick.

Leaving the terrace doors open, she walked into the living area. Other than a few gifts, she'd chosen each and every piece herself. She hadn't wanted a decorator, but had enjoyed the adventure of hunting down every pillow and lamp.

It certainly reflected her taste, she thought with a wry smile. Eclectic. Hell, she corrected—scattered. An antique curio cabinet crowded with Limoges boxes and Steuben glass. The japanned chest that served as coffee table was topped with a huge Waterford compote that was in turn filled with colorful handblown fruit.

There were Tiffany lamps, Art Deco ones, even a Doulton Flambe that featured a seated Buddha and had cost her some ridiculous amount at auction just to sit there and look ugly.

Every room of the two-bedroom flat was crammed with more. Inkwells she'd collected during some passing stage. Russian boxes, paperweights, vases, bottles—all purchased for no other reason than that they were what she had been acquiring at the time.

Still, it made a lovely, cluttered, and homey place, she thought, as she settled down on the deeply cushioned sofa. The paintings were good. She'd been told she had an eye for art, and the street scenes that lined her walls were clever and lovely and brought the world into her rooms.

Her world. Her rooms. Temporarily, at any rate, Margo thought and lighted a cigarette. But she wasn't going to be able to hide in them for much longer.

Maybe she would take the offer from *Playboy* and drive the wolf back, away from her door. Her eyes narrowed in consideration, she drew in smoke. Why not? Why not sell her pathetic story to the tabloids that called daily to clutter her answering machine tape? Either way, she'd have money again. Either way, she would strip herself naked for the grinning world.

What were those few shreds of pride really doing for her?

Hell, maybe she should shock the civilized world and drag all her furnishings out onto the street for one wild, goes-to-the-highest-bidder bazaar.

Laughing, she envisioned how it would distress her very polite and proper doorman, her elegant neighbors. And how it would delight the ever-hungry press.

So what if she spread herself out on the centerfold of a glossy men's magazine with a couple of strategically placed staples? Who would care if she prostituted her pride to whine about her troubles in a Sunday supplement or supermarket paper?

No one expected any more or any less from her. Perhaps, she thought, tiredly crushing out the cigarette, neither did she.

But to sell her possessions, to publicly barter things for money, that was so . . . middle-class.

Well, something had to be done. The bills were piling up, and she wouldn't have a roof over her head much longer if she didn't pass over considerable lire.

She supposed the logical step would be to find a discreet and reputable jeweler and sell her glitters. It would hold her level until she decided what step to take next. She toyed with the square-cut sapphire on her hand; she didn't have a clue what she had paid for it.

It hardly mattered, did it? she decided. Kate had calculated the worth, and it was what she could get for it now that mattered. She pushed herself up and hurried into the bedroom. After unlocking the safe built into the cedar chest at the foot of her bed, she began pulling out boxes and pouches. In moments, the lamplight beamed on a pile of glittering treasures worthy of Ali Baba's cave.

Dear God, did she really own a dozen watches? What was wrong with her? And what had possessed her to buy that jeweled collar? It looked like something out of *Star Trek*. Marcasite hair combs. She never wore hair combs.

The tension began to ease from her shoulders as she examined, separated, began to make decisions. There were dozens of pieces, she discovered, that she could part with without a qualm. Certainly she would reap enough to keep her head above water until she had time to think.

And clothes.

With manic energy she leapt up, scattering jewelry and dashing to her closet. It was enormous, lined with dresses, suits, jackets. Lucite shelves held shoes, bags. Built-in drawers were packed with scarves and belts. A triple mirror ringed with lights reflected her image as she frantically pushed hangers to and fro.

There were secondhand shops that specialized in designer clothes, she knew. Indeed, she had purchased her first Fendi bag at one in Knightsbridge a lifetime ago. If she could buy from a secondhand shop, then by God, she could sell to one.

She tossed jackets, blouses, skirts, slacks over her arm, rushed out to drop them on the bed, dashed back for more.

She was giggling when the doorbell rang, and she ignored it until the constant buzz cut through what she realized abruptly was the edge of hysteria. It was a struggle to swallow the next bubble of laughter, and for the life of her she couldn't remember the deep breathing exercises from her yoga class.

"Maybe I'm having a breakdown." The sound of her own voice was tight and nervy. The doorbell continued to buzz like a swarm of angry bees. "All right, all right, all right!" she snapped as she stepped over suede boots that had fallen out of her arms. She would face whoever was at the door, get rid of them, and then deal with the latest mess she'd created.

Ready to fight, she yanked the door open and stared. "Josh!" Why, she wondered, was he always the last person she expected to see?

He took a quick survey of the tousled hair, the flushed face, the robe that was slipping off her shoulder. His first jealous thought was that he'd interrupted sex. "I was in the neighborhood."

She folded her arms. "You're checking up on me."

"Laura made me." The charming smile flirted around his mouth, but his eyes were hot. Who the hell was in the flat? Who'd been touching her? "I had a little problem to iron out at Templeton Milan, so I promised her I'd swing by, see how you were." He angled his head. "So, how are you?"

"Tell Laura I'm fine."

"You could tell her yourself if you'd answer the phone occasionally."

"Go away, Josh."

"Thanks, I'd love to come in for a while. No, no," he continued as he nudged by her, "I can't stay long." When she stood firm and left the door open, he shut it himself. "All right, but just one drink."

God, he was gorgeous, she thought. Arrogance fit him as sleekly as his linen shirt. "Maybe I'll call security and have you tossed out."

His quick laugh had her clenching her fists. As he wandered the room, she measured him. In leather bomber jacket and snug jeans, he looked tougher than she would have expected. She wondered if cheerful little Marco, who manned the door, could bite him on the ankle.

"This oil of the Spanish Steps is new since I was here last," he commented, eyeing her painting with mild avarice. "It's not bad. Sixty-five hundred for the French Quarter watercolor."

She arched a brow. "You go up five hundred every time you make an offer. I'm still not going to sell it to you."

It belonged in the lobby of Templeton New Orleans. He shrugged off her refusal. He would pry it away from her sooner or later. He picked up a paperweight, icy white shapes swimming inside icy white glass, passed it from hand to hand. He hadn't missed the way she kept glancing back toward the bedroom.

"Something else on your mind, Josh?"

Murder. Mayhem. But he smiled easily. "Hunger. Got anything to eat around here?"

"There's a nice trattoria just down the street."

"Good, we'll walk down later, but I'd love a little wine and cheese now. Don't trouble yourself," he added when she didn't budge. "I'll just make myself at home." Still carrying the paperweight, he headed for the bedroom.

"The kitchen's back here," Margo began, panicked.

His mouth turned grim. He knew exactly where her kitchen was. He knew where everything was in her flat, and whoever was in the bedroom was going to discover that Joshua Templeton had staked prior claim.

"Damn it." She caught at his arm and was dragged along with him. "I'll get you a glass of wine. Just stay out of —"

But it was too late. She let out a frustrated groan as he strode over the threshold and stopped dead.

Looking at the scene now, she could hardly believe it herself. Clothes were in a stream from closet to bed, sequins piled on denim, cashmere heaped on cotton. Jewelry was spread in a sparkling lake on the rug. It looked, she realized, like some bad-tempered child had thrown a tantrum. But Josh's observation was closer to the mark.

"It looks like Armani and Cartier went to war."

One of those tricky bubbles of laughter tickled her throat. She nearly managed to clear it away, but her voice stuttered dangerously. "I was just . . . sort of . . . organizing."

The look he sent her was so dry and bland, she lost her slippery hold on control. Holding her stomach, she stumbled to the chest and collapsed onto it in a wild explosion of laughter. Casually, Josh reached down to pick up a slate-blue jacket, fingered the material.

"The man is a god," he said, before tossing the Armani onto the bed.

That sent her off into fresh peals. "Joshua." She managed to hitch in enough breath to speak. "You have to be the only living soul I know who could look at this and not run for the butterfly net." Because she loved him for it, she held out a hand to invite him to sit beside her. "It was a temporary episode," she said and let her head tilt against his shoulder. "I think I'm over it."

With an arm draped around her, he surveyed the chaos. "This is all your stuff?"

"Oh, no." She chuckled. "I have a closet in the second bedroom, too. It's packed."

"Of course it is." He pressed a kiss to the top of her head, frowned at the scattered gems. "Duchess, how many earrings do you figure you own?"

"I haven't the foggiest. I didn't get into the costume stuff yet." Feeling better, she sighed. "Earrings are like orgasms. You can never have too many."

"I never thought about it quite that way."

"Well, you're a man." She gave his knee a friendly pat. "Why don't I get that wine?"

She was wearing nothing under the robe, and his fingertips were beginning to tingle against the thin silk. "Why don't I get it?" Distance, he told himself, was the key. The last thing she needed him to do just then was to lose his mind and start to slobber.

"The kitchen—"

"I know where the kitchen is." He flashed a grin at her narrow-eyed stare. "I was hoping to come in here and intimidate your lover."

"I don't have a lover at the moment."

"That's handy, isn't it?" He strolled out, certain that he'd given her something to mull over. When he came back, pleased to have found an excellent Barola in her wine rack, she was kneeling on the floor, carefully putting jewelry back in boxes.

The robe was flirting off her shoulder again. Josh was tempted to tug the sash tight himself, double-knot it so the fabric wouldn't continue to slip and slide so devastatingly.

When she saw him and rose, he couldn't avoid seeing the flash of long, slim leg. Every muscle in his body groaned.

The worst of it was she wasn't trying to drive him to his knees. If she had been, he could have, without qualm, tossed her onto the bed and finally fulfilled his fantasies.

But that careless sexuality was pure Margo.

She took the glass he held out, smiled at him. "I suppose I have to thank you for interrupting the insanity."

"Want to tell me what started the insanity?"

"Just a stupid idea." She walked to the doors of the bedroom terrace, threw them open. Night poured in, full of sound and scent. She drew it in as she drew in the wine. "I really love Milan. Almost as much as . . ."

"As?"

Annoyed with herself, she shook her head. "Doesn't matter. I'm working on ways to stay here, with some level of comfort. Going home to Templeton House isn't an option."

"You're going to let Peter lock you out?"

She bristled at that, turning. The fairy lights on the terrace twinkled around her and dazzled through the thin silk of her robe. "I don't give a gold-plated shit about Peter Ridgeway, but I'm not going to complicate things for Laura."

"Laura can manage. She doesn't let Peter dust her around the way she used to. If you had bothered to hang around, you'd have seen that for yourself."

She felt her hackles rise again. Damn him. But she spoke smoothly: "Regardless, she's got a marriage to worry about. For some ridiculous reason, marriage is what matters to her. Christ knows why she wants to be tied down to one man, especially a pompous jerk like Peter."

Josh took a contemplative sip. "Weren't you planning on marrying Alain, the slick, lying drug smuggler?"

She tried for dignity. "I didn't know he was a smuggler."

"Just a slick liar."

"All right, fine. You can say that experience gave me a fresh viewpoint on and a general dislike for the institution. The point is, Laura is married and I'm not going to make it more difficult for her."

"It's your home too, Margo."

Now her heart swelled, and broke just a little. "He can't change that. But you can't always go home. Besides, I've been happy here, and I can be again."

He moved closer, wanting to read her eyes. "Kate says you're considering selling your flat."

Her eyes were simple to read. They were filled with annoyance. "Kate talks too much." She turned around to study those last gilding lights. He turned her back again.

"She's worried about you. So am I."

"You don't have to be. I'm working on a plan."

"Why don't I take you to dinner? You can tell me about it."

"I'm not sure I'm up to the telling stage, but I could probably eat. We don't have to go out. The trattoria will deliver."

"And that way you don't risk bumping into anyone who knows you," he concluded and shook his head. "Don't be a coward."

"I like being a coward."

"Then you'd better get dressed." Deliberately, he skimmed his fingertip over the bare skin of her shoulder, up her throat. And watched her eyes go dark and wary. "Because you're asking for trouble right here."

She nearly tugged her robe into place before she stopped herself. Odd how the skin could tingle. "You've already seen me naked."

"You were ten." He slid the robe into place himself, gratified when he felt her quick shiver. "It doesn't count." To test her reaction, he hooked his fingers in the belt of the robe, gave one gentle tug. "Want to risk it, Margo?"

Danger had snapped into the air, abruptly, unexpectedly, fascinatingly. Struggling to be cautious, she stepped back. "I'll get dressed. We'll go out."

"Safe choice."

But she didn't feel safe when he walked out and closed the door behind him. She felt . . . stirred.

HE'D DONE IT to push her into going out. That was the simple, rational conclusion Margo came to. It seemed the only conclusion when he settled into the busy little restaurant and dived into his first-course selection of *antipasto di funghi crudi* with exuberance.

"Try one." He held a marinated mushroom to her lips, nudged it through. "Nobody does vegetables like the Italians."

"Nobody does anything edible like the Italians." But she toyed with her salad of tomato and mozzarella. She'd grown so accustomed to denying herself full meals that eating heartily still felt like cheating.

"You need a good five pounds, Margo," he said. "Ten wouldn't hurt."

"Ten and I'd have a whopping bill from the dressmaker for alterations in my wardrobe."

"Eat. Live dangerously."

She nibbled on cheese. "You're sort of a businessman," she began and made him laugh.

"Oh, if you stretch the point."

"That wasn't meant to be an insult. It's hard for me to picture you as an executive, making corporate decisions. Your father's always had this aura of power. You're more—"

"Feckless?" he suggested.

"No. Relaxed." Impatient with herself, she huffed out a breath. "I'm really not trying to insult you, Josh. What I should say is that whatever it is you do, you make it seem easy. Take Peter."

"No, thanks."

"In comparison," she continued. "He's tense and driven. 'Successful yet ambitious corporate man' is etched onto his face."

"And I, on the other hand, the scion of the Templeton fortune, am relaxed, was it? And carefree, jetting my way around the world's hot spots, seducing women in between squash matches. Or is it playing squash in between seducing women?"

"I'm not entirely sure," Margo said evenly, "but that's beside the point."

"And the point of this deathless observation is . . . ?"

"I have insulted you." Too used to him to be concerned, she shrugged. "You have to have some talent for business because your parents aren't fools. However much they love you, they wouldn't give you free rein to poke into the hotels. They'd just let you drain your trust fund and be a wastrel."

"Your confidence in me is touching." With a sneer, he topped off their glasses. "I think I need another drink."

"And you have that law degree."

"Yes, the one they gave me after I'd finished racketing around Harvard."

"Don't be so sensitive." She patted his hand. "It occurs to me that you must know something about managing . . . things. I've had a few interesting offers," she began. "The most lucrative and least complicated is from *Playboy*."

His eyes went so sharp, so flinty, it surprised her that they didn't strike sparks off the silverware. "I see."

"I've posed naked before—or the next thing to it." Wary of his enigmatic response, she sliced off a bit of cheese. "European magazines aren't as puritanical as American ones."

"And you consider an arty ad in Italian *Vogue* on the same level as a centerfold in a skin magazine?" There were murderous thoughts rocketing through his head, making him feel ridiculously like the cuckolded lover.

No, she didn't, and felt incredibly foolish. "Same body," she said with a careless shrug. "The point is, I've made my living in front of the camera in varying stages of dress and undress. This is a way to continue to do so. A one-shot deal, anyway, that would put some distance between me and the creditors. With what they're offering me I could get back on my feet. Well, one foot anyway."

His eyes never left her face. Nearby, a waiter dropped a tray of dishes with a resounding crash, and Josh didn't so much as blink. "Are you asking me to look over the offer?"

It had been her thought, but she reconsidered, and reconsidered quickly, at the razor-edged tone in the question. "No, I was simply mentioning one of my alternatives."

"Is that what you want to be, Margo? Some sweaty-palmed adolescent's wet dream? This month's pinup in the auto mechanic shop, a visual aid at the fertility clinic?"

"I think that's in very poor taste," she said stiffly.

"That's in poor taste?" The way he exploded with it had several diners jerking their heads around and murmuring.

"Don't shout at me," she said under her breath. "You've never had any respect for what I do. I don't know why I thought you might have some sensible comment about this."

"You want a sensible comment. Terrific." He gulped down wine to force the bile back down his throat. "Go right ahead and do it, duchess. Take the money and run. Don't worry about embarrassing your family. Why should you care? So they snicker the next time your mother's standing in line at the supermarket. If the kids tease Ali at school, it's not your problem. Just make sure you're well paid."

"That's enough," she said quietly.

"Is it?" he tossed back. "I'm just warming up."

"I said it was an option. I didn't say I was going to accept." With impatient fingers she rubbed at a headache brewing at her left temple. "Goddamn it, it's just a body. My body."

"You're connected to people. I'd hoped you'd begun to realize that what you do affects them."

"I have." Wearily she let her hand drop. "All right, I have. Judging from your reaction, it wouldn't go over very well."

Inch by inch he reeled in his temper and studied her. "Is that what this was about? Testing the waters with me?"

She managed a smile. "Yes. Bad idea." Sighing, she pushed her plate away. "On to the next. We won't bother with the German producer who's offering a considerable pile of marks if I let him showcase me in his latest adult film."

"Jesus Christ, Margo—"

"I said we wouldn't bother with that. So what do you do when you decide to redecorate one of your hotels?"

He rubbed a hand over his face. "While I'm trying to make that leap of thought, we'll order the pasta course." He signaled the waiter, ordered tagliolini for himself and risotto for Margo.

Bracing her chin on her palm, she began to think through that next option. "Your Italian's much better than mine. That might be helpful, too."

"Margo darling, don't go off on another tangent until I've caught up." His blood was still hot at the idea of her being spread out in full, glorious color for any man with pocket change to drool over. "Are you asking me for decorating advice?"

"No. No, of course not." The very idea made her snicker. The headache and unsteady stomach his temper had caused began to ease. "I'm curious about what you do with the furnishings when you redo suites."

"You want furniture?"

"Josh, just answer the question. What do you do when you change the decor?"

"Okay, fine. We rarely do that in one of our established hotels, as the clientele appreciates the tradition." What the hell was going through that fascinating mind of hers now? he wondered, but shrugged. It wouldn't take long to find out. "However, when we buy out another hotel, we will usually revamp the rooms in the Templeton style, using the locale for inspiration. We'll keep whatever is suitable or up to our standards, sometimes shipping pieces off to another location. What doesn't suit is normally sold at auction, which is where the decorator and buyer would pick up replacements. We also buy at antique shops and through estate sales."

"Auction," she murmured. "It might be best. Simplest. Auctions, antique shops, estate sales. They're all really just secondhand stores, aren't they? I mean, everything there has been owned before, used before. Sometimes people value things more if they've belonged to someone else."

She beamed up at the waiter, nearly causing him to jostle the plates as his blood pressure spiked. "*Grazie, Mario. Ho molta fame.*"

"*Prego, signorina. Mia piacere. Buona appetite.*" He bowed away from the table, narrowly avoiding a collision with a busboy.

"Your Italian's fine," Josh said dryly. "You don't even need words."

"He's a sweetheart. He has a lovely wife who presents him with a bambina every year. And he never looks down my blouse." She paused, considered. "Well, hardly ever. Anyway," she said, digging into the risotto with genuine enthusiasm, "speaking of secondhand shops."

"Were we?"

"Yes. What sort of percentage of the value is customary when you sell?"

"It would depend on several factors."

"What are they?"

Deciding he'd been patient and informative long enough, he shook his head. "No, you first. Why do you want to know?"

"I'm thinking of—what's the term?—downsizing." She speared a shrimp from his plate.

"Actually, rightsizing has become the more politically correct term."

"Okay. I like that better anyway. Rightsizing." She chuckled over the idea. "I've been collecting things for ten years. I thought I might unload some of them. My apartment's entirely too crowded, and I've never taken the time to weed out my wardrobe. Since I've got some free time, I thought . . ."

She trailed off. He hadn't said a word, but she knew he understood she was scrambling for pride. "I need the money," she said flatly. "It's stupid of me to pretend otherwise. Kate thinks liquidation is the best option." She tried to smile again. "And since *Playboy* is out . . ."

"You don't want me to offer you a loan," he murmured. "You just want me to sit back and do nothing while you sell your shoes for grocery money."

"And my bags, and my porcelain boxes, and my candlesticks." He wasn't going to feel sorry for her, she determined. By God, no one was going to feel sorry for her. "Look, Streisand did it a couple years ago, didn't she? Not that she needed the money, but what's the difference? She sold things she'd collected over the years, and I doubt she turned up her nose at the money. It doesn't appear that I'm going to be able to sell my face for the foreseeable future, and I don't intend to sell my body, so I've whittled the options down to my things."

She didn't want sympathy, he determined. So he wouldn't offer it. "Is that what you were doing tonight when I came by? Inventory?"

"In an impulsive, semihysterical sort of way. But now I'm calm and rational, and I see that the plan—actually Kate's plan—has value." She covered his hand with hers. "Josh, when you saw me back home, you asked if I needed help. I'm telling you I do. I'm asking you for it."

He looked down at her hand, the glint of sapphire and diamonds against creamy white skin. "What do you want me to do?"

"First, keep this between us for now."

He turned his hand over, linked his fingers with hers. "All right. What else?"

"If you could help me figure out how and where to sell what I have to sell. How to get the best price. I haven't managed my money well. Hell, I haven't done such a hot job with my life either, but I'm going to start now. I don't want to get fleeced because I'm not sure what something's worth, or because I'm in too much of a hurry."

He picked up his wine with his free hand, considered. Not just what she was asking, but what it meant, and what could be done. "I can help you, if you're sure it's what you want."

"I'm sure."

"You've got a couple of choices, as I see it. You can get an agent." Keeping his eyes on hers, he topped off their wine. "I know an outfit here in Milan that's very trustworthy. They'll come in, appraise what you've selected, give you around forty percent."

"Forty? But that's terrible."

"It's actually a bit on the high side, but we do a lot of business with them and you'd probably get it."

Grimly, she set her teeth. "What are my other choices?"

"You could try one of the auction houses. You could go with an appraiser and then contact some of the antique or collectible shops and see what you'd get there." He leaned closer, watching her face. "But, if you ask me, you should sell yourself."

"Excuse me?"

"Margo Sullivan can sell anything. What else have you been doing for the last ten years but hawking someone else's products? Sell yourself, Margo."

Baffled, she sat back. "Excuse me. Aren't you the one who just finished rapping my knuckles for mentioning doing just that?"

"Not your picture. You. Open a shop, stock it with your own possessions. Advertise it. Flaunt it."

"Open a shop?" Her laugh bubbled out as she reached for her glass. "I can't open a shop."

"Why not?"

"Because I . . . I don't know why," she murmured and deliberately pushed her glass aside. "I've had too much wine if I don't know why."

"Your flat's already a small-scale department store."

"There are dozens of reasons why it wouldn't work." Her head spun just thinking about it. "I don't know anything about running a business, keeping books."

"Learn," he said simply.

"There's taxes, and fees. Licenses. Rent, for Christ's sake." Flummoxed, she began to run her fingers up and down the jeweled chain she wore. "I'm trying to eliminate bills, not make more of them. I'd need money."

"An investor, someone who would be willing to pump in the startup money."

"Who'd be stupid enough to do that?"

He lifted his glass. "I would."

CHAPTER 7

SHE SPENT MOST of the night picking the idea apart, tossing in bed and reciting all the sane objections she should have thought of in the first place.

It was a ridiculous notion. Reckless and foolish. And it had come along just when she was trying so hard to stop being ridiculous and reckless and foolish.

When tossing in bed frustrated her enough, she rose to pace in the dark. Obviously Josh knew little more about business than she did, or he would never have suggested such a preposterous plan.

She wasn't a shopkeeper, for God's sake. Appreciating lovely things only meant she had expensive taste. It didn't mean she could turn herself into a merchant. And maybe she did know how to sell, but being the Bella Donna Woman and urging some tourist to write a traveler's check for a Daum goldfish were two entirely different matters.

Certainly people would come, at first. Out of curiosity, out of glee to see the once famous, now notorious Margo Sullivan hawking her wares. She would probably make a few sales too, initially. And some society matron with too many face-lifts could gesture to her curio cabinet to point out the antique snuff bottle she'd bought from that poor model who'd fallen on hard times.

Margo set her teeth. Well, she'd have that snooty matron's money in her pocket, wouldn't she?

Catching herself, she shook her head. No, it was an impossible idea. Starting a business was simply too complicated, and maintaining one would be beyond her. She would only be setting herself up for another failure.

Coward.

"Just shut up, Josh. It wouldn't be your butt on the line. Just your money."

And she wasn't going to take his money anyway. The idea of being indebted to him was more than her pride could stand. Even if she swallowed her pride, she didn't think her nerves could handle working with him. He'd undoubtedly be popping up even more than usual, checking on her, checking on his investment.

Looking at her the way he looked at her. Absently she rubbed a hand between her breasts. Had he always looked at her that way? Had she just begun to notice? She recognized hunger in a man's eyes when she saw it. Was used to seeing it. There was no reason for her mouth to go dry and her pulse to start jittering because they were Josh's eyes.

His eyes were as familiar to her as her own. She'd known those eyes, known him, all of her life. It had to be her imagination—imagination skewed by her emotional upheaval. It was just that she'd been feeling so unwanted, she'd mistaken kindness and concern from an old friend for desire.

That was it, of course.

But she knew she hadn't mistaken her own reaction when he touched her, when his fingers skimmed over her shoulder. Flesh to flesh. And for an instant, just a quick flash, she'd actually fantasized that his fingers would dip lower, part her robe, cup her breasts and . . .

And she had to be skirting madness to wind an erotic daydream around Josh Templeton.

He was a friend, practically family. And at the moment, the least of her worries.

She had to concentrate on practicalities, not sexual intrigues. After Alain she'd decided that sex, romance, even the whisper of relationship were going to the bottom of her priority list. The most reasonable thing for her to do would be to contact Josh in the morning and ask him for the name of the agent he'd mentioned. She would cull out everything she didn't need for basic survival, take the forty percent, and go on.

She'd sell the car as well. And her furs. Her standing twice-monthly appointment at Sergio Valente in Rome was out, as was her biannual jaunt to Les Pres et les Sources in France. There would be no more strolling down the Montenapoliane with careless forays into Valentino and Armani.

She would make do with what she had, or what she had left, and find a job.

Damn him for making her too ashamed to snatch up a quick six figures for one harmless photo shoot.

Besides, what kind of shop would it be? she asked herself as her mind stubbornly circled back. People didn't go into a store expecting to buy a Gucci bag and a Steuben bird in the same place. It wouldn't be secondhand clothing, or curios, or leather goods. It would be a hodgepodge; confusing, unfocused.

It would be unique.

It would be hers.

With her hands pressed to her mouth, Margo let herself imagine it. Busy shelves with an elegant yet friendly clutter of pretty, useless things. Glass cabinets gleaming with jewelry. Tables and chairs and fussy ottomans. For relaxing, and all for sale. A room fashioned like a huge walk-in closet for clothes. Another little seating area where she would serve tea and flutes of champagne. China and crystal also priced to sell.

It could work. Not only could it work, it could be fun. An adventure. The hell with the details, the fine print, the sanity. She'd figure it out somehow.

With a reckless laugh, she dashed into the bedroom and threw on some clothes.

JOSH WAS DREAMING, and dreaming well. He could even smell her, that straight-to-the-glands fragrance that always seeped through her pores. She was murmuring his name, almost sighing it as he stroked his hands over her. God, her skin was like satin, smooth and white, that glorious, generous goddess body growing damp as she clung to him.

Arched back, trembling and—

"Ow. Goddamn it." Pinched him.

He opened his eyes, blinked at the dark. He would have sworn his shoulder ached where fingers had dug. And he could swear that her scent was in the air.

"Sorry. You were sleeping like the dead."

"Margo? Are you crazy? What time is it? What are you doing here? Jesus!" He continued to swear, viciously, as the light she turned on speared into his eyes. "Turn that goddamn thing off or I'll kill you."

"I'd forgotten how surly you are when you wake up." Too cheerful to take offense, she switched off the light, then moved to the drapes, opening them to the lovely muted glow of sunrise. "Now, to answer your questions: I think I may be. It's about quarter after dawn. I'm here to thank you."

She smiled at him as he stared groggily at the coffered ceiling. The bed was a lake of rumpled linen sheets and the slick royal blue satin of the spread. The headboard was a fantasy of cherubs and fruit, all carved and gilded. Rather than looking ridiculous tucked in all that splendor, he looked just right.

"Gosh, you're cute, all heavy-eyed and grumpy, and that sexy stubble." She leaned over to give it a teasing rub, then squealed when he yanked her onto the bed with him. Before she could gather the next breath, she was pinned under a long, hard male body.

A fully aroused male body. There was no possible way to attribute that to imagination this time. Her hips arched in response before she could prevent it. And his eyes went opaque. Instinctively she pried a hand free and slapped it to his chest.

"I didn't come to wrestle."

"Then why are you here, and how'd you get into the suite?"

"They know me downstairs." Good God, she was out of breath, and shaky. And hot. "I just said you were expecting me, and said you might be in the shower, so . . . the front desk gave me a key." His gaze lingered on her mouth, made her burn. "Ah, listen, I seem to have interrupted one of your prurient dreams, so I can just wait in the parlor until . . ."

She trailed off, deciding it was best not to continue the thought, when he caught her wrist and pulled her arm back over her head.

"Until?"

"Whenever." His mouth was close. She could almost feel it on hers. Hard and hungry. "I wanted to talk to you, but obviously I should have waited. Until."

"You're trembling," he murmured. And her eyes were delicately shadowed from lack of sleep. Her hair, those sexy miles of it, spread wildly over the tumbled sheets. "Nervous?"

She could hear her own labored breaths, knew no one could mistake the desire in the sound. "Not exactly."

He lowered his head, scraped his teeth lightly over her jaw. When she moaned, he hoped he was making her suffer for even one of the nights he'd burned for her. "Curious?"

"Yes."

He cruised up to her ear, and her eyes crossed with lust. "Ever wonder why we haven't ended up like this before?"

She was having a hard time keeping a coherent thought in her head as he nibbled along her neck. "Maybe, once or twice."

He lifted his head. The light from the rising sun showered over him. With his hair tousled, his eyes dark, his face shadowed, he looked rough and reckless, dangerously and delectably male.

"Don't." She didn't know where the denial came from when every nerve in her body was primed to beg for more.

"Don't what?"

"Don't kiss me." She let out a shaky breath, drew in another. "If you do, we're going to have sex. I'm just turned inside out enough to jump in without giving a damn about an hour from now."

"You don't have to give a damn about an hour from now." His mouth skimmed along her temple, teased the corner of her lips. "This is going to take longer. A lot longer."

"Please. A few hours ago . . . Jesus, Josh . . . you convinced me that what I do affects other people."

"Believe me," he murmured, "I'm affected."

Her heart drummed in her ears, insistently. "I can't afford to ruin another part of my life. I need a friend. I need you to be my friend."

Cursing her, he rolled off. "No offense, Margo, but go to hell."

"No offense taken." She didn't touch him. She was certain that if she did one or both of them would go off like a rocket. For a moment they lay there on the rumpled satin spread in silence, not moving, barely breathing. "I'm just saving us both a lot of trouble."

His gaze shifted, pinned hers. "You're only postponing it. We'll get back to this."

"I've been choosing my own bedmates for some time."

He moved fast, snagging her wrist and hauling her against him. "You want to be careful, duchess, about throwing your lovers in my face just now."

It was exactly what she needed to break the spell. Her chin angled.

"Don't get pushy. I'll let you know if and when I want to play." She saw the change in his eyes and flashed her own. "Try it, just try it, and I'll shred the skin from your bones. You aren't the first man who thought he could shove me on my back and make me enjoy it."

He let her go because it was a wiser course than strangling her. "Don't compare me to the wimps and washouts you've wasted your time with."

Knowing her temper was ready to snap, she got off the bed. "I didn't come here to tear up the sheets with you, or to fight. I'm here to discuss business."

"Next time make an appointment." No longer worried about the niceties, he tossed back the sheets. Her eyes didn't flicker as he strode naked into the adjoining bath. "Since you're here, order up some breakfast."

She waited until she heard the shower running before she let out a long, relieved breath. Another minute, she admitted, and she might have eaten him alive. With a hand pressed to her jumpy stomach, she told herself they were both lucky she'd forced them to avoid that mistake.

But as she glanced back at the bed, she didn't feel lucky. Only deprived.

WHILE JOSH DRESSED, Margo enjoyed the first cup of coffee and picked over the silver basket of baked goods on the linen-decked table in the window nook of the dining area. She relaxed with the view of the piazza, the statues of gods and winged horses in white marble.

As did any suite in any Templeton, it offered a sumptuous interior as well as the view. A massive Oriental carpet spread over a floor of ivory tile. The walls were papered with roses with golden leaves, the fancy work of cornices and textured ceilings added to the opulence. Curvy settees rich with brocade and tasseled pillows, entertainment centers discreetly concealed in intricately carved cabinets, the little touches of statuary, antique lamps, heavy crystal ashtrays, giant urns filled with flowers, the full ebony bar curved in front of a glass wall—all bespoke that distinct Templeton flair.

The Art Nouveau style was just rich enough, just decadent enough to make even the most jaded guest sigh. She sighed herself.

But with Templeton, style went hand in glove with efficiency. A touch of a button on the streamlined white phone in every room of the suite could summon anything from fresh towels to tickets to *La Scala* or a bottle of perfectly chilled Cristal in a silver bucket. There was a basket of fruit on the pond-size coffee table, the grapes plump, the apples glossy. Behind the bar, the mini fridge would be stocked with unblended Scotch, Swiss chocolates, French cheeses.

The flowers, abundant even in the bath and dressing rooms, were fresh, watered and replaced daily by one of the well-trained and always amenable staff.

She sniffed at the pink rose on the breakfast table. It was long-stemmed, fragrant, and just opening. Perfect, she mused, just as anything with the Templeton name was expected to be.

Including, she thought as Josh stepped into the room, the Templeton heir.

Because she was feeling just a little guilty about invading his rooms at dawn, she poured him a cup from the heavy silver pot, adding the generous dollop of cream she knew he preferred.

"Service at Templeton Milan is still the best in the city. So's the coffee." She passed him the cup when he joined her at the table.

"I'll be sure to pass your comments along to the manager—after I fire him for letting you in."

"Don't be cranky, Josh." She slanted her most persuasive smile his way, only slightly annoyed when she saw it didn't make a dent. "I'm sorry I woke you up. I wasn't thinking about the time."

"Not thinking is one of your most highly honed skills."

She plucked a berry from the bowl, popped it into her mouth. "I'm not going to fight with you, and I'm not going to apologize for not sleeping with you just because your ego's bruised."

His smile was thin and sharp as a scalpel. "Duchess, if I'd gotten your clothes off, you not only wouldn't have to apologize, you'd be thanking me."

"Oh, I see I'm mistaken. Your ego's not bruised, it's just painfully swollen. Let's clear the air here, Joshua." She leaned forward, the confidence in her eyes sultry. "I like sex. I think it's an excellent form of entertainment. But I don't have to be entertained every time someone suggests a party. I select the time, the place, and my playmates."

Satisfied, she sat back and lazily chose a tiny cake from the basket. That, she was sure, should settle that.

"You might be able to get away with that." She was right, he thought. The coffee was excellent, and put him in a better mood. "If you hadn't been trembling and moaning under me half an hour ago."

"I was not moaning."

He smiled. "Oh, yes. You were." Yes, indeed, he was feeling much, much better. "And on the verge of writhing."

"I never writhe."

"You will."

She bit neatly into the cake. "Every boy should have his dreams. Now if we're finished jousting over sex—"

"Darling, I haven't even picked up my lance."

"That's a very weak double entendre."

She had him there. "It's early. Why don't you tell me why I'm having breakfast with you."

"I was up all night."

The comment that occurred to him was not only weak, but crude. He let it pass. "And?"

"I couldn't sleep. I was thinking about the spot I'm in, the options you'd suggested. The first seems the most sensible. Having an agent come in and make me an offer on the furnishings, my jewelry. It would probably be the quickest solution, and the least complicated."

"Agreed."

She pushed away from the table, rubbing her hands together as she paced. Her soft suede boots were as soundless on the tile as they were on the thick carpet. "It's probably time I learned to be sensible. I'm twenty-eight, unemployed, with the wolf snarling at the door. I was feeling sorry for myself at first, but now I realize I had an incredible run of luck. I got to go places and do things, be things that I'd always dreamed of. And why?"

She stopped in the center of the room, turned a slow circle under the ornate gold and crystal chandelier. In tight jodhpur-style pants and a drapey white blouse, she looked voluptuous and vibrant.

"Why?"

"Because I have a face and a body that translate well through the camera. That's all. A good face, a killer body. Not that I didn't have to work hard, be clever and stubborn. But the core of it, Josh, is luck. The luck of the draw from the gene pool. Now, through circumstances that may or may not have been beyond my control, that's done. I'm through whining about it."

"You've never been a whiner, Margo."

"I could give lessons. It's time for me to grow up, take responsibility, be sensible."

"Talk to life insurance salesmen," Josh said dryly. "Apply for a library card. Clip coupons."

She looked down her nose. "Spoken like a man born with not only a silver spoon but the whole place setting stuck in his arrogant little mouth."

"I happen to have several library cards," he muttered. "Somewhere."

"Do you mind?"

"Sorry." He waved her on, but he was worried. She looked eager and happy, but she wasn't talking like Margo. Not his delightfully reckless Margo. "Keep going."

"Okay, I can probably weather this, eventually I could wrangle some shoots, get a spot on the catwalk in Paris or New York. It would take time, but I could come around." Struggling to think clearly, she traced a finger down a candlestick in the form of a maiden in flowing robes flanked by twin cups holding gold tapers. "There are other ways to make money modeling. I could go back to catalogs, where I started."

"Selling teddies for Victoria's Secret?"

She whirled, fire in her eyes. "What's wrong with that?"

"Nothing." He broke open a small roll. "I appreciate a well-sold teddy as much as the next guy."

She took a slow breath. He would not annoy her, not now. "It wouldn't be easy in my current situation to get bookings. But I did it before."

"You were ten years younger," he pointed out helpfully.

"Thank you so much for reminding me," she said between her teeth. "Look at Cindy Crawford, Christie Brinkley, Lauren Hutton, for God's sake. They're not teenagers. And as far as your brilliant solution, the idea of opening a shop is ludicrous. I thought of half a dozen valid reasons against it last night. Over and above the fact that I don't have a clue how to run a business is the larger fact that if I was crazy enough to try I could very well make my situation—a very unstable situation—worse. It's more than likely I'd be bankrupt within six months, faced with yet another public humiliation and forced to sell myself on street corners to traveling salesmen looking for cheap thrills."

"You're right. It's out of the question."

"Absolutely."

"So when do you want to start?"

"Today." With a jubilant laugh, she dashed to him, threw her arms around his neck. "Do you know what's better than having someone who knows you inside out?"

"What?"

"Nothing." She gave him a noisy kiss on the cheek. "If you're going to go down—"

"Go down swinging." He caught her hair in his hand and pulled her laughing mouth to his.

It wasn't a laughing matter. She discovered that very quickly. His lips were hot and clever and had hers parting in sighing response. The lazy sweep of his tongue sent shock waves of need vibrating out to her fingertips.

It should have been familiar. She'd kissed him before, tasted him before. But those casual brotherly embraces hadn't prepared her for the instant, undeniable jolt of pure animal lust.

Part of her mind tried to draw back, to remember that this was Josh.

Josh who had scorned her prized collection of dolls when she was six. Who had dared her to scramble with him on the cliffs when she was eight, then had carried her back to the house when she gashed her leg on a rock.

Josh who had smirked at her adolescent crushes on his friends, who had patiently taught her to handle a five-speed. Josh who had always been somewhere right around the corner wherever she had gone in her life.

But this was like kissing someone new. Someone dangerously exciting. Painfully tempting.

He'd been expecting it. Hadn't he dreamed, hundreds of times, of tasting her like this? Of having her go taut in his arms, her mouth answering his with a kind of banked fury?

He'd been willing to wait, just as he'd been willing to dream. Because he knew she would be his. He knew she needed to be.

But he wasn't going to make it easy.

He drew back, pleased that when her lashes slowly lifted, her eyes were dark and clouded. He hoped to God the same jittery desire that was churning in his gut was churning in hers.

"You're awfully good at that," she managed. "I'd heard rumors." She realized she was in his lap but wasn't sure if he'd pulled her there or if she'd simply crawled onto him. "I believe they might have been understated. Actually I did sneak outside one night and watch you put the moves on Babs Carstairs out by the pool. I was impressed."

Nothing she could have said could have been more perfectly designed to make desire wilt. "You spied on me and Babs?"

"Just once. Or twice. Hell, Josh, I was thirteen. Curious."

"Jesus." He remembered exactly how far things had gone with Babs out by the pool on one pretty summer night. "Did you see— No, I don't want to know."

"Laura and Kate and I all agreed she was overmammaried."

"Over—" Before he could laugh at the term, he winced. "You *and* Laura *and* Kate. Why didn't you just sell tickets?"

"I believe it's perfectly natural for a younger sister to spy on her older brother."

His eyes glinted. "I'm not your brother."

"From where I'm sitting, I'd say that fact saves our immortal souls."

The glint turned into a grin. "You may be right. I want you, Margo. There are all manner of incredible, nasty, unspeakable things I want to do to you."

"Well." She let out a breath she hadn't realized she'd been holding. "So much for our immortal souls. Listen, I have to say this change is a little abrupt for me."

"You haven't been paying attention."

"Obviously not." She couldn't take her eyes off his. It would be wiser to, she knew. She had survived all the games men and women play by always, without exception, staying in control. Those eyes, gray and cool and confident, warned her that that wouldn't be an option with him. Not for long. "I'm paying attention now, but I'm not ready for the starting gun."

"It went off years ago." His hands skimmed up her sides, brushed her breasts. "I'm way ahead of you."

"I have to decide if I want to catch up." She laughed and scrambled off his lap. "It's just too weird, the whole concept of you and me and sex." Then she rubbed a hand over her heart because it was plunging like a mare in heat. "And it's surprisingly tempting. There was a time, not that long ago, I'd have said what the hell, it'll be fun, and raced you to the bed."

When he rose, she laughed again and put the table between them. "I'm not being coy. I don't believe in it."

"What are you being?"

"Cautious, for once in my life." Suddenly, her eyes were sober, her mouth soft instead of teasing. "You matter too much. And I've just figured out that I matter, too. Not just out here," she said, gesturing toward her face. "Inside. I've got to straighten out my life. I've got to do something with it I can be proud of. I have all these new plans, all these new dreams. I want to make them work. No." She closed her eyes a moment. "I *have* to make them work. To do that I need to take time and effort. Sex is distracting if you do it right." She smiled again. "We would."

He tucked his thumbs in his pockets. "What are you going to do? Take a vow of celibacy?"

Her smile spread slowly. "That's an excellent idea. I can always count on you for a viable solution."

His jaw dropped. "You're kidding."

"I'm perfectly serious." Delighted with both of them, she walked over and patted his cheek. "Okay, I'm celibate until my life is in order and my business is up and running. Thanks for thinking of it."

He circled her throat with his hand, but was more inclined to throttle himself. "I could seduce you in thirty seconds flat."

Now he was getting cocky. "If I let you," she said silkily. "But it's not going to happen until I'm ready."

"And I'm supposed to enter a monastery until you're ready?"

"Your life's your own. You can have anyone you want." She turned to wander back toward the cakes, looked over her shoulder. "Except me."

But the idea didn't sit very well. Nibbling on the cake, she contemplated. "Unless, of course, you'd like to make it a kind of bet."

She was licking those crumbs off her bottom lip on purpose, he thought. He knew when a woman was trying to drive him crazy. "What kind of bet?"

"That I can abstain longer than you. That I can make an adult commitment to control my hormones and seriously pursue a career."

His face bland, he added hot coffee to his cup, then hers. Inside he was snickering. She hadn't a clue how long it would take to open the doors to this shop she was planning. It could be months. She would never last that long, he mused as he lifted his cup, watched her over the rim. He'd see to it.

"How much?"

"Your new car."

He choked on coffee. "My car? My Jag?"

"That's right. I have to sell my car and I don't know when I'll be able to replace it. You succumb first, I get the Jag. Clear title. You ship it to Italy."

"And if you succumb first?" When she gestured, dismissing the possibility, he grinned. "I get your art."

"My street scenes." Her heart actually fluttered at the thought. "All of them?"

"Every last one. Unless you're afraid to risk it."

She lifted her chin, held out a hand. "Done."

He closed his hand over hers, then brought it up, brushed his lips over her wrist, nibbled lightly to her palm.

"Nice try," she murmured, and shook free. "Now I've got business to tend to. I'm going to go sell my car."

"You're not going to take it to a dealer," he objected as she grabbed her bag and jacket. "They'll scalp you."

"Oh, no." She paused at the door, her smile sly and irresistible. "No, they won't."

CHAPTER 8

IT AMAZED MARGO how quickly she got into the spirit. She'd never realized how much fun, how simply exhilarating wheeling and dealing could be. The car started it all.

It hadn't shamed her a bit to use every ounce of charm, all of her sex appeal and generous dollops of femininity, not merely as bargaining chips, but as weapons, God-given and well honed. She was at war.

After choosing the car dealer, she had ambushed her quarry with flattery and smiles, fencing expertly with claims of her inexperience in busi-

ness dealings, her trust in his judgment. She batted her eyes, looked helpless, and slowly, sweetly annihilated him.

And had squeezed lire out of him until he was gasping for breath.

The jeweler, being a woman, had been more of a challenge. Margo had
selected two of her best and most expensive pieces, and after sizing up her
opponent as a clever, hardheaded, unsentimental businesswoman, she had
adopted the same pose.

It had been, she thought, *mano a mano*, female style. They'd negotiated,
argued, scorned each other's offers, insulted one another, then come to
terms each of them could live with.

Now, adding the take from her furs, she had enough ready cash to hold
her more impatient creditors off for a few weeks.

With the breathing room, she buckled down and completed a tentative
cataloging of her possessions, and began to pack them up, knowing the
sooner she thought of them as inventory, the easier it would be. No longer
were they her personal possessions. Now they were business assets.

Each morning she studied the paper for available space to rent. The
prices made her wince and worry and eventually concede that she wouldn't
be able to afford a prime location. Nor would she be able to advertise by
conventional means if she wanted her money to last. Which left her a
second-rate location that she would have to make work, and unconven-
tional means.

Comfortable in leggings and a T-shirt, she stretched out in a chair and
surveyed her living space. Tables had been ruthlessly cleared off. A good
many of them were stacked alongside packing boxes and crates. Her paintings remained on the walls. A symbol, she thought, of what she was risking in so many areas of her life just now.

She'd gone to work elsewhere in the flat as well. Her wardrobe had been
cut down to a quarter of its original size. The other seventy-five percent
was carefully packed away. She'd been merciless in her selections, with an
eye to her new lifestyle rather than sentiment. Not that she intended to
dress down as a merchant. She would dress as she would run her business.
With flair and style and bold pride.

With luck, one of the three locations she had arranged to view that afternoon would be just the one she was looking for.

She was anxious to begin before the press got a firm hold on her situation. There were already dribbles in the papers about La Margo selling her
jewelry to pay her mounting debts. She'd taken to sneaking out of the service entrance to avoid the reporters and paparazzi who so often ambushed
her outside the building.

She'd begun to wonder if she should just give up the flat after all. Kate had been right—trying to keep it was whittling her already meager resources to nothing. If she found a good location for the shop, she could simply move in there. Temporarily.

At least, she thought with a laugh, that way she would have her things around her.

She wished she had Josh to play the idea off of. But he was in Paris. No, she remembered, by now it was Berlin, and after that Stockholm. There was no telling when she would hear from him again, much less see him.

The few days they'd spent together in Milan, that jarring and exciting morning in his suite, were more like a dream now than a memory. She might have wondered if she'd actually ached when he'd kissed her, but whenever she thought of it, she ached again.

He was probably nibbling some Fräulein's ear right now, Margo thought and kicked at the corner of the sofa as she rose. He'd never be able to keep those clever hands of his off a willing female. The jerk.

At least she was going to get a car out of the whole mess. If nothing else, Josh Templeton was a man of his word.

She didn't have time to think about him—swilling beer and tickling some statuesque German goddess. She had to change for her appointments, adopt the appropriate image. As she dressed she practiced the technique she would employ with the Realtor. Picky, she mused, braiding her hair. No enthusiasm.

"Questa camera . . ." A dismissive look, a gesture of the hand. *"Piccola."* Or, it would be too large to suit her needs. She would make unhappy noises as she wandered around and let the Realtor try to convince her. Of course, she would remain unconvinced. She would say the rent was absurd. She would ask to see something else, say she had another appointment in an hour.

She stepped back, studied herself. Yes, the black suit was businesslike but had the flair the Italian eye recognized and appreciated. The smooth French braid was feminine, flattering but not fussy, and the oversized Bandalino bag was tailored like a briefcase.

Odds were, her opponent—and she thought of everyone on the other side of her business deals as opponents now—would have recognized her name. He would certainly recognize her face. So much the better. In all likelihood he'd assume he was meeting a flighty, empty-headed bimbo. And that would give her not only the advantage but the sizzling satisfaction of proving him wrong.

Drawing a long breath, she stared at herself. Margo Sullivan was not a bimbo, she insisted to the reflection. Margo Sullivan was a businesswoman, with brains, ambition, plans, goals, and determination. Margo Sullivan was not a loser. She was a survivor.

She closed her eyes for a moment, struggling to absorb the self-administered pep talk, needing to believe it. Doesn't matter, she thought with an inner quaver, as long as I can make everyone else believe it.

Damned if she wouldn't.

The phone was ringing as she shouldered her bag and headed out. "Just leave your name and a brief message," she told the insistent two-toned bell, "and I won't get back to you."

It was Kate's impatient voice that stopped her.

"Damn it all to hell and back, Margo. Are you ever going to answer this thing? I know you're there. I know you're standing right there sneering at the phone. Pick it up, will you? It's important."

"It's always important," Margo muttered and kept right on sneering.

"Goddamn it, Margo. It's about Laura."

Margo pounced on the phone, jerking the receiver to her ear. "Is she hurt? What's wrong? Was there an accident?"

"No, she's not hurt. Take off your earring, it's clinking on the phone."

Disgusted, Margo worked it off. "If you're yanking my chain just to get me to talk to you—"

"Like I've got nothing better to do at five A.M. on April fifteenth than make crank phone calls. Listen, pal, I haven't slept in twenty-six hours and I've burned off most of my stomach lining with caffeine. Don't start with me."

"You called me, remember? I'm on my way out the door."

"And Laura's on her way to see a lawyer."

"A lawyer? At five A.M.? You said there wasn't an accident."

"She's not literally on her way. She has an appointment at ten. I wouldn't have even known about it, but her lawyer's a client of the firm and he thought I knew. He said he was sorry she was upset, and—"

"Just nail it down, Kate."

"Sorry, I'm strung out. She's divorcing Peter."

"Divorcing?" Since the chair that had been by the phone was now in the inventory section, she sat down abruptly on the floor. "Oh, Christ, Kate, it's not because they fought over me?"

"The world doesn't revolve around you, Margo. Hell, sorry. It's not your fault," she said more gently. "I didn't get much out of her when I went over, but the deciding factor seemed to be that she walked in on him and his secretary. And he wasn't dictating a letter."

"You're kidding. That's so . . ."

"Ordinary?" Kate suggested dryly. "Trite? Disgusting?"

"Yes."

"Well, that sums it up. If it's happened before, she's not saying. But I can tell you she's not giving him another turn at bat. She's dead serious."

"Is she all right?"

"She seems very calm, very civilized. I'm so bogged down here, Margo, I can't work on her. You know how she is when she's really upset."

"Sucks it all in," Margo murmured, jiggling the earring impatiently in her hand. "The kids?"

"I just don't know. If I could get out of here I would. But I've got another nineteen hours before flash point. I'll corner her then."

"I'll be there inside of ten."

"That's what I was hoping you'd say. I'll see you at home."

"I DON'T KNOW why I'm surprised you'd fly six thousand miles for something like this, Margo." Laura competently sewed stars onto Ali's tutu for her daughter's ballet recital. "It's just like you."

"I want to know how you are, Laura. I want to know what's going on."

Margo stopped pacing the sitting room and slapped her hands on her hips. She was past exhaustion and into the floaty stage of endless travel. Ten hours had been typically optimistic. It had taken her closer to fifteen to manage all the connections and layovers. Now, she was cross-eyed with fatigue, and Laura just sat there calmly plying needle and thread.

"Would you put that silly thing down for a minute and talk to me?"

"Ali would be crushed if she heard you call her fairy tutu silly." But her daughter was in bed, Laura thought. Safe and innocent. For the moment. "Sit down, Margo, before you collapse."

"I don't want to sit." If she did, she was certain she would simply fade away.

"I didn't expect you to be so upset. You were hardly fond of Peter."

"I'm fond of you. And I know you, Laura. You're not chucking a ten-year marriage without hurting."

"I'm not hurting. I'm numb. I'm going to stay numb as long as I possibly can." Gently she smoothed a hand over the net of the ballet skirt. "There are two little girls down the hall who need someone in their life to be strong and stable. Margo . . ." She looked up then with baffled eyes. "I don't think he loves them. I don't think he cares at all. I could handle him not loving me. But they're his children." She stroked the tulle again, as if it were her daughter's cheek. "He wanted sons. Ridgeways. Boys to become men and carry on the family name. Well"—she set the skirt aside—"he got daughters."

Margo lighted a cigarette with a quick jerk, made herself sit. "Tell me what happened."

"He stopped loving me. I'm not sure he ever did, really. He wanted an important wife." She moved her shoulders. "He thought he got one. In the past couple of years we began to disagree over quite a lot of things. Or I began to disagree with him out loud. He didn't care for that. Oh, it's no use going over all the details." She waved her hands with self-directed impatience. "Basically we grew apart. He began to spend more time away from home. I thought he was having an affair, but he was so uncharacteristically furious when I accused him, I believed I was wrong."

"But you weren't."

"I'm not sure, about then. It doesn't matter." Laura jerked a shoulder, picked up the tulle again to give herself something to do with her hands. "He hasn't touched me in more than a year."

"A year." It was, perhaps, foolish to be shocked at the idea of marriage without intimacy, but Margo was shocked nonetheless.

"At first, I wanted us to go to a counselor, but he was appalled by the idea. Then I thought I should try some therapy, and he was beyond appalled." Laura managed a quick, thin smile. "It would get out, and then what would people think, what would they say?"

No sex. None. For a year. Margo fought her way past the block and concentrated. "That's just ridiculous."

"Maybe. But I stopped caring. It was easier to stop caring and concentrate on my children, the house. My life."

What life? Margo wanted to ask, but held her tongue.

"But I could see in the last few weeks that it was affecting the children. Ali in particular." Gently, she replaced the tutu, folded her hands in her lap to keep them still. "After you left, I decided we had to straighten things out. We had to fix what was wrong. I went to the penthouse. I thought it would be best if we talked there, away from the children. I was willing to do whatever had to be done to put things back together."

"You were willing," Margo interrupted, leaping up and puffing out an angry stream of smoke. "It sounds to me like—"

"It doesn't matter what it sounds like," Laura said quietly. "It's what is. Anyway, it was late. I'd put the girls to bed first. All the way over I practiced this little speech about how we'd had a decade together, a family, a history."

It made her laugh to think of it now. She rose, deciding she could indulge in a short brandy. As she poured two snifters, she related the rest. "The penthouse was locked, but I have a key. He wasn't in the office." Calmly she handed Margo a glass, sat down again with her own. "I was annoyed at first, thinking he'd gone out for a late dinner meeting or some such thing and I'd geared myself up for nothing. Then I noticed the light under the bedroom door. I nearly knocked. Can you imagine how pathetic the situation was, Margo, that I nearly knocked? Instead, I just opened the door." She took a sip of brandy. "He was having a dinner meeting, all right."

"His secretary?"

Laura gave a snorting laugh. "Like a bad French farce. We have the philandering husband sprawled over the bed with his jazzy redheaded secretary and a bowl of chilled shrimp."

Barely, Margo managed to strangle a giggle. "Shrimp?"

"And what appeared to be a spiced-honey sauce, with a bottle of Dom to wash it down. Enter the unsuspecting, neglected society wife. The tableau freezes. No one speaks, only the strains of *Bolero* can be heard."

"*Bolero*. Oh, Jesus." Her breath hitching, Margo dropped into a chair. "I'm sorry. I'm sorry, I can't help it. I'm too tired to fight back."

"Go ahead and laugh." Laura felt a smile breaking through herself. "It is laughable. Pitifully. The wife says, with incredible and foolish dignity, 'I'm terribly sorry to interrupt your dinner meeting.'"

It was an effort, but Margo managed to wheeze in a breath. "You did not."

"I did. They just goggled at me. I've never seen Peter goggle before. It was almost worth it. The fresh young secretary began to squeak and try to cover herself, and in her rush for modesty upended the shrimp sauce on Peter's crotch."

"Oh. Oh, God."

"It was a moment." Laura heaved a sigh, wondering which of the three of them had felt more ridiculous. "I told them not to get up, I would see myself out. And I left."

"Just like that?"

"Just like that."

"But what does he say? How is he handling it?"

"I have no idea." Those soft gray eyes hardened into a look that was pure Templeton—tough, hot, and stubborn. "I'm not taking his calls. That stupid electric gate of his has finally paid off." As her gentle mouth hardened as well, Margo thought it was like watching silk turn to steel. "He can't get in because I've instructed the staff not to admit him. In any case, he's only tried once."

"You're not going to even talk to him?"

"There's nothing to talk about. I could and did tolerate indifference. I could and did tolerate his utter lack of affection and respect for me and my feelings. But I won't tolerate, not for an instant, his lying and his lack of fidelity. He might think that boinking his secretary is simply his *droit de signor*. He's going to find out different."

"Are you sure it's what you want?"

"It's the way it's going to be. My marriage is over." She looked down into her brandy, saw nothing. "And that's that."

The stubborn streak was classic Templeton, Margo thought. Carefully, she tapped out her cigarette, touched a hand to Laura's rigid one. "Honey, you know it won't be that easy—legally or emotionally."

"I'll do whatever I have to do, but I won't play the easily deceived society wife any longer."

"And the girls?"

"I'll make it up to them." Somehow. Some way. "I'll make it right for them." Little tongues of fear licked at her, and she ignored them. "I can't do anything else."

"All right. I'm behind you all the way. Look, I'm going to go down and scare up some food. Kate's going to be starving when she gets here."

"Kate's not coming here tonight. She always falls into bed for twenty-four hours after the tax deadline."

"She'll be here," Margo promised.

"You'd think I was on my deathbed," Laura muttered. "All right, I'll make sure her room's ready. And yours. We'll put some sandwiches together."

"I'll put some sandwiches together. You worry about the rooms." Which would, Margo thought as she hurried out, give her enough time to pump her mother for information.

She found Ann exactly where she'd expected to, in the kitchen, already arranging cold cuts and raw vegetables.

"I don't have much time," Margo began and headed directly for the coffeepot. "She'll be down in a minute. She's not really all right, is she?"

"She's coping. She won't talk about it, hasn't yet contacted her parents."

"The scum, the slime." Her legs wobbled with fatigue and made it hard to storm around the kitchen, but Margo gave it her best shot. "And that little slut of a secretary putting in overtime." She broke off when she caught her mother's eye. "All right, I wasn't much better when it came to Alain. And maybe believing he was working out a divorce isn't any excuse, but at least his wife's family wasn't cutting my paychecks." She drank the coffee black to fuel her system. "You can lecture me on my sins later. Right now I'm concerned about Laura."

A mother's sharp eye noted the signs of exhaustion and worry. "I'm not going to lecture you. It never did any good when you were a child and it would hardly do any good now. You go your own way, Margo, you always did. But your way has brought you here when a friend needs you."

"Does she? She was always the strong one. The good one," she added with a wry smile. "The kind one."

"Do you think you're the only one who feels despair when the world falls apart around you? Who wants to pull the covers over her head instead of facing tomorrow?"

A quick flare of temper made Ann slam down the loaf of bread. Oh, she was tired, and heartsick, and her emotions were bouncing like a rubber ball from joy that her daughter was home, misery for Laura, and frustration at not knowing what to do for either of them.

"She's afraid and full of guilt and worry. It's only going to get worse for her." She pressed her lips together but couldn't settle herself. "Her home is broken, and whether you can see it or not, so is her heart. It's time you paid back some of what she's always given to you, and help her mend it."

"Why do you think I'm here?" Margo tossed back. "I dropped everything I was doing and flew six thousand miles to help her."

"A noble gesture." Ann's sharp, accusing eyes pinned her daughter. "You've always had a knack for the grand gesture, Margo, but holding fast takes something more. How long will you stay this time? A day, a week? How long before you're too restless to stick it out? Before the effort of caring for someone else becomes an inconvenience? Before you rush back to your glamorous life, where you don't have to think about anyone but yourself?"

"Well." Because her hand was unsteady, Margo set the cup down. "Why don't you get the rest of it out, Mum? Sounds like you've stored plenty."

"Oh, it's easy for you, isn't it, to come and go on a whim? Sending post-cards and presents, as if that made up for your turning your back on every-thing real you've been given."

Ann's own worries acted as an impetus for resentments harbored for years. They spewed out before she could stop them, splattering them both with bitterness.

"You grew up in this house pretending you weren't the daughter of a servant, and Miss Laura treated you always as a sister. Who sent you money after you'd run off? Who used her influence to get you your first photo shoot? Who was there for you, always?" she demanded, stacking slices of bread like an irate cardsharp. "But have you been there for her? These past few years when she's been struggling to hold her family to-gether, when she's been lonely and sad, were you there for her?"

"How could I have known?"

"Because Miss Kate would have told you. And if you hadn't been so wrapped up in Margo Sullivan, you'd have listened."

"I've never been what you wanted," Margo said wearily. "I've never been Laura. And I can't be."

Now guilt layered onto weariness and worry. "No one's asked you to be someone you're not."

"Haven't you, Mum? If I could have been kinder, more generous like Laura, more sensible, more practical like Kate. Do you think I didn't know that, didn't feel that from you every day of my life?"

Shocked and baffled, Ann shook her head. "Maybe if you'd been more satisfied with what you had and what you were, instead of running away from it, you'd have been happier."

"Maybe if you'd ever looked at me and been satisfied with what I was, I wouldn't have run so far, and so fast."

"I won't take the blame for how you've lived your life, Margo."

"No, I'll take it." Why not? she thought. There was so much on her debit side already, a little more would hardly matter. "I'll take the blame and the glory. That way I don't need your approval."

"I've never known you to ask for it." Ann strode out of the room and left Margo to stew.

SHE GAVE IT three days. It was odd. They had never actually lived together in the house as adults. At eighteen Laura had gotten married, Margo had run to Hollywood, and Kate, always struggling to leap over that single year's age difference, had graduated early and bolted to Harvard.

Now they settled in. Kate used the excuse that she didn't have the energy to drive back to her apartment in Monterey, and Margo claimed to be marking time. She decided her mother had been right about some things. Laura was coping. But the difficult situation was only going to get worse. Already visitors were dropping by. Mostly the country club set, Margo noted, sniffing for gossip on the breakup of the Templeton-Ridgeway merger.

One night Margo found Kayla camped outside Laura's bedroom door because she was afraid her mama might go away too.

That was when she stopped believing it would settle down and she would go back to Milan. Her mother was right about something more, she'd decided. It was time for Margo Sullivan to hold fast and to pay back what had been given to her. She called Josh.

"It's six o'clock in the morning," he complained when she tracked him down at Templeton Stockholm. "Don't tell me you've become that monster of civilized society, Margo—the morning person."

"Listen up. I'm at Templeton House."

"That's all right then. It's the shank of the evening there. What do you mean you're at Templeton House?" he demanded when his brain cleared. "What the hell are you doing in California? You're supposed to be putting a business together in Milan."

She took a moment. It would be, she realized, the first time she'd said it aloud. The first time she would acknowledge the loss of one part of her life.

"I'm not going back to Milan. At least not anytime soon." As his voice exploded in her ear with questions, accusations, she watched one dream fade away. She hoped she could replace it with another. "Just be quiet a minute, would you?" she ordered with a snap. "I need you to do something, whatever it is that needs to be done, to have my things shipped here."

"Your things?"

"Most of it's boxed up anyway, but the rest will have to be packed. Templeton must have a service for that kind of thing."

"Sure, but—"

"I'll pay you back, Josh, but I don't know who to call and I just can't handle the extra expense just now. The plane fare cut into my resources."

Typical, Josh thought and jammed a pillow behind his back. Just typical. "Then why the hell did you buy a plane ticket to California?"

"Because Peter was diddling his secretary and Laura's divorcing him."

"You can't just go flying off whenever— What the hell did you say?"

"You heard me. She's filed for divorce. I don't think he's going to fight it, but I can't imagine the whole thing is going to be friendly, either. She's trying to handle too much of it on her own, and I've decided I'm not going to let her."

"Let me talk to her. Put her on."

"She's asleep." If Laura had been wide awake and standing by her side, she wouldn't have handed the phone over. The icy violence in Josh's voice stabbed over the line. "She had another session with the lawyer today, and it upset her. The best solution all around is for me to stay here. I'm going to ask her to help me find the right location for the shop. It'll take some of this off her mind. Laura's always better at worrying about someone else than she is at worrying about herself."

"You're going to stay in California?"

"I won't have to worry about the VAT tax or Italian law, will I?" She felt hateful tears of self-pity sting her eyes and ruthlessly blinked them back. To ensure that her voice remained brisk and steady, she set her teeth. "Speaking of law, can I give you power of attorney, or whatever it's called? I need you to sell my flat, transfer funds, all those little legal details."

Details of what she was planning ran through and boggled his mind. Had he thought *typical*? he mused. Nothing about Margo was ever typical. "I'll draft one up and fax it there. You can sign it, fax it back to me at Templeton Milan. Where the hell is Ridgeway?"

"Rumor is he's still at the penthouse."

"We'll soon fix that."

Personally, she appreciated the cold viciousness in his voice, but . . . "Josh, I'm not sure Laura would want you rousting him out at this point."

"I outrank Laura in the Templeton feeding chain. I'll take care of the shipment as soon as I can. Are there any surprises I should be prepared for?"

Her American Express bill had arrived just before she'd left. She decided he didn't need another shock just then. "No, nothing worth mentioning. I'm sorry to dump this on you, Josh. I mean that, but I don't know how else to stay here with Laura and get this shop up and running before I'm shipped off to debtors' prison."

"Don't worry about it. Chaos is my business." He imagined her leaving everything in that chaos to rush off to support a friend. Loyalty, he thought, was and always had been her most admirable quality. "How are you holding up?"

"I'm good. And still untouched," she added. "Are you alone in that bed?"

"Except for the six members of the all-girl Swedish volleyball team. Helga's got a hell of a spike. Aren't you going to ask what I'm wearing?"

"Black Speedos, sweat, and a big smile."

"How'd you guess? So, what are you wearing?"

Slowly, she ran her tongue around her teeth. "Oh, just this little . . . very little . . . white lace teddy."

"And stiletto heels."

"Naturally. With a pair of sheer hose. They have little pink roses around the tops. It matches the one I'm tucking between my breasts right now. I should add I've just gotten out of the tub. I'm still a little . . . wet."

"Jesus. You're too good at this. I'm hanging up."

Her response was a long, throaty laugh. "I'm going to love driving that Jag. Let me know when to expect the shipment."

When the phone clicked in her ear, she laughed again, turned, and found herself nearly face-to-face with Kate. "How long have you been standing there?"

"Long enough to be confused. Were you just having phone sex with Josh? Our Josh?"

Carelessly, Margo brushed her hair behind her ear. "It was more fore-play really. Why?"

"Okay." She'd have to give that one some thought. "Now what is this about getting a shop up and running?"

"My, my, you do have big ears, don't you?" Margo tugged on them hard enough to make Kate yelp. "Well, sit down. I might as well tell you the master plan."

Kate listened, her only comments the occasional grunt, snort, or mutter. "I suppose you've calculated start-up costs?"

"Ah—"

"Right. And you've looked into licenses, fees, applied for a tax number."

"I have a few details to iron out," Margo muttered. "And it's just like you to toss cold water in my face."

"Gee, and here I thought it was cool common sense."

"Why shouldn't I make a business out of selling my things?" Margo de-manded. "What's wrong with turning humiliation into an adventure? Just because I hadn't thought about applying for some stupid tax number doesn't mean I can't pull this off."

Sitting back, Kate tapped her fingertips together. It wasn't an entirely insane idea, she mused. In fact, it had some solid financial merit. Liquida-tion of assets tied to old-fashioned free enterprise. Kate decided she could help iron out some of the details if Margo was truly set on giving capital-ism a try. It would be risky, certainly, but then Margo had always been one for taking risks.

"You're going to be a shopkeeper?"

Eyes bland, Margo studied her manicure. "I'm thinking of it more as a consultant position."

"Margo Sullivan," Kate marveled, "selling used clothes and knickknacks."

"Objets d'art."

"Whatever." Amused, Kate stretched out her legs, crossed them at the ankles. "It looks like hell has finally frozen over."

CHAPTER 9

MARGO STOOD IN front of the storefront on busy Cannery Row and knew this one was it. The wide display window glinted in the sun and was protected from the elements by a charming little covered veranda. Its door was beveled glass decorated with an etched bouquet of lilies. Old-fashioned brass fittings gleamed. The peaked roof was topped by rows of Spanish tile softened to pink by time and weather.

She could hear the tinny tune from a carousel, the harsh cry of gulls, and the busy chatter of tourists. Scents of cooking from the stands and open-air restaurants of Fisherman's Wharf carried on the strong breeze flying off the water. Bicycles built for two clattered by.

Street traffic was a constant snarl, cars desperately seeking a parking spot they were unlikely to find in this busy tourist haven. Pedestrians strolled along the sidewalks, many with children who were either all eyes and grins or whining crankily.

There was movement everywhere. People and noise and action. The little shops lining the street, the restaurants and attractions, drew them day after day, month after month.

All the other buildings, the narrow storefronts, the empty storage rooms she'd viewed had just been steps, she thought, leading to this.

"It's perfect," she murmured.

"You haven't even been inside," Kate pointed out.

"I know it's perfect. It's mine."

Kate exchanged a look with Laura. She had a pretty good idea what property rented for in this location. If you're going to dream, she thought, dream big. But then, Margo always had.

"The Realtor's probably inside by now." Arriving late was part of Margo's strategy. She didn't want to appear too eager. "Just let me do the talking."

"Let her do the talking," Kate muttered and rolled her eyes at Laura. "We're going to have lunch after this one, right?" She could smell the frying fish and spicy sauces, aromas wafting down from Fisherman's Wharf. Dull, nagging hunger pangs attacked her stomach. "This is the last one before lunch."

"This is the only one." Shoulders squared for battle, Margo stepped up to the door. She had to force herself not to snatch the For Rent sign away. Little frissons of possession were already sprinting along her spine. She didn't question them, or the fact that she had certainly walked past this building countless times before and felt nothing.

She felt it now, and that was enough.

The main room was wide and empty. Scars were dug into the hardwood floor where counters and display cases had been ripped out. The paint had faded from white to something resembling old paste and was pocked with small holes where the previous tenant had hung wares.

But she saw only a lovely archway leading into an adjoining space, the charm of a set of iron tightwinder stairs spiraling toward the second level, the airy, circling balcony. She recognized the signs in herself, the quickening of her pulse, the sharpening of vision. She often felt the same when she walked into Cartier and saw something that seemed to be waiting just for her.

Sensing trouble, Laura put a hand on her arm. "Margo."

"Can't you see it? Can't you just see it?"

"I see it needs a ton of manual labor." Kate wrinkled her nose. The air smelled of . . . incense? Pot? Old candles? "And fumigating."

Ignoring her, Margo walked over to a peeling door and opened it. Inside was a tiny bathroom with an aging pedestal sink and chipped tile. It thrilled her.

"Hello?" The voice echoed down from the second floor, following by the quick tap of high heels on wood. Laura winced.

"Oh, God, not Louisa. Margo, you said your appointment was with a Mr. Newman."

"Well, it was."

The voice called out again, and if there had been anywhere to dive for cover, Laura would have used it.

"Ms. Sullivan, is that you?" The woman appeared at the top of the stairs. She was all in pink from her flowing swing jacket to her clicking heels. Her hair was the careful ash blond that hairdressers often chose to hold off gray, and it was styled ruthlessly into a helmet that curved around pink cheeks. Gold rattled on her wrists, and an enormous sunburst pin exploded over her left breast.

Mid-fifties, Margo estimated with an experienced eye, and holding desperately on to forty. Very decent face-lift, she mused, smiling politely as the woman picked her way down the circling stairs, chattering all the way. Regular aerobic classes to keep her in shape, possibly aided by a tummy tuck and lipo.

". . . just refreshing my memory," Louisa continued, bubbling like a brook. "I haven't been in here for several weeks. Dear Johnny was supposed to show you through, but he had a teeny little accident with his car this morning." When she reached the bottom, slightly out of breath, she offered a hand. "So delighted to meet you. I'm Louisa Metcalf."

"Margo Sullivan."

"Yes, of course you are." Her raisin-colored eyes glinted with interest and carefully applied bronze shadow. "I recognized you right away. I had no idea my one o'clock was *the* Margo Sullivan. And you're just as lovely as all your photographs. They're so often touched up, aren't they? Then you meet someone whose face you've seen just hundreds of times and it's such a disappointment. You've led such an interesting life, haven't you?"

"And it's not over yet," Margo said and had Louisa tittering with laughter.

"Oh, no, indeed. How fortunate to be so young and lovely. I'm sure you can overcome any little setback. You've been in Greece, haven't you?"

"Hello, Louisa."

She turned, laying a hand over her heart. "Why, Laura dear. I didn't see you there. What a delightful surprise."

Knowing the routine, Laura met her halfway and the women exchanged quick air kisses. "You look wonderful."

"Oh, my professional mode." Louisa smoothed her jacket, under which her bosom was heaving happily in anticipation of gossip. "I so enjoy dabbling a few days a week in my little hobby. Real estate takes you into such interesting places, and you meet so many people. With Benedict so busy with his practice and the children grown, I have to have something to do with my time." Those glinting eyes sharpened. "I don't know how you manage, dear, with those two lovely children, all your charity work, the social whirl. I was just telling Barbara—you remember my daughter, Barbara—how amazing I thought you were. Managing all those committees and functions, raising two children. Especially now that you're going through such a trial. Divorce." She whispered it as though it were a dirty word. "Such a heartbreak for everyone involved, isn't it? How are you bearing up, dear?"

"I'm fine." More out of desperation than manners, Laura tugged Kate forward. "This is Kate Powell."

"Nice to meet you."

Kate didn't bother to tell her that they'd met at least half a dozen times before. Women like Louisa Metcalf never remembered her.

"Are you interested in the building, Laura?" she continued. "I understood that the caller was looking to rent, but if you're wanting an investment now that you're on your own, so to speak, this would be perfect for you. A woman alone needs to think about her future, don't you agree? The owner is willing to sell."

"Actually, it's Margo who—"

"Oh, of course. I do beg your pardon." She pivoted toward Margo like a cannon bearing to aim from the top of a tank. "Seeing an old friend again, you understand. And the two of you have been friends for years, haven't you? So nice you can be close by during our Laura's time of trouble. It's a wonderful building, isn't it? A clever location. You wouldn't have

the least trouble finding a suitable tenant. And I can recommend a very reliable management company."

Buy it? To own it. Margo had to swallow the saliva that pooled in her
mouth. Afraid that Louisa might see the territorial light in her eyes, she
turned away and wandered. "I haven't actually decided whether to rent or
buy." She rolled her eyes gleefully at Kate and Laura. "Who were the last
tenants?"

"Oh, well, that was a bit unfortunate. Which is why the owner is considering selling out. It was a New Age shop. I don't understand that business myself, do you? Crystals and odd music and gongs. It came out that
they were also selling drugs." She whispered the last word, as if saying it
might addict her. "Marijuana. Oh, my dear, I hope that doesn't upset you,
with your recent troubles."

Margo sent her an arch look. "Not at all. Perhaps I could see upstairs."

"Certainly. It's quite roomy. It's been used as a little apartment and has
the most adorable doll's house of a kitchen, and of course the view."

She picked her way back up, chattering about the delights of the building while the others trailed after her.

"You can't be serious," Kate hissed, grabbing Margo's arm. "You
couldn't afford the rent in this location, much less the purchase price."

"Just shut up. I'm thinking."

It was hard to think with Louisa's incessant chirping, so Margo shut it
out. Shut out everything but sheer delight. It was roomy, surprisingly so.
And if the banister circling the second level was shaky, so what? And the
pentagram painted on the floor could be removed.

Maybe it was hot as a furnace, and the kitchen alcove was only big
enough for one of the Seven Dwarfs. But there were quaint eyebrow windows peeking out, offering teasing glimpses of the sea.

"It has wonderful potential," Louisa went on. "A bit of cosmetic work,
some pretty paper or paint. Of course you know that property in this area
rents by the square foot." She opened the briefcase she'd left on the narrow
kitchen counter, took out a file. "This building has six hundred and
twenty-eight." She offered papers to Margo. "The owner has kept the rent
very reasonable, considering. Of course, the utility fees are the responsibility of the tenant."

Kate turned on the tap, watched gray water sputter out. "And the repairs?"

"Oh, I'm sure something can be worked out there." Louisa dismissed
Kate with a wave of her hand and a jangle of bracelets. "You'll want to
look over the lease, of course. I don't want to pressure you, but I feel
obliged to let you know we have another interested party coming through

tomorrow. And once it's officially known that the building's for sale, well . . ." She let that lay, smiling. "I believe the asking price is only two hundred seventy-five thousand."

Margo felt her dream pop—an overinflated red balloon. "That's good to know." She managed a shrug, though her shoulders felt weighted. "As I said, I'm not sure if it's just what I'm looking for. I have several properties I'm considering."

Scanning the lease, she saw that Kate—damn her—had been right. Even the rent was well out of her reach. There had to be a way, she thought.

"I'll be in touch within a day or two." She smiled again, politely and dismissively. "Thank you so much, Mrs. Metcalf, for your time."

"Oh, no trouble at all. I so enjoy showing off places. Homes are more fun, of course. You've been living in Europe, haven't you? Terribly exciting for you. If you're thinking of buying a second home here in the area, I have the most fabulous ten-bedroom on Seventeen Mile. An absolute steal. The owners are in the middle of a vicious divorce, and . . . oh." She looked around to make a tittering apology to Laura, but her eyes continued to gleam. "She must have gone back downstairs. I wouldn't want to upset her by talking about divorce. Such a shame about her and Peter, isn't it?"

"Not really," Margo said dryly. "I think he's scum."

"Oh." Her color fluctuated. "You're just being loyal to your old friend, aren't you? Actually, no one could have been more surprised than I was when I heard they had separated. Just the most charming couple. He's so well mannered, so attractive and gentlemanly."

"Well, you know what they say about appearances? They lie. I think I'll just poke around for a bit longer, if you don't mind, Mrs. Metcalf." Firmly, Margo took her arm to lead her back to the stairs. "It might help me make up my mind if I spend a little time alone."

"Of course. Take all the time you like. Just lock the door behind you. I have the key. Oh, and let me give you my card. You be sure to call if you want to breeze through again, or if you'd like to see that wonderful house on Seventeen Mile."

"I certainly will." Margo didn't see either Kate or Laura on the first floor and kept marching Louisa toward the door.

"Oh, do tell Laura good-bye for me, won't you? And her young friend. I'm sure I'll see you and Laura at the club soon."

"Absolutely. 'Bye now. Thank you so much." Margo closed the door with a quick rattle. "And do be a stranger," she muttered. "Okay, where are you two hiding?"

"We're up here," Kate called out. "In the bathroom."

"Jesus, it's really tacky for two grown women to hide in a bathroom."

Once she'd climbed the steps again, she found them. Laura sat on the edge of the old clawfoot tub with Kate facing her from her perch on the john. In any other setting, Margo would have said they were deep in some intense and serious discussion. "I really appreciate you leaving me alone with that nosy magpie."

"You wanted to do the talking," Kate reminded her.

"Nothing really to talk about." Discouraged, Margo joined Laura on the edge of the tub. "I could probably squeeze out the rent, if I didn't eat for the next six months. Which isn't that much of a problem. But I wouldn't have enough left over to handle the start-up costs. I want to buy it," she said with a sigh. "It's exactly what I'm looking for. There's just something about it that tells me I could be happy here."

"Maybe it's the leftover aroma of stale pot."

Margo sent Kate a withering look. "I only smoked it once when I was sixteen. And you had several hits yourself on that memorable evening."

"I didn't inhale," she said with a grin. "That's my story and I'm sticking to it."

"Then explain why you claimed you were doing a *pas de deux* with Baryshnikov."

"I have no recollection of that event—and he told me to call him Misha."

"It's a damn good thing I only wheedled two joints out of Biff." Margo blew out a breath. "Well, this, unfortunately, is reality. I can't afford this place."

"I can," Laura said.

"What do you mean, you can?"

"I mean I can buy it, and I can rent it to you, and we'll be in business."

Margo nearly threw her arms around Laura before sanity, and pride, prevailed. "Oh, no. I'm not starting off this next section of my life that way." She dug in her bag for a cigarette, lighted it with a violent flick. "You're not bailing me out. No one's bailing me out. Not this time."

"Tell her what you told me, Kate, when I suggested it."

"Okay. First I asked her if she was out of her mind. Not that I don't think you couldn't pull off this plan of yours, Margo, but I don't think you can pull it off."

Eyes narrowed, Margo huffed out smoke. "Thanks so much."

"It's an admirable idea," Kate soothed. "But starting a new business is a risky venture at any time, with anyone. The vast majority go tits up in the first year. Basic economics, even if the people have some training and education in retail. Not to mention that Monterey and Carmel are already lousy with gift shops and boutiques. But," Kate continued, holding up a hand before Margo could snarl at her, "some succeed, even thrive. Now, putting your part of it aside for the moment, we look at Laura's current situation. Having been married at the ridiculous age of eighteen, she's never invested on her own. There is the Templeton organization, of course, in which she shares. But she has no personal, individual stocks, bonds, or property beyond her interest in Templeton. As she's just filed for divorce, and is solvent financially, it makes good economic sense for her to seek investments."

"I've never bought anything on my own," Laura interrupted. "Never owned anything that wasn't through the family or with Peter. And when I was looking around this place, I thought, why not? Why shouldn't I buy it? Why shouldn't I take a gamble on myself? On us."

"Because if I screw it up—"

"You won't. You've got something to prove here, don't you, Margo?"

"All right, yes, but it doesn't include taking you down with me."

"Listen to me." Eyes serious and soft, Laura laid a hand on Margo's knee. "All my life I've done what I was told, taken the quiet, well-tended path. Now I'm going to do something just for the hell of it." She felt a giddy little thrill at the thought. "I'm buying this building, Margo, whether you want a piece of it or not."

Margo took a deep gulp, discovered it wasn't pride she was swallowing. It was excitement. "So, how much are you going to gouge out of me for rent?"

THE FIRST SHOCK came at the bank. A cashier's check for ten percent of the asking price was Kate's advice, not only to nail down a contract but to help negotiate that price down by twenty-five thousand.

The money wasn't there.

"There must be some mistake. I should have at least twice this amount liquid."

"Just a moment, please, Mrs. Ridgeway." The teller hurried off while Laura tapped her fingers.

As a sick feeling began to stir in her gut, Margo laid a hand on her shoulder. "Laura, this is a joint account with Peter?"

"Sure. We use it primarily as a checking account, to run the household. I'm taking out less than half, so there shouldn't be a problem. We're a community property state. My lawyer explained all of that."

The vice president of the bank came out into the lobby, shook her hand. "Laura, would you come back to my office for a moment."

"Frank, I'm in kind of a hurry. I just need a cashier's check."

"Just for a moment." He slipped an arm around her shoulders.

Margo gritted her teeth as Laura was guided away. "You know what that bastard did?"

"Yeah. Yeah, I do." Furious, Kate pressed her fingers to her eyes. "I should have thought of it. Christ, I should have known. It's all happened so fast."

"They'd have money scattered around, wouldn't they? In another bank. Stocks, bonds, a portfolio through a broker."

"They'd have to. Laura might have let Peter take over the finances, but neither of them is foolish enough to put all their eggs in one basket. And there's the insurance limit on funds in a bank. This is a drop in the bucket." But she had a sick feeling. "Shit. He never let me near their books. Here she comes," Kate muttered. "Goddamn it, it's all over her face."

"Peter cleaned out the account." Face pale, eyes dazed, Laura headed for the doors. "The morning after I found him in bed with his secretary, he came in here and took out all but a couple of thousand." She had to stop, press a hand to her stomach. "We had started little savings accounts for the girls, so they could put money in themselves. He took that, too. He took their money."

"Let's find a place to sit down," Margo murmured.

"No. No, I have to make calls. I have to contact the broker. I don't even know his name." She covered her face with her hands and tried to breathe. "So stupid. So stupid."

"You're not stupid," Kate said furiously. "We're going home. We'll find the numbers and we'll call. We'll arrange to have the rest of your assets frozen."

There wasn't much to freeze.

"Fifty thousand." Kate sat back, slipped off her reading glasses, and rubbed her eyes. "Well, it was damn generous of him to leave you that much. From what I can figure, that's about five percent of your joint holdings." Thoughtfully, she unrolled her package of Tums. "The good news is he wasn't able to touch your stock in Templeton and he doesn't have any claim on the house."

"Their college funds," Laura said weakly. "He closed Ali's and Kayla's college funds. How could money have meant so much to him?"

"Money's probably only part of it. He's teaching you a lesson." Margo poured another glass of wine. It might help them all to be a little drunk. "And he got away with it because you'd never have thought of doing the same thing. I would have, but I wasn't thinking at all. Maybe your lawyer can get some of it back."

"Odds are it's all tucked away in the Caymans by now." Kate shook her head in disgust. "The way it looks, he's been busily transferring stock and cash and mutuals out of your joint accounts into a personal one for quite a while. He just made a quick final sweep." She bit her tongue before she could chastise Laura for signing anything Peter had handed her. "But you've got the paperwork, copies of the transactions and withdrawals, so you'll be able to fight when you get to court."

Laura sat back, closed her eyes. "I'm not fighting him for money. He can have it. Every lousy penny."

"The hell with that," Margo erupted.

"No, the hell with him. The divorce is going to be hard enough on the girls without the two of us battling over dollars and cents in court. I've still got fifty thousand cash—which is a lot more than most women start with. He can't touch the house because it's in my parents' name."

She picked up her glass but didn't drink. "I'm the one who was stupid enough to sign whatever he put in front of me without questioning him. I deserved to get fleeced."

"You've got the Templeton stock," Kate reminded her. "You could sell part of your shares."

"I'm not touching the family stock. It's a legacy."

"Laura." To calm her, Kate laid a hand on Laura's. "I'm not saying to put the stock on the market. Either Josh or your parents would buy it, or margin you a loan against it until everything's sorted out."

"No." Closing her eyes, Laura willed herself to settle down. "I'm not running to them." She drew in a deep breath and opened her eyes again. "And neither is either of you. I made the mistakes, I'll fix the mistakes. Kate, I need you to figure out how to liquidate enough money for the deposit on the building."

"No way you're going to take more than half of what you have left in cash and buy that place."

She smiled thinly at Margo. "Yes, I am. Oh, yes, I am. I'm still a Templeton. It's time I started to act like one." Before she could change her mind, she picked up the business card Margo had tossed on the table and dialed the phone. "Louisa, it's Laura Templeton. Yes, that's right. I want to make an offer on the building we looked at this afternoon."

When she hung up, she pulled off her wedding and engagement rings. Guilt and liberation twisted inside her. "You're the expert, Margo. How much can I expect to get for these?"

Margo eyed the five-carat round-cut and the band with sparkling channel-set diamonds. At least, she mused, there was some small justice in the world. "Kate, don't worry about liquidating anything. It looks like we got the down payment out of Peter after all."

Later that night Margo sat in her room scribbling figures, drawing rough sketches, making lists. She needed to think about paint and paper and plumbing. The shop space had to be remodeled to include a dressing room, and that meant carpenters.

She could move in on the top floor as it was, which would save her the drive down to Monterey every day to check on progress. In fact, she could cut corners if she painted it herself rather than hiring professionals.

How hard could it be to roll paint on a wall?

"Yes, come in," she called at the knock on her door and wondered if carpenters charged by the hour or the job.

"Margo?"

Distracted, she glanced up, blinked at her mother. "Oh. I thought it was one of the girls."

"It's nearly midnight. They're sleeping."

"I lost track of the time." She pushed at the papers scattered over the bed.

"You always did. Daydreaming." Ann skimmed her gaze over the papers, amused at the numbers her daughter had added and subtracted. It had taken bribes and threats and shouts to get Margo to do the simplest arithmetic homework when she was a child. "You forgot to carry the five," Ann said.

"Oh. Well." Margo shoved the paper aside. "I really need one of those little calculators Kate's always got in her pocket."

"I was talking to Miss Kate before she left. She said you're going into business."

"And that's laughable for someone who doesn't remember to carry the five." Margo pushed herself off the bed and picked up the wineglass she'd brought up with her. "Would you like a drink, Mum, or are you still on duty?"

Saying nothing, Ann moved into the adjoining bath and came out with a tumbler. She poured wine. "Miss Kate thinks you've thought it through fairly well, and though the odds are against you, it may work."

"Kate's always so blindly optimistic."

"She's a sensible woman, and she's given me fine financial advice over the years."

"Kate's your accountant?" With a little laugh, Margo sat again. "I should have known."

"You'd be wise to use her services if you go through with this business of yours."

"I'm going through with this business of mine." Prepared to see doubt and derision on her mother's face, Margo flicked her eyes up. "Number one, I don't have many options. Number two, selling things people don't need is what I do best. And number three, Laura's counting on me."

"Those are three good reasons." There was nothing on Ann's face but a small, enigmatic smile. "Miss Laura is footing the bill."

"I didn't ask her," Margo said, stung. "I didn't want her to. She got the idea in her head to buy the building, and there was no shaking it out." When Ann remained silent, Margo crumpled up a sheet of paper and heaved it. "Damn it, I'm putting everything I have into this. Everything I own, everything I worked for. It's not a lot of cash, but it's everything I have."

"Money's not so important as time and effort."

"It's pretty damn important right now. We don't have a lot to start with."

Nodding as she wandered about, looking for something to straighten, Ann considered. "Miss Kate told me what Mr. Ridgeway has done." Ann took a long, deep gulp of wine. "The cold, blackhearted bastard should rot in everlasting hell. Please God."

With a laugh, Margo lifted her glass. "Finally, something we can agree on. I'll drink to it."

"Miss Laura believes in you, and Miss Kate, too, in her fashion."

"But you don't," Margo countered.

"I know you—you'll make some fancy place out of it, where people with no sense at all will come and toss their money around."

"That's the idea. I've even got a name for it. 'Pretenses.'" Margo's laugh was quick and amused. "It suits me, doesn't it?"

"That it does. You're doing this here in California to be with Miss Laura."

"She needs me."

"Yes, she does." Ann looked down into her glass. "I said some things the night you came back that I'm sorry for. I was hard on you, maybe I've always been. But you were wrong when you said I wanted you to be like Miss Laura or Miss Kate. Perhaps I wanted you to be what I could understand, and you couldn't do that."

"We were both tired and upset." Margo shifted on the bed, not quite sure how to handle an apology from her mother. "I don't expect you to understand this whole idea about a shop, but I hope you'll believe I'm going to try to make something real out of it."

"Your aunt ran a trinket shop in Cork. You've some merchant in your blood." Ann moved her shoulders, her decision made. "It will cost considerable, I imagine."

In agreement, Margo indicated her papers. "I just have to rob Peter to pay Paul for a while. It would help if I could sell my soul. If I still have one to sell."

"I'd feel better if you kept it." Ann reached into the pocket of her skirt, took out an envelope. "Use this instead."

Curious, Margo took the envelope, opened it, then dropped it on the bed as if it had sprouted fangs and bitten her. "It's a brokerage account."

"That's right. Miss Kate recommended the firm. Very conservative investments, as I prefer. But they've done well enough."

"It's almost two hundred thousand dollars. I won't take your savings. I can do this on my own."

"I'm pleased to hear you say so, but it's not my savings in there. It's yours."

"I don't have any savings. Hasn't that been the problem all along?"

"You could never hold on to a penny in a clutched fist. You sent me money, and I banked it for you."

A little amazed, Margo stared down at the brokerage statement. Had she sent so much, had so much to send? It had seemed so little at the time. "I sent the money for you."

"I had no need for it, did I?" Brow arched, Ann angled her head. It pleased her to see the pride in her daughter's face. "I have a good job, a fine roof over my head, enough for a nice vacation twice a year because Miss Laura insists I need it. So the money you sent I banked. And there it is."

Ann took another sip of wine because that wasn't how she'd meant to say it. "Listen to me, Margo, for once. The fact that you did send the money was appreciated. Perhaps I'd have gotten sick and unable to work and needed it. But that didn't happen. Sending it was a loving thing to do."

"No, it wasn't." It shamed her as much to know it as to admit it. "I did it out of pride. I did it to show you I was successful, important. That you were wrong about me."

Understanding, Ann inclined her head. "There's not so much of a difference, and the result's the same. It was your money, and it still is. I had the comfort that you thought to send it, that you had it to send. You'd have frittered it away if you hadn't passed it to me, so we've done each other a favor." She reached out to stroke Margo's hair, then, faintly embarrassed by the show of affection, dropped her hand back to her side. "Now take it and do something with it."

When Margo said nothing, Ann clucked her tongue. She set down her glass, then cupped Margo's chin in her palm. "Why are you so contrary, girl? Did you earn the money with honest work or not?"

"Yes, but—"

"Do what your mum tells you for once. You might be surprised to find she's right. Go into this business venture on equal terms with Miss Laura, and take pride in that. Now clean up this mess you've made before you go to bed."

"Mum." Margo picked up the papers as her mother paused at the door. "Why didn't you send this to me in Milan when you knew I was scraping bottom?"

"Because you weren't ready for it. Be sure you are now."

CHAPTER 10

MINE. HOLDING OUT her arms, Margo circled the empty main room of the shop on Cannery Row. Technically it wasn't hers quite yet. Settlement was still two weeks away, but the offer had been accepted, the contract signed. And the loan, with the Templeton name behind it, had gone off without a hitch.

She'd already had a contractor in to discuss alterations. It was going to cost big, and in her new frugal fashion she had indeed decided to do the simple cosmetic improvements herself. Research was under way on the rental of floor sanders, the purchase of caulking guns. She'd even looked into something wonderful called a paint sprayer. More coverage, faster. More efficient.

And the building wouldn't actually be hers, she reminded herself. It would be theirs. Hers, Laura's, and the bank's. But in two weeks' time, she would be sleeping in that little room upstairs. In a sleeping bag if need be.

Then by midsummer, the doors of Pretenses would open.

And the rest, she thought with a laugh, would be history.

She turned at the tap on the glass and saw Kate.

"Hey, open up, will you? I'm on my lunch hour. Thought I'd find you here gloating," she said when Margo opened the door. "It still smells," she added after a testing sniff.

"What do you want, Kate? I'm busy."

Kate studied the clipboard and the pocket calculator on the floor. "Did you figure out how to work that thing?"

"You don't have to be a CPA to use a calculator."

"I meant the clipboard."

"Ha ha."

"You know, the place grows on you." Hands tucked in her trouser pockets, Kate wandered. "It's a nice busy area, too. Should pull in some walk-in traffic. And people on vacation are always buying things they don't have any use for. The secondhand clothes, though. Everything's going to be a size eight."

"I've already thought of that. I'm working on some other stock. I know a lot of people who ditch their wardrobes every year."

"Smart people buy classics—seasonless classics—then they don't have to worry."

"How many navy blue blazers do you own, Kate?"

"Half a dozen," she said and grinned, then thumbed a Tums out of the roll in her pocket. Her idea of lunch. "But that's just me. Here's the deal, Margo. I want in."

"In what?"

"In on the building." She popped the antacid, crunched it. "I've got some money to invest, and I don't see why you and Laura should have all the fun."

"We don't need a partner."

"Sure you do. You need someone who knows the difference between black ink and red." Bending down, she scooped up the calculator and began to run figures. "You and Laura put in twelve-five apiece, cash. Now you'll have the settlement costs, points, insurance, taxes. Which should bring it up to somewhere around, oh, eighteen each, which makes it thirty-six." Taking glasses out of her breast pocket, she put them on as she continued to work. "Divide that by three, and it makes twelve each, which is less than you've already shelled out."

She paced as she cleared figures, added more. "Now, you've got repairs, remodeling, maintenance, utilities, business license fees, more taxes, book-keeping—I can set the books up for you, but I don't have time to take on another client right now so you'll have to hire someone or learn to add."

"I can already add," Margo said, stung.

Kate merely took out a small electronic memo and entered a reminder to herself to earmark time to give Margo a course in basic bookkeeping. The cellular phone in her briefcase rang, and she ignored it. Her service would have to deal with that until her current business was concluded.

"There's the overhead for shopping bags, tissue paper, boxes, cash register tape," she continued. "That'll bump things back up into six figures in no time. You'll have fees to the credit card companies since your clientele will be using primarily plastic." Tipping the glasses down, she peered at Margo over the tops. "You do intend to accept all major credit cards, don't you?"

"I—"

"See, you need me." Satisfied, she bumped up the glasses again. No joint venture between Laura and Margo was going to exclude her, no matter how many funds she had to juggle. "Of course, I'll just be a silent partner, as I'm the only one of the three of us who has a real job."

Margo narrowed her eyes. "How silent?"

"Oh, just a peep now and then." All the practicalities were already ordered in her tidy mind. "You'll have to figure out how and when to replace your stock once it starts to sell, what your markup percentage needs to be to ensure your profit margin. Oh, then there's legal fees. But we can talk Josh into handling that. How did you get him to let you use his Jag? That is his new Jag out front, isn't it?"

Margo's expression turned smug. "You could say I'm test-driving it."

Lifting her brows, Kate slipped her glasses off and back into her pocket. "Are you test-driving him?"

"Not yet."

"Interesting. I'll write you a check for the twelve thousand. We'll have a partnership agreement drawn up."

"A partnership agreement."

"Jesus, you do need me." She caught Margo by the shoulders and kissed her dead on the lips. "The three of us love each other, trust each other. But you've got to make a business legal. Right now the stock is all yours, but—"

"Laura's added to it," Margo interrupted, and wicked humor glinted. "We're selling everything in Peter's office."

"Good start. How's she holding up?"

"Pretty well. She's worried about Ali. The kid took it hard when Peter didn't show up for her ballet recital. Word is he's in Aruba."

"I hope he drowns. Nope, I hope he gets eaten by sharks and then drowns. I'll get over to the house this weekend and spend some time with the girls." She took out a check, already written and signed. "There you go, partner. I've got to get back."

"We haven't cleared this with Laura."

"I did," Kate said breezily, as she opened the door and plowed into Josh. "Hi." She kissed him. "Bye."

"Nice to see you too," he called after her, then cautiously closed the door.

Laura had warned him not to expect much. It was a good thing. "Have you and Kate been smoking grass in here?"

"That's all she ever does on her lunch hour. We really have to get her into a program." Thrilled with herself, Margo spread her arms. "So, what do you think?"

"Uh-huh. It's a building, all right."

"Josh."

"Give me a minute." He walked past her into the adjoining room, came back, looked into the bath, gazed up the pretty, and potentially lethal, staircase. He wiggled the banister, winced. "Want a lawyer?"

"We're going to have that fixed."

"I don't suppose it occurred to you that sometimes dipping your toe in is smarter than diving headfirst."

"It's not as much fun."

"Well, duchess, I'm sure you could have done worse." He walked over, lifted her pouting face to his. "Let's just get this out of the way, shall we? I've been thinking about it across two continents."

He pulled her close, covered her mouth greedily with his. After a moment of token disinterest, she let herself melt into a kiss that tasted of frustrated lust. So unexpected. So thrilling, the way his mouth fit on hers, the way all those hard lines and planes of his body met and meshed so perfectly with the curves of hers.

It didn't give her time to think whether it was simply that she had missed that glorious sensation of being held by a man, or if it was Josh. But because it was Josh, she needed to think.

"I don't know how I missed how potent you were all these years." She drew away, flashed a quick, teasing smile.

His system was straining like an engine revved too high. "That was just a free sample. Come back here and we'll go for the full treatment."

"I think we'll take it in stages." She walked away, opened her bag, and took out a pack of cigarettes. Her elegant case was already boxed into inventory. "I'm learning to be a cautious woman."

"Cautious." He scanned the room again. "Which is how you got from renting a little shop in Milan to clear your debts and make a reasonable living to buying a building on Cannery Row and adding to those debts."

"Well, I can't change overnight, can I?" She eyed him through a haze of smoke. "You're not going to get all lawyerly on me, are you, Josh?"

"Actually I am." He picked up the briefcase he'd set aside, opened it. "I have some papers for you." He looked around for a place to sit and settled on the bottom step of the staircase. "Come here. Come here," he repeated and patted the narrow space beside him. "I can manage to keep my hands off you."

She picked up a little tin ashtray and joined him. "I'm getting good at papers. I'm thinking of buying a file cabinet."

He didn't sigh. It wouldn't have made any difference. "Is your Italian good enough to wade through this?"

She frowned at the papers he offered. "It's a contract of sale on my flat."

Emotions whirled up inside her, regret warring with relief. "You work fast," she murmured.

"It's a very decent offer." He tucked her hair behind her ear. "Are you sure it's what you want?"

"It's the way it is. Reality doesn't always chew well, but I'm trying to acquire a taste." She closed her eyes and leaned her head on his shoulder. "Just let me feel sorry for myself a minute."

"You're entitled."

"Self-pity's a bad habit of mine. It's hard to shake. Damn it, Josh, I loved that place. Sometimes I'd just stand on the terrace and think: Look where you are, Margo. Look who you are."

"Well, now you're someplace else." It wasn't sympathy she needed, he decided, but a good boot in the butt. "And you look the same to me."

"It's not the same. It's never going to be the same again."

"Toughen up, Margo. You're starting to wallow in it."

She jerked up. "Easy for you to say. Joshua Conway Templeton, the bright star of the Templeton empire. You never lost anything. You never groped your way sweating to get a grip on something everyone told you you couldn't have. No one ever told you you couldn't have anything and everything you wanted."

"That's the breaks, isn't it?" he said easily. "You played, duchess, and you lost. Whining about it isn't going to change a thing, and it's very unattractive."

"Thanks so much for your support." Fuming, she snatched the contract out of his hand. "When do I get the money?"

"There's time, and there's Italian time. If you're lucky, you may have it settled in sixty days. The bottom line's on the next page."

He watched her flip it over. Her eyes were hot as they skimmed down, the heat clouded with distress. "That's it?"

"You didn't have a lot of equity built up. The bank gets theirs first, then the government takes its share."

"It's better than a stick in the eye," she muttered. "Barely."

"I drew on your account to square your American Express bill. I don't suppose it occurred to you to fly back here coach." When she only stared coolly, he shook his head. "I don't know why I said that. You're back under the max on your Visa card, but I'd go easy on it. After you distribute the net from the sale of the flat, you'll only be about a hundred and fifty thousand in the hole, excluding interest and penalties."

"Pin money," she said dryly.

"You shouldn't plan on buying any pins for a while. Now, as your representative, I'm willing to clear your debts, and assist you in dealing with any you incur while initiating your business. You got a name for this place yet?"

"Pretenses," she said between her teeth as he flipped out more papers.

"Perfect. I've drawn up the necessary agreements."

"Have you?" she said slowly. "In triplicate?"

Warned by the tone, he looked up, met her icy stare equally. "Naturally."

"And just what would I be agreeing to, Counselor Templeton?"

"To pay back this personal loan in regular installments beginning six months after the date of signing. That gives you some breathing space. You also agree to live within your means during the term of the loan."

"I see. And what are my means, in your legal opinion?"

"I've worked up a budget for personal expenses. Food, lodging, medical."

"A budget?"

He'd expected an explosion. Even, perversely, hoped for one. Margo's tantrums were always so . . . stimulating. It didn't appear that he was going to be disappointed.

"A budget?" she repeated, storming to him. "Of all the unbelievable, bloody nerve. You arrogant son of a bitch. Do you think I'm going to stand here and let you treat me like some sort of brainless bimbo who needs to be told how much she can spend on face powder?"

"Face powder." Deliberately, he scanned the papers, took a pen out of his pocket, and made a quick note. "That would come under 'Miscellaneous Luxuries.' I think I've been very generous there. Now, as to your clothing allowance—"

"Allowance!" She used both hands to shove him back a step. "Just let me tell you what you can do with your fucking allowance."

"Careful, duchess." He brushed the front of his shirt. "Turnbill and Asser."

The strangled sound in her throat was the best she could do. If there had been anything, anything at all to throw, she'd have heaved it at his head. "I'd rather be picked apart, alive, by vultures than let you handle my money."

"You don't have any money," he began, but she barreled on as she whirled around the room. Watching her, he all but salivated.

"I'd rather be gang-raped by midgets, staked naked to a wasp nest, be force-fed garden slugs."

"Go three weeks without a manicure?" he put in and watched her hands curl into claws. "You go after my face with those, I'll have to hurt you."

"Oh, I hate you."

"No, you don't." He moved very fast. One instant he was leaning lazily on the wobbly banister and the next he'd flashed out, grabbed her. He took a moment to enjoy the dark fury on her face, the lethal glint in her eyes, before he crushed her snarling mouth under his. It was like kissing a lightning bolt—that heat, the jolt of deadly power, the sizzling sting of fury.

He knew that when he finally got her into bed, it would be a full-blown storm.

She didn't resist. That would have given him too much satisfaction. Instead, she met him force for force and pleased herself. Until they both stepped back, gasping.

"I can enjoy that and still hate you." She tossed her hair back. "And I can make you pay for it."

Maybe she could. There were women in the world who had the innate gift of knowing just how to make a man suffer and burn and beg. All of them could have taken lessons from Margo Sullivan. But he wasn't fool enough to let her know it. He walked back to the stairs, picked up the papers.

"Just so we know where we stand, darling."

"I'll tell you just where we stand, *darling*. I don't need your insulting offer. I'm running my life my way."

"And that's been such a rousing success so far."

"I know what I'm doing. Take that ridiculous smirk off your face."

"I can't. It sticks there every time you say you know what you're doing." But he tucked all the papers back in his briefcase, closed it. "I'll say this, I don't think it's an entirely moronic idea—this place."

"Well, I'll sleep easy now, knowing I have your approval."

"Approval's a little strong. It's more like hopeful resignation." He gave the banister a last wiggle. "But I believe in you, Margo."

Temper died into confusion. "Damn you, Josh. I can't keep up with you."

"Good." He strolled over, flicked a finger down her cheek. "I think you're going to make something out of this shop that'll surprise everyone. Especially you." He leaned down, and when he kissed her this time it was light and friendly. "Got cab fare?"

"Excuse me?"

Grinning, he pulled keys out of his pocket. "Fortunately, I had a spare set to the Jag. Don't work too late, duchess."

She didn't smile until he was well out of sight. Then she gathered up her bag, her clipboard. She was going to put her newly healed Visa card to use and buy a paint sprayer.

IT TOOK JOSH less than two weeks at Templeton Monterey to fine-tune his strategy for dealing with Peter Ridgeway. He had already made it clear with a single phone call from Stockholm that it would be best for his brother-in-law, personally and professionally, to take a brief leave of absence from Templeton.

Until, as he'd put it, all reason and bonhomie, they'd gotten this little domestic matter ironed out.

He had always steered clear of his sister's marriage. As a bachelor, he hardly felt that he qualified to hand out marital advice. And as he adored his sister, and had mildly despised her husband, he'd also had to consider the indisputable fact that his advice would have been heavily one-sided.

Since Peter had always performed well as a Templeton executive, there'd been no cause for complaint there. He was, perhaps, a bit rigid in his view of hotel management, more than a bit distant from the staff and the day-to-day problems and triumphs, but he'd had a fine hand with the corporate groups and foreign businesses that poured money into Templeton coffers.

Still, there came a time when professional efficiency had to be weighed against personal disgust. Because nobody, but nobody, messed with Joshua Templeton's family and walked away whole.

He'd considered taking the corporate route, simply amputating Peter from any connection with Templeton hotels and using his connections and influence to see to it that the son of a bitch never managed so much as a roadside motel in Kansas.

But that was so easy, so . . . bloodless.

He agreed with Kate that the sensible route, and the most straightforward, was to—in Kate's words—drag Ridgeway's sorry flat ass into court. Josh knew a half a dozen top family lawyers who would rub their hands together in glee at the prospect of nailing the greedy, adulterous husband who had cleaned out his own daughters' little savings accounts.

Oh, that would be sweet, Josh mused as he drew in the early-morning scents of sea and oleander blossoms. But it would also be a painful and public humiliation for Laura. And again, he thought, bloodless. .

Still, such matters were best handled in a civilized fashion. Josh decided the most civilized place to balance the scales was the country club. So he waited, patient as a cat, for Peter to return to California.

Peter accepted his invitation for a morning set of tennis without hesitation. Josh had expected no less. He imagined Peter calculated that being seen exchanging lobs with his brother-in-law would quell some of the rumors over Peter's position with Templeton.

Josh was happy to oblige him.

Golf was Peter's game, but he considered himself a fair hand at the net. He'd dressed for the match in spotless whites, his shorts pressed with lethal pleats. Josh wore a similar uniform, if slightly less formal, with the addition of a Dodgers fielder's cap to shade his eyes from the dazzling morning sun.

Later, Minn Whiley and DeLoris Solmes, who'd been playing their regular Tuesday morning set on the adjoining court, would sip after-match mimosas and comment on what a picture the men had made, golden and bronzed and fit, muscular legs pumping as they thwacked the bright yellow ball back and forth.

Of course, Minn would tell Sarah Metzenbaugh after she joined them for a steam, that had been before The Incident.

"I don't take time to do this often enough," Peter commented as they unzipped their rackets. "Eighteen holes of golf twice a week is all I can squeeze in."

"All work and no play," Josh said affably, and didn't miss Peter's smirk of disdain. He knew exactly what Ridgeway thought of him. The pampered golden boy who spent all his time jetting from party to party. "I feel deprived if I don't get at least one decent set in every morning."

Taking his time, Josh set out a bottle of Evian. "I'm glad you could manage to meet me. I'm sure that between us we can straighten this uncomfortable business out. You're staying at the resort now that you're back from Aruba?"

"It seemed best. I'd hoped that if I gave Laura a little time and space she'd see reason. Women." He spread his elegant hands, uncluttered now by the gold band of his marriage. "Difficult creatures."

"Tell me about it. Let's warm up." Josh took his place behind the line, waited for Peter to set. "Volley for serve," he called out and hit the ball easily. "How was Aruba?"

"Restful." Peter returned, pacing himself. "Our hotel there has a few kinks. It should be looked into."

"Really?" Josh had done a complete check on it less than eight months before and knew it ran brilliantly. "I'll make a note of that." Deliberately he fumbled a backhand, sending it wide of the line. "Rusty," he said with a shake of his head. "Your serve. Tell me, Peter, do you plan to contest the divorce?"

"If Laura insists on going through with it, I hardly see the point. It would only add fuel to the gossip. She's dissatisfied with my responsibilities to Templeton. A woman like Laura doesn't understand the demands of business."

"Or a man's relationship with his secretary." Teeth flashing in a feral grin, Josh sent the ball whizzing by Peter's ear.

"She misinterpreted a situation. My point." Testing a fresh ball, Peter shook his head. "Frankly, Josh, she'd become unreasonably jealous over the time it was necessary for me to spend at the office. I'm sure you're aware of the recent influx of conventions, and the ten-day visit last month of Lord and Lady Wilhelm. They took two floors and the presidential suite. We couldn't offer them less than perfection."

"Naturally not. And Laura didn't understand the pressure you were under to deliver." She'd only been nursed at the breast of the grande dame of hoteliers.

"Exactly." Puffing a little as Josh mercilessly worked him cross court, Peter missed the return. "It only got worse when that ridiculous, foul-mouthed Margo showed up on the doorstep. Naturally, Laura would take her in without a thought to the consequences."

"Softhearted, our Laura," Josh said easily, and let the conversation lag until he'd taken the first set 5–3.

"It wasn't exactly gallant, old man, cleaning out the bank accounts."

Peter's lips hardened. He'd expected Laura to have more pride than to go whining to her brother. "On my lawyer's advice. Simple self-preservation, as she had no sense about finances. The move has certainly been justified now that she's proved her lack of sense by going into partnership with Margo Sullivan. Shopkeepers, for God's sake."

"As bad as innkeepers," Josh murmured.

"What was that?"

"I said who knows what puts ideas in a woman's head."

"She'll have lost her capital within six months—if Margo doesn't abscond with it before that. You should have tried to talk her out of the whole insane notion."

"Oh, who listens to me?" He thought about letting Peter win the second set, then decided he was bored and wanted it over. He played it out for a while and, just to make it interesting, allowed Peter to break his serve.

"Bad luck." The pleasure of beating his brother-in-law at his own game pumped through Peter's blood like fine wine. "You'll have to work on your backhand."

"Mmm." Josh jogged to the sideline, mopped his face, glugged down Evian. As he recapped the bottle, he flashed a smile toward the women in the next court. He was darkly pleased at the idea of an audience for the show he had in mind. "Oh, before I forget, I've been doing some spot-checking at the hotel. There's been an unusual number of staff turnovers in the last eighteen months."

Peter arched a brow. "It isn't necessary for you to involve yourself with Templeton Monterey, or the resort. That's my territory."

"Oh, don't mean to trespass, but I was here, and you weren't." He tossed his towel aside, plunked the plastic bottle onto it, then went back behind the net. "It's odd, though. Templeton has a tradition of long-term employee loyalty."

Interfering bastard, pampered fool, Peter thought, carefully controlling his temper as he walked in the opposite direction. "As you can see if you read the reports, lower management made several errors of judgment in hiring. Weeding out was necessary to continue our standard of service and appearance."

"I'm sure you're right."

"I'll be back at the helm tomorrow, so there's no need to concern yourself."

"Not concerned at all. Just curious. Your serve, isn't it?" Josh's smile was as lazy as a nap in a hammock.

They resumed play. Peter faulted his first serve, then bore down on his irritation and slammed the next cleanly. Biding his time, Josh entertained himself by bouncing Peter back and forth across the court, forcing him to dig and pump. Barely winded himself, he kept up a steady flow of conversation as he took the next game, forty-love.

"I noticed a few other things while I was fiddling around. Your expense account, for instance. Seventy-five thousand in the last five months for client entertainment."

Sweat dripped into Peter's eyes, infuriating him. "My expense account records have never been questioned in the fifteen years I've worked for Templeton."

"Of course not." All easy smiles, Josh gathered balls in preparation for the next game. "You've been married to my sister for two-thirds of that time. Oh, and there was that bonus to your secretary." Idly, he bounced a ball on the heart of his racket. "The one you were fucking. Ten thousand's very generous. She must make a hell of a cup of coffee."

Stopping, bending with his hands on his knees to catch his breath, Peter squinted over the net. "Bonuses and financial incentives are Templeton policy. And I don't appreciate your innuendos."

"That wasn't an innuendo, Peter. Listen up. It was a statement."

"And a pathetically hypocritical one coming from you. Everyone knows how you spend your time, and the family money. Cars and women and gambling."

"You're right about that." With a friendly smile, Josh stepped behind the serving line, bounced the ball lightly. "And you could say it was hypocritical of me even to mention it." He tossed the ball up as if to serve, then caught it, scratched his head. "Except for one little detail. No, no, it would be two really minor details. One, it's my money, and two, I'm not married."

He tossed the ball up, swung and served an ace. Straight into Peter's nose. As Peter dropped to his knees, blood gushing out from between his fingers, Josh strolled over, twirling his racket.

"And three, it's my sister you're fucking with."

"You son of a bitch." Peter's voice was muffled and thick and breathless with pain. "You crazy bastard, you've broken my nose."

"Be grateful I didn't aim for your balls." Crouching down, Josh jerked Peter up by the collar of his blood-splattered Polo. "Now listen to me," he murmured while the women on the next court squealed and shouted for the tennis pro. "And listen carefully because I'm only going to say this once."

There were stars wheeling in front of Peter's eyes, nausea welling in his stomach. "Get your damn hands off of me."

"You're not listening," Josh said quietly. "And you really want to pay close attention here. Don't you even speak my sister's name in public. If I decide you've so much as had a thought about her I don't like, you'll pay with more than your nose. And if you ever talk about Margo again the way you've talked about her to me, I'll twist off your nuts and feed them to you."

"I'll sue you, you bastard." Pain radiated through his face like sunbursts; humiliation darted after it. "I'll sue you for assault."

"Oh, please do. Meanwhile, I suggest you take another trip. Go back to Aruba, or try St. Bart's, or go to hell. But I don't want to see you anywhere near me or mine." He let Peter go in disgust and as an afterthought wiped his blood-smeared hand on the front of Peter's shirt. "Oh, and by the way, you're fired. That's game, set, and fucking match."

Well satisfied with the morning's work, he decided to treat himself to a steam.

CHAPTER 11

MIRACLES COULD HAPPEN, Margo thought. They only took six weeks, aching muscles, and somewhere in the neighborhood of three hundred and fifty thousand dollars to create.

Six weeks before, she had become the official one-third owner of the empty building on Cannery Row. Immediately after glasses of Templeton sparkling wine had been passed around, she'd rolled up her sleeves.

It was a new experience, dealing with contractors, surrounding herself with the sounds of saws and hammers and men with tool belts. She spent nearly every waking moment of those weeks in the shop or on shop business. The clerks at the supply stores began to weep with joy when she walked through the door. Her carpenters learned to tolerate her.

She debated paint samples with Laura, agonized over the choice between Dusty Rose and Desert Mauve until the slight variance in shades became a decision of monumental proportion. Recessed lighting became an obsession for days. She learned the joy and terror of hardware, spending hours picking through hinges and drawer pulls the way she had once perused the jewelry displays at Tiffany.

She painted, learning to love and despise the eccentricities of her variable-speed Sears-brand paint sprayer. Growing neurotically possessive, she refused to allow Kate or Laura to try their hand with it. And once after a particularly long session, she jumped at the reflection in the mirror.

Margo Sullivan, the face that launched a million bottles of alpha hydroxy, stared back, her glorious hair bundled messily under a dirty white cap, her cheeks flecked with deep-rose freckles, her eyes naked and a little wild.

She didn't know whether to shudder or scream.

But the shock sent her straight into the clawfoot tub for a hot, frothy soak in sea salts and urged her to give herself a full treatment—facial, hot oil, manicure, just to prove she hadn't completely lost her mind.

Now, after six weeks of insanity, she had begun to believe that dreams could be made. The floors gleamed, sanded smooth and slicked with three satiny coats of varnish. The walls, her personal pride and joy, were a soft, warm rose. Windows she'd washed herself in her mother's secret solution that relied heavily on vinegar and elbow grease, sparkled in their frame of new trim. The iron stairs and circling banisters had been securely bolted and shimmered with fresh gilt.

Tiles in both bathrooms had been regrouted and ruthlessly scrubbed and were now accented with fancy fingertip towels with lace edging.

Everything was rose and gold and fresh.

"It's like Dorian Gray," Margo commented. She and Laura were huddled in the sitting area of the main showroom, struggling to price the contents of a crate.

"It is?"

"Yeah. The shop keeps getting prettier and shinier." She pinched her tired cheeks and laughed. "And I'm the picture in the closet."

"Oh, that explains those warts."

"Warts?" Instant panic. "What warts?"

"Easy." It was Laura's first good laugh in days. "Just joking."

"Christ, next time just shoot me in the head." As her blood pressure returned to normal, Margo held up a faience vase painted with stylized flowers. "What do you think? It's Doulton."

It was no use asking Margo what she'd paid for it, Laura knew. She wouldn't have a clue. Following routine, Laura glanced at the stack of price guides and catalogs they'd collected. "Did you look it up?"

"Sort of." Over the past weeks, Margo had developed a love-hate relationship with price guides. She loved the idea of marking prices, hated the knowledge that so much money had already slipped through her fingers. "I think a hundred fifty."

"Go for it."

Tongue caught between her teeth, Margo slowly tapped the keys on the laptop Kate had insisted they couldn't live without. "Stock number 481 . . . G for glassware or C for collectibles?"

"Um, G. Kate's not here to argue the point."

"481-G. Damn it, I said *G*." She deleted, tried again. "One hundred fifty." Though it was probably inefficient, which Kate would have pointed out, Margo tagged the vase, rose to carry it to the glass étagère that was already filling up, then came back to light a cigarette. "What the hell are we doing, Laura?"

"Having fun. What made you buy something like this?"

Smoking contemplatively, Margo eyed an undoubtedly ugly urn with wing handles. "I must have been having a bad day."

"Well, it's Stinton, and signed, so maybe . . ." She flipped busily through a price book. "About forty-five hundred."

"Really?" Had she really once been in the position to pay so much for so little? She nudged the laptop toward Laura. "They're coming to paint the sign on the window tomorrow. And the crew from *Entertainment Tonight* is supposed to be here by two."

"Are you sure you want to do that?"

"Are you kidding? All that free publicity?" Margo stretched her arms up. Her shoulders were aching, a sensation she'd gotten used to. "Besides, it'll give me a chance to deck myself out, get in front of the camera. I'm thinking the sage green Armani or the blue Valentino."

"We've already tagged the Armani."

"Right. Valentino it is."

"As long as it doesn't make you uncomfortable."

"Valentino never makes me uncomfortable."

"You know what I mean." Laura hefted the urn, decided it looked slightly less unattractive on the corner shelf. "All those questions about your private life."

"I don't have a private life at the moment. You've got to learn to shrug off the gossip, honey." She tapped out her cigarette and knelt to explore the crate. "If you let every whisper and snicker about you and Peter sting, the wasps will know and they'll keep after you."

"He came back to town last week."

Her head jerked up. "Is he hassling you?"

"No, but . . . Josh had an incident with him a few days ago. I didn't hear about it until this morning."

"An incident?" Amused, Margo studied a little Limoges box replicating a French flower stall. Christ, she loved these little bits of nonsense. "What did they do, draw their Mont Blancs and duel?"

"Josh broke Peter's nose."

"What?" Staggered between shock and glory, she nearly bobbled the box. "Josh *punched* him?"

"He broke it with a tennis ball." When Margo collapsed into hoots of laughter, Laura scowled. "There were people in the next court. It's all over the club. Peter had to be taken to the hospital, and he might very well file charges."

"What, assault with a forehand lob? Oh, Laura, it's too delicious. I haven't given Josh enough credit." She pressed a hand on her stomach as her ribs began to ache.

"It had to be deliberate."

"Well, of course it was deliberate. Josh can bean a speeding car at fifty yards with his backhand. He could have played center court if he'd taken himself seriously. Damn, I wish I'd seen it." Wicked delight sparkled in her eyes. "Did he bleed a lot?"

"Profusely, I'm told." It was wrong, Laura had to continually remind herself, it was wrong to enjoy the image of bright red blood geysering out of Peter's aristocratic nose. "He's gone to Maui to recuperate. Margo, I don't want my brother smashing tennis balls into the face of the father of my children."

"Oh, let him have his fun." Without remembering to tag or log it, Margo placed the Limoges in a curved-front cabinet where a dozen others were already displayed. "Ah, is Josh seeing anyone?"

"Seeing anyone?"

"You know, as in dating, escorting, having hot sex with?"

Baffled, Laura rubbed at her tired eyes. "Not that I know of. But then, he stopped bragging about having hot sex around me years ago."

"But you'd know." As if it were vital to world peace, Margo rubbed at a smudge on the display glass. "You'd have heard, or sensed."

"He's awfully busy just now, so I'd say probably not. Why?"

"Oh." She turned back, smiling widely. "Just a little wager we have going. I'm starving," she realized abruptly. "Are you starving? I think we should order something in. If Kate comes by after work and we're not done with this shipment, she's going to lecture us on time management again."

"I don't have time for lectures on time. I'm sorry. I have to pick up the girls. It's Friday," she explained. "I promised them dinner and a movie. Why don't you come with us?"

"And leave all this luxury?" Margo spread her arms wide to encompass boxes, heaps of packing material, half-empty cups of cold coffee. "Besides, I have to practice my gift wrapping. Everything I do still looks like it was wrapped up by a slow-witted three-year-old. I don't mind, really—"

She broke off as the door swung open and Kayla burst through. "Mama! We came to visit." With a beaming smile, she launched herself into Laura's arms, clung just a little too hard.

"Hello, baby." Laura squeezed back, worrying how long these small reassurances would be necessary. "How did you get here?"

"Uncle Josh picked us up. He said we could come and look at the shop 'cause we should take an interest in our legacy."

"Your legacy, huh?" Laughing now, Laura set Kayla down and watched her older daughter come more cautiously, less happily into the room. "Well, Ali, what do you think?"

"It looks different than it did before." She walked unerringly to the jewelry case.

"A girl after my own heart," Margo declared and wrapped an arm around Ali's shoulder.

"They're so beautiful. It's like a treasure chest."

"It is. Not Seraphina's dowry this time, but mine."

"We got pizza," Kayla called out. "Uncle Josh bought lots and lots of pizza so we can eat here instead of in a restaurant. Can we, Mama?"

"If you like. Do you want to, Ali?"

Ali shrugged, continued to stare at the bracelets and pins. "It doesn't matter."

"And here's the man of the hour." Margo crossed the room as Josh elbowed the door open, his arms loaded with pizza boxes. She leaned over them and gave him a smacking kiss on the mouth.

"Just for pizza? Hell, I could've gone for the bucket of chicken."

"Actually, that was a reward for your tennis prowess."

She kept her voice low, and at the answering gleam in his eyes, she took the boxes from him. "Still sleeping alone, darling?"

"Don't remind me." He arched a brow. "You?"

She grinned and trailed a finger down his cheek. "I've been much too busy for sports of any kind. Ali, I think there's a bottle of Pepsi in the refrigerator upstairs."

"Got that covered, too," he said, torturing himself with the scent of her perfume. "Can you handle getting the drinks out of the car, Ali Cat?"

"Me, too." Kayla bulleted for the door. "I can help. Come on, Ali."

"Well, well." Josh tucked his hands in his pockets and scanned the room as his nieces slammed the door. "You have been busy." He wandered toward the adjoining room, had to smile. It looked very much like Margo's closet back in Milan, except that all the clothes were now discreetly tagged.

"Lingerie and nightclothes are upstairs," Margo told him. "In the boudoir."

"Naturally." Idly, he picked up a gray suede pump, turned it over. The sole was barely scraped and the price was ninety-two fifty.

"How are you pricing?"

"Oh, we have our little system."

He set the shoe back, glanced at his sister. "I didn't think you'd mind if I brought the girls by."

"No, not at all. What I do mind is you taking it upon yourself to fight with Peter."

He didn't bother to look contrite. "Heard about that, did you?"

"Of course I heard about it. Everyone from Big Sur to Monterey's heard about it by now." She refused to warm when he walked over and kissed her. "I can deal with my marital problems myself."

"Sure you can. That ball just got away from me."

"Like hell," Margo muttered.

"Actually, I was aiming for his caps. Listen, Laura," he continued when she bristled under his hands, "we'll talk about it later, okay?"

She had little choice, since at that moment her daughters came back, carrying bags from the car.

He'd thought of paper plates as well, and napkins and silly party cups for soda and a good red Bordeaux. There seemed to be very little, Margo mused as they spread the makeshift picnic on the floor, that Josh Templeton didn't think of.

It was a little lowering to realize she had underestimated him all these years. He would be a formidable foe, which he'd proved by one swing of the racket. And she was certain he would be a memorable lover.

Josh caught her staring and passed her a plate. "Problem, duchess?"

"More than likely."

But she enjoyed herself, listening to the children. Ali seemed to brighten shade by shade under Josh's teasing and attention. Poor thing wants a father, Margo mused. She understood the need, the empty ache of it. It had been Thomas Templeton who had helped fill that void for her, and who at the same time, simply by being kind and caring, had made her constantly aware that he was not hers.

She had never had her own—or had had him so briefly she couldn't remember him. Her mother had always been so closemouthed about the man she had married and lost that Margo had been afraid to ask questions. Afraid, she realized, that there had been nothing there, for any of them.

No love, she mused. Certainly no passion.

One more tepid marriage in the world hardly made a difference to anyone. Even those, she thought, involved in it. A good Irish Catholic girl married and had children, as was expected of her. Then accepted God's will with a bowed head. Ann Sullivan wouldn't have mourned and tossed herself, cursing God, into the sea as Seraphina had done. Ann Sullivan had picked herself up, moved on, and forgotten.

And so easily, Margo mused, that there had likely been little to remember. It was as if she had never had a father at all.

And hadn't she sought to fill that lifetime gap with men? Often older men, like Alain, men who were successful and established and always safely beyond commitment. Married men, or oft-married men, or loosely married men with wives who turned a blind eye to an affair as long as their husbands turned a blind eye to theirs.

There had always been a cozy cushion with men who looked at her as a lovely prize to be pampered and fussed over. Displayed. Men who would never stay, which of course only made them more attractive, only more forbidden.

Her stomach shuddered, and she gulped wine to steady it. What a horrible realization, she thought. What a pathetic one.

"Are you all right?" Concerned, Laura laid a hand on her arm. "You've gone pale."

"It's nothing. Just a little headache. I'm going to take something." She rose and used every ounce of control she had to walk up the stairs rather than run.

In the bathroom she riffled through the medicine bottles. Her fingers rested on tranquilizers before she shifted them firmly to aspirin. Too easy, she told herself as she ran the water cold. Too easy to pop a pill and make it all go away.

"Margo." Josh came up behind her, took hold of her shoulders. "What's got you?"

"Demon dreams." She shook her head, swallowed aspirin. "It's nothing, just a nasty little epiphany."

She would have turned, but he held her firm so that their faces reflected back at them. "Nervous about opening the shop next week?"

"Terrified."

"Whatever happens, you've already accomplished something important. You've taken this place and made it shine. It's beautiful and elegant and unique. Very much like you."

"And filled with pretenses, priced to sell?"

"So what?"

She closed her eyes. "So what. Be a friend, Josh, and hold on to me for a minute."

He turned her, gathered her close. He heard her loose a long, shuddering breath, and he stroked her hair. "Do you remember that winter when you went on a search for Seraphina's dowry?"

"Umm. I dug up the rose garden and part of the south lawn. Mum was furious and mortified and threatened to ship me off to my aunt Bridgett in Cork." She sighed a little, comforted by the feel of him, the scent of him. "But your father laughed and laughed. He thought it was a great joke and that I showed an adventurous spirit."

"You were looking for something you wanted, and you went after it." His lips brushed her hair to soothe. "That's what you've always done."

"And I've always wanted the unattainable?"

"No." He eased back, tipped up her chin. "The interesting. I'd hate to think you'd stop digging up rosebushes, duchess."

Sighing again, she snuggled her head on his shoulder. "I really hate to admit this, but you're good for me, Josh."

"I know." And he thought it was long past time that she figured that out.

SHE HADN'T EXPECTED to be nervous. There'd been so much to do in the past three months—appointments, meetings, decisions to make, stock to sort through. The decorating, the planning. Even the choice of shopping bags and boxes had prompted hours of debate.

There'd been so much to learn. Inventory, profit-and-loss ratios, tax forms. Sales tax, business tax, property tax.

Interviews to give. The spread in *People* had just hit the stands, and *Entertainment Weekly* had run a blurb on her and her shop. A snide blurb, but it was print.

It was all falling into place, so she had expected the actual opening to be rather anticlimactic. The attack of nerves twenty-four hours before Pretenses' grand opening was both unexpected and unwelcome.

Over the years, Margo had taken various courses to deal with nerves. A glass of wine, shopping, a pill, sex. None of those seemed a viable option now, nor did they fit in with the new direction her life was taking.

She was giving sweat a try instead.

The exercise facilities at the country club were, she supposed, top of the line. She had through her career played with free weights and pranced through a few aerobic classes. But she'd been blessed with a killer metabolism, long legs, long torso, and generous breasts that weren't echoed in hips, and she had smugly scorned the fitness craze.

Now she struggled through the programming of a StairMaster, wondering how anyone could get excited about climbing steps to nowhere. She could only hope it would turn her busy mind to mush—and keep the weight she'd put back on properly distributed.

The huge room was ringed with windows that offered views of the golf course or the pool. For those who weren't interested in the great outdoors, there were individual television sets affixed above treadmills, so one could walk or trot to health while watching Katie and Bryant or CNN. Various pieces of what she considered rather terrifying equipment were placed here and there.

Beside her, a woman in red spandex doggedly climbed flight after flight while reading the latest Danielle Steele. Margo struggled to get her rhythm and focus on the bobbing print of the business section of the *Los Angeles Times*.

But she couldn't concentrate. This was a whole new world, she realized. One that had been bumping, jogging, and grunting along while she'd been wrapped up in her own. A man with a gorgeous body and biceps like bricks watched himself carefully in a mirror while lifting brutal-looking weights. A bevy of women, trim or pudgy, pumped on stationary bikes. Some of them chattered together, others rode to the tune on headsets.

People crunched, twisted, bent, and punished their bodies, mopped sweat from their faces, glugged down mineral water, then went back for more.

It was, to her, amazing.

For her, this was a lark, a momentary diversion. But for them, all these damp, straining bodies, it was a serious lifestyle choice.

Perhaps they were all slightly insane.

Still . . . weren't these the very people she would need to appeal to? The businesspeople, the clever rich. The women who worked out in hundred-dollar bike shorts and two-hundred-dollar shoes. After straining and stretching their bodies, wouldn't they enjoy a bit of pampering? Beyond the Swedish massages, the Turkish baths, the whirlpools, surely they would enjoy strolling into a classy shop to browse, be offered a cup of cappuccino, a glass of chilled champagne, while an attractive woman helped them select the perfect bauble or a tasteful gift.

Of course, the challenge would be to convince them that the fact that the bauble or gift was secondhand only made it more interesting and unique.

Calculating, she slanted a look at the woman beside her. "Do you do this every day?"

"Hmm?"

"I was wondering if you do this every day." With a friendly smile, Margo sized up her companion. Mid-thirties, carefully groomed. The channel-set diamonds on her wedding band were excellent quality and weighed in at about three carats. "I've just started."

"Three days a week. It's really all you need to maintain." Obviously willing to be distracted, she skimmed a glance over Margo. "Losing weight isn't your goal."

"I've gained seven pounds in the last three months."

With a laugh, the woman lifted the towel she'd slung over the bar and blotted her throat. Margo noted the watch was a slim Rolex. "We should all be able to say that and look like you. I've lost thirty-three over the last year."

"You're kidding."

"If I put it back on, I'll kill myself. So now I'm on maintenance. I'm back to a size eight, and by God, I'm staying there."

"You look wonderful." Size eight, she thought. Perfect. "Do you like working out?"

The woman smiled grimly as her stepper pumped up the pace. "I hate every fucking minute of it."

"Thank God," Margo said sincerely as her calves began to burn. "Sanity. I'm Margo Sullivan. I'd offer my hand, but I'm afraid I'd fall off."

"Judy Prentice. Margo Sullivan," she repeated. "I thought you looked familiar. I used to hate you."

"Oh?"

"When I was cruising toward a size sixteen, and I'd flip through a magazine. There'd you'd be, curvy and perfect. I'd head straight for the Godivas." She offered a quick grin. "It's rewarding to know you sweat just like a human being."

Deciding Judy was likable as well as a potential customer, Margo grinned back. "Isn't there supposed to be something about endorphins?"

"Oh, that's a lie. I think Jane Fonda started it. You grew up here, didn't you?"

"Big Sur," Margo confirmed, puffing now. "I'm back. I have a shop in Monterey. Pretenses, on Cannery Row. We're having our grand opening tomorrow. You should drop in, look around." She gritted her teeth. "I'll make sure we have Godivas."

"Bitch," Judy said with a quick laugh. "I might just do that. Well, that's my twenty minutes of hell. Fifteen with the free weights and a short session on the Nautilus torture chamber and I'm out of here." She grabbed her towel, glanced toward the entrance. "Oh, here comes the diva."

"Candy Litchfield," Margo muttered as she spotted the redhead in a floral unitard.

"Know her?"

"Too well."

"Hmm. If you have the good taste to loathe her, I might just check out that shop of yours. Oops, she's heading this way, and she's all yours."

"Listen, don't—" But it was too late. Candy let out a squeal that had every head swiveling.

"Margo! Margo Sullivan! I just can't believe it."

"Hello, Candy." To Margo's despair, Candy bounced up to the stepper.

Candy bounced everywhere. It was just one of the many reasons to despise her. She was bandbox pretty, all perky features and tumbling red hair. In their high school days, Candy had been head cheerleader, and head pain in the ass. She'd married well—twice—had two perfect children, one from each marriage, and spent her days, as far as Margo knew, planning perfect tea parties and indulging in discreet affairs.

Under the surface, past the perky face and well-toned body, was the heart of a viper. To Candy, other women weren't simply members of the same sex and species. They were the enemy.

"I heard you were back, of course." With a perfect pink nail she tapped in her choice of time and program on the machine Judy had vacated. "I've been meaning to call, but I've been so busy." The diamond studs in her ears winked as she smiled at Margo. "How are you, Margo? You look wonderful. No one would ever know."

"Wouldn't they?"

"All those terrible stories." Delighted malice flitted around her Kewpie-doll lips. "Why it must have been just dreadful for you. I just can't imagine the terror of being arrested—and in a foreign country, too." Her voice was just loud enough to catch the interest of several morning athletes.

"Neither can I." Margo struggled not to puff and wished violently for a cigarette. "I wasn't arrested. I was questioned."

"Well, I was sure the stories were exaggerated." Her tone was a bright brew of sympathy laced with doubt. "All those horrible things they said about you. Why, when I heard, I told several of the girls over lunch that it was just nonsense. But the stories just kept coming. The press is so heartless. You were wise to get out of Europe until the scandal dies down. It's so like Laura to overlook all the talk and take you in."

There was nothing to say to that but "Yes."

"It's such a shame about Bella Donna. I'm sure your replacement won't be nearly as effective. You're so much more photogenic than Tessa Cesare." Bouncing perkily, Candy sharpened her lance. "Of course, she's younger, but she doesn't have your . . . experience."

It was a shaft to the heart, well aimed and well honed. Margo's fingers tightened on the bar, but she kept her voice easy. "Tessa's a beautiful woman."

"Oh, of course. And very exotic. That golden skin, those wonderful black eyes. I'm sure the company felt they had to go with a contrast." Her smile was calculatedly tinged with amused disdain. "You'll make a comeback, Margo. Don't you worry."

"Not if I'm serving time for murder," she said under her breath.

"So, tell me everything. I heard the most hilarious story about you going into retail."

"I laugh about it all the time. We open tomorrow."

"No! Really?" Her eyes popped wide on a titter. "Then poor Laura Ridgeway did buy you a building. That's so touching."

"Laura, Kate Powell, and I bought the building together."

"The three of you always did stick together." Candy's smile turned sharp. She'd always detested them for their unshakable friendship. "I'm sure it'll be great fun for you, and poor Laura certainly needs a distraction just now. There can't be anything more painful and distressing than seeing your marriage fail."

"Unless it's seeing your second marriage fail," Margo returned with a cheery smile. "Is the divorce final, Candy?"

"Next month. You never did marry any of those . . . men, did you, Margo?"

"No, I just had sex with them. Most of them were already married anyway."

"You've always had such a European attitude. I suppose I'm just too American. I don't think I could ever be comfortable being a mistress."

Temper shot little lights of red in front of Margo's eyes. "Darling," she drawled, "it's blissfully comfortable. Believe me. But then, you're probably right. You're not suited for it. No alimony."

She stepped off the machine, grateful that her session with Candy had taken her mind off nerves and screaming muscles. Maybe her legs felt like limp strings of linguini, but she wouldn't give Candy the satisfaction of seeing them buckle. Instead, she carefully wiped off the machine as she had seen Judy do.

"Do come by the shop, Candy. We're having our grand opening tomorrow. You've always wanted what I had. This is your chance to get it. For a price."

As Margo flounced out, Candy drew a breath up her pert, tip-tilted nose and turned to the interested woman puffing behind her. "Margo Sullivan always pretended to be something she wasn't. Why, if it wasn't for the Templetons, she wouldn't be allowed through the front gates of this club."

The woman blinked the sweat out of her eyes. She'd admired Margo's style. And her sapphire tennis bracelet. "What was the name of her shop?"

CHAPTER 12

NINE-FORTY-FIVE, July twenty-eighth. Fifteen minutes to zero hour and Margo was sitting on the bed in the ladies' boudoir. The bed she had once slept in, made love in. Dreamed in. Now she was perched on the edge of it, holding her stomach and praying for the nausea to pass.

What if no one came? What if absolutely no one so much as stepped through those freshly washed glass doors? She would spend the next eight hours trembling, staring out the display window now so painstakingly arranged with her charcoal silk taffeta St. Laurent—worn only last year to the Cannes film festival—its skirts draped over a Louis XIV hall chair. That flowing skirt was surrounded by once prized possessions. A Baccarat perfume bottle, rhinestone-studded evening slippers, sapphire drop earrings, a black satin purse with a jeweled clasp in the shape of a panther. The Meissen candlestick, the Waterford champagne flute, a display of her favorite trinket boxes, and the silver-backed dresser set that had been a gift from an old lover.

She'd placed every piece personally, as a kind of ritual, and now she feared that those things she had once owned and loved would draw no more than scorn from passersby.

What had she done?

Stripped herself. Stripped herself raw, and in public. She thought she could handle that, live through that. But she had dragged the people she cared about most into the morass with her.

Wasn't Laura downstairs right now waiting for that first customer? And

Kate would dash over on her lunch hour, eager to see a sale rung up on the vintage cash register she'd hauled in from an antique shop in Carmel.

And Josh would probably swing by toward evening, strolling in with a smile on his face to congratulate them on their first day's success.

How could she possibly face them with failure? When the failure was all hers?

What she wanted most at that moment was to bolt downstairs and out the door. And just keep running.

"Stage fright."

With one arm still wrapped around her queasy stomach, she glanced up. Josh was in the doorway. "You talked me into this. If I could stand up right now, I'd kill you."

"Lucky for me those gorgeous legs of yours aren't steady." He gave her a quick, appraising look. She'd chosen a simple and perfectly tailored suit in power red with a short, snug skirt that gave those stunning, unsteady legs plenty of exposure to do their work. Her hair was braided, with just a few tendrils calculatingly free to frame her face. Pale as marble now, eyes glassy with fear.

"You disappoint me, duchess. I figured to find you downstairs revved up to kick ass. Instead you're up here shaking like a virgin on her wedding night."

"I want to go back to Milan."

"Well, you can't, can you?" His tone was hard as he crossed the room, took her by the arm. "Stand up, get a grip on yourself." Those big blue eyes were swimming, and he was afraid that if the first tear fell, he would break and carry her off anywhere she wanted to go. "It's a damn store, for Christ's sake, not a capital trial. It's just like you to blow it out of proportion."

"It's not just a store." Her voice hitched, mortifying her. "It's all I've got."

"Then go down and do something about it."

"I don't want to go down. What if no one comes? Or if they only come to stare and snicker."

"What if they don't? What if they do? There are plenty of people who'll be interested enough to breeze by just to see you fall on your face. Keep this up and that's all they're going to see."

"I shouldn't have started out so big."

"Since that applies to every aspect of your life, I don't see why you're complaining now." He studied her face, angry with her for letting him see the fear, angry with himself for wanting to protect her. "Look, you've got five minutes, and you'll make up your own mind. I've got my own problems to deal with." He brought out the single red rose he'd held behind his back and curled her fingers around the stem. "Let me know how you deal with yours."

He closed his lips over hers impatiently and didn't wait for her reaction.

He could have offered a little sympathy, she fumed and stalked into the bathroom to retouch her makeup. Just a little understanding and support. No, not Josh. She slammed her blusher back into the cabinet. All she got from him was insults and surly remarks. Well, that was fine. That was good. It reminded her that she had no one to lean on but herself.

Five minutes later, she made herself walk downstairs. Laura was beaming at the big, ornate cash register as its bells chimed.

"You've got to stop playing with that thing."

"I'm not playing." Face flushed with excitement, she turned to Margo. "I've just rung up our first sale."

"But we're not open."

"Josh bought the little Deco lamp before he left. He said to box it up and ship it." Reaching across the counter, she grabbed Margo's hands and squeezed. "Box it up and ship it, Margo. It's our first box it up and ship it. You can always depend on Josh."

Margo let out a shaky laugh. Damn him, it was just like him. "Yeah, you can, can't you?" The mantel clock behind the counter chimed the hour. Zero hour. "Well, I guess we'd better . . . Laura, I'm—"

"Me, too." Laura drew a long, cleansing breath. "Let's open for business, partner."

"Yeah." Margo straightened her shoulders and angled her chin as she crossed to the door. "And fuck them if they can't take a joke."

TWO HOURS LATER, she wasn't sure if she was thrilled or punch-drunk. She couldn't claim they were jammed with customers, particularly of the paying variety. But they'd enjoyed a small, steady stream almost from the first minute. She had, with her own trembling hands, rung up the second sale of the day barely fifteen minutes after opening the doors. Both she and the tourist from Tulsa had agreed that the silver cuff bracelet was an excellent buy.

With some amazement and no little admiration, she'd watched Laura steer a trio of browsers toward the wardrobe room like a veteran shop clerk and flatter them into reaching for their credit cards.

When Kate arrived at twelve-thirty, Margo was closing the sapphire earrings from the display window into one of the bright gold boxes with silver lettering that she'd chosen for the shop's trademark.

"I know your wife's going to love them," she said as she slipped the box into a tiny gold bag. Her hands weren't trembling, but they wanted to. "I did. And happy anniversary."

The minute the customer stepped away from the counter, she snagged Kate's hand and pulled her into the powder room. "That was fifteen hundred and seventy-five dollars, plus tax." Grabbing Kate around the waist, she led her into a quick, clattering dance. "We're selling things, Kate."

"That was the idea." It had killed her not to be there, with Laura and Margo, to open the doors for the first time. But responsibility at Bittle took priority. "You own a store, you sell things."

"No, we're really selling them. Liz Carstairs was in and bought the set of Tiffany wineglasses for her daughter's shower gift, and this couple from Connecticut bought the gateleg table. We're shipping it. And, oh, more. We're not going to be paying that storage bill for the rest of the stock much longer."

"Are you logging the sales?"

"Yeah—well, I might have made a couple of mistakes, but we'll fix that. Come on, you can ring something up." She paused with a hand on the door. "It's sort of like sex. There's this attraction, and you build on it, then there's foreplay, little thrills of anticipation, then there's this big bang."

"Want a cigarette?"

"I'm dying for one."

"You're really getting into this, aren't you?"

"I had no idea that sales could be so . . . stimulating. Give it a shot."

Kate glanced at her watch. "I've only got forty-five minutes, but, hey, I'm all for cheap thrills."

Margo snagged her wrist, studied the clean lines of the practical Timex. "You know, we could get a good price for this."

"Control yourself, Margo."

She tried. But every now and again throughout the day she had to find some quiet corner and simply gloat. Maybe her emotions were swinging high and wide like a batter too eager to score, but she just didn't care. If there was a pang now and then when one of her treasured trinkets slipped away in a gold-and-silver box, there was also a sense of triumph.

People had come. And for every one who snickered there was another who admired, and another who bought.

By three, when there was a lull, she poured two cups of the tea they'd offered to customers throughout the morning. "I'm not hallucinating, am I?"

"Not unless we both are." Laura winced as she wriggled her toes. "And my feet hurt too much for this to be a dream. Margo, I think we've actually done it."

"Let's not say that yet. We could jinx it." Carrying her cup, she walked over to straighten a vase of roses. "I mean, maybe this is just fate's way of sneering at us. Giving us a few hours of success. We're open for three more hours, and . . . the hell with that." She whirled around. "We're a hit. We're a smash!"

"I wish you'd be more enthusiastic—and I wish I could stay and ride the next wave with you." Wincing, Laura looked at her watch. "But the girls have dance class. I'll wash out the cups before I go."

"No, I'll take care of them."

The door opened, letting in a group of teenage girls who made a beeline for the jewelry counter.

"We have customers," Laura murmured and gathered up the cups herself. "We have customers," she repeated, grinning. "I'll try to be here tomorrow by one." There were so many obligations to juggle, and she worried about how long it would be before she started dropping balls. "Are you sure you can handle working the shop by yourself?"

"We agreed from the start that you'd have to be part time. I'm going to learn how to handle it. Get going."

"As soon as I wash these." She stopped, turned. "Margo, I don't know the last time I had this much fun."

Nor did she, Margo thought. As she measured her young customers, a smile began to bloom. Teenage girls who wore designer shoes had generous allowances—and parents with gold cards. She crossed to the counter, took her place behind it.

"Hello, ladies. Can I show you something?"

JOSH DIDN'T MIND long hours. He could handle being chained to a desk and being buried under paperwork. Though it wasn't as appealing as zipping across continents to fine-tune the workings of a busy hotel chain and its subsidiaries, he could deal with it cheerfully enough.

But what really pissed him off was being played for a fool.

The longer he remained in the penthouse and studied the files generated from the California Templetons, the more certain he was that Peter Ridgeway had done just that.

He'd done his job. There was no way to accuse him, legally, of mishandling funds or staff, of cutting corners. Though he had done precisely those things, Peter had documented it all, in terms of his rationale, his position, and the increase in profit that his alterations had generated.

But Templeton had never been an organization that was motivated exclusively by profit. It was a family-owned operation steeped in two hundred years of innkeeping tradition that prided itself on its humanity, on its commitment to the people who worked in it and for it.

Yes, Ridgeway had increased profits, but he had done so by changing staff, cutting back on full-time employees in favor of part-time ones. And thereby squeezing people out of benefits and slicing their pay stubs.

He'd negotiated a new deal with wholesalers, produce distributors, and as a result had lowered the quality in the staff kitchens. Employee discounts in reservations and in Templeton hotel boutiques had been cut back, reducing the incentive that had always been traditional for Templeton people to use Templeton services.

In the meantime, his own expense account had increased. His bills for meals, laundry, entertainment, flowers, travel, had steadily grown. He'd even had the gall to charge his trip to Aruba to Templeton as a business expense.

It gave Josh great pleasure to cancel Peter's corporate credit cards. Even if he did consider it too little, too late.

Should have aimed for his balls after all, he thought, and leaned back to rub his tired eyes.

It would take months to rebuild trust among the staff. A huge bonus and a mountain of flattery would be necessary to lure back the head chef who had quit in a huff at Ridgeway's interference. Added to that was the resignation from the longtime concierge at Templeton San Francisco that he'd found buried in Peter's files. There were others as well. Some could be lured back, others were lost to competitors.

None of them had come to him, Josh mused, or to his parents. Because they'd believed, justifiably, that Peter Ridgeway was a trusted, highly placed member of the Templeton group.

He tugged at his tie, trying not to think about the amount of work that still lay before him. Someone was going to have to take over his responsibilities in Europe, at least temporarily. He wasn't going anywhere.

Already the penthouse suite was more his than Ridgeway's. The fussy furniture had been replaced with Josh's preference for the traditional. American and Spanish antiques, with deeply cushioned, generous chairs were more in keeping with the scheme of Templeton Monterey. After all, the hotel and its decor followed the history of the area. The resort was more truly of California Spanish design, but the hotel echoed it in the ornate facade, the musical fountains, and lush gardens. The lobby was done in deep reds and golds, offering heavy chairs, long, high tables, winking brass, and glossy tiled floors.

There were potted palms, like the one he'd chosen for the corner of his office, in a huge hand-thrown clay pot that took two men with beefy arms to lift.

He'd always thought Templeton Paris more feminine, with its mix of the airy and the ornate, and Templeton London more distinguished, so British with its two-level lobby and cozy tearoom.

But Monterey was perhaps closest to his heart after all. Not that he'd ever pictured himself settling behind a desk here, even if it was a Duncan Phyfe, with an eye-blurring view of the coast he loved only a head's turn away.

It didn't bother him for outsiders to consider him the globe-trotting trust fund baby. Because he knew better. The Templeton name wasn't simply a legacy, it was a responsibility. He'd worked long and hard to meet that responsibility, to learn the craft of not simply owning but managing and expanding a complex organization. He'd been expected to learn hotels from the ground up, and he had done just that. By doing so he'd developed respect and admiration for the people who worked in the kitchens, picked up wet towels from bathroom floors, calmed the tired and frazzled incoming guests at the front desks.

He appreciated the hours that went into public relations and sales and the frustrations of dealing with oversized conventions and harried conventioneers.

But there was a bottom line, and that line was Templeton. Whatever went wrong, whatever needed to be fixed, smoothed over, or polished up was up to him. And there was a great deal of fixing, smoothing over, and polishing up to be done in California.

He thought about getting up and brewing coffee, or just calling down to room service. But he didn't have the energy for either. He'd sent the temp home because she'd gotten on his nerves, scrambling around like an eager puppy desperate to please.

If he was going to be stuck behind a desk for the foreseeable future, he would need an executive assistant who could match his pace and not go wide-eyed with terror every time he gave an order. He was going to have to toss the temp back into the pool and go fishing.

But for now he was on his own.

He swiveled to his keyboard and began to compose a memo to all department heads, with a copy to his parents and the rest of the board of directors. It took him thirty minutes to perfect it. He faxed a copy, with the addition of a personal note, to his parents, printed out the others, and arranged for them to be messengered or overnighted.

Seeing no reason to waste time, he set up a full staff meeting at the hotel for eleven A.M., another at the resort at two. Though it was already after six, he contacted legal and left a message on voice mail outlining the urgency of a meeting and setting it up for nine sharp in his penthouse office.

It was highly probable that Ridgeway would sue over his abrupt termination. Josh wanted his bases covered.

Shifting back to the keyboard, he began another memo, reinstating the previous employee discounts. That, he thought, was something they would be able to see immediately, and, hopefully, it would build morale.

Standing in the open doorway, Margo watched him. It was a delightful shock to discover that watching him work made her juices flow. The loosened tie, the hair disarrayed by restless fingers, the dark and focused intensity of his eyes had her all but vibrating.

Odd, she'd never thought of Josh taking work of any kind seriously. And she had never realized that a serious man at work could be quite so arousing.

Maybe it was the months of self-imposed celibacy, or the heady success of the day. Maybe it was Josh himself—and had been all along. She didn't, at the moment, give a damn. She'd come here for one thing—a good, hot, sweaty bout of sex. She wasn't leaving without it.

Quietly, she closed the doors at her back, flipped the locks. "Well, well," she murmured, her pulse leaping when his head shot up like a wolf scenting his mate. "The scion at work. Quite a picture."

Knowing exactly the kind of picture she made—God knew she'd worked on it—she swaggered to his desk. After setting a frosty bottle of Cristal on the blotter, she eased a hip onto the edge. "Am I interrupting?"

His mind had gone blank the moment she'd stepped toward him. He did his best to snap it back. "Yeah, but don't let that stop you." He glanced down at the bottle, back into her glowing face. "So, how was your day?"

"Oh, nothing worth mentioning." She leaned over the desk, all but slithered over it, and gave him a tantalizing glimpse of pearly lace and cleavage. "Just fifteen thousand dollars in sales." She screamed, reaching out to tug his hair. "Fifteen thousand, six hundred and seventy-four dollars, eighteen cents in sales."

She sprang back off the desk, whirled in a giddy circle. "Do you know how I felt the first time I saw my face on the cover of *Vogue*?"

"No."

"Just like this. Insane. I closed the doors at six, and there was half a bottle of champagne left. I drank it all myself, right from the damn bottle. Then I realized I didn't want to drink alone. Open the bottle, Josh. Let's get drunk and crazy."

He rose, began to rip the foil. He should have known that gleam in her eye had been helped along by bubbly. "From what you've just said, you're already there."

"I'm only half drunk."

The cork popped celebrationally. "This should fix that." He went to the kitchen, setting the bottle on the counter of granite-colored tile and reaching into a glass-front oak cabinet for glasses.

"That's what you do, isn't it? Fix things. You fixed me, Josh. I owe you."

"No." That was one thing he didn't want. "You did it yourself."

"Made a start on it. I'm not finished yet." She clinked her glass to his. "But, oh, it's a hell of a start."

"To Pretenses, then."

"You bet your adorable ass. I know it won't be like this every day. It can't be." Fueled with energy, she prowled back into the office. "Kate says we can expect sales to dip, then level off. But I don't care. I watched this incredibly ugly woman waltz out with one of my Armanis, and I just didn't care."

"Good for you."

"And I—" Her voice hitched, strangled, and he set his glass down in pure panic.

"Don't do that. Don't cry. I'm begging you."

"It's not what you think."

"Don't give me that shit about happy tears. They're all the same to me. They're wet and make me feel like slime."

"I can't get hold of myself." As a defense, she gulped down more champagne, sniffled. "I've been like this all day. Dancing on the ceiling one minute, bawling in the bathroom the next. I'm selling my life away, and it makes me so sad. And people are buying it, and that makes me so happy."

"Jesus." Frustrated, he rubbed his hands over his face. "Let's trade in the champagne for some coffee, shall we?"

"Oh, no." Spurting up again, she danced away from him. "I'm celebrating."

"Okay." When she folded, he would pour her drunk, sexy body into his car and drive her to Templeton House. But for now, she had the right to celebrate, to gloat and be ridiculous. He sat on the desk, picked up his glass again. "To ugly women in secondhand Armani."

She tossed back the champagne and let it fizz down her throat. "To teenage girls with rich, indulgent parents."

"God love them."

"And tourists from Tulsa."

"Salt of the earth."

"And hawk-eyed old men who appreciate long legs in a short skirt." When he only frowned into his glass, she laughed and poured them both more. "And who plunk down cash for Meissen tea sets and harmless flirtation."

Before she could drink again, he caught her wrist. "How harmless?"

"I let him cluck my chin. If he'd bought the raku vase, he could have pinched any and all of my cheeks. It's such a rush."

"The clucking."

"No." She giggled happily. "The selling. I had no idea I'd find it so exciting. So . . . arousing." She spun back, sprinkling them both with champagne before he could pluck the glass from her hand and set it safely aside. "That's why I came to find you."

"You came to find me," he repeated, too cautious to move forward, too needy to move back.

With a low laugh she slid her hands up his shirt front, over his shoulders, into his hair. "I thought you could finish the job."

She was more than half drunk, he calculated, and told himself to remember the rules. He just couldn't think of them. "What do you want me to sell?"

She laughed again, dragged his mouth to hers for a steamy kiss. "Whatever it is, I'm ready to buy it."

He came up for air, tried for reason. "You've got champagne on your brain, duchess. This might not be the time to do business."

She made quick work of his tie, slinging it over her shoulder while her mouth went to war with his. "It's the perfect time. I could eat you alive, in great . . . big . . . bites."

"Jesus." It was hard to focus on reason when all the blood was draining out of his head. "In about ten seconds . . ." His mouth clashed with hers again as she dragged his shirt clear of his waistband. "I'm not going to give a damn if you're drunk or sober."

"I told you I'm only half drunk." She tossed her head back so that he could see her eyes. They were filled with laughter and desire. "I know exactly what I'm doing and who I'm going to do it with. What would you say if I suggested we consider that little bet of ours a draw?"

He was busy tugging her buttons free before he realized his hands had moved. "How about 'Thank you, God'?"

"It's probably a mistake." She attacked his throat with her teeth. "A terrible, terrible mistake. Jesus, put your hands on me."

"I'm trying." He managed to drag her jacket off while they stumbled toward the bedroom.

"Try harder." She wriggled out of her shoes, tripped, and sent them both crashing into the wall. When his hands streaked under her skirt, hiking it high as they greedily cupped her bottom, she arched back. "Don't stop," she panted, "whatever you do, don't stop."

"Who's stopping?" Desperate, he lifted her off her feet so that his mouth could close over her lace-covered breast.

She moaned once, grasping his hair for balance. "This could ruin our friendship."

He mumbled, his mouth busy with soft, hot flesh. "I don't want to be friends anymore."

"Me either," she managed as they fell onto the bed.

She'd always thought of sex as one of the quirky bonuses life had to offer, with the act itself rarely measuring up to the anticipation. There was certainly nothing dignified about two people panting like dogs and groping each other frantically. It was, if you discounted all the fripperies, a laughable, if temporarily satisfying, experience.

But she'd never made love with Josh Templeton.

There was panting, plenty of groping, even some laughter. But she was about to discover that reality could occasionally outdistance anticipation.

The minute her body was pinned under his, it shifted into overdrive. She was wild for him, wild to feel strong male hands stroke over her, to taste the heat and reckless lust of a hungry mouth, to hear that animal sound of flesh slapping against flesh.

The light from the office slanted in, cut across the bed so that they rolled from brightness to shadow and back again. But there was nothing innocent in the wrestling. It was ripe with purpose, desperation, and edgy greed. She could see the dark intensity of his eyes, the restless smoke of them focused on hers. She could feel the taut muscles of his shoulders under her hands before she tore his shirt aside and reared up to taste.

When he tugged her skirt impatiently down her hips, she thought, now. Thank God, now, and arched to meet him. But he dragged her to her knees and battered her senses with mouth on mouth.

Hot, voracious kisses lashed with tongue and teeth, the frantic strain of torso against torso with one thin layer of silk between dampening flesh. She rocked against him, sizzling, as those clever hands soothed, abraded, tormented her skin. She thought she might burn from the inside out and fumbled desperately at his waistband.

Then he cupped her, fingers streaking under silk, plunging inside velvet fire to drive her hard and mercilessly over the edge. She came like a geyser, release spurting out of her, shooting out shock waves that made her nails bite viciously into his back.

Before she could gulp in air, he shoved her on her back to devour.

He'd wanted her like this—just like this—mindless and frantic and burning for him. He'd dreamed of it, the way she would move under him, the sounds she would make, even the scent of her skin as desire shot to quivering need.

Now he had it, and even that wasn't enough.

He wanted to unravel her inch by inch, to watch her come apart. To hear her scream for him. His own needs were brutal, unreasonable, pumping through his blood like fiery little demons on their way to hell.

She clutched at him, wrapped those glorious long arms and legs around him, and slammed him through the wall of his own sanity.

He yanked her chemise down, baring her breasts for ravenous mouth and bruising hands, and filled himself with her.

It was a war now, fought with moans and gasps and needs that clashed like swords. She rolled, slithered, tearing at his slacks until with a cry of triumph she wrapped long, smooth fingers around him.

His vision grayed. He feared for a moment that he might simply erupt like a novice at that first jolt of pleasure. Then he focused on her face, saw that slow, sly smile, and was damned if he'd let her win.

"I want you inside me." She all but purred it, even though her pulse was pounding like a wound. "I want you inside me. Come inside me." Dear God, he was huge, and iron hard, and she wanted, wanted, wanted. Her smile spread as he lowered his mouth to hers.

"Not yet." Even as she drew breath to curse him, he drove her up and over. Climax slapped into climax like battling tidal waves that left her floundering and gasping for air. And as she scrambled frantically toward the next peak, he plunged into her.

Fresh, outrageous energy blasted through him, fired by new, unspeakable greed. A feral snarl vibrated in his throat as he yanked her hips higher, arrowed deeper. In response, she locked her legs around him, arched back like a bow. Each thrust was like a hammer to the heart, battering them both.

He could no longer see her. He desperately wanted to see her face, to watch her face as they met and mated. But the animal had taken over, and it was blind and deaf and insatiable.

He could see nothing but the red haze that was as much fury as passion. Then even that vanished as the vicious climax ripped through him and emptied him.

CHAPTER 13

S HE THOUGHT SHE'D seen stars. Of course that had probably been her imagination, some latent romantic streak she hadn't been aware of possessing.

More likely it had been a physical reaction due to near unconsciousness.

What they'd done, Margo decided with lazy pleasure, had been to nearly fuck each other to death.

They were sprawled over the bed, two casualties of war, limp and sweaty and scarred. What an intriguing surprise, she mused, running a hand over her damp torso, that Josh should have been the most worthy of opponents.

Stirring up the energy to move, she turned her head and smiled affectionately at him. He was stretched out flat on his stomach, facedown. He hadn't moved since he'd groaned, rolled off her, and plopped there like a landed trout.

Probably asleep, snoring any minute, she decided. Men were so predictable. But then, she was feeling much too lazy and satisfied to be irked. After all, she wasn't the kind of woman men cuddled, particularly after sex. Draining them of all signs of life was just one of her little skills.

She grinned, stretched. Still, he'd surprised her. She'd never had a man come so close to making her beg. The rough, reckless sex had left her feeling very much like a cat with a mouthful of cream-drenched feathers, but there had been a few moments there—perhaps more than a few—when she'd been almost frightened of what he was able to pull out of her.

Good old Josh, she thought. Then her gaze skimmed down his long, naked body and her pulse went to fast shuffle. Gorgeous, sexy, fascinating Josh. Time to move on, she told herself, before she got wound up for something he wouldn't be able to deliver.

She sat up, gave him a friendly slap on the butt, then let out a squealing laugh as his arm snaked out and tumbled her back.

"I'm finished with you, pal." She pressed a kiss to his shoulder. "Gotta go."

"Uh-uh." To her surprise, he pulled her close, shifting until she was curled against him. "I'm getting sensation back in my toes again. Who knows what could be next?"

"We're lucky we lived through it." He nuzzled her hair, moving her in new and lovely ways. After a brief hesitation, she curled an arm over his chest. "Your heart's still pounding."

"Thank Christ. I was afraid it had stopped." Lazily he stroked a hand up her leg, down again. "Margo?"

Her eyes were nearly closed. It was so sweet to be held, to be murmured to. "Hmm?"

"You definitely writhed."

She opened one eye balefully and found him grinning down at her. "I didn't want to hurt your feelings. It seemed so important to you."

"Uh-huh. Not that I was counting . . ." He twirled her tumbled hair around his finger. "But you came five times."

"Only five?" She patted his cheek. "Don't blame yourself, I've had a long day."

He rolled on top of her, watched surprise flicker into her eyes. "Oh, I can do better."

"Think so?" Lips curved, she linked her arms around his neck. "I dare you to try."

"You know the Templetons." He nipped that curved bottom lip. "We can't resist a dare."

WHEN SHE WOKE, the room was dark and she was alone. It surprised her that he was out of bed. They hadn't let loose of each other for more than five minutes all night. When she glanced over and saw the red glow of the alarm clock, she realized she hadn't been asleep much longer than that. It was barely after six, and the last time they'd collapsed it had been quarter to.

Whatever the press gleefully reported on her exploits, she'd never actually made love all night before. She hadn't believed it was physically possible. As she shifted to sit up and every muscle of her body wept, she realized it was certainly possible but not necessarily wise.

Because she had to crawl out of bed, literally, she was grateful not to have an audience. Josh would surely have made some snide remark—then jumped her.

As lowering as it was, she was ready to toss in the towel. Another orgasm might kill her.

And she was a businesswoman now. Time to put fun and games aside and get ready to face the day. She heard herself moan as she limped across the room. A press of a button had the drapes swinging open to admit a dazzling view of the coast, the curve of beach, the rocky inclines. The milky dawn light flowed in—and saved her from a painful encounter with a ficus tree planted in a toe-bruising copper pot.

There were two of them, she noted, a little bleary-eyed. Two delicate-leaved trees flanking the wide window, adding a homey touch to the sheen of the framed elbow chairs done in ivory brocade. The high gloss of oak tables reflected back the little pieces of him. Cuff links, loose change, keys.

He'd tossed a comb on the bureau, she noted. Beside it stood a bottle of men's cologne and a thick black appointment book. She imagined there were women's names and numbers from every time zone around the globe noted in it.

She caught a glimpse of herself in the mirror, naked, still glowing from the aftermath of good sex. Well, she mused, she was here now, wasn't she? And they weren't.

Her gritty eyes popped wide as she noticed the bed reflected behind her. How could she have been so involved with Josh that she hadn't noticed the bed? They had made love throughout the night on a lake-sized mattress framed with glinting brass head- and footboards, subtly curved to embrace jade green sheets.

But then, the elegant simplicity of the jade-and-white room, the shining touches of brass and copper, suited Templeton. The man, and the hotel.

She found one of the plushy white robes the hotel provided in the closet and wrapped it around her. The thought of a long, hot shower almost made her whimper, but curiosity drew her to the door first, and she cracked it open.

Josh was wearing nothing but wrinkled slacks that he hadn't bothered to fasten. He'd opened the shades so the fragile light crept into the room, and he held a portable phone to one ear while he paced the room in his bare feet.

He was speaking French.

God, he was gorgeous, she thought. Not just that wonderful gold-tipped hair, the long, lithe body, the elegant, surprisingly capable hands. It was the way he moved, the timbre of his voice, that aura of power around him that she'd always been too close to see.

Her French was spotty at best, so she understood little of what he said. It didn't matter. It was the way he said it, the warm, liquid sounds, the hand gestures he unconsciously added to emphasize.

She watched those smoke gray eyes narrow—irritation, impatience—before he rattled off what could have been orders or oaths. Then he laughed, and his voice simply creamed over lovely, exotic words.

Suddenly she realized she was holding her breath, that she had a hand pressed to her heart, like some dreamy-eyed teenager over the captain of the football team.

It's just Josh, she reminded herself and deliberately drew in air, firmly dropping her hand to her side. It was a matter of pure ego that made her lean provocatively against the door to wait until he'd finished.

"Ça va, Simone. Oui, oui, oui, c'est bien. Ah, nous parlerons dans trois heures." Pausing, he listened, wandered to the window. "Parce que ils sont les idiots." He chuckled. "Non, non, pas de quoi. Au revoir, Simone."

He clicked the phone off, turned toward the desk, before he spotted her. Tumbled blond hair, witchy blue eyes, and a white robe loosely belted. His glands went on full alert.

"A little loose end I left dangling in Paris."

"Simone." Watching him, Margo ran a hand down the soft lapel of the robe. "Tell me, is she as . . . intriguing as her name?"

"Oh, more so." He walked over, slid his hands inside the robe. "And she's crazy about me."

"Pig," Margo murmured against his mouth.

"And she does whatever I tell her," he added, walking her backward toward the bed.

"Aren't you lucky?" Margo shifted, jabbed her elbow into his gut. When he grunted, she slipped out of his arms, smoothed her hair. "I need a shower."

"Just for that I'm not going to tell you she's fifty-eight, has four grandchildren, and is the associate director of marketing, Templeton Paris."

She shot a look over her shoulder. "I didn't ask. Why don't you order up some breakfast? I want to be in the shop by eight-thirty."

He obliged her, ordering room service to deliver it in an hour. That should give him just enough time, he decided as he joined her in the shower. She frowned at him when he blocked the best part of the spray.

"It's lukewarm," he complained.

"It's better for the skin. And I like privacy when I shower."

"Templeton's a green company." He nudged up the hot water even when she slapped at his hand. Steam began to rise satisfactorily along the glossy black walls of the stall. "As vice president it's my corporate duty to conserve our natural resources." Reaching out, he worked up the lather in the hair she'd just begun to wash.

The shower was large enough for a party of four, she reminded herself. There was no reason for her to feel crowded. "You're just in here because you think you can get lucky again."

"God, the woman sees right through me. It's mortifying." When she turned away to finish the job herself, he contented himself with washing her back. "How long does it take to dry all that hair? There's miles of it."

"It's not the length, it's the thickness," she said absently. It was foolish, she knew. He'd already run and rubbed and stroked those hands over every inch of her body. But this . . . cleansing ritual was uncomfortably intimate.

She'd spoken no less than the truth. She didn't bathe with her lovers. She only slept with them in the literal sense, when she chose. It wasn't just a matter of control, though that was part of it. It was a matter of maintaining image and illusion.

Now with Josh she had not only spent the night with him without intending to, but she was sharing the shower with him. It was time, she decided, to lock a few parameters in place.

She tipped her face under the spray, let it stream the suds from her hair. When he handed her the soap and turned his back to her, she stared blankly.

"Your turn," he told her.

Her eyes narrowed, then lighted with wicked purpose. He hissed between his teeth when she slapped lather on his back.

"Oh, sorry. Those scratches must sting some."

Hands braced on the tile, he looked back at her. "It's all right. I've had my shots."

Without realizing it, she gentled her strokes. It was such a nice back, she mused. Muscled, broad at the shoulder, tapering to the waist, with all that smooth, tasty skin between. On impulse, she pressed a light kiss between his shoulder blades before stepping out of the shower.

"You know, Josh, I was only teasing about Simone." Bending at the waist, she turbaned her hair in a towel, then reached for another. "We've both had other relationships, and are free to continue to have them. We're not going to tangle each other up with strings at this point in our lives." After securing the towel between her breasts, she made do with the complimentary body cream in Templeton's spiraled bottle on the counter. Setting a foot on the padded vanity stool, she smoothed fragrant lotion onto her legs. "Neither one of us is looking for complications, and I'd hate for us to ruin a simple affair by making promises we'd never keep."

She slicked cream down her other leg, humming a little. "We have an advantage here that most people don't. We know each other so well, we don't need to play all those games or juggle all the pretenses." She flicked a glance toward the shower, mildly troubled by his lack of response.

He could handle the anger that simmered up to his throat. That was simply a matter of control. But the hurt, the little slashing knives that her careless words had dueling in his gut were another matter. For those, he could have cheerfully murdered her.

He turned off the water with a snap of his wrist, stepped through the double glass doors that separated the shower from the rest of the bath.

"Yeah, we know each other, duchess," he said as he flicked a towel from the heated bar. She was standing front and center of the eight-foot-long bath counter, looking perfect in the stark and sophisticated black-and-white decor, her skin glowing from the lotion she still held in one hand. "Inside and out. What would two shallow sophisticates like us want with mixing romance with our sex?"

She rubbed her arms. Despite the billowing steam, the room seemed abruptly chilly. "That's not entirely what I meant. You're angry."

"See, you do know me. Okay, no strings, no games, no pretenses." He walked over, slapped his hands on the counter, and caged her. "But I've got a hard and fast rule of my own. I don't share. As long as I'm fucking you, no one else is."

She balled her hands at her sides. "Well, that's clear enough. And crude enough."

"Your call. Why cloud the issue with euphemisms?"

"Just because you're angry that I said it first is no reason to—"

"There you go, seeing right through me again."

She took a steadying breath. "There's no reason for either of us to be angry. First, I don't like to fight before I've had at least one cup of coffee. And second, I didn't mean that I would stroll out of here and jump into someone else's bed. Contrary to popular belief, I don't juggle men like flaming swords. I simply meant that when either of us is ready to move on, there won't be any nasty scenes."

"Maybe I like nasty scenes."

"I'm beginning to see that. Have we finished with this one?"

"Not quite." He caught her by the chin. "You know, duchess, this is the only time since you first picked up a mascara wand that I've seen you without makeup." With his free hand, he tugged the towel off her hair so that it tumbled wet and wild over breasts and shoulders. "Without all that sheen and polish."

"Cut it out." She tried to jerk her chin free, furious that he'd reminded her she was without her accustomed shield.

"You're so goddamn beautiful." But there was grim purpose rather than admiration in his eyes. "They'd have burned you at the stake a few hundred years ago. They'd never have believed you'd gotten that face, that body, without seducing the devil."

"Stop it." Was that her voice? she wondered. So weak, ready to melt on words she didn't mean. Her unsteady hands were an instant too late to stop the second towel from sliding to the floor. "If you think I'm going to let you—"

"Let me, hell." He slipped his hand between her legs and felt her hot and wet and ready. "You said no pretenses, Margo. So if you tell me you don't want me, right now . . ." He gripped her hips, braced her as he eased slowly inside her. "If you tell me, I'll believe you."

She felt the avalanche of need carrying her under. Saw by the dark triumph in his eyes that he knew it. "Damn you, Josh."

"Well, that makes two of us."

* * *

SHE SKIPPED BREAKFAST. She'd simply felt too raw and unsteady to share a civilized meal with him after they'd savaged each other in a steamy bathroom. Still, she'd gotten back to the shop, changed into a fresh suit, and brewed both coffee and tea.

The coffee she attacked herself, drinking half a pot before it was time to open the doors. Revving on nerves and caffeine, she faced her first day alone as a merchant.

By midday, despite several bolstering sales, both her spirits and her energy were flagging. A night without sleep certainly explained the fatigue, and she knew exactly where to point the finger of blame for her sulks. Right at Josh Templeton's calculating heart.

She hated the way he had shrugged and bid her an absent good-bye that morning. Sitting down to his breakfast as if there hadn't been wild sex and angry words between them. It hardly mattered that his attitude was exactly what she had outlined. That didn't stop her from worrying over the nagging certainty that he was playing some game she hadn't been informed of. And he kept shifting the rules to suit himself.

There had been a cold gleam in his eyes as he glanced up from his coffee, she thought. And she was sure she'd seen a calculating smirk on his mouth before she'd shut the door. Well, slammed it—but that was beside the point.

Just what was he up to? She knew him well enough to be sure . . . Damn it, she was beginning to wonder if she knew him at all.

"Miss, I'd like to see this pearl choker."

"Yes, of course." It made her feel brisk and efficient to fetch the keys, unlock the display, spread the gleaming pearls on black velvet. "They're lovely, aren't they? Beautifully matched."

A present, she remembered, from a shipping magnate old enough to be her grandfather. She'd never slept with him, though the press had beat war drums about their affair. He'd only wanted someone young and attractive to talk to, someone to listen while he spoke of the wife he'd lost to cancer.

He had been, in the two years she had known him, a rare thing in her life. A male friend. The pearls had been nothing more than a gift from a friend who was pining away from a broken heart and who soon died from it.

"Is this clasp eighteen-karat?"

Suddenly Margo wanted to snatch them back, to scream at the woman that she couldn't have them. They were hers, a reminder of one of the few unselfish and loving things she'd ever done in her life.

"Yes." She forced herself to speak through a smile so stiff it ached. "Italian. It's stamped. Would you like to try them on?"

She did, and hemmed, hawed, preened, and stroked. In the end, she handed them back with a shake of her head. Margo locked the pearls into the display like a guilty secret.

Tourists came in, poking through the treasures, carelessly clanking porcelain against glass, china against wood. Margo lost three potential customers when she testily informed them not to handle the merchandise unless they were prepared to buy it.

That cleared the shop long enough for her to run upstairs and pump some aspirin into her system. On her way down again, she caught a glimpse of herself in the mirror.

Her face was set and angry, her eyes deadly. She felt her stomach jitter with repressed temper.

"Want to scare all the customers away, Margo?"

She closed her eyes, breathed deep, visualized a cool white screen. It was a technique she'd often used in modeling when a session had dragged on, with hairstylist and makeup artist poking, photographer waiting, assistants whining.

All she had to do was go away for a minute, remind herself that she could, and would, fill the blank screen with whatever image they wanted.

Calmer, she opened her eyes, watched her face smooth out. If her head still throbbed, no one had to know but herself. She walked downstairs ready to greet the next customer.

She was delighted when Judy Prentice dropped in, bringing a friend with her. She poured them tea, then excused herself to show another customer into a fitting room. At two, she opened the first bottle of complimentary champagne and wondered what was keeping Laura.

By two-thirty, she was feeling frazzled, struggling with the gift wrap she was afraid she would never get the hang of. And Candy breezed in.

"Oh, what an adorable little shop." She clapped her pretty hands together and bounced over to the counter, where Margo was sweating over a tape dispenser. "I'm so sorry I couldn't make it by for your opening, Margo. I just couldn't squeeze it into my day. But I made a special point of coming by today."

Particularly since the shop and its owners had been the hot topic at brunch.

"I'm just going to poke around, but don't you worry, I'll be sure to buy something. Isn't this fun," she said to the woman waiting for the package. "Just like a big yard sale. Oh, what a nice little bowl." She danced over, running her fingers over the frosted glass, looking for chips. "The price is a little high for secondhand." Still holding the bowl, she turned a sharp-edged smile on Margo. "I suppose you inflate it to give your customers room to bargain."

Keep cool, Margo warned herself. Candy was just trying to get her goat, the same way she had in high school. "We consider our merchandise priced to sell."

"Well." With a careless shrug, Candy set the bowl down. "I suppose I don't know very much about cost. I just know what I like." She eyed a pair of enameled candlesticks. "These are . . . unusual, aren't they?"

"You have lovely things," the waiting customer commented as Margo slipped the wrapped box into a bag.

"Thank you." Margo shuffled through her tired mind for the name on the credit slip. "Thank you very much, Mrs. Pendleton. Please come again."

"I certainly will." She accepted the bag, hesitated. "Do you mind if I say I only came in today because I've seen your photograph so many times? I spend a lot of time in Europe. La Margo's face is everywhere."

"Was everywhere. No, I don't mind."

"I switched to the Bella Donna line of skin-care products primarily because of your advertisements."

She winced before she could prevent herself. "I hope you're satisfied with the products."

"It's an excellent line. As I said, I came in because I wanted to see you in person. I'll come back because you have beautiful things imaginatively presented." She slid the bag onto her arm as she stepped back from the counter. "I think you're a very brave and adventurous woman." Mrs. Pendleton flicked a glance toward Candy, who was frowning over a paperweight. "And an admirable one." She leaned back over the counter, her eyes dancing. "Make sure that one doesn't stick something in that Chanel bag of hers. She looks shifty."

Chuckling, Margo waved her now favorite customer off and walked over to deal with Candy. "Champagne?"

"Oh, such a clever idea. I imagine the offer of free drinks lures in a certain type of clientele. Just a tiny glass. How are you managing, darling?"

"Well enough."

"I was just admiring your jewelry." Coveting it. "It must be heartbreaking for you to have to sell it."

"My heart's cold steel, Candy, remember?"

"When it comes to men," Candy said breezily and turned to the jewelry case. "But diamonds? I wouldn't think so. What did you have to do for those earrings?"

"Things better not spoken of in polite company. Would you like to see them? Considering your last divorce settlement, they're within your price range. Unless, of course, dumping a husband doesn't earn a woman what it used to."

"Don't be snide, Margo. You're the one peddling your wares. And no, I'm not interested in secondhand jewelry. In fact, I'm having a hard time finding anything I can use at all. Your taste is more . . . let's say, emancipated than mine."

"Not enough gold leaf? I'll be sure to keep your taste in mind when we restock."

"You're actually planning on keeping this place running?" She sipped her champagne and giggled. "Margo, that's so sweet. Everyone knows you never finish anything. A few of us were having a wonderful time over brunch at the club, speculating on how long you'd last."

The customer, Margo thought, was not always right. "Candy, do you remember that time all your clothes were stolen from gym class and you were shoved into a locker and stayed trapped in there until Mr. Hansen from Maintenance sawed off the lock and got you out, naked and hysterical? You, not Mr. Hansen."

Candy's eyes narrowed to lethal slits. "You. I knew it was you, but I couldn't prove it."

"Actually it was Kate, because I lost the draw. But it was my idea. Except for calling Mr. Hansen. That was Laura's. Now would you like to leave quietly, or should I knock you down, rip off that Laura Ashley blouse—which doesn't suit you, by the way—and send you out of here naked and hysterical?"

"To think I actually felt sorry for you."

"No, you didn't," Margo corrected, nipping the flute out of Candy's hand before it could be hurled.

"You're nothing but a second-rate slut who spent all her life begging for scraps and pretending to be something she never could be," Candy spat out.

"Funny, most people consider me a first-rate slut. Now get the hell out of here before I stop pretending to be what I'm not and rip off the nose your parents bought you when you were twelve."

Candy shrieked, curled her fingers into talons. She might have leaped, but the sound of the door opening stopped her from making a public display.

One brow lifted, Laura assessed the scene. "Hello, Candy, you're looking healthy. Sorry I'm late, Margo, but I brought you a present."

Candy whirled, intending to give Laura a taste of the temper both of her ex-husbands could attest to. But Laura wasn't alone. Candy shuddered back the venom and beamed a delighted smile.

"Mr. and Mrs. Templeton—how wonderful to see you both."

"Ah, Candace Litchfield, isn't it?" said Susan Templeton, knowing full well. "Margo." Easily ignoring Candy's outstretched hand, Susan glided into Margo's open arms. She kissed both of Margo's cheeks lavishly, then winked. "We didn't even take time to unpack. We just couldn't wait to see you."

"I've missed you." She clung hard, enveloped by the familiar scent of Chanel. "Oh, I've missed you. You look wonderful, beautiful."

"Doesn't give me the time of day," Thomas Templeton complained, giving his daughter's shoulder a quick squeeze. He nodded absently to Candy as she stalked out, then grinned as Margo raced across the room. She bounded into his arms. "Now that's more like it."

"I'm so glad to see you. I'm so glad you're here. Oh, I'm so sorry." And she buried her face in his shoulder and wept like a child.

CHAPTER 14

"Better?"

"Mmm." Leaning over the sink in the upstairs bath, Margo splashed water on her face. "I guess I've been a little on edge."

"Nothing like a good cry to smooth out those edges." Susan offered her a fingertip towel and a quick, supportive rub on the shoulder. "And you always cried well."

"Poor Mr. T." As much for comfort as to dry her skin, Margo buried her face in the towel. "What a greeting. Two seconds and I'm blubbering all over his shoulder."

"He loves having his girls blubber on him. It makes him feel strong. Now—" Susan put her ring-studded hands on Margo's shoulders, turned her around. "Let's have a look." She pursed her pretty mouth, narrowed her pale blue eyes. "A little blush, a couple coats of mascara, and you'll do. Do you have your arsenal up here?"

In answer, Margo opened the mirror cabinet over the sink. Inside were neatly arranged bottles and tubes. "Emergency kit."

"That's my girl. Still using Bella Donna," she commented when Margo took out a small tube. "I threw mine out."

"Oh, Mrs. T."

"They made me mad." Susan jerked an athletic shoulder. She was a small woman, delicate-boned and slim like her daughter. She kept in shape in her own style. She skied like a demon, played a vicious game of tennis, and swam laps as though competing in the Olympics. To fit her lifestyle, her sable-colored hair was cut short and sleek to cap a bright, interesting face that she cared for religiously.

"I screwed up," Margo reminded her.

"Which was hardly enough cause to dump you as the Bella Donna Woman. Which is an irritatingly redundant title in the first place. All in all, you're better off without them."

Margo smiled into the mirror, smoothed on a light base. "I really have missed you."

"What I'd like to know is why you didn't contact Tommy and me the minute you found out you were in trouble." With her hands on her hips, Susan strode to the tub, then back to the sink. "It was weeks before we heard a thing. The photographic safari kept us out of touch, but Josh and Laura knew how to reach us."

"I was ashamed." She couldn't explain why she could admit it so easily to Susan. She just could. "I'd made such bad choices. I was having a seedy affair with a married man, I let him use me. No, worse—I was too stupid to realize he was using me. I ruined my career, destroyed what little repu-tation I had, and nearly bankrupted myself in the process."

"Well." Susan angled her head. "That's quite an accomplishment. How busy you must have been to do all that by yourself."

"I did do it myself." She chose taupe shadow to accent her eyes, brush-ing it on with a deft and practiced hand.

"This man you were involved with had nothing to do with it, I suppose. Did you love him?"

"I wanted to." Even that was easier to admit now. "I wanted to have someone, to find someone I could build a life with. The kind of life I thought I wanted. Fun, games, and no responsibilities."

"And that's past tense?"

"It is. Has to be." Margo carefully darkened her eyebrows. "Naturally, I chose someone completely inappropriate, someone who could never offer me permanence. That's my system, Mrs. T."

Susan waited a moment, watching as Margo dashed on eyeliner and mascara with the skill of a master. "Do you know what's always worried me about you, Margo? Your self-esteem."

"Mum always said I thought too much of myself."

"No, on that Annie and I have always disagreed, and we disagreed rarely. Your self-worth is too tied up in your looks. You were a beautiful child, dazzlingly beautiful. Life is different for children with dazzling looks. More difficult in some ways, because people tend to judge them by their beauty, and then they begin to judge themselves by that same standard."

"It was my only skill. Kate had the brains, Laura had the heart."

"It makes me sad that you believe that, and that too many people pointed you in that direction."

"You were never one of them." She replaced the makeup carefully, as a master carpenter would store his tools. "I'm trying to go in a new direction now, Mrs. T."

"Well, then." Slipping a bolstering arm around Margo's waist, Susan led her back into the boudoir. "You're young enough to take a dozen different directions. And smart enough. You've wasted your brains for a while, made foolish mistakes and poorly considered choices."

"Ow." With a sheepish smile, Margo rubbed her heart. "You've always been able to sneak those jabs in."

"I haven't finished. You've worried and disappointed your mother. A woman, I'll add, who deserves not only your love and respect but your admiration. There aren't many who at the tender age of twenty-three and still grieving could leave behind everything familiar and cross an ocean with a small child to build a new life. But that's not the point." Susan waved that away and nudged Margo onto the edge of the bed. "You squandered your money and danced your way to the edge of a very high and dangerous cliff. But," she lifted Margo's chin with a finger, "you didn't jump. Unlike our little Seraphina, you stepped back, you squared your shoulders, and you showed you were willing to face what life had dealt you. That takes more courage, Margo—much more—than leaping into the void."

"I had people to turn to."

"So do we all. It's only fools and egotists who think no one will be there to lend a hand. And bigger fools and bigger egotists who don't reach out." She held out a hand. Without hesitation Margo took it, then pressed it to her cheek.

"Better?" Laura asked in an echo of her mother as she came to the door. It took only an instant to survey the scene and feel relief.

"Much." After a long breath, Margo rose, smoothed down her skirt. "Sorry to leave you in the lurch down there."

"No problem. Actually, Dad's having the time of his life. He's made three sales. And the way he's charming Minn Whiley right now, I think we can count on four."

"Minn's downstairs?" Amused, Susan flicked her fingers through her boyish hair. "I'll go add my charm. She'll walk out loaded down with bags and won't know what hit her." She paused at the doorway to rub a hand over Laura's back. "You girls have a lovely place here. You've made a good choice."

"We're worrying her," Laura murmured when her mother's greeting to Minn floated upstairs. "You and I."

"I know. We'll just have to show her how tough we are. We are tough, aren't we, Laura?"

"Oh, sure. You bet. The disgraced celebrity and the betrayed trophy wife."

Temper snapped into Margo's eyes. "You're nobody's trophy."

"Not anymore. Now, before I forget—why was Candy looking at me as if she was hoping to grind up my liver for pâté?"

"Ah." Remembering the scene put a sneaky smile on her face. "I had to tell her whose idea it was to call Mr. Hansen when she was trapped naked in her locker."

Laura closed her eyes, tried not to think of the next meeting of the Garden Club. She and Candy were co-chairs. "Had to tell her?"

"Really had to." Margo smiled winningly. "She called you 'poor Laura.' Twice."

Laura opened her eyes again, set her teeth. "I see. I wonder how difficult it would be to stuff her bony butt into a locker at the club?"

"For tough babes like you and me? A snap."

"I'll think about it." Automatically she checked her watch. Her life now ran on packets of time. "Meanwhile, we're having a family dinner tonight. A real one this time. Kate's meeting us at the house, and I left a message for Josh."

"Ah, Josh." As they started for the stairs, Margo linked her fingers together, pulled them apart. Wished desperately for a cigarette. "There's probably something I should tell you."

"Mmm-hmm. Look, Margo." Chuckling, she leaned on the rail. "Dad's playing with the cash register and Mama's packing boxes. Aren't they wonderful?"

"The best." How could she tell Laura she'd spent the night ripping up the sheets at Templeton Monterey with her brother? Better left alone, she decided. In any case, the way they had parted, it was unlikely to happen again.

"What did you want to tell me?"

"Um . . . only that I sold your beaded white sheath."

"Good. I never liked it anyway."

MARGO FELT SHE'D made the right decision when Josh arrived at Templeton House. He joined the family in the solarium, exchanged warm embraces with both his parents, then helped himself from the hors d'oeuvres tray. He entertained his nieces, argued with Kate over some esoteric point of tax law, and fetched mineral water for Laura.

As for the woman with whom he'd spent the night committing acts that were still illegal in some states, he treated her with the absent, vaguely infuriating affection older brothers reserved for their pesky younger siblings.

She thought about stabbing him in the throat with a shrimp fork.

She restrained herself, even when she was plunked down between him and Kate at the glossy mahogany table at dinner.

It was, after all, a celebration, she reminded herself. A reunion. Even Ann, who considered it a breach of etiquette for servants to sit at the family table, had been cajoled into joining in. Mr. T.'s doing, Margo thought. No one, particularly if it was a female, could say no to him.

Surely part of Josh's problem was that he resembled his father so closely. Thomas Templeton was as tall and lean as he'd been in his youth. The man Margo had frankly adored for twenty-five years had aged magnificently. The lines that unfairly made a woman look worn added class and appeal as they crinkled around his smoky gray eyes. His hair was still thick and full, with the added dash of glints of silver brushed through the bronze.

He had, she knew, a smile that could charm the petals off a rose. And when roused, a flinty, unblinking stare that chilled to the bone. He used both to run his business, and his family, and with them he incited devotion, unswerving love, and just a little healthy fear.

It was rumored that he had cut a wide, successful, and memorable swath through the ladies in his youth, romancing, seducing, and conquering at will. Until thirty, when he'd been introduced to a young Susan Conway. She had, in her own words, hunted him down like a dog and bagged him.

Margo smiled, listening to him build stories for his goggle-eyed granddaughters of herds of elephants and prides of lions.

"We have the *Lion King* video, Granddaddy." Kayla toyed with her Brussels sprouts, hoping a miracle would make them disappear.

"You've watched it a zillion times," Ali said, tossing her hair back in the way she'd seen Margo do.

"Well, we'll have to make it a zillion and one, won't we?" Thomas winked at Kayla. "We'll have ourselves a moviethon. What's your favorite video, Ali?"

"She likes to watch kissy movies." Striking back, Kayla pursed her lips and made smacking noises. "She wants Brandon Reno to kiss her on the mouth."

"I do not." Mortified, Ali flushed scarlet. It proved there was no secret safe with a little sister. "You're just a baby." She dug for her deepest insult. "A baby pig-face."

"Allison, don't call your sister names," Laura said wearily. Her two little angels had been sniping at each other for weeks.

"Oh, and she can say whatever she wants. Just because she's the baby."

"I am not a baby."

"I thought you were my baby." Thomas sighed sadly. "I thought you were both my babies, but I guess if you're all grown up and don't need me anymore . . ."

"I'll be your baby, Granddaddy." Eyes wide and sincere, Kayla gazed up at him. Then she saw, to her delight, that a miracle had happened. The dreaded Brussels sprouts were gone from her plate. They'd made the leap to his. Love swarmed through her. "I'll always be your baby."

"Well, I'm not a baby." Far from ready to surrender, Ali jutted out her chin. But her lip was quivering.

"No, I suppose you're not." Laura cocked a brow at her daughter's mutinous face. "And since you're not, you won't fight with your sister at the table."

"Oh, I don't know." Margo picked up her wineglass. The fairy light of crystal chandeliers and flickering candlelight shot through it in red and gold glints. "I always fought with Kate at the table."

"And you usually started it," Kate added, forking up a bite of lamb.

"You always started it."

"No, I always finished it." Kate peered around Josh to grin. "You always got sent to your room."

"Only because Mum felt sorry for you. You were so outgunned."

"Outgunned, my butt. When it came to a verbal showdown, you were always playing with blanks. Even when I was Ali's age, I could—"

"Isn't it nice to be home, Tommy?" Susan lifted her glass in a toast. "It's so comforting to see that no matter how life goes on, little changes. Annie, dear, how are you managing all our girls without me?"

"It's a trial, Mrs. T. Now, my ma, she kept a switch in the kitchen. A good hickory switch."

War forgotten, Ali gaped at Ann. "Your mother hit you with a stick?"

"Once or twice she did indeed, and sitting down after was a punishment itself. Mostly just seeing it there on the peg by the door was enough to keep a civil tongue in your head."

"Your weapon of choice was a wooden spoon." Remembering, Margo shifted in her seat.

"A fine deterrent it was to a sassy mouth, too."

"You walloped me once with it, Annie, remember?" It was Josh who spoke.

"Really?" Intrigued, Susan studied her son. "I never heard about that."

Josh sampled his wine and watched Ann squirm out of the corner of his eye. "Oh, Annie and I decided it would be our little secret."

"And so it has been," Annie muttered. "Until now." She cleared her throat, dropped her hands into her lap. "I beg your pardon, Mrs. T. It was hardly my place to spank the boy."

"What nonsense." Intrigued, Susan leaned forward. "I want to know what he did to deserve it."

"I might have been innocent," Josh objected, to which his mother merely snorted.

"You never had an innocent day in your life. What did he do, Annie?"

"He'd been hounding me." Even after all the years that had passed, Ann could remember the insistence in his voice, the demon in his eye. "I tell you the truth, I've never known a child so tenacious as Master Josh. He could devil you beyond death, and that's the truth."

"Persistence." He grinned at Annie, then glanced at his father. "It's a trait of the Templeton males, right, Dad?"

"And plenty the times I earned a warm rear end because of it," Thomas agreed.

"I'd love to hear about Josh's." Margo tipped back her glass, sent him a smoldering look. "In fact, I'm dying to. How many whacks did you give him, Mum?"

"I didn't count. It was—"

"I did. Five. In rapid and shocking succession." He met Margo's look sneer for sneer. "I still say it was Margo's fault."

"Mine? Oh, that's so typical."

"He was teasing you unmercifully," Ann put in. "And picking on Miss Laura. And as Miss Kate had just come to us, he had a new target there. He was twelve, I believe, and acting like a bully."

"It was just high spirits," Josh claimed. "And I still say Margo—"

"Four years your junior," Ann said in a tone that made him feel twelve again. "And you, who should have known better, daring her and the other girls to clamber down those cliffs looking for that foolish treasure chest. Calling them names, too. And going out there after I'd told you to stay in the yard with them for one blessed hour. One blessed hour," she repeated, shrinking him with a look, "so I could finish the ironing in some peace. But off you went, and if I hadn't caught sight of you, the lot of you might have dashed yourselves on the rocks."

"Oh, that time." Margo smiled. "I'd like to know how that was my fault."

Josh cleared his throat because his tie suddenly felt too tight. Annie, he realized, hadn't lost her touch. "You said you knew where it was. That you'd seen it, and even had a gold doubloon."

"So," she shrugged, "I lied."

"Which would have earned you a swat if I'd known that part of it."

Satisfied, Josh poured more wine. "See?"

"Took it like a man, did you?" Thomas reached over to slap his son on the back. "And didn't drag a lady's name into it."

"He yelped like a scalded dog." Ann's dry comment brought a burst of laughter around the table. "But it hurting me more than him was never truer. I was sure I would be fired on the spot, and rightfully so for spanking the master's son."

"I'd have given you a raise," Susan said easily.

"Nothing like a mother's love," Josh muttered.

"Well, he came up to me about an hour later. Seemed he had thought it through well enough." Now the look Ann sent Josh was full of warmth. "He apologized as neat as you please, then asked if we couldn't keep the matter between us."

"Smart boy." Thomas slapped him on the back again.

LATER, WHEN LAURA was up putting the children to bed, they lounged in the parlor. It was, Margo realized, moments like this, rooms like this, that had spurred her quest for more.

Soft, rich lights from jewel-hued lamps bathed the glossy walls, played over the dark windows where drapes had been left open wide. The faded colors in the Oriental rugs seemed to highlight the gleam of the wide-planked chestnut floors.

A perfect room in a perfect house, she thought, with the old, heirloom furniture more a statement of permanence than wealth. Fresh flowers lovingly arranged by her mother's hands speared out of china and crystal. Terrace doors, flung open, welcomed a quiet, fragrant night with just the right touch of moonlight.

It was a room that breathed elegance and warmth and welcome. And, she understood now that when she had run from it to make her own, she had focused only on the elegance. Warmth and welcome had been neglected for too long.

Josh sat at the baby grand improvising blues with Kate. Lazy, blood-stirring music, she mused. That suited him. He didn't play often. Margo had nearly forgotten how clever he was with the keys. She wished it didn't remind her how clever those hands had been last night.

She wished that hearing the companionable way he and Kate laughed together, seeing the intimate way their heads bent close, didn't shoot a burning blast of jealousy through her blood.

Ridiculous reaction, she told herself. Knee-jerk. Which certainly suited the occasion, as he'd been a complete and utter jerk all evening. But he wasn't going to spoil it for her, she decided. She was going to enjoy her time with the Templetons, her evening in the house she'd always loved, and the hell with him.

Couldn't he at least look at her when she was despising him?

She was too wrapped up in her own foul thoughts to notice the tacit look that passed between the Templetons. With a nod, Susan rose. She would go upstairs, corner Laura, and find out exactly how her daughter was feeling.

Thomas poured a brandy, lighted the single cigar his wife now allowed him per day, and sat on the curved settee. Catching Margo's eye, he patted the cushion beside him.

"Aren't you afraid I'll start bawling again?"

"I've got a fresh handkerchief."

She did sit, brushed her fingers over the edge of white in his top pocket. "Irish linen. Mum tricked me into learning to iron with your handkerchiefs. They always felt so soft and smelled so good when they came out of the wash. I never see Irish linen without remembering standing at the ironing board in the laundry room, pressing your handkerchiefs into perfect white squares."

"Ironing's becoming a lost art."

"It would have been lost years ago if men had had to do it."

He laughed and patted her knee. "Now tell me about this business you're running."

She'd known he would ask, known she'd fumble for an explanation. "Kate could give you a better, more organized rundown."

"I'll get the fine print and bottom line from our Kate. I want to know what you're looking to get out of it."

"A living. I let the one I had get away."

"You fucked up, girl. No use prettying it up, or moping over it. What are you doing now?"

It was one of the reasons she loved him. No sentimentalizing over mistakes. "Trying to make people buy what I want to sell. I collected a lot of things over the years. It was one of the things I did best. You know, Mr. T., I realized when I was packing up that I might not have deliberately surrounded myself with the interesting or the potentially valuable, but that's what I did. I think I have an eye for buying."

"I won't argue with that. You always had a sense of quality."

"Even when I didn't have any other kind of sense. I tossed my money away on things, and now I've found a way that I don't have to be sorry about it. Buying the building instead of renting was a risk, I know."

"If it hadn't been a good investment, Kate wouldn't have let you do it, and she damn well wouldn't have anted up her own money."

"Including repair, remodeling, and startup, six hundred and thirty-seven dollars a square foot," Kate said over her shoulder. "And some loose change."

"A good price." Thomas puffed on his cigar. "Who did the renovations?"

"Barkley and Sons handled the carpentry and subcontracted out the plumbing and wiring." Margo took his snifter for a sip. "I did most of the painting myself."

"Did you now?" He grinned around his cigar. "Advertising?"

"I'm using my checkered past to get print space with interviews, some television. Kate's going to try to squeeze out time to look things over and see if we can budget in advertising money."

"And how are you going to replace your stock?"

Looking forward made her nervous, but Margo answered briskly. "I'll have to try auctions and estate sales. I thought I could contact some of the models and designers I know, negotiate to buy used clothes that way. But I'll have to expand from that, because we've already gotten a lot of requests for larger sizes."

She scooted around on the settee, curled her legs under her. If anyone would understand the thrill of business dealings, it would be Mr. T. "I know we've only been open for two days, but I really think we can make it work. No one else has anything like it."

She forgot to be worried, and her voice began to bubble with excitement. "At least I don't know of any shop that offers secondhand designer clothes along with fashion and fine jewelry, furniture, glassware, antiques."

"Don't forget kitchen appliances and art," Josh put in.

"My cappuccino maker isn't for sale," she shot back. "And neither are my paintings. But the rest"—she shifted back to Thomas—"hell, I'd sell my underwear for the right price."

"You are selling your underwear," Kate reminded her.

"Pegnoirs," Margo corrected. "Negligees. Laura has already added to the stock. Of course, Kate won't part with a bedroom slipper."

"I'm still wearing them."

"But we're drawing people in, and a lot of them are buying."

"And you're happy."

"I don't know about happy yet, but I'm determined."

"Margo." He patted her knee. "In business that's the same thing. Why don't you have a display set up in the hotel lobby?"

"I—"

"We have half a dozen up for boutiques and jewelry stores, gift shops. Why don't we have one from our own girls?" He jabbed the air with his cigar, spilling ashes that Margo automatically brushed from his knee. "Josh, I'd have expected you to take care of that. Templeton takes care of its own, and it has a policy of supporting small businesses."

"I've already arranged it." Josh continued to noodle out boogie-woogie. "Laura's going to select the pieces for the hotel, and for another display at the resort."

Margo opened her mouth, then set her teeth. "You might have mentioned it to me."

"I might have." He shot a look over his shoulder, his fingers never faltering. "I didn't. Laura knows what works best for Templeton clientele."

"Oh, and I wouldn't know anything about that."

"Here she goes," Kate murmured.

"I know as much as you do about Templeton clientele," Margo fumed, unfolding her legs to get to her feet. "Damn it, I've *been* Templeton clientele. And if you're interested in displaying merchandise from Pretenses, then you talk to me."

"Fine." He stopped playing to glance at his watch. "I've got a tennis match with Mom at seven. I've set up the board meeting for nine-thirty. Does that suit you?"

"Well enough." Thomas settled back with his brandy. "We'll meet at eight-forty-five, to discuss those other matters beforehand."

"Good." Josh flicked his eyes back to Margo. "Annie's got your bag packed by now. Why don't you go up and get it?"

"My bag?" She found herself teetering between unfinished temper and bafflement. "Why do I need a bag?"

"So you won't have to rush back to the shop to change every morning. It makes more sense to have your clothes where you sleep."

Her cheeks flushed, not from embarrassment but from fury. "I sleep here, or at the shop."

"Not anymore." He walked over, took her hand in a firm grip. "Margo's staying with me at the hotel, for the time being."

"Look, you jerk, just because I made the regrettable mistake of sleeping with you once—"

"Neither of us got any sleep," he reminded her. "But we'll have to tonight. I've got a full day coming up. Let's get going."

"Oh, I'll go all right." Her toes bumped into his. "I'll be delighted to go with you so I can have the time and the privacy to tell you exactly what I think of you."

Appreciating good timing, Kate waited until the door had closed behind them before she swiveled on the piano bench. "Okay, Uncle Tommy, which one is going to be found in the morning in a pool of their own blood, and which one will be holding the blunt instrument? My money's on Margo," she decided. "She's vicious when she's cornered."

He sighed, trying to compute the new development. "Have to go with my boy, Katie girl. Never known him to lose a fight unless he wanted to."

CHAPTER 15

SHE DIDN'T SPEAK on the drive to the hotel. She had a great deal to say, but she was saving it up. When he carried her garment bag into the bedroom and hung it in the closet, she pounced.

"If you're laboring under some egotistical delusion that I came here to have sex with you—"

"Not tonight, honey." He loosened his tie. "I'm beat."

The only sound she could make was a strangled growl in her throat as she used both hands to shove him back.

"Okay, okay, if you insist. But I won't be at my best."

"Don't you put your hands on me! Don't even think about it." Because her feet were tired, she pulled off her shoes. She kept one handy as a weapon, tapping it restlessly against her palm as she paced. "It wasn't bad enough that you told your family I'd been with you last night, you had the nerve to tell my mother to pack my clothes."

"I asked her," Josh corrected, hanging his jacket over the valet. "I asked if she would mind putting what she thought you'd need for a day or two in a bag. Until you had a chance to take care of the rest yourself."

"And that makes it all right? Because you said please and thank you? Which is certainly more than you said to me."

He flicked open the buttons of his shirt, worked out kinks in his shoulders. "I have no intention of sneaking around the way you did with your last choice of bedmates, duchess. If we're sleeping together, we do it, metaphorically speaking, in the open."

His shoes went next, then socks, while she fumbled through her mind for the right retort. "I haven't decided if I'm going to sleep with you again."

His gaze flicked up to her face, filled with both amusement and challenge. "Well, you should have said so."

It was her good luck that he was sitting on the edge of the bed. So much easier to look down her nose at him. "I didn't care for the way you behaved before I left here this morning."

"That makes us even." He rose, unhooked his trousers, and walked into the bath to turn on the water in the oversized whirlpool tub. "Now that we've settled that, let's stop playing the games you claimed we weren't going to play. We haven't finished with each other yet." Off went his briefs, on went the jets. "Now I want to work out some kinks before I go to bed. You're welcome to join me."

"You think I'm just going to pop into the tub with you? After you spent most of the evening ignoring me?" Men never ignored her, she fumed. Never. He was going to pay for that, if for nothing else. "And the way you were flirting with Kate?"

"Kate?" Genuinely surprised, he blinked at her. "Jesus, Margo, Kate's my sister."

"No more than I am."

Unsure whether he was amused or just plain tired, he stepped down into the tub, lowered himself, and let the hot bubbling water do its job. "You're right, she's not. Let's put it this way. I've always thought of Kate as my sister." His eyes rested on hers before he laid his head back and sank down. "I never thought of you that way. But, if you're jealous . . ." He trailed off with a shrug.

"I'm not jealous." The very idea was appalling to the pride. "I'd have to give two good damns to be jealous. I'm making a statement. Will you open your eyes and pay attention to me?"

"I'm paying attention. I'm too damn tired to open my eyes. Christ, for someone who couldn't wait to throw down warning flags about not getting too serious, not tangling each other up with strings, you're acting more like a nagging wife than a casual lover."

"I am not nagging." Then she closed her mouth, afraid she might have been close to doing so. "And I'm certainly not acting like a wife. From what I've observed about wives, any one of them worth her salt would have booted you out on your pointy head by now."

He merely smiled, dipped down a little lower. "It's my penthouse, baby. If anyone gets booted out on anything pointy, it'll be you."

Her hand clamped down on his head. From the advantage of surprise and leverage, she managed to hold him under the churning water for ten glorious seconds. It was even worth the water splashing out on her white linen suit when he surfaced, sputtering.

"I believe I'll get my bag and check into another room."

He caught her wrist, hard, threw her off balance enough that she had to stoop down to brace on the ledge of the tub. Their eyes met, locked.

"You wouldn't—" She stopped herself before uttering the D word, but already implied, it was too late. He yanked her into the tub and, as she hissed and spat like a cat, wrapped his arms around her and shoved her under.

He contemplated the ceiling for a few seconds as she kicked, hummed a few seconds more as she thrashed. Then pulled her up by the hair.

"You bastard. You goddamn—"

"Whoops, not done yet." He cheerfully dunked her again. The tub was big enough for four, which was handy because she was slippery and he needed room to maneuver. By the time she was gasping and trying to drag her sopping hair out of her eyes, he'd already dealt with her jacket. He was working on removing the clinging wet blouse.

"What the hell do you think you're doing?"

"I'm getting you naked." He flicked open the front hook of her bra. "I'm not feeling tired anymore."

Eyes narrowed, she shifted quickly so that her knee was pressed dangerously close to his crotch. "Do you have some sort of incredibly lame, essentially male idea that being manhandled arouses me?"

It was a tricky one, he thought. "Yeah—in a manner of speaking."

She increased the pressure. "Whose manner of speaking?"

"Ah . . ." He took a chance, reached out to rub his thumb gently over her nipple. It was pebble hard. "I might have resisted if you hadn't dared me." The pressure eased off slightly, and he figured it was safe to breathe again. "I want you to stay with me, Margo." His voice was soft now, barely a murmur as he stroked a hand up her leg. "If you'd rather book another room until you've thought about it, that's fine. If you're not in the mood for sex, that's fine, too."

For a moment she simply studied him. All innocence, she mused, except for that wicked glint in his eye. All patient reason—except for the challenging quirk at the corner of his mouth.

"Who said I wasn't in the mood?" She pushed back her dripping hair, slanted him that killer look under her lashes. "Are you going to help me out of the rest of these wet clothes, or do I have to do it myself?"

"Oh, allow me."

* * *

IT WAS AN interesting experience, living with a man. She'd never done so before because she hadn't been willing to share her space or privacy with anyone for longer than a weekend trip to the mountains, a jaunt to the seaside, or perhaps an extended cruise.

But it worked well enough with Josh. Perhaps, she supposed, because they had lived under the same roof for years, and because the one that currently covered their heads was a hotel.

It made it all seem less structured, more like an arrangement than a commitment. They merely shared rooms, she thought, business rooms at that. The flowers were freshened, the furniture polished, the towels replaced by staff rarely seen. That kept it impersonal, almost like an extended holiday.

Fun and games, she decided, was exactly what she and Josh wanted, and expected from each other.

No one in the family questioned her new accommodations. After days stretched into a week, then two, she began to wonder why they didn't.

Her mother at least should have been outraged, or tight-lipped. But she seemed completely unconcerned. Neither of the Templetons so much as lifted an eyebrow. And though she caught Laura watching her with a worried frown now and then, Laura also said nothing.

It was Kate who made the single pithy comment. "Break his heart and I'll break your neck," she said. And it was such a ridiculous statement that Margo had chosen to ignore it rather than rise to the bait.

She had too much to do to worry about Kate's snippy temperament. Echoes of the nastiness that Candy was spreading bounced back to her—the merchandise at Pretenses was inelegant and overpriced, the service lax, rude, and inexperienced. Laura had overextended herself to bail out her reckless, undeserving friend, and they would be bankrupt within the month. The clothing was gray market knockoffs fashioned from inferior materials.

Brooding over Candy's vindictiveness and the inevitable fallout ate into Margo's time. The shop took up at least ten hours a day, six days a week. On the one day she closed it, she struggled with paperwork until she was cross-eyed from trying to learn the fine points of bookkeeping. Though she had resented every minute she'd been forced to sit in a classroom, she now considered signing up for a course on business management.

There she was on a balmy Sunday morning, a cigarette burning in the ashtray beside her, pecking at the keys of the computer—the desktop Kate had insisted they couldn't live without—and struggling to make sense out of a spreadsheet.

Why were there so many bills? she wondered. There were more eating away at her pockets than there had been when she was unemployed. How was anyone supposed to remember how and when and whom to pay and stay sane? Life had been so much simpler when she'd had a manager seeing to all the irritating financial details of life.

"And look where that got you, Margo," she muttered. "Concentrate. Take charge."

"I told you it was serious."

At the sound of the voice, Margo shrieked and jerked back in the chair. The computer manual on her lap went flying.

"I see what you mean," Kate agreed. "I only hope we're not too late."

"Why don't you just shoot me next time?" Margo crossed her hands over her breasts and pressed to keep her heart in place. "What the hell are you doing here?"

"Rescuing you." Laura darted over in time to catch the cigarette before it finished rolling to the floor and igniting the papers spread around Margo's chair. She tapped it out neatly. "Talking to yourself, drinking alone."

"It's coffee."

"Closed up in your little room counting your money like Silas Marner," Laura finished.

"I'm not counting my money—though I have been able to pay off another five thousand, despite Candy Litchfield's plot to see me dragged off in chains—I'm—"

"She'll start gibbering any minute," Kate put in. "Told you we should have brought the nets."

"Such wit." Margo grabbed her cigarettes, lighted a fresh one. "Since you're so bright and sharp, explain all this insurance to me again. How come we have to pay these—what are they?"

"Premiums," Kate said dryly. "They're called premiums, Margo."

"I think they should be called extortion. I mean, look at this. There's fire and theft, there's mortgage insurance, earthquake insurance, comprehensive—whatever that means, because it's incomprehensible to me. And this umbrella. Is that some cute insurance-speak for flood protection?"

"Oh, yeah, that's it." Kate rolled her eyes. "Insurance companies are filled with jokers. Those boys are a laugh a minute. You'll see that for yourself the first time you file a claim."

"Look, smart-ass, if you'd just explain how it works again."

"No, no, I'm begging you." Laura grabbed Kate's shoulders. "Please, don't explain how it works again. And don't get into the thing again."

"The thing?" Kate repeated.

"You know the thing."

"Yeah, the thing." Shifting in her chair, Margo jabbed at the air with her cigarette. "I'd like to talk about the thing, actually."

"Oh, that thing." Kate sniffed at Margo's coffee, decided it was probably palatable, and picked up the cup. "Okay, here's the thing. Estimated tax payments are split into quarters—" She broke off, staring blandly at Laura. "That's a very good scream. I see where Kayla gets it." With a sigh, she leaned over and to Margo's distress and envy, batted a few keys and had the screen blinking off. "There, all gone. Feel better now?"

"Much." Laura shuddered. "But it was close."

"Well, the two of you are in a rare mood." Margo snatched her coffee back from Kate. "Now run along and play. Some of us have work to do."

"It's worse than I thought." Laura heaved a sigh. "Okay, Sullivan, come quietly, or we'll have to get tough. It's for your own good."

Margo wasn't sure whether to laugh or call for help when they flanked her and took her arms. "Hey, what's the idea?"

"Shock therapy," Kate said grimly.

AN HOUR LATER, Margo was naked and sweating. Lying on her back, she let out a long, heartfelt moan. "Oh, God. God. *God*."

"Just roll with it." Sympathetically, Laura patted her hand. "It'll be better soon."

"Mum? Is that you?"

With a chuckle, Laura leaned back. Steam billowed in clouds and drained some of her own tension away. Maybe she'd come up with the idea of a day in the spa facilities of the resort for Margo's sake, but it wasn't doing her any harm either.

"How do you all just lie here like this?" From her perch on the second-level bench, Kate rolled over, stared down at Margo. "I mean, are we really having fun?"

"I could weep," Margo murmured. "I'd forgotten, actually forgotten what it was like." She reached out to pat Laura's naked knee. "My life for you. I'm getting a facial, and a fango, and a pedicure."

"You know, honey, you're staying right at the hotel. The facilities there aren't as extensive as here, but you could use the sauna, get a massage. And they give very good facials in the beauty salon."

"She's too busy boffing Josh."

Laura winced. "Do you mind? That's an image I'd just as soon not have in my head."

"I kinda like it." Kate peeked over the edge. "It's like something on the

Discovery Channel. Two sleek golden animals mating." When Laura moaned, Kate's grin widened. "So is he good, or what? Like on a scale of one to ten."

"We're out of high school. I don't rate men," Margo said primly and rolled onto her stomach. "Twelve," she muttered. "Maybe fourteen."

"Really?" The idea perked Kate up. "Good old Josh. Our Josh."

My Josh. Margo nearly said it before she caught herself. "Ignore the idiot in the balcony," she told Laura. "Does it really bother you? Josh and me?"

"Not bother." Uncomfortable, Laura shifted. "It's just weird. My brother and one of my closest friends and sex. It's just . . . weird. It's none of my business."

"She's worried you'll toss him out like an old Ferragamo pump when you're done with him."

"Shut up, Kate. And I don't throw my shoes out anymore. I sell them. Laura, Josh, and I understand each other. I promise you."

"I wonder if you do," Laura murmured, and whatever else might have been said was interrupted as the door to the steam room opened.

"Look who's here," Kate said brightly. "It's Candy Cane." Because her teeth threatened to grind together, she set them in a feral smile. "Won't this just be cozy?"

With her turbaned head erect, Candy sat down on the bench opposite Laura. "The three of you still travel in a pack, I see."

"Like rabid dogs," Kate agreed. "And since you're the one who's been trying to steal our bone, be careful we don't bite."

"I have no idea what you're talking about."

"Inferior, overpriced merchandise, my ass," Kate shot out. "You'd better watch your mouth, Candy, before you find yourself in the middle of a slander suit."

"Expressing an opinion isn't slander." She'd checked with her second husband, the lawyer, to be sure. "It's a matter of taste." Proud of the body her first husband, the plastic surgeon, had helped create, Candy spread her towel open. "One might have thought you had more, Laura. But apparently bloodlines and breeding aren't always enough to ensure taste in companions."

"You know, I was just thinking that." Margo sat up. "Both of your exes had such sterling pedigrees. Go figure."

With some dignity, Candy crossed her naked legs. "I wanted to speak to you, Laura, about the Garden Club. Under the circumstances, I think it would be best if you resigned as co-chair." When Laura only lifted a brow, Candy dabbed at her throat with the edge of her towel. "There's gossip brewing, about you and Peter, about your association with . . ." She skimmed her eyes over Margo. "Certain unsuitable elements."

"I'm an unsuitable element," Margo told Kate.

"That's nothing. I'm an undesirable element. Aren't I, Candy?"

"You are simply detestable."

"See?" Grinning, Kate leaned over, staring into Margo's upturned face. "I'm detestable. It's because I'm the poor and distant relation. The Powells were a questionable offshoot of the Templetons, you know."

"I'd heard that."

"And I'm an accountant," Kate went on. "Which is much worse than a shopkeeper. We actually talk about money."

"That's enough," Laura said quietly. "You want the chair to yourself, Candy, it's all yours." She only regretted she wasn't able to break it over Candy's empty head. "That'll give me more time to associate with unsuitable and undesirable elements."

The easy capitulation was disappointing. Candy had so hoped for a fight. "And how is Peter enjoying Hawaii?" she said with a sneer. "I heard he took that clever little secretary of his with him this time. Though now that I think of it, they did take several . . . business trips before. It must be devastating to find yourself replaced by an employee of your own company. She's quite young too, isn't she?"

"Candy likes them young," Kate said, as fury bubbled through her. "How old is the pool boy you're bumping, Candy? Sixteen?"

"He's twenty," she snapped, then seethed at the way she had stepped into the trap. "At least I can get a man. But then, you don't want a man, do you, Kate? Everyone knows you're a lesbian."

Margo snorted, had to slap a hand over her mouth to hold the next one in. "Oh-oh, Kate, secret's out."

"It's a relief." Kate scooted forward on the bench so that she could leer at Candy's body. "I've had my eye on you for years, Sugar Lips, but I was too shy to tell you."

"It's true." Conspiratorially, Margo leaned toward Candy. "She's been afraid of her love for you."

Unsettled, unsure, Candy shifted. "That's not amusing."

"No, it's been painful, wrenching." Kate swung her legs over the bench, slid down. "But now that you know the truth, I can make you mine at last."

"Don't touch me." Squeaking, Candy jumped up, fumbled with her towel. "Don't come near me."

"I think they want to be alone," Laura commented and wrapped her towel over her breasts.

"I hate you. I hate all of you."

"God." Kate gave a quick shudder. "Isn't she the sexiest little thing?"

"You're revolting." Fearing for her life, Candy dashed out of the steam room, leaving her towel behind.

"Pervert," Margo said mildly when Kate collapsed on the bench.

"Careful, you might get me hot. If I was a lesbian, I'm sure you'd be more my type." Catching her breath, she looked over at Laura. "Honey, don't let her get to you."

"Hmm?" Distracted, Laura glanced back. "I was just thinking—how much do you think she paid for that boob job?"

"Not enough." Margo rose and tucked the towel in place. "Come on, let's go stuff her in a locker. For old time's sake."

"I DO LIKE men," Kate insisted, fidgeting as her toenails were painted. The salon's cotton-candy-pink and spun-sugar-white decor was designed to put a woman into a relaxed and festive mood. It made Kate itchy. "I just don't have a lot of time for them."

"You won't need time after Candy gets done," Laura said. She sipped her sparkling mineral water and relaxed in the deep cushions of the high-backed swivel chair. "By the time she gets through spreading the word, any man within a hundred-mile radius is going to avoid you like a vasectomy."

"Well, maybe it's a blessing." Kate flipped through the stack of fashion magazines on the table beside her and found nothing of interest. "It might discourage that jerk Bill Pardoe from calling me all the time."

"Bill is a very sweet and decent man."

"Then you go out with him, let him tickle your knee under the table and call you honeybunch."

"She's always been too picky." Margo kept her eyes closed, nearly purring as her feet were massaged. "She'd have had more fun in her life if she'd gone looking for Mr. Goodbar instead of Mr. Perfect."

"I look for more in a date than a fat portfolio and a penis."

"Girls, girls." Laura picked up her mineral water again. "We have to stick together now. If Candy follows through and files charges for assault, it could get sticky."

"But, officer," Margo cooed, batting her lashes. "It was just high-spirited, girlish fun. Shit, she'd never humiliate herself by admitting in public that for the second time in her life she'd been trapped naked in a gym locker. She'll be more subtle than that. I say within a week we all have new identities. The slut, the shrew, and the dyke."

"I might like being the shrew," Laura decided. "Being the wimp gets old fast."

"You were never the wimp," Margo said loyally.

"Oh, yes, I've been a practicing wimp for years. It's going to take some doing to make the leap to shrew. But I might give it a shot. Josh?" She blinked as her brother walked into the salon, looking hot and harassed.

"Ladies." He plopped down in a vacant chair, picked up Margo's glass of water, and guzzled it down. "Well don't you all look . . ." He paused, skimmed his eyes over three faces packed in green goo. "Hideous. Been having fun?"

"Go away." Living with a man didn't mean he had to see you in a seaweed pack, Margo thought. "This is a girl thing."

He set her empty glass down, picked up Kate's, and guzzled that too. "I was into my second set with Carl Brewster on the courts here. You know Carl Brewster, television journalist, investigative reporter, and anchor on *Informed*, that long-running, highly rated, and revered newsmagazine."

The tone of his voice had Laura biting her lip. "I've heard of it. How is Carl?"

"Oh, fit and sassy, not that I wasn't whipping his ass, but I digress. *Informed* is planning to do a series of reports on the fine hotels of the world, with Templeton, of course, as a highlight. I've spent weeks arranging for various crews to film our hotels, interview staff, certain guests. All to show the viewing public the fine, upstanding, sophisticated, and unrivaled class and hospitality of Templeton, worldwide."

He set aside Kate's glass. Laura wordlessly handed him hers. "I'm sure they got some wonderful footage."

"Oh, they did. Naturally when Carl suggested we get some clips of the two of us playing tennis at our landmark resort here in Monterey, I agreed. A nice, human touch, the VP of Templeton enjoying the pleasant surroundings where his guests are always pampered and satisfied."

He paused, smiled charmingly at the hovering beauticians. "Would you mind giving us a moment?" After they'd moved away a discreet distance, his smile turned to a snarl. "Imagine my surprise, my distress, when one of our regular patrons raced screaming into camera range, her Templeton Spa robe flapping open, her eyes wild as she sputtered accusations about being attacked—bodily attacked—by Laura Templeton Ridgeway and her cohorts."

"Oh, Josh, I'm so sorry." Laura turned her head away, hoping he'd take it for shame. It would never, never do to laugh.

He showed his teeth. "One snicker, Laura. Just one."

"I'm not snickering." Composed, she turned back. "I'm terribly sorry. It must have been very embarrassing for you."

"And won't it just be a laugh riot when they run that little scene? Of course, they'll beep out most of the dialogue to conform to Standards and Practices, but I think the viewing audience, the millions of people who tune in to *Informed* each week will get the gist."

"She started it," Kate said, then winced when he turned flinty eyes on her. "Well, she did."

"I'm sure Mom and Dad will understand that completely."

Even the stalwart Kate could be cowed. "It was Margo's idea."

Margo hissed through her teeth, "Traitor. She called Kate a lesbian."

Shaking his head, Josh covered his face with his hands and rubbed, hard. "Oh, well, then, get the rope."

"I suppose you'd have let her get away with it. She's been trying to damage the shop. She said nasty things to Laura," Margo went on, heating up. "And just the other day she came into the shop and called me a slut. A second-class slut."

"And your answer was to gang up on her, three to one, smack her around, strip her naked, and shove her into a locker?"

"We never smacked her. Not once." Not, Margo thought, that she wouldn't have liked to. "As for the locker business, it was a matter of tradition. We did nothing more than embarrass her, which is no more than she deserved after the way she insulted us. And anyway, a real man would applaud our actions."

"Unlike you, and your idiot sisters here, pitiful insults from crazy women don't bother me. And your timing was rare and perfect." He leaned forward, pleased to be able to pay her back, in spades, for the "real man" comment. "I'd just begun to get Carl to nibble at the idea of doing a sidebar story on the latest innovation of a Templeton heir. Laura Templeton Ridgeway's partnership with old and dear friends Margo Sullivan— yes, *the* Margo Sullivan, and Kate Powell. Smart, savvy women creating and running a smart, savvy business."

"We're going to get air on *Informed*? That's fabulous."

He shot Margo a disgusted look. "Christ, you are an idiot. What you're going to get, unless I can do some fast and sweet talking, is sued and very possibly charged in a criminal action. She's claiming assault, verbal and physical abuse—and now that I know Kate's a lesbian, that explains the sexual abuse she tossed in."

"I am not a lesbian," Kate fumed. "Though the way she said it was an insult to any rational person who supports freedom of sexual preference." From his expression she realized it wasn't the time to get up on any liberal or feminist soapbox. Instead, she shifted, sulked. "And I never touched her in any sexual way. This is completely out of proportion, Josh, and you know it. She gave us grief, and we gave her some back. That's all."

"That's not all. The Templeton Resort isn't second-period gym class. This is the adult world. Didn't any of you remember her second husband was a litigator? A litigator who delights in pursuing and winning just this sort of nuisance suit. She could go after the shop."

Every ounce of blood in Margo's face drained. "That's ridiculous. She'd never get it. No court would take her that seriously."

"Maybe not." His voice was a cold snap, an unmerciful whip. "But the time and expense you'd have to put into fighting her off could go a long way toward draining your capital." He rose, shook his head at the three of them. "If you haven't been paying attention the last decade or so, school's out. So, you sit here and enjoy having your toenails painted while I go back to work and try to save your sorry butts."

"He's really steamed," Kate murmured as he stormed out. "One of us should go talk to him." She looked from Margo to Laura. "One of you should go talk to him."

"I'll go." Laura rose, feeling ridiculous in her little paper slippers and cotton balls.

"No, you'd better warn your parents, tell them we've put our foot in it." Margo sighed, struggled not to be terrified. "I'll do what I can with Josh."

SHE GAVE HIM an hour. It took her nearly that long to put herself together, in any case. When facing a furious man, she thought it wise to look her best.

He was on the phone at the desk in the office when she walked in, and he didn't so much as flick a glance at her. So much, she thought, for a five-hundred-dollar session at the spa. Saying nothing, she crossed to the desk and waited for him to complete his call.

He'd frightened her, he noted. And he'd meant to. Her wild temperament was part of what he found so appealing about her. But in the past weeks, he'd watched her channel that temperament, all that passion and energy into building something for herself. It infuriated him that with one careless tantrum, she'd risked damaging it.

"Yes, I said for a full year. Any and all services. I'll draft a memo to that effect. You'll have it by tomorrow." He hung up the phone, drummed his fingers on the desk.

"Tell me what I have to do," she said quietly. "If an apology will help, I'll go over and apologize to her right now."

"Give me a dollar."

"What?"

"Give me a goddamn dollar."

Baffled, she opened her purse. "I don't have a single. I have a five."

He snatched it out of her fingers. "I'm now your legal counsel, and as such I'm advising you to admit nothing. You're not going to apologize for anything because you didn't do anything. You don't know what she's talking about. Now if you tell me there were six other naked women and three attendants hanging around who saw you shove her into the locker, I'll have to kill you."

"There was nobody else there. We're not idiots." She grimaced. "I know you think we are, but we're not stupid enough to have done it in front of witnesses. Actually, we timed it that way so she'd be stuck in there longer." She smiled weakly. "It seemed like a good idea at the time." When he said nothing, she felt her temper simmer again. "Aren't you the one who broke Peter's nose?"

"I could afford to indulge myself."

"Oh, that's typical. The Templeton heir can behave any way he pleases and damn the consequences."

His eyes flashed, a dangerous, edgy glint. "Let's just say I pick my battles."

She forced herself to stop. Josh's attitude and position were hardly the point. "How much trouble am I in?" she demanded. "I know you're not a trial lawyer, so that five bucks isn't going to do me much good if this actually goes to court."

"It depends on how stubborn she is." With an effort, he calmed himself. Her little jab at his character was nothing new. "Templeton's official stand will be shock and distress that such an incident occurred while she was a guest. We're compensating her for her inconvenience and stress with a year's complementary services at any of our Spa Resorts. That, and the fact that publicizing the incident will be embarrassing for her, might do it."

He ran the five-dollar bill through his fingers, laid it on the desk blotter. "She might be satisfied with bad-mouthing you and the shop and using her influence to have her friends boycott. And since she does have a wide range of acquaintances, a boycott will likely sting."

"We'll get over that." Calmer, she pushed her hands through her hair. She'd come to apologize, and intended to do it right. "I'm sorry. I know the whole thing was—is—embarrassing for you and your family."

He braced his elbows on the desk, his brow on his fists. "She came shrieking across the court. I'd just hit a line drive, barely missed beaning her. Cameras rolling, and there I am trying to look my sixth-generational-hotelier best, the athletic yet intelligent, the world-traveled yet dedicated, the dashing yet concerned heir to the Templeton name."

"You'd be good at that," Margo murmured, hoping to placate him.

He didn't even look at her. "Suddenly I've got my arms full of this half-naked, spitting, swearing, clawing mass who's screaming that my sister, her lesbian companion, and my whore attacked her." He pinched the bridge of his nose, hoping to relieve some pressure. "I figured out right away who my sister was. Though I didn't appreciate the term, I deduced you must be my whore. The lesbian companion might have stumped me, but for process of elimination." He lifted his head. "I was tempted to belt her, but I was too busy trying to keep her from ripping off my face."

"It's such a nice face, too." Hoping to soothe, she walked around the desk and sat on his lap. "I'm sorry she took it out on you."

"She scratched me." He turned his head to show her the trio of angry welts on the side of his throat. Dutifully, Margo kissed them. "What am I going to do with you?" he said wearily and rested his cheek on her head. Then he chuckled. "How the hell did you stuff her into one of those skinny lockers?"

"It wasn't easy, but it was fun."

He narrowed his eyes. "You're never going to do it again, no matter what the provocation—unless you sedate her first."

"Deal." Since the crisis seemed to have passed, she slipped a hand under his shirt, stroked it over his chest, watched his brow lift. "I've been waxed and polished. If you're interested."

"Well, just so the day isn't a complete loss." He picked her up and carried her to the bed.

CHAPTER 16

IT DIDN'T TAKE long for the fallout. Sales and traffic fell off sharply during the following week. Sharply enough to have Margo's stomach jittering as she wrote out checks for the monthly bills. Oh, there were still plenty of tourists and walk-ins, but a great many of the ladies who lunch, the very clientele Pretenses required in order to move the high-end merchandise, were giving the shop a wide berth.

If things didn't pick up within the next thirty days, she would have to dip into her dwindling capital just to stay open.

She wasn't panicked, just uneasy. She'd told Josh they could wait it out, and she believed it. The loyalty of Candy's country club pals could be measured in their demitasse cups with room to spare.

But that didn't mean her business didn't need a jolt of adrenaline. She didn't want the shop merely to struggle along, she wanted it to thrive. Perhaps, she realized, she wanted it to be as she had once been. In the spot-light, admired, successful.

As she arranged and rearranged displays, she wracked her brains to come up with a workable concept to turn Pretenses from an intriguing lit-tle secondhand shop into a star.

When the door opened, she had a bright—and, she was afraid, desperate—smile waiting. "Mum. What are you doing here?"

"It's my day off, isn't it?" Ann pursed her lips as she scanned the show-room. "And I haven't come by here since the first week you opened. It's awful quiet."

"I'm being punished for my sins. You always said I would be."

"I heard of it." She clucked her tongue. "Grown women behaving like hoydens. Though I never liked that woman, not even when she was a girl. Always with her nose in the air."

"This time I put it out of joint. She's managed to slice a chunk out of sales. Though Kate says it's also part of the natural correction of a new business after its initial opening weeks." Margo scowled at an amber globe. "You know how she talks when she's wearing her accountant hat."

"I do, yes. More often than not I listen to her when she's going on about my investments, and just nod soberly without a clue as to what the devil she's talking about."

For the first time all day, Margo indulged in a long laugh. "I'm glad you came in. There haven't been many friendly faces in here today."

"Well, you'll have to do something about that." Out of habit, Ann checked for dust on a table, nodded in approval when she found the sur-face smooth and glossy. "Have a sale, give away prizes, hire a marching band."

"A marching band—good one, Mum."

"Well, what do I know about shopkeeping? It's getting people in that's the trick, isn't it?"

Absently, Ann picked up a pretty glass bottle. Not to put things in, she mused, perplexed as always with fripperies. Just to sit about the house.

"Your uncle Johnny Ryan back in Cork had himself a pub," she contin-ued. "He would hire musicians now and then—the Yanks liked it especially and would come in to hear the music and buy pints while they did."

"I don't think an Irish jug band is the answer to traffic flow in here."

The dismissive tone was an insult as far as Ann was concerned. "I'm speaking of fine, traditional music. You've never respected your heritage."

"You never gave me the chance to," Margo shot back. "What you've told me about Ireland and my family there could fit into one paragraph."

It was true enough. Ann tightened her lips. "So, you couldn't pick up a book, I suppose, or take a bit of a detour on your gallivanting through Europe?"

"I've been to Cork twice," Margo said and had the satisfaction of seeing Ann's mouth fall open. "Surprise. And to Dublin and Galway and Clare." She shrugged her shoulders, annoyed with herself for admitting she had once gone searching for her roots. "It's a pretty country, but I'm more interested in the one I'm living in now."

"No one wrote me, told me you'd gone to see them."

"I didn't see anyone when I was there. What would have been the point? Even if I'd gone around digging up Ryans and Sullivans, we wouldn't have known each other."

Ann started to speak, then shook her head. "No, I suppose you're right."

For a moment she thought she saw regret in her mother's eyes, and was sorry for it. "I have problems now, ambitions now," she said briskly, "that have to be dealt with now. Reminiscing about pennywhistles and pints of Guiness won't help get the business moving the way I want it to move."

"Music and drink appeal to more than the Irish," Ann pointed out. "What's wrong with offering a bit of entertainment?"

"I need customers," Margo insisted. "I need a hook to lure the platinum-card set in past Candy's boycott and set a standard for Pretenses."

"So, you'll have a sale." Suddenly Ann wanted badly to help. "You've pretty things in here, Margo. People want pretty things. You've only to get them in the door."

"Exactly my point. What I need is . . . Wait."

Margo pressed a hand to her head as an idea tried to form. "Music. A harpist, maybe. An Irish harpist, maybe, in traditional dress. Music and drink. A reception. Champagne and little trays of canapés like at a gallery opening. Prizes."

She grabbed her mother's shoulders, surprising Ann with the quick hug. "A prize, just one. It's more alluring to have just one. No, no, no, not a prize," Margo continued, circling the shop. "An auction, on one piece. The diamond brooch. No, no, the pearl choker. Proceeds to charity. What's a good charity? Oh, Laura will know. A charity reception, Mum, it'll get them in here."

The girl's mind whirled like a dervish, Ann thought, running and spinning from one point to the next. That, she saw, hadn't changed a wit. "Well, then, you'd better get to it."

*   *   *

SHE GOT TO it with a vengeance. Within a week, invitations to the charity reception and auction benefiting Wednesday's Child, a program for handicapped and underprivileged children, were being printed. Laura was delegated to handle interviews, and Margo went to work trying to charm liquor distributors into donating cases of champagne.

She auditioned harpists, begged Josh to select waiters from Templeton staff to serve, and flattered Mrs. Williamson into making the canapés.

It was just the beginning.

When Josh came back to the penthouse after a long day trip to San Francisco, he found his lover in bed. But she wasn't alone.

"What the hell is this?"

Margo tossed back her hair, turned on a smile. Creamy curves of white breasts rose above glossy red-satin sheets. Those same slick sheets were artfully twisted to showcase a long, shapely leg.

The camera flashed.

"Hello, darling. We're nearly done here."

"Hold the sheet between your breasts," the photographer ordered, crouching at the foot of the bed on which Margo was sprawled seductively. "A little lower. Now tilt your head. That's it, that's it. You're still the best, baby. Let's sell the goods."

Josh set down his briefcase, stepped over a cable, and earned a mutter from the photographer's assistant. "What are you wearing?"

"Pearls." She skimmed her fingers down them, ran her tongue invitingly over her lips as the camera clicked. "The choker we're auctioning off. I thought photos would help bump up the bids."

Since she appeared to be wearing nothing else, Josh had to agree with her.

"Just a couple more. Give me the look. Oh, yeah, that's the one. Got it." He stood, an agile, sharp-eyed man with a flowing red ponytail. "Great working with you again, Margo."

"I owe you, Zack."

"Not a thing." He handed off his camera to his assistant, then leaned over the bed to kiss Margo warmly. "I've missed seeing that billion-dollar face in my viewfinder. Glad I could help." He glanced at Josh. "Be out of your way in a shake."

"Josh, be a doll and get Zack and Bob a couple of beers." Without a flicker, she dropped the sheet, then reached for a robe to cover her lovely breasts.

"A couple of beers." His smile was quick and feral. "Sure, why not?"

"We met before." Leaving his assistant to pack up, Zack followed Josh back into the office. "In Paris—no, no, Rome. You dropped by one of Margo's shoots."

The green lights of jealousy faded a bit. It was hard to forget a man with a foot-long red ponytail. "Yeah. I think she was dressed at the time."

Zack took the beer. "Just to clear the air here, I've seen more naked women than a bouncer in a strip joint. It's just part of the job."

"Not that you enjoy it."

"I'm willing to sacrifice for my art." He grinned winningly. "Pal, I fucking love it. But it's still part of the job. If you want a professional's opinion, you've got yourself the top of the line. Some women you have to know how to shoot, what angle, what lighting, so the camera'll love them. Doesn't matter if they're beautiful—the camera's fickle, and it's picky." He took a long, satisfying gulp of beer. "It don't matter a damn how you shoot Margo Sullivan. It just don't matter a damn. The camera fucking worships her."

He looked toward the bedroom as her warm, throaty laugh flowed out. "And I'll tell you, if she wasn't set on running this store of hers, I'd talk her into coming back to L.A. with me and giving fashion photography a try."

"Then I'd have to break all the bones in your fingers."

Zack nodded. "I thought you might. And since you're bigger than me, I think I'll take Bob his beer to go."

"Good choice." Josh decided a beer might go down well and was just tipping a bottle back when Margo came into the room.

"God, it was good to see Zack again. Is there a split of champagne in there? I'm parched. I'd forgotten how hot you get under the lights."

Her face was glowing as she tilted her head back and ran her fingers through her hair. She'd done something curling and sexy with it, he noted, so that it spiraled wildly.

"And how much I love it," she went on. "There's just something about the whole process. Looking into the camera, the way it looks at you. The lights, the sound of the shutter."

When she let her hair fall and opened her eyes, he was staring at her in a way that made her heart stutter. "What is it?"

"Nothing." His eyes never left hers as he held out the glass of wine he'd poured. "I didn't realize you were thinking of going back to it."

"I'm not." But she sipped, knowing that for a moment it had been a tantalizing thought. "I don't mean I'd never pose again or take an intriguing offer, but the shop's my priority now and making it a success is number one on my list."

"Number one." Had he carried this mood back with him from San Francisco, he wondered, or had it dropped on him like a cloud when he'd walked into the suite and seen her? "Tell me, duchess, just what position do you and I rate on that list?"

"I don't know what you mean."

"Simple question. Are we five, seven? Have we even made it to the list yet?"

She looked into her glass, watched the wine bubble like dreams. "Are you asking me for something?"

"I think it's about time I did. And that, I imagine, is your cue to exit stage right." When she said nothing, he set down his beer. "Why don't we try something different? You stay and I'll go."

"Don't." She still didn't look at him, but kept staring at the bubbles rising and dancing in her glass. "Please don't. I know you don't think much of me. You care about me, but you don't think much of me. And maybe I deserve that."

"We're even there, aren't we? You don't think much of me either."

How could she answer when she wasn't at all sure just what she thought of Joshua Templeton? She turned then. He was waiting, and she was grateful for that. Halfway across the room, but waiting.

"You're important to me," she told him. "More important than I expected or wanted you to be. Isn't that enough?"

"I don't know, Margo. I just don't know."

Why was her hand shaking? It was civilized, wasn't it? Just as it was supposed to be. "If you're . . . if this has run its course for you, I'll understand." She set her glass down. "But I don't want to lose you altogether. I don't know what I'd do if you weren't in my life."

This wasn't what he wanted, this calm, gentle understanding. He wanted her to rage, to throw the wine at his head, to scream at him for having the nerve to think he could walk out on her.

"So if I walk out, we'll be friends again?"

"Yes." She squeezed her eyes shut as her heart contracted. "No."

Relieved, he crossed back to her. "You'll hate me if I go." Gathering her hair in his hand, he drew her head back until their eyes met. "You need me. I want to hear you say it."

"I'll hate you if you go." She reached up, framed his face with her hands. "I need you." She pulled his mouth to hers. "Come to bed." It was the best way to show him, the only way.

"The easy answer," he murmured.

"Yes, it should be easy. Let's make it easy." The moment he lifted her into his arms, she tugged at his jacket, whispered hot promises in his ear.

But he didn't intend to make it easy this time, for either of them. He stood her next to the bed, let her undress him with quick, eager hands. When she would have pulled him down with her to the sheets still warm from the lights and her body, he gathered her close and began his assault.

One long, lazy meeting of lips that spun out and trembled and shimmered with something new. Simple tenderness. He took her hands, drew them down to her side, behind her back, and cuffed them there so that his free hand could stroke over her face, down her throat, into her hair while his mouth continued to seduce.

"Josh." Her heartbeat echoed slow and thick in her head. "Touch me."

"I am." He feathered kisses over her cheeks, her jaw. "Maybe for the first time I'm touching you. It's hard to feel when there's only heat. But you're feeling now, aren't you?" When her head fell weakly back, he nuzzled her throat. "No one's ever made you feel what I'm going to make you feel."

It was frightening, this weakness weighing down her limbs, clouding her brain. She wanted the flash, the fire. There was simplicity in that. And even in dangerous heat, safety. But mixed with the fear was the dark, dizzying thrill of being taken slowly, so slowly that each touch, each brush of lips lasted eons.

He could swear he felt her bones melting inside that sleek, pampered flesh. The drum of her turgid pulse thudded against his fingers. Low, baffled whimpers sounded in her throat where pearls glowed against her skin. He slid the robe aside so she wore nothing but them, luminous white orbs circling a long, slim neck.

"Lie down with me." She lifted her arm to take him. "Lie down on me."

Her voice alone, that husky flow of it, could have brought a man to his knees. And had, he thought, too often. He stroked his hands down her back, up, a teasing fingertip caress that had her shuddering, had her lips parting on what might have been a plea before his closed over them and swallowed it.

When she was limp against him, when her hands slid weakly back to her sides, he lay her on the bed, on the slick, slippery satin. But he didn't cover her. Again, he braceleted her wrists, lifted them above her head. Sigh layered over sigh as he began a slow, thorough trail down her body.

She thought the air had turned gold. How else could every breath she took be so rich? His mouth was so gentle, yet it exploited weaknesses she hadn't known were hidden inside her. His hands were impossibly tender and patient, yet they made her burn. And they made her weep.

It was more than pleasure. She had no words for it. It was soft, stronger than lust, and lovelier than any dream she'd ever held in her heart. Her body simply wasn't hers any longer, not hers alone.

He could feel her opening for him, that pliant surrender that was beyond passion and more exciting. Her skin hummed as his tongue teased over it, her muscles tensed in anticipation of climax. Lazily he backed off and left them quivering.

And when he met her lips with his again, emotions poured like wine. He slipped inside her like a wish.

"No." He used his weight to pin her as she moved restlessly. "It won't be fast this time." Even as the blood pounded in his brain, he nipped at her mouth in small, torturous bites. "It's me who's filling you, Margo. As no one else has. No one else could." He moved in her, long, slow strokes. Shattering.

She could see nothing but his face, feel nothing but that glorious friction. Then the gradual, the delicious, the aching build of luxurious orgasm.

Her hands slid bonelessly off his shoulders.

"No one knows you like I do. No one can love you like I do."

But she was beyond words.

SHE WAS AFRAID of him. It was a staggering realization, especially in the middle of the night when she lay wakeful beside him. He'd changed something between them, Margo thought. Shifted the balance so that she felt vulnerable.

And he'd done it by showing her what it was like to feel cherished.

Cautious and quiet, she slipped out of bed, left him sleeping. The champagne was still on the table. Flat now, but she drank it just the same. She found a cigarette, lit it, and told herself to calm down.

She was terrified.

It had been a risk, certainly, to sleep with him. But one she'd been willing to take. But she'd never counted on falling in love with him. That was a dare she would have turned down cold.

Still could, she assured herself and drew deep on the cigarette. Her emotions were still her own. No matter how often or how quickly her life seemed to be changing, she was still in charge of her emotions.

She wasn't going to be in love with anyone, most particularly Josh. She didn't know anything about love, not this kind. And didn't want to.

Pressing a hand to her head, she let out a quiet laugh. Of course—that was it. She didn't know anything about love, so why was she so sure that was what she was feeling? More than likely it was just surprise that he could be so sweet and that she could be so susceptible to sweetness.

And it was the first time she'd been involved with a man she'd cared for as deeply as she did Josh. The closely twined history they shared, the memories, the affection.

It was easy, and foolish of her, to twist that all up inside and come out with love. More settled, she crushed out the cigarette, took a deep breath.

"Can't sleep?"

She jumped like a cat, made him laugh.

"Sorry, didn't mean to startle you." The light from the bedroom pooled behind him as he stepped closer. She stepped back. "Problem?"

"No."

He cocked his head and, as his eyes adjusted, got a good look at her face. His smile spread, arrogant and male. "Nervous?"

"Of course not."

"I'm making you nervous."

"I don't like being stalked when I'm trying to think." She stepped aside, evading him. "I've got a lot on my mind with the reception and . . ." She trailed off, going blank when his hand skimmed down her arm.

"You're tense," he murmured. "Jittery. I like it."

"You would. I need a clear mind and a good night's sleep. I'm going to take a sleeping pill."

"Let's try something else." He shook his head when she eyed him balefully. "Can't you think of anything but sex? I'm going to rub your back."

Doubt mixed with interest. "You are?"

"Guaranteed to beat off tension and chase away insomnia," he promised as he led her back to the bed. "Lie down on your stomach, duchess, close your eyes, and leave it to me."

Wary, she twisted her head to look at him. "Just my back?"

"Neck and shoulders, too. That's a girl." He eased her down, straddled her, and grinned when all those long lovely muscles bunched into wires. He pressed the heels of his hands just at the base of her neck. "What's worrying you, baby?"

"Things."

"Name one."

You was the first answer on her tongue, but she bit that one off. "Those quarterly tax things are almost due, and sales are down."

"How down?"

"We've never matched the sales from the first two weeks. Kate says Candy hasn't done that much damage—it's just the natural leveling off of a new business. But I'm afraid I might have made a mistake funneling money into this reception when I should be using it for day-to-day expenses. God, you have wonderful hands."

"That's what they all say."

"The necklace I'm contributing was priced at eighty-five hundred. It's a big chunk out of inventory."

"It'll also be an excellent deduction."

"That's what Kate said." Her voice thickened as he stroked the tension out of her shoulders. "I'm tired of being afraid, Josh."

"I know."

"I never used to be afraid of anything. Now everything scares me."

"Including me."

"Hmm." She was drifting off, too tired to deny it. "I don't want to mess things up again."

"I'm not going to let you." He leaned down to touch his lips to her shoulder. "Go to sleep, Margo. Everything's on the right track."

"Don't go away," she managed before she sank.

"When have I ever?"

CHAPTER 17

I T HAD TO be perfect. Margo was determined that every detail of the night would go off flawlessly. It took hours of rearranging stock before she was satisfied that she had achieved just the right presentation, the best traffic pattern, the most attractive corner for the harpist, who was even now tuning up.

She had redressed the window, highlighting the pearl choker with just a few carefully selected bottles and trinket boxes and silk scarves to add color.

The gilded banister that ringed the second floor was sparkling with fairy lights. Vases and decorative urns were filled with fall flowers and hothouse roses, culled from the Templeton gardens and greenhouse and elegantly arranged by her mother. On the tiny veranda, still more flowers bloomed lusciously out of copper pots and glazed pottery.

She had personally buffed, polished, and scrubbed every surface of the shop until it shined.

It was just a matter of controlling every detail, she told herself as she puffed manically on a cigarette. Of making sure everything was first class and overlooking nothing.

Had she overlooked something?

Turning, she studied herself in the wall of decorative mirrors. She wore the little black dress she'd chosen for her first dinner back at Templeton

House. The neckline, that low square, was the perfect canvas for the choker. It had seemed a smart sales pitch to remove it from the window and display it against soft, female flesh. And she realized she'd chosen well when she'd selected that piece to auction.

Not just because it was elegant and lovely, she mused. Because it reminded her of a time of her life that would never come again. And a lonely old man she had had enough heart to care for.

So rare, she thought, for Margo Sullivan to have heart, to do something out of kindness rather than calculation.

Dozens of Margos, she mused. It had taken her almost twenty-nine years to realize that there were dozens of Margos. One who would throw caution to the winds, another who would worry endlessly. There was the Margo who knew how to hot-wax an antique table and the one who could laze away the day with a fashion magazine. The one who understood the rich pleasure of buying an art nouveau bottle for no more reason than seeing it sit on a shelf. And the one who'd learned to thrill at selling it. The one who could flash a smile and turn men to jelly, no matter what their age.

And the one who was suddenly able to think of only one man.

Where was he? Sick with nerves, she lit yet another cigarette. It was nearly time, nearly zero hour. He should have been there. This was a crisis point in her life. Josh was always there at the crisis points.

Always there, she thought, with a dull jolt of surprise. How odd that he should always be there at her turning points.

"Why don't you just chew that pack up, swallow it, and get it over with?" Kate suggested as she came through the door.

"What?"

"If you're going to eat that cigarette, you might as well use your teeth. Traffic's murder out there," she added. "I had to park three blocks away, and I don't appreciate the hike in these stupid shoes you made me buy." Shrugging out of her practical coat, she lifted her arms. "Well, am I going to pass the audition?"

"Let's have a look." Margo crushed out the cigarette and with lips pursed circled her finger so Kate would turn around. The long sweep of the simple black velvet suited the angular frame, and the flirty scoop-necked bodice added softness. The back dipped alluringly.

"I knew it would be perfect for you. Despite being all skin and bones and flat-chested, you look almost elegant."

"I feel like an impostor, and I'm going to freeze." Kate didn't mind the critique of her body nearly as much as the inconvenience of bare shoulders. "I don't see why I couldn't wear my own clothes. That dinner suit I have is fine."

"That dinner suit is fine for the next accountant convention you go to." Margo knit her well-shaped eyebrows. "Those earrings."

"What?" Protectively, Kate closed her hands over earlobes decorated with simple gold swirls. "They're my best ones."

"And so department store. How could we have been raised in the same house?" Margo wondered and marched over to the jewelry display. After sober study, she chose jaw-length swings of rhinestones.

"I'm not wearing those chandeliers. I'll look ridiculous."

"Don't argue with the expert. Put them on like a good girl."

"Oh, I hate playing dress-up." Bad-temperedly, Kate strode to a mirror and made the exchange. She hated more that Margo was right. They added dash.

"Kitchen's under control." Laura started down the winding steps balancing a silver tray with three flutes of champagne. "I thought we'd have our own private toast before—" She paused at the bottom, grinned. "Wow! Don't we look fabulous?"

Margo studied Laura's slim black evening suit, trimmed in satin, winking with buttons of rhinestone and pearl. "Don't we just?"

"I don't see why we all had to wear black," Kate complained.

"We're making a statement." Margo took her glass, lifted it. "To partners." After one sip, she pressed a hand to her stomach. "My system's gone haywire."

"Want a Tums?" Kate asked.

"No. Unlike you, I don't consider antacids a member of the four major food groups."

"Oh, yeah, you'd rather hit the Xanax, chase it with a little Prozac."

"I am not taking tranquilizers." But she had one in her bag, just in case. No need to mention it. "Now take that thing you call a coat into the back room before it scares off the guests. You sure I shouldn't check upstairs?" she asked Laura.

"Everything's fine. Don't worry so much."

"I'm not worried. This little party's only costing us about ten thousand dollars. Why should I be worried? Did I overdo it with the fairy lights?"

"They look charming. Get a grip, Margo."

"I'm getting one. But maybe a little Xanax wouldn't hurt. No, no." She tugged another cigarette out of the pack on the counter. "I'm handling this without chemical assistance." She caught Laura's bland look at the wine and tobacco and hissed out a breath. "Don't expect miracles."

But she made herself put the cigarette back. "I know I'm obsessing."

"Well," Laura said with a bland smile, "as long as you know."

"What I don't know is how this event got to be worse than the opening. Maybe it's because your parents put off going back to Europe to stay for it."

"And because rubbing Candy's nose in a bust-out success wouldn't hurt," Kate added as she came back from the storeroom.

"There is that," Margo agreed and found some comfort in it. "Bottom line, the shop isn't a means to an end the way I expected it to be. And I'm not just worried that we'll all lose what we put into it. It's gotten to be more important than money." She glanced around at the setting where what had been hers was offered. "And I'm feeling a little guilty, I realize, that I've dragged this charity, this children's charity into it just so I can keep the doors open."

"That's just plain dumb," Kate said flatly. "The charity is going to benefit. Without fundraisers and patrons eyeing the tax deduction, it would have to close its doors."

"Be sure to tell me that whenever I get a greedy gleam in my eye." And she had one now. "Damn, I want to empty some deep pockets tonight."

"That's more like it." Kate lifted her glass in approval. "You were starting to worry me." She looked around as the door opened. "Oh, God, my heart." She patted her hand against her chest. "There's nothing like a man in a monkey suit to start it fluttering."

"You look nice, too." Josh, sleeked into black tie, held out three white roses. "Actually, the three of you would knock the breath out of the Seventh Fleet."

"Let's get this charming man some champagne, Kate." Taking her friend firmly by the hand, Laura tugged her toward the steps.

"It doesn't take two of us."

"Get a clue."

Kate glanced back, noted the way Josh and Margo were staring at each other, and shook her head. "Jesus, isn't knowing they're sleeping together enough without having to watch them smolder? People should have some control."

"You have enough for everybody," Laura murmured and pulled her up the rest of the way.

"I was afraid you wouldn't be here in time."

Josh lifted Margo's hand to his lips, then angled his wrist to look at his watch. "Fifteen minutes to spare. I figured if I made a fashionably late entrance, you'd kill me in my sleep."

"Good guess. What do you think? Does everything look right?"

"You really expect me to look at anything but you?"

She laughed even as her pulse jittered. "Boy, I must be in bad shape when a shopworn line like that hits the mark."

"I mean it," he said and watched her smile fade. "I adore looking at you." Laying a hand on her cheek, he leaned down and buckled her knees with a long, slow, thorough kiss. "Beautiful Margo. Mine."

"Well, you're certainly taking my mind off my . . . kiss me again."

"Glad to."

Deeper this time, longer, until everything but him drained from her mind. When she eased away, his hand remained gentle on her cheek. "It's different," she managed.

"You're catching on."

"It's not supposed to be." New nerves, different nerves, jittered. "I don't know if it can be."

"Too late," he murmured.

There was the panic again, spurting up through mists of pleasure. "I have to—" She nearly shuddered with relief when the door opened.

"Thought we'd beat the rush," Thomas claimed. "Take your hands off the girl, Josh, and give someone else a chance." When Margo rushed into his arms, he wiggled his brows teasingly at his son. "She was mine first."

First didn't mean a damn, Josh thought as he leaned negligently on the counter. Last was what counted.

At least, he was trying to believe that.

BY TEN, TWO hours after the doors opened for Pretenses's First Annual Reception and Charity Auction, Margo was in her element. This was something she understood—beautifully dressed people chatting, bumping silk-covered elbows as they sipped wine or designer water.

It was a world she had focused her life on entering. And this time, they'd come to her.

"We thought a week or two in Palm Springs would do the trick."

"I don't know how she continues to turn a blind eye to his affairs. They're so blatant."

"I haven't seen him since the last time we were in Paris."

Small talk among the privileged, Margo thought, and she knew how to chat right back. Entertaining had been one of her hobbies in Milan. She knew how to juggle three conversations, keep an eye on the roving waiters, and pretend she had nothing on her mind but the next sip of champagne.

She also knew how to ignore, when necessary, the catty and sly snippets that came to her ears.

"Imagine having to sell everything. I mean, darling, even your shoes."

". . . just last week that Peter asked her to file for the divorce so that she could save face. The poor thing's frigid. The doctors haven't been able to help her."

Margo wouldn't have ignored that one, if she could have found the source, but before she could ease away and try to locate it, there was more.

"So clever, the way it's all set up like some interesting European flat. And I simply adore the collection of compacts. I must have the little elephant."

"There's a Valentino in the other room, darling, that just screamed your name. You really should see it."

Let them talk as much as they wanted, Margo decided and pasted a smile back on her face. And let them buy.

"Great party." Judy Prentice slipped up to Margo's side.

"Thanks."

"I guess Candy had a prior commitment."

Matching the gleam in Judy's eye, Margo smiled. "She wasn't invited."

"Really?" Judy leaned closer to Margo's ear. "That'll burn her ass."

"I do like you."

"In that case, you won't mind putting that flora minaudière aside for me until I can get in to pick it up?"

"The Judith Leiber? Consider it yours. There's a matching lipstick case, and a compact too. It makes a really fabulous set."

"Your middle name's Satan, right?" Judy tossed up a hand. "Put them all aside for me. I'll be in next week."

"We appreciate your patronage." She laid a hand on Judy's shoulder as she eased by. "Oh, and don't forget to save something to bid on the choker. I heard it screaming your name."

"You are the devil."

With a laugh, Margo moved on to the next group. "So nice to see you. What a gorgeous bracelet."

"She's a natural, isn't she?" Susan murmured to her son. "No one would know there's a nerve in her body."

"See the way she's running her fingers up the stem of her glass. She can't keep her hands still when she's tense. But she's pulling it off."

"So well that I just had Laura put aside two jackets, a bag, and a jeweled snuff bottle for me." Tucking her arm through Josh's, Susan laughed at herself. "They were Laura's jackets, for God's sake. I'm buying my own daughter's castoffs."

"She comes by her excellent taste honestly. Except in men."

Susan patted his hand. "She was too young to know any better, too much in love to be stopped." Laura was older now, Susan thought, and hurting. "You'll keep your eye on her and the girls once your father and I leave, won't you?"

"I guess I haven't been doing my brotherly duty very well lately."

"You've been distracted, and you've earned your own life." Her eyes, sharp and maternal, scanned the room until they found Laura. "I'm a little worried that she's holding up too well."

"You'd rather she fell to pieces."

"I'd rather be sure that if and when she does, someone's there for her." Then she smiled, watching Kate and Margo grab a quick moment with Laura. "They will be."

"WE'VE GO TO make some sort of list," Margo whispered. "Otherwise, we're going to be promising the same things to different people. I'll never keep it all in my head."

"I told you to keep the cash register open," Kate grumbled.

"It would be tacky."

She sent Margo a withering look. "It's a store, pal."

"Margo's right—you don't go ringing up sales and making change at an affair like this."

"God save me from delicate tastes." Kate blew out a breath that fluttered her bangs. "I'll duck into the storeroom and log the promised merchandise. What the hell was it you said, a minatoe?"

"A minaudière," Margo said with a superior smirk. "Just put down 'jeweled evening bag.' I'll know what it is. And don't start playing with the computer. You have to mingle."

"I'm mingled out. Except there's this one guy. He's kind of cute." She craned her head, zeroed in. "There, the one with the moustache and shoulders. See him?"

"Lincoln Howard." Laura identified him easily. "Married."

"Figures." Muttering, Kate walked off.

"You ought to make her keep that dress," Laura commented. "I've never seen her look better."

"She'd look better yet if she didn't walk as though she was late for an audit." Margo caught herself before she pressed a hand to her jumpy stomach again. "We're going to have to start the auction, Laura." She gripped her friend's hand. "Christ, I need a cigarette."

"Make it fast, then. The rep from Wednesday's Child has been giving me the high sign for ten minutes."

"No, I'll suck it in and make another pass so people can cast avaricious looks at the pearls. Then I'll work my way over to Mr. T., and tell him to start the auction."

She started the glide, pausing here and there to touch someone's arm, share a quick laugh, to note who needed a refill of champagne. The minute she saw Kate come back out of the storeroom, she stepped up to Thomas.

"It's showtime. I want to thank you again for helping us out."

"It's a good cause, and good business." He patted her head affectionately. "Let's hose 'em."

"Damn right." She kept her hand in his as they stepped to the front of the room. She knew the murmurs would grow as people turned their heads to study them, knew how to let them play out as she, in turn, sized up the room. From close by, she caught a curious whisper.

"I don't know what Candy was talking about. She doesn't look debilitated or desperate."

"Tommy Templeton wouldn't have let things go so far with his son if she was the conniving whore Candy claims she is."

"Darling, if men recognized conniving whores when they saw them, it wouldn't be the oldest profession."

She felt Thomas's hand tense in hers and looked up at him with an easy smile and hot eyes. "Don't worry." Rising on her toes, she kissed his cheek. "They got the conniving part right, after all."

"If I wasn't a man, I'd punch that jealous cat in the nose." His eyes lit up. "I'll get Susie to do it."

"Maybe later." She gave his hand another squeeze, turned to the crowd. "Ladies and gentlemen, if I could interrupt for a moment." She waited while conversations ebbed, flowed, then politely tapered off. "I'd like to thank you all for coming to Pretenses's first reception."

The speech had been in her head, the one she and Laura and Kate had fine-tuned, but it was slipping away. Using her nerve, she skimmed her gaze over faces.

"We'd especially like to thank you for staying even after you'd had your fill of champagne. Most of you are aware of my . . . checkered career, the way it ended with the kind of delectable little scandal we all love to read about."

She caught Laura's eye and the concern in it. Just smiled. "When I left Europe and came back here, it wasn't because I was thinking of America as the land of opportunity and free enterprise. I came back because home is where you go when you're broken. And I was lucky, because the door was open." She picked her mother out in the crowd, kept her eyes on Ann's. "I don't have anyone to blame for the mistakes I made. I had family who loved me, cared for me, watched over me. That isn't the case with the children who so desperately need what Wednesday's Child offers. They're broken because they weren't loved and cared for and watched over. Because they weren't given the same chances as those of us in this room. Tonight, with my partners, Laura Templeton and Kate Powell, I'd like to take a small step toward giving a few of those children a chance."

She reached back, unclasped the choker, and let it slide through her fingers. "'Bye, baby," she murmured. "I hope you'll bid generously. Remember, it's only money." After draping the pearls over a velvet stand, she turned to Thomas. "Mr. Templeton."

"Miss Sullivan." He took her hand, kissed it. "You're a good girl. Now, then." He turned a cagey eye on the audience as Margo slipped to the rear of the room. His voice boomed out, challenging as he described the single item up for bid, and ordering the bidders, many of whom he called by name, to keep their wallets open.

"That was better than the script," Laura murmured.

"Much better." In agreement, Kate slipped an arm around Margo's waist. "Let's hope it inspires some of these tightwads."

"All right," Thomas called out. "Who's going to get this ball rolling and open the bid?"

"Five hundred."

"Five hundred." Thomas's brows lowered. "Jesus, Pickerling, that's pitiful. If it wasn't against the rules I'd pretend I didn't hear that."

"Seven-fifty."

He huffed and shook his head. "We have a miserly seven-fifty. Do I hear a thousand?" He nodded at a raised hand. "There's a thousand, now let's get serious."

The bidding continued, some called out, others signaled—a lift of the finger, a sober nod, a careless wave. Margo began to relax as they slipped over five thousand. "That's better," she murmured. "I'm going to try to think of anything else as gravy."

"It's making me nuts." Kate fumbled in her bag for her roll of Tums.

"We have six thousand two," Thomas continued. "Madam, you have the throat of a swan. These pearls might have been made for you."

His quarry laughed. "Tommy, you devil. Six-five."

"How much did you say those were worth?" Kate wanted to know.

"Retail at Tiffany? Maybe twelve-five." Delighted, Margo tried to see through the crowd as hands went up. "They're still getting a bargain."

When the bidding topped nine thousand, she wanted to dance. When it hit ten, she wished she had a chair so she could see the bidders. "I never expected it to go this high. I underestimated their generosity."

"And their competitive spirit." Kate balanced on her toes. "It seems to be between two or three people, but I can't see."

"And it's serious now," Margo murmured. "No called bids."

"That's twelve thousand, looking for twelve-five." His sharp eyes darting back and forth, Thomas guided the bidding. "Twelve-five is bid. Thirteen?" At the head shake response, he zeroed in on another bidder. "Thirteen? Yes, we have thirteen. Thirteen is bid, will you bid thirteen-five? The call is for thirteen thousand five hundred. And we have it. Thirteen-five. Will you go fourteen? There's a man who knows his mind. Fourteen is bid. Calling fourteen-five. Fourteen is the bid on the floor. That's fourteen thousand going once, and going twice. Sold for fourteen thousand to the man with exquisite taste and an eye for value."

There was polite applause, pleasant laughter. Margo was too busy trying to see through the now milling crowd to notice the looks aimed her way. "We should go congratulate the winner. Make sure the paper gets a picture. Whoever gets up there first, make sure to hold on to him."

"Margo, dear."

She hadn't made it two steps before her arm was snagged. Staring into the woman's face, Margo searched desperately for a name, then settled on the usual out. "Darling, how wonderful to see you."

"I've had the best time. Such a delightful affair, and a charming little shop. I would have been in weeks ago, but I was so . . . swamped. If I'm asked to serve on another committee, I'll simply slit my wrists."

One of Candy's friends, Margo remembered. Terri, Merri . . . Sherri. "I'm delighted you were able to shuffle us into your schedule."

"Oh, so am I. I've had a wonderful evening. And I've got my heart set on those darling earrings. The little ruby-and-pearl ones. They're just so sweet. Can you tell me how much you're selling them for? I'm going to insist that Lance buy them for me since he lost the choker to Josh."

"I'll have to check the— To Josh." Her mind stopped searching for price tags and went blank. "Josh bought the choker?"

"As if you didn't know." Sherri's eyes glittered as she tapped Margo's arm again. "So clever of you to have him buy it back for you."

"Yes, wasn't it? I'll put a hold on the earrings, Sherri. Come in anytime next week during business hours and take a look at them. You'll have to excuse me."

She worked her way through the crowd, bid good night to dozens while struggling to keep that bright, careless smile on her face. She found Josh flirting ruthlessly with the teenage daughter of one of his board members.

"Josh, I have to steal you away for a minute," she began as the girl went automatically to a pout. "If you could just help me with this little thing in the storeroom." She all but shoved him inside, shut the door. "What have you done?"

"Just giving the kid something to dream about tonight." All innocence, he lifted his hands, palms out. "Never laid a hand on her. I have witnesses."

"I'm not talking about your pathetic flirtation with a child young enough to be your daughter."

"She's seventeen. Give me a break. And I was letting her flirt with me. Just target practice."

"I said I wasn't talking about that, though you should be ashamed of yourself. What do you mean buying the choker?"

"Oh, that."

"Oh, that," she repeated. "Do you know what it looks like?"

"Yeah, it's three strands, beautifully matched pearls with a bow-shaped pavé diamond clasp on eighteen-karat."

She made a sound like expelling steam. "I know what the damn choker looks like."

"Then why did you ask?"

"Don't play lawyer games with me."

"It's really more politics than law."

Now she held up her hands, closing her eyes until she thought she had a shaky hold on her temper. "It looks as though I wheedled you into buying it—and paying more than it's worth on the retail market—just so I could have my cake and eat it too."

He decided that telling her she hadn't served any cake would not result in an amused chuckle. "I was under the impression that the proceeds went to charity."

"The proceeds do, but the necklace—"

"Was offered to the highest bidder."

"People think that I asked you to buy it."

Interested, he angled his head. Yes, her face was definitely flushed, he noted. Her eyes bright and hot. Embarrassment was a new, and not unattractive, look on her. "Since when do you care what people think?"

"I'm trying to learn to care."

He considered. "Why?"

"Because . . ." She closed her eyes again. "I have no idea. I have no earthly idea."

"All right, then." He slipped the pearls out of his pocket, running them through his hand as he studied them. "Just grains of sand, hunks of carbon, tricked into something lovely by time and nature."

"Spoken like a man."

His gaze lifted, locked on hers, made her stomach tremble. "I made up my mind to buy it when I was inside you, and this was all you were wearing, and you looked at me as if nothing else existed but us. That's spoken like a man, too. A man who loves you, Margo. And always has."

Terrified and thrilled, she stared at him. "I can't breathe."

"I know the feeling."

"No, I really can't breathe." Quickly, she dropped into a chair and put her spinning head between her knees.

"Well, that's quite a reaction to a declaration of love." He slid the pearls back into his pocket so he could rub her back. "Is it your usual?"

"No."

His grim mouth curved a little. "That's something, then."

"I'm not ready." She drew in air slowly, tried to let it out molecule by molecule. "I'm just not ready for this. For you. I love you too, but I'm not ready."

Of all the scenarios he'd imagined when she would finally tell him she loved him, none of them had included her saying the words with her head between her knees.

"Would you mind sitting up and telling me that again. Just the 'I love you' part."

Cautious, she lifted her head. "I do love you, but— No, don't touch me now."

"The hell with that." He hauled her out of the chair and crushed his mouth to hers with more impatience than finesse.

CHAPTER 18

KATE OPENED THE door of the storeroom and let out a long, windy sigh at the sight of Josh and Margo locked in a passionate embrace. Maybe it did warm her heart, but there was no reason to let them know that.

"Do you two mind putting your glands on hold so we can finish out the evening with some sense of decorum?"

Josh tore his mouth from Margo's long enough to suck in a breath. "Scram," he ordered and got back to business.

"I will not scram. There are still over a dozen people out there who expect to be bid a fond farewell by the owners. All three owners. And that includes the woman you're currently performing an emergency tonsillectomy on."

Josh gave her a brief glance over the top of Margo's head. "Kate, you're such a romantic fool."

"I know, it's a weakness of mine." She stepped up and pried them apart. "I'm sure the two of you can remember where you left off. Come on, partner. Oh, and Josh, you might want to stay in here until you're a little more . . . presentable."

He damned near blushed. "Sisters aren't supposed to notice that sort of thing."

"This one sees all, knows all." She whisked Margo through the door. "What's the matter with you?" she muttered. "You look like you've been poleaxed."

"I have been. Give me one of those damn Tums you're so crazy about."

"Soon as I can get to my purse." Concerned, she rubbed her hand over Margo's back. "Tell me what's wrong, honey?"

"I can't now. Tomorrow." And because she understood her job, she curved her lips into a bright smile and held out both hands to the woman approaching them. "So glad you could come. I hope you enjoyed the evening."

She repeated those sentiments, with variation, for nearly an hour before the last lingerer trickled out. Necessity, along with aspirin and antacids, kept her functioning. She wanted a quiet room, a moment to herself to sort out all the emotions whirling through her, but she was swept along when the Templetons insisted on taking the family out to celebrate.

IT WAS NEARLY one before she walked into the penthouse with Josh. She should have had it all figured out by now, she thought. She should know exactly what to say and do. But when the door closed behind them and they were alone, she didn't have a clue.

"I'm going to miss them—your parents—when they go back to Europe."

"So am I." There was an easy smile on his face. His formal tie was loose now, as were the studs on his tuxedo shirt. Margo thought he looked like an elegantly male ad for an outrageously expensive and sexy cologne. "You've been quiet."

"I know. I've been trying to think, to figure out what to say when we talk about this."

"You shouldn't have to think that hard." He stepped toward her, began to slide the pins from her hair. "I've been thinking about being alone with you. Finally." As her hair tumbled free, he tossed the pins on the dresser. "It didn't take much effort."

"One of us has to be sensible."

"Why?"

At any other time, she would have laughed. "I'm not sure why, I just know one of us has to be. And it doesn't look as though it's going to be you. Josh, I'm not sure either of us knows how to handle this."

"I've got a pretty good idea how to start." His arms slipped around her, raced up her back to cup her shoulders and pull her into him.

"This part's easy, maybe too easy for both of us. I don't think we want that to change."

"Why should it?" He skimmed his mouth along her jaw. And the taste of her was warm and silky.

"Because we've muddied up the waters." How did he expect her to think when he was sampling her as if she was a delicacy he'd chosen from under glinting crystal? "Because I've never really been in love before, and I don't think you have either." Her pulse was already stuttering. "We don't know what we're doing."

"So, we'll improvise." His mood was soaring too high and too free to let her sudden attack of logic dampen it. He tugged on the zipper at the back of her dress, and when the silk parted, he slid his hands along her skin.

"Are you saying things don't have to change?" Bubbles of relief warred against flickers of need as her dress slipped down.

He wanted to tell her everything had already done so. But he knew her so well, understood that if he spoke of change, of commitment, of forever, she'd balk or evade, or simply bolt. "Nothing that we don't want to change. This, for instance," he murmured, skimming his thumbs along the soft white swell of her breasts. They rose, full and white, out of the strapless lace of a black body skimmer. Her stockings stopped high on the thigh, another seductive contrast of black against white. He let his fingers trail from stocking to flesh to lace, and thrilled at each sharply defined texture. All the while, his eyes stayed on hers.

"The minute you touch me, I want you. It's something I can't seem to control." And it worried her, worried her enough that she purposely pushed all rational thought aside and eased open his stark white shirt to caress the pale gold tint of the flesh beneath. "I've never had a lover who stirred me up so much just by being in the same room. How long can that last?"

"Let's find out." He eased her onto the bed—pale hair spilling, milk-white skin against black silk and lace. She was all promising scents and luscious curves, long, limber limbs that reached out to enfold.

She held him against her, reveling in the feel of his weight pinning her, imprisoning sex under sex with slow friction. All she had to know, for this moment, was that she wanted him. And her mouth sought his eagerly for that dreamy mating of tongues.

When had she come to need the flavor of him, the scent and texture of his skin? After so many years, how had friendship and family shot into passion and longing? And why, when their bodies meshed so perfectly, should it matter?

Her skin hummed under his hands, those long, gliding strokes that shifted in a pulsebeat to rough and possessive. What spurted to life inside of her was too layered and complex to analyze. She let the heat take her.

He felt every shift and sigh, knew when nerves had melted into acceptance. Here, in this big, soft bed, there were no questions. She was, and always had been, everything he wanted.

Long, lean limbs, sumptuous curves, sleek, perfumed skin. Her body had been designed to take and give pleasure. And no one else, he thought as his mouth fused to hers, would take it from or give it to her again. No one else understood her heart, her mind, and her dreams as he did.

No one else.

Her heart leapt, then stuttered as his mood turned urgent. Desperate hands, a ravenous mouth raced over her. Sighs deepened into moans as she matched him beat for beat, flame for flame.

How delicious was madness.

She rolled over, her hands as quick and fast as his, to drive him as he was driving her. Dangerous heights. Pleasure that was a shuddering kin to pain. She rose up. In the shadowed lights her skin gleamed like damp silk. Her eyes, wildly blue, locked on his. One heartbeat. Two.

Now. The demand seemed to shimmer in the air around them. In answer he gripped her hips, fingers digging in. In one fluid move, she took him deep, deep, holding there, holding them both trembling. On a long, feline moan, she arched back, skimming her hands over her own body, from center over torso to breast, where she felt her heart thundering. Slow, very slow, acutely aware of every tremor of her body, acutely aware that his eyes were following her movements, she trailed her hands down until they covered, caressed that mating of bodies.

Glorying in every breath, she sleeked her hands up again, lifted her hair. And began to ride.

The pace she set was hard and fast and merciless. He watched as she drove herself to the peak, shuddered over it. Sensations battered him like an avalanche, blurring his vision. But he knew he'd never seen anything more glorious than Margo lost in her own passion.

When she cried out, flinging herself forward, her hands braced on his shoulders, her hair curtaining his face, he had no choice but to lose himself with her.

* * *

"WHY DO I always feel as if I've dived off a mountain whenever I make love with you?" Margo didn't really expect an answer. She thought Josh was asleep, or at least comatose, but he shifted, his lips brushing over the curve of one breast, then the other.

"Because you and I together, duchess, are a dangerous pair. And I want you again already." He nibbled his way up to her throat, found her warm, swollen mouth.

She was ready to float again, her arms light and limber as they lifted to circle him. "It's never been like this for me before." Through the daze of sensations building fresh, she felt the change. And understood the reason for it. "I know how that sounds."

"It doesn't matter." He didn't want to think about it. Only wanted to have her, to hold her.

"It does. To both of us." Suddenly unsure here, where she had always felt so confident, she cupped his face in her hands to raise it. His eyes were heavy with desire, a hint of irritation now working through. "I think we have to talk about it."

"Neither one of us took a vow of chastity."

That was true enough. She also knew that though she had taken lovers before, the press had gifted her with a libido and a trail of broken hearts that was well beyond reality.

"We need to talk about it," she repeated.

"I haven't asked you any questions, Margo. Whoever, how many ever, have been in your life before, there's only one now. There's only me."

The cool, possessive tone might have annoyed her under other circumstances. It was so Joshua Templeton—I see, I want, I take. But they were still linked, still warm from each other. "There haven't been as many as you might think. Josh, I didn't sleep with every man I dated."

"Fine. I didn't sleep with every woman I took to dinner." He snapped it out as he turned over on his back to drag the hair off his face. "It's now that matters, in any case. Are we straight about this?"

She wanted them to be. It was his anger, the cold control of it, that told her differently. "Josh, my reputation's never really mattered to me before. In fact, it only added to my bank account. But now . . . it matters now." Suddenly chilled, she sat up, wrapped her arms around herself. "It matters now because you matter now. And I don't know how to handle it. I don't know how either of us is going to handle it. When it was just sex—"

"It was never just sex for me."

"I didn't know that," she said quietly. "I didn't know how you felt, or how I felt, until it was just there. And it's so big, so important. So scary."

It surprised him, not just what she said but the way she said it. Nerves, regrets, confusion. All those things were so rare in Margo when it came to the games men and women played.

"You're scared?"

"Terrified." She hissed out a breath and rose to yank a robe out of the closet. "And I'm not happy about it."

"So am I."

With the beginnings of temper simmering in her eyes, she looked at him over her shoulder. A long, lean male animal, she mused, his hands tucked behind his head now, the start of a smirk on that gorgeous mouth. She wasn't sure whether to slug him or jump on him.

"So are you what?"

"Terrified, and not happy about it."

She tugged the belt on the robe, kept her hands in place as she turned. "Really?"

"You know what I figure, duchess?"

"No." It was the smirk that drew her, had her going back to sit on the side of the bed. "What is it that you figure?"

"It's all been so easy for us before. Too easy."

"And this isn't going to be."

He took her hand, linking fingers casually. "Doesn't look like it. Maybe I've got a little problem, a hitch, when it comes to other men. After all, the woman I'm in love with has been engaged five times."

"Three." She jerked her hand free, aware that her past was constantly going to sneak up and slap her in the face. "The other two were products of an overeager press. And the three were . . . quickly rectified mistakes."

"The point being," he said, with what he considered admirable patience, "that none of my relationships ever progressed that far."

"Which could be taken as a fear of commitment on your part."

"Could be," he murmured. "But the simple fact is I've been in love with you nearly half my life. Nearly half my life," he said again, sitting up so that his eyes, dark as shadows, were level with hers. "Every woman I touched was a substitute for you."

"Josh." She only shook her head. There was nothing she could say, nothing that could rise above the wave of emotion that swamped her.

"It's demoralizing, Margo, to watch the woman, the only woman you really want, turn to anyone but you. To wait and to watch."

It was thrilling, and panicking, to think it. To know it. "But why did you wait?"

"A man has to use what advantage he has. Mine was time."

"Time?"

"I know you, Margo." He skimmed a finger down the curve of her cheek. "Sooner or later you were going to get in over your head, or just get bored with the high life."

"And you'd be right there to pick up the pieces."

"It worked," he said lightly and snagged her wrist before she could jump out of the bed. "No reason to get frosted."

"It's a perfect reason. You arrogant, egotistical son of a bitch. Just wait till Margo fucks up and then step in." She'd have taken a swing at him if he hadn't anticipated her and grabbed her other wrist.

"I wouldn't have put it exactly that way, but . . ." He smiled winningly. "You did fuck up."

"I know what I did." She tugged her arms outward and only succeeded in performing a warped rendition of patty-cake. "I also got out of that mess with Alain on my own." It was the flicker in his eyes that stopped her. It was there and gone quickly, but she knew every nuance of his face. "Didn't I?"

"Sure you did, but the point is—"

"What did you do?" Incensed, she batted her trapped hands against his chest. "You weren't in Greece. I'd have known if you were. How did you fix it?"

"I didn't fix it. Exactly." Hell. "Look, I made a few calls, pulled in a few markers. Christ, Margo, did you expect me to sit around on the beach while they were toying with tossing your butt in jail?"

"No." She spoke quietly because she was afraid she might scream. "No. I have a crisis, you ride to the rescue. Let go of my hands."

"I don't think so," he said, judging the temper in her eyes. "Listen, all I did was make it go away faster. They didn't have anything on you, didn't want to have anything on you. But there wasn't any point in you cooling your heels in custody longer than necessary. All you'd done was have the bad taste and poor sense to hook up with some slick con artist who was using you for cover."

"Thank you very much."

"Don't mention it."

"And since you have mentioned it, yet again, I'll admit that I've had plenty of experience with bad taste and poor sense." She jerked her arms, fuming when he held firm. "But I'm over it now. I took charge of my own life, damn you. And I put it back together, piece by piece. Which is something you've never had to do. I took the risk, I did the work, I—"

"I'm proud of you." Deflating her completely, he brought her fisted hands to his lips.

"Don't try to turn this around."

"Proud of the way you faced what had to be done and turned it all into something unique and exciting." He opened her fingers, pressed his lips to her palm. "And moved by you. By the way you stood there tonight, by the things you said."

"Damn you, Josh."

"I love you, Margo." His lips curved. "Maybe it was my poor sense that made me love you before. But I'm even more in love with the woman I'm with now."

Defeated, she rested her brow against his. "How do you do this, wind me up, spin me out? I can't remember why I was mad at you."

"Just come here." He drew her into his arms. "Let's see what else we can forget."

LATER WHEN SHE lay curled beside him, the weight of his arm around her, the sound of his heart beating slow and steady under her ear, she remembered it all. They had, she realized, resolved nothing. She wondered if two people who had known each other so long and so well could understand each other's hearts so little.

Until tonight, she'd never been ashamed of the men she had let into her life. Fun, excitement, romance had been everything she'd looked for, dreamed of. Most women had viewed her as competition. Even as a child she had had few female friends other than Laura and Kate.

But men . . .

She sighed and closed her eyes.

She understood men, had at an early age deduced the power that beauty and sex could wield. She'd enjoyed wielding it. Never to hurt, she thought. She had never played the game with the risk of genuine pain on either side. No, she'd always been careful to choose game partners who understood the rules. Older men, experienced men, men with smooth manners, hefty wallets, and guarded hearts.

None of them would interfere with her career, her ambitions, because the rules were simple and always followed.

Fun, excitement, romance. With no spills, no tangles, no hard feelings when she moved on.

No feelings at all. But plenty of poor judgment.

Now there was Josh. With him her power was different, her dreams were different. The rules were different. Oh, the fun was there, and the excitement, and the romance. But there had already been spills and tangles.

Didn't it follow that someone was going to get hurt?

However much he loved her, she hadn't yet earned his trust. And inches behind trust, she thought, was his respect.

He loved the woman he was with now, she remembered. But she wondered if he was waiting to see whether she would stay or run. And she wondered, deep down wondered, if she was waiting too.

After all, he'd been born to a life of privilege, had the in-the-blood advantage of being able to choose and discard anything—and anyone—at his leisure. If it was true that he'd wanted her for so long, he'd waited and watched, and, being Josh, he'd reveled in the challenge.

Now that the challenge had been met . . .

"I'll hate you for it," she murmured and pressed her lips to his shoulder. "Whoever does the hurting, I'll hate you for it." She curled closer, wishing he would wake, wake and make her mindless again so she wouldn't have to worry and wonder.

"I love you, Josh." She laid her palm over his heart and counted the beats until hers matched them. "God help both of us."

CHAPTER 19

THE CLIFFS WERE always the place Margo went for thinking. All of her major decisions had been made there. Who should be invited to her birthday party? Did she really want to cut her hair? Should she go to the homecoming dance with Biff or Marcus?

Those decisions had seemed so monumental at the time. The crash of waves, the smell of the sea and wildflowers, the jagged sweep of rocks from dizzying heights had both soothed and aroused her. The emotions she felt here went into all those decisions.

It was here she had come the day before she ran away to Hollywood. Just after Laura's wedding, she thought now. She was eighteen and so certain that life with all its mysteries was passing her by. She was desperate to see what was out there, to see what she could make of it. Make from it.

How many arguments had she had with her mother during those last weeks? she wondered. Too many to count, she thought now.

You've got to go to college, girl, if you want to make something out of yourself.

It's boring. It's useless. There's nothing for me there. I want more.

So you always have. More what this time?

More everything.

And she'd found it, hadn't she? Margo mused. More excitement, more attention, more money. More men.

Now that she had come full circle, what did she have? A new chance. Something of her own. And Josh.

She threw her head back, watched a gull swoop, skim the air, and bullet out to sea. Far out on the diamond-blue water a boat glided, glossy and white, the sun just catching the brasswork to wink and flash. The wind swirled up and spun like a dancer, teasing her hair, whipping at the draping silk of her white tunic.

She felt shockingly alone there, small and insignificant on the high, spearing cliffs, with destruction or glory only a few small steps away.

A metaphor for love? she thought, amused at herself. Deep thoughts had never been her forte. She was alone without him, solitary. If commitment to Josh was like a leap from a cliff, would a woman like her fly up or tumble and crash?

If it was a risk she was willing to take, what would it do to him? Would he trust her? Could he? Would he believe in her, stand with her? Would he, most of all, be willing to hold through all the ups and downs of a life together?

And how, in God's name, had she leaped from love to marriage? Jesus, she was actually thinking of marriage.

She had to sit down.

Shaky, she eased down onto a rock, waited for her breath to come back. Marriage had never been a goal in her life. The engagements had simply been a lark, a tease, no more serious to her than a wink and a smile.

Marriage meant promises that couldn't be broken with a shrug. It meant a lifetime, a sharing of everything. Even children. She shivered once, pressed her hand to her stomach. She wasn't the motherly type. No, no, white picket fences and car pools were light-years out of her realm.

No—she nearly laughed at herself—it wasn't even to be considered. She would live with him. The situation as it was now was perfect. Naturally, it was the way he wanted it as well. She couldn't understand why she'd gotten so worked up over it. The penthouse suite suited their needs, their lifestyles, gave them each a chance to fly off, together or separately, when the whim struck.

Nothing permanent, nothing that hinted at obligation. Of course, that had been the answer all along. Hotel life was in his blood, and it was part of her choice of living. Tired of looking at the same view? Pack up your clothes and find another.

Of course that was what he would want. And what she would be comfortable with.

Then she turned and looked up, higher still, at the house with its rock-solid permanence, its strength and its beauty. Towers added by new generations, colorful tiles set by the old. She knew that memories made there lasted forever. Dreams dreamt there never really faded away. Love spoken there bloomed as free and as wild as the tangled vines of bougainvillea.

But it wasn't hers. A home of her own was something that had always eluded her. She turned away again, looked out to sea, surprised that her eyes were stinging.

What do you want, Margo? What in God's name do you want?

More. More everything.

"Figured you'd be here." Kate dropped down on the rocks beside her. "Good day for sea gazing."

"You must be feeling jazzed this morning." Laura laid a hand on her shoulder. "Last night was a smash, beginning to end."

"She's brooding." Kate rolled her eyes at Laura. "Never satisfied."

"I'm in love with Josh." Margo stared straight ahead when she said it, as if speaking to the wind.

Kate pressed her lips together, considered. Because she couldn't see Margo's eyes behind the shaded lenses, she tipped them down on Margo's nose. "Lowercase or uppercase 'l'?"

"Kate, it's not high school," Laura murmured.

"It's still a relevant question. What's the answer?"

"I'm in love with Josh," Margo repeated. "And he's in love with me. We've lost our minds."

"You mean it," Kate said slowly and shifted her gaze from Margo's eyes to Laura's. "She means it."

"I've got to walk." Margo rose quickly and began to follow the curving line of the cliffs. "I've got all this energy I don't know what to do with. And all these nerves that keep circling around from my head to my gut and back again."

"That doesn't have to be a bad thing," Laura told her.

"You were in love with Peter, weren't you?"

Laura looked down at her feet, told herself it was necessary to watch her step. "Yes. Yes, I was. Once."

"There's my point. You were in love with him, started a life together, and then it all fell apart. Do you have any idea how many relationships I've watched unravel or just rip? I couldn't count them. Nothing lasts forever."

"My parents?"

"Are the shining example of an exception to the rule."

"Wait a minute. Wait a minute." Kate grabbed at her arm. "Are you and Josh thinking of getting married?"

"No. Good God, no. Absolutely not. Neither of us is the 'till death do us part' type." Needing to be closer to the sea, Margo picked her way down some rocks.

"Do you want to be in love with him?"

At Kate's question she looked over, annoyed, impatient. "It's not a choice."

"Of course it is." Kate didn't believe that love, or any other emotion, was uncontrollable.

"Love isn't a spring suit," Laura put in, "that you try on for size."

Kate merely moved her shoulders and scrambled agilely down to the ledge. "If it doesn't fit, you put it aside, as far as I'm concerned. So, Margo, does it fit or not?"

"I don't know. But I'm wearing it."

"Maybe you'll grow into it." Or, Laura worried, grow out of it.

It was the tone that made Margo stop. Concern was a layer over doubt. "I really do love him," she said quietly. "I don't know exactly how to handle it yet, but I do. We don't seem to be able to talk it through sensibly. I know, I can see that part of him is hung up on the way I've lived. The men I've been with."

"Oh, right. Like he's been in a monastery copying scripture for the last ten years." Kate squared her shoulders, her feminist flag waving high. "It's none of his damn business if you've taken on the Fifth, Six, and Seventh fleets. A woman has just as much right as a man to be stupidly and irresponsibly promiscuous."

Margo opened her mouth, but for a moment she could only laugh at the cleverly insulting support. "Thank you so much, Sister Immaculata."

"Anytime, Sister Slut."

"My point is," Margo continued dryly, "that it's not just garden-variety jealousy with Josh. I could overlook that, or be annoyed by that. In this case, he has cause to doubt, and I'm not sure how long it will take to prove to both of us that that part of my life is over."

"I think you're being too easy on him," Kate muttered.

"And too hard on myself?"

Kate smiled cheerfully. "I didn't say that."

"Then I will," Laura said with an elbow jab to Kate's ribs.

"It's more than the men." Staring out to sea, Margo tried to make sense of it all. "That's just a kind of symptom, I suppose. He says he's proud of me, what I've done to put my life back in order. I'd say he's more surprised than anything else. And because of that," she said slowly, "I realize that it's unlikely he really expects me to follow it all the way through, to stand and to stay. Why should he?" she murmured, remembering his sharp reaction to her recent photo shoot. "He's waiting for me to take off again, to run to something bigger, easier."

"I'd say you don't have enough faith in him." Frowning, Kate studied Margo's face. "Are you planning to run?"

"No." It was something, at last, that she could be absolutely certain of. "I've finished running. But with my track record—"

"The two of you better start concentrating on now," Laura interrupted. "Where you are now and what you feel for each other now. All the rest, well, that just brought you to where you're standing, and who you're standing with."

It sounded so simple, so clean. Margo struggled to believe it. "Okay. I think it's best if we take it one step at a time," Margo decided. "Like a recovery program, in reverse." Reaching down, she picked up a pebble, tossed it out to sea. "Meanwhile, we're in meanwhile. It might be fun."

"Love's supposed to be." Laura smiled. "When it's not hell."

"You're the only one of the three of us who's been there." Margo glanced at Kate for confirmation.

"Affirmative."

"If it doesn't bother you, would you mind telling me how you came out the other side. I mean how did you fall out?"

It did bother her. It scraped her raw inside and left her a failure. But she would never admit it. "It was gradual, like water against rock gradually wears it down. It wasn't a flash, like waking up one morning and realizing I wasn't in love with my husband. It was a slow, nasty process, a kind of calcifying of emotions. In the end, I felt nothing for him at all."

A terrifying thought, Margo decided. Not to feel anything for Josh. She was sure she'd rather hate him than feel nothing for him. Or worse, much worse, she realized, to have him feel nothing for her. "Could you have stopped it?"

"No. We might have been able to stop it, but I couldn't. Not alone. He never loved me." And oh, that stung. "That makes it entirely different than you and Josh."

"I'm sorry, Laura."

"Don't be." Easier, Laura leaned against Margo's supporting arm. "I have two beautiful daughters. That's a pretty good deal all around. And you have a chance for something special, and uniquely yours."

"I might take that chance." She plucked another pebble, tossed it.

"Well, if you're looking to start a love nest, an account I have is unloading a property about half a mile south of here." Getting into the spirit, Kate scooped up pebbles herself. "A beauty, too. California Spanish."

"We're perfectly happy in the suite." Safe in the suite, a small voice whispered in her head. In limbo.

"Whatever works for you," Kate shrugged. She believed strongly in the investment value of real estate. A home was one thing—it couldn't be measured in terms of short- or long-term capital gains. But property, well chosen, was a necessary addition to any well-rounded portfolio. "But it's got a killer view."

"How would you know?"

"I delivered some forms there once." She caught Margo's smirk. "Gutter mind. The client is female. She got the house in the divorce settlement and wants to sell it and buy something smaller, lower-maintenance."

"Is that Lily Farmer's house?" Laura asked.

"One and the same."

"Oh, it's beautiful. Two stories. Stucco and tile. They had it completely restored about two years ago."

"Yep. Finished it up just in time to say 'adios.' He got the boat, the BMW, the Labrador retriever, and the coin collection. She got the house, the Land Rover, and the Siamese cat." Kate grinned. "There are no secrets from your CPA."

"That's just the sort of thing I'm talking about, and why I don't want a house, a four-wheel-drive, or a dog." The very idea made Margo's stomach hurt. "I've simplified my life. Streamlined it, anyway, and I'll be damned if I'm going to fuck it up again." She had a handful of stones now and was shooting them over the edge like bullets. "What was it my mother always said? Begin as you mean to go on? Well, that's just what I'm doing. Begin simple, keep it simple. Josh doesn't want all those responsibilities any more than I do. We'll leave it—"

"Wait!" Laura grabbed her wrist before she could heave the next stone. "What is that? It's not a rock."

Frowning, Margo began to rub it with her thumb. "Someone must have dropped some change. I didn't notice. It's just a . . . Oh, my Jesus."

As she brushed off the dirt and sand, it gleamed at her, a small disk nestled in the palm of her hand.

"It's gold." Kate closed her hand over Laura's, and the three of them were linked. "It's a doubloon. Holy God, it's a gold doubloon."

"No, no." Breathless, Margo shook her head. "It's got to be one of those fake tokens they give away at the arcade in town." But it had weight. And such a fine gleam. "Doesn't it?"

"Look at the date," Laura managed. "1845."

"Seraphina." Margo pressed a hand to her head as it revolved like a carousel. "Seraphina's dowry. Could it be?"

"It has to be," Kate insisted.

"But it was just lying there. We've walked along here hundreds of times. We even searched here when we were kids. We never found anything."

"I guess we never looked in the right place." Kate's eyes danced with excitement as she leaned up to give Margo a hard, smacking kiss. "Let's look now."

As laughingly eager as the girls they had once been, they crawled over the dirt and rocks, ruining manicures, nicking fingers.

"Maybe she didn't leave it hidden after all," Margo suggested. "Maybe when he didn't come back and she decided she wouldn't live without him, she just chucked it all. Scattering coins into the sea."

"Bite your tongue." Kate wiped sweat from her brow with a dusty forearm. "The three of us always swore we'd find it, and now that we've actually got a piece, you want to have her taking the treasure into the sea with her!"

"I don't think she'd do that." Muffling a yelp as she scraped a knuckle on rock, Laura sat back on her heels. "The dowry wasn't important to her anymore. Nothing was. Poor thing, she was just a child." She blew hair out of her eyes. "And speaking of children . . . look at us."

It wasn't the order that made Kate and Margo stop. It was the laughter that rolled out of her. Such a rare sound these days, Laura's low, gurgling laugh.

And getting a good look at one of society's most respected matrons with her hair flying, her face streaked with dirt, her once well-pressed cotton shirt soiled with sweat and grime, Margo laughed with her.

Then she clutched her stomach and pointed at Kate, who was on her hands and knees staring at them. She managed to clutch a rock before the next spurt of laughter rolled her off the cliff.

"Jesus, Kate! Jesus, even your eyebrows are dirty."

"You're not exactly bandbox-fresh yourself, pal. Only you would go treasure hunting in white silk."

"Oh, shit, I forgot." Wincing, Margo looked down at herself. The once spotless and fluid tunic was now filthy and stuck to her skin. She let out a low moan. "This used to be an Ungaro."

"Now it's a rag," Kate said smartly. "Next time try jeans and a T-shirt like the rest of the peasants." Kate rose and brushed the dirt off her denim. "We're never going to find anything this way. We need to organize. We need a metal detector."

"That's actually a good idea," Margo decided. "Where do we get one?"

* * *

By THE TIME Margo got back to the penthouse it was dark. She limped through the front door and began stripping as she aimed directly for the whirlpool.

Josh halted in the act of pouring a glass of Poully Fuisse. "What in God's name have you been doing?" Glass cracked against wood as he rushed to her. "Was there an accident? Are you hurt?"

"No accident, and I hurt everywhere." She whimpered as she reached to turn on the hot water. Her fingers cramped painfully. "Josh, if you really do love me, you'll get me a glass of whatever you were pouring and you won't, no matter how much you want to, laugh at me."

He couldn't spot any blood as she eased her body into the water. Relieved, he went back and brought two glasses filled with pale gold wine. "Tell me this—did you fall off a cliff?"

"Not exactly." She took a glass from him and downed the wine in a few greedy swallows. She took a breath, handed him the empty glass, then took the full one. "Thanks."

He only lifted a brow, then went back for the bottle. "I know, you took the girls to the beach and let them bury you in your clothes."

She leaned back, groaned. "I work out regularly now. How can there still be muscles I haven't been using? How can they hurt this much? Can you order me a massage?"

"I'll give you one myself if we can stop playing guess what."

She opened her eyes. She wanted to see if he laughed. If she spotted so much as a quiver, he'd have to die. "I was with Laura and Kate."

"And?"

"And we were treasure hunting."

"You were . . ." He ran his tongue around his teeth. "Hmm."

"Was that a chuckle?"

"No, it was a hmm. You spent the afternoon and a good part of the evening treasure hunting?"

"On the cliffs. We got a metal detector."

"You got a—" He tried manfully to disguise the laugh with a cough, but her eyes narrowed. "Did you figure out how to work it?"

"I'm not an idiot." But she pouted and, as the water level rose, hit the button for jets. "Kate did. And before you make any other smart comments, go check the pocket of my slacks out there." She sank deeper, sipped wine, and felt as though she might live after all. "Then you can apologize."

Willing to play along, he set his glass down on the ledge of the tub and sauntered into the other room. Her slacks were near the door, less than a foot in front of where she'd stepped out of her shoes. And they were filthy enough to have him lifting them gingerly with two fingertips.

"You're going to need a new treasure-hunting outfit, honey. This one's shot."

"Shut up, Josh. Look in the pocket."

"Probably found a diamond that fell out of somebody's ring," he muttered. "Thinks she's hit the mother lode."

But his fingers closed over the coin. With a puzzled frown he drew it out. Spanish coin, more than a century old and bright as summer.

"I don't hear any laughing out there," she called out. "Or any apology, either." She began to hum to herself as the churning water loosened her muscles. Sensing him in the doorway, she flicked him a glance from under her lashes. "You don't have to grovel. A simple 'Please forgive me, Margo. I was a fool' will do nicely."

He flipped the coin and caught it neatly before sitting on the ledge. "One doubloon does not a treasure make."

"Rudyard Kipling?"

He had to grin. "J. C. Templeton."

"Oh, him." She closed her eyes. "I always thought he was cynical and overblown."

"Take a breath, darling," he warned, and dunked her.

When she surfaced, sputtering, he turned the coin over in his hand. "I admit it's intriguing. Where exactly did you find it?"

She was pouting and blinking water out of her eyes. "I don't see why I should tell you. Seraphina's dowry is a girl thing."

"Okay." He shrugged and picked up his wine. "So, what else did you do today?"

"At least you could wheedle," she said in disgust.

"I've cut way back on my wheedling." He passed her the soap. "You really need this."

"Oh, all right, then." One long, gorgeous leg shot out of the water. She soaped it lavishly. "It was on the cliffs in front of the house. Kate put a pile of stones up to mark the spot. But we searched there for hours after I found the coin and didn't find so much as a plug nickel."

"And what exactly is a plug nickel? Just a rhetorical question," he said when she hissed at him. "Look, duchess, I'm not going to spoil your fun. You've got yourself a nice little prize here. And the date's right. Who knows?"

"I know. And Kate and Laura know." She dragged her fingers through her wet hair. "And I'll tell you something else. It meant something to Laura. She lost that look in her eyes, that wounded look that always seems to be there if she doesn't know you're watching."

When his face went grim, she was sorry she'd said it. She covered his hand with hers. "I love her too."

"Firing the bastard wasn't enough."

"You broke his nose."

"There was that. I don't want her hurting. I don't know anyone who deserves it less than Laura."

"Or who seems to handle it better," she added, giving his hand a quick squeeze. "You should have seen her today. She was laughing and excited. We even got the girls in on it. I haven't seen Ali smile like that in weeks. It was so much fun. Just the anticipation of what might be there."

He eyed the coin again before setting it down to gleam on the ledge. "So when are you going back?"

"We decided to make it a regular Sunday outing." She wrinkled her nose at the water. "I might as well be taking a mud bath." And pulled the plug. "I'm starved. Do you mind eating in tonight? I have to shower off and wash my hair."

He watched her rise up, water sluicing off creamy skin in streams. "Can we eat naked?"

"Depends." She laughed as she padded toward the shower. "What's on the menu?"

THE NEXT MORNING, loose with love, she stretched as Josh maneuvered through traffic. "You didn't have to drive me in," she told him, "but I appreciate it."

"I want to drop by the resort anyway. Check on a few things."

"You haven't mentioned any travel coming up."

"Things are covered."

She glanced out the window, as if engrossed in the passing scenery. "Once you replace Peter you'll have to go back to Europe, I imagine."

"Eventually. I'm handling things from here well enough for now."

"Is that what you want?" She needed to keep the question easy, for both of them. "To stay here?"

He was as cautious as she. "Why do you ask?"

"You've never stayed in one place for long."

"There was never a reason to."

Her lips curved. "That's nice. But I don't want you to feel tied down. Both of us have to understand that the other's business has demands. If Pretenses continues to do well, I'll have to start making buying trips."

He'd considered that, had already begun working on a solution. "Where did you have in mind?"

"I'm not sure. Local estate sales won't do. And for the clothing end of it, I want to try my contacts first. I could probably pitch a better ball in person. L.A. certainly, and New York, Chicago. And if it all keeps rolling, back to Milan, London, Paris."

"Is that what you want?"

"I want the shop to shine. Sometimes I miss Milan, the being there, the feeling of being in the center of something. Of having it all buzzing around me." She sighed a little. "It's hard to let go completely. I'm hoping that if I can visit there a couple of times a year, do business there now and again, it'll be enough. Don't you miss it too?" She turned to face him. "The people, the parties?"

"Some." He'd been too busy changing his life, and hers, to think about it. But now that he did think, he could admit that the whirl was in his blood. "There's no reason we couldn't coordinate your buying trips with my business. Just takes a little planning."

"I'm getting better at planning." When he pulled to the curb in front of Pretenses, she leaned over to kiss him. "It's good, isn't it? This is good."

"Yeah." He cupped her neck to linger over the kiss. "It's very good."

All they had to do, she thought, was keep it that way. "I'll take a cab back. No, I mean it." She kissed him again before he could protest. "I should be there by seven, so try not to work too late. I'd love to go somewhere fabulous for dinner and neck over champagne cocktails."

"I think I can arrange that."

"I've never known you to fail."

He caught her hand as she started to alight. "I do love you, Margo."

She tossed him a brilliant smile. "I know."

CHAPTER 20

IT WAS A smug feeling, spending the day in her own shop, among her own things, reaping the rewards of her first successful reception. And so she told her mother when Ann dropped by in the middle of the day with a box of Margo's old favorite. Chocolate chip cookies.

"I just can't believe it all happened," Margo said over a greedy bite. "People have been coming in all day. This is the first break I could manage. Mum, I really think I have a business. I mean I wanted to believe it all along. I nearly believed it after the first day went so well. But Saturday night." She closed her eyes and shoved the rest of the cookie into her mouth. "Saturday night I really believed it."

"You did a good job." Ann sipped the tea she'd brewed in the upstairs kitchen. Though she raised an eyebrow at Margo's choice of champagne—champagne at lunchtime!—she didn't comment. "You've done a good job. All these years . . ."

"All these years I've squandered my life, my time, my resources." Margo shrugged her shoulder. "The old ant and grasshopper story again, Mum?"

Despite herself Ann felt a smile tug at her lips. "You never listened to that story, never stored your larder for winter. Or so I thought." She rose to walk to the doorway, glanced into the tastefully decorated boudoir. "It looks as if you've been storing up after all."

"No. That's a different adage. Necessity being the mother of invention. Or maybe it's desperation." Since she was working hard on honesty in the new Margo, she might as well start here. "I didn't plan it this way, Mum. Or want it this way."

Ann turned back, studied the woman who sat on the fussy ice cream chair with its hot-pink cushion. Softer than she'd been, Ann thought. Around the eyes and mouth. She wondered that Margo, who had always been so aware of every inch of her own face, didn't seem to notice the change.

"So you didn't," Ann said at length. "And now?"

"Now I'm going to make it work. No, that's wrong." She picked up another cookie, tapped it against her glass like a toast. "I'm going to make it fabulous. Pretenses is going to grow. In another year or two, I'll open a branch in Carmel. Then—who knows? A tastefully elegant little storefront in San Francisco, a funky shop in L.A."

"Still dreaming, Margo?"

"Yes, that's right. Still dreaming. Still going places. Just different places." She tossed her hair back and smiled, but there was an edge to it. "Under it all, I'm still the same Margo."

"No, you're not." Ann crossed over, cupped her daughter's chin in her hand. "You're not, but there's enough of the little girl I raised that I recognize you. Where did you come from?" she murmured. "Your grandfathers caught fish to live. Your grandmothers scrubbed floors and hung out the wash with wooden pegs in high winds." She picked up Margo's hand, studied the long, narrow palm, the tapering fingers accented with pretty rings. "My mother's hand would have made two of yours. Big and hard and capable it was. Like mine."

She saw the surprise in Margo's eyes that she should speak so freely, so casually of people she had never spoken of at all. From selfishness, Ann had come to realize. Because if she didn't speak of them, it didn't hurt so deeply to be without them.

Oh, she'd made mistakes, Ann berated herself. Big and bad mistakes with the one child God had given her. If it stung to try to fix them, it was only just.

"My mother's name was Margaret." She had to clear her throat. "I didn't mention that to you before because she died a few months after I left Ireland. And I felt guilty about leaving her when she was ailing, and about being unable to go back and say good-bye. I didn't talk to you of her, or to anyone. She would have been sad to know that."

"I'm sorry," was all Margo could say. "I'm sorry, Mum."

"So am I—for that and for not telling you sooner how she doted on you in the little time she had with you."

"What—" The question was there, but Margo was afraid to ask it, afraid it would be brushed off again.

"What was she like?" Ann's lips curved in a quiet smile. "You used to badger me with questions like that when you were a small thing. Then you stopped asking, because I never answered. I should have."

She turned away, crossed to the pretty eyebrow windows that offered the sounds and sights of busy streets. Her sin, she realized, had been one of cowardice, and self-indulgence. If the penance was the pain of remembering, it was little enough.

"Before I answer, I want to tell you that I never did before because I told myself not to look back." With a small sound of regret, she turned and walked to her daughter. "That it was more important to raise you up right than to fill your head with people who were gone. Your head was always filled with so much anyway."

Margo touched the back of her mother's hand briefly. "What was she like?"

"She was a good woman. Hardworking, but not hard. She loved to sing, and she sang when she worked. She loved her flowers and could grow anything. She taught us to take pride in our home, and in ourselves. She wouldn't take any nonsense from us, and she doled out whacks and hugs in equal measure. She'd wait for my father to come home from the sea with a look in her eye I didn't understand until I was grown."

"My grandfather? What was he like?"

"A big man with a big voice. He liked to swear so that my mother would scold him." A smile ghosted around Ann's mouth. "He'd come home from the sea smelling of fish and water and tobacco, and he'd tell us stories. Grand stories he could tell."

Ann steadied herself, brushed a few crumbs from the table. "I named you for my mother. My father called her Margo when he was teasing with her. Though I can't see her in you, nor much of myself when it comes to it. The eyes sometimes," she continued while Margo sat silently staring. "Not the color of them, but the shape and that stubborn look that comes into them. That's me right enough. But the color's your father's. He had eyes a woman could drown in. And the light of them, sweet Jesus, such a light in them it could blind you."

"You never speak of him."

"It hurt me to." Ann dropped her hand and sat again, tiredly. "It hurt, so I didn't, then I got out of the habit, and robbed you of him. It was wrong of me not to share him with you, Margo. What I did was keep him for myself," she said in an unsteady voice. "All for myself. I didn't give you your father."

Margo took a shaky breath. It felt as though a huge, hard weight was pressing on her chest. "I didn't think you loved him."

"Didn't love him?" Shock came first, followed by a long, rolling laugh. "Mother of God, girl, not love him? I had such a love for him my heart couldn't hold it. Every time I looked at him it flopped around like one of the fish he'd toss on the table after a catch. And when he'd sweep me up as he liked to do and swing me around, I wouldn't be dizzy from the spinning, but just from the smell of him. I can still smell him. Wet wool and fish and man."

She tried to picture it, her mother young and laughing, caught up in strong arms and wildly in love. "I thought . . . I assumed that you'd married him because you had to."

"Well, of course I had to," Ann began, then stopped, eyes wide. "Oh, *had* to. Why, my father would have thrashed him within an inch of his mortal life. Not that he didn't try, my Johnny," she added with a quick smile. "He was a man, after all, and had his ways. But I had mine, as well, and went to my wedding bed a proper, if eager virgin."

"I wasn't—" Margo picked up her glass, took a bracing sip. "I wasn't the reason he married you?"

"*I* was the reason he married me," Ann said with a lilt of pride in her voice. "And I'm sorrier than I can say that you had that thought planted in your head, that I didn't realize it until this very moment."

"I thought—I wondered . . ." How to put it, Margo wondered, when there were so many emotions spinning? "You were so young," she began again. "And in a strange country with a child to raise on your own."

"You were never a burden to me, Margo. A trial many a time," she added with a wry curve of her lips. "But never once a burden. Nor were you a mistake, so get that idea out of your head for good. We had to get married, Margo, because we loved each other. We were desperate in love. Sweet and desperate and so young, and it was all that sweet and desperate love that made you."

"Oh, Mum, I'm so sorry."

"Sorry? I had more in those four years God gave us than a less fortunate woman could pack into two lifetimes."

"But you lost him."

"Yes, I lost him. And so did you. You didn't have much time with him, but he was a good father, and, God, he adored every inch of you. He used to watch you sleeping and touch your face with his fingertip, as if he was afraid he'd break you. And he'd smile so it seemed his face would split open with it." She pressed a hand to her mouth because she could picture it too well, still. Feel it too well, still. "I'm sorry I never told you that."

"It's all right." The weight was off her chest now, but it welled full of tears. "It's all right, Mum. You've told me now."

Ann closed her eyes a moment. How could she explain that grief and love and joy could carry in a heart for a lifetime? "He loved us both, Margo, and he was a fine man, a kind one, full of dreams for us, for the other children we were going to have." She fumbled in her pocket for a tissue and wiped away her tears. "Silly to cry over it now. Twenty-five years."

"It's not silly." To Margo it was a revelation, a beautiful, wrenching one. If there was grief after a quarter of a century, then there had been love. Sweet and desperate. And more, enduring. "We don't have to talk about it anymore."

But Ann shook her head, blinked her eyes dry. She would finish and give her child, her Johnny's child, what should have been her birthright. "When they came back that night in the storm. Oh, God, what a storm it was, wailing and blowing and the lightning breaking the sky into pieces." She opened her eyes then, met her daughter's. "I knew—I didn't want to believe but I knew he was lost before they told me. Because something was gone. In here." She pressed a hand to her heart. "Just gone, and I knew he'd taken that part of my heart with him. I didn't think I could live without him. Knew I didn't want to live without him."

Ann linked her fingers together tight, for the next would be harder still to speak of. "I was almost three months along with another baby."

"You—" Margo wiped at tears. "You were pregnant?"

"I wanted a son for Johnny. He said that would be fine because we already had the most beautiful daughter in all the world. He kissed us goodbye that morning. You, then me, then he laid his hand on me where the baby was growing. And smiled. He never came back. They never found him so I could look at him again. One last time to look at him. I lost the baby that night, in the storm and the grief and the pain. Lost Johnny and the baby, and there was only you."

How did anyone face that and manage to go on? Margo wondered. What kind of strength did it take? "I wish I had known." She took her mother's clasped hands in hers. "I wish I had known, Mum. I would have tried to be . . . better."

"No, that's nonsense." After all these years, Ann realized, she was still doing it wrong. "I'm not telling you enough of the good things. There wasn't only grief and sorrow. The truth is I had him in my life for so many years. I first set my eyes on him when I was six, and he was nine. A fine, strapping boy he was then, Johnny Sullivan, with a devil's laugh and an angel's eyes. And I wanted him. So I went after him, putting myself in his face."

"You?" Margo sniffled. "You flirted with him?"

"Shamelessly. And by the time I was seventeen, I'd broken him down, and I snapped up his proposal of marriage before he could finish the words." She sighed once, long and deep. "Understand and believe this. I loved him, Margo, greedily. And when he died, and the baby died inside me, I wanted to die too, and might have, but for you. You needed me. And I needed you."

"Why did you leave Ireland? Your family was there. You must have needed them."

She could still look back to that, to rocky cliffs and tempestuous seas. "I'd lost something I'd thought I would have forever. Something I loved, something I'd wanted all my life. I couldn't bear even the air there without him. I couldn't breathe it. It was time for a fresh start. Something new."

"Were you frightened?"

"Only to death." Her lips curved again, and suddenly she had an urge for a taste of champagne herself. She took her daughter's glass, sipped. "I made it work. So maybe there's more of me in you than I thought. I've been hard on you, Margo. I haven't understood how hard until just recently. I've done some praying over it. You were a frighteningly beautiful child, and willful with it. A dangerous combination. There was a part of me that was afraid of loving you too much because . . . well, to love so full again was like tempting God. I couldn't show you, didn't think I could dare, because if I lost you I'd never have been able to go on."

"I always thought . . ." Margo trailed off, shook her head.

"No, say it. You should say what's inside you."

"I thought I wasn't good enough for you."

"That's my fault." Ann pressed her lips together and wondered how she could have let so many years slip away with that between them. "It was never a matter of that, Margo. I was afraid of and for you. I could never understand why you wanted so much. And I worried that you were growing up in a place where there was so much, and all of it belonging to others. And maybe I don't understand you even now, but I love you. I should have told you more often."

"It's not always easy to say it, or to feel it. But I always knew you loved me."

"But you haven't known that I'm proud of you." Ann sighed. It was her own pride, after all, that had kept her silent. "I was proud the first time I saw your face in a magazine. And every time after." She drank again, prepared to confess. "I saved them."

Margo blinked. "Saved them?"

"All your pictures. Mr. Josh sent them to me and I put them in a book. Well, books," she corrected. "Because there got to be so many." She smiled foolishly at the empty glass. "I believe I'm just a little tipsy."

Without thinking, Margo rose to get the bottle from the refrigerator, took off the silver cap, and poured her mother more. "You saved my photos and put them in scrapbooks?"

"And the articles, too, the little snips of gossip." She gestured with her glass. "I wasn't always proud of those, I'll tell you, and I have a feeling that boy held back the worst of them."

Margo understood that Josh was "that boy," and smiled. "He would only have been thinking of you."

"No, he's always thought of you." Ann inclined her head. "There's a man blind in love if ever there was one. What are you made of, Margo? Are you as smart as your mother to latch on to a strong, handsome man who'll make you dizzy in bed and out?" She caught herself when Margo snorted, and she struggled for dignity. "It's the drink. It's sinful to be drinking in the middle of the day."

"Have another and take a cab home."

"Maybe I will, at that. Well, what's your answer then? Are you going to leave the man dangling or reel him in proper?"

Dangling had seemed a fine idea, the best idea. And now she wasn't sure. "I'm going to have to give that some thought. Mum, thank you for giving my father to me."

"I should have—"

"No." A little surprised at herself, Margo shook her head. "No, let's not worry about 'should haves.' We'll be here all day pitching them back and forth between us. Let's start with now."

Ann had to use her tissue again. "I did a better job with you than I've given either one of us credit for. I have a fine daughter."

Touched, Margo pressed her lips to her mother's cheek. "Let's say you still have a work in progress. And speaking of work," she added, knowing both of them were about to start weeping again, "you enjoy the rest of your wine. My lunch break's over, and I have to go down and open up."

"I have photographs." Ann swallowed hard. "I'd like to show you sometime."

"I'd like to see them. Very much like to see them." Margo walked to the doorway, paused. "Mum, I'm proud of you, too, and what you've made of your life."

JOSH HEARD THE sound of girlish laughter as he circled the east terrace toward the pool. The squeals and splashing lightened his heart. As the curved sweep of water came into view, he grinned. A race was on.

Obviously Laura was holding back, keeping her strokes small and slow. When she was serious about her pace, no one could beat her. It used to infuriate him, having his little sister outdistance him. But then as captain of her swim team, she'd gone All-State and had even flirted with the Olympics.

Now she was letting her daughters overtake her, all but crawling to the edge as Ali put on a furious burst of speed.

"I won!" Ali bounced in the water. "I beat you to the side." Then her bottom lip poked out. "You let me."

"I gave you a handicap." Laura ran a hand over Ali's slicked-back hair, then smiled as Kayla surfaced, her mouth working like a guppy's. "Just like you gave your sister a handicap because you're bigger and faster and stronger."

"I want to win on my own."

"The way you're going, you will." She bent to kiss Kayla between the eyes. "Both of you swim like mermaids."

The thought of that made the mutiny die out of Ali's eyes and Kayla swim backward with a dreamy smile. "I'm a mermaid," Kayla claimed. "I swim all day with the dolphins."

"I'm still faster." Ali started to push off, then caught a movement out of the corner of her eye. She saw a man, tall, the suit, the glint of hair. Her heart speared up. But when she blinked her eyes clear of water, she saw it wasn't her father after all. "Uncle Josh!"

"Uncle Josh! Uncle Josh is here." Kayla kicked her feet to send water flying. "Come in and swim with us. We're mermaids."

"Anyone could see that. I'm afraid I'm not dressed to play with mermaids. But they're fun to watch."

To entertain him, Kayla did handstands, somersaults. Not to be out-done, Ali rushed to the board to show him how her diving had improved. He whistled and applauded, offered advice as Laura climbed out and tow-eled off.

She'd lost weight. Even a brother could see that. He had to concentrate on keeping his smile in place for the girls and not allowing his teeth to grind together.

"Got a minute?" he asked her when she'd bundled into a terry-cloth robe.

"Sure. Girls, shallow end." That brought groans and complaints, but both of them paddled in. "Is there a problem at work?"

"Not precisely. You mentioned you wanted to take a more active part." The frown came as he wandered toward a gardenia bush. He wanted to be out of the girls' hearing. "You've got a lot on your plate, Laura."

"I don't want your job, Josh." She smiled and combed her fingers through hair that the water had curling wildly. "I just think it's time I paid attention. I let things slide by me before. It's never going to happen again."

"You'll piss me off if you start blaming yourself."

"It takes two people to make a marriage." Laura sighed, making sure she kept her daughters in view as they walked along the edge of the garden. In the distance were the stables, the lovely old stucco and dark-beamed build-ing, tucked behind the slope of the uneven land. She wished there were horses inside, or frisking in the paddock. She wished she had the time to tend to them as she did when she was a girl.

"I'm not taking it on, Josh. What Peter did was inexcusable. It was bad enough that he ignored his children, but then to take what was theirs—"

"And yours," he reminded her.

"Yes, and mine. I'm going to make it back. It's going to take a while, but I'm going to make it back."

"Honey, you know if you need money—"

"No." She shook her head. "No, I'm not taking money from you or Mom and Dad, I'm not using Templeton money I haven't earned to pay for my life. Not as long as the girls aren't doing without." She smiled a lit-tle, running a hand over his arm as they walked. "Let's be realistic, Josh. The three of us have a beautiful home, food on the table. Their tuition's paid. There are plenty of women who find themselves in my position and have nothing left."

"It doesn't make your situation any less rotten. How long are you going to be able to pay the servants, Laura, and the tuition if you're determined to use only your share of profits from the shop?"

She'd worried about the servants. How could she let them go when most of them had been at Templeton House for years? What would Mrs. Williamson or old Joe the gardener do if she had to cut the staff?

"Pretenses is bringing in money, and I have the dividends from Templeton stock—which I intend to start earning. I've got time on my hands, Josh, and I'm tired of filling it up with committees and lunches and fundraisers. That was Peter's lifestyle."

"You want a job?"

"Actually, I thought I might be able to work part time. It's not that I'm destitute, it's that it's long past time that I started to make my own way. I look at Kate and the way she's always worked toward what she wanted. And Margo. Then I look at me."

"Just stop it."

"I've got something to prove," she said evenly. "And I'm damn well going to do it. You're not the only Templeton in this generation who knows hotels. I know about putting events together, catering, entertainment. I'd have to juggle time with the shop and the girls, of course."

"When can you start?"

She stopped dead. "Do you mean it?"

"Laura, you have just as much interest in Templeton as I do."

"I've never done anything for it, or about it. Not for years, anyway."

"Why?"

She grimaced. "Because Peter didn't want me to. My job, as he told me often, was being Mrs. Peter Ridgeway." It would, she understood, always humiliate her to admit it. "You know what finally occurred to me a year or so ago, Josh? My name was nowhere in there. I was nowhere in there."

Uncomfortable, he looked over toward the pool where his nieces were having a contest to see who could hold her breath longer. "I guess marriage is a loss of identity."

"No, it isn't. It shouldn't be." It was salt in a raw wound to admit it, but . . . "I let it be. I always wanted to be perfect. Perfect daughter, perfect wife, perfect mother. It's been a hard slap in the face to realize I couldn't be any of those things."

He laid his hands on her shoulders and gave her a little shake. "How about perfect sister? You won't hear any complaints from me."

Touched, she rested her hands on top of his. "If I were the perfect sister, I'd be asking you why you haven't asked Margo to marry you." She tightened her grip when he would have slipped his hands away. "You love each other, understand each other. I'd say you have more in common than any two people I know, including fear of taking the next step."

"Maybe I like the step I'm on."

"Is it enough, Josh? Really enough for you, or for Margo?"

"Damn, you're pushy."

"That's only one required element of the perfect sister."

Restless, he moved away, stopped to toy with a pale pink rosebud. "I've thought about it. Marriage, kids, the whole package. Pretty big package," he murmured. "Lots of surprises inside."

"You used to like surprises."

"Yeah. But one thing Margo and I have in common is an appreciation for being able to pick up and move whenever we like. I've lived in hotels for the last dozen years because I like the transience, the convenience. Hell." He broke off the bloom, handed it absently to Laura. "I've been waiting for her all my life. I always figured after the wait was over, I'd bide my time. A year or two of fun and games—which is exactly what she expects of me. How she thinks of me. Then I'd sneak the idea of marriage in on her."

With a half laugh, Laura shook her head. "Is this a chess game or a relationship, Josh?"

"It's been a chess game until recently. Move and countermove. I finessed her into falling in love with me."

"Do you really think so?" Laura clucked her tongue and slid the rosebud into the lapel of his jacket. "Men are such boobs." She rose on her toes to kiss him lightly. "Ask her. I dare you."

He had to wince. "I wish you hadn't put it like that."

"One more element of the perfect sister is knowing her brother's deepest weakness."

BLISSFULLY IGNORANT OF the plans afoot, Margo watched a satisfied customer walk out the door. The way her feet were aching she was relieved that Laura would be putting in a half day tomorrow. As it was five-forty-five, she considered cashing out for the day, maybe nipping out just a few minutes early to go back to the suite and make herself beautiful for the fabulous dinner Josh had promised her.

The advantages to her new life were just piling up, she decided as she swung around the counter and slipped out of her shoes. Not only was she proving that she had a brain as well as a body, but she had discovered a whole new aspect of her background to explore.

Her parents had loved each other. Perhaps it was foolish for a grown woman to find such comfort and joy in that. But she knew it had opened something in her heart. Some things do last forever, she thought. Love held.

And tonight, she was going to tell Josh what she knew, what she believed, and what she wanted. A real life, a full life.

A married life.

It made her laugh to imagine his face when she proposed to him. She would have to be clever in her phrasing, she mused while she transferred cash out of the till into the bag for deposit. A subtle challenge, she decided. But not too subtle.

She would make him happy. They would travel the world together, go to all those exciting places they both loved. And always come back here. Because here was home for both of them.

It had taken her much too long to accept that.

She glanced up as the door opened, pushed back impatience with a shopkeeper's smile. Then squealed.

"Claudio!" She was around the counter in a dash, her hands flung out toward the tall, handsomely distinguished man. "This is wonderful." She kissed both of his cheeks before drawing back to arm's length to beam at him.

He was, of course, as stunning as ever. Silver wings flew back from his temples into thick black hair. His face was smooth and tanned, set off by his long Roman nose and the light in his chocolate-brown eyes.

"*Bella.*" He brought both of her hands to his lips. "*Molta bella*. I was set to be angry with you, Margo *mia*, but now, seeing you, I'm weak."

Appreciating him, she laughed. "What is Italy's most successful film producer doing in my little corner of the world?"

"Looking for you, my own true love."

"Ah." That was nonsense, of course. But they had always understood each other perfectly. "Now you've found me, Claudio."

"So I have." And he could see immediately that he need not have worried. She was glowing. "And the rumors and buzzing I heard when I returned from location were true after all. La Margo is running a shop."

With a challenging gleam in her eye, she lifted her chin. "So?"

"So?" He spread his hands expressively. "So."

"Let me get you a glass of champagne, darling, and you can tell me what you're really doing in Monterey."

"I tell you I come to search for my lost love." But he winked at her as he accepted the glass. "I had a bit of business in Los Angeles. How could I come so close without seeing you?"

"It was sweet of you. And I am glad to see you."

"You should have called me when there was trouble for you."

It seemed a lifetime ago. She only shrugged. "I got through it."

"That Alain. He's a pig." Claudio stalked around the shop in the long, limber strides he used to stalk a soundstage. His burst of gutter Italian termed Alain as a great deal more, and less, than a mere pig.

"I cannot but agree," Margo said when he had run down.

"If you had called my offices, the studio, they would have gotten word to me. I would have swept down on my winged charger and saved you."

She could picture it. Claudio was one of the few men who wouldn't look foolish on a winged charger. "I saved myself, but thanks."

"You lost Bella Donna. I'm sorry for it."

"So was I. But now I have this."

His head angled, his mouth quirked. "A shopkeeper, Margo *mia*."

"A shopkeeper, Claudio."

"Come." He took her hand again, and though his voice was teasing, his eyes were serious. "Let me whisk you away from this. To Roma, with me. I have a new project to begin in a few months. There's a part perfect for you, *cara*. She's strong, sexy, glamorous. Heartless."

She laughed delightedly. "Claudio, you flatter me. Six months ago I'd have snapped it up, without worrying that I'm not an actress. Now I have a business."

"So, let someone else see to it. Come with me. I'll take care of you." He reached out, toyed with her hair, but his eyes were serious. "We'll have that affair we always meant to have."

"We never got around to that, did we? That's why we still like each other. No, Claudio, though I am very, very touched and very, very grateful."

"I don't understand you." He began to prowl again. "You weren't meant to make change and box trinkets. This is not the— *Dio!* These are your dishes." He stopped at a shelf and gawked. "You have served me pasta on these plates."

"Good eye," she murmured.

That eye was dazed as he turned back, began to recognize other things he had admired as a guest in her home in Milan. "I thought it was a joke, a poor one, that you were selling your possessions. Margo, it should not have come to this."

"You make it sound as though I'm living out of a shopping cart in an alley."

"It's humiliating," he said between his teeth.

"No, it's not." She bristled, then calmed herself. He was only thinking of her. Or the woman he had known. She, Margo realized, would have been humiliated. "It's not. I thought it would be, but I was wrong. Do you want to know what it is, Claudio?"

He swore again, ripely, and gave serious thought to hauling her over his shoulder and carrying her off. "Yes, I want to know what it is."

She came close to him, until they were eye to eye. "It's fun."

He nearly choked. "Fun?"

"Great, wonderful, giddy fun. And do you know what else? I'm good at it. Really good at it."

"You mean this? You're content?"

"No, I'm not content. I'm happy. It's mine. I sanded the floors. I painted the walls."

He paled a little, pressed a hand to his chest. "Please, my heart."

"I scrubbed the bathrooms." She laughed and gave him a bracing kiss. "And I loved it."

He tried to nod, but couldn't quite pull it off. "I'd have some more wine, if you please."

"All right, but then you have to browse." She filled his glass and her own before tucking her arm through his. "And while we're browsing, I'll tell you what you can do for me."

"Anything."

"You know a lot of people." Her mind was working quickly as she led him toward the stairs. "People who grow tired of last year's fashions or the trinkets they bought. You could give them my name. I'd like first shot at the discards."

"Jesus" was all he could say as they climbed the stairs.

THE FIRST THING Josh noted when he walked into the shop was the deposit bag. He shook his head at her carelessness, then locked the door. Going behind the counter, he tucked the bag back into the till—and noticed her shoes.

He was going to have a little talk with her about basic precautions, but it could wait. In his pocket was his grandmother's ring. He was still rolling with the excitement he'd felt when he'd lifted it out of the safety deposit box. The square-cut Russian white diamond might have been fashioned with Margo in mind. It was sleek and glamorous and full of cold fire.

He was going to dazzle her with it. He would even go so far as to get down on one knee—after he had plied her with a little champagne. A man needed an edge with Margo.

She would probably balk at the idea of marriage, but he would sweet-talk her into it. Seduce her into it if necessary. It wouldn't be such a sacrifice. The image of her wearing nothing but his ring was alluring enough to calm the nerves in the pit of his stomach.

Enough fun and games, he told himself. Time for serious business.

He started up the steps, nearly called out to her when he heard her laughter drift out like smoke. Nearly smiled before he heard the low male chuckle that followed.

A customer, he told himself, furious at the instant knee jerk of jealousy. But when he walked to the doorway of the boudoir, the knee jerk jolted into a full, vicious kick.

She was locked in a man's arms, and the kiss had enough smolder to singe him where he stood.

He thought of murder, bloody, bone-breaking, brain-splattering murder. His hands clenched into ready fists, the snarl already in his throat. But pride was nearly as violent an emotion as vengeance. It iced over him in a gale wind as Margo drew back.

"Claudio." Her voice was a silky purr. "I'm so glad you came. I hope we can—" She spotted Josh then, and myriad emotions flickered over her face. Surprise, pleasure, guilt, amusement. The amusement didn't last. His eyes were hard and cold and much too easy to read. "Josh."

"I wasn't expected," he said coolly. "I know. But I don't think an apology for the interruption's in order."

"This is a friend from Rome," she began, but he cut off her explanation with a look that sliced to the bone.

"Save the introductions, Margo. I won't keep you from entertaining your friend."

"Josh." He was halfway down the stairs before she reached the landing. "Wait."

He shot her one last, lethal look as he flipped open the lock on the front door. "Stay healthy, Margo. Stay away from me."

"*Cara.*" Claudio laid a hand on Margo's shoulder where she stood shivering at the base of the stairs. "I'm surprised he let us live."

"I have to fix it. I have to make him listen. Do you have a car?"

"Yes, of course. But if I could suggest giving him a little time to calm—"

"It doesn't work that way with Josh." Her hand was shaking as she reached for her purse, forgetting her shoes. "Please, Claudio. I need a ride."

CHAPTER 21

SHE'D WORKED UP a fine head of steam by the time she burst into the penthouse. Being angry, being furious was better than being terrified.

And she had been terrified when she'd read that cold disgust in his eyes, heard the icy dismissal in his voice. She wasn't going to tolerate that. No, sir, not for one New York minute. He was going to have to crawl.

"Josh Templeton, you bastard!" She slammed the door at her back and darted toward the bedroom in bare feet. "How dare you walk out on me that way! How dare you embarrass me in front of my friend!"

Her breath caught with a jerk of a heartbeat when she saw him at the closet calmly transferring clothes into a garment bag. "What are you doing?"

"Packing. I have to make a run to Barcelona."

"The hell with that. You're not just walking out." She'd taken two strides forward with the intent of ripping the clothes free when he whirled on her.

"Don't do it," was all he said, and it shocked her anger back to fear.

"This is childish," she began, but her teeth chattered as panic shot frozen fingers up her spine. "You don't even deserve an explanation, but I'm willing to overlook your filthy attitude and give you one. Claudio and I—"

"I didn't ask for an explanation." In quick jerks, he zipped the bag.

"No," she said slowly. "You've already made up your mind what you saw, what it meant. What I am."

"I'll tell you what I saw." He dipped his hands into his pockets to keep them off her throat. But his fingers brushed the velvet box he carried and doubled his fury and pain. "I saw you in the bedroom, a couple of glasses of champagne, nice soft light coming in through the lace curtains. A very romantic setting. You had your mouth on another man—your usual type, too, if I'm not mistaken. Fiftyish, rich, foreign."

He lifted the bag from the hanger, folded it. "What it meant, Margo, is that I walked in on the first act. You should be able to figure out what that makes you."

She would rather he'd used his fists on her. Surely there would have been less pain in that. "You believe that?"

He hesitated. How could she sound so hurt? How dare she sound hurt after she'd ripped out his heart and stomped on it while it was still beating. "You've sold sex your whole life, duchess. Why should you change?"

What little color that was left in her cheeks drained. "I suppose that's true. It looks like my mistake was giving it to you for free."

"Nothing's free." He bit off the words like stringy meat. "And you had your fun as well. I fit most of the requirements, didn't I? I'm not old enough to be your father, but I qualify for the rest. Rich, restless, irresponsible. Just another social piranha living off the family fortune."

"That's not true," she said, furious with panic. "I don't think—"

"We know what we think of each other, Margo." He spoke calmly now, had to speak calmly. "You've never had any more respect for me than you do for yourself. I thought I could live with that. I was wrong. I told you in the beginning I don't share, and I don't want a woman who thinks I'm stupid enough, or shallow enough, to overlook her old friends."

"Josh." She stepped forward, but he slung the bag over his arm.

"I'd like you out by the end of the week."

"Of course." She stood where she was as he brushed by her. She didn't cry, not even when she heard the door close. She simply sank to the floor and rocked.

"BYRON DE WITT agreed to take over Ridgeway's position. He'll be ready to make the move to California in six to eight weeks."

"That's fine." Thomas sipped his after-dinner coffee and exchanged a look with his wife as their son prowled the drawing room of their villa. "He's a good man. Sharp. Tough-minded."

"You'll go back." Susan crossed her legs. "Through the transitional period."

"It's not really necessary. Things are again in running order. I wasn't able to lure our old chef back." He flashed a fleeting grin. "But the one I stole from the BHH is working out well."

"Hmm." He needed to go back, Susan thought, but she would work on that. "How's Laura doing in Conventions?"

"She's a Templeton." He started toward the brandy, reminded himself that was too easy, and settled for coffee. "She's got a knack for handling people."

Susan lifted a brow, a signal that she was tossing the ball back into her husband's court. He picked it up smoothly.

"And she's putting in time at the shop? Not overdoing, is she?"

"Kate says not. She's a reliable source."

"I'd feel better if one of us could keep an eye on her for a while yet. She's in a rough patch."

"Dad, she's handling it. I can't go play baby-sitter."

"You look tired," Susan said mildly. "That's probably why you're so cranky. Remember, Tommy, how he'd squall if he missed his nap?"

"Jesus. I'm not cranky. I'm trying to get business settled. I have to be in Glasgow tomorrow afternoon. I don't have time to . . ." He caught himself as his parents watched him indulgently. There was nothing worse than being smiled at like a fretful child. Unless it was being a fretful child. "Sorry."

"Don't give it a thought." Thomas rose, slapped him on the back. "What you need's a drink, a cigar, and a nice game of billiards."

Josh rubbed his tired eyes. When was the last time he'd slept, really slept? Two weeks? Three? "It couldn't hurt," he decided.

"You go ahead, Tommy, and set things up for your man hour." She patted the cushion beside her. "I want Josh to keep me company for a few more minutes."

Understanding, Tommy strolled off. "Fifty bucks a ball," he called out.

"He'll trounce me," Josh muttered as he sat. "He always does."

"We all have our game." She patted his knee. Hers was a deft and merciless knack for interrogation. "Now, are you going to tell me what happened between you and Margo?"

"Hasn't Kate given you a full report?"

She ignored the annoyance in his tone, was sorry for the bitterness underneath it. "Reports are spotty. Apparently Margo is being stubbornly closemouthed. All Kate can drag out of her is that the two of you decided to call it a day."

"Well, then."

"And you expect me to believe it's as simple as that when you're sitting here looking mean and miserable?"

"I caught her with another man."

"Joshua." Susan set her cup down with a snap. "No," she said positively, "you didn't."

"I walked into the goddamn bedroom, and there they were."

She hurt for him, couldn't help but hurt for him. Still, she shook her head. "You misinterpreted something."

"What the hell is there to misinterpret?" he shot back and sprang up to pace again. "I walked in and she was kissing another man. Fucking Claudio."

"Josh!" She wasn't so much shocked by the word, but she had taken his statement literally. "I don't believe that."

"No, I didn't mean—" Frustrated, he dragged both hands through his hair. "It hadn't gotten that far yet. I meant, she called him Claudio."

"Oh." Her heart settled a little. "Well, what was her explanation?"

He stopped his pacing to stare at her. "Do you really think I waited around for explanations?"

On a long sigh, she picked up her coffee again. "No, of course you didn't. You stormed out, wishing them both to go to hell. I'm surprised you didn't toss him out the window on your way."

"I thought about it," he said with relish. "I thought about tossing both of them. It seemed . . . more civilized to leave."

"More pigheaded," she corrected. "Oh, sit down, Joshua. You're making me tired just watching you. You know you should have given her a chance to explain."

"I didn't—don't—want excuses and explanations. Damn it, I overlooked the hordes of men from before, but—"

"Ah," Susan said with a satisfied nod. Now they had nailed it. "Did you now? Did you really?"

"I was working on it." He found he did want a brandy after all and poured a generous snifter before he obeyed her command to sit. "When I came home and found her posing naked in our bed, I took it in stride." He caught his mother's eye. "Pretty much in stride. That was business. And when we go out to a restaurant or to the club and every man within half a mile has drool running down the side of his chin, I shrug it off. Mostly."

"Shame on me. I've raised a jealous fool."

"Thanks for your support."

"You listen to me. I understand it must be difficult on one level to love a woman who looks like Margo. The kind of woman who attracts men, inspires fantasies."

"Good." He gulped at the brandy. "I feel better now."

"The point is, that's the woman you fell in love with. Now, let me ask you. Did you fall in love with her because she has a beautiful face and a stunning body? Is that all you see when you look at her?"

"It's the sort of thing that drills between the eyes." But he sighed, surrendered. "No, that's not all I see. That's not why I fell in love with her. She's warm and reckless and stubborn. She's got more guts and brains than she realizes. She's generous and she's loyal."

"Ah, loyal." Susan smiled smugly. "I'd hoped you wouldn't overlook that. It's one of her most admirable traits. And a woman with Margo's sense of loyalty would not have done what you accused her of doing. Go home, Josh, and deal with this."

He set the snifter down, closed his eyes. "It wasn't just the men. It was seeing her that way and realizing when I did what we had together, and didn't have. Telling her I loved her didn't seem to be enough. Showing her didn't seem to be enough. She doesn't want what I want, and she'd be shocked speechless if she knew what I wanted."

"What do you want?" She smiled and brushed at his hair. "I won't be shocked speechless."

"Everything," he murmured. "Usually Margo understands everything just fine, but not this time. She doesn't see marriage and family and commitment when she looks at me. She sees a pampered idiot who's more interested in fine-tuning his backhand than in making a contribution to his legacy or building a life."

"I think you're underestimating both of you. But if you're right, you only proved her point by walking away before you sorted it out."

"I'd have killed her if I'd stayed. I didn't know she could hurt me like this. I didn't know anyone could."

"I know. I'm sorry. When you were little and you were hurt, I could make it better by sitting you in my lap and holding on."

He looked at her, loved her. "Let's try this." He lifted her into his lap and held on. "I think it'll work."

KATE SAUNTERED INTO the shop at midafternoon. She'd had to take an hour off, but she loved being the messenger. "How's it going, troops?"

Laura glanced up as she slid the credit card machine back under the counter. Automatically she glanced at her watch to be certain she hadn't lost a couple of hours. The girls had to be picked up from dance class at six-thirty sharp.

"It's going pretty good. What are you doing here this time of day?"

"Taking a break. Where's Margo?"

"She's in the wardrobe room with a couple of customers. Kate . . ." Lowering her voice, Laura leaned over the counter. "We sold my rubies."

Kate's mind shuffled back. "The necklace. Oh, but Laura, you loved that necklace."

She only shrugged. "Peter gave it to me for our fifth anniversary— bought it, naturally, with my money. I'm glad it's gone." And her share would go a long way toward paying next year's tuition for her daughters. "And there's more. My supervisor called me in this morning and gave me a raise."

Kate waited a beat. "The daughter of the owners has a supervisor and gets a raise. I don't understand life."

"I wanted to start at an entry position. It's only fair."

"Okay. Okay." Kate held up a hand to hold her off. She understood the need to prove oneself, had been scrambling to do just that all her life. "Congratulations, pal. So I guess everybody's happy."

Laura had to sigh as she glanced back toward the wardrobe room. "Not everybody."

"She still being stoic and stubborn?"

"I could shake her," Laura said fiercely. "She flits around here all day as if nothing in the world is wrong. And as if a couple of layers of polished ivory base coat can hide the shadows under her eyes."

"Still refusing to move back into the house?"

"The resort has everything she needs. She loves it there." Laura sucked air through her nose. "I'm going to hit her the next time she says that. And she's already making excuses for skipping the treasure hunt this weekend. Sunday's the only time she can squeeze in for a manicure. It's such bullshit."

"Ooh, you are pissed. Good, you're going to love what happens when I get hold of her."

With surprising speed and strength, Laura reached across the counter and grabbed Kate's hand. "What's up? What do you have? Can we double-team her?"

"That's a thought. Listen, I— Whoops, here she comes. Just follow my lead."

Margo spotted Kate, gave her a raised-eyebrow look even as she continued to chat up her customers. "I don't think you could have found anything more perfect for you. That red St. Laurent is going to draw every eye."

The woman currently clutching it gnawed on her lip. "Still, it's a little early to be shopping for holiday parties."

Margo only smiled, and Laura caught the steel in her eyes. "It's never too early. Not for something that special."

"It is a wonderful price." As she laid it on the counter, she ran a loving hand over the satin skirt. "I've never owned a designer anything."

"Then you're overdue. And that's just what Pretenses is for. To give everyone a chance to feel lush."

"You can't waffle," the woman's companion ordered, giving her friend an encouraging nudge. "You couldn't pry this green velvet away from me with a crowbar." She laughed as she handed it to Margo. "Well, just ring it up and box it. But don't seal the box," she ordered. "I'm going to have to drool over it in the car."

"That's the spirit." Margo took the plastic card, and her eyes softened. "It really did look fabulous on you. I'm sorry we didn't have any shoes that worked."

"I'll find some—or go barefoot." Flushed with the pleasure of the hunt, the woman elbowed her friend. "Give her your credit card, Mary Kay, and live a little."

"Okay, okay. The kids can always get new shoes next month." When Margo snatched back her hand, appalled, Mary Kay let out a long, cheerful laugh. "Only kidding. But if you want to take an extra ten percent off . . ."

"Not on your life." She rang up both sales while Laura competently wrapped and boxed the gowns. "I ought to charge you an extra ten for making my heart stop."

"How about we call it even and I tell you I love it in here. When my conscience is clear again, I'm coming back for that silver evening bag shaped like an elephant."

"Buy it now and take the ten percent."

"I—" Mary Kay's mouth worked for a moment, then she shut her eyes tight. "Ring it up. Go ahead, but I can't watch."

A few minutes later, Margo watched the door close, then dusted her hands together. "Another satisfied victim—I mean customer."

"Right, killer." Laura filed the credit slips. "You gave her a hell of a deal."

"Yeah, but they'll both be back—and the formal wear is slow to move. What's going on, Kate? Did you run out of red ink?"

"Oh, I can always find a fresh supply. Actually I had a couple of errands to run, so I slipped out a little early. And I like to check up on my investment."

"Going to audit the books?"

"Not until the first of the year," she said blithely. "How much is my partner's discount on those wineglasses there, the ones rimmed with gold? My boss's grandson is getting married."

Margo decided to sneak a cigarette. "You pay the full shot and get your share out of the profits."

"God, you're tough. Well, box them up pretty, but I want Laura to wrap them. You still screw it up."

Margo smiled sweetly. "Sorry, I'm on my break. Box them yourself."

"Can't get decent help anymore," Kate muttered. But she ran her tongue around her teeth as she took the box Laura handed her and carefully began to pack the glasses. "Oh, guess who called the office right before I left?"

"Donald Trump, looking for a new accountant."

"I wish." She glanced casually at Margo and brought the box to the counter. "Josh."

Out of the corner of her eye she watched Margo's hand freeze on the way to her lips, jerk, then continue. Smoke billowed out in a shaky stream. "I'd better straighten up the other clothes Mary Kay and her pal tried on." She started to crush out her cigarette in nervous taps, and Kate continued.

"He's back in town."

"Back?" The cigarette kept smoldering as Margo's hand dropped away. "Here?"

"Well, at the hotel. I want the silver bells, Laura, with a silver ribbon. He said he had some business to finish up." She smiled sweetly at Margo. "Something he left . . . hanging."

"And you just had to rush right over here to rub my face in it."

"Nope. I rushed right over here to slap your face in it."

"A rude but effective wake-up call," Laura commented and earned a shocked stare.

"I expected better from you."

"You shouldn't have." Hands brisk and competent, she affixed a shiny silver bow to the box. "If you don't want to tell us what happened between you and Josh, fine. But you can't expect us to sit around quietly while you mope."

"I have not been moping."

"We've been cleaning up the blood spilling out of your heart for weeks." Kate passed Laura her credit card. "Face it, pal, you're just no fun anymore."

"And that's all this friendship is about? Fun? I thought I might get a little support, a little sympathy, a little compassion."

"Sorry," Laura imprinted the card with a steady sweep. "Fresh out."

"Well, the hell with you." She snatched up her purse. "The hell with both of you."

"We love you, Margo."

That stopped her. She whirled back to glare at Kate. "That's a lousy thing to say. Bitch." When Kate grinned, she tried to grin back. Instead she dropped her purse back behind the counter and burst into tears.

"Oh, shit." Shocked, Kate leaped forward to gather her close. "Oh, hell. Oh, shit. Lock the door, Laura. I'm sorry, Margo. I'm sorry. Bad plan. I thought you'd just get mad and go tearing off to fix his butt. What did the bastard do to you, honey? I'll fix his butt for you."

"He dumped me." Thoroughly ashamed, she sobbed wretchedly on Kate's shoulder. "He hates me. I wish he were dead. I wish I had slept with Claudio."

"Wait. Whoa." Firmly, Kate drew her back while Laura brought over a cup of tea. "Who's Claudio and when didn't you sleep with him?"

"He's a friend, just a friend. And I never slept with him." The tears were so hot it felt as though her eyes were on fire. "Especially not when Josh found us in the bedroom."

"Uh-oh." Kate rolled her eyes at Laura. "Is it a French farce or a Greek tragedy? You be the judge."

"Shut up, Kate. Come on, Margo. Let's sit down. This time you tell us everything."

"CHRIST, I FEEL like a fool." Now that everything had poured out, she felt not only foolish but empty.

"He's the fool," Laura corrected. "For jumping to conclusions."

"Give the guy a break." Kate handed Margo another tissue. "The evidence was pretty damning. Not that he should have taken off before he listened," she added quickly when Margo sniffled. "But you have to look at it from his side a little."

"I have looked at it from his side." And she was finished weeping. "I really can't blame him."

"I wouldn't go that far," Kate began.

"No, I can't. The history was there. Why should he trust me?"

"Because he loves you," Laura put in. "Because he knows you."

"That's what I told myself when I was busy hating him. But now, saying it all out loud, it's hard for me to believe me. He thinks I look at him and the whole relationship as one more exciting amusement. And it's probably better that it happened before I . . ."

"Before you . . . ?" Kate prompted.

"Before I asked him to marry me." Suddenly she covered her face with her hands, but this time it was laughter that poured out. "Can you believe it? I was going to propose. I was going to set the scene—candlelight, wine, music—and when I had him wrapped around my finger, I was going to pop the question. What a brainstorm!"

"I think it's wonderful! I think it's perfect." This time it was Laura's eyes that overflowed.

Kate tugged a tissue free for herself. "And I think you should go get him."

"Go get him." Margo snorted. "He can't even look at me."

"Pal, you go fix your face, get yourself back in gear, and he won't have a chance."

IT WAS SUCH a huge risk. Margo told herself he wouldn't even come, and if he did he wouldn't listen. But she was willing to dream, one more time. Fingering the gold coin in her pocket, she wandered the sloped lawn in front of the house.

It was everything Kate had said, a magnificent example of California Spanish at its best, with the elegant arched windows, the dull red of hand-rolled tile on the roof. The recessed doorway of the entrance tower was framed in floral tiles. Bougainvillea climbed riotously.

And the view. She turned to it, drew in a long, greedy breath. All sea and cliffs beyond the sweeping road. Perhaps Seraphina had stood there, walked there, mourning her lost love. But Margo wanted to believe she had walked there with him, when hope and dreams were still vivid. She needed that hope now as she saw Josh's car zip down the road and swing up the snaking drive.

Oh, God, just one more chance. All or nothing now.

Her heart was pounding like the surf when he stepped out of his car. The wind blew through his hair, the sun shot light off the dark glasses he wore. And she couldn't see his eyes. But his mouth was set and cold.

"I wasn't sure you'd come."

"I said I would." He was still reeling from her call, one that had come even as he'd cursed himself and reached for the receiver to call her. "These your new digs?"

"No, I haven't risen back up in the world quite that much. It belongs to a client of Kate's. She's moved out. It's empty." Her breath was almost steady, and she was pleased with the easy, measured tone. "I thought neutral ground would be best."

"Fine." He wanted to touch her, just touch her, so badly his hands ached with it. "Do we start with small talk? How are you? How's business?"

"No." It was easier to walk than to look at him looking at her. She could already feel the humiliation, and she accepted it. She'd already lost him once. She could live through anything now. "I'll just say this straight out so we can get it done with. I didn't sleep with Claudio. In fact, I never slept with him. He's one of those rare finds. A true male friend. I'm not telling you this to put things back the way they were. I don't want them the way they were. But I don't want you believing I was unfaithful."

"I apologize," he said stiffly. He still wanted to touch her, if only to wrap his hands around her throat. He'd come knowing he would beg her to take him back, to forgive him for being a jealous, insensitive idiot, and she was already telling him she didn't want him.

"And I don't want an apology. I might have reacted the same way if the situation had been reversed." She turned her head toward him and smiled. "After I'd torn her eyes out and stomped on your throat."

"It was a close call," he said, struggling to match her light tone.

"I know." Her smile warmed. "I've known you long enough to recognize murder in your eyes when I see it." She only wished she could see his eyes now. "And I think I understand that you left the way you did before you did something or said something neither of us could live with."

"I said more than I should have, certainly more than was warranted. I'll apologize for that, too."

"Then I'll say I'm sorry for kissing Claudio, even though it was a kiss of friendship and gratitude. He'd come to offer me his help, and a part in his next movie."

It took him only a moment. "Oh, that Claudio." Emotions swirled and tightened and threatened to strangle him. "Well, that's a break for you."

"Could be," she said with a careless shrug and started walking again. "In any case, in retrospect, I can see just how it looked and why you reacted the way you did."

He swore lightly. "Just how guilty do you want me to be?"

"That's probably guilty enough." She turned, and this time she laid a hand on his arm. "But I need to tell you that you were wrong about something else. I don't think about you the way you seem to believe. I know you're not spoiled and careless. Maybe I used to think that, and maybe I once resented the fact that you were born to all the advantages I thought I wanted. Hell, I did want them," she corrected with a quick smile. "It used to irritate me that you didn't have to fight for them."

"You always made that clear."

"I suppose I did. But what I haven't made clear is how much I admire the man you've made of yourself. I know how important you are to Templeton, and how important Templeton is to you. I've come to understand just how much responsibility you have, and how seriously you take it since we—well, since we've been together. It's important to me that you believe that."

"You make me feel like an idiot." He had to walk away from her, crossing the tiled terrace to look out to the cliffs. "It matters," he managed. "What you think of me matters." He turned back. "I was fascinated, and often irritated by the girl you were, Margo."

She cocked a brow. "*You* always made that clear."

"I still am, fascinated and often irritated, but I admire the woman you've made of yourself, Margo. I admire her a great deal."

So there was hope, she thought, closing her eyes briefly. And where there was hope, there could be trust and respect, and certainly love. "I want us to be friends again, Josh. You're too important to my life to do without. We managed to be friends before. I want us to be friends again."

"Friends." It threatened to choke him.

"I think both of us forgot that part of our history along the way. I wouldn't want that to happen again."

She was smiling at him, the wind making a sexy mess of her fancy braid, the sun slanting in her eyes as it drifted lazily down in the west. "You can stand there and tell me you think friendship is the answer."

"It's one of them. An important one."

He couldn't start all over again. It would kill him. The rage of love inside him would never settle for something as patient as friendship. Slowly, he crossed back to her. "One of us has lost his or her mind."

"Let's give it some time. We can start with you giving me some friendly advice." Smooth as silk, she tucked her hand through his arm and guided him around the side of the house. "Isn't this place fabulous? Wait until you see the fountain in the back. It's charming. Of course, I think it should have a pool. There's enough land for a small free-form. And the view from that upper balcony—that must be the master suite, don't you think? It's got to be incredible. I guess there's at least two fireplaces. I haven't been inside yet, but I'm hoping there's one in the master bedroom."

"Wait a minute. Hold on." His mind was spinning. Her perfume was clouding his brain, and her words jammed into his consciousness.

"And look at this bougainvillea. It really should be cut back, but I love it wild. The terrace is perfect for entertaining, isn't it? And the location couldn't be better. Just up the coast from the shop and all but next door to Templeton House."

"I said, hold it." He turned her around, took a firm grip on her shoulders. "Are you thinking of buying this place?"

"It's a once-in-a-lifetime chance." Her only chance. "Kate says it's a fabulous deal, a solid investment, and you know how pessimistic she is. It isn't even going on the market until next week—there was some problem with clearing the deed—so it's ground floor."

"Jesus, duchess, you never change."

Her heart lightened a bit at the amused exasperation in his tone. "Should I?"

"Listen, this place has got to run at least three hundred K."

"Three hundred fifty, but Kate thinks three hundred will close it."

"Dream on," he muttered.

"I am."

"You've been in business less than a year, a month before that you were sniffing at bankruptcy. There isn't a bank on the planet that's going to approve a loan of this size. Margo, you just can't afford it."

"I know." She aimed her best smile, the one that had earned her fleeting fame and fortune. "But you can."

He did choke. "You want me to buy a damn house for you?"

"Sort of." She toyed with the button of his shirt, shot a look up from under her lashes. "I thought if you bought it, and married me, we could both live here."

He couldn't get a word out. When his vision hazed, he realized he wasn't breathing either. "I have to sit down."

"I know how you feel." She linked her hands together, found them damp, as he lowered himself to a bench.

"You want me to buy a house and marry you so you can live in it?"

"So we can live in it," she corrected. "Together. When we're not traveling."

"You just got finished telling me you didn't want things back the way they were."

"I don't. It was too easy before. Too easy to dive in, too easy to walk. I want to make it hard. I want to make it very, very hard. I love you." Because her eyes were filling, she turned away. "I love you so much. I can live without you. You don't have to worry that I'll jump off a cliff like Seraphina if you walk. But I don't want to live without you. I want to be married to you, have a family with you, build something here with you. That's all I have to say."

"That's all you have to say," he repeated. His heart had settled back in place, but it seemed to be taking up too much room. So much that it hurt his chest. Just as the grin was so wide it hurt his face. "I guess it's my turn to say something."

"I'd never cheat on you."

"Shut up, Margo. You lost your chance to see me crawl over that one. I was wrong, I was stupid and I was careless with you, and it won't happen again. And I'm going to add that I always thought a hell of a lot more of you than you thought of yourself. That's all I have to say."

"All right, then." She struggled to find a dignified exit. But he laid a hand on her shoulder and put what he had in his hand under her nose.

The ring caught fire and light and promise. She covered her mouth with her hand as it shot out dreams that dazzled her eyes. "Oh, my God."

"Grandmother Templeton's engagement ring. You remember her."

"I— Yes. Yes."

"It came to me. I got it out of the safe deposit box, had it in my pocket the day I walked in on you and your Italian friend."

"Oh. Oh."

"No, you're not going to sit down." He jerked her upright and into his arms. "I want your knees weak. I wouldn't mind if you babbled too, since you've spoiled my romantic plans of giving you this on one knee in candlelight."

"Oh." She dropped her head on his chest. "Oh."

"Don't cry. I can't stand it when you cry."

"I'm not." To prove it, she lifted her face and showed him she was laughing. "I was going to ask you."

"Ask me what?"

"Jesus, why can't we keep up with each other?" She mopped at tears with her fingers. "That night, I was going to ask you to marry me. I figured it was going to take a lot of work and flare to talk you into it. So I had it all planned. I was going to dare you."

"You're kidding."

"Take off those damn glasses." She snatched them off herself, tossed them recklessly over her shoulder, heard them shatter on the terra-cotta. "I still beat you to it. I still asked you first." Before he could move, she snatched the ring out of his hand. "And you said yes. This proves it."

"I didn't say anything yet," he corrected and made a grab for her. "Damn it, Margo, come here. If I don't get my hands on you, I'll explode."

"Say yes." She danced out of reach, holding the ring aloft like a torch. "Say yes first."

"All right, yes. What the hell. I'll take you on."

He caught her on the fly, whirled her around. And she felt something swirl inside her. No, it's not the spinning, Mum, she thought. It is the man.

His mouth was on hers before her feet touched the ground. "For life," he murmured, cupping her face.

"No. Forever." She tipped her mouth to his again. "I want forever."

He took her hand, holding her gaze as he slipped the ring on her finger. It fit like a dream. "Done," he said.

HOLDING THE DREAM

CHAPTER 1

HER CHILDHOOD HAD been a lie.

Her father had been a thief.

Her mind struggled to absorb those two facts, to absorb and analyze and accept. Kate Powell had trained herself to be a practical woman, one who worked hard toward goals, earned them step by careful step. Wavering was not permitted. Shortcuts were not taken. Rewards were earned with sweat, planning, and effort.

That, she had always believed, was who she was; a product of her heredity, her upbringing, and her own stringent standards for herself.

When a child was orphaned at an early age, when she lived with the loss, when she had, essentially, watched her parents die, there seemed little else that could be so wrenching.

But there was, Kate realized as she sat, still in shock, behind her tidy desk in her tidy office at Bittle and Associates.

Out of that early tragedy had come enormous blessings. Her parents had been taken away, and she'd been given others. The distant kinship hadn't mattered to Thomas and Susan Templeton. They had taken her in, raised her, given her a home and love. Given her everything, without question.

And they must have known, she realized. They must have always known.

They had known when they took her from the hospital after the accident. When they comforted her and gave her the gift of belonging, they had known.

They took her across the continent to California. To the sweeping cliffs and beauty of Big Sur. To Templeton House. There, in that grand home, as gracious and welcoming as any of the glamorous Templeton hotels, they made her part of their family.

They gave her Laura and Josh, their children, as siblings. They gave her Margo Sullivan, the housekeeper's daughter, who had been accepted as part of the family even before Kate.

They gave her clothes and food, education, advantages. They gave her rules and discipline and the encouragement to pursue dreams.

And most of all, they gave her love and family and pride.

Yet they had known from the beginning what she, twenty years later, had just discovered.

Her father had been a thief, a man under indictment for embezzlement.

Caught skimming from his own clients' accounts, he had died facing shame, ruin, prison.

She might never have found out but for the capricious twist of fate that had brought an old friend of Lincoln Powell's into her office that morning.

He was so delighted to see her, remembered her as a child. It warmed her to be remembered, to realize that he had come to her with his business because of the old tie with her parents. She'd taken the time, though she had little to spare during those last weeks before the April 15 tax deadline, to chat with him.

And he just sat there, in the chair on the other side of the desk, reminiscing. He'd bounced her on his knee when she was little, he said, had worked in the same ad firm as her father. Which was why, he told her, since he'd relocated to California and now had his own firm, he wanted her as his accountant. She thanked him and mixed her questions about his business and his financial requirements with queries about her parents.

Then, when he spoke so casually of the accusations, the charges, and the sorrow he felt that her father had died before he could make restitution, she had said nothing, could say nothing.

"He never intended to steal, just borrow. Oh, it was wrong, God knows. I always felt partially responsible because I was the one who told him about the real estate deal, encouraged him to invest. I didn't know he'd already lost most of his capital in a couple of deals that went sour. He would have put the money back. Linc would have found a way, always did. He was always a little resentful that his cousin rode so high while he barely scraped by."

And the man—God, she couldn't remember his name, couldn't remember anything but the words—smiled at her.

The whole time he was speaking, making excuses, adding his own explanations to the facts, she simply sat, nodding. This stranger who'd known her father was destroying her very foundations.

"He had a sore spot where Tommy Templeton was concerned. Funny, when you think it turned out that he was the one to raise you after it all. But Linc never meant any harm, Katie. He was just reckless. Never had a chance to prove himself, and that's the real crime, if you ask me."

The real crime, Kate thought, as her stomach churned and knotted. He had stolen, because he was desperate for money and took the easy way out. Because he was a thief, she thought now. A cheat. And he had cheated the justice system by hitting an icy patch of road and crashing his car, killing himself and his wife and leaving his daughter an orphan.

So fate had given her as a father the very man her own father had been so envious of. Through his death, she had, in essence, become a Templeton.

Had it been deliberate? she wondered. Had he been so desperate, so reckless, so angry that he'd chosen death? She could barely remember him, a thin, pale, nervous man with a quick temper.

A man with big plans, she thought now. A man who had spun those plans out into delightful fantasies for his child. Visions of big houses, fine cars, fun-filled trips to Disney World.

And all the while they lived in a tiny house just like all the other tiny houses on the block, with an old sedan that rattled, and no trips to anywhere.

So he stole, and he was caught. And he died.

What had her mother done? Kate wondered. What had she felt? Was that why Kate remembered her most as a woman with worry in her eyes and a tight smile?

Had he stolen before? The idea made her cold inside. Had he stolen before and somehow gotten away with it? A little here, a little there, until he'd become careless?

She remembered arguments, often over money. And worse, the silences that followed them. The silence that night. That heavy, hurting silence in the car between her parents before the awful spin, the screams and the pain.

Shuddering, she closed her eyes, clenched her fists tight, and fought back the drumming headache.

Oh, God, she had loved them. Loved the memory of them. Couldn't bear to have it smeared and spoiled. And couldn't face, she realized with horrid shame, being the daughter of a cheat.

She wouldn't believe it. Not yet. She took slow breaths and turned to her computer. With mechanical efficiency she accessed the library in New Hampshire where she'd been born and had lived for the first eight years of her life.

It was tedious work, but she ordered copies of newspapers for the year before the accident, requested faxes of any article mentioning Lincoln Powell. While she waited, she contacted the lawyer back east who had handled the disposition of her parents' estate.

She was a creature comfortable with technology. Within an hour she had everything she needed. She could read the details in black and white, details that confirmed the facts the lawyer had given her.

The accusations, the criminal charges, the scandal. A scandal, she realized, that had earned print space because of Lincoln Powell's family connection to the Templetons. And the missing funds, replaced in full after her parents were buried. Replaced, Kate was certain, by the people who had raised her as one of their own.

The Templetons, she thought, who had been drawn into the ugliness, had quietly taken the responsibility, and the child. And, always, had protected the child.

There in her quiet office, alone, she laid her head on the desk and wept. And wept. And when the weeping was done, she shook out pills for the headache, more for the burning in her stomach. When she gathered her briefcase to leave, she told herself she would bury it. Just bury it. As she had buried her parents.

It could not be changed, could not be fixed. She was the same, she assured herself, the same woman she had been that morning. Yet she found she couldn't open her office door and face the possibility of running into a colleague in the corridor. Instead, she sat again, closed her eyes, sought comfort in old memories. A picture, she thought, of family and tradition. Of who she was, what she had been given, and what she had been raised to be.

AT SIXTEEN, SHE was taking an extra load of courses that would allow her to graduate a full year ahead of her class. Since that wasn't quite enough of a challenge, she was determined to graduate with honors as well. She had already mentally outlined her valedictorian speech.

Her extracurricular activities included another term as class treasurer, a stint as president of the math club, and a place in the starting lineup of the baseball team. She had hopes of being named MVP again next season, but for now her attention was focused on calculus.

Numbers were her strong point. Sticking with logic, Kate had already decided to use her strengths in her career. Once she had her MBA—more than likely she would follow Josh to Harvard for that—she would pursue a career in accounting.

It didn't matter that Margo said her aspirations were boring. To Kate they were realistic. She was going to prove to herself, and to everyone who mattered to her, that what she had been given, all she had been offered, had been put to the best possible use.

Because her eyes were burning, she slipped off her glasses and leaned back in her desk chair. It was important, she knew, to rest the brain periodically in order to keep it at its keenest. She did so now, letting her gaze skim around the room.

The new touches the Templetons had insisted she choose for her sixteenth birthday suited her. The simple pine shelves above her desk held her books and study materials. The desk itself was a honey, a Chippendale kneehole with deep drawers and fanciful shell carving. It made her feel successful just to work at it.

She hadn't wanted fussy wallpaper or fancy curtains. The muted stripes on the walls and the simple vertical blinds fit her style. Because she understood her aunt's need to pamper, she'd chosen a pretty, scroll-sided settee in deep green. On rare occasions she actually stretched out on it to read for pleasure.

Otherwise, the room was functional, as she preferred.

The knock on her door interrupted her just as she was burying her nose in her books again. Her answer was a distracted grunt.

"Kate." Susan Templeton, elegant in a cashmere twin set, entered, her hands on her hips. "What am I going to do with you?"

"Nearly finished," Kate mumbled. She caught the scent of her aunt's perfume as Susan crossed the room. "Midterm. Math. Tomorrow."

"As if you weren't already prepared." Susan sat on the edge of the tidily made bed and surveyed Kate. Those huge and oddly exotic brown eyes were focused behind heavy-framed reading glasses. Hair, sleek and dark, was tugged back into a stubby ponytail. The girl cut it shorter every year, Susan thought with a sigh. Plain gray sweats bagged over a long, thin frame down to the bare feet. As Susan watched, Kate pursed her wide mouth into something between a pout and a frown. The expression dug a thinking line between her eyebrows.

"In case you haven't noticed," Susan began, "it's ten days until Christmas."

"Umm. Midterm week. Nearly done."

"And it's six o'clock."

"Don't hold dinner. Want to finish this."

"Kate." Susan rose and snatched Kate's glasses away. "Josh is home from college. The family's waiting for you to trim the tree."

"Oh." Blinking, Kate struggled to bring her mind back from formulas. Her aunt was watching her owlishly, her dark blond hair curled smoothly around her pretty face. "I'm sorry. I forgot. If I don't ace this exam—"

"The world as we know it will come to an end. I know."

Kate grinned and rolled her shoulders to loosen them. "I guess I could spare a couple of hours. Just this once."

"We're honored." Susan set the glasses on the desk. "Put something on your feet, Kate."

"Okay. Be right down."

"I can't believe I'm going to say this to one of my children, but . . ." Susan started toward the door. "If you open one of those books again, you're grounded."

"Yes, ma'am." Kate crossed to her dresser and chose a pair of socks from an orderly pile. Beneath the carefully folded socks was her secret stash of

Weight-On, which had done pitifully little to put more pounds onto her bones. After tugging the socks on, she downed a couple of aspirin to kick back the headache that was just beginning to stir.

"It's about time." Margo met her at the top of the stairs. "Josh and Mr. T. are already stringing the lights."

"That could take hours. You know how they love to argue whether they should go clockwise or counterclockwise." Tilting her head, she gave Margo a long study. "What the hell are you all dolled up for?"

"I'm simply being festive." Margo smoothed the skirt of her holly-red dress, pleased that the scoop neckline hinted at cleavage. She'd slipped on heels, determined that Josh should notice her legs and remember she was a woman now. "Unlike you, I don't choose to trim the tree wearing rags."

"At least I'll be comfortable." Kate sniffed. "You've been into Aunt Susie's perfume."

"I have not." Lifting her chin, Margo fluffed at her hair. "She offered me a spritz."

"Hey," Laura called from the bottom of the staircase, "are you two going to stand up there arguing all night?"

"We're not arguing. We were complimenting each other on our attire." Snickering, Kate started down.

"Dad and Josh are nearly finished with their debate over the lights." Laura shot a look across the spacious foyer toward the family parlor. "They're smoking cigars."

"Josh smoking a cigar?" Kate snorted at the image.

"He's a Harvard man now." Laura affected an exaggerated New England accent. "You've got shadows under your eyes."

"You've got stars in yours," Kate countered. "And you're all dressed up too." Annoyed, Kate pulled at her sweatshirt. "What's the deal?"

"Peter's dropping by later." Laura turned to the foyer mirror to check the line of her ivory wool dress. Busy dreaming, she didn't notice the winces that Margo and Kate exchanged. "Just for an hour or so. I can't wait till winter break. One more midterm, and then freedom." Flushed with anticipation, she beamed at her friends. "It's going to be the best winter vacation ever. I have a feeling Peter's going to ask me to marry him."

"What?" Kate yelped before Laura could shush her.

"Quiet." She hurried back across the blue-and-white-tiled floor toward Kate and Margo. "I don't want Mom and Dad to hear. Not yet."

"Laura, you can't seriously be thinking of marrying Peter Ridgeway. You barely know him, and you're only seventeen." A million reasons against the idea whirled through Margo's mind.

"I'll be eighteen in a few weeks. It's just a feeling, anyway. Promise me you won't say anything."

"Of course not." Kate reached the bottom of the curving staircase. "You won't do anything crazy, will you?"

"Have I ever?" A wistful smile played around Laura's mouth as she patted Kate's hand. "Let's go in."

"What does she see in him?" Kate mumbled to Margo. "He's old."

"He's twenty-seven," Margo corrected, worried. "He's gorgeous and treats her like a princess. He has . . ." She searched for the word. "Polish."

"Yes, but—"

"Ssh." She spotted her mother coming down the hallway, wheeling a cart laden with hot chocolate. "We don't want to spoil tonight. We'll talk later."

Ann Sullivan's brow furrowed as she studied her daughter. "Margo, I thought that dress was for Christmas Day."

"I'm in a holiday mood," Margo said breezily. "Let me take that, Mum."

Far from satisfied, Ann watched her daughter roll the cart into the parlor before she turned to Kate. "Miss Kate, you've been overworking your eyes again. They're bloodshot. I want you to rest them later with cucumber slices. And where are your slippers?"

"In my closet." Understanding the housekeeper's need to scold, Kate hooked her arm through Ann's. "Come on now, Annie, don't fuss. It's tree-trimming time. Remember the angels you helped us make when we were ten?"

"How could I forget the mess the three of you made? And Mr. Josh teasing the lot of you and biting the heads off Mrs. Williamson's gingerbread men." She lifted a hand to touch Kate's cheek. "You've grown up since. Times like this I miss my little girls."

"We'll always be your little girls, Annie." They paused in the parlor doorway to survey the scene.

It made Kate grin, just the look of everything. The tree, already shining with lights, soared a good ten feet. It stood in front of the tall windows that faced the front. Boxes of ornaments brought out of storage sat ready to be opened.

In the lapis hearth decked with candles and fresh greenery a sedate fire flickered. Scents of apple wood and pine and perfume filled the room.

How she loved this house, she thought. Before the decorating was done, every room would have just the right touches of holiday cheer. A bowl of Georgian silver filled with pinecones would be flanked by candles.

Banks of poinsettias in gilt-trimmed pots would crowd all the window seats. Delicate porcelain angels would be placed just so on glossy mahogany tables in the foyer. The old Victorian Santa would claim his place of honor on the baby grand.

She could remember her first Christmas at Templeton House. How the grandeur of it had dazzled her eyes and the constant warmth had soothed that ache just under her heart.

Now half of her life had been lived here, and the traditions had become her own.

She wanted to freeze this moment in her mind, make it forever and unchangeable. There, she thought, the way the firelight dances over Aunt Susie's face as she laughs at Uncle Tommy—and the way he takes her hand and holds it. How perfect they look, she thought, the delicate-framed woman and the tall, distinguished man.

Christmas hymns played quietly as she took it all in. Laura knelt by the boxes, lifting out a red glass ball that caught the light and tossed it back. Margo poured steaming chocolate from a silver pot and practiced her flirting skills on Josh.

He stood on a ladder with the lights from the tree glinting in his bronze hair. They played over his face as he grinned down at Margo.

In this room filled with shining silver, sparkling glass, polished old wood and soft fabrics, they were perfect. And they were hers.

"Aren't they beautiful, Annie?"

"That they are. And so are you."

Not like them, Kate thought, as she stepped into the room.

"There's my Katie girl." Thomas beamed at her. "Put the books away for a while, did you?"

"If you can stop answering the phone for an evening, I can stop studying."

"No business on tree-trimming night." He winked at her. "I think the hotels can run without me for one night."

"Never as well as they run with you and Aunt Susie."

Margo lifted a brow as she passed Kate a cup of hot chocolate. "Somebody's bucking for another present. I hope you've got something in mind other than that stupid computer you've been drooling over."

"Computers have become necessary tools in any business. Right, Uncle Tommy?"

"Can't live without them. I'm glad your generation's going to be taking over, though. I hate the blasted things."

"You're going to have to upgrade the system in Sales, across the board,"

Josh put in as he climbed down the ladder. "No reason to do all that work when a machine can do it for you."

"Spoken like a true hedonist." Margo smirked at him. "Be careful, Josh, you might actually have to learn how to type. Imagine, Joshua Conway Templeton, heir apparent to Templeton Hotels, with a useful skill."

"Listen, duchess—"

"Hold it." Susan cut off her son's testy remark with an upraised hand. "No business tonight, remember. Margo, be a good girl and pass Josh the ornaments. Kate, take that side of the tree with Annie, will you? Laura, you and I will start over here."

"And what about me?" Thomas wanted to know.

"You do what you do best, darling. Supervise."

It wasn't enough to hang them. The ornaments had to be sighed over and stories told about them. There was the wooden elf that Margo had thrown at Josh one year, its head now held on its body with glue. The glass star that Laura had once believed her father had plucked from the sky just for her. Snowflakes that Annie had crocheted for each of the family members. The felt wreath with silver piping that had been Kate's first and last sewing project. The homey and simple hung bough by bough with the priceless antique ornaments Susan had collected from around the world.

When it was done, they held their collective breath as Thomas turned off the lamps. And the room was lit by firelight and the magic of the tree.

"It's beautiful. It's always beautiful," Kate murmured and slipped her hand into Laura's.

LATE THAT NIGHT when sleep eluded her, Kate wandered back downstairs. She crept into the parlor, stretched out on the rug beneath the tree, and watched the lights dance.

She liked to listen to the house, the quiet ticking of old clocks, the sighs and murmurs of wood settling, the crackle of spent logs in the hearth. Rain was falling in little needle stabs against the windows. The wind was a whispering song.

It helped to lie there. The nerves over her exam the following day slowly unknotted from her stomach. She knew everyone was tucked into bed, safe, sound. She'd heard Laura come in from her drive with Peter, and sometime later Josh returned from a date.

Her world was in order.

"If you're hanging out for Santa, you've got a long wait." Margo came into the room on bare feet and settled down beside Kate. "You're not still obsessing over some stupid math test, are you?"

"It's a midterm. And if you paid more attention to yours, you wouldn't be skimming by with C's."

"School's just something you have to get through." Margo slipped a pack of cigarettes out of her robe pocket. With everyone in bed, it was safe to sneak a smoke. "So, can you believe Josh is dating that cross-eyed Leah McNee?"

"She's not cross-eyed, Margo. And she's built."

Margo huffed out smoke. Anyone not struck blind could see that compared to Margo Sullivan, Leah was barely female. "He's only dating her because she puts out."

"What do you care?"

"I don't." She sniffed and smoked and sulked. "It's just so . . . ordinary. That's something I'm never going to be."

Smiling a little, Kate turned to her friend. In a blue chenille robe, with her tumbled blond hair, Margo looked stunning and sultry and sleek. "No one would ever accuse you of being ordinary, pal. Obnoxious, conceited, rude, and a royal pain in the ass, yes, but never ordinary."

Margo raised a brow and grinned. "I can always count on you. Anyway, speaking of ordinary, how stuck do you think Laura really is on Peter Ridgeway?"

"I don't know." Kate gnawed on her lip. "She's been dreamy-eyed over him ever since Uncle Tommy transferred him out here. I wish he was still managing Templeton Chicago." Then she shrugged. "He must be good at his job or Uncle Tommy and Aunt Susie wouldn't have promoted him."

"Knowing how to manage a hotel has nothing to do with it. Mr. and Mrs. T. have dozens of managers all over the world. This is the only one Laura's gone over on. Kate, if she marries him . . ."

"Yeah." Kate blew out a breath. "It's her decision. Her life. Christ, I can't imagine why anyone would want to get tied down that way."

"Neither can I." Stubbing the cigarette out, Margo lay back. "I'm not going to. I'm going to make a splash in this world."

"Me, too."

Margo slanted Kate a look. "Keeping books? That's more like a slow drip."

"You splash your way, I'll splash mine. This time next year I'll be in college."

Margo shuddered. "What a hideous thought!"

"You'll be there, too," Kate reminded her. "If you don't tank your SAT."

"We'll see about that." College wasn't on Margo's agenda. "I say we find Seraphina's dowry and take that trip around the world we used to talk about. There are places I want to see while I'm still young. Rome and Greece, Paris, Milan, London."

"They're impressive." Kate had seen them. The Templetons had taken her—and would have taken Margo as well if Ann had allowed it. "I see you marrying a rich guy, bleeding him dry, and jet-setting all over."

"Not a bad fantasy." Amused by it, Margo stretched her arms. "But I'd rather be rich myself and just have a platoon of lovers." At the sound in the hall, she shoved the ashtray under the folds of her robe. "Laura." Blowing out a breath, she sat up. "You scared the wits out of me."

"Sorry, couldn't sleep."

"Join the party," Kate invited. "We were planning our future."

"Oh." With a soft, secret smile, Laura knelt on the rug. "That's nice."

"Hold on." Eyes sharp, Margo shifted and took Laura's chin in her hand. After a moment's study, she let out a breath. "Okay, you didn't do it with him."

Flushing, Laura batted Margo's hand away. "Of course I didn't. Peter would never pressure me."

"How do you know she didn't?" Kate demanded.

"You can tell. I don't think you should have sex with him, Laura, but if you're seriously thinking marriage, you'd better try him on first."

"Sex isn't a pair of shoes," Laura muttered.

"But it sure as hell better fit."

"When I make love the first time, it's going to be with my husband on our wedding night. That's the way I want it."

"Uh-oh, she's got that Templeton edge in her voice." Grinning, Kate tugged on a curl falling over Laura's ear. "Unbudgable. Don't listen to Margo, Laura. In her head, sex is equated with salvation."

Margo lit another cigarette. "I'd like to know what tops it."

"Love," Laura stated.

"Success," Kate said at the same time. "Well, that sums it up." Kate wrapped her arms around her knees. "Margo's going to be a sex fiend, you're going to search for love, and I'm going to bust my ass for success. What a group."

"I'm already in love," Laura said quietly. "I want someone who loves me back, and children. I want to wake up each morning knowing I can make a home for them and a happy life for them. I want to fall asleep each night beside someone I can trust and depend on."

"I'd rather fall asleep at night beside someone who makes me hot." Margo chuckled when Kate poked her. "Just kidding. Sort of. I want to go places and do things. Be somebody. I want to know when I wake up in the morning that something exciting is right around the corner. And whatever it is, I want to make it mine."

Kate rested her chin on her knees. "I want to feel accomplished," she said quietly. "I want to make things work the way I think they should work. I want to wake up in the morning knowing exactly what I'm doing next, and how I'm going to do it. I want to be the best at what I do so that I know I haven't wasted anything. Because if I wasted it, it would be like . . . failing."

Her voice broke, embarrassing her. "God, I must be overtired." Because her eyes were stinging, she rubbed them hard. "I have to go to bed. My exam's first thing in the morning."

"You'll breeze through it." Laura rose with her. "Don't worry so much."

"Professional nerds have to worry." But Margo rose as well, and patted Kate's arm. "Let's get some sleep."

Kate paused at the doorway to look back at the tree. For a moment she'd been shocked to discover that a part of her wished she could stay here, just like this, forever. Never have to worry about tomorrow or the next day. Never have to concern herself with success or failure. Or change.

Change was coming, she realized. It was barreling down on her in the dewy look in Laura's eyes, the edgy one in Margo's. She turned off the lights. There was no stopping any of it, she realized. So she'd better get ready.

CHAPTER 2

SHE GOT THROUGH the days and the nights and the work. There was no choice but to cope. And for the first time in her life, Kate felt there was no one she could talk to. Each time she felt herself tipping, needing to reach for the phone or run to Templeton House, she yanked herself back.

She could not—would not—pour out this misery, these fears to the people who loved her. They would stand by her, there was no doubt about that. But this was a burden she had to carry herself. And one she hoped she could hide in some dark corner of her mind. Eventually she would be able to let it rest, to stop feeling compelled to pick it up, again and again, and examine it.

She considered herself practical, intelligent, and strong. Indeed, she couldn't understand how anyone could be the latter without the two formers.

Until this, her life had been exactly as she wanted it. Her career was cruising along at a safe and, yes, intelligent speed. She had a reputation at Bittle and Associates as a clearheaded, hardworking CPA who could handle complex accounts without complaint. Eventually she expected to be offered a full partnership. When that time came, she would ascend yet another rung on her personal ladder of success.

She had family she loved and who loved her. And friends . . . well, her closest friends were family. And what could be more convenient than that?

She adored them, had loved growing up at Templeton House, overlooking the wild, sweeping cliffs of Big Sur. There was nothing she wouldn't do for Aunt Susie and Uncle Tommy. That included keeping what she had learned weeks before in her office to herself.

She wouldn't question them, though questions burned inside her. She wouldn't share the pain or the problem with Laura or Margo, though she had always shared everything with them.

She would suppress, ignore, and forget. That, she had to believe, would be best for everyone.

Her entire life had been focused on doing her best, being the best, making her family proud. Now, she felt she had more to prove, more to be. Every success she had enjoyed could be traced back to the moment when they had opened their home and their hearts to her. So she promised herself to look forward rather than back. To go on with the routine that had become her life.

Under ordinary circumstances, treasure hunting wouldn't be considered routine. But when it involved Seraphina's dowry, when it included Laura and Margo and Laura's two daughters, it was an event. It was a mission.

The legend of Seraphina, that doomed young girl who had flung herself off the cliffs rather than face a life without her true love, had fascinated the three of them all of their lives. The beautiful Spanish girl had loved Felipe, had met him in secret, walked with him along the cliffs in the wind, in the rain. He had gone off to fight the Americans, to prove himself worthy of her, promising to come back to marry her and build a life with her. But he had not come back. When Seraphina learned he had been killed in battle, she had walked these cliffs again. Had stood on the edge of the world and, overcome with grief, had flung herself over it.

The romance of it, the mystery, the glamour had been irresistible to the three women. And of course, the possibility of finding the dowry that Seraphina had hidden away before she leapt into the sea added challenge.

On most Sundays Kate could be found on the cliffs, wielding a metal detector or a spade. For months, ever since the morning that Margo, at a crossroads in her life, had found a single gold doubloon, the three had met there to search.

Or maybe they gathered not so much in hopes of uncovering a chest of gold as simply to enjoy each other's company.

It was nearly May, and after the jangled nerves she had suffered leading up to April 15 and the income tax deadline, Kate was thrilled to be out in the sun. It was what she needed, she was sure. It helped, as work helped, to keep her mind off the file she had hidden in her apartment. The file on her father that she had carefully organized.

It helped to block out the worries, and the ache in her heart, and the stress of wondering if she'd done the right thing by hiring a detective to look into a twenty-year-old case.

Her muscles protested a bit as she swept the metal detector over a new section of scrub, and she sweated lightly under her T-shirt.

She wouldn't think of it, she promised herself. Not today, not here. She wouldn't think of it at all until the detective's report was complete. She had promised the day to herself, for her family, and nothing would get in the way.

The gorgeous breeze ruffled her short cap of black hair. Her skin was dusky, an inheritance from the Italian branch of her mother's family, though beneath it was what Margo called "accountant's pallor." A few days in the sun, she decided, would fix that.

She'd lost a little weight in the last few weeks of crunch time—and yes, because of the shock of discovering what her father had done—but she intended to put it back on. She always had hopes of putting some meat on her stubbornly thin bones.

She didn't have Margo's height or stunning build, or Laura's lovely fragility. She was, Kate had always thought, average, average and skinny, with an angular face to match her angular body.

Once she had hoped for dimples, or the dash of a few charming freckles, or deep-green eyes instead of ordinary brown. But she'd been too practical to dwell on it for long.

She had a good brain and skill with figures. And that was what she needed to succeed.

She reached down for the jug of lemonade Ann Sullivan had sent along. After a long, indulgent drink, Kate cast a scowl in Margo's direction.

"Are you just going to sit there all afternoon while the rest of us work?"

Margo stretched luxuriously on her rock, her sexpot body draped in what, for Margo Sullivan Templeton, was casual wear of red leggings and a matching shirt. "We're a little tired today," she claimed and patted her flat belly.

Kate snorted. "Ever since you found out you're pregnant you've been finding excuses to sit on your butt."

Margo flashed a smile and tossed her long blond hair behind her shoulders. "Josh doesn't want me to overdo."

"You're playing that one for all it's worth," Kate grumbled.

"Damn right I am." Delighted with life in general, Margo crossed her long, gorgeous legs. "He's so sweet and attentive and thrilled. Jesus, Kate, we've made ourselves a baby."

Maybe the idea of two of her favorite people being blindly in love, starting their own family, did bring Kate a warm glow. But she was bound by tradition to snipe at Margo whenever possible. "At least you could look haggard, throw up every morning, faint now and again."

"I've never felt better in my life." Because it was true, Margo rose and took the metal detector. "Even giving up smoking hasn't been as hard as I thought it would. I never imagined I wanted to be a mother. Now it's all I can think about."

"You're going to be a fabulous mother," Kate murmured. "Just fabulous."

"Yes, I am." Margo studied Laura, who was giggling and digging at a patch of scrubby earth with her two little girls. "I've got an awfully good role model right there. This past year's been hell for her, but she's never wavered."

"Neglect, adultery, divorce," Kate said quietly, not wanting the fitful breeze to carry her words. "Not a lot of fun and games. The girls have helped keep her centered. And the shop."

"Yeah. And speaking of the shop—" Margo turned the detector off, leaned on it. "If these past couple of weeks are any indication, we may have to hire some help. I'm not going to be able to give Pretenses ten and twelve hours a day after the baby comes."

Always thinking of budget, Kate frowned. The upscale secondhand boutique they had opened on Cannery Row was primarily Margo's and Laura's domain. But as the third partner in the fledgling enterprise, Kate crunched numbers for it when she could squeeze out the time.

"You've got over six months left. That hits holiday shopping time. We could think about hiring seasonal help then."

Sighing, Margo handed the metal detector back to Kate. "The business is doing better than any of us anticipated. Don't you think it's time to loosen up?"

"No." Kate switched the machine back on. "We haven't been open a full year yet. You start taking on outside help, you've got social security, withholding, unemployment."

"Well, yes, but—"

"I can start helping out on Saturdays if necessary, and I've got my vacation time coming up." Work, she thought again. Work and don't think. "I can give Pretenses a couple of weeks full time."

"Kate, a vacation means white-sand beaches, Europe, a sordid affair—not clerking in a shop."

Kate merely raised an eyebrow.

"I forgot who I was talking to," Margo muttered. "The original all-work-and-no-play girl."

"That was always to balance you, the quintessential all-play girl. Anyway, I'm a one-third owner of Pretenses. I believe in protecting my investments." She scowled at the ground, kicked it. "Hell, there's not even a bottle cap to give us a little beep and thrill here."

"Are you feeling all right?" Margo's eyes narrowed, looked closer. "You look a little washed out." And frail, she realized. Frail and edgy. "If I didn't know better I'd say you were the one who was pregnant."

"That would be a good trick since I haven't had sex in what feels like the last millennium."

"Which could be why you seem edgy and washed out." But she didn't grin. "Really, Kate, what's going on?"

She wanted to say it, spill out all of it. Knew if she did she would find comfort, support, loyalty—whatever she needed. My problem, she reminded herself.

"Nothing." Kate made herself look down her nose disdainfully. "Except I'm the one doing all the work and my arms are falling off while you sit on your rock and pose for a *Glamorous Mothers-to-Be* photo shoot." She rotated her shoulders. "I need a break."

Margo studied her friend for another moment, tapping her fingers on her knee. "Fine. I'm hungry anyway. Let's see what Mum packed." Opening the nearby hamper, Margo let out a long, heartfelt moan. "Oh, God, fried chicken."

Kate peeked in the hamper. Five minutes more, she decided, then she was digging in. Mrs. Williamson's chicken was bound to erase the nagging hunger pains. "Is Josh back from London?"

"Hmm." Margo swallowed gamely. "Tomorrow. Templeton London did a little remodeling, so he's going to bring back some stock for the shop. And I asked him to check with some of my contacts there, so we may have a nice new supply. It would save me a buying trip."

"I remember when you couldn't wait to get on a plane."

"That was then," Margo said smugly. "This is now." She bit into the drumstick again, then remembered something and waved a hand. "Umm, forgot. Party next Saturday night. Cocktails, buffet. Be there."

Kate winced. "Do I have to dress up?"

"Yes. Lots of our customers." She swallowed again. "Some of the hotel brass. Byron De Witt."

Pouting, Kate turned off the machine and grabbed a chicken thigh out of the hamper. "I don't like him."

"Of course not," Margo said dryly. "He's gorgeous, charming, intelligent, world-traveled. Absolutely hateful."

"He knows he's gorgeous."

"And that takes a lot of nerve. I don't really give a damn whether you like him or not. He's taken a lot of the weight off Josh here at the California hotels, recovered a lot of the ground Peter Ridgeway lost for us."

She caught herself and glanced over toward Laura. Peter was Laura's exhusband, the girls' father, and whatever she thought of him, she wouldn't criticize him in front of Ali and Kayla.

"Just be civil."

"I'm always civil. Hey, guys," Kate called out and watched Ali and Kayla's pretty blond heads pop up. "We've got Mrs. Williamson's fried chicken over here, and Margo's eating it all."

With shouts and scrambling feet, the girls dashed up to join the picnic. Laura came after them and sat cross-legged at Margo's feet. She watched her daughters squabble over one particular piece of chicken. Ali won, of course. She was the older of the two and in recent months the more demanding.

Divorce, Laura reminded herself as Ali smugly nibbled her chicken, was very, very hard on a ten-year-old girl. "Ali, pour Kayla a glass of lemonade too."

Ali hesitated, considered refusing. It seemed, Laura thought as she kept cool, calm eyes on her daughter's mutinous ones, that Ali considered refusing everything these days. In the end, Ali shrugged and poured a second glass for her sister.

"We didn't find anything," Ali complained, choosing to forget the fun she'd had giggling and digging in the dirt. "It's boring."

"Really?" Margo selected a cube of cheese from a plastic container. "For me, just being here and looking is half the fun."

"Well . . ." Whatever Margo said was, to Ali, gospel. Margo was glamorous and different; Margo had run away to Hollywood at eighteen, had lived in Europe and had been involved in wonderful, exciting scandals. Nothing ordinary and awful like marriage and divorce. "I guess it's kinda fun. But I wish we'd find more coins."

"Persistence." Kate flipped a finger from Ali's chin to her nose. "Pays. What would have happened if Alexander Graham Bell had given up before he put that first call through? If Indiana Jones hadn't gone on that last crusade?"

"If Armani hadn't sewed that first seam?" Margo put in and earned a fresh giggle.

"If *Star Trek* hadn't gone where no one had gone before," Laura finished, and had the pleasure of seeing her daughter flash a smile.

"Well, maybe. Can we see the coin again, Aunt Margo?"

Margo reached in her pocket. She'd fallen into the habit of carrying the old Spanish gold coin with her. Ali took it gingerly, and because she was awed, as always, held it so that Kayla could coo over it too.

"It's so shiny." Kayla touched it reverently. "Can I pick some flowers for Seraphina?"

"Sure." Leaning over, Laura kissed the top of her head. "But don't go near the edge to throw them over without me."

"I won't. We always do it together."

"I guess I'll help her." Ali handed Margo the coin. But when she stood up, her pretty mouth went thin. "Seraphina was stupid to jump. Just because she wasn't going to be able to marry Felipe. Marriage is no good anyway." Then she remembered Margo and blushed.

"Sometimes," Laura said quietly, "marriage is wonderful and kind and strong. And other times it isn't wonderful enough, or kind enough or strong enough. But you're right, Ali, Seraphina shouldn't have jumped. When she did that, she ended everything she could have become, threw away all those possibilities. It makes me feel very sorry for her." She watched her daughter, head drooping, shoulders hunched, walk away. "She's so hurt. She's so angry."

"She'll get through this." Kate gave Laura's hand a bracing squeeze. "You're doing everything right."

"It's been three months since they've seen Peter. He hasn't even bothered to call them."

"You're doing everything right," Kate repeated. "You're not responsible for the asshole. She knows you're not to blame—inside she knows that."

"I hope so." Laura shrugged and picked at a piece of chicken. "Kayla just bounces and Ali broods. Well, I guess we're a textbook example that kids can grow up in the same house and be raised by the same people and turn out differently."

Kate's stomach wrenched.

"True." Margo had a low-grade urge for a cigarette, quashed it. "But we're all so fabulous. Well . . ." She smiled sweetly at Kate. "Most of us."

"Just for that, I'm eating the last piece of chicken." Kate popped a couple of Tums first. Medication helped her to eat when she had no desire for food. Nervous heartburn, she thought of the low burn just under her breastbone. Insisted on thinking of it that way. "I was telling Margo that I'd be able to pitch in at the shop on Saturdays."

"We could use the help." Laura shifted so she could continue the conversation and keep an eye on her daughters. "Last Saturday was a madhouse, and I could only give Margo four hours."

"I can put in a full day."

"Wonderful." Margo plucked some glossy grapes from a bunch. "You'll be hunkered over the computer the whole time, trying to find mistakes."

"If you didn't make them, I wouldn't have to find them. But . . ." She held up a hand, not so much to avoid the argument as to make a point. "I'll stay at the counter, and I have twenty bucks that says I make more sales than you by the time we close."

"In your dreams, Powell."

ON MONDAY MORNING, Kate wasn't thinking about dreams or treasure hunts. At nine sharp, with her third cup of coffee at her elbow, her computer booted, she was behind her desk in her office at Bittle and Associates. Following her daily routine, she had already removed her navy pin-striped jacket, draped it behind her chair, and rolled up the sleeves of her starched white shirt.

The sleeves would be rolled back down and the jacket neatly buttoned into place for her eleven o'clock meeting with a client, but for now it was just Kate and numbers.

And that was how she liked it best.

The challenge of making numbers dance and shuffle and fall neatly into place had always fascinated her. There was a beauty in the ebb and flow of interest rates, T-bills, mutual funds. And a power, she could privately admit, in understanding, even admiring, the caprice of finance, and confidently advising clients how best to protect their hard-earned money.

Not that it was always hard-earned, she thought with a snort as she studied the account on her screen. A good many of her clients had earned their money the old-fashioned way.

They'd inherited it.

Even as the thought crossed her mind, she cringed. Was that her father in her, sneering at those who had inherited wealth? Taking a deep breath, she rubbed a hand over the tense spot in the back of her neck. She had to stop this, seeing ghosts around every thought in her head.

It was her job to advise and protect and to ensure that any account she handled through Bittle was served well. Not only was she not envious of her clients' portfolios, she worked hand in glove with lawyers, bookkeepers, brokers, agents, and estate planners to provide each and every one of them the very best in short- and long-term financial advice.

That, she reminded herself, was who she was.

What she reveled in was the numbers, their stoic and dependable consistency. For Kate two and two always and forever equaled four.

To realign herself, she skimmed through a spreadsheet for Ever Spring Nursery and Gardens. In the eighteen months since she had taken over that account, she'd watched it slowly, cautiously expand. She believed strongly in the slow and the cautious, and this client had taken her direction well. True, the payroll had swelled, but the business justified it. Outlay for the health plan and employee benefits was high and nipped at the profit margin, but as a woman raised by the Templetons, she also firmly believed in sharing success with the people who helped you earn it.

"A good year for bougainvillea," she muttered, and made a note to suggest that her client ease some of the last quarter's profits into tax-free bonds.

Render unto Caesar, sure, she thought, but not one damn penny more than necessary.

"You look beautiful when you're plotting."

Kate glanced up, her fingers automatically hitting the keys to store her data and bring up her screen saver. "Hello, Roger."

He leaned against the doorjamb. Posed, was Kate's unflattering thought. Roger Thornhill was tall, dark, and handsome, with classic features reminiscent of Cary Grant in his prime. Broad shoulders fit beautifully under a tailored gray suit jacket. He had a quick, brilliant smile, dark-blue eyes that zeroed in flatteringly on a woman's face, and a smooth baritone that flowed like melted honey.

Perhaps it was for all of those reasons that Kate couldn't abide him. It was only coincidence that they were on the same fast track for partnership. That, she assured herself often, had nothing to do with why he annoyed her.

Or just a very little to do with it.

"Your door was open," he pointed out and strolled in without invitation. "I figured you weren't very busy."

"I like my door open."

He flashed that wide, toothy smile and eased a hip onto the corner of her desk. "I just got back from Nevis. A couple of weeks in the West Indies sure clears out the system after the tax crunch." His gaze roamed over her face. "You should have come with me."

"Roger, when I won't even have dinner with you, why would you think I'd spend two weeks frolicking with you in the sand and surf?"

"Hope springs eternal?" He took one of the pencils, sharpened like swords, from her Lucite holder, slid it idly through his fingers. Her pencils were always sharpened and always kept in the same place. There was nothing in her office that didn't have a proper slot. He knew all of them. An ambitious man, Roger made use of what he knew.

He also made use of charm, keeping his eyes on hers, smiling. "I'd just like us to get to know each other again, outside the office. Hell, Kate, it's been almost two years."

Deliberately, she raised an eyebrow. "Since?"

"Okay, since I messed things up." He put the pencil down. "I'm sorry. I don't know how else to say it."

"Sorry?" Voice mild, she rose to refill her coffee, though the third cup wasn't sitting well. She sat again, watching him as she sipped. "Sorry that you were sleeping with me and one of my clients at the same time? Or that you were sleeping with me in order to get to my client? Or that you seduced said client into moving her account from my hands to yours? Which of those are you apologizing for, Roger?"

"All of them." Because it invariably worked with females, he tried the smile again. "Look, I've already apologized countless times, but I'm willing to do it again. I had no business seeing Bess, ah, Mrs. Turner, much less sleeping with her, while you and I were involved. There's no excuse for it."

"We agree. Good-bye."

"Kate." His eyes stayed on hers, his voice flowing, just the way she remembered it had when she had moved under him, climbing toward climax. "I want to make things right with you. At least make peace with you."

She cocked her head, considered. There was right and there was wrong. There were ethics and there was the lack of them. "No."

"Damn it." With his first sign of temper, he stood up from the desk, the movement jerky and abrupt. "I was a son of a bitch. I let sex and ambition get in the way of what was a good, satisfying relationship."

"You're absolutely right," she agreed. "And you didn't know me well the first time around if you have any hope that I'd let you repeat the performance."

"I stopped seeing Bess months ago, on a personal level."

"Oh, well, then." Leaning back in her chair, Kate enjoyed a good, rolling laugh. "Jesus Christ, you're a case, Roger. You think because you've cleared the field, I'm going to suit up and jump into the game? We're associates," she told him, "and that's all. I'm never going to make the mistake of getting involved with someone at work again, and I'm never—repeat, never—going to give you another shot."

His mouth thinned. "You're afraid to see me outside the office. Afraid because you'd remember how good we were together."

She had to sigh. "Roger, we weren't that good. My appraisal would put us at adequate. Let's just close the books on this one." In the interest of sanity, she rose, held out her hand. "You want to put it behind us, let's. No hard feelings."

Intrigued, he studied her hand, then her face. "No hard feelings?"

No feelings at all, she thought, but decided not to say it. "Fresh sheet," she said. "We're colleagues, marginally friendly. And you'll stop pestering me about having dinner or taking trips to the West Indies."

He took her hand. "I've missed you, Kate. Missed touching you. All right," he said quickly when he saw her eyes narrow, "if that's the best I can do, I'll take it. I appreciate your accepting my apology."

"Fine." Struggling to be patient, she tugged her hand away. "Now I've got work to do."

"I'm glad we worked this out." He was smiling again as he walked to the door.

"Yeah, right," she muttered. She didn't slam the door behind him. That would have indicated too much emotion. She didn't want Roger the slime Thornhill, to get the idea there was any emotion inside her where he was concerned.

But she did close the door, quietly, purposefully, before sitting back down at her desk. She took out a bottle of Mylanta, sighed a little, and chugged.

He had hurt her. It was demoralizing to remember just how much he had hurt her. She hadn't been in love with him, but with a little more time, a little more effort, she could have been. They had had the common ground of their work, which she believed could have served as a strong foundation for more.

She had cared for him, and trusted him, and enjoyed him.

And he had used her ruthlessly to steal one of her biggest clients. That was almost worse than discovering he'd been jumping from her bed to her client's bed and back again.

Kate took another swig from the bottle before recapping it. She had, at the time, considered going to Larry Bittle with a formal complaint. But her pride had outweighed whatever satisfaction she might have gleaned from that.

The client was satisfied, and that was the bottom line at Bittle. Roger would have lost some ground, certainly, if she'd filed a complaint. Others in the office would have distrusted him, pulled back from him.

And she would have looked like the whining, betrayed female, sniveling because she had mixed sex and business and had lost.

Better that she'd kept it to herself, Kate decided and put the Mylanta back in her drawer. Better that she'd been able to say, straight to his face, that she had put the whole incident behind her.

Even if it was a lie, even if she would detest him for the rest of her life.

With a shrug, she recalled her data. Better by far to avoid slick, smart, gorgeous men with more ambition than heart. Better, much better, to stay in the fast lane on the career track and avoid any and all distractions. Partnership was waiting, with all the success it entailed.

When she had that partnership, had climbed to that next rung, she would have earned it. And maybe, she thought, just maybe, when she reached that level of success, she would be able to prove to herself that she was not her father's daughter.

She smiled a little as she began to run figures. Stick with numbers, pal, she reminded herself. They never lie.

CHAPTER 3

THE MINUTE KATE walked into Pretenses, Margo scowled. "You look like death."

"Thanks. I want coffee." And a moment alone. She headed up the curving stairs to the second floor, found the pot already brewing.

She knew she hadn't slept more than three hours, not after poring over every detail in the report from the detective back east. And every detail had confirmed that she was the daughter of a thief.

It was all there—the evidence, the charges, the statements. And reading through those papers had killed the faint hope she'd hidden even from herself that it had all been some sort of mistake.

Instead, she had learned that her father had been out on bail at the time of the accident and had instructed his lawyer to accept the plea bargain he'd been offered. If he hadn't been killed that night on that icy stretch of road, he would have been in prison within the week.

Telling herself to accept it, to get on with her life, she drank her coffee hot and black. She needed to go back down, get to work. And face a friend who knew her too well to miss signs of stress.

Well, she thought, carrying her cup with her, she had other excuses for a poor night's sleep. And there was nothing to be gained by obsessing over facts that couldn't be changed. From this moment, Kate promised herself, she would cease to think about it.

"What's going on?" Margo demanded when Kate wound her way down the stairs. "I want an answer this time. You've been jumpy and out of sorts for weeks. And I swear you're losing weight with every breath. This has just gone on long enough, Kate."

"I'm fine. Tired." She shrugged. "A couple of accounts are giving me some problems. On top of that it's been a weird week." Kate opened the cash register, counted out the bills and coins for morning change. "Monday, that scum Thornhill came slinking into my office."

Margo turned from setting up the teapot. "I hope you kicked his ass right out again."

"I let him think we've made up. It was easier," she said before Margo could comment. "He's more likely to leave me alone now."

"You're not going to tell me that's what's keeping you up at night."

"It gave me some bad moments, okay?"

"Okay." Margo smiled in sympathy. "Men are pigs, and that one is a blue ribbon hog. Don't waste your beauty sleep on him, honey."

"Thanks. Anyway, that was only the first weird thing."

"The wacky life of a CPA."

"Wednesday, I got tossed this new account. Freeland. It's a petting zoo, kiddie park, museum. Very strange. I'm learning all about how much it costs to feed a baby llama."

Margo paused. "You lead such a fascinating life."

"You're telling me. Then yesterday, the partners all huddled together for most of the afternoon. Even the secretaries were barred. Nobody has a clue, but the rumor is somebody's about to be canned or promoted." Kate shrugged and closed the cash register. "I've never seen them powwow like that. They had to make their own coffee."

"Stop the presses."

"Look, my little world has just as much intrigue and drama as anyone else's." She stepped back as Margo advanced on her. "What?"

"Just hold still." Grabbing Kate's lapel, Margo pinned on a crescent-shaped brooch dangling with drops of amber. "Advertise the merchandise."

"It's got dead bugs in it."

Margo didn't bother to sigh. "Put some lipstick on, for God's sake. We open in ten minutes."

"I don't have any with me. And I'll tell you right now, I'm not going to work with you all day if you're going to be picking on me. I can sell, ring up, and box just fine without painting my face."

"Fine." Before Kate could evade her, Margo picked up an atomizer and spritzed her with perfume. "Advertise the merchandise," she repeated. "If anyone asks what you're wearing, it's Bella Donna's Savage."

Kate had just worked up a snarl when Laura burst in. "I thought I was going to be late. Ali had a hair emergency. I was afraid one of us would kill the other before it was over."

"She's getting more like Margo every day." Wishing it were coffee, Kate strolled over to pour herself tea and used it to wash down a palm full of pills she didn't want either of her friends to see. "I meant that in the worst possible way," she added.

"A young girl becoming interested in appearance and grooming is natural," Margo shot back. "You were the changeling in the family. Still are, as you constantly prove, by going around like a scarecrow dressed in navy blue serge."

Unoffended, Kate sipped at her tea. "Navy serge is classic because it's serviceable. There is only a very small percentage of the population who feel honor bound to fart through silk."

"Jesus, you're crude," Margo managed over a laugh. "I don't even want to argue with you."

"That's a relief." Hoping to keep it that way, Laura hurried over to turn the Open sign around. "I'm still cross-eyed from arguing with Allison. If Annie hadn't intervened, it would have been hairbrushes at ten paces."

"Mum always could defuse a good fight," Margo commented. "Okay, ladies, remember, we're pushing Mother's Day. And in case it slipped both of your minds, expectant mothers also warrant gifts."

Kate braced for the onslaught and struggled to ignore the viselike clamp on her temples that was usually the sign of a migraine on the boil.

Within an hour Pretenses was busy enough to keep all three of them occupied. Kate boxed up a Hermès bag of dark-green leather, wondering what anyone needed with a green leather purse. But the slick slide of the credit card machine kept her cheerful. She was, by her calculations, neck and neck with Margo on sales.

It was a fine feeling, she thought as she wrapped the gold and silver box in elegant floral paper, watching the business progress. And the combo of competition and medication had eased the headache that had been threatening.

She had to give Margo full credit for it. Pretenses had been a dream rising like smoke from the ashes of Margo's life.

Just over a year ago, Margo's career as a popular model in Europe, her exposure and financial rewards as the Bella Donna Woman, had been rudely cut off. Not that Margo was blameless, Kate thought, smiling as she handed the purchase to her customer. She'd been reckless, foolish, head-strong. But she hadn't deserved to lose everything.

She'd come back from Milan broken and nearly bankrupt, but in a mat-ter of months, through her own grit, she had turned her life around.

Opening a shop and selling her possessions in it had been Josh Temple-ton's idea originally. His idea, Kate mused, to keep Margo from sinking, since he was blindly in love with her. But Margo had expanded the idea, nurtured it, polished it.

Then Laura, reeling from her husband's deceit, betrayal, and greed, had taken the bulk of what he'd left of her money and helped Margo buy the building for Pretenses.

When Kate had insisted on acquiring a one-third interest, thus making herself a partner, it had been because she believed in the investment, be-cause she believed in Margo. And because she didn't want to be left out of the fun.

Of all of them, she understood the risks best. Nearly forty percent of new businesses failed within a year, and almost eighty percent went under within five.

And Kate worried over it, gnawed on it at night when she couldn't sleep. But Pretenses, Margo's conception of an elegant, exclusive, and unique secondhand shop that offered everything from designer gowns to teaspoons, was holding its own.

Kate's part in it might have been small, and her reasons for getting in-volved certainly straddled the practical and the emotional, but she was en-joying herself. When she wasn't obsessing.

Here was proof, after all, that life could be what you made of it. She badly needed to hang on to that idea.

"Is there something I can show you?" The man she smiled at was thirty-ish, attractive in a rugged, lived-in manner. She appreciated the worn jeans, the faded shirt, the dashing reddish moustache.

"Ah, well, maybe. This necklace here."

She looked down into the display, zeroed in on his choice. "It's pretty, isn't it? Pearls are so classic."

Not regular pearls, she thought as she lifted the necklace out. What the hell were they called? She continued to search through her mind as she draped the necklace over a velvet form.

"Seed pearls," she remembered and beamed at him. He really was awfully cute. "It's called a lariat," she added. She'd gotten that off the tag. "Three strands, and the clasp, or the slide thing has a . . ." Give me a minute. "A mabe pearl set in gold. Tradition with a flair," she added, enjoying the ad lib.

"I wondered how much . . ." Hesitating, he flipped the tiny, discreet price tag over. To his credit, he winced only slightly. "Well," he smiled a little, "it hits the top of my price range."

"It's something she'll wear for years. Is it for Mother's Day?"

"Yeah." He shifted his feet, running a calloused finger over the strands. "She'd go nuts over it."

She melted toward him. Any man who would take such time and trouble for a gift for his mother earned top points from Kate Powell. Especially when he looked just a little bit like Kevin Costner. "We have several other really nice pieces that aren't quite so expensive."

"No, I think . . . maybe . . . Could you put it on so I could get a better picture?"

"Sure." Happy to oblige, she fastened it around her neck. "What do you think? Is it great?" She angled the counter mirror so that she could judge for herself and added, laughing, "If you don't buy it, I might have to snap it up myself."

"It looks awfully pretty on you," he said with a shy, quiet smile that made her want to scoop him up and bundle him into the back room. "She's got dark hair like you. Wears it longer, but the pearls look good with dark hair. I guess I'll have to take it. Along with that box over there, the silver one with all the fancy scrolling."

Still wearing the necklace, Kate scooted out from behind the counter to get the trinket box he'd pointed to. "Two presents." She reached up to undo the necklace clasp. "Your mother must be a very special woman."

"Oh, she's great. She's going to like this box. She sort of collects them. The necklace is for my wife, though," he added. "I'm getting all my Mother's Day shopping done at one time."

"Your wife." Kate forced herself to keep her lips cheerily curved at the corners. "I guarantee she'll love it. But if she or your mother prefers something else, we have a thirty-day exchange and return policy." With what she considered admirable restraint, Kate laid the necklace down. "Now, will that be cash or charge?"

Ten minutes later she watched him saunter out. "The cute ones," she muttered to Laura, "the nice ones, the ones who love their mothers are all married."

"There, there." Laura patted Kate's arm before reaching under the counter to select the proper box. "It looked like a very good sale."

"Puts me at least two hundred up on Margo. And the day's young."

"That's the spirit. But I should warn you, she's got one back in the wardrobe room now, and she's definitely leaning toward Versace."

"Shit." Kate turned to scan the main showroom for prey. "I'm going for the blue-haired lady with the Gucci bag. She's mine."

"Reel her in, tiger."

Kate didn't break for lunch and told herself it was because she wanted to keep up her momentum, not because her stomach was acting up again. She had tremendous success in the second-floor ladies' boudoir and racked up two peignoirs, a stained-glass accent lamp, and a tasseled footstool.

Maybe she did sneak into the back room a couple of times to boot up the computer and check Margo's bookkeeping. But only when her lead was comfortable. She corrected the expected mistakes, rolled her eyes over a few unexpected ones, and tidied up the files.

She was forced to admit, in the end, that accountant's lapse was what cost her the victory. When she came back, smug, already preparing the lecture she intended to deliver to Margo on the cost of careless accounting, her rival was closing a sale.

A whopper.

Kate knew antiques. A child didn't grow up at Templeton House and not learn to recognize and appreciate them. Her heart sank even as dollar signs revolved in her head when she recognized the piece Margo was cooing over.

Louis XVI, Kate recited in her head. A *secrétaire-à-abattant*, probably near 1775. The marquetry panels, typical of that era, included vases and garlands of flowers, musical instruments and drapery.

Oh, it was a stunner, Kate thought, and one of the remaining pieces from Margo's original stock.

"I'm sorry to lose it," Margo was telling the dapper white-haired gentleman who leaned on a gold-headed cane and studied the *secretaire* and the woman who described it with equal admiration. "I bought it in Paris several years ago."

"You have a wonderful eye. In fact, you have two wonderful eyes."

"Oh, Mr. Stiener, that's so sweet of you." In her shameless style, Margo trailed a finger down his arm. "I do hope you'll think of me, now and again, when you're enjoying this."

"I can promise you I will. Now, as to shipping?"

"Just come over to the counter and I'll take all the necessary information." Margo crossed the room, hips swinging, and shot Kate a triumphant look.

"I think that crushes you for the day, ace," she said when her customer strolled out.

"The day's not over," Kate insisted. "We still have two hours until closing. So until the fat lady sings—which will be you in a few months—don't count your chickens."

"Such a sore loser." Margo clucked her tongue and was ready to pounce when the door jangled. It wasn't a customer, but she pounced anyway. "Josh!"

He caught her, kissed her, then pulled her to a chair. "Off your feet." He kept one hand on her shoulder and turned to glare at Kate. "You're supposed to be keeping an eye on her, making sure she doesn't overdo."

"Don't hang this on me. Besides, Margo doesn't stand when she can sit and doesn't sit when she can lie down. And I made her drink a glass of milk an hour ago."

Josh narrowed his eyes. "A whole glass?"

"What she didn't spit at me." Because it amused and touched her to see her big brother worry and fuss, Kate decided to forgive him. She stepped over and kissed him. "Welcome home."

"Thanks." He stroked a hand over her hair. "Where's Laura?"

"Upstairs with a couple of customers."

"And there's another one in the wardrobe room," Margo began, "so—"

"Sit," Josh ordered. "Kate can handle it. You're looking pale."

Margo pouted. "I am not."

"You're going home and taking a nap," he decided. "No way you're going to work all day, then run around giving a party. Kate and Laura can finish out here."

"Sure we can." Kate shot Margo a smug look. "A couple of hours should do it."

"Keep dreaming, Powell. I've already won."

"Won?" Always interested in a bet, Josh looked from woman to woman. "Won what?"

"Just a friendly wager that I could outsell her."

"Which she's already lost," Margo pointed out. "And I'm feeling generous. You can have the two-hour handicap, Kate." Taking Josh's hand, she rubbed it against her cheek. "And when you've lost, officially, you wear the Ungaro slip dress, the red, to the party tonight."

"The thing that looks like a nightgown? You might as well be naked."

"Really?" Josh wiggled his eyebrows. "No offense, Kate, hope you lose. Come on, duchess, home, bed."

"I'm not wearing a red slip to any party," Kate insisted.

"Then don't lose," Margo said with a careless shrug as she walked with Josh to the door. "But when you do, have Laura pick out the accessories."

SHE WORE A hammered-gold collar and triangular earrings that danced below her lobes. Her complaints that she looked like a slave girl captured by the Klingons fell on deaf ears. Even the shoes had been forced on her. Red satin skyscrapers that had her teetering at three and a half inches over her normal five seven.

She sipped champagne and felt like a fool.

It didn't help matters that some of her clients were there. Margo and Josh's acquaintances ran toward the rich, the famous, and the privileged. And she wondered how she was going to maintain her image as a clear-headed, precise, and dedicated accountant when she was dressed like a bimbo.

But a bet was a bet.

"Stop fidgeting," Laura ordered when she joined Kate on the terrace. "You look stunning."

"This from a woman tastefully garbed in an elegant suit that covers her extremities. What I look," she said after another gulp of champagne, "is desperate. I might as well be wearing a sign. 'Single Woman, HIV negative, apply in person.'"

Laura laughed. "As long as you're hiding out here, I don't think you have to worry about it." With a sigh, she leaned back on the decorative banister. "God, it's a beautiful night. Half-moon, starlight, the sound of the sea. A sky like that, it doesn't seem like anything bad could ever happen under it. This is a good house. Can you feel that, Kate? Margo and Josh's house. It's good."

"Excellent investment, prime location, excellent view." She smiled at Laura's bland stare. "Okay, yeah, I can feel it. It's a good house. It has heart and character. I like thinking of them here, together. Of them raising a family here."

Relaxed now, she leaned back with Laura. There was music drifting through the open doors and windows, the friendly sound of conversation, the tinkle of laughter. She could smell flowers, the sea, a mix of feminine perfumes, exotic tidbits being passed around on silver trays. And she could, simply by standing there, feel the permanence and the promise.

Like Templeton House, she mused, where she had spent so much of her life. Maybe that was why she had never been driven to make a home of her own, why an apartment convenient to work was all she'd wanted. Because, she thought with a faint smile, she could always go home to Templeton House. And now she could always come here as well.

"Oh, hello, Byron. I didn't know you were here."

At Laura's easy greeting Kate's pretty mood popped. She opened her eyes, straightened up from the banister and squared her shoulders. Something about Byron De Witt always made her feel confrontational.

"I just got here. I had some business that ran over. You look lovely, as always." He squeezed Laura's offered hand lightly before turning his gaze to Kate. The shadows were deep enough that she didn't notice his deep-green eyes widen slightly. But she did catch the quick, amused grin. "Nice to see you. Can I get either of you a fresh drink?"

"No, I have to get back inside." Laura stepped toward the terrace doors. "I promised Josh I'd charm Mr. and Mrs. Ito. We're in hot competition for their banquet business in Tokyo."

She was gone too quickly for Kate to scowl at her.

"Would you like another glass of champagne?"

Kate scowled down into her glass instead. It was still half full. "No, I'm fine."

Byron contented himself by lighting a thin cigar. He knew Kate's pride wouldn't permit her to bolt. Normally, he wouldn't have stayed with her any longer than manners dictated, but at the moment he was a little tired of people and understood that ten minutes with her would be more interesting than an hour with the party crowd. Especially if he could irritate her, as he seemed so skilled at doing.

"That's quite a dress, Katherine."

She bristled, as he'd expected, at his use of her full name. Grinning around the cigar, he leaned back and prepared to enjoy the diversion.

"I lost a bet," she said between her teeth.

"Really?" He reached out to toy with and tug up the thin strap that had slid off her shoulder. "Some bet."

"Hands off," she snapped.

"Fine." Deliberately he moved the strap down again so that she was forced to pull it up. "You've got a good eye for real estate," he commented and nodded at the surroundings when she frowned at him. "You steered Josh and Margo to this place, didn't you?"

"Yeah." She watched him, waited, but he seemed content to puff on his cigar and study the view.

He was just the type she'd decided to dislike. Poster-boy gorgeous, she termed it derisively. Thick brown hair that showed hints and streaks of gold waved with careless attraction around a heart-stopping face. What would have been charming dimples in his youth had deepened to creases in his cheeks that were now designed to incite a woman's sexual fantasies. The firm, hero's chin, the straight, aristocrat's nose, and those dark, dark green eyes that could, at his whim, slide over you as if you were invisible or pin you shuddering to the wall.

Six two, she judged, with the long limbs and strong shoulders of a long-distance runner. And of course, that voice, with its faint, misty drawl that hinted of hot summer nights and southern comfort.

Men like him, Kate had decided, were not ever to be trusted.

"That's new," he murmured.

Caught staring and appraising as his sharp green eyes shifted to hers, Kate looked quickly away. "What?"

"That scent you're wearing. It suits you better than the soap and talc you seem so fond of. Straight up sexy," he continued, smiling when she gaped at him. "No games, no illusions."

She'd known him for months, ever since he had transferred from Atlanta to Monterey to take over Peter Ridgeway's position at Templeton. He was, by all accounts, a savvy, experienced, and creative hotelier, one who had worked his way to the top of the Templeton organization over a period of fourteen years.

She knew he came from money, polite southern wealth, steeped in tradition and chivalry.

She had disliked him on sight and had been confident, despite his unflagging manners, that her feelings were reciprocated.

"Are you coming on to me?"

His eyes, still on hers, filled with humor. "I was commenting on your perfume, Katherine. If I were coming on to you, you wouldn't have to clarify."

She tossed back the rest of her wine. A mistake, she knew, with a migraine lurking. "Don't call me Katherine."

"That always seems to slip my mind."

"Like hell."

"Exactly. And if I were to tell you you're looking particularly attractive tonight, that would be an observation, not an overture. Anyway . . . Kate. We were discussing real estate."

She continued to scowl. Even Margo's favored Cristal champagne didn't sit well on a nervous stomach. "We were?"

"Or were about to. I'm considering buying a home in the area. Since my six-month trial period is almost over—"

"You had a trial period?" It cheered her considerably to picture him on probation at Templeton California.

"I had six months to decide if I wanted to be based here permanently or go back to Atlanta." Reading her mind easily, he grinned. "I like it here— the sea, the cliffs, the forests. I like the people I work with. But I don't intend to continue to live in a hotel, however well run and lovely it may be."

She shrugged, irritated by the way the wine seemed to be sitting like lead under her breastbone. "Your business, De Witt, not mine."

He would not, he told himself patiently, allow her prickly nature to divert him from his objective. "You know the area, you have contacts and a good eye for quality and value. I thought you could let me know if you hear about any interesting property, particularly in the Seventeen Mile Drive area."

"I'm not a Realtor," she muttered.

"Good. That means I don't have to worry about your commission."

Because she appreciated that, she bent. "There is a place—might be a little big for your needs."

"I like big."

"Figures. It's near Pebble Beach. Four or five bedrooms, I can't remember. But it's back off the road, a lot of cypress trees and a nice established yard. Decks," she continued, squinting her eyes as she tried to remember. "Front and back. Wood—cedar, I think. Lots of glass. It's been on the market about six months and hasn't moved. There's probably a reason for that."

"Might be it was waiting for the right buyer. Do you know the Realtor?"

"Sure, they're a client. Monterey Bay Real Estate. Ask for Arlene. She shoots straight."

"I appreciate it. If it works out, I'll have to buy you dinner."

"No, thanks. Just consider it a—" She broke off as pain stabbed into her stomach, then, like a sick echo, erupted in her head. The glass slipped out of her hand and shattered on the tile even as he grabbed her.

"Hold on." He picked her up, had a moment to notice she was little more than bones and nerves, before he eased her onto the cushions of a chair. "Jesus Christ, Kate, you're dead white. I'll get someone."

"No." Biting back on the pain, she grabbed at his arm. "It's nothing. Just a twinge. Sometimes alcohol—wine on an empty stomach," she managed, regulating her breathing. "I should know better."

His brow knit, his voice thrummed with impatience. "When did you eat last?"

"I was kind of swamped today."

"Idiot." He straightened. "There's enough food around here for three hundred starving sailors. I'll get you a damn plate."

"No, I—" Ordinarily that vicious look wouldn't have quelled her, but at the moment she was feeling shaky. "Okay, thanks, but don't say anything. It'll only worry them, and they've got all these people here. Just don't say anything," she repeated, then watched him, after one last, smoldering look, stride off.

Her hand trembled a bit as she opened her bag and swigged from a small medicine bottle. All right, she promised herself, she would take better care of herself. She'd start trying those yoga exercises Margo had shown her. She'd stop drinking so much damn coffee.

She would stop thinking.

By the time he came back she was feeling steadier. One look at the plate he carried and she let out a laugh. "How many of those starving sailors do you intend to feed?"

"Just eat," he ordered and popped a small, succulent shrimp into her mouth himself.

After a moment's deliberation, she scooted over on the cushion. A distraction, even in the form of Byron De Witt, was what she needed. "I guess I have to ask you to sit down and share."

"You're always so gracious."

She chose a tiny spinach quiche. "I just don't like you, De Witt."

"Fair enough." He dipped into some crab soufflé. "I don't like you either, but I was taught to be polite to a lady."

YET HE THOUGHT of her. Odder still, he dreamed of her, a fog-drenched, erotic dream he couldn't quite remember in the morning. Something about the cliffs and the crash of waves, the feel of soft skin and a slim body under his hands, those big, dark, Italian eyes staring into his.

It left him uncomfortably amused with himself.

Byron De Witt was sure of many things. The national debt would never be paid, women in thin cotton dresses were the best reason for summer, rock and roll was here to stay, and Katherine Powell was not his type.

Skinny, abrasive women with more attitude than charm didn't appeal to him. He liked them soft, and smart, and sexy. He admired them simply for being women and delighted in the bonuses of quiet conversation, hardheaded debate, outrageous laughter, and hot, mindless sex.

He considered himself as much of an expert on the female mystique as any man could be. After all, he'd grown up surrounded by them, the lone son in a household with three daughters. Byron knew women, and knew them well. And he knew what he liked.

No, he wasn't remotely attracted to Kate.

STILL, THE DREAM nagged at him as he prepared for the day. It followed him into the executive weight room, tugged at the back of his mind as he pushed himself through reps and sets and pyramids. It lingered while he finished off his routine with twenty minutes of the *Wall Street Journal* and the treadmill.

He struggled to think of something else. The house he intended to buy. Something close to the beach so that he could run on the sand, in the sun instead of on a mechanical loop. Rooms of his own, he mused, done to his own taste. A place where he could mow his grass, turn his music up to earsplitting levels, entertain company, or enjoy a quiet, private evening.

There had been few quiet, private evenings in his childhood. Not that he regretted the noise, the crowds he had grown up with. He adored his sisters, had tolerated their ever-increasing hordes of friends. He loved his parents and had always considered their busy social and family life normal.

Indeed, it had been the uncertainty as to whether he could bear to be so far away from his childhood home and family that had made him put the six-month-trial-period clause into his agreement with Josh.

Though he did miss them, he'd realized he could be happy in California. He was nearly thirty-five, and he wanted his own place. He was the first De Witt to move out of Georgia in two generations. He was determined to make it the right move.

If nothing else, it would stop the not-so-subtle family pressure for him to settle down, marry, start a family. The distance would certainly make it difficult for his sisters to continually shove women they considered perfect for him under his nose.

He had yet to meet a woman who was perfect for him.

As he stepped into the shower back in his penthouse office suite, he thought of Kate again. She was definitely wrong.

If he'd dreamed about her, it was only because she'd been on his mind. Annoyed that she continued to be, Byron turned up the radio affixed to the tiles until Bonnie Raitt bellowed out the challenge to give them something to talk about.

He was merely concerned about her, he decided. She'd gone so pale, become so quickly and unexpectedly vulnerable. He'd always been a sucker for a damsel in distress.

Of course, she was an idiot for not taking care of herself. Health and fitness weren't an option in Byron's mind but a duty. The woman needed to learn to eat properly, cut back on the caffeine, exercise, build up some flesh, and jettison some of those jangling nerves.

She wasn't half bad when she lost the attitude, he decided, stepping out of the shower with Bonnie still blasting. She'd given him a decent lead on the kind of property he was interested in, and they'd even managed to have a reasonable conversation over a shared plate.

And she had looked . . . interesting in that excuse for a dress she'd been wearing. Not that he was interested, Byron assured himself as he lathered up to shave. But she had a certain gamine appeal when she wasn't scowling. Almost Audrey Hepburn-ish.

He swore when he nicked his chin with the razor, put the blame for his inattention directly on Kate's head. He didn't have time to analyze some bony, unfriendly numbers cruncher with a chip on her shoulder. He had hotels to run.

CHAPTER 4

KATE KNEW IT was a mistake even when she set up the appointment. It was, she admitted, like picking at a scab, ensuring that a wound would never heal cleanly. Her father's friend Steven Tydings was more than willing to meet her for lunch. She was, after all, his new CPA, and he'd told her he was a man who liked to keep his finger on the pulse of his finances.

She was sure she could work with him, do her job. Yet every time Kate had opened his file, she'd fought off a sick feeling in her stomach, flashback memories of her father. Bitter complaints about bills, about just missing that big break.

She had forgotten all of that, forged her memories of her parents more out of need, she realized now, than reality. Hers had not been a happy home, nor had it been a stable one. Though she had woven it as such in her dreams.

Now that it was impossible to pretend otherwise, she realized it was equally impossible not to probe, not to poke. Not to know.

She had nearly balked when Tydings insisted on meeting at Templeton Monterey. The dining room there was the best in the area, the view of the bay superb. None of the excuses that she came up with had changed his mind. So at twelve-thirty sharp, she sat across from him at a window seat with a chef's salad in front of her.

It didn't matter where she was, Kate told herself as she picked at her meal. Laura was working at Pretenses. If anyone recognized her and mentioned it, it would be a simple matter to tell Laura she'd been lunching with a client. It was, after all, true.

For the first half hour, Kate guided the conversation to business. Strictly business. Whatever the circumstances, his account was entitled to and would receive her best. And he was pleased, telling her so often as she constantly eased her dry throat by sipping Templeton mineral water.

"Your dad had a way with numbers too," Tydings told her. He was a toughly built, compact man in his middle fifties who beamed at her out of dark-brown eyes. Success sat as stylishly on him as his suit.

"Did he?" Kate murmured, staring down at Tydings's hands. Well-manicured, businessman's hands. No flash, but a simple gold band on his finger. Her father had liked flash—heavy gold watches, the small diamond ring he wore on his pinky. Why should she remember that now? "I don't remember."

"Well, you were just a little thing. But I'll tell you, Linc had a gift for numbers. He could run figures in his head. You'd have thought he had a calculator in there."

It was her opening, and she had to take it. "I don't understand how someone that good with numbers could make such an enormous mistake."

"He just wanted bigger things, Katie." Tydings sighed, eased back in his chair. "He had a run of bad luck."

"Bad luck?"

"Bad luck, and bad judgment," Tydings qualified. "The ball got away from him."

"Mr. Tydings, he embezzled funds. He was going to prison." She took a deep breath, braced herself. "Was money so important to him that he would steal, that he would risk everything he risked just to have it?"

"You have to see the whole picture, understand the frustrations, the ambitions . . . well, the dreams, Katie. Linc always felt he was overshadowed, outclassed by the Templeton branch of the family. No matter what he did, how hard he tried, he could never measure up. That was a hard pill for a man like him to swallow."

"Just what kind of a man was he that he would be so envious of someone else's success?"

"It wasn't like that, exactly." Obviously uncomfortable, Tydings shifted in his seat. "Linc had a powerful need to succeed, to be the best."

"Yes." She struggled against a shudder. Tydings might have been describing the daughter rather than the father. "I understand that."

"He just felt that if he could catch a break, just one break, he could build on it. Make something. He had the potential, the brains. He was a smart, hardworking man. A good friend. With a weakness for wanting more than he had. He wanted the best for you."

Tydings's smile spread again. "I remember the day you were born, Katie, how he stood there looking at you through the glass and making all these big plans for you. He wanted to give you everything, and it was hard for him to always settle for less."

She hadn't needed everything, Kate thought later when she sat alone at the table. She had only needed parents who loved her and loved each other. Now she would have to live knowing that what her father had loved most was his own ambition.

"Something wrong with your lunch?"

She glanced over, and the hand she had pressed protectively against her stomach fisted as Byron slid into the chair that Tydings had vacated. "Are you on dining room detail? I thought the brass stayed up in the lofty regions of the penthouse."

"Oh, we mingle with the lower floors occasionally." He signaled to a waitress. He'd been watching Kate for ten minutes. She had sat completely still, staring out of the window, her meal untouched, her eyes dark and miserable. "The chicken bisque," he ordered. "Two."

"I don't want anything."

"I hate to eat alone," he said smoothly, as the waitress cleared the dishes. "You can always play with it like you did your salad. If you're not feeling well, the bisque should perk you up."

"I'm fine. I had a business lunch." Under the table she pleated her napkin in her lap. She wasn't ready to get up, wasn't sure her legs were strong enough. "Who eats at business lunches?"

"Everyone." Leaning forward, he poured two glasses of mineral water. "You look unhappy."

"I have a client with an imbalance of passive income. That always makes me unhappy. What do you want, De Witt?"

"A bowl of soup, a little conversation. You know, I developed this hobby of conversation as a child. I've never been able to break it. Thank you, Lorna," he said when the waitress set a basket of warm rolls between them. "I've noticed that you often have a bit of trouble in that area. I'd be happy to help you, as I'm sort of a buff."

"I don't like small talk."

"There you are. I do." He held out a roll he'd broken apart and buttered. "In fact, I'm interested in all manner of talk. Large, small, meaningless, profound. Why don't we start this particular session with me telling you that I've got an appointment to view that house you recommended."

"Good for you." Since the bread was in her hand now, she nibbled.

"The Realtor speaks highly of you." When Kate only grunted, then scowled down at the bowl of soup that was slipped under her nose, Byron smothered a grin. Damned if she wasn't too much of a challenge to resist. "I may just solicit your services myself, as I'll be staying in Monterey. Hardly practical to keep my accountant back in Georgia."

"It's not necessary to have an accountant in the same location. If you're satisfied with his or her work, there's no need to change."

"That's the way to drum up business, kid. I also have a habit of eating," he continued. "If you need help along those lines, I can tell you that you start by dipping your spoon into the soup."

"I'm not hungry."

"Think of it as medicine. It might put some color back in your cheeks. You not only look unhappy, Kate, you look tired, beaten down, and closing in on ill."

Hoping it would shut him up, she spooned up some soup. "Boy, now I'm all perked up. It's a miracle."

When he only smiled at her, she sighed. Why did he have to sit there, acting so damn nice and making her feel like sludge?

"I'm sorry. I'm lousy company."

"Was your business meeting difficult?"

"Yes, as a matter of fact." Because it was soothing, she sampled the bisque again. "I'll deal with it."

"Why don't you tell me what you do when you're not dealing with difficult business problems?"

The headache at the edges of her consciousness wasn't backing off, but it wasn't creeping closer. "I deal with simple business problems."

"And when you're not dealing with business?"

She studied him narrowly, the mild, polite eyes, the easy smile. "You *are* coming on to me."

"No, I'm considering coming on to you, which is entirely different. That's why we're having a basic conversation over a bowl of soup." His smile widened, flirted. "It also gives you equal opportunity to consider whether or not you'd like to come on to me."

Her lips twitched before she could stop them. "I do appreciate a man who believes in gender equality." She also had to appreciate that for a few minutes he'd taken her mind off her troubles. That he knew it, yet didn't push the point.

"I think I'm beginning to like you, Kate. You are, I believe, an acquired taste, and I've always enjoyed odd flavors."

"That's quite a statement. My heart's going pitty-pat."

He laughed, a quick, full-throated, masculine sound that appealed, however much she would have preferred otherwise.

"Yeah, it's definite. I like you. Why don't we expand this conversation thing over a full meal? Say, dinner. Tonight?"

She was tempted to agree, for the simple reason that being around him made her think about something other than herself. But . . . She set her napkin beside her bowl. She thought it would be best to err on the side of caution with a man like Byron De Witt. "I don't want to form habits too quickly. I have to get back to the office."

She rose, amused when he automatically got to his feet. Gender equality or not, she decided, he was southern gentleman through and through. "Thanks for the soup."

"You're welcome." He took her hand, held it lightly and enjoyed the faint line that popped up between her brows. "Thanks for the conversation. We will have to do it again."

"Hmm," was her best response as she slid the strap of her briefcase over her shoulder and walked away.

He watched her go and wondered what problem, business or otherwise, had made her look so devastated. And so alone.

THE RUMOR MILL was working overtime at Bittle and Associates. Every tiny, underripe fruit plucked from the grapevine was chewed lavishly at the water cooler, the copy room, the storage closet.

Larry Bittle and his sons, Lawrence Junior and Martin—just call me Marty—continued their closed-door meetings with the other partners every morning. Copies of accounts were delivered regularly to the group by Bittle Senior's tight-lipped, sharp-eyed executive assistant.

If she knew anything, went the wisdom of the water cooler, she wasn't saying.

"They're working their way through every account," Roger told Kate. He'd hunted her down in the stockroom when she went to replenish her supply of computer paper. "Marcie in Accounts Receivable said they're even going over internal ledgers. And Beth, the Dragon Lady's assistant, says they've been on the hot line with the lawyers."

Lips pursed, Kate grabbed a handful of Ticonderoga number 2's. "Are all your sources female?"

He grinned. "No, but Mike in the mail room is coming up dry. What's your take?"

"Gotta figure internal audit."

"Yeah, that's mine. But here's the question, Kate. Why?"

In truth, that very question had been on her mind for days. She considered. Smart, ambitious, ruthless people had the best gossip. Since Roger fit all the requirements, she decided to share her thoughts in hopes of priming his pump.

"Okay, we've had a couple of really good years. In the past five we've increased our client base by fifteen percent. Bittle's growing, so I'm thinking expansion, maybe a new branch. They'd put Lawrence in charge, add more associates, and give some of us the option of relocating. A big step like that would take a lot of thought and planning, and the partners would want to focus hard on the bottom line."

"Could be. There's been noises before about opening in the L.A. area, snagging more media accounts. But I've been hearing other grumblings, too." He leaned closer, lowered his voice, and his eyes were bright with excitement. "Larry's been thinking about passing the torch. Retiring."

"Why would he?" Kate whispered in response. They sounded like conspirators. "He's only sixty."

"Sixty-two." Roger glanced over his shoulder. "And you know how his wife likes those cruises. She's always bugging him to take one to Europe, around the Med, that sort of thing."

"How do you know that?"

"Beth. Assistant to the assistant. She got brochures for the old man. The Bittles' fortieth anniversary is coming up this year. If he retires early, there's going to be a partnership slot up for grabs."

"A new partner." It made sense. Perfect sense. All the meetings, the account checks. The current partners would have to weigh and judge, debate and discuss who would be most qualified to move up. She barely stopped herself from dancing a jig. She had to remember who it was she was talking to. Roger was her toughest competitor.

"Maybe." She shrugged, though inside, glee was spreading like a lovely pink balloon. "But I don't see Larry sailing off into the sunset yet. No matter how much his wife nags him."

"We'll see." Roger kept a sly smile on his face. "But something's going to happen, and it's going to happen soon."

Kate walked sedately back to her office, closed the door, put her supplies neatly away. Then she danced her jig.

She didn't want to get ahead of herself, didn't want to start projecting. The hell she didn't. Dropping into her chair, she spun herself around once, twice, and a giddy third time.

She had an MBA from Harvard, had graduated in the top ten percent of her class. In the five years she'd worked for Bittle, she had brought in twelve new accounts through client recommendations. And had lost only one. To that jerk Roger.

But even that hadn't gone out of house. She personally generated over two hundred thousand a year in billing. So did Roger, she admitted. She kept an eye on him. But when Marty had awarded her a raise last year, he'd told her she was considered the cream of Bittle's associates. Larry Bittle called her by her first name, and his wife and daughters-in-law had been known to drop by Pretenses to shop.

A partnership. At twenty-eight, she would be the youngest partner ever at Bittle. She would have exceeded by years her own rigid expectations of herself.

And wouldn't it, in some way, erase this taint she felt? This secret she had buried inside. If she was a success, it would overshadow all the rest.

She allowed herself to dream about it—the new office, the new salary, the new prestige. She would be consulted on policy, her opinion would be weighed and respected. Giggling, she leaned back in the chair and spun again. She would have a private secretary.

She would have everything she'd ever wanted.

Kate imagined picking up the phone, calling the Templetons in Cannes. They'd be so happy for her, so proud of her. Finally, she would be able to believe that everything they'd done for her was deserved.

She'd have a celebration with Margo and Laura. Oh, that would be sweet. At long last Kate Powell had come into her own, had done something important and solid. Years and years of work and study, of aching shoulders, tired eyes, and a burning stomach would have paid off.

All she had to do was wait.

Forcing herself to push the dream to the back of her mind, she swiveled to her computer and got to work.

She hummed as she ran figures, calculated expenditures, logged tax deductions, clucked over capital gains, and figured depreciation. As usual, she tuned in to the work and lost track of time. Kate came up blinking when the beep from her watch told her it was five o'clock.

Another fifteen minutes to close the file, she decided, then glanced up in mild annoyance at the knock on her door. "Yes?"

"Ms. Powell." Lucinda Newman—or the Dragon Lady, as she was unaffectionately called among the rank and file—stood imposingly in the doorway. "You're wanted in the main conference room."

"Oh." Kate's heart gave a wild, joyful leap, but she kept her face composed. "Thanks, Ms. Newman. I'll be right there."

Well aware that her hands were trembling with anticipation, Kate pressed them together in her lap. She had to be cool and professional. Bittle wasn't going to offer a partnership to a giddy, giggling woman.

She had to be what she always was, what they expected her to be. Practical, levelheaded. And, oh, she was going to savor the moment, remember every detail. Later, when she was out of sight and earshot, she would scream all the way to Templeton House.

Kate rolled down her sleeves, shrugged into her jacket, and smoothed it into place. She hesitated over taking her briefcase, then decided it only made her look more dedicated to the job.

With measured steps she took the stairs to the next floor, walked past the partners' offices toward the executive conference room. No one who chanced to see her in the quiet corridor would have realized her feet weren't touching the tasteful tan carpet. She thumbed an antacid out of the roll in her pocket, knowing it would do little to calm her jittery stomach.

She wondered if a bride on her wedding night could feel any more nervous and thrilled than she did as she raised a hand to knock politely on the thick paneled door.

"Come in."

She lifted her chin, put a polite smile on her face as she turned the knob. They were all there, and her heart gave another skipping leap. All the partners, the five powers of the firm, were seated around the long, glossy table. Large tumblers of water stood by each place.

She skimmed her gaze over each of them, wanting to remember this moment. Fusty Calvin Meyers with his usual suspenders and red bow tie. Elegant and terrifying Amanda Devin, looking stern and beautiful. Marty, of course, sweet and homely and rumpled. Lawrence Junior, steady, balding, and cool.

And of course, the senior Bittle. She had always thought he looked like Spencer Tracy—that lived-in face, the sweep of white hair, the stocky, powerful little body.

Her pulse bumped, aware that all eyes were on her.

"You wanted to see me?"

"Sit down, Kate." From his seat at the head of the table, Bittle gestured to one at the foot.

"Yes, sir."

He cleared his throat as she took her chair, settled. "We thought it best to meet at the end of the workday. You're aware, I'm sure, that we've been involved for the past several days in a check of our accounts."

"Yes, sir." She smiled. "Speculation's been racing down the corridors." When he didn't smile back, she felt a nervous tickle at the back of her throat. "It's hard not to get on the rumor train, sir."

"Yes." He let out a breath, folded his hands. "A discrepancy in an income tax payment came to Mr. Bittle Junior's attention last week."

"A discrepancy?" Her gaze shifted to Lawrence.

"In the Sunstream account," he clarified.

"That's one of mine." The nervous tickle at the back of her throat changed to a nervous dread in her stomach. Had she made some sort of stupid error in the chaos of the tax crunch? "What kind of discrepancy?"

"The client's copy of the tax form indicates a federal payment due of seven thousand six hundred and forty-eight dollars." Lawrence opened a file, took out a thick stack of papers. "Is this your work, Ms. Powell?"

He was the only Bittle who called her Ms. Powell. Everyone in the firm was accustomed to his formality. But it was the clipped manner of his speech that put her on alert. Carefully she took out her glasses and slipped them on as the papers were passed down to her.

"Yes," she said after a quick glance. "It's my account, I did the tax work. This is my signature."

"And as with several of our clients, the firm cuts the checks for tax payments for this one."

"Some prefer it." She dropped her hands into her lap. "It distances them, a bit, from the sting. And it's more convenient."

"Convenient," Amanda commented and drew Kate's eye. "For whom?"

This was trouble, was all Kate could think. But from what and where? "Many clients prefer to come into the office, discuss the tax situation and the results—argue and vent." They all knew this, she thought, scanning the table again. Why did she have to explain? "The client will sign the necessary forms and the account exec will issue the check out of escrow."

"Ms. Powell." Lawrence took another stack of papers from his file. "Can you explain this?"

As smoothly as possible, Kate wiped her damp palms on her skirt, then studied the forms passed to her. Her mind went momentarily blank. She blinked, focused, swallowed hard.

"I'm not sure I understand. This is another copy of the 1040 filed for Sunstream, but the tax due amount is different."

"Twenty-two hundred dollars less," Amanda pointed out. "This is the form and the payment made on April fifteenth of this year to the IRS. The check drawn out of escrow was for this amount."

"I don't understand when or how the other copy was generated," Kate began. "All work sheets are filed, of course, but any excess forms are shredded."

"Kate." Bittle drew her attention with one quiet word. "The excess money was transferred via computer out of the client's escrow account in cash."

"In cash," she repeated, blank.

"Since this came to our attention, we initiated a check on all accounts." Bittle's face was grave as he watched her. "Since late March of this year, amounts that total seventy-five thousand dollars have been withdrawn from escrow accounts, seventy-five thousand in excess of tax payments. Computer withdrawals, in cash, from your accounts."

"From my clients?" She felt the blood drain out of her face, couldn't stop it.

"It's the same pattern." Calvin Meyers spoke for the first time, tugging on his bright red tie. "Two copies of the 1040s, small adjustments on various forms, to total excess on the client's copy in amounts ranging from twelve hundred to thirty-one hundred dollars." He puffed out his cheeks. "We might not have caught it, but I golf with Sid Sun. He's a whiner about taxes and kept after me to look over his form and be certain there was nothing else he could use to cut his payment."

Embezzlement. Were they accusing her of embezzlement? Was this some awful nightmare? They knew about her father and thought . . . no, no, that was impossible. While her hand flexed nervously in her lap, she kept her voice even.

"You examined one of my accounts?"

Calvin lifted an eyebrow. The last thing he'd expected from steady-as-she-goes Kate Powell was blank-eyed panic. "I did so to get him off my back, and in examining his copy, I found several small errors. I thought it best to look further and pulled out our file copy of his latest return."

She couldn't feel anything. Even her fingertips had gone numb. "You think I stole seventy-five thousand dollars from my clients. From this firm."

"Kate, if you could just explain how you think this might have happened," Marty began. "We're all here to listen."

No, her father had stolen from clients. Her father. Not her. "How could you think it?" Her voice shook, shamed her.

"We haven't come to any firm conclusion," Amanda countered. "The facts, the numbers, however, are here, in black and white."

Black and white, she thought as the print blurred, as it overlapped with visions of newspaper articles from twenty years past. "No, I—" She had to lift a hand, rub her eyes to clear them. "It's not. I didn't."

Amanda tapped one scarlet nail on the tabletop. She'd expected outrage, had counted on the outrage of the innocent. Instead, what she saw was the trembling of the guilty.

"If Marty hadn't gone to bat for you, if he hadn't insisted we search for some rational explanation, even incompetence on your part, we would have had this meeting days ago."

"Amanda," Bittle said quietly, but she shook her head.

"Larry, this is embezzlement, and over and above the legal ramifications, client trust and confidence have to be considered. We need to clear this matter up quickly."

"I've never taken a penny, not a penny from any client." Though terrified that her legs would buckle, Kate shot to her feet. She would not be sick, she told herself, though her stomach was heaving into her throat. "I couldn't." It seemed to be all she could say. "I couldn't."

Lawrence frowned at his hands. "Ms. Powell, money is easily hidden, laundered, spent. You've assisted a number of clients in investments, accounts in the Caymans, in Switzerland."

Investments. Bad investments. She pressed a hand to her throbbing temple. No, that had been her father. "That's my job. I do my job."

"You recently opened a business," Calvin pointed out.

"I'm a one-third partner in a secondhand boutique." Grief and fear and nausea swirled inside her, made her hands shake. She had to be coherent, she ordered herself. Shaking and weeping only made her look guilty. "It took almost all my savings to do it."

She drew in a breath that burned, stared straight into Bittle's eyes. "Mr. Bittle—" But her voice broke, and she had to begin again. "Mr. Bittle, I've worked for you for five years. You hired me a week out of graduate school. I've never given this firm anything but my complete loyalty and dedication, and I've never given a client anything but my best. I'm not a thief."

"I find it difficult to believe you are, Kate. I've known you since you were a child and always considered my decision to hire you one of my best judgment calls. I know your family."

He paused, waiting for her to rebound, to express her fury at being used. To demand to assist the firm in finding the answers. When she did nothing but stare blindly, he had no choice.

"However," he said slowly, "this matter can't be ignored. We'll continue to investigate, internally for now. It may become necessary to go outside the firm with this."

"To the police." The thought of it dissolved her legs so that she had to brace herself with a hand on the table. Her vision grayed and wavered. "You're going to the police."

"If it becomes necessary," Bittle told her. "We hope to resolve the matter quietly. Bittle and Associates is responsible, at this point, for adjusting the escrow accounts." Bittle studied the woman standing at the end of the table, shook his head. "The partners have agreed that it is in the firm's best interest for you to take a leave of absence until this is cleared up."

"You're suspending me because you think I'm a thief."

"Kate, we need to look into this carefully. And we have to do whatever is in the best interest of our clients."

"A suspected embezzler can't handle accounts." The tears were going to come, but not yet. She could hold them back just a little longer. "You're firing me."

"A leave of absence," Bittle repeated.

"It's the same thing." Accusations, disgrace. "You don't believe me. You think I've stolen from my own clients and you want me out of the office."

He saw no other choice. "At this time, yes. Any personal items in your office will be sent to you. I'm sorry, Kate. Marty will escort you out of the building."

She let out a shuddering breath. "I haven't done anything but my best." Picking up her briefcase, she turned stiffly and walked to the door.

"I'm sorry. Christ, Kate." With his lumbering stride, Marty caught up with her. "What a mess, what a disaster." He started huffing when she took the stairs down to the main level. "I couldn't turn them around."

She stopped, ignoring the pain in her stomach, the throbbing in her head. "Do you believe me? Marty, do you believe me?"

She saw the flicker of doubt in his earnest, myopic eyes before he answered. "I know there's an explanation." He touched her gently on the shoulder.

"It's all right." She made herself push through the glass doors on the lobby level, walk outside.

"Kate, if there's anything I can do for you, any way I can help . . ." He trailed off lamely, standing by the door as she all but ran to her car.

"Nothing," she said to herself. "There's just nothing."

AT THE LAST minute she stopped herself from running to Templeton House. To Laura, to Annie, to anyone who would fold her in comforting arms and take her side. She swung her car to the side of the road rather than up the steep, winding drive. She got out and walked to the cliffs.

She could stand alone, she promised herself. She had had shocks, survived tragedies before. She'd lost her parents, and there was nothing more devastating than that.

There had been boys she'd dreamed over in high school who had never dreamed back. She'd gotten over it. Her first lover, in college, had grown bored with her, broken her heart and moved on. She hadn't crumbled.

Once, years before, she had fantasized about finding Seraphina's dowry all alone, of bearing it proudly home to her aunt and uncle. She had learned to live without that triumph.

She was afraid. She was so afraid.

Like father, like daughter. Oh, dear God, would it come out now? Would it all come out? And how much more damning then? What would this do to the people who loved her, who had had such hopes for her?

What was it people said? Blood will tell. Had she done something, made some ridiculous mistake? Christ, how could she think clearly now when her life had been turned upside down and shattered at her feet?

She had to wrap her arms tight around her body against the spring breeze, which now seemed frigid.

She'd committed no crime, she reminded herself. She'd done nothing wrong. All she'd done was lose a job. Just a job.

It had nothing to do with the past, nothing to do with blood, nothing to do with where she had come from.

With a whimper, she eased down onto a rock. Who was she trying to fool? Somehow it had to do with everything. How could it not? She'd lost what she had taught herself to value most next to family. Success and reputation.

Now she was exactly what she'd always been afraid she was. A failure.

How could she face them, any of them, with the fact that she'd been fired, was under suspicion of embezzling? That she had, as she always advised her clients not to, put all of her eggs in one basket, only to see it smashed.

But she would have to face them. She had to tell her family before someone else did. Oh, and someone would. It wouldn't take long. She didn't have the luxury of digging a hole and hiding in it. Everything she was and did was attached to the Templetons.

What would her aunt and uncle think? They would have to see the parallel. If they doubted her . . . She could stand anything, anything at all except their doubt and disappointment.

She reached in her pocket, chewed viciously on a Tums, and wished for a bottle of aspirin—or some of the handy tranqs Margo had once used. To think she'd once been so disdainful of those little crutches. To think she had once considered Seraphina a fool and a coward for choosing to leap rather than stay and face her loss.

She looked out to sea, then rose and walked closer to the edge. The rocks below were mean. That was what she'd always liked best about them, those jagged, unforgiving spears standing up defiantly to the constant, violent crash of water.

She had to be like the rocks now, she thought. She had to stand and face whatever happened next.

Her father hadn't been strong. He hadn't stood, he hadn't faced it. And now, in some twisted way, she was paying the price.

BYRON STUDIED HER from the side of the road. He'd seen her car whiz past as he was leaving Josh's house. He wasn't sure what impulse had pushed him to follow her, still wasn't sure what was making him stay.

There was something about the way she looked, standing there at the edge of the cliff, so alone. It made him nervous, and a little annoyed. That vulnerability again, he supposed, a quiet neediness that called to his protective side.

He wouldn't have pegged her as the type to walk the cliffs or stare out to sea.

He nearly got back into his car and drove off. But he shrugged and decided that since he was here, he'd might as well enjoy the view.

"Hell of a spot," he said as he walked up to her. It gave him perverse pleasure to see her jolt.

"I was enjoying it," she muttered and kept her back to him.

"Plenty of view for two to enjoy. I saw your car, and . . ." When he got a look at her, he saw that her eyes were damp. He'd always been compelled to dry a woman's tears. "Bad day?" he murmured and offered her a handkerchief.

"It's just windy."

"Not that windy."

"I wish you'd go away."

"Ordinarily I try to comply with women's requests. Since I'm not going to in your case, why don't you sit down, tell me about it?" He took her arm, thinking the tension in it was edgy enough to cut glass. "Think of me as a priest," he suggested, dragging her with him. "I wanted to be one once."

"To use some clever phrasing, bullshit."

"No, really." He pulled her down on a rock with him. "I was eleven. Then puberty hit, and the rest is history."

She tried and failed to tug free and rise. "Did it ever occur to you that I don't want to talk to you? That I want to be alone?"

To soothe, because her voice was catching helplessly, he stroked a hand over her hair. "It crossed my mind, but I rejected it. People who feel sorry for themselves always want to talk about it. That, next to sex, was the main reason I decided against the seminary. And dancing. Priests don't get lots of opportunity to dance with pretty women—which, I suppose, is the same thing as sex. Well, enough about me."

He put a determined hand under her chin and lifted it. She was pale, those long, spiky lashes were wet and those deep, doe's eyes damp. But . . .

"Your eyes aren't red enough for you to have had a good cry yet."

"I'm not a sniveler."

"Listen, kid, my sister highly recommends a good cry, and she'd deck you for calling her a sniveler." Gently, he rubbed his thumb over Kate's chin. "Screaming's good, too, and throwing breakables. There was a lot of that in my house."

"There's no point—"

"Venting," he interrupted smoothly. "Purging. There aren't any breakables around here, but you could let out a good scream."

Emotions welling up inside her threatened to choke her. Furiously she jerked her face free of his hand. "I don't need you or anyone to charm me out of a mood. I can handle my own problems just fine. If I need a friend, all I have to do is go up to the house. Up to the house," she repeated as her gaze focused on the towering structure of stone and wood and glass that held everything precious to her.

Covering her face with her hands, she broke.

"That's a girl," he murmured, relieved by the natural flow of tears. "Come here now." He drew her close, stroking her hair, her back. "Get it all out."

She couldn't stop. It didn't matter who he was, his arms were strong, his voice understanding. With her face buried against his chest, she sobbed out the frustration, the grief, the fear, let herself for one liberating moment be coddled.

He rested his cheek on her hair, held her lightly. Lightly because she seemed so small, so fragile. A good grip might shatter those thin bones. Tears soaked through his shirt, cooled from hot to cold on his skin.

"I'm sorry. Damn it." She would have pulled away, but he continued to hold her. Humiliated, she squeezed her aching eyes shut. "I never would have done that if you'd left me alone."

"You're better off this way. It's not healthy to hold everything in." Automatically, he kissed the top of her head before easing her back to study her face.

Why it should have charmed him, wet, blotchy, streaked with mascara as it was, he couldn't have said. But he had a terrible urge to shift her onto his lap, to kiss that soft, sad mouth, to stroke her again, not quite so consolingly.

Bad move, he cautioned himself, and wondered how any man faced with such sexy distress could think like a priest.

"Not that you look better." He took the handkerchief she'd balled up in her fist and mopped at her face. "But you should feel better enough to tell me why you're so upset."

"It has nothing to do with you."

"So what?"

She could feel another sob bubbling in her chest and blurted out the words before it could escape. "I got fired."

He continued calmly cleaning and drying her face. "Why?"

"They think—" Her voice hitched. "They think I—"

"Take a breath," he advised, "and say it fast."

"They think I stole money out of client escrow. Embezzled. Seventy-five thousand."

Watching her face, he stuck the ruined linen back in his pocket. "Why?"

"Because—because there are duplicate 1040s, and money missing. And they're my clients."

And my father—my father. But she couldn't say that, not out loud.

In fits and starts she babbled out the gist of her meeting with the partners. A great deal of it was incoherent, details crisscrossing and overlapping, but he continued to nod. And listen.

"I didn't take any money." She let out a long, unsteady breath. "I don't expect you to believe me, but—"

"Of course I believe you."

It was her turn to gather her wits. "Why?"

Leaning back a little, he took out a cigar, shielding the flame on his lighter with a cupped hand. "In my line of work, you get a handle on people quickly. You've been around the hotel business most of your life. You know how it is. There are plenty of times with a guest, or staff, that you have to make a snap judgment. You'd better be accurate." Puffing out smoke, he studied her. "My take on you, Katherine, in the first five minutes, was—well, among other things—that you're the type of woman who would choke on her integrity before she loosened it to breathe."

Her breath came out shaky, but some of the panic eased. "I appreciate it. I think."

"I'd have to say you worked for a bunch of shortsighted idiots."

She sniffled. "They're accountants."

"There you go." He smiled, ran a finger down her cheek when she glared. "A flash there in those big brown eyes. That's better. So, are you going to take it lying down?"

Rising, she straightened her shoulders. "I can't think about how or what I can take now. I only know I wouldn't work at Bittle again if they came crawling on their hands and knees through broken glass."

"That's not what I meant. I meant someone's embezzling and pointing the finger at you. What are you going to do about it?"

"I don't care."

"You don't care?" He shook his head. "I find that hard to believe. The Katherine Powell I've seen is a scrapper."

"I said I don't care." And her voice hitched again. If she fought, looked too close, demanded too much, they might uncover what her father had done. Then it would be worse. "There's nothing I can do."

"You've got a brain," he corrected.

"It doesn't feel like it at the moment." She put a hand to her head. Everything inside was mushy and aching. "They can't do anything else to me because I don't have the money, and they'd never be able to prove I do. As far as I'm concerned right now, finding who's skimming is Bittle's problem. I just want to be left alone."

Surprised at her, he stood up. "I'd want their ass."

"Right now, I just want to be able to get through the next few hours. I have to tell my family." She closed her eyes. "Earlier today, I actually thought, hoped, that I was going to be called in and offered a partnership. Signs indicated," she said bitterly. "I couldn't wait to tell them."

"Brag?" But he said it gently, with hardly any sting.

"I suppose. 'Look at what I did. Be proud of me because . . . ' Well, that's done. Now I have to tell them that I lost it all, that the prospects of getting another position or finessing any clients are nil for the foreseeable future."

"They're family." He stepped toward her and laid his hands on her shoulders. "Families stand by each other."

"I know that." For a moment, she wanted to take his hand. He had such big, competent hands. She wanted to take it and press it to her cheek. Instead she stepped back, turned away. "That makes it worse. I can't begin to tell you how much worse. Now, I'm feeling sorry for myself all over again."

"It comes and goes, Kate." Well aware that they were doing a little dance and dodge of physical contact, he draped an arm around her shoulders. "Do you want me to go up with you?"

"No." She was appalled, because for an instant she'd wanted to say yes. To lean her head against that broad shoulder, close her eyes, and let him lead. "No, I have to do it." She slipped away from him again, but faced him. "This was awfully nice of you. Really. Nice."

He smiled, his dimples deepening. "That wouldn't have been insulting if you hadn't sounded quite so surprised."

"I didn't mean to be insulting." She managed a smile of her own. "I meant to be grateful. I am grateful . . . Father De Witt."

Testing, he lifted a hand, skimmed his fingers through her short cap of hair. "I decided I don't want you to think of me as a priest after all." His hand slid down the back of her neck. "It's that sex thing again."

She felt it herself—inconvenient little hormonal tugs. "Hmm." It seemed as good a response as any. And certainly safe. "I'd better go get this done." Eyes warily on his, she backed up. "I'll see you around."

"Apparently you will." He stepped forward, she backed up again.

"What are you doing?"

Amused at both of them, he raised his eyebrows. "Going to my car. I'm parked behind you."

"Oh. Well." As casually as possible, she turned and walked to the car as he fell into step beside her. "I, ah, have you seen the house yet, the one on Seventeen Mile?"

"I have an appointment to view it tonight, as it happens."

"Good. That's good." She jangled her keys in her pocket before pulling them out. "Well, I hope you like it."

"I'll let you know." He closed a hand over hers on the door handle. When her gaze flew suspiciously to his, he smiled. "My daddy taught me to open doors for ladies. Consider it a southern thing."

She shrugged, slid into the car. "Well, 'bye."

"I'll be in touch."

She wanted to ask what that was supposed to mean, but he was already walking toward his own car. Besides, she had a pretty good idea.

CHAPTER 5

"IT'S OUTRAGEOUS. IT'S insulting."

In a rare show of temper, Laura stormed around the solarium. Thirty minutes before, Kate had interrupted homework time, and Laura had shifted from solving the mysteries of punctuation and multiplication tables with her daughters to the shock of hearing Kate's story.

Watching her friend, Kate was glad she'd had the presence of mind to ask to speak to Laura privately. The flash in the gray eyes, the angry flush staining those cool ivory cheeks, and the wild gestures might have frightened the children.

"I don't want you to be upset," Kate began.

"You don't want me to be upset?" Laura rounded on her, the curling swing of chin-length bronze hair flying, the soft, pretty mouth pulled back into a snarl. "Then what exactly should I be when my sister gets plugged between the eyes?"

Oh, yeah, Kate thought, this definitely would have given the girls a jolt. If she hadn't been so miserable, she would have laughed. Laura the Cool had metamorphosed into Laura the Enraged. Despite being five two, she looked capable of going ten rounds with the champ.

"Don't want me to be upset!" Laura repeated, her small, almost fairylike frame revving high as she stalked around the lush glass-walled room. "Well, I'm not upset. I'm past upset and heading beyond pissed. How dare they? How dare those pinheaded idiots think for one minute, for one instant, that you'd steal money?"

She slapped at the swaying fronds of a potted palm. "When I think how many times the Bittles have been guests in this house, it makes my blood boil. Treating you like a common criminal. Escorting you out of the building. I'm surprised they didn't bring out the cuffs and the SWAT team." Sun pouring through the glass walls glinted fiercely in her eyes. "Bastards, idiot bastards."

She pounced, all five feet two inches of raging fury, on the slim white phone beside the padded chaise. "We're calling Josh. We're suing them."

"Hold it. No, hold it, Laura." Torn between tears and laughter, Kate slapped a hand over her friend's. For the life of her, Kate couldn't remember why she'd hesitated to come here, to Templeton House. This was exactly what she'd needed to snap her back. "I can't tell you how much I appreciate the tirade, but—"

"You haven't begun to see a tirade."

"I've got nothing to sue them about. The evidence—"

"I don't give a fuck about evidence." At Kate's bubble of laughter, her eyes narrowed. "Just what the hell are you laughing at?"

"I'll never get used to hearing you say 'fuck.' It's just not natural." But she swallowed because the laugh had come perilously close to hysteria. "And seeing you storm around this elegant room with all the hibiscus and ferns is quite a show." She caught her breath. "I didn't come here to send you on a rampage, though it's doing wonders for my bruised ego."

"This isn't about ego." Laura struggled to get a grip on her temper. She lost it rarely because it was a powerful thing, a dangerous thing. "It's about defamation of character, loss of income. We're not going to let them get away with this, Kate. We've got a lawyer in the family, and we're going to use him."

There was no use in pointing out that Josh wasn't a litigator. She certainly wouldn't have told Laura that the very thought of pursuing the matter, particularly through the legal system, had her feeling nauseated again. Instead, she struggled to keep it light.

"Maybe we could have him tack on loss of consortium, just for kicks. I always liked that one."

"How can you joke?"

"Because you've made me feel so much better." Suddenly she felt like crying again, and hugged Laura tight instead. "I knew in my heart you'd stand behind me, but in my head, in my gut . . . I was just so shattered. Oh, God." She eased away to press a hand to her stomach. "I'm going to start again."

"Oh, Kate. Oh, honey, I'm so sorry." Gently now, Laura slipped a hand around her waist. "Let's sit down. We'll get some tea, some wine, some chocolate, and figure this out."

Kate sniffed back the tears, nodded. "Tea's good. Alcohol hasn't been agreeing with me lately." She managed a smile. "Chocolate never fails."

"Okay. Just sit right here." Normally she would have gone to the kitchen herself, but she didn't want to leave Kate alone. Instead she crossed the glossy fieldstone floor to the intercom by the doorway—the system Peter had insisted they install to summon the servants. After a few murmured instructions, she came back to Kate and sat down.

"I feel so useless," Kate said. "So stripped. I don't think I appreciated, really, how Margo must have felt last year when she had the rug pulled out from under her."

"You were there for her. Just like Margo and I, and everyone, will be here for you. Anyone who knows you won't believe you did anything wrong."

"Even one who doesn't," she murmured, thinking of Byron. "Still, plenty will believe it. It's going to get out, I can promise you that. I'm used to defending myself," she continued. "Skinny girls with more brains than charm tend to hide through high school, or fight through it."

"And you always fought."

"I'm out of practice." She closed her eyes and leaned back. The room smelled like a garden, she thought. Peaceful, calm. She badly needed to find calm again. "I don't know what I'm going to do, Laura. It's probably the first time in my life I don't have a plan." She opened her eyes again, met the concern in Laura's. "I know it's going to sound foolish, but everything I am and wanted to be was tied up in my career. I was good at it. More than good. I needed to be. I chose Bittle because it was an old, established firm, there was plenty of room and opportunity for advancement, because it was close to home. I liked the people there—and I don't like that many people. I felt comfortable and appreciated."

"You'd feel comfortable and appreciated at Templeton," Laura said quietly and took her hand. "You know there's no question that you could have a position there tomorrow. Mom and Dad wanted you in the organization."

With a taint on her, she thought, that stretched back a generation. No, that she would not ask. "They've done enough for me."

"Kate, that's ridiculous."

"Not to me. I can't go crawling to them now. I'd hate myself." It was the only thing she felt capable of standing firm on. Maybe it was pride, but it was all she had left. "It's going to be hard enough to call them and tell them about this."

"You know exactly what their reaction will be, but I'll do it if you like."

Would they remember? Kate wondered. Just for an instant, remember? And doubt. That she had to face as well. Alone. "No, I'll call them in the morning." She ran a hand over her slim navy skirt and tried to be practical. "I've got a little time to weigh my options. Money isn't an immediate problem. I've got some set aside, and there's the income, meager though it is, from the shop." Her hand jerked. "Oh, God. Oh, my God, is this going to affect the shop?"

"Of course not. Don't worry."

"Don't worry?" Kate sprang up. Her stomach began doing flip-flops again. " 'Pretenses's third partner suspected of embezzlement.' 'CPA skimming client accounts.' 'Former Templeton ward under investigation.' "

She squeezed her eyes shut, terrified of what that investigation might uncover. Blood will tell. Think of now, she ordered herself. One step at a time.

"Jesus, Laura, it never occurred to me until this second. I could ruin it. A lot of my clients shop there."

"Just stop it. You're innocent. I wouldn't be surprised if a great many of your clients dismiss this whole business as nonsense."

"People have a funny attitude about their money, Laura, and about the people they hire to handle it for them."

"That may be, but you're going to start handling mine. Don't even think about arguing," Laura said before Kate could open her mouth. "I don't have a lot to work with since Peter scalped me in the divorce, but I expect you to fix that. And it's about time you started pulling your weight at the shop. Margo and I are adequate bookkeepers, but—"

"That's a matter of opinion."

Pleased, Laura cocked a brow. "Well, then, you'd better get busy protecting our investment. You were too busy before, but now you've got time on your hands."

"So it seems."

"And by putting in some time behind the counter as well, you can take some of the pressure off Margo and me."

Kate's mouth fell open. "You expect me to clerk? Regularly? Damn it, Laura, I'm not a saleswoman."

"Neither was Margo," Laura said placidly. "And neither was I. Circumstances change. Bend or break, Kate."

She wanted to remind Laura that she had an MBA from Harvard. She'd graduated with honors a full year early. She'd been within a breath of a partnership at one of the most respected firms in the area, had handled millions of dollars a year in accounts.

She closed her mouth again because none of it was worth a damn at the moment. "I don't know an Armani from . . . anything."

"You'll learn."

It was self-indulgent, but she pouted anyway. "I don't even like jewelry."

"The customers do."

"I don't understand why people need to clutter up their house with dust catchers."

Laura smiled. If Kate was arguing, she thought, she was coming around. "That's easy. To keep us in business."

"Good point," Kate conceded. "I haven't done too badly the few Saturdays I've been able to help out. It's just dealing with people, day after day."

"You'll learn to live with it. We really need you on the books. We didn't push it before because we didn't want to pressure you. Actually Margo did, but I talked her out of it."

One of the many wounds she'd been planning to lick healed over. "Really?"

"No offense, Kate, but we've been open about ten months. Margo and I decided after about ten days that we really hate accounting. We hate spreadsheets. We hate percentages. We hate figuring the sales tax we have to send off every month."

Laura let out a sigh, lowered her voice. "I shouldn't tell you, she asked me not to, but . . ."

"What?"

"Well, Margo . . . We didn't think we could add to our overhead with a full-time bookkeeper, not yet anyway. So Margo's been looking into taking classes."

"Classes." Kate blinked. "Accounting classes? Margo? Jesus Christ."

"And business management, and computers." Laura winced. "Now, with the baby coming along, it seems like a lot to handle. I'm fairly computer-literate," she added, hoping to press her point. "I have to be, working conventions and special events at the hotel. But retail's a different matter entirely." Knowing the value of timing, she waited a beat, let it sink in. "I just don't see how I could squeeze any classes in myself, between working at Templeton, the shop, the girls."

"Of course not. You should have told me you were having that rough a time. I'd have picked up the ball."

"You've been cross-eyed with work for six months. It didn't seem fair."

"Fair? Hell, it's business. I'll come in first thing in the morning and take a good look at the books."

Laura managed to keep her smile pleasant rather than smug as Ann Sullivan wheeled in a tea cart. "The girls have finished their homework," Ann began. "I brought extra cups and plates so they could join you. I thought you might enjoy a little tea party."

"Thank you, Annie."

"Miss Kate, it's good to see—" Her smile of greeting faded the minute she looked into Kate's swollen, red-rimmed eyes. "What's the matter, darling?"

"Oh, Annie." Kate caught the hand Ann had lifted to her cheek, soothed herself with it. "My life's a mess."

"I'll get the girls," Laura said, rising. "And another cup," she added, nodding at Ann. "We'll have our tea party, and work on straightening it out."

Because Kate had always been the awkward one, and the feisty one, she held a special place in Ann's heart. After pouring two cups, selecting two chocolate-frosted cakes, Ann sat down and draped an arm around Kate's shoulder.

"Now, you drink your tea and eat some sweets and tell Annie all about it."

Sighing, Kate burrowed. Dorothy from Kansas was right, she decided. There really was no place like home.

"I DON'T LIKE the way she keeps talking about software." Behind the counter of Pretenses, Margo muttered into Laura's ear. "The only software I want to know about is cashmere."

"We don't have to know," Laura muttered right back. "Because she knows. Think about all the Sunday evenings we sweated over the books."

"Right." But Margo pouted. "Actually, I thought I was getting pretty good at it. The way she talks, it's like I was brain-dead."

"Want to go into the back room and help her out?"

"No." That was definite. Margo scanned a browsing customer, calculated nine more seconds before the next subtle sales pitch. "But I don't like the way she's taking this whole mess. No way our Kate walks away from a fight."

"She's hurt, shaken." Though Laura was worried over it herself. "This is just recovery time."

"It better be. I'm not going to be able to hold Josh back from storming into Bittle much longer." A martial light glowed in her Mediterranean blue eyes. "I'm not going to be able to hold myself back, for that matter. Creeps, jerks."

She continued to mutter as she approached the customer, but her face underwent a metamorphosis. Easy, sophisticated beauty. "That's a gorgeous lamp, isn't it? It belonged to Christie Brinkley." Margo trailed a finger down the mother-of-pearl shade. "Confidentially, it was a gift from Billy, and she didn't want to keep it around any longer."

Truth or fiction? Laura wondered, muffling a laugh. The ownership was fact, but the little sidebar was probably fantasy.

"Laura." With the long-suffering look she'd worn after the first hour with the books, Kate stepped out of the back office. "Do you realize how much money you're wasting by short-ordering boxes? The more you order at a time, the less each costs. The way we go through them—"

"Ah, yes, you're right." Out of defense and necessity, Laura looked at her watch. "Oops, piano lessons. Gotta go."

"You're buying tape at the dime store rather than through a wholesaler," Kate added, dogging Laura to the door.

"I should be shot. 'Bye." And she escaped.

Her foot tapping, Kate turned, with the intent of nagging Margo. But her partner was busy fussing with a customer over some silly little lamp that didn't look as if it could light a closet, much less a room.

It helped to nag. It felt good to take charge. Even if it was over boxes and tape.

"Miss. Oh, miss." Another woman came out of the wardrobe room carrying a pair of white spangled pumps. "Do you have these in an eight narrow?"

Kate looked at the shoes, looked at the woman, and wondered why anyone would want a pair of shoes covered with iridescent sequins. "Everything's out that's in stock."

"But these are too small." She all but wailed it, thrusting the shoes at Kate. "They're perfect with the dress I've chosen. I have to have them."

"Look," Kate began, then ground her teeth together as Margo caught her eye with a fiery warning look. She remembered the routine Margo had drummed into her head. Hated it, but remembered. "Pretenses is almost exclusively one of a kind. But I'm sure we can find something that works for you." Already missing her computer, she guided the customer back into the wardrobe room.

It took a great deal of control not to yelp. Shoes were tumbled everywhere, rather than neatly arranged on the shelves. Half a dozen cocktail dresses were tossed haphazardly over a chair. Others had slipped to the neat little Aubusson.

"Been busy, haven't we?" Kate said with a frozen smile.

The woman let out a trill of laughter that cut right through the top of Kate's skull. "Oh, I'm just in love with everything, but I'm very decisive once I've made up my mind."

That was a statement for the books. "Okay, which dress have you become decisive about?"

It took twenty minutes, twenty hemming and hawing, oohing and ahing minutes, before the customer settled on a pair of white slingbacks with satin bows.

Kate struggled to arrange the yards of white tulle in the skirt of the dress the woman couldn't live without. Tulle, Kate thought as she finally zipped it into a bag, that would certainly make the woman resemble an oversized wedding cake.

Her work complete, Kate handed over dress, shoes, and sales receipt and even managed a smile. "Thanks so much for shopping at Pretenses."

"Oh, I love it here. I just have to see these earrings."

"Earrings?" Kate's heart sank.

"These. I think they'd be wonderful with the dress, don't you? Could you just take it out of the bag again so I could see?"

"You want me to take the dress out of the bag." With a fierce smile, Kate leaned over the counter. "Why don't you—"

"Oh, the Austrian crystals just make those earrings, don't they?" Dashing around the counter, Margo gave Kate a shove that knocked her a full foot sideways. "I have a bracelet that's just made to go with them. Kate, why don't you take the dress back out while I unlock the case?"

"I'll take the damn dress back out," Kate muttered with her back turned. "But I'm not putting it in again. No one can make me." Spoiling for a fight, she scowled as the door jingled open. Her scowl only deepened at Byron's quick smile.

"Hello, ladies. I'll just browse until you're free."

"You're free," Margo said meaningfully to Kate. "I'll finish up here."

One devil was the same as another, Kate supposed and walked reluctantly out from behind the counter. "Looking for something?"

"Mother's Day. I bought my mother's birthday present in here a couple of months ago, and it made me a hero. I figured I'd stick with a winner." He reached out, skimmed a knuckle along her jaw. "How are you feeling?"

"Fine." Embarrassed at the memory of sobbing in his arms, she turned stiffly away. "Did you have anything specific in mind?"

In answer, he put a hand on her shoulder, turned her around. "I thought we'd parted on semi-friendly terms at least."

"We did." She reeled herself in. There was no point in blaming him, though it was more satisfying. "I'm just a little wired. I nearly punched that customer."

Lifting an eyebrow, Byron glanced over Kate's head at the woman currently sighing over a bracelet. "Because?"

"She wanted to see earrings," Kate said between her teeth.

"Good God, what is the world coming to? If you promise not to hit me, I swear I won't even look at a pair of earrings in here. I may never look at a pair anywhere again."

She supposed that deserved at least a smile. "Sorry. It's a long story. So, what does your mother like?"

"Earrings. Sorry." He let out a rumbling chuckle. "Hard to resist. She's an internist with nerves of steel, a wicked temper, and a sentimental streak for anything that has to do with her children. I'm thinking hearts and flowers. Anything that falls into that basic symbolism."

"That's nice." She did smile. She was a sucker for a man who not only loved his mama but understood her. "I don't know the stock very well. It's my first week on the job."

She looked neat as a pin, he mused, in her tidy little gray suit with a Windsor-knotted striped tie. The sensible shoes shouldn't have led him to think about her legs. Surprised that that was exactly what he was doing, he cleared his throat.

"How's it going?"

She glanced back at Margo. "I think my coworkers are plotting my demise. Other than that, good enough. Thanks." But when he continued to study her, she shifted. "You did come in for a gift, right—not to check up on me or anything?"

"I can do both."

"I'd rather you—" The door opened again, heralding the entrance of three laughing, chattering women. Kate grabbed Byron's arm in a steely grip. "Okay, I'm with you. You need my undivided attention. I'll give you ten percent off if you take up all my time until they leave."

"A real people person, aren't you, Katherine?"

"I'm a desperate woman. Don't screw with me." She kept her hand firmly on his arm as she steered him to a corner of the shop.

"Your scent's different again," he commented, indulging himself with a sniff close to her hair. "Subtle, yet passionate."

"Something Margo squirted on me when I was distracted," she said absently. This was her new life, she reminded herself. The old was gone, and she was going to make the best of what she had left. "She likes us to push the merchandise. She'd have hung jewelry all over me if I hadn't escaped." From her safe distance, she glanced back and made a face at her partner. "Look, she made me wear this pin."

He glanced down at the simple gold crescent adorning her lapel. "It's very nice." And drew the eye to the soft swell of her breasts. "Simple, classic, subdued."

"Yeah, right. What do pins do but put holes in your clothes? Okay, back to business. It so happens, there's this music box that might make you a hero again."

"Music box." He brought himself back to the business at hand. "Could work."

"I remember it because Margo just picked it up at an estate sale in San Francisco. She'd know the circa this and the design that. I can tell you it's lovely."

She lifted it, a glossy mahogany box large enough for jewelry or love letters. On its domed lid was a painting of a young couple in medieval dress, a unicorn, and a circle of flowers. The lid opened to deep-blue velvet and the charming strains of "Für Elise."

"There's a problem," he began.

"Why?" Her back went up. "It's beautiful, it's practical, it's romantic."

"Well." He rubbed his chin. "How am I going to take up all your time when you've shown me the perfect gift first thing?"

"Oh." Kate glanced over her shoulder again. The three fresh customers were in the wardrobe room making a lot of female-on-the-hunt noises. Trying not to feel guilty, she looked over at Margo, who was expertly re-bagging the tulle. "Want to buy something else? It's never too early to shop for Christmas."

He angled his head. "You've got to learn to gauge your clientele, kid. Here's a man coming in to buy a Mother's Day gift three days before the mark. A gift that he will now have to have shipped overnight to Atlanta. That type doesn't shop for Christmas until sometime after December twenty-first."

"That's very impractical."

"I like to use up my practicality at work. Life is different."

When he smiled at her, the creases in his face deepened. She liked the look of them, caught herself wondering how it would feel to trace her finger along those charming dents. Surprised at herself, she blew out a breath. Steady, girl.

"Then maybe you should look at something else, to like, compare."

"No, this is it." It intrigued him to see that he was making her uncomfortable, and that the discomfort was sexual. Deliberately, he put his hands over hers so that they held the box together. "Why don't I dawdle over the wrapping paper?"

That, she decided, was definitely a come-on. She'd have to think about whether or not she liked it later. "Okay, that'll work." She sent Margo a beaming smile as they crossed paths, then set the music box carefully on the counter.

Margo closed the door behind her now-satisfied customer and aimed an automatically flirtatious smile at Byron. "Hello, Byron. It's wonderful to see you."

"Margo." He caught her hand, brought it to his lips. The gesture was as automatic as her smile. "You look incredible, as always."

She laughed. "We just don't get enough men in here, particularly handsome, gallant ones. Have you found something you like?"

"Kate saved my life with a Mother's Day gift."

"Did she?" As Kate studiously boxed Byron's selection, Margo leaned over the counter, caught Kate by her red-and-blue-striped tie, and tugged viciously. "I'm going to kill you later. Excuse me, Byron. I have customers."

Kate kept her hot eyes on Margo's retreating back. "See, I told you. She wants me dead."

"One definition of family is a constant state of adjustment."

Kate lifted a brow. "From *Webster*'s?"

"From De Witt's. Let's try the paper with the little violets. Margo's a remarkable woman."

"I've never known a man who didn't think so. No, that's wrong," she said as she measured wrapping paper. "Laura's ex-husband couldn't stand her. Of course, that was because she's the housekeeper's daughter, and he's a puss-faced snob. And I think it was because he wanted her. Men do. And it irritated him."

Intrigued by the brisk way she worked, the almost mathematical manner in which she aligned the box and folded corners on the gift wrap, he leaned on the counter. Her hands were really quite lovely, he noted. Narrow, competent, unadorned.

"How did he feel about you?"

"Oh, he hated me, too, but that didn't have anything to do with sexual fantasy. I'm the poor relation who has the nerve to say what she thinks." When her stomach jittered, she glanced up and frowned. "I don't know why I told you all that."

"Could be repressed conversation urges. You don't talk to people for long periods, then you get caught in a conversation and forget you don't like to talk to people. I told you, it can be a pleasant hobby."

"I don't like to talk to people," she muttered. "Most people. You want purple ribbon or white?"

"Purple. You interest me, Kate."

Wary, she looked up again. "I don't think that's necessary."

"Just an observation. I assumed you were cold, prim, rude, annoying, and self-involved. I'm not ordinarily that far wrong with people."

She jerked the ribbon into a knot, snipped off the ends. "You're not this time, either. Except for the prim."

"No, the rude and annoying probably stick, but I've been reevaluating the rest."

She chose a large, elaborate bow. "I don't want an evaluation."

"I didn't ask. It's another hobby of mine. Gift card?"

Frowning again, she found the one to match the paper and slapped it on the counter in front of him. "We can overnight it."

"I'm counting on it." He handed her his credit card, then took out a pen to write on the card. "Oh, by the way, I made an offer on the house you recommended. Like the music box, it's exactly what I was looking for."

"Good for you." After a brief search, she found the shipping form, set it down beside the box. She suppressed the urge to ask him about it, the house, what had appealed to him, the terms. Damn conversation.

"If you'll fill in the name and address where you want it shipped, we'll have FedEx pick it up in the morning. She'll get it with twenty-four hours to spare and save you a whining phone call."

His head lifted. "My mother doesn't whine."

"I was referring to you." Her smug smile faltered when two more customers came in.

"Isn't that handy?" Byron dashed off his mother's name and address. "We're all done, just in time for you to help some new customers."

"Listen, De Witt. Byron—"

"No, no, don't bother to grovel. You're on your own." He pocketed his card, the receipt, then tore off his copy of the shipping form himself. "See you around, kid."

He strolled toward the door. The sound of "Miss, could you show me these earrings?" was music to his soul.

CHAPTER 6

BYRON DIDN'T LIKE to interfere with his department heads, but he knew—and wanted them to know—that at Templeton problems rose to the top. His interest in hotels and all their crosshatched inner workings had begun during a summer stint at Atlanta's Doubletree. Three months as a bellman had taught him more than the proper way to handle a guest's luggage and had earned him more than enough cash to buy his first vintage car.

He'd learned there were dramas and tragedies playing out daily, not just behind the closed doors of rooms and suites, but behind the front desk, in sales and marketing, in housekeeping and engineering. In fact, everywhere within the buzzing hive of a busy hotel.

It had fascinated him, had pushed him toward sampling other aspects, from desk clerk to concierge. His curiosity about people, who they were, what they expected, what they dreamed of, had given him a career.

He wasn't the doctor his parents had not so secretly hoped he would be. Nor had he been the travel-weary trust-fund kid his circumstances could have made him. He had a career he enjoyed, and the constant variety of life in a big hotel continually intrigued him.

He was a problem solver, one who considered the individual as well as the big picture. His choice of moving into the Templeton organization had been a simple one. He'd spent a great deal of time studying hotels— the luxurious, the opulent, the small and tidy, the chains with their brisk pace, the old Europeans with their quiet charm, the Las Vegas ones with their flash and gaudiness.

Templeton had appealed to him because it was family-run, traditional without being stodgy, efficient without sacrificing charm, and above all, personable.

He didn't have to make it his business to know the names of the people who worked with and under him. It was simply a part of his makeup to take an interest, to retain information. So when he smiled at the woman currently checking in a guest, called out a casual, "Good morning, Linda," he wasn't aware that her pulse picked up several beats or that her fingers fumbled on the keyboard as she watched him pass through on his way to the offices.

Another section of the beehive was here. Ringing phones, clicking faxes, humming copiers, the clack of keyboards. He passed stacks of boxes, crowded desks. He exchanged a few greetings as he went, causing several pairs of shoulders to straighten and more than a few female employees to wish they'd checked their lipstick.

The door to his destination was open, and he found Laura Templeton with a phone to her ear. She offered him a harried smile and gestured to a chair.

"I'm sure we can arrange that. Mr. Hubble in Catering . . . Yes, yes, I understand how important it is. Mr. Hubble—" She broke off, rolled her eyes at Byron. "How many extra chairs would you like, Ms. Bingham?" She listened patiently, a small smile playing at the corners of her mouth. "No, of course not. And I'm sure you'll have plenty of room if you make use of the terrace. No, I don't believe it's calling for rain. It should be a lovely evening, and I'm sure your reception will be elegant. Mr. Hubble—" Now she gritted her teeth. "Why don't I talk to Mr. Hubble for you and get back to you? Yes, by noon. I will. Absolutely. You're welcome, Ms. Bingham." She hung up. "Ms. Bingham is insane."

"Is she the orthodontist convention or the interior decorating?"

"Decorating. She has decided, at the last minute, that she simply must give a reception tonight for sixty of her closest friends and associates. For reasons I can't explain, she doesn't trust Bob Hubble to pull it off."

"Templeton," Byron said and smiled at her. "The trouble is, your name is Templeton. Which puts you in a lofty position."

You wouldn't know it from her office, he thought. It was tiny, cramped and windowless. He knew she'd chosen the position and the work space herself when she had decided to squeeze out time for a part-time job at the hotel.

Byron didn't know how she managed—her family and home, the shop, the hotel. But she seemed to him to be the soul of serenity and quiet efficiency. Until you looked close enough, at the eyes. There, shadowed in their lake-gray depths, were doubt and worry and grief. Remnants, he thought, of a shattered marriage.

"You didn't have to come down here, Byron." She finished scribbling notes to herself as she spoke. "I would have made it up to your office this morning."

"It's all right. Problem with the tooth soldiers?"

"You'd think orthodontists would have a little decorum, wouldn't you?" With a sigh, she pulled papers out of a file. "We've had complaints from both bars, but that's nothing I can't handle."

"I've yet to come across anything you can't handle."

"I appreciate that. But there's a delicate situation. One of the doctors apparently was having a, let's say, intimate moment with one of the other doctors when her husband decided to pay an unannounced surprise visit."

"God, I love this job." Byron settled back. "It's like a long-running soap opera."

"Easy for you to say. I spent an hour this morning dealing with the penitent woman. She sat where you are, spilling out tears and the whole sordid story of her marriage, her affairs, her therapy."

Weary with the memory, Laura pressed her fingers to the inside corner of her eye, almost relieving the tension that was living there. "This is her third husband, and she claims to be addicted to adultery."

"She should go on *Oprah*. Women who are addicted to adultery, and the men who love them. Do you want me to talk to her?"

"No, I think I sent her off steady enough. Our problem is, the husband wasn't too thrilled to find his wife and his"— she winced—"his brother-in-law wrapped in matching Templeton robes."

"It just gets better. Don't stop now."

"The husband popped his brother-in-law—who, I should add for clarification, is married to our heroine's sister—in the mouth. Knocked out several thousand dollars' worth of caps and so forth. There was some damage to the room, nothing major. A couple of lamps and crockery." She waved that away. "But our problem is that the guy with the broken mouth is threatening to sue the hotel."

"Another victim." If he hadn't been so amused with the scenario, he would have sighed. "What's his rationale?"

"That the hotel is responsible for letting the husband in. He—the husband—called room service from a house phone, ordered champagne and strawberries for his wife's room. He had a dozen roses with him," she added. "Then he waited until the wine arrived, slipped into the room behind the waiter, and—well, the rest is history."

"I don't think we've got any real problem here, but I'll take the file."

"I appreciate it." Relieved, Laura passed the torch. "I'd talk to the man myself, but I get the impression he's not too keen on women in authority. And, to be honest, I'm swamped. The orthodontists have their banquet tonight, and the cosmetic people are coming in tomorrow."

"And, of course, Ms. Bingham."

"Right." She checked her watch and rose. "I'd better get down to Catering. There was one other little thing."

Standing up himself, he raised an eyebrow. "The decorators are wrestling in the atrium?"

"Not yet." Because she appreciated him, she smiled. It was second nature to Laura to hide nerves. "It was an idea I had for the shop, but since it involves the hotel, I wanted to run it by you."

"Laura, it's your hotel."

"No, at the moment I work here, and you're the boss." She picked up her clipboard and passed it from one of her hands to the other. "Last fall we put on a reception and charity auction at the shop. We intend to do it every year. But I was thinking we could plan another event. Straight advertising, really. A fashion show, using clothes and accessories from the shop, during the holiday season. The White Ballroom would be ideal, and it's not booked for the first Saturday in December. I thought we could feature gala attire, formals, ballgowns, in addition to accessories, all from the shop. We'd advertise it in both the hotel and the resort, with percentage-off certificates issued to Templeton employees and guests."

"You've got marketing in the blood. Listen, Laura, you work conventions and special events." He put an arm around her shoulders as they left the office. "You don't need my go-ahead."

"I like to dot my i's, so to speak. After I've talked it over with Margo and Kate, I'll work up a proposal."

"Fine." She'd given him the opening he'd been hoping for. "So how is Kate?"

"She's holding up. Of course, she occasionally drives Margo and me crazy. A born salesman Kate isn't," Laura said with feeling. "But she's competitive enough to make it work." Her smile softened, spread. "And if Margo or I so much as breathes on the books, she hisses. So that's a blessing. Still . . ."

"Still?"

"They damaged something inside her. I don't know how seriously yet, but she's too together, too controlled. She won't talk about it, won't even discuss what should be done. Just closes up when any of us try to draw her out. Kate used to be a champion tantrum thrower."

Now her fingers fidgeted restlessly, tapping a pencil, plucking at papers on her clipboard. "She's taking this without a fight. When Margo's career blew up and she lost her spot as the spokeswoman for Bella Donna, Kate wanted to organize a protest. She actually talked about going down to L.A. and picketing on Rodeo Drive."

Remembering put a smile back on Laura's face. "I never told Margo, because I managed to talk Kate out of it, but that's the way she is. She spits and claws and slaps when she's up against a personal problem. But not this time. This time she's pulled in, and I don't understand it."

"You're really worried about her," Byron realized.

"Yes, I am. So's Margo, or she would have strangled Kate half a dozen times by now. She wants us to fill out a sheet in something called a columnar pad every day."

"Once an accountant," he said.

"She carries one of those electronic memo pads in her pocket all the time. She's starting to talk about co-linking and getting on-line. It's terrifying." When he laughed, Laura caught herself and shook her head. "Ask a simple question . . ." she began. "Does everybody dump on you this way?"

"You didn't dump. I asked."

"Josh said you were the only man he wanted in this job. It's easy to see why. You're so different from Peter—" This time she didn't just catch herself, she clenched her teeth. "No, I'm not getting started on that. I'm already behind schedule and Ms. Bingham's waiting. Thanks for taking the orthodontists off my hands."

"My pleasure. You might not hear it very often, but you're an asset to Templeton."

"I'm trying to be."

As she walked away, Byron turned in the opposite direction, studying her careful and precise report as he went.

AT THE END of the day he met with Josh at Templeton Resort. The office there was a sprawling room on the executive level, with windows offering a view of one of the resort's two lagoonlike pools, surrounded by hibiscus in riotous bloom and a patio with redwood tables under candy-pink umbrellas.

Inside, it was built for comfort as well as business with deeply cushioned leather chairs, Deco lamps, and a stylish watercolor street scene of Milan.

"Want a beer?"

At the offer Byron merely sighed low and deep. He accepted the bottle from Josh, tipped it back. "Sorry to hit you at the end of the day. It's the first I could get away."

"There is no end of the day in the hotel business," Josh said.

"Your mother said that." Byron grinned. Susan Templeton was one of his favorite people. "You know if your father would just step aside like a gentleman, I'd beg her to marry me." He drank again, then nodded at the file he'd put on Josh's desk. "I started to fax this business over, then thought I'd just swing by personally."

Instead of going behind the desk, Josh picked up the file and stretched out in the chair opposite Byron. He skimmed the reports with varying reactions. A chuckle, a groan, a sigh, an oath.

"That sums up my feelings," Byron concurred. "I had a talk with Dr. Holdermen myself a few hours ago. He's still a guest. He's got temporary caps on and a real beaut of a black eye. My take is he doesn't have a case, but he's pissed off enough, and embarrassed enough, to pursue it."

Josh nodded, came to his own conclusions. "And your recommendation?"

"Let him."

"Agreed." Josh tossed the file onto his desk. "I'll pass it along to Legal with that recommendation. Now . . ." Josh settled back, the beer bottle cupped loosely in his hand, his eyes curious. "Why don't you tell me why you're really here? You can handle this kind of nuisance in your sleep."

Byron rubbed his chin. "We know each other too well."

"Ten years on and off should be enough. What's on your mind, By?"

"Kate Powell."

Josh's brows shot up. "Really?"

"Not in that context," Byron said, a bit too quickly. "It was something Laura said today that got me thinking about the whole situation. Bittle made some serious allegations against her, yet they haven't pursued it. And neither has she. It's going on three weeks now."

"I'm going to get pissed off again." Feeling his temper bubbling, Josh rose and paced it off. "My father used to play golf with Larry Bittle. I don't know how many times he's been over to the house. He's known Kate since she was a kid."

"Have you talked to him?"

"Kate almost took my head off when I threatened to." Scowling, Josh gulped down his beer. "That was okay, but then she just shut down. She seemed so shaky over the whole thing, I didn't push. Hell, I've been so wrapped up in Margo and the baby, I let it slide. We did this heartbeat thing at the doctor's today. It was so cool. You could just hear it, beating away, this quick little bopping." He stopped when he caught Byron's grin. "Kate," he began again.

"That's okay, you can indulge in obsessive expectant fatherhood for a minute."

"There's more. It's not an excuse for letting my sister dangle." He sat again, with a muscle in his cheek twitching. "We've decided to settle with Ridgeway. Goddamn bastard cheats on Laura, scalps her, ignores his children, alienates half the staff at the hotel, and we end up cutting him a check for a quarter million just to avoid a premature termination suit."

"It's rough," Byron agreed. "But he'll be gone."

"He better stay gone."

"You could always break his nose again," Byron suggested.

"There is that." Willing himself to relax, Josh rolled his shoulders. "You could say I've been a little distracted the last few weeks. And Kate, she's always been so self-reliant. You begin to take it for granted."

"Laura's worried about her."

"Laura worries about everyone but Laura." Josh brooded for a minute. "I haven't been able to get through to Kate. She won't talk about it, at least not to me. I hadn't considered going over her head to Bittle. Is that what you're getting at?"

"It's none of my business. The thing is . . ." Byron studied his beer for a moment, then lifted those calm, clear eyes to Josh. He'd thought it through, as he did any problem, and had come to one conclusion. "If Bittle does decide to pursue a case against her, wouldn't she be better off to take the offensive now?"

"The threat of a nice fat libel suit, an unjustified suspension, loss of income, emotional distress."

Byron smiled and finished off his beer. "Well, you're the lawyer."

IT TOOK HIM the best part of a week, but Josh was hotly pleased when he strolled into Pretenses. He'd just come from a meeting with the partners of Bittle and Associates.

He caught his wife around the waist and kissed her thrillingly, to the delight of the customers milling about the shop.

"Hi."

"Hi, yourself. And what are you doing in my parlor in the middle of the day?"

"I didn't come for you." He kissed her again and barely restrained himself from laying a hand on her stubbornly flat stomach. He couldn't wait for it to grow. "I need to talk to Kate."

"Captain Queeg is in the office, rolling marbles and talking about strawberries."

Josh winced. "I thought you were calling her Captain Bligh these days."

"He wasn't insane enough. She's redoing the filing system. Color-coded."

"Good God. What's next?"

Margo narrowed her eyes. "She put up a bulletin board."

"She must be stopped. I'll go in." He drew a deep breath. "If I'm not out in twenty minutes, remember, I've always loved you."

"Very funny," she muttered, and managed to hold the smile back until he'd slipped into the rear office.

Josh found Kate mumbling over files. Her hair stood up in spikes, and the first two fingers of her right hand were covered with rubber tips.

"Less than a year," she said without turning around, "and you and Laura have managed to misfile half of everything. Why the hell is a fire insurance invoice in the umbrella file?"

"Someone should be flogged."

Unamused, she turned, eyed him. "I don't have time for you, Josh. Your wife's making my life a living hell."

"Funny, she says the same thing about you." Despite her ferocious glare, he walked over and kissed the tip of her nose. "I hear you're color-coding the files."

"Somebody has to. The software I installed keeps clean records, but you're better off backing up with hard copy in retail. I told Margo to do this months ago, but she's more interested in selling trinkets."

"God knows how you can expect to keep a retail business running by selling things!"

She drew in a breath, refusing to hear how foolish she sounded. "My point is you can hardly keep any business successful if you don't concern yourself with the details. She's been logging shoes under wardrobe instead of accessories."

"She needs to be punished." He grabbed Kate's shoulders. "Let me do it."

Chuckling, she shoved him back. "Go away. I don't have time to laugh right now."

"I didn't come by for laughs. I need to talk to you." He pointed to a chair. "So sit."

"Can't this wait? I have to be back in the showroom in an hour. I want to get the files in shape first."

"Sit," he repeated and gave her a brotherly nudge. "I just had a meeting at Bittle."

The impatience drained out of her eyes, leaving them cold and blank. "Excuse me?"

"Don't take that tone with me, Kate. It's past time this was dealt with."

She continued to take that tone, quiet and icy, as fear clawed at her insides. "And you decided you were the one to deal with it?"

"That's right. As your attorney—"

"You're not my attorney," she shot back.

"Who went to court to get you out of that speeding ticket three years ago?"

"You, but—"

"And who looked over your lease for your apartment before you signed it?"

"Yes, but—"

"Who wrote your will?"

Her face turned mutinous. "I don't see that that has anything to do with it."

"I see." Idly, he studied his manicure. "Just because I've handled all the pesky little legal details of your life doesn't make me your lawyer."

"It doesn't give you the right to go behind my back and talk to Bittle. Particularly since I asked you to leave it alone."

"Fine, it doesn't. Being your brother does."

Bringing up family loyalty was, in Kate's opinion, hitting below the belt. She sprang to her feet. "I'm not the inadequate, incapable little sister, and I won't be treated like one. I'm handling this."

"How?" Primed to fight, he got to his feet as well. "By color-coding the files in here?"

"Yes." Since he was shouting now, Kate matched her voice to his. "By making the best of the situation. By getting on with my life. By not whining and crying."

"By backing down and doing nothing." He poked his finger against her shoulder. "By going into denial. Well, it's gone on long enough. Bittle and company know that they're facing legal action."

"Legal action?" The blood drained out of her face. She could feel every drop flow. "You told them I was going to sue? Oh, my God." Dizzy, she leaned on the desk.

"Hey!" He grabbed her in alarm. "Sit down. Catch your breath."

"Leave me alone. Leave me the hell alone. What have you done?"

"What needed to be done. Now come on, honey, sit down."

"Jesus Christ." She exploded, and rather than a poke on his shoulder, she landed a punch on it. "How dare you?" Her color was back, flaming. "How dare you threaten legal action?"

"I didn't tell them you were going to sue. I merely left them chewing over that impression."

"I told you to leave it. This is my business. Mine." She threw up her arms, spun around. "What gave you this brainstorm, Joshua? I'm going to kill Margo."

"Margo didn't have anything to do with it, though if you would open your beady eyes for five minutes, you'd see how worried she is about you. How worried everyone is."

Because he might poke her again, he decided his hands were safer in his pockets. "I shouldn't have let it go this long, but I've had things on my mind. If By hadn't dropped by and given me a push, it would have taken me longer, but I'd have gotten to it."

"Stop." Breathing hard, she held up a hand. "Playback. Byron De Witt talked to you about me?"

Realizing his misstep, Josh tried a quick retreat. "Your name came up in conversation, that's all. And it started me—"

"My name came up." Now she was breathing between clenched teeth— teeth that matched the fists ready at her sides. Anger was better, she realized, than panic. "Oh, I just bet it did. That son of a bitch. I should have known he couldn't keep his mouth shut."

"About what?"

"Don't try to cover up. And get out of my way." Her shove was fierce enough and unexpected enough to knock him back. Before he could make the grab, she was sailing past him.

"Just a damn minute. I haven't finished."

"You go to hell," she shot back over her shoulder, causing several customers to glance around nervously as she stormed out of the office. She sent Margo one seething glare before slamming the front door behind her.

"Well." Struggling with a smile, Margo handed a bagged purchase to a wide-eyed customer. "That's thirty-eight fifty-three out of forty." Still smiling, she handed over the change. "And the show was free. Please come again."

With the wariness of a man who understood trouble when it stared at him from sultry blue eyes, Josh approached the counter. "Sorry about that."

"We'll deal with sorry later," she said under her breath. "What did you do to upset her?"

Just like a woman, he thought, to take the woman's side. "I tried to help her."

"You know how she hates that. Why, instead of taking your head off, did she storm out of here looking like she was going to take someone else's head off?"

He sighed, scratched his chin, shuffled his feet. "She'd finished taking my head off. Now she's going for Byron's. He sort of suggested that I help her."

Margo tapped coral-tipped nails on the glass counter. "I see."

"I really ought to call him, give him some advance warning." But when Josh reached for the phone on the counter, Margo laid a firm hand over his.

"Oh, no. I don't think so. We wouldn't want to spoil Kate's advantage."

"Margo, it's only fair."

"Fair has nothing to do with it. And you're going to be too busy waiting on customers to make personal calls."

Now he stuck his hands in his pockets. "Duchess, I've got a meeting in a couple of hours. I don't have time to help you out around here."

"Thanks to you, I'm shorthanded." Knowing that that wouldn't get her very far, she let her shoulders slump. "And I'm feeling a little tired."

"Tired?" Panic came on wings. "You should get off your feet."

"You're probably right." Though she felt strong as a horse, she scooted a stool over to the cash register and perched on it. "I'll just sit here and ring up sales for the next hour. Oh, Josh, darling, be sure to offer the customers champagne."

Enjoying herself, she slipped off her shoes and prepared to watch her adorable husband handle a storeful of customers.

The only show she would have preferred to witness was the one that would be starting shortly in the penthouse office of Templeton Monterey.

* * *

THE FIRST ANALOGY that came to Byron's mind was that of a wild, possibly rabid, deer charging.

Kate cut through his shocked, protesting assistant like a sharp knife through quivery jelly, snarled like a feral she-wolf, and might very well have delivered the knockout punch of a flyweight champ if Byron hadn't signaled his assistant to retreat.

"Well, Katherine." He barely missed a beat when she slammed the door with a resounding *crack*. "What an unexpected pleasure."

"I'm going to kill you. I'm going to rip off your meddling nose and stuff it in your flapping mouth."

"As much fun as I'm sure that'll be, would you like a drink first? Some water? You're a bit flushed."

"Who the hell do you think you are?" She sprang toward the desk, smashed her palms down on its polished, and just now crowded, surface. "What possible right do you have to mix in my business? Do I strike you as some weak-willed, empty-headed woman who needs a man to defend her?"

"Which one of those questions would you like me to answer first? Why don't I take them in order?" he said before she could shout again. "You know exactly who I am. I didn't mix in your business any more than any tentative and concerned friend would, and no, no indeed, I don't see you as weak-willed or empty-headed. I see you as stubborn, rude, and potentially dangerous."

"You haven't got a clue how dangerous, pal."

"That threat might have more weight if you'd take off those filing tips. They spoil the image."

A strangled sound erupted from her throat as she looked down and discovered the brown rubber tips still on her fingers. Smooth and quick, she ripped them off and threw them at him. Just as smooth, just as quick, he caught them both before they hit his face.

"Good arm," he commented. "I bet you played ball in school."

"I thought I could trust you." For reasons she didn't want to analyze, thinking of that made her eyes sting. "I even, for one brief, foolish moment, thought I could learn to like you. Now I see that my first impression of you as an arrogant, self-important, sexist jerk was totally on the mark." Her sense of betrayal was every bit as keen as her fury. "I was reeling when you found me on the cliffs, I was vulnerable. Everything I said there I said to you in confidence. You had no right to run to Josh with it."

He set the rubber tips on his desk. "I didn't say anything to Josh about that day on the cliffs."

"I don't believe you. You went to him—"

"I don't lie," he said sharply. She glimpsed the steel beneath the polish.

"Yes, I went to him. Sometimes it takes someone outside the family to put things on the table. And your family is torn up about what happened to you, Kate. More worried about the way you're behaving."

"My behavior isn't—"

"Any of my business," he finished for her. "Odd that something as harmless as my speaking with Josh sends you into a tailspin of revenge and retribution, but being questioned about embezzlement makes you curl up in the fetal position and suck your thumb."

"You don't know what I'm doing, what I'm feeling. And you have no right to pass judgment."

"No, that's all quite true. If you weren't so self-involved, you'd see that no one's passing judgment. But as an outsider I can tell you that your family is hurting for you."

Her flush died until her cheeks were bone-white. "Don't lecture me about my family. Don't you dare. They're the most important people in the world to me. I'm handling this my way because of my family."

He cocked his head. "Which means?"

"Which means that, too, is none of your business." She pressed her fingers to her eyes, fighting for control. "Nothing and no one is more on my mind than my family."

He believed that without hesitation, and only felt more sorry for her. "Your way of handling this situation isn't working."

"How the hell do you know?"

"Because people talk to me." His voice was gentle now, and the edge of temper had smoothed out of it. "Margo, Laura, Josh. Because I know how worried and angry I'd be if it was my sister."

"Well, it isn't your sister." The anger snapped back into her voice, but her cheeks stayed white. "I'm capable of dealing with this. Josh has enough on his plate without being guilted into taking this on."

"Do you really think guilt has anything to do with it?"

She fumbled, recovered. "Don't twist my words around, De Witt."

"Those were your words, Powell. Now, if you've finished with your tantrum, we can discuss this."

"Tantrum—"

"I'd heard you were good at them, but now that I've had a firsthand demonstration, I see the reports were understated."

He'd never thought that dark, glossy brown could turn to fire until he watched it happen in her eyes. "I'll show you a tantrum." With one swipe she sent most of the papers on his desk flying, then raised her fist. "Come out from behind that desk."

"Oh, you tempt me." His voice was ominously quiet, his eyes danger-ously cool. "I've never hit a woman in my life. And never have I found it necessary to make that statement before. But you tempt me, Katherine, to break all kinds of records. Now either sit down or get out."

"I'm not sitting down, and I'm not getting out until we—" She broke off, strangling a cry as she pressed a hand under her breasts.

Now he did come around the desk, cursing all the way. "Damn it. Damn it! What are you doing to yourself?"

"Don't touch me." The burning pressure made her eyes water, but she struggled when he led her to a chair.

"You're going to sit down. You're going to try to relax. And if you don't have your color back in thirty seconds, I'm hauling your skinny butt to the hospital."

"Just leave me alone." She fumbled out her antacids, knowing it was like trying to put out a forest fire with a water pistol. "I'll be fine in a minute."

"How often does this happen?"

"None of your business." She yelped in pain and shock when he pressed two fingers to her abdomen.

"Do you have your appendix?"

"Keep your hands off me, Dr. Feelgood."

He only continued to frown and moved his fingertips to the inside of her wrist. "Been skipping meals again?" Before she could evade, he caught her face in his hands and took a long, objective look. Her color was seeping back, slowly, and her eyes were filled with temper again rather than pain. But he saw other things. "You're not sleeping. You're tired, overstressed and undernourished. Is that how you're handling this?"

Her stomach quivered, an echo of pain and nerves. "I want you to leave me alone."

"You don't always get what you want. You're exhausted, Kate, and until you start taking better care of yourself, someone else will have to do it for you. Be still," he ordered in an absent murmur, holding a hand on her shoulder as he checked his watch. "I'm tied up here until after six. I'll pick you up at seven. Will you be at the shop or at home?"

"What the hell are you talking about? I'm not going anywhere with you."

"I realize I'm annoyed with myself for handling this matter badly. You do seem to bring out the worst in me," he added, mostly to himself. "So, you're going to get a decent meal and the opportunity to discuss these gripes of yours in a civilized manner."

It was frightening her, the casual manner he assumed, the glint of heat in his eye that warned he could shift out of casual mode at any moment.

"I don't want to have dinner with you, and I'm not feeling civilized."

Considering, he rocked back on his heels, so that their eyes were level. "Let's try it this way. You go along with this or I pick up the phone and call Laura. It should take her about two minutes to get up here, and when she does, I'll tell her that twice now I've seen you go white and double over."

"You have no right."

"No, Kate, what I have here is the hammer. That beats the hell out of rights." He checked his watch again. "I have a conference call coming through in about five minutes, or we'd finish more of this now. Since the reasonable thing for you to do is go home and get some rest, I assume you'll go back to the shop. I'll pick you up at seven."

Trapped, she nudged him aside and got to her feet. "We close at six."

"Then you'll have to wait, won't you? And don't slam the door on your way out."

Of course she did, and he found he had to smile. But the smile faded when he picked up the phone and hurriedly punched in a number. "Dr. Margaret De Witt, please. It's her son." Another look at his watch brought out a mild oath. "No, I can't wait. Would you ask her to call me when she's free? The office before six, at home after seven. Thanks."

He hung up, then began to put in order the papers Kate had scattered. Almost amused, he pocketed the filing tips she'd left behind. He doubted that Kate would appreciate him calling his mother the internist for an over-the-phone diagnosis of her symptoms.

But somebody had to look out for her. Whether she wanted it or not.

CHAPTER 7

SHE WAS GOING to be calm. Kate promised herself that. She'd made a fool of herself, barging into Byron's office, shouting and raging. She wouldn't have minded that so much—if it had worked. There was nothing worse than having a good temper fit snuffed out by reason, patience, and control.

It was more than humiliating.

She didn't much care for taking orders either. Frowning, she looked around the shop she'd just closed. She could simply walk out, she considered, drumming her fingers on the counter. She could just stroll right out, go anywhere she wanted. Home, for a drive, to Templeton House for dinner. That might be the best option, she thought, rubbing a hand absently over the grinding ache in her stomach. She was hungry, that was all. A good meal at Templeton House, an evening with Laura and the girls would soothe all the pangs and nerves.

It would serve Byron right if she wasn't there when he came gunning for her. For that, she was sure, was his intention. Soothe the victim with reason, with promises of calm discussions, then, *pow*, shoot her between the eyes.

And that, she knew, was the reason she was staying put. Kate Powell never walked away from a challenge.

Let him come, she told herself grimly as she began to wander about the shop. She could handle Byron De Witt in her sleep. Men like him were so used to getting their own way with a quick smile, a murmured word, they didn't know how to act with a woman who stood firmly on her own feet.

Besides, now that her finances were a little strained, she acknowledged the advantage of a free meal.

The grinding came back, like a sneering echo. Nerves, she thought again. Of course she was nervous. She knew better than anyone that Pretenses could barely support three incomes and stay afloat. They were lucky to have made it through the first year. But the odds were still against them.

She frowned down at a stylish glass rhinoceros in pale gold. How long, she wondered, were they going to be able to sell things quite that foolish? The price tag made her laugh. Nine hundred dollars? Who in their right mind would plunk down nearly a thousand dollars for something so ridiculous?

Margo, she decided, and her lips curved up again. Margo had a keen eye for the expensive, the ridiculous, and the salable.

If Pretenses went down the toilet, Margo would be fine. She had Josh now, a baby on the way, a beautiful home. A far cry from her circumstances a year ago, Kate mused, and was glad for her.

But there was Laura to worry about, and the girls. They wouldn't starve, Kate knew. The Templetons wouldn't allow it. They would live in Templeton House, which would give them far more than a roof over their heads. It would give them a home. Since Laura was too proud to touch the income from her Templeton stocks, she could work at the hotel and earn a living, a good one. But how badly would her ego be bruised if the business she started herself failed?

Kate had discovered a great deal about the difficulties of functioning with a scraped ego.

They had to make the shop work. It was Margo's dream, and it had become Laura's. It was all Kate had to hold on to. All her neat little plans were ruined. There would be no partnership at Bittle, no possibility of striking out with her own firm at some future date. No pretty brass plaque on her office door. No office, she thought, and sat down on a painted wooden bench.

Right now she had sleepless nights, headaches that never quite faded, a stomach that refused to behave, and Pretenses.

Pretenses, she thought with a thin smile. Margo had named it well. The three owners were just full of them.

The knock on the door made her jolt, then swear, then straighten her shoulders as she rose and went to unlock it. She nudged Byron aside, stepped out onto the little flower-decked veranda, and locked up again.

Pedestrian and street traffic churned past with all the noise and bustle that usually accompanied it. Tourists, she thought absently, searching for just the right spot to enjoy a vacation dinner. Members of the workforce heading home after a long day. Couples out on dates.

Just where did Kate Powell fit in?

"I'm not going because you told me I was going," she said without pre-amble, "I'm going because I want the opportunity to speak calmly and clearly about the situation, and because I'm hungry."

"Fine." He cupped a hand under her elbow. "We'll take my car. I managed to find a space in the lot across the street. It's a busy area."

"It's a good location," she began as he led her to the curb. "A stone's throw from Fisherman's Wharf and the water. Tourists are a big part of our business, but a lot of the locals come here to shop too."

Two young boys on a rented tandem bike whizzed by behind her, laughing like hyenas. It was a beautiful evening, full of soft light and soft scents. A night for beach walking, she mused, or for tossing hunks of bread to the gulls as the couple by the water was doing just now. A night, she thought, for couples. Kate nibbled her lip as Byron guided her across the street.

"I can follow you. There are a dozen restaurants within walking distance, for that matter."

"We'll take my car," he repeated, gently and firmly maneuvering through the crowded parking lot. "And I'll bring you back to yours when we're finished."

"It would save time and be more efficient if —"

"Kate." He turned and looked at her, really looked, and scotched the annoyed remark hovering on his tongue. The woman was exhausted. "Why don't you try something new? Go with the flow."

He opened the passenger door of his vintage Mustang and waited with some amusement for her bad-tempered shrug. He wasn't disappointed.

She watched him round the hood. He'd ditched his tie and jacket, she noted, opened his collar. The casual, easy look suited those lineman's shoulders, she supposed, the beachcomber hair. She decided to realign her strategy and wait until they were at dinner before beginning the lecture she'd been planning.

She could, when necessary, manage small talk with the best of them.

"So, you're into classic cars."

He settled behind the wheel. The minute he turned the key the radio exploded with Marvin Gaye. Byron turned it down to a murmur before cruising through the lot.

"Sixty-five Mustang with a 289 V-8. A car like this isn't just a mode of transportation. It's a commitment."

"Really?" She liked the creamy white bucket seats, the trained-panther ride, but couldn't think of anything more impractical than owning a car older than she was. "Don't you have to spend a lot of time babying it, finding parts?"

"That's the commitment. Runs like a dream," he added with an affectionate stroke to the dash as he merged into traffic. "She was my first."

"First what? First car?"

"That's right." He grinned at her baffled stare. "Bought her when I was seventeen. She's got over two hundred thousand miles on her and still purrs like a kitten."

Kate would have said it was more "roars like a lion," but that wasn't her problem. "Nobody keeps their first car. It's like your first lover."

"Exactly." He downshifted, eased around a turn. "As it happens, I had my first lover in the backseat, one sweet summer night. Pretty Lisa Montgomery." He sighed reminiscently. "She opened a window to paradise for me, God bless her."

"A window to paradise." Unable to resist, Kate craned her neck and studied the pristine backseat. It wasn't very difficult to imagine two young bodies groping. "All that in the back of an old Mustang."

"Classic Mustang," he corrected. "Just like Lisa Montgomery."

"But you didn't keep her."

"You can't keep everything, except memories. Remember your first time?"

"In my college dorm room. I was a slow starter." Marvin Gaye had given way to Wilson Pickett. Kate's foot began to keep time. "He was captain of the debate team and seduced me with his argument that sex, next to birth and death, was the ultimate human experience."

"Good one. I'll have to try it sometime."

She slanted a look at his profile. Hero perfect, she judged, with just a hint of rugged. "I don't imagine you need lines."

"It never hurts to keep a few in reserve. So what happened to the captain of the debate team?"

"He was used to getting his point across inside of three minutes. That ability bled over into the ultimate human experience."

"Oh." Byron fought back a grin. "Too bad."

"Not really. It taught me not to build up unrealistic expectations and not to depend on someone else to fulfill basic needs." Kate scanned the scenery. Her foot stopped tapping as she tensed up again. "Why are we on Seventeen Mile?"

"It's a pretty drive. I enjoy taking it every day. Did I mention that I was able to arrange renting the house I'm buying until we settle?"

"No, you didn't." But she was getting the drift. "You said we were going to have dinner and a civilized discussion."

"And we are. You can take a look at the favor you did for me at the same time."

Even as she formulated several arguments against, Byron turned into a driveway and pulled up behind a dramatically glossy black Corvette.

"It's a '63, first year the Stingray rolled out of Detroit," he said with a nod toward the car. "Three hundred sixty horsepower, fuel-injected. An absolute beauty. Not that the original 'Vette wasn't a honey before the redesign. They don't make bodies like that anymore."

"Why do you need two cars?"

"Need isn't the issue. Anyway, I have four cars. The other two are back in Atlanta."

"Four," she murmured, and found this little quirk of his amusing.

"Fifty-seven Chevy, 283-cubic-inch V-8. Baby blue, white sidewalls, all original equipment." There was affection in his voice. Kate thought the southern heat of it flowed over the words like a man describing a lover. "Every bit as classy as the songs they wrote about her."

"Billie Jo Spears." Kate knew her music trivia. "Fifty-seven Chevrolet.'"

"That's the best." Surprised and impressed, he grinned at her. "Keeping her company is a '67 GTO."

"'Three deuces and a four speed'?"

"Right." His grin widened. "And a 389."

She grinned back. "Just what the hell are three deuces, automotively speaking?"

"If you don't know already, it would take a little time to explain. Just let me know if you ever want a serious lesson."

Then he put a hand over Kate's and shifted his gaze to the house. She was relaxed enough not to pull away. "It's great, isn't it?"

"It's nice." All wood and glass, she mused, bilevel decks, flowers already blooming riotously, that wonderful cypress bent and magical. "I've seen it before."

"From the outside." Knowing she'd never wait for him to come around to her door, he leaned across her to open it. And inhaled the simple scent of soap. Enjoying it, he let his gaze wander lazily from her mouth to her eyes. "You'll be another first."

"Excuse me?"

God, was he losing his mind or was he actually starting to look forward to that edgy tone? "My first guest." He got out of the car, retrieved his briefcase and jacket. As they started up the walk, he took her hand in a friendly gesture. "You can hear the sea," he pointed out. "It's just close enough. I've caught a couple of glimpses of seals, too."

It was charming—almost too charming, she thought. The setting, the sounds, the scent of roses and night-blooming jasmine. What was left of the setting sun spread vivid, heartbreaking color across the western sky. The twisted shadows from the trees were long and deep.

"A lot of tourists drive along here," she said, fighting the spell. "Isn't that going to bother you?"

"No. The house is set back from the road, and the bedrooms face the water." He turned the key in the lock. "There's just one problem."

She was glad to hear it. Perfection made her nervous. "What?"

"I don't have much in the way of furniture." He opened the door and proved his point.

It shouldn't have delighted her. Bare floors, bare walls, bare space. Yet she found it delightful, the way the entranceway flowed into a room. The simplest of welcomes. The wide glass doors on the facing wall exploded with that stunning sunset, almost demanded to be opened wide to it.

The yellow pine floors gleamed under her feet as she stepped inside, crossed over them. There was no rug, as yet, to tame that ocean flood of shine.

He would get one, she imagined. It was practical, sensible. But, she thought, it would also be a shame.

From her outside survey of the house, she hadn't guessed that the ceilings were so high or that the stairs leading to the next level were open, as open as the carved pickets in the ornate railing that skirted the second story.

She could see how cleverly, how simply one room became another, so that the house appeared to be one large living space. White walls, golden floors, and the beautiful bleeding light from the west.

"Great view," she managed and wondered why her palms were damp. Casually she wandered to a crate on which stood an elaborate stereo system. The only piece of furniture was a ratty recliner with duct tape holding the arms together. "You've got the essentials, I see."

"No point in living without music. I picked up the chair at a yard sale. It's so awful it's wonderful. Want a drink?"

"Just some club soda, or water." Alcohol was off the list for a couple of reasons, and he was one of them.

"I've got some Templeton mineral water."

She smiled. "Then you've got the best."

"I'll take you on a tour after I've gotten dinner started. Come in the kitchen and keep me company."

"You know how to cook?" It was the shock of it that made her follow him.

"Actually, I do. You like grits and chitlins, right?" He waited a beat, turned, and wasn't disappointed with the look of sheer horror on her face. "Just kidding. How about seafood?"

"Not those crawfish things."

"I make a hell of a crawfish étouffée, but we'll save that for when we're better acquainted. If the rest of the house hadn't already sold me, this would have done it."

The kitchen was done in dramatic maroon and white tiles, with a center island that gleamed like an iceberg. A built-in banquette curved in front of a wide window that looked out on blooming flowers and the deep-green lawn.

"Subzero," Byron commented, running a loving hand over the stainless-steel front of a wide refrigerator. "Convection oven, Jenn-Air range, teak cabinets."

There was a big blue bowl of fresh, glossy fruit on the counter. The grinding in Kate's stomach told her if she didn't eat soon, she'd die. "You like to cook?"

"It relaxes me."

"Okay, why don't you relax? I'll watch."

She had to admit it was an impressive show. She sipped chilled water while he sliced an array of colorful vegetables. His movements were brisk and, as far as she could tell, professional. Intrigued, she moved closer, watched his hands.

Very nice hands, now that she took a good look. Long fingers, wide palms, with a neat manicure that didn't take away from the basic masculinity.

"Did you, like, take a course or something?"

"Or something. We had this cook. Maurice." Byron turned a red bell pepper into long, neat strips. "He told me he'd teach me how to box. I was tall and skinny, regularly got the shit beat out of me at school."

Kate stepped back, did a slow survey. Broad shoulders, trim waist, narrow hips. Long limbs, certainly. And with his sleeves rolled up for cooking, she could see forearms that looked just a bit dangerous. "What happened? Steroids?"

He chuckled and went briskly to work on an onion. "I grew into my arms and legs after a while, started working out, but I was about twelve and pathetically awkward."

"Yeah." Kate sipped, remembering her own adolescence. The trouble was, she'd never grown into anything. Still the runt of the litter, she mused. "It's a rough age."

"So Maurice said he'd teach me to defend myself, but I had to learn to cook. It was, according to him, just one more way to become self-sufficient." Byron drizzled oil into a large cast-iron pan already heating on the stove. "In about six months I whipped Curt Bodine's bad ass—he was the bane of my existence at the time."

"I had Candy Dorall, now Litchfield," Kate put in conversationally. "She was always my bane."

"The terminally pert Candace Litchfield? Redhead, smug, foxy face, annoying little giggle?"

Anyone who described Candy so accurately deserved a smile. "I think I might like you after all."

"Did you ever punch Candy in her sassy nose?"

"It's not her nose. She had rhinoplasty." Kate snacked on a strip of pepper. "And no, but we did stuff her naked into a locker. Twice."

"Not bad, but that's girl stuff. Me, I just beat the hell out of Curt, salvaged masculine pride while earning the appropriate macho rep. And I could produce a chocolate soufflé to die for."

When she laughed, he paused and turned to face her. "Do that again." When she didn't respond, he shook his head. "You really ought to laugh more, Katherine. It's a fascinating sound. Surprisingly full and rich. Like something you'd expect to hear floating out of the window of a New Orleans brothel."

"I'm sure that's a compliment." She lifted her water glass again, made herself keep her eyes level with his. "But I rarely laugh on an empty stomach."

"We'll fix that." He tossed minced garlic into the hot oil. The scent was immediate and wonderful. The onion went in next, and she began to salivate.

He pried the lid off a covered bowl, slid shelled shrimp and scallops into the pan. She thought it was a bit like watching a mad scientist at work. A glug of white wine, a pinch of salt, a slight grating of what he told her was ginger. Quick stirs and shakes to mix all those pretty strips of vegetables.

In less time than it might have taken her to peruse a menu, she was sitting down to a full plate.

"It's good," she said after her first bite. "It's really good. Why aren't you in food services?"

"Cooking's a hobby."

"Like conversation and old cars."

"Vintage cars." It pleased him to see her eat. He'd decided on the menu because he'd wanted to get something healthy into her. He imagined her snatching junk food when she remembered to eat at all, snacking on antacids. No wonder she was too thin. "I could teach you."

"Teach me what?"

"To cook."

She speared a shrimp. "I didn't say I couldn't cook."

"Can you?"

"No, but I didn't say I couldn't. And I don't need to as long as there's takeout and microwave ovens."

Because she'd refused his offer of wine, he stuck with water himself. "I bet there's a place reserved for you at McDonald's drive-through window."

"So? It's quick, it's easy, and it's filling."

"Nothing wrong with the occasional french fry, but when it's a dietary staple—"

"Don't start with me, Byron. This is why I'm here in the first place." Remembering her plan, she got down to business. "I don't like people, particularly people I barely know, interfering in my life."

"We have to get to know each other better."

"No, we don't." It was weird, she realized, how easily she'd become distracted, and interested, and at ease. Time had slipped by when all she'd meant to do was give him the sharpest edge of one piece of her mind. "Your intentions might have been good, but you had no business going to Josh."

"Your eyes are fabulous," he said and watched them narrow with suspicion. "I don't know if it's because they're so big, so dark, or because your face is narrow, but they really pack a punch."

"Is that one of your reserved lines?"

"No, it's an observation. I happen to be looking at your face, and it occurs to me that it has all these contrasts. The snooty New England cheekbones, the wide, sexy mouth, angular nose, the big, doe eyes. It shouldn't work, but it does. It works better when you're not pale and tired, but that adds a rather disconcerting fragile quality."

She shifted. "I'm not fragile. I'm not tired. And my face has nothing to do with the subject under discussion."

"But I like it. I liked it right away, even when I didn't like you. Now I wonder, Kate," he continued, laying a hand over hers, twining fingers.

"Why did you put so much effort into making sure I didn't look twice in your direction?"

"I didn't have to put any effort into that. I'm not your type any more than you're mine."

"No, you're not," he agreed. "Still, I occasionally enjoy sampling something . . . different."

"I'm not a new recipe." She pulled her hand free, pushed her plate aside. "And I came here to have, as you termed it, a civilized discussion."

"This seems civilized to me."

"Don't pull out that reasonable tone." She had to squeeze her eyes shut and count to ten. She made it to five. "I hate that reasonable tone. I agreed to go to dinner with you so that I could make myself clear, so that I could do so without losing my temper the way I did earlier today."

For emphasis, she leaned forward a little, was distracted by discovering that there was a thin gold halo around his pupils. "I don't want you meddling in my life. I don't know how to make it any more plain than that."

"That's plain." Since they seemed to have finished the meal, he picked up the plates and carried them to the counter. Sitting again, he took a cigar from his pocket, lit it. "But there's a problem. I've developed an interest in you."

"Yeah, right."

"You find that difficult to believe?" He puffed out smoke, considered. "So did I initially. Then I realized what kicked it off. I'm driven to solve problems and puzzles. Answers and solutions are essential to me. Do you want coffee?"

"No, I don't want coffee." Didn't he know it drove her crazy the way he could slide from one topic to the next in that slow, southern drawl of his. Of course he did. "And I'm not a problem or a puzzle."

"But you are. Look at you, Kate. You white-knuckle your way through life." He reached out, deliberately uncurled her fist. "I can almost see whatever fuel you bother to put inside you being sucked away by nerves. You have a loving family, a solid base, an excellent mind, but you pick at details as if they were knotted threads. You never consider just snipping one off. Yet when you're faced with the injustice, the insult of being fired from a job that was a huge part of your life, you sit back and do nothing."

It grated and hurt and shamed. And because she couldn't explain to him, or to those who cared for her, it festered. "I'm doing what works for me. And I didn't come here for an analysis."

"I haven't finished," he said mildly. "You're afraid to be vulnerable, even ashamed of it. You're a practical woman, yet you're aware you're physically run-down and you're doing nothing about that either. You're an honest woman, but you're putting all of your energy into denying there might be even a mild hint of attraction between us. So you interest me." He took a last drag on his cigar, tamped it out. "The puzzle of you interests me."

She got to her feet slowly to prove to both of them she was still in control. "I realize it might be difficult—no, next to impossible—for you to realize that I'm not interested in you. I'm not vulnerable, I'm not ill, and I'm not even mildly attracted."

"Well." He unfolded himself and rose. "We can put at least one of those statements to the test." His eyes stayed watchful on hers as he cupped a hand behind her neck. "Unless you're afraid you're wrong."

"I'm not wrong. And I don't want—"

He decided it was simpler not to let her finish. The woman could argue with the dead. He covered her mouth with his quietly, with barely a whisper of pressure and promise. When her hands jerked up to his chest, he scooped an arm around her waist and brought her gently closer.

For his own pleasure, he skimmed his tongue over her lips, then dipped inside when they parted. He thought, foolishly, that he could hear a new window to a new paradise begin to creak open.

Then she trembled, and he forgot to be amused at both of them. When he eased back he saw that she was still pale, her eyes dark and clouded. Testing, he pressed light kisses on either side of her mouth and watched her lashes flutter.

"I don't—I can't—God." The hand pressed against his chest balled into a fist. "I don't have the time or the inclination for this."

"Why?"

Because her head was spinning, her pulse was pounding, and her juices were running in a way they hadn't in—ever. "You're not my type."

That clever mouth curved. "You're not mine either. Go figure."

"Men who look like you are always scum." She knew better, absolutely knew better, but she couldn't stop her hands from streaking up his chest and grabbing all that wonderful gold-tipped hair. "It's like the law."

His lips curved. "Whose law?"

She could have had a snappy comeback for that, if she'd just been able to concentrate. "Oh, the hell with it," she muttered and dragged his mouth back to hers.

Nerves and needs seemed to pulse from her in fast, greedy waves. He couldn't stand against them, could barely stand at all once her mouth started its assault. He should have known she wouldn't believe in the slow and the gradual, or the easy sweetness of a lazy seduction. But he hadn't considered that the fire-drenched demands of that mobile mouth would undermine his innate sense of reason.

In the space of a heartbeat he went from enjoying her to devouring her.

His arms banded around her, forgot about her long, fragile bones and soft, spare flesh. He used his teeth because that mouth, that wide, sultry mouth seemed to have been made for him to ravish. The scent of soap was absurdly sexy. He could almost taste it as he ran hot, wild kisses down her throat.

"It's only because I haven't had sex in so long." She gasped out the rationale even as her eyes crossed.

"Okay. Whatever." He curled his hands around her tiny, tight butt and muffled a moan against her throat.

"A year," she managed. "Okay, it's been nearly two, but after the first few months you hardly . . . Jesus, touch me. I'm going to scream if you don't touch me."

Where? He nearly panicked. He was unable to tell one part of her from another. He was steeped in all of her. Instinct had him tugging her crisp white shirt out of the waistband of her skirt, fumbling with buttons.

"Upstairs." He swore ripely as the buttons refused to yield. He didn't have enough sanity left to be appalled at how his fingers shook. "We should go upstairs. I've got a bed."

Desperate, she grabbed his hand and pressed it to her breast herself. "You've got a floor right here."

He managed a laugh. "I'm beginning to love practical women."

"You haven't seen anything—" Then it hit her. The first wave of pain was followed so swiftly by a second she barely managed a choked gasp.

"What? What is it? Did I hurt you?"

"No, it's nothing." He was trying to straighten her up as she doubled over. "It's just a twinge. It's—" But the burning was spreading like wildfire, and the fear burst through with it as she felt her skin break out in a cold, clammy sweat. "Just give me a minute." Blindly she reached out for something to balance her and would have fallen if he hadn't scooped her up.

"The hell with this." The words exploded between gritted teeth. "The hell with it. I'm taking you to the hospital."

"No. Stop it." Desperate for relief, she hooked an arm under her breasts and pressed. "Just take me home."

"In a pig's eye." Like a warrior hoisting his conquest, he carried her out of the house. "Save your breath and yell at me later. Right now you're doing what you're told."

"I said take me home." She didn't bother to fight him when he strapped her into the car. All of her energy had to focus on dealing with the pain.

He backed out of the drive, saying nothing as she tore Tums out of the roll habitually in her pocket. Instead, he snatched up the car phone and punched in a number. "Mom." He drove fast, whipping the car around curves, and interrupted his mother's apology for not returning his call. "It's okay. Listen, I've got a friend, a woman, five sevenish, maybe a hundred and five pounds, mid-twenties." He swore lightly, cradling the phone on his shoulder as he shifted gears. "It's not that," he said at the inevitable chuckle. "I'm taking her to the hospital right now. She's got abdominal pain. It seems to be habitual."

"It's just stress," Kate managed between shallow breaths. "And your lousy cooking."

"Yes, that's her. She can talk, and she's lucid. I don't know." He glanced briefly at Kate. "Any abdominal surgery, Kate?"

"No. Don't talk to me."

"Yeah, I'd say she lives with a lot of stress, brings most of it on herself. We'd eaten about forty-five, fifty minutes before," he said in response to his mother's brisk questions. "No, no alcohol, no caffeine. But she lives on goddamn coffee and eats Tums like chocolate drops. Yeah? Is there a burning sensation?" he demanded of Kate.

"It's just indigestion," she muttered. The pain was backing off. Wasn't it? Please, wasn't it?

"Yes." He listened again, nodded. He was grimly aware of where his mother's questions were heading. "How often do you get that gnawing ache, under the breastbone?"

"None of your business."

"You don't want to piss me off right now, Kate. You really don't. How often?"

"A lot. So what? You're not taking me to any hospital."

"And the grinding in the stomach?"

Because he was describing her symptoms with pinpoint accuracy, she closed her eyes and ignored him.

He spoke to his mother another moment, punched up the gas. "Thanks, that's what I figured. I'm going to take care of it. Yeah, I'll let you know. I will. 'Bye." He hung up, kept his eyes firmly on the road. "Congratulations, you idiot. You've got yourself a nice little ulcer."

CHAPTER 8

NO WAY DID she have an ulcer. Kate comforted herself with that thought, and the image of how foolish Byron was going to look for rushing her to the hospital with a case of nervous heartburn.

Ulcers were for repressed wimps who didn't know how to express their emotions, who were afraid to face what was inside them. Kate figured she expressed her emotions just fine, and at every opportunity.

She was simply dealing with more stress than usual. Who wouldn't have a jittery stomach after the two months she'd just had? But she was handling it, she told herself, shutting her eyes tight against the incessant burning pressure. She was handling it her way.

The minute Byron stopped the car, she would explain yet again, calmly, that Kate Powell took care of Kate Powell.

She would have, too. If she could have caught her breath. But he jerked to a halt in front of the emergency room, slammed out of the car, and plucked her out of her seat before she could so much as squeak.

Then it was worse, because she was inside, with all the sounds and scents of a hospital. Emergency rooms were all the same, everywhere. The air inside was thick with despair and fear and fresh blood. Antiseptics, alcohol, sweat. The slap of crepe-soled shoes and the whisper of wheels on linoleum. It paralyzed her. It was all she could do to keep herself from curling into a ball in the hard plastic chair where he'd dumped her.

"Stay," he ordered curtly before marching over to the admitting nurse.

She didn't even hear him.

Flashes of memory assaulted her. She could hear the high, desperate scream of sirens, see the red lights pulsing and spinning. She was eight years old again, and the dull throb deep inside her ached like a wound. And blood—she could smell it.

Not hers. Or very little of her blood. She'd barely had a scratch. Contusions, they had called them. Minor lacerations. A mild concussion. Nothing life-threatening. Nothing life-altering.

But they had wheeled her parents away, even while she'd screamed for her mother. And they had never come back.

"It's your lucky night," Byron said when he came back to her. "Not much going on. They're going to take a look at you now."

"I can't be here," she murmured. "I can't be in a hospital."

"That's the breaks, kid. This is where the doctors are." He lifted her to her feet, surprised when she went along like an obedient puppy. He passed her off to a nurse, then settled down to wait.

Kate told herself the more she cooperated, the quicker they would let her go. And they had to let her go. She wasn't a child now who had no choice. She stepped into the narrow examining area, shuddering once at the sound of the curtain being drawn closed behind her.

"Let's see what we've got here."

The doctor on duty was young and pretty. A round face, narrow eyes behind wire-framed glasses, dark hair scooped back at the side with simple bobby pins.

It had been a man before, Kate remembered. He'd been young, too, but his eyes had been exhausted and old. Mechanically, Kate answered the standard questions. No, she didn't have any allergies, she'd had no surgery, she was taking no medication.

"Why don't you lie back, Ms. Powell? I'm Dr. Hudd. I'm going to check you out. Are you having pain now?"

"No, not really."

The doctor lifted an eyebrow. "No or not really?"

Kate closed her eyes and struggled to steep herself in the here and now. "Some."

"Tell me when it increases."

Soft hands, Kate thought as they began to probe her. Doctors always seemed to have soft hands. Then she hissed as the doctor applied pressure under her breastbone.

"That's the spot, huh? How often does this happen?"

"It happens."

"Do you find the discomfort occurs after a meal, say, an hour or so after a meal?"

"Sometimes." She sighed. "Yes."

"And when you drink alcohol?"

"Yes."

"Is there any vomiting?"

"No." Kate swiped a hand over her clammy face. "No."

"Dizziness?"

"No. Well, not really."

Dr. Hudd's unpainted mouth pursed as she pressed her fingers to Kate's wrist. "Your pulse is a little fast."

"I don't want to be here," Kate said flatly. "I hate hospitals."

"Yeah, I know the feeling." The doctor continued as she made notations on a chart, "Describe the pain for me."

Kate stared up at the ceiling, pretended she was talking aloud to herself. "It's a burning in the torso, or an aching." She wouldn't stay here, she reminded herself calmly. On this table, behind these curtains. "More like sharp hunger pains in my stomach. They can get pretty intense."

"I bet. How have you been dealing with it?"

"My heartburn," Kate said dully. "Mylanta."

The doctor chuckled, patted Kate's hand. "Are you under a lot of stress, Ms. Powell?"

My father was a thief, I've lost my job, and the cops could be knocking on my door any minute. There's nothing I can do about it, nothing, that won't make it worse.

"Who isn't?" She tried not to jerk when the doctor lifted her eyelid and shined a light to check her pupils.

"How long have you been having these symptoms?"

"Somewhere around forever. I don't know. They've gotten worse in the last couple of months."

"Sleeping well?"

"No."

"Taking anything for that?"

"No."

"How about headaches?"

"No, thanks. I have plenty of them. Nuprin," she said, anticipating the question. "Excedrin. I switch off."

"Mm-hmm. When was your last physical?" When Kate didn't answer, the doctor eased back, pursed her lips again. "That long ago, huh? Who's your regular doctor?"

"I go see Minelli once a year for a pap. I don't get sick."

"You're doing a good imitation of it now. I'll follow that up with my imitation of an exam. Let's check your blood pressure."

Kate submitted to it. She was calmer now, certain that the ordeal was almost over. She imagined the doctor would dash off a prescription and be done with it.

"Blood pressure's a little high, heart's strong. You're underweight, Ms. Powell. Dieting?"

"No. I never diet."

"Lucky you," Hudd said, with a considering look in her eye. It was a look Kate recognized, one that made her sigh.

"I don't have an eating disorder, doctor. I'm not bulimic, not anorexic. No binging, no purging, no pills. I've always been thin."

"So you haven't lost any weight lately?"

"A few pounds, maybe," Kate admitted. "My appetite's been kind of sporadic. Look, I've had some problems at work and it's stressed me out. That's all. Believe me, if I had a choice, I'd rather have curves than angles."

"Well, when we solve this problem, you should put them back on. After we run a few tests—"

Kate's hand shot out, curled around the doctor's wrist. "Tests? What kind of tests?"

"Nothing that involves torture chambers, I promise. We need some X-rays, a barium certainly. And I recommend an upper G.I. These are to pinpoint and to eliminate."

"I don't want any tests. Give me a pill and let me out of here."

"Ms. Powell, it's not quite that simple. We'll get you in and out of X-ray as quickly as possible. I'll try to schedule the G.I. for first thing in the morning. Once we get you admitted—"

Panic was white, Kate realized. White rooms and women in white uniforms. "You're not keeping me here."

"Just overnight," the doctor soothed. "It's not that I don't respect your boyfriend's diagnosis . . ."

"He's not my boyfriend."

"Well, I'd work on that if I were you, but in any case, he's not a doctor."

"His mother is. He talked to his mother on the way over. Ask him. I want you to get him back here. I want you to get him."

"All right. Try to calm down. I'll go talk to him. Just lie down here and try to relax." The doctor eased Kate's shoulders back.

Once she was alone, Kate struggled to breathe deeply, evenly. But terror was circling.

"Still arguing," Byron began when he stepped into the room.

Kate popped up like a spring. "I can't stay here." She snatched at his shirt front with trembling hands. "You have to get me out."

"Now, listen, Kate—"

"I can't stay here overnight. I can't spend the night in a hospital. I can't." Her voice lowered to a broken whisper. "My parents."

Confusion came first. Did she expect him to call the Templetons in France to back her up? Then he remembered—her own parents were dead. Had been killed in an accident. Hospital.

And he saw that what he had taken for pain and bad temper in her eyes was sheer terror.

"Okay, baby." To soothe her, he pressed his lips to her brow. "Don't worry. You're not going to stay."

"I can't." She felt her breath hitch, felt the simmering hysteria start its greasy rise.

"You won't. I promise." He cupped her face until her swimming eyes met his. "I promise, Kate. I'm going to talk to the doctor now, then I'll take you home."

Hysteria receded, replaced by trust. "All right. Okay." She closed her eyes. "All right."

"Just give me a minute." He stepped to the other side of the curtain with the doctor. "She's got a phobia. I didn't realize it."

"Look, Mr. De Witt, most people don't like spending time in hospitals. There are times I don't like it myself."

"I'm not talking about ordinary resistance." Frustrated, he dragged a hand through his hair. "That's all I thought it was. But it's a lot more. Listen, her parents were killed in some sort of accident when she was a kid. I don't know the details, but there must have been some hospital time. She's panicked at staying here, and she isn't the panicking type."

"She needs these tests," the doctor insisted.

"Dr. . . . Hudd, is it? Dr. Hudd, she's got an ulcer. Textbook symptoms. We both know it."

"Because your mother said so?"

"My mother's chief of internal medicine at Atlanta General."

Hudd's brows shot up. "Dr. Margaret De Witt?" She sighed again. "Impressive. I've read a number of her papers. Though I tend to agree with her diagnosis, I'm sure she'd agree with my procedure. Signs point to a duodenum ulcer, but I can't discard other possibilities. These tests are standard."

"And if the patient is so distressed, emotionally wrecked, that the idea of the tests aggravates the preexisting condition?" He waited a beat. "Neither one of us is going to be able to force her to have them. She'll just walk out of here, go on popping Tums until she's got a hole in her stomach you could sink a putt through."

"No, I can't force her to have the tests," Hudd said irritably. "And I can give her medication, in exchange for a promise that she comes back as an outpatient for a barium X-ray if symptoms recur."

"I'll see that she does."

"You'd better. Her blood pressure's up, her weight's down. She's hoarding stress. I'd say she's got a breakdown on the boil."

"I'll take care of her."

Dr. Hudd hesitated a moment, measuring him. Then nodded. "I'm sure you will." She reached for the curtain, glanced back. "Is your father Dr. Brian De Witt?"

"Thoracic surgery."

"And you're—"

"In hotels." He smiled charmingly. "But my sisters are doctors. All three of them."

"There's one in every family."

"I'M SORRY," KATE murmured. She kept her head back, resting it against the car's seat. Kept her eyes closed.

"Just follow doctor's orders. Take your medicine, get your rest. Cut back on the jalapeños."

She knew he said it to make her smile, and tried to oblige him. "And I was just craving some. I didn't want to ask until I was sure we'd managed the great escape, but how did you talk her out of admitting me?"

"Reason, charm, compromise. And by invoking my mother's name. She's a big deal."

"Oh."

"And a promise," he added, "that if it happens again, you go in for X-rays—as an outpatient." He laid a hand over hers, squeezed. "This isn't something you can ignore, Kate. You have to take care of this, and yourself."

She fell silent again. It was all too embarrassing. And there were still little hot licks of panic flickering in her stomach.

When she opened her eyes again, she saw the moon-kissed sweep of Big Sur, the rise of cliffs, the flash of forests, the wild curve of the road with thin mists of fog hovering. Tears stung her eyes. She'd asked him to take her home, and he'd understood. Home was Templeton House.

The lights were glowing against the windows. Glowing in a warmth and welcome that was as dependable as sunrise. She could smell the flowers, hear the sea. Even before he had fully stopped the car at the top of the drive, the door swung open. Laura raced out.

"Oh, honey, are you all right?" Her robe swirling around her legs, Laura wrenched open the car door and all but absorbed Kate into her arms. "I've been so worried!"

"It's all right. It's so silly. I—" Then she spotted Ann hurrying out and nearly broke.

"There, darling girl." Crooning, Ann tucked an arm around Kate's waist. "Let's get you inside now."

"I—" But it was too easy to just let her head rest on Ann's shoulder. Here were memories of warm cookies and sweet tea. Of soft sheets and cool hands.

"Byron." Laura cast a distracted look back at him. "I'm so grateful you called. I—" She looked toward Kate, already halfway to the house with Ann. "Please come in. Let me get you some coffee."

"No, I'll head on home." It was obvious that Laura was oblivious to everyone but Kate. "I'll come by later and see how she is. Go ahead."

"Thank you. Thank you so much." She dashed away.

He watched her catch up and flank Kate on the other side. The three of them slipped into the house as one.

SHE SLEPT FOR twelve hours and awakened rested and dazed. She was in the room of her middle childhood. The wallpaper was the same, the subtle pastel stripes. The blinds of her late adolescence had been replaced by lace curtains that swayed at the open windows. They had been Kate's grandmother's. Had hung in her own mother's bedroom. Aunt Susie had thought they would bring her comfort when she had first settled in Templeton House, and she'd been right.

They brought her comfort now.

There had been many a morning Kate had lain in the big, soft four-poster and watched those curtains flutter. And felt her parents close.

If she could just talk to them now, she thought. Just try to understand why her father had done what he had done. But what comfort would there be in that? What excuse could possibly justify it?

She had to concentrate on the now. Had to find a way to live in the now. And yet how could she not drift back?

It was the house, most of all, she supposed. It held so many memories. There was history here, eras, people, ghosts. Like the cliffs, the forests, those wildly shaped cypress trees, it held magic.

She turned her face into the pillow, encased in Irish linen. Ann always saw to it that the bed linen was scented lightly with lemon. There were flowers on the night table, a Waterford vase filled with sweet-smelling freesia. A note was propped against it. Recognizing Laura's handwriting, she stirred herself to reach out.

Kate, I didn't want to wake you when I left. Margo and I are at the shop this morning. We don't want to see you there. Annie has agreed to lock you in your room if necessary. You're to take your next dose at eleven sharp, unless you sleep through it. One of us will come home at lunchtime. You're expected to stay in bed. If you ever scare us like this again . . . I'll threaten you in person. I love you, Laura.

Just like her, Kate mused, and set the note aside. But she couldn't very well stay in bed all day. Too much thinking time in bed. No, she decided to call it by its name: brooding time. So she would find something to keep her from brooding. Her briefcase had to be somewhere, she decided. She'd just—

"And what do you think you're about, young lady?" Ann Sullivan stood in the doorway with a tray in her hand and a hard light in her eyes.

"I was going to . . . go to the bathroom. That's all." Cautiously Kate finished climbing out of bed and ducked into the adjoining bath.

Smiling, Ann set down the tray and moved to fluff the pillows. All her girls thought they could lie when the chips were down, she mused. And only Margo was any good at it. She waited, her back soldier straight, until Kate came back in. Then Ann merely pointed at the bed.

"Now, I'm going to see to it that you eat, take your medicine, and behave yourself." With smooth efficiency, Ann fit the tray over Kate's lap. "An ulcer, is it? Well, we're not putting up with that. No, indeed. Now Mrs. Williamson has fixed you some nice soft scrambled eggs and toast. And there's herb tea. She says chamomile will soothe your innards. You'll eat the fruit too. The melon's very mild."

"Yes, ma'am." She felt as though she could eat for hours. "Annie, I'm sorry."

"For what? For being knotheaded? Well, you should be." But she sat on the edge of the bed and, in the time-honored fashion, laid her hand over Kate's brow to test for fever. "Working yourself up until you're sick. And look at you, Miss Kate, nothing but a bag of bones. Eat every bite of those eggs."

"I thought it was heartburn," she murmured, then bit her lip. "Or cancer."

"What is this nonsense?" Appalled, Ann snagged Kate's chin in her hand. "You were worrying you had cancer and did nothing about it?"

"Well, I figured if it was heartburn I could live with it. And if it was cancer, I'd just die anyway." She grimaced at the violent glare. "I feel like such a fool."

"I'm glad to hear it, for you are." Clucking her tongue, Annie poured Kate's tea. "Miss Kate, I love you, but never in my life have I been more angry with anyone. No, you don't. Don't you dare tear up while I'm yelling at you."

Kate sniffled, took the tissue Ann held out, and blew her nose fiercely. "I'm sorry," she said again.

"Be sorry, then." Exasperated, she handed over another tissue. "I thought Margo was the only one of you who could make me crazy. You may have waited twenty years to do it, my girl, but you've matched her. Did you once tell your family you were feeling poorly? Did you once think what it would mean to us if you ended up in the hospital?"

"I thought I could handle it."

"Well, you couldn't, could you?"

"No."

"Eat those eggs before they're cold. There's Mrs. Williamson down in the kitchen, fretting over you. And old Joe the gardener cutting his precious freesia so you could wake to them. That's to say nothing of Margo, who kept me on the phone thirty minutes or more this morning, so worked up over you, she is. And Mr. Josh, who came by and looked in on you before he would go on to his work. And do you think Miss Laura got a wink of sleep last night?"

As she lectured, Ann piled toast with raspberry preserves and handed it to Kate. "That's to say nothing of how the Templetons are going to feel when they hear."

"Oh, Annie, please don't—"

"Don't tell them?" Ann said, with a fierce look at Kate. "Is that what you were going to say, missy? Don't tell the people who loved and cared for you, who gave you a home and a family?"

No one, Kate thought miserably, piled on jam or shame like Ann Sullivan. "No. I'll call them myself. Today."

"That's better. And when you're feeling more yourself, you're going to go and thank Mr. De Witt in person for taking care of you."

"I . . ." Foreseeing fresh humiliation, Kate toyed with her eggs. "I did thank him."

"And you'll thank him again." She glanced up as a maid knocked quietly on the open door.

"Excuse me. These just arrived for Miss Powell." She carried in a long white florist's box and set it on the foot of the bed.

"Thank you, Jenny. Wait just a moment and we'll see what vase we'll use. No, you finish eating," Ann continued. "I'll open this."

She undid the bow, opened the lid, and the room was filled with the scent of roses. Two dozen long-stemmed yellows bloomed against a bed of glossy green. She allowed herself one quiet, feminine sigh.

"Fetch the Baccarat, will you, Jenny? The tall one in the library breakfront."

"Yes, ma'am."

"Now I know I'm sick." Cheered, Kate plucked up the envelope. "Imagine Margo sending me a bunch of flowers." But when she tore out the card, her jaw dropped.

"Not from Margo, I take it." With the privilege of time and affection, Ann slipped the card out of Kate's fingers and read, " 'Relax, Byron.' Well, well, well."

"It's nothing to 'well' about. He's just feeling sorry for me."

"Two dozen yellow roses are something aside from sympathy, girl. That's moving toward romance."

"Hardly."

"Seduction, anyway."

Kate remembered the wild embrace in his kitchen. Hot, intense, rudely interrupted. "Maybe. Sort of. If I was the seducing type."

"We all are. Thank you, Jenny. I'll take it from here."

Ann took the vase from the maid and went into the bathroom to fill it. She wasn't surprised, and not just a little pleased, to see Kate sniffing thoughtfully at one of the blooms when she came back.

"Drink your tea now while I arrange these. It's a relaxing thing, arranging flowers."

She took a pair of scissors from the old kneehole desk, spread the tissue that had covered the flowers on the dresser, and got to work. "Something you take your time about, enjoy. Plunking them by the handful into a handy vase doesn't bring any joy."

Kate dragged her thoughts away from detailing a list of Byron De Witt's qualities. Confident, kind, interfering, sexy, meddlesome. Sexy. "It gets the job done."

"If that's all you're after. In my opinion, Miss Kate, you've always been in a hurry to get the job done, whatever it may be. You've forgotten the pleasure of doing. Rushing through something to get to the next something might be productive, but it's not fun."

"I have fun," Kate muttered.

"Do you now? From what I've seen, you've even turned your weekly treasure hunts into a scheduled chore. Let me ask you this. If you were, by some wild chance in your quest for efficiency, to stumble over Seraphina's dowry, what would you do with it?"

"Do with it?"

"That's what I asked. Would you take the riches and sail around the world, lie on some lazy beach, buy a fancy car? Or would you invest it in mutual funds and tax-free bonds?"

"Properly invested, money makes money."

Ann slipped a stem gently into the vase. "And for what? So it can pile up neatly in some vault? Is that the only means to the end, or end to the means? Not that you haven't done a tidy job with helping me build up a fine nest egg, darling, but you've got to have dreams. And sometimes they have to be beyond your immediate reach."

"I have plans."

"I didn't say plans. I said dreams." Wasn't it odd, Ann mused. Her own daughter had always dreamed too much. Miss Laura had dreamed simple dreams that had broken her heart. And little Miss Kate had never let herself dream enough. "What are you waiting for, darling? To be as old as me before you indulge yourself, enjoy yourself?"

"You're not old, Annie," Kate said softly. "You'll never be old."

"Tell that to the lines that crop up on my face daily." But she smiled as she turned. "What are you waiting for, Katie?"

"I don't know. Exactly." Her gaze shifted to the crystal vase behind Ann, filled to bursting with yellow flowers that glowed like sunlight. She could, if she bothered to, count on one hand the number of times a man had sent her roses. "I haven't really thought about it."

"Then it's time you did. Top of the list is what makes Kate happy. You're good at list making, God knows," she said briskly, then went to the closet for the robe Kate always left in her room at Templeton House. "Now you can sit out on the terrace in the sun for a while. You sit there and do nothing but dream for a bit."

CHAPTER 9

A WEEK OF pampering was excellent medicine. For Kate it was also nearly an overdose. Yet anytime she made noises about going home and getting back to work, everyone within earshot ganged up on her.

Telling herself she would turn over a new leaf if it killed her, she struggled to let it ride, to go with the flow, to take life as it came.

And wondered how anyone could live that way.

She reminded herself that it was a gorgeous evening. That she was sitting in the garden with a child snuggled in her lap, another at her feet. Her ulcer—if it was an ulcer—hadn't given her any real trouble in days.

And she had found there, in the home of her childhood, a peace that had been missing.

"I wish you could live with us forever and ever, Aunt Kate." Kayla looked up, her gray eyes soft in her angel's face. "We'd never let you get sick or worry too much."

"Aunt Margo says you're a professional nitpicker." Ali giggled at the term and carefully brushed pink polish on Kate's toenails. "What's a nit?"

"Aunt Margo." Wasn't it bad enough, Kate thought, that she was going to have hot-pink toenails, without adding insult to injury? "Good thing for her I happen to like nits."

"If you didn't go back to your apartment, we could play with you every day." For Kayla, this was the ultimate bribe. "And you and Mama could have tea parties like Annie said you used to when you were little."

"We can all have tea parties when I come visit," Kate reminded her. "That's more special."

"But if you lived here, you wouldn't have to pay rent." Ali capped the polish and looked entirely too wise for a ten-year-old. "Until you regain your financial feet."

A fresh smile flitted around Kate's mouth. "Where'd you get that?"

"You're always saying stuff like that." Ali smiled and pressed her cheek against Kate's knee. "And Mama's working a lot now and nothing's the way it used to be. It's better with you here."

"I like being with you, too."

Touched and torn, Kate stroked Ali's curly hair. A sunshine-yellow butterfly flitted through the air and landed gracefully in the cup of a red petunia. For a moment, Kate caressed the child and watched the butterfly's wings gently open and close as it fed.

How hard would it be, she wondered, to simply stay here, like this, forever? Just drift. Forget everything. Not hard at all, she realized. And wasn't that part of the reason it wasn't possible for her?

"I have to go back to my own place. That doesn't mean I won't spend lots of time with you. Every Sunday for sure, so we can find all of Seraphina's gold."

She looked up in relief at the sound of footsteps. If this kept up, she'd be ready to agree to anything her nieces wanted. "There's the nit now."

Margo only raised an elegant eyebrow as the girls giggled. "I'll consider that a private joke. I'm too jazzed to be annoyed with you. Look!" After tugging up her sleek linen tunic, she pulled out the elastic waist of her slacks. "I couldn't get my skirt zipped this morning. I'm starting to show." Her face glowing, she turned to the side. "Can you tell?"

"You look like a beached whale," Kate said dryly, but Kayla bounced up and rushed over to press an ear against Margo's tummy.

"I can't hear him yet," she complained. "Are you sure he's in there?"

"Absolutely sure, but I can't guarantee the *he* part." Abruptly her lips trembled, her eyes filled. "Kate, it moved. This afternoon I was helping a customer decide between an Armani and a Donna Karan, and I felt this, this fluttering. I felt the baby move. I felt—I felt—" She broke off and burst into wild tears.

"Oh, Jesus." Jolting up, Kate gathered the goggle-eyed girls and nudged them toward the flagstone path. "This is a good thing," she assured them. "She's crying because she's happy. Tell Mrs. Williamson we want a whole jug of lemonade, the kind she makes that fizzes."

Whirling back to Margo, she hugged her close. "I was only kidding before. You're not fat."

"I want to be fat," Margo sobbed. "I want to waddle. I want to stop being able to sleep on my stomach."

"Okay." Torn between amusement and concern, Kate patted her. "Okay, honey, you will. In fact, I think you're already starting to waddle. A little."

"Really?" Margo sniffed, caught herself. "Oh, shit, listen to me. I'm crazy. I'm doing this kind of thing all the time these days. I felt the baby move, Kate. I'm going to have a baby. I don't know anything about being a mother. I'm so scared. I'm so happy. Hell, I've wrecked my mascara."

"Thank God, she's coming back." A little shaky herself, she eased Margo into a chair. "What does Josh do when you have one of these crying jags?"

"Passes the tissues."

"Great." Without much hope, Kate searched her pockets. "I don't have any."

"I do." Margo sniffed and blew and sighed. "Wacky hormones." She used a fresh tissue to dab, then ran an expert hand over her fancy French braid. "I came out here to see how you were feeling."

"Unlike you, there doesn't seem to be anything going on in my stomach. It's fine. I think that ulcer business was just bullshit."

Recovered, Margo lifted a brow. "Oh, do you? Do you really?"

Because she recognized that tone, Kate braced for a fight. "Don't start on me."

"I've waited for days to start on you. But you're feeling fine now. So I can tell you, you're an insensitive, selfish idiot. You sent everyone who has the poor judgment to care about you into a tailspin of worry."

"Oh, and it would have been sensitive and selfless of me to whine and complain—which you're an expert at—and—"

"Take care of yourself," Margo finished. "See a doctor. No, not you, you're too smart for that, too busy for that."

"Get off my back."

"Pal, I've just climbed on, and I'm staying there like that monkey in the story. You've had a week of everyone patting your head and stroking you. Now you can take your dose of reality. Mr. and Mrs. T. are on their way back here."

Guilt heaped on Kate's head. "Why? There's no need for them to come all this way. It's just a stupid ulcer."

"Ah, now you admit it's an ulcer." Margo popped up again, whirled around the chair. "If this was a twelve-step program, you'd have made it to step one. They'd have been on the first plane the minute Laura called them, but she and Josh convinced them everything was under control and to finish up their business first. But nothing would stop them from seeing for themselves that their Kate was well."

"I talked to them myself. I told them it was nothing major."

"No, no, nothing major. You get suspended under suspicion of embez-zlement, end up in the ER. Nothing for them to worry about." She propped her hands on her hips. "Who the hell do you think you are?"

"I—"

"Josh is furious, blaming it all on Bittle, and beating himself up because he didn't jump on them the minute they axed you."

"That has nothing to do with it." Kate sprang up as well, her shouts matching Margo's decibel for decibel. "Josh has nothing to do with it."

"That's just like you. That's just perfectly like you. Nobody has anything to do with anything when it applies to you. That's why Laura's been blam-ing herself for not paying attention to how you were feeling, what you were doing. That doesn't mean a damn to you."

With fizzing lemonade sloshing in a glass pitcher, Laura all but ran toward the sounds of battle. "What's going on here? Margo, stop yelling at her."

"Shut up," Margo and Kate shouted in unison as they faced off.

"I could hear you all the way in the kitchen." Struggling not to slam glass on glass, Laura set the pitcher down on the table. Wide-eyed and fas-cinated, her daughters watched the three-way bout.

"I have to yell," Margo insisted. "To get the sound through that thick head of hers. You're too busy feeling sorry for her to yell."

"Don't drag Laura into this." But even as she said it, Kate whirled on Laura. "And you have no business blaming yourself for my problems. You are not responsible for me."

"If you took better care of yourself," Laura snapped back, "no one would have to be responsible for you."

"Ladies." Not sure whether he should be amused or wary, Josh stepped behind his nieces, took the glasses they carried out of their hands. "Is this any way to throw a party?"

"Stay out of this." Kate's voice vibrated with fury. "All of you stay out of my life. I don't need to be watched over and worried over. I'm perfectly capable—"

"Of making yourself sick," Margo finished.

"Everybody gets sick," Kate roared. "Everybody has pain."

"And those who are capable, seek help." Laura put her hands on Kate's shoulders and firmly shoved her into a chair. "If you'd had any sense, you'd have gone to the doctor, gone into the hospital for tests. Instead, you act like an idiot and send the entire family into an uproar."

"I couldn't go to the hospital. You know I can't . . . I can't."

Remembering, Laura rubbed her hands over her face. This is where temper got you, she thought. Sniping at a hurting friend. "Okay." Her voice gentle now, she eased onto the arm of Kate's chair. When her eyes met Margo's, she saw that Margo had also remembered Kate's shuddering childhood fear. "That's done now. You have to start taking care so it doesn't happen again."

"Which means you have to start practicing to be human," Margo said, but there wasn't any sting in it.

"Are they still mad?" Kayla whispered, still clutching Josh's trouser leg with one hand.

"Maybe a little, but I think it's safe now."

"Mama never yells." Unsettled, uneasy, Ali chewed on her nails. "She never yells."

"She used to yell at me. It takes a lot to make her yell. It has to really, really matter. And once she hit me right in the nose," Josh said.

Fascinated, Kayla reached up and rubbed her fingers over Josh's nose as he bent down. "Did it bleed and everything?"

"And everything. Kate and Margo had to pull her off me. Then she felt really bad." Then he grinned. "Even though I started it. What do you say we have some of that lemonade?"

Ali walked behind her uncle and studied her mother with a curious and considering eye.

It had to be done, Kate reminded herself. It was Sunday morning. Her aunt and uncle were expected by mid-afternoon. Before she faced them, she had to face Byron.

It was her new plan for a healthy life. Deal with your personal and emotional problems as carefully as you dealt with the practical ones. Why, she wondered, was it so much harder?

She'd secretly hoped he wouldn't be home. A lot of people went to brunch on Sunday mornings, or to the beach. Somewhere. But both of his cars were in the drive. Even parked behind them, she could hear the music pounding out of the windows. Creedence Clearwater Revival. She spent a moment listening to John Fogerty's fervent warning about a bad moon on the rise.

She hoped it wasn't an omen.

It was difficult to reconcile a man with his looks—smooth, elegant—and his obvious preference for down-and-dirty rock and edgy Motown. Well, she wasn't here to analyze his musical tastes. She was here to thank him and then turn the page on this awkward chapter in her life.

Prompting herself as she went, Kate got out of the car, started toward the house. She would be casual, brief, friendly, cheerful. She would turn the whole matter into a joke on herself, show the proper appreciation for his consideration and concern. And get out.

She drew a breath, rubbed her hands over the thighs of her jeans, then knocked. And laughed at herself. Superman wouldn't have heard a knock over the blast of CCR. She pressed the doorbell hard. At the tinny notes of "Hail, Hail, the Gang's All Here" she gaped in shock, then shook with laughter. Enjoying the absurdity, she pressed it again, then a third time.

He came to the door, sweaty and incredibly sexy in tattered shorts and a sweatshirt with the sleeves torn off. "The doorbell tune isn't mine," he said immediately. "I can't change it until after the settlement."

"I bet that's what you tell everyone." She indulged herself with a long, thorough look. "Did I interrupt a wrestling match?"

"Weight lifting." He stepped back. "Come on in."

"Look, I can come back when you're not busy pumping iron." Christ, he had amazing muscles. Everywhere. How had she missed that?

"I was nearly finished anyway. Gatorade?" He held up the bottle in his hand, and when she shook her head, glugged from it himself. "How are you feeling?"

"Fine. That's why I dropped by. To—" He leaned close, closed the door behind her, and made her jump. "To tell you I was fine. And to thank you for . . . things. The flowers. They were nice."

"Any flare-ups?"

"No. It's not a big deal. Really." Nervous, she shrugged her shoulders, rubbed her palms together. "One out of ten people ends up with a peptic ulcer. All socioeconomic levels, too. There's no clear evidence that they hit on, you know, people with a lot of stress and harried schedules."

"Been researching, have we?" A smile flirted around his mouth.

"Well, it seemed the logical thing to do. All in all."

"Uh-huh. And did your research also reveal that people with chronic anxiety tend to be more susceptible and to aggravate the condition?"

She dipped her restless hands in her pockets. "Maybe."

"Sit down." He gestured to the single chair before he walked over to turn down the music.

"I can't stay. My aunt and uncle are coming in today."

"Their flight's not due until two-thirty."

He'd know, of course. She caught herself twisting her fingers together, and made herself stop. "Yes, but I have things to do, and so do you. So, I'll just . . ."

She was saved by a scrabbling sound and the surprising sight of two running balls of yellow fur. "Oh, God." Automatically, she went down on her knees and caught the deliriously happy puppies in her arms. "Oh, you're so cute. Aren't you sweet? Aren't you wonderful?"

In unanimous agreement, they bathed her face with eager tongues, yipped and wiggled, crawling over each other to get closer.

"That's Nip and Tuck," Byron informed her as he got down on the floor with them.

"Which is which?"

He sent one puppy into slant-eyed ecstasy by scratching a furry belly. "I don't know. I figured we'd work it out with time. I've only had them a couple of days."

Kate picked one up to nuzzle and forgot she'd been anxious to get in and out. "What are they?"

"A little of this and a little of that. Some golden retriever, some Lab."

Before the second puppy could desert her, she kissed his nose. "Followed you home, right?"

"I adopted them from the animal shelter. They're eight weeks old." Byron found the remnants of a well-chewed rawhide bone on the floor and skidded it over the polished wood for the pups to chase.

"Mind if I ask what you're going to do with two puppies when you're at work?"

"Take them with me—for a while. I figure I can fence in part of the backyard, and they'll have each other for company when I'm not here." They came barreling back, jumped him. "I was only going to get one, but then . . . well, they're brothers and it seemed only fair." He glanced over, found her smiling at him. "What?"

"You wouldn't know it to look at you."

"Wouldn't know what?"

"You're a sucker."

He shrugged, tossed the bone again. "I'd think a practical woman like you would see the value of taking both. A backup dog is a sensible plan."

"Yeah, right."

"Jesus, Kate, have you ever been in one of those shelters? They break your heart." He tolerated wet, sloppy kisses from the rebounding puppies. "They're doing a great job—don't get me wrong—but all those cats and dogs, just waiting for somebody to come along and take them. Or . . ."

"Yeah. Or." She reached over, rubbing her hand over the dog in his lap. "You saved them." Her gaze came back to his. "You're good at that."

He reached out, curled a hand around her calf and slid her over until their knees bumped. "I tend to get attached to things I save. You look good." Anticipating her, he kept his hand on her leg and kept her from scooting back. "Rested."

"I didn't do much more than rest all week. And eat." She smiled a little. "I gained three pounds."

"Well, strike up the band."

"It may not seem like much to you, ace, but I've spent most of my life trying to develop something resembling a figure. I tried everything you read about in the back of magazines and Sunday supplements."

He had to grin. "Get out of here."

"No, really. There I was, faced with Margo—who I think was born built—and Laura's feminine little body. I always looked like their under-nourished younger brother."

"You don't look like anyone's younger brother, Kate. Believe me."

Feeling foolishly flattered, she shrugged. "Anyway—"

"Despite the amazing weight gain and the lack of symptoms," he interrupted, "you are going to see your regular doctor."

"I don't have much choice. My family's ganged up on me."

"That's what family's for. You gave us a scare."

"I know. I've been lectured by experts on my careless, selfish ways."

He smiled and patted her legs. "Sting?"

"Big-time. I'm thinking about just having 'I'm sorry' tattooed on my forehead so I don't have to keep repeating myself. And speaking of apolo-gies." She blew out a breath, fluttered her bangs. "I was going to try to get out of here without bringing this up, but I'm trying to reform."

Her brows knit, as they did whenever she had to face a thorny problem or unsettling task. This qualified for both. "The other night, before I had my little . . . attack, we were . . ."

"On our way to the floor, as I remember." He reached over the puppy that had fallen asleep in his lap, brushed at the hair above her ear. "Looks like we got there after all."

"What I want to say is that things got out of hand. My fault as much as yours," she added.

"Fault's assigned when there's a mistake."

"That's my point." She should have known it wouldn't be simple. Nip or Tuck was draped across her thigh, snoring. She busied herself with stroking his head. "We don't—I don't jump into bed with men I hardly know."

"It was going to be the floor," he reminded her. He still had a hard time going into his own kitchen without imagining what might have been. "And I never assumed you did. Otherwise, it wouldn't be two years since you've had sex."

Her mouth dropped open. "Where did you get an idea like that?"

"You mentioned it," he said easily, "when I was trying to get your clothes off."

She closed her mouth, let air out her nose. "Oh. Well, that only strengthens my point." Uneasy, she watched him gently lift the puppy from his lap and set it aside, where it curled deeper into sleep. "What happened was just a moment." He repeated the procedure with the second puppy. Kate's heart began to thud. "A hormone burst."

"Uh-huh." He didn't even touch her, just leaned forward until his mouth slid expertly over hers.

Kate could almost feel her mind tilt and her brains flow out. Well, she needed a distraction, didn't she? An outlet for all this tension. It seemed like the most sensible thing in the world to unfold her legs, wrap them around his waist and dive in.

"This only proves it," she murmured. She threaded her hands through his hair and gripped. "Proves I'm right."

"Shut up, Kate."

"Okay."

It was wonderfully, brutally hot. She hadn't known until that instant how cold she had been. Until his unshaven cheeks rubbed roughly over her skin, she hadn't known how soft she could be. Or how gratifying it could be to be the soft one.

She let out a long, grateful moan when his hands streaked under her T-shirt to stroke her back, slid around to cup and squeeze her tingling breasts. The flick of his thumbs over her nipples shot a bolt of heat through her center that vibrated achingly in her crotch. Arching back, she pulled his head down until his mouth replaced his hands.

He suckled through cotton, tormenting himself with fantasies of what her flesh would feel like, taste like, sliding under his tongue. She was so . . . slight. That neat, almost boyish torso should never have appealed to him. There was no womanly flare of hip, and her breasts were small.

And firm, and warm.

The way she moved against him, that edgy eagerness of a woman already teetering on the edge, was viciously arousing. He wanted, needed, to shove her back, rip aside that denim and drive himself inside her until they were both screaming.

Instead he dragged his mouth back to hers, slid a hand between their bodies and sent her free-falling over the edge. He shuddered himself when she convulsed, ordered himself to breathe when her head dropped limply on his shoulder.

Well, he thought, that should hold one of us.

It took her a moment to realize that he'd stopped, was just holding her. "What?" she managed. "Why?"

The dazed questions nearly made him smile. "I decided I didn't want it to be a hormone burst. For either of us." He eased her back, studied her flushed face, the heavy, glazed eyes. "Better now?"

"I don't think—" Couldn't think. "I don't know—Don't you want to—?"

He crushed his mouth to hers in a kiss that tasted of dark and swirling frustration. "Does that answer your question?" Taking her by the shoulders, he gave her a quick, satisfying shake.

"You're trying to confuse me." Part of her brain was starting to regenerate, and with it, temper. "This is some kinky version of *Gaslight*."

This time he did smile. "God, you're a pain in the ass. Listen to me, Katherine, I want you. I haven't the smallest clue why, but I just want the hell out of you. If I'd followed my first instinct, you'd be flat on your back, naked, and I'd be feeling a lot better than I do right now. But I'll be goddamned if you're going to pick yourself up afterward and claim I just helped you end your sexual drought."

Her eyes snapped back into focus. "That's a hideous thing to say."

"Yeah, it is. And that's just how you'd have rationalized it. I'm not giving you the chance. What I am doing is giving you the chance to get used to the idea of having me as a lover."

"Of all the—"

"Just keep quiet for once," he said mildly. "We're going to take this slow, go out together in public, have a few reasonable conversations, take some time to figure each other out."

"In other words, it's going to be all your way."

He angled his head, nodded. "Yeah, that sums it up." When she tried to wriggle free, he simply sighed and held her in place. "Honey, I'm as stubborn as you are, and a hell of a lot stronger. That puts me one up."

"You're not going to keep me here when I don't want to be here."

He gave her a friendly kiss on the nose. "You may be a scrapper, but you've got toothpick arms. We can work on that," he added, ignoring the strangled sounds she made. "In fact, there's no time like the present."

She thought she'd had all the shocks she could handle for one morning, but she got a fresh one when he hauled her up and slung her over his shoulder. "Are you insane? Put me down, you muscle-bound son of a bitch. I'll have you hauled in for assault."

"It's muscles we're going to deal with," he said mildly, as he carted her into an adjoining room. "Believe me, there's nothing like a good workout to relieve tension. Considering your ulcer and your desire to gain weight, this is something you should add to your daily routine." He set her down, caught the fist she swung at him in his hand, gave it an affectionate squeeze. "You want to be able to put some power behind that punch. We'll work on your biceps."

"This isn't happening," she said and closed her eyes. "I'm not even here."

"We need to work on diet and nutrition, too, but we'll get to that." They were going to get to a lot of things, he thought, as soon as she didn't look as if he could knock her flat with one exhale. "Right now, I think you should start off with three-pounders." He took two metal dumbbells from a rack. "You'll work up to five. You're going to want to go buy yourself some girl weights."

She opened her eyes again. "Did you say girl weights?"

"No offense. They make these nice plastic-coated sets of free weights in colors." He put a weight into each of her hands, curled her fingers around them. The only thing that stopped her from dropping them on his feet was curiosity.

"Why are you doing this?"

"You mean besides because I find myself oddly attracted to you?" He smiled into her eyes as he positioned her elbows at her waist. "I think I'm starting to like you. Now pretend you're lifting and lowering these through mud. Concentrate on your biceps and keep your elbows in place."

"I don't want to lift weights." Hadn't this man just minutes ago taken her to rough and blistering orgasm? "I want to hit you."

"Just think about how much harder you'll be able to hit me once you've got some muscle." He guided her arms down, then up. "Just like that, but resist both ways."

"These are too light. It's silly."

"They won't feel so light after a few sets. You're going to work up a nice sweat before I'm finished with you."

She sent him a sweet smile. "Yeah, that's what I thought before." Pleased with herself, she lowered the weights, lifted them. Then her brain flashed. "Goddamn you, Byron, are you saving me again?"

He stepped behind her, positioned her shoulders. "Just pump iron, kid. We'll work out the details later."

CHAPTER 10

IT WAS ALWAYS good to have Aunt Susan and Uncle Tommy home. Kate had worried that something would show in her face—or worse, that there would be something in theirs. The knowledge of crimes past, the doubt of her own innocence. But there had been only concern, and acceptance.

Their visit also meant extending her stay at Templeton House. It was difficult seeing them every day with the questions she tried to ignore drumming in the back of her mind. Questions she couldn't bring herself to ask.

She used the routine to carve out the path she intended to follow. Days at the shop—work to challenge the brain and keep it busy. Evenings with her family to soothe the heart. The occasional date with Byron to keep her on her toes.

He was a new element. Seeing him, wondering about him helped keep her from brooding about the turn her life had taken. She'd decided to think of him as a kind of experiment. Kate preferred that term to "relationship." And it wasn't an altogether unpleasant experiment. A few dinners, a movie now and again, perhaps a walk on the cliffs.

Then there were those long, stirring kisses he apparently loved to indulge in. Kisses that had her heart flopping in her chest like a landed trout, sent her senses cartwheeling into each other. Then ended, leaving her aching and baffled. And itchy.

The entire relationship—no, *experiment*, she corrected—left him far too much in control. Now that she was feeling a little steadier—all right, healthier—she was going to work on balancing the power.

"That's good to see." Susan Templeton stood at the doorway, her arm tucked through her husband's. "Our Kate never did enough daydreaming, did she, Tommy?"

"Not our sensible girl." He closed the door to the office behind them. He and his wife had worked out the logistics of this maneuver, and following their plan, they flanked the small desk where Kate had been pretending to work.

"I was trying to calculate our advertising budget for the next quarter." She flipped the screen saver onto her monitor. "If you're smart, you two will hide in here before Margo can put you to work."

"I promised her a couple of hours." Thomas winked. "She thinks she charmed me into it, but I get a kick out of working that old cash register."

"Maybe you'll give me some tips on salesmanship. I can't quite get the knack of it."

"Love what you sell, Katie girl, even if you hate it." He cast an experienced eye around the office, noted the tidy shelves, the organized work space. "Somebody's been streamlining in here."

"Nobody puts things, and people, in their place better than Kate." Susan laid a hand over Kate's, kept her soft blue eyes level. "Why haven't you put Bittle in his?"

Kate shook her head. Because she'd been waiting for days for one of them to bring it up, she didn't panic. She had her rationale ready. "It's not important." But Susan's eyes stayed on hers, calm, patient, waiting. "It was too important," she corrected. "I'm not going to let it matter to me."

"Now you listen here, girl—"

"Tommy," Susan murmured.

"No." He cut his wife off with a snap of sizzling temper. In contrast to Susan, his slate-gray eyes were sizzling. "I know you wanted to soft-pedal this business, Susie, but damned if I will."

He loomed over the desk, a tall man, powerfully built, well used to taking control, be it in business or family. "I expected better of you, Kate. Letting yourself get run roughshod over, giving up without a fight. Turning your back on something you worked for your whole life. Worse, getting yourself sick over it instead of standing up to it. I'm ashamed of you."

Those were words he'd never said to her before. Words she'd worked her entire life to keep him from saying. Now they struck her like a backhanded slap. "I—I never took any money."

"Of course you didn't take any money."

"I did the best I could. I know I let you down. I'm sorry."

"We're not talking about me," he shot back. "We're talking about you. You've let yourself down."

"No, I—" Ashamed of her. He was ashamed of her. And angry. "I put everything I had into my job. I tried to—I thought I was on the fast track to partner, and then you'd—"

"So the first time you take a knock, you crumble?" He leaned forward, poking his finger at her. "Is that your answer?"

"No." Unable to face him, she stared at her hands. "No. They had evidence. I don't know how, because I swear to you I never took any money."

"Give us some credit, Katherine," Susan said quietly.

"But they had the forms, my signature." The breath was backing up in her lungs. "If I'd pushed, they might have filed charges. It might have gone to court. I'd have to . . . You'd have to . . . I know people are whispering about it, and that's embarrassing for you. But if we just leave it alone, it'll pass. It'll just pass."

This time Susan held up a hand before her husband could interrupt. She, too, was accustomed to control. "You're concerned that we're embarrassed."

"It all reflects. It's all of a piece, isn't it?" She squeezed her eyes tightly shut. "I know that what I do reflects on you. If I can just wait it out, build something here with the shop. I know I owe you."

"What bullshit is this?" Thomas exploded.

"Hush, Tommy." Susan sat back, folded her hands. "I'd like Kate to finish. What do you owe us, Kate?"

"Everything." She looked up then, eyes swimming. "Everything. Everything. I hate disappointing you, knowing I've disappointed you. I had no way to stop it, to prepare for it. If I could fix it, if I could go back and fix—"

She broke off, shuddering as she realized she was mixing past and present. "I know how much you've given me, and I wanted to pay you back. Once I'd made partner . . ."

"It would have been a proper return on our investment," Susan concluded. She got slowly to her feet because every muscle in her body was tingling. "That is insulting, arrogant, and cruel."

"Aunt Susie—"

"Be quiet. Do you actually believe we expect payment for loving you? How dare you think such a thing?"

"But I meant—"

"I know what you meant." All but shaking with fury, she clutched her husband's shoulder. "You think we took you into our home, into our lives, because we felt pity for the poor orphaned child? Do you think it was charity—worse, the kind of charity that comes with strings and expectations? Oh, yes," she continued, fired up now. "The Templetons are known for their charitable works. I assume we fed you, clothed you, educated you because we wanted the community to witness our largesse. And we loved you, comforted you, admired you, disciplined you because we expected you to grow into a successful woman who would then pay us back for our time and effort with the importance of her position."

Rather than interrupt what he couldn't have said better himself, Thomas handed Kate a handkerchief so she could wipe her streaming eyes.

Susan leaned over the desk. Her voice was low, had remained low even in anger. "Yes, we pitied the little girl who had lost her parents so tragically, so brutally, so unfairly. Our hearts ached for the child who looked so lost and so brave. But I'll tell you something, Katherine Louise Powell, the minute you stepped through the door of Templeton House you became ours. Ours. You were my child then, and you still are. And the only things any of my children owe me or their father is love and respect. Don't you ever, *ever* throw my love in my face again."

She turned on her heel, sailed out of the room, and let the door click quietly behind her.

Thomas huffed out a long breath. His wife's tirades were few and far between, but they were brilliant. "Put your foot in it, didn't you, Katie girl?"

"Oh, Uncle Tommy." She could see the world she'd tried to piece back together shattered in her hands. "I don't know what to do."

"Start by coming over here." When she'd crawled into his lap and buried her face in his chest, he rocked her. "Never knew such a bright child could be so stupid."

"I'm screwing everything up. I don't know what to do. I just don't know how to fix it. What's wrong with me?"

"Plenty, I'd say, but nothing that can't be mended."

"She was so angry with me."

"Well, that can be mended too. You know one of your problems, Kate? You've focused on figures so long you think everything has to add up and be equal. It's just not true with people and feelings."

"I never wanted to bring either of you into this. To hurt you, remind you—" She broke off, shook her head fiercely. "I always wanted to be the best for you. The best in school, in sports. Everything."

"And we admired your competitive spirit, but not when it eats a hole in your gut."

Exhausted from tears, she laid her head against his shoulder. It was cowardice, she thought, that had eaten that hole in her gut. Now she had to face it all, what had been, what was, and what would come.

"I'm going to fix things, Uncle Tommy."

"Take my advice and give Susie a little time to cool off. She gets hard of hearing when her temper's on boil."

"Okay." Kate drew a deep breath and sat up. "Then I guess I'll start with Bittle."

His face broke into a huge grin. "Now that's my Kate."

IN THE PARKING lot of Bittle and Associates, Kate flipped down her rearview mirror to take one last critical look at her face. Margo had performed a little miracle. She'd dragged Kate upstairs and with cold compresses, eyedrops, lotions, and makeup had erased all traces of damage. Kate decided she no longer looked as though she had spent twenty minutes bawling like a scolded child. She looked efficient, composed, and determined.

That was perfect.

She told herself it didn't bother her that conversations stopped when she sailed into the first-floor lobby. She didn't mind the stares and murmurs, the strained smiles and curiosity-laced greetings. They were, in fact, an eye-opener.

The few people who greeted her warmly, who detoured to stop her on her march to the second floor and offer support, showed her that she'd made more friends at Bittle than she'd realized.

It took only one twist of the corridor to bring Kate face to face with the dragon. Newman raised a brow, gave Kate one brief, chilly stare. "Ms. Powell. May I help you?"

"I'm on my way to see Marty."

"Do you have an appointment?"

Kate angled her chin. The fingers gripping the handle of her briefcase tightened. "I'll take that up with Marty and his secretary. Why don't you go tell Mr. Bittle Senior that the disgraced associate has invaded the hallowed halls?"

Like a Swiss guard protecting royalty, Newman shifted her stance. "I see no reason for you to—"

"Kate." Roger poked his head out of his office, rolled his eyes behind Newman's back, and beamed a smile. "Good to see you. I was hoping you'd make it by. Oh, Ms. Newman, I've got that report Mr. Bittle Senior needed." Like a magician pulling a rabbit out of his hat, Roger produced a sheaf of papers. "He was anxious to see it."

"Very well." She shot Kate one last warning glance, then hurried down the hallway.

"Thanks," Kate murmured. "I think we might have come to blows."

"My money was on you." He put a supportive hand on her shoulder. "This situation really sucks. I'd have called you, but I didn't know what to say." He dropped his hand, stuck it in his pocket. "How to act."

"It doesn't matter. I didn't have anything to say myself." Until now. Now, she had plenty to say.

"Listen." He nudged her toward his office door but didn't, Kate noted wryly, invite her inside. "I don't know how much pressure your lawyer's putting on."

"My lawyer?"

"Templeton. The partners went into a powwow after he came in and stirred them up. Maybe that's a good thing, I don't know. You've got to handle it the way you think best. I can tell you that it looks like the partners are divided over whether or not to pursue and prosecute."

His brow creased and his voice, like a conspirator's, was low and dramatic. "Amanda's leading the charge, and Bittle Junior's behind her. My take is that Calvin and Senior are on the fence, with Marty solidly against."

"It's always good to know who's in your corner and who's going for your throat," Kate murmured.

"All this craziness over a lousy seventy-five K," Roger said in disgust. "It's not like you killed anyone."

Kate stepped back, studied his face. "Stealing is stealing, seventy-five cents or seventy-five K. And I didn't take any money."

"I didn't say you did. I didn't mean it that way." But there was doubt in his voice even as he took her hand to squeeze it. "I meant everybody over-reacted. I get the impression that if you came up with the money, it would all go away."

Slowly, firmly, she drew her hand free. "Would it?"

"I know it's a lousy deal either way, but hell, Kate, the Templetons sneeze that much money away every day. It would offset the chance of you being charged, ruining your whole damn life. Sometimes you've got to choose between the rock and the hard place."

"And sometimes you've got to stick. Thanks for the advice."

"Kate." He took a step after her, but she didn't stop or look back. With a shrug, he went back into his office.

Word was already out. Marty came to his door personally to meet her. He offered his hand, shook hers in a friendly, professional manner. "Kate, I'm glad you came by. Come inside."

"I should have come before," she began as she followed him past his secretary, who was doing her best to look busy and disinterested.

"I thought you would. Want anything? Coffee?"

"No." It was the same old Marty, she thought as she took her seat. From the wrinkled shirtsleeves to the affable smile. "I'm cutting back. I want to say first that I appreciate you seeing me like this."

"I know you didn't skim any funds, Kate."

The quiet statement stopped the neat little opening speech she'd pre-pared. "If you know that, why . . . Well, why?"

"I know it," he said, "because I know you. The signatures, the forms in-dicated otherwise, but I'm sure as I'm sitting here that there's another ex-planation." He wagged a finger, signaling her that he wasn't finished but was formulating his thoughts. The gesture nearly made her smile, it was so familiar. So Marty. "Certain people, ah, believe that I feel so strongly in this matter because I'm . . . attracted to you."

"Well, that's just silly."

"Actually I am—was. Am." Stopping himself, he rubbed his hands over his rapidly coloring face. "Kate, I love my wife. I would never . . . that is, other than the occasional thought, which I would never act on, I would never . . . Never," he finished, leaving her quite literally speechless.

"Um," was all she could think of in response.

"I'm not bringing that up to embarrass either one of us. Though it seems to have done just that." He cleared his throat as he rose, and with nervous hands poured two mugs of coffee. As he handed her one, he re-membered. "Sorry, you said you didn't want any."

"I'll take it." What was a little afterburn in comparison with staggered shock? "Thanks."

"I only mentioned that because people who know me well have sort of noticed that I— Not that you've done anything to encourage, or that I would have done anything even if you had."

"I get the picture, Marty." She allowed a breath to ease quietly through her lips, studied his wide, harmless, homely face. "I'm flattered."

"It muddies the waters, so to speak. I'm sorry for that. But I feel your record with this firm stands for itself. I'll continue to do everything I can to prevent formal charges being filed and to get to the bottom of this situation."

"I don't think I appreciated you enough when I worked here." She set her mug aside and rose. "Marty, I want to talk to the partners. All of them. I think it's time I took a stand."

He nodded as though he'd merely been waiting for her to say so. "I'll see if I can arrange it."

It didn't take him long. He might have been considered the puppy dog of Bittle, but he knew what buttons to push. Within thirty minutes, Kate was again seated at the long, polished table in the conference room.

In keeping with the strategy she'd outlined on the drive over, she made eye contact with each partner, then settled her gaze firmly on Bittle Senior. "I've come here today, without my lawyer, in an effort to keep this meeting informal. Even personal. I realize your time is valuable, and I appreciate each of you taking that time to listen to what I have to say."

She paused, once again glanced at the faces around the table, once again addressed herself to the senior partner and founder. "I worked for this firm for nearly six years. I dedicated my professional, and a good deal of my personal, life to it. My goals were not selfless. I worked very hard to bring in accounts, to keep accounts assigned to me satisfied and viable in order to increase Bittle's revenue and reputation, with the ultimate aim of sitting at this table as a partner. Not once during my employment here did I ever take one penny from an account. I was raised, as you know, Mr. Bittle, by people who value integrity."

"It is your accounts that remain in question, Ms. Powell," Amanda put in briskly. "Your signature. If you've come here today with an explanation, we are prepared to hear it."

"I haven't come here for explanations. I haven't come to answer questions or to ask them. I've come here to make a statement. I have never done anything illegal or unethical. If there is a discrepancy in the accounts, I am not responsible for it. I'm prepared to make this same statement, if necessary, to each client involved. Just as I am prepared to go to court and defend myself against these charges."

Her hands were beginning to shake, so she gripped them tightly together under the table. "If charges are not brought, and this matter is not satisfactorily resolved within thirty days, I will advise my attorney to file suit against Bittle and Associates for unjustified termination and slander."

"You would dare to threaten this firm." Though his voice was quiet and clipped, Lawrence fisted a hand on the table.

"It's not a threat," she said coolly, even as her stomach jittered and churned. "My career has been sabotaged, my reputation impugned. If you believe I would sit idly by and do nothing about that, then I'm not surprised that you believe I would embezzle from my accounts. Because you don't know me at all."

Bittle leaned back in his chair. He steepled his hands, considered. "It's taken you some time to come around to this position, Kate."

"Yes, it has. This job meant everything to me. I'm starting to believe that everything is just too much. I couldn't have stolen from you, Mr. Bittle. You of all people know me well enough to be sure of that."

She waited a moment, wanting him to remember her, personally. "If you want a question to ponder," she continued, "ask yourselves this: Why would I have pilfered a measly seventy-five thousand when if I had needed or wanted money, I would only have had to go to my family? Why would I have worked my butt off for this firm all these years when I could have taken a top position in the Templeton organization at any time?"

"We have asked ourselves those questions, Kate," Bittle told her. "And those questions are the very reason this matter hasn't been resolved."

She rose, slowly. "Then I'll give you the answer. I'm not sure it's an attractive one, but I know the answer is pride. I'm too goddamn proud to have taken a dollar from this firm that wasn't mine. And I'm too proud to do nothing when I'm accused of embezzlement. Ms. Devin, gentlemen, thank you for your time." She shifted her gaze, smiled. "Thanks, Marty."

Not a single murmur followed her out the door.

SHE STOPPED SHAKING when she hit Highway 1 and realized where her instincts were taking her. Even before she pulled her car to the shoulder, got out to walk toward the cliffs, she was calm again.

There were fences to mend, work to do, responsibilities to handle. But for a moment, there was just Kate and the soothing roar of the sea. Today it was sapphire, that perfect blue that called to lovers and poets and pirates. The foam, far below the lapped shale and rock was like the froth of lace on the hem of a woman's velvet skirt.

She climbed down a ways, enjoying the swirl of wind, the taste of salt and sea that flavored it. Wild grasses and flowers defied the elements and grew, fighting their way out of thin soil and cracks in stone. Gulls wheeled overhead, their breasts as white as moonlight, the golden sun flashing off their spread wings.

Diamonds glittered on the water, and farther out, whitecaps rode the sea like fine horses. The music never stopped, she thought. The ebb and flow, the crash and thunder, the eerily female screams of the gulls. How often had she come here to sit, to watch, to think? She couldn't count the number of hours.

Sometimes she was pulled here simply to be, other times to sit in solitude and work out some thorny problem. In her early years at Templeton House she had come here, to these cliffs, above this sea, under this sky, to quietly grieve for what she had lost. And to struggle with guilt over being happy in her new life.

She didn't dream here, had always told herself to wait for that until next year, or the next. The present had always taken priority. What to do now.

She stood on the comfortably wide ledge and asked herself what to do now.

Should she call Josh and tell him to go ahead with preparation for a suit against Bittle? She thought she had to. As difficult and potentially dangerous as such an action was, she could no longer ignore—or pretend to ignore—what had been done to her life. She hadn't been born a coward, nor had she been raised as one. It was time she dealt with that part of herself that was constantly in fear of failure.

In a way, she supposed, she had acted like Seraphina, metaphorically tossing her life over a cliff rather than working with the hand she'd been dealt.

That was over now. A little late, she admitted, but she had done the right thing. The Templeton thing, she thought with a smile as she picked her way down a rough and crooked incline. Uncle Tommy had always said that you couldn't be stabbed in the back if you faced your attackers.

The first step she needed to take was to face her aunt. Somehow she had to make things right there again. Kate looked back, and though she was too far down the slope to see the house, she could picture it.

Always there, she mused, tall and strong and waiting. Offering shelter. Hadn't it been there for Margo when her life had smashed around her? For Laura, and her girls, during the most difficult period of their lives?

It had been there for her, Kate thought, when she had been lost and afraid and numb with grief. Just as it was there now.

Yes, she'd done the right thing, Kate thought again as she looked back out to sea. She hadn't given up. She'd finally remembered that a good noisy fight was better than a quiet, dignified surrender.

She laughed a little and drew a deep breath. The hell with surrender, she decided. It was no more palatable than a cowardly plunge off the cliffs. The loss of a job, a goal, a man wasn't an ending. It was just another beginning.

Byron De Witt was another step she needed to take, she decided. Time for another beginning there. The man was driving her crazy with his patience, and it was past time for her to take control again. Maybe she would just ride over there later and jump him.

The thought of that had her laughing loud and long. Imagine his reaction, she mused, clutching her stomach. What did a proper Southern gentleman do when a woman threw him down and tore off his clothes? And wouldn't it be fascinating to find out?

She wanted to be held and touched and taken, she realized as the laughter in her stomach melted into warm, liquid need. But not by just anyone. By someone who could look at her the way he did, the way he looked deep, as though he could see places inside her that she hadn't dared to explore yet.

She wanted the mystery of that, wanted to match herself against a man strong enough to wait for what he wanted.

Hell, she admitted, she wanted him.

If she was strong enough to screw up her courage and face the partners at Bittle, if she had enough left inside her to deal with the damage she'd done to the aunt she adored, then she damn well had enough grit to handle Byron De Witt.

It was time she stopped planning and started doing.

Turning, she started back up the narrow path.

It was right there, as if it had been waiting. At first she simply stared, sure that she was imagining things. Hadn't she just come that way? Hadn't she and Laura and Margo combed every inch of this section of the cliffs over the past months?

Slowly, as if her bones were old and fragile, she bent down. The coin was warm from the sun, glinting like the gold it surely was. She felt the texture, the smooth face of the long-dead Spanish monarch. She turned it over in her palm twice, each time reading the date as if she expected it to change. Or simply vanish like a waking dream.

1845.

Seraphina's treasure, that small piece of it, had been tossed at her feet.

CHAPTER 11

KATE BROKE RECORDS on the drive back to Pretenses. Even the state trooper who stopped her to issue a lecture on traffic laws and a speeding ticket didn't dampen her spirits—or slow her down. She made it into Monterey in under twenty minutes.

Too wired to cruise for a legal parking space, she zipped through traffic, double-parked, and raced through the strolling wall of tourists.

She spun to the left, narrowly avoiding a collision with a kid on a skateboard, and all but stumbled through the door of the shop.

Her eyes were more than a little wild.

"I started to call from the car." Gasping, she pressed both hands to her thudding heart as Margo gaped at her. "I'm winded," she realized. "I'm going to have to take those workouts Byron's come up with more seriously."

"You had an accident." Margo bolted from the customer she'd been waiting on and made it to Kate seconds before Thomas got there. He was calling for Susan as he hurried over to take Kate's arm.

"Are you hurt? You'd better sit down." He halfway carried her to a chair.

"I'm not hurt. There wasn't an accident." Her adrenaline was so high, she was surprised everyone couldn't see it bouncing off the walls. "Well, there was the skateboard incident, but we both escaped unharmed. I didn't call because it wouldn't have seemed dramatic enough over the phone."

Then she began to laugh, so hard and so deep she was forced to clutch her ribs. Margo's hand snaked out and pushed Kate's head between her knees.

"Get your breath back," Margo ordered. "Maybe she had a flare-up. Maybe we should call the doctor."

"No, no, no." Still laughing, Kate dug into her pocket and held up the coin like a trophy. "Look."

"Damn it, Kate, how'd you get my coin?"

"It's not yours." Kate nipped it back before Margo could make the grab. "This one's mine." She bolted up and kissed Margo hard on the mouth. "Mine. I found it on the cliffs. It was just lying there, out in the open. Look, it didn't even have any sand or salt on it. It was just there."

After deciding the glowing flush on Kate's face didn't jibe with an ulcer attack, Margo exchanged a quiet look with Thomas. "Sit down, Kate, catch your breath. Let me finish up here."

"She doesn't believe me." Kate grinned hugely as Margo moved off to her customer. "She thinks I snatched hers and went crazy. It's all the stress I'm under." Letting her head fall back, she laughed like a loon. "Stress is a killer."

"Maybe some water," Thomas murmured, and looked up in relief as his wife hurried down the stairs. "Kate seems to be a little hysterical."

Calmly efficient, Susan took the bottle of champagne from the ice bucket and poured half a glass. "Drink," she ordered. "Then breathe."

"Okay." Kate obeyed, but she couldn't stop snickering. "You're all looking at me as if I'd grown another head. I haven't snapped, Uncle Tommy. I promise. I just found part of Seraphina's dowry. I was walking on the cliffs and it was right there. Bright as a penny and a lot more valuable."

"Just sitting there," Margo hissed as she walked by carrying a Limoges box in the shape of a sun hat. "Like hell. Take her upstairs, will you, Mrs. T.? I'll be up as soon as I can."

"Good idea," Kate agreed. "There's more champagne up there. We're going to need a lot of it." She tucked the coin back in her pocket, toyed with it as she climbed the winding stairs. First things first, she ordered herself, and turned as she stepped into the kitchen. "I need to talk to you, Aunt Susie."

"Hmm." Her back stiff, Susan crossed to the stove and put a kettle on to boil. The pretty little eyebrow windows were open to the breeze and all the bells and whistles that were summer on Cannery Row. But Susan said nothing.

"You're still angry with me." Kate sucked in both breath and triumph. "I deserve it. I don't know how to apologize, but I hate knowing that I hurt you."

"I hate knowing you feel the way you do."

Kate shifted her feet. Staring at the pretty footed glass bowl filled with fresh fruit that sat on the counter, she tried to find the right words.

"You never gave anything to me with strings attached. I put them there." Susan turned, met Kate's eyes. "Why?"

"I'm no good at explaining things that don't add neatly up. I'm better with facts than with feelings."

"But I already know the facts, don't I?" Susan said quietly. "You'll have to make an attempt at explaining your feelings if we're going to settle this, Kate."

"I know. I love you so much, Aunt Susie."

The words, and the simple emotion in them neatly sliced away a layer of Susan's anger. But the bafflement was still there, and under it, the hurt. "I've never doubted that, Kate. I wonder why you should doubt how very much I love you."

"I don't. It's just . . ." Knowing she was already fumbling it, Kate slid onto a stool, folded her hands on the counter. "When I came to you, you were already a unit. Whole. Templeton House, you and Uncle Tommy, all so open and perfect. Like a fantasy. A family."

Her words stumbled over each other in their hurry to get out. "There was Josh, the crown prince, the heir apparent, the clever, golden son. Laura, the princess, sweet and lovely and kind. Margo, the little queen. Stunning, dazzling really, and so sure of her place. Then me, bruised and skinny and awkward. I was the ugly duckling. That makes you angry," she said when Susan's eyes fired. "I don't know how else to describe it."

Deliberately, she made herself slow down, choose her words with more care. "You were all so good to me. I don't mean just the house, the clothes, the food. I don't mean the things, Aunt Susie, though they were staggering to a child who'd come from my barely middle-class background."

"Do you think we would have treated you differently if we hadn't had certain advantages?"

"No." Kate shook her head briskly. "Absolutely not. And that was only more staggering." Pausing, she stared down at her hands. When she lifted her eyes again, they were glossy with threatening tears. "All the more staggering," she repeated, "now, because . . . I found out about my father."

Susan simply continued to stare, her head angled attentively. "Found out?"

"About what he did. About the charges against him." Sick and terrified, Kate watched her aunt's brow crease, then slowly clear.

"Oh." She let out a long, long sigh. "God, I'd forgotten."

"You—you'd forgotten?" Stunned, Kate ran a hand through her hair. "You'd forgotten he was a thief? You'd forgotten that he stole, was charged, that you paid off his debts and took his daughter into your home? The daughter of a—"

"Stop it." It was a sharp order rather than the sympathy Susan would have preferred. But she knew her Kate. "You're in no position to judge what a man did twenty years ago, what was in his mind or heart."

"He stole," Kate insisted. "He embezzled funds. You knew all of it when you took me in. You knew what he'd done, what he was. Now I'm under suspicion for essentially the same thing."

"And it becomes clear why you sat back and took it, and made yourself ill. Oh, you poor, foolish child." Susan stepped forward, cupped Kate's face in her hands. "Why didn't you tell us? Why didn't you let us know what you were thinking, feeling? We would have helped you through it."

"Why didn't you tell me? Why didn't you tell me what he had done?"

"To what purpose? A grief-stricken child has burden enough. He made a mistake, and he would have paid for it."

"You paid for it." She tried to swallow, couldn't. "You took your own money and made restitution for him. For me."

"Do you think that matters, that Tommy or I gave that part of it even a moment's thought? You mattered, Kate. Only you mattered." She smoothed back Kate's hair. "How did you find out?"

"A man, a client who came in. He was a friend of my father's. He thought I knew."

"I'm sorry you found out that way." Susan dropped her hands, stepped back. "Maybe we should have told you when you were older, but after a while, it just passed away. What timing," she murmured, heartsick. "You found this out shortly before the business at Bittle?"

"A couple of months before. I looked into it, found articles from newspapers, hired a detective."

"Kate." Susan wearily pressed her fingers to her eyes. "Why? If you'd needed to know, to understand, we would have explained. You had only to ask."

"If you'd wanted to talk about it, you would have."

After a moment Susan nodded. "All right. All right, that's true."

"I just needed to know, for certain. Then I tried to put it aside. I tried, Aunt Susie, to forget it, to bury it. Maybe I could have, I don't know. But then, all of a sudden, I was in the middle of this. The discrepancy of funds from my clients' accounts, what was my explanation, internal investigations, suspension." Her voice broke like glass, but she made herself go on. "It was a nightmare, like an echo of what must have happened to my father. I just couldn't seem to function or fight back or even think. I've been so afraid."

Kate pressed her lips together. "I didn't think I could tell you. I was ashamed to tell you, and afraid that you might think—even for just a second you might think that I could have done it. Because he'd done it. I could stand anything but that."

"I can't be angry with you again, even for such foolishness. You've had a rough time of it, Kate." Susan gathered her close.

"It'll come out," Kate murmured. "I know it will, and people will talk. Some will assume I took money because my father took money. I didn't think I could stand that. But I can." She sat back, scrubbed away her tears. "I can stand it, but I'm sorry. I'm so sorry it touches you."

"I raised my children to stand on their own feet and to understand that family stands together. I think you forgot the second part of that for a while."

"Maybe. Aunt Susie . . ." She had to finish, finish all of it. "You never made me feel like an outsider, not from the first moment you brought me home. You never treated me like a debt or an obligation. But I felt the debt, the obligation, and wanted, always, to be the best. I never wanted you to question whether you'd done the right thing by taking me, by loving me."

With her own heart still aching, Susan folded her arms. "Do you think we measure our love by the accomplishments of the people we care for?"

"No. But I did—do. It's my failing, Aunt Susie, not yours. At first, I'd go to bed at night wondering if you'd change your mind about me in the morning, send me away."

"Oh, Kate."

"Then I knew you wouldn't. I knew you wouldn't," she repeated. "You'd made me part of the unit, part of the whole. And I'm sorry if it makes you angry or hurts you, but I owe you for that. I owe you and Uncle Tommy for being who and what you are. I'd have been lost without you."

"Did you ever consider, Kate, what you did to complete our lives?"

"I considered what I could do to make you proud of me. I couldn't be as beautiful as Margo, as innately kind as Laura, but I could be smart. I could work hard, plan things out, be sensible and successful. That's what I wanted for myself, and for you. And . . . there's something else you should know."

Susan turned to switch off the spurting kettle, but didn't pour the hot water over the waiting tea. "What, Kate?"

"I was so happy at Templeton House, and I would think that I wouldn't be there with you, with everyone, if the roads hadn't been icy that night, if we hadn't gone out, and the car hadn't skidded and crashed. If my parents hadn't died."

She lifted her eyes to Susan's. "And I wanted to be there, and as the years passed, I loved you so much more than I could remember loving them. And it seemed horrible to be glad I was with you instead of them."

"And you've nurtured that ugly little seed all these years." Susan shook her head. She wondered if parents and their children ever really understood each other. "You were a child, barely eight years old. You had nightmares for months, and you grieved more than any child should have to. Why should you go on paying for something over which you had no control? Kate." Her fingers stroked gently over Kate's temples. "Why shouldn't you have been happy? Would you have been better off clinging to the pain and the grief and the misery?"

"No."

"So you chose guilt instead?"

"It seemed that the best thing that had ever happened in my life had grown out of the worst. I could never make sense of it. It was as if my life began the night they died. I knew if a miracle had happened and my parents had come to the door of Templeton House, I would have run to you and begged you to keep me."

"Kate." Susan shook her head, smoothed Kate's hair back from her face. "If God Almighty had come to the door, I'd have fought Him tooth and nail to keep you with me. And I don't feel the least bit guilty about it. What happened wasn't your fault or mine. It doesn't make sense. It just is."

Nearly believing it, Kate nodded. "Please say you'll forgive me."

Susan stepped back, eyed her. Her child, she thought. A gift given to her out of tragedy. So complicated, so layered. So precious. "If you feel you have to owe me for—how did you put it—making you part of the unit, the payment is that you accept who you are, what you've made yourself. We'll be even then."

"I'll work on it, but in the meantime . . ."

"You're forgiven. But," she continued as Kate sniffled, "we're going to work on the rest of this together. Together, Kate. When Bittle deals with one Templeton, he'll deal with all of them."

"Okay." Kate knuckled a tear away. "I feel better."

"I'm sure you do." Susan's lips curved. "So do I."

Eyes wide and a little wild, Margo burst into the kitchen. "Let me see that coin," she demanded, and thrust a hand into Kate's pocket before Kate could move.

"Hey!"

"Oh, my God." Margo goggled at it, then goggled at the matching doubloon she held in her other hand. "I checked my purse. I really thought you were playing some sort of idiotic joke on me. They're the same."

And the world somehow settled neatly back into place. "I was trying to tell you," Kate began, then grunted when Margo grabbed her and squeezed.

"They're the same!" Margo shouted and held the coins in front of Susan's face. "Look, Mrs. T.! Seraphina."

"They're certainly from the right place and the right time." Struggling to switch gears, Susan frowned over the coins. "You just found this one, Kate."

"No, this one." In a proprietary move, Kate snatched the coin from Margo's left hand. "Mine," she stated.

"I can't believe it. All these months since I found the first one. All these months we've been searching and scraping and hauling that silly metal detector around. And you just stumble over it."

"It was just there."

"Exactly." Margo crowed in triumph. "Just like the first one was just there. It's a sign."

Kate rolled her eyes. "It's not magic, Margo. It's luck. There's a difference. I just happened to be there after the coin got kicked up or washed up or whatever."

"Hah," was all Margo had to say to that. "We've got to tell Laura. Oh, who the hell can remember where she is with that insane schedule of hers?"

"If you'd bother to look at the weekly schedule I've posted in the office, you'd know exactly where she is." Feeling superior, Kate glanced at her watch. "If memory serves, she's at the hotel for the next thirty minutes, then she has a meeting with Ali's teacher. After that—"

"We don't need after that. We'll just—" Margo stopped short. "Hell, we can't just close the shop in the middle of the afternoon."

"Go ahead," Susan told her. "Tommy and I can mind the store for an hour."

"Really?" Margo beamed at her. "I wouldn't ask, but this is so exciting, and we're in it together."

"You've always been in it together," Susan said.

"IT PERKED HER up." Margo loitered in the lobby after their brief contact with Laura. "It's frustrating to have to wait until Sunday to go back and look, but with her schedule we're lucky to manage that."

"Don't you think she's taken on an awful lot?"

Kate scanned the sweeping lobby with its elaborate potted plants, half hoping to see Byron breeze by on some executive mission. Instead she saw wandering guests, bustling bellmen, a group of women standing near the revolving doors with shopping bags heaped at their feet and a look of happy exhaustion on their faces.

"I know she likes to fill her time," Kate continued. "And it probably helps keep her mind off . . . things. But she barely has a minute in the day just for herself."

"Ah, you finally noticed." Then Margo shook her head and sighed. "I can't nag her about it anymore. When I suggested that the shop could probably swing a part-time clerk and that she could cut back there, she almost took my head off." Absently she rubbed a soothing hand over her belly as the baby kicked. "I know the bulk of her salary here at the hotel is earmarked for the kids' tuition."

"That bastard Peter." Kate's teeth began to grind even as she thought of it. "He was a slimy creep for taking Laura's money, but taking his own children's . . . that makes him whatever's lower than slime. She could have fried his sorry ass in court."

"That's what I'd have done," Margo agreed. Amused, she noted that two men in one of the lobby's plush seating areas were trying to catch her eye. "What you'd have done. Laura has to handle this her own way."

"And her way is to hold down two jobs, raise two children on her own, support a full staff because she's too softhearted to lay anyone off. She can't keep working twenty out of twenty-four hours, Margo."

"You try telling her." Out of long habit, she sent the hopeful men a quick, flirtatious smile.

"Stop playing with those insurance salesmen," Kate ordered.

"Is that what they are?" Carelessly, Margo scooped her long hair back. "Anyway, Josh and I have pushed Laura as far as we can push. She's not budging. Nobody could tell you to take a vacation, could they? To see a doctor?"

"Okay, okay." That was the last thing Kate wanted to hash over. "I had reasons, and I'll explain it to you when we have a little more time. I should have told you before."

"What?"

"We'll talk about it," she promised, then baffled her friend by leaning in and kissing her. "I love you, Margo."

"Okay, what have you screwed up?"

"Nothing. Well, everything, but I'm starting to fix it. Now, back to Laura. We'll just have to do more to pick up the slack. Maybe take the girls off her hands a few hours every week. Or run some of the errands she's always got a million of. And worrying about this is spoiling my mood." She pulled the coin out of her pocket, watched it glint. "Once we find Seraphina's dowry, the rest will be irrelevant."

"Once we do, I'm going to open a new branch of Pretenses. In Carmel, I think."

Surprised, Kate swept her gaze up to Margo's face. "I'd have figured you for a cruise around the world, or a new haute couture wardrobe."

"People change." Margo shrugged. "But I might add in a short cruise and a swing down Rodeo Drive."

"It's a relief to know people don't change too much." But maybe they could, Kate mused. Maybe they should. "Look, there's something I want to do. Can you handle the shop until closing?"

"With Mr. and Mrs. T. there, I don't have to go back myself." With a chuckle, Margo dug out her car keys. "If I could keep them in the shop for a month, we'd double our profits. Oh, say hi to Byron for me."

"I didn't say I was seeing Byron."

Margo sent a sly smile over her shoulder as she walked away. "Sure you did, pal."

It was demoralizing to realize she was so obvious. Demoralizing enough that Kate nearly talked herself out of going up to the penthouse. She was still arguing with herself when she stepped out of the elevator. When she was told Mr. De Witt was in conference, she decided it was for the best.

At loose ends, she rode back down, but rather than heading to her car, she wandered out to the pool. Leaning on the stone wall that skirted it, she watched the play of the courtyard fountain, the people who sat at the pretty glass tables sipping colorful drinks under festive umbrellas. She spotted name tags pinned to lapels that identified conventioneers taking a break from seminars.

In striped lounge chairs around the curving tiled pool lounged bodies slicked with sunscreen. Magazines and best-sellers were being read, headphones were in place. Waitpeople in cool pastel uniforms delivered drinks and snacks from the poolside bar and grill. Other guests splashed and played in the water, or simply floated, dreaming.

They knew how to relax, Kate thought. Why had she never acquired this simple skill? If she were to stretch out in one of those lounge chairs, she'd be asleep in five minutes. That was how her body was trained. Or if sleep refused to come, restlessness would have her up and gone, with her mind ordering her not to waste time.

Since this appeared to be a red-letter day in the life of Kate Powell, she decided to give wasting time a try. She slid onto a seat at the bar and ordered something with the promising name of Monterey Sunset. She lingered over it for nearly half an hour, watching people come and go, catching snatches of conversation. Then she ordered another.

It wasn't so bad, this time wasting, she decided. Especially when she felt so hollowed out inside. A good feeling, she realized. As if she'd purged herself of something that had been gnawing at her too long.

It was time to repair those rents in her life, or perhaps to ignore some of them and move on. There was promise in this hollow feeling, in the possibilities of how to fill it.

Carrying her drink, she wandered through the hotel gardens, reminding herself to enjoy the scents of camellia, jasmine, to appreciate the vivid shades of the tumbling bougainvillea. She sat on a stone bench near a pair of cypress and wondered how people managed to do nothing and not go insane.

It was probably best to try it in stages, she decided. Like exercise, an hour the first time out was probably overdoing. She rose, with the idea of going back to the shop and checking inventory, then she heard his voice.

"Be sure to cross-check the details with Ms. Templeton tomorrow. She'll need to be aware of these changes."

"Yes, sir, but it will require more staff—at least two more waitpeople and an extra bartender."

"Three more waitpeople. We want this smooth. I think Ms. Templeton will agree that this is the best position for the third bar setup. We don't want staff running through the guests with ice buckets, do we? Now, Lydia, Ms. Templeton has her finger on this particular pulse."

"Yes, sir, but these people keep changing their minds."

"That's their prerogative. It's our problem to accommodate them. What I wanted to discuss with you, Lydia, is the complimentary coffee setup on the east terrace every morning. We refined that a bit at the resort a couple of weeks ago, and it's working out well."

He came around the path as he spoke, caught sight of Kate sitting on the stone bench with a pretty drink in her hand and a quiet smile on her lips. And lost his train of thought.

"Mr. De Witt?" Lydia prompted. "The coffee setup?"

"Ah, right. Check with my assistant for the memo. It's all laid out. Let me know what you think." He didn't precisely push her along, but the intent was there. "We'll go over all of this with Ms. Templeton in the morning."

Once Lydia was on her way, he stopped at the bench, looked down at Kate. "Hi."

"Hi. I'm practicing."

"Practicing what?"

"Doing nothing."

He thought it was like coming across a fawn in an enchanted garden—those dark, deep, oddly slanted eyes, the warm and humid scent of flowers. "How's it going?"

"It's not as easy as it looks. I was about to give up."

"Let's give it another minute," he suggested and sat beside her.

"I didn't think the brass worried about little things like complimentary coffee setups."

"Every detail is a piece, every piece makes up the whole. And speaking of details"—he turned her face toward his, touched his lips to hers—"you look wonderful. Really. I'd say revived."

"I feel revived. It's a long story."

He grinned. "I'd like to hear it."

"I think I might like to tell you." She thought he was someone she could tell. No, she realized, she knew he was. "I came by to tell Laura a portion of it, then decided to hang around and try the nothing experiment."

He struggled with disappointment. The way he'd found her, sitting there, it had been as though she'd been waiting for him. "Want to go into the details, over dinner?"

"I'd love to." She rose, held out a hand. "If you're cooking."

He hesitated. He'd been very careful to avoid being completely alone with her. When he was alone with her he seemed to forget little things like timing and finesse. Now she was standing there, holding out her hand, with her lips curved in a way that let him know she understood his dilemma. And was enjoying it.

"Fine. It'll give me a chance to try out the barbecue grill I picked up a couple days ago."

"Tell you what, I'll bring dessert and meet you there."

"Sounds like a plan."

Testing both of them, she stretched onto her toes and closed her mouth softly, lingeringly over his. "I'm a terrific planner."

He stood where he was, his hands firmly tucked in his pockets, while she walked away. He decided one of them was about to have their plans tumbled. It would certainly be interesting to see which one it was.

FLAKY, CREAMY, DECADENT chocolate eclairs had seemed the perfect choice. Kate set the bakery box on the table in his kitchen and watched him through the window. He'd left the door unlocked, in invitation. She'd accepted it, had come in to a blast of searing Bruce Springsteen, noted he'd added a couple of pieces of furniture to complement the ratty recliner.

The low coffee table with the checkerboard inlay looked expensive and unique, as did the stained-glass lamp and the thick geometric-patterned area rug. She admitted she was dying to see the rest of the house, but she made herself go into the kitchen.

And there he was in the backyard, wrestling the puppies over a sock. He looked as at home in jeans and a T-shirt as he had earlier in his tailored suit and silk tie. It made her wish she'd taken the time to swing by home and change into . . . anything, she thought, but this tidy pin-striped suit and sensible shoes. In compromise, she took off her jacket and undid the top button of her shirt before she went out to join him.

She stepped onto the redwood deck. A deck, she noticed, that he'd made his own with the simple addition of pottery planters filled with geraniums and pansies and trailing vines. A complex and somewhat terrifying gas grill stood shiny and new near the double glass doors, and a pair of redwood chairs, deeply cushioned in navy, were positioned to offer a view of the lawn leading down to the sea.

He'd had the yard fenced in, she noted, with wooden pickets to keep his precious pets in but still leave it all open to the view. A gate stood by the beach steps, offering easy access to the sea.

He'd planted something at regular intervals along the fencing. She could see tender young plants and the carefully packed mulch around them. She imagined he'd done the digging there himself. Some sort of trailing flowering vine, she supposed, that would, in time, grow and tumble color over the fence.

A patient man, Byron De Witt, she mused. One who would enjoy watching those vines grow and bloom and tangle year after year.

And she knew he would experience a quiet satisfaction when the first bud blossomed. Then he would tend it. The man enjoyed tending things.

Puppies yapped, the sea murmured, and the wind trailed lightly through the fluttering cypress leaves. As the sky deepened from blue to indigo splashed with scarlet, she felt a quick flutter around her heart. There were, she supposed, perfect spots in the world. It seemed Byron had found one of them and claimed it.

And so did he look perfect, she realized, with the wind in his hair, puppies at his feet. That long, mouthwatering, muscular build was tucked snug and sexy into denim and cotton. Her reaction to it, to him, completely unprecedented, was to grab hold and tear in with fingers and teeth. She wanted to taste and take. She wanted to be taken.

She wanted.

With legs less than steady, she descended the short flight of steps to the yard. The puppies dashed up to her, yipping and leaping. Even as she crouched to welcome them, she kept her eyes on Byron.

"What did you plant along the fence?"

"Wisteria. It'll take a little while to establish." He looked over to the fence line. "But it'll be worth the wait. There was always some growing on a trellis outside my bedroom back in Georgia. It's a scent that stays with you."

"You've already done a terrific job with the place. It's gorgeous out here. Must take a lot of time to add all these touches."

"When you find what you're looking for, you take care of it." He crossed to her. "We can take a walk down to the beach after dinner if you like." He stroked a hand over her hair, much as he had done to the dogs' fur. Then he stepped back. "Catch this." He snapped his fingers twice. "Sit."

Butts wiggling frantically, both dogs sat. He had them offer their paws, and after some confusion, lie down. Though their bodies quivered with suppressed excitement.

"Very impressive," Kate commented. "Does everyone do what you tell them?"

"It's just a matter of asking often enough in the right way." He pulled two dog biscuits out of his back pocket. "And bribery usually works." The dogs took the treats and raced away to feast. "I've got a nice red Bordeaux breathing. Why don't I get it, and you can tell me about this interesting day of yours?"

She lifted a hand, laid it on his chest. Felt the heat, the rhythm. "There's something I think I want to say to you."

"All right. Let's go inside." He thought it was best to get into the brightly lit kitchen, away from the sumptuous sunset and seductive night air.

But she kept her hand on his chest and stepped closer. It must have been their color, Byron thought, that made her eyes glow so erotically through the twilight shadows.

"I was going to avoid men like you, on a personal level," she began. "It was to be a kind of principle, a rule of thumb. I'm very fond of rules and principles."

He arched a brow. "And generalities?"

"Yes, and generalities, because they usually have some basis in fact, or they wouldn't have gotten to be generalities. I'd decided after a couple of unfortunate experiences that when something, or someone, looked too good, it was probably bad for me. You may be bad for me, Byron."

"Have you been working on this theory long?"

"Actually I have, but it may need some further adjustments. In any case, I didn't like you when I first met you."

"Now there's a surprise."

She smiled and disconcerted him by moving closer. "I didn't like you because I started wanting you the first minute. That was uncomfortable for me. You see, I prefer wanting things that are tangible and that can be acquired through time, planning, and effort. I don't like being uncomfortable, or wanting someone I don't understand, who is in all probability bad for me, and who doesn't fit my requirements."

"You have requirements too?" He didn't care for the sensation of being annoyed and aroused at the same time.

"Absolutely. One of the main requirements is a lack of demand. I don't think you're an undemanding man, and that's, undoubtedly, going to be my biggest mistake. One of the other things I really, really hate to do is make mistakes. But I'm working on being more tolerant of myself."

"Is that something else you're practicing, like doing nothing?"

"Exactly."

"I see. Well, now that we've established that this fledgling relationship with me is practice for your personal tolerance, I'll start dinner."

She laughed and put her other hand on his chest. "I irritate you. I don't know why I find that so funny."

"It doesn't surprise me, Katherine. You have an abrasive, contrary nature and like nothing better than stirring things up."

"You're right, absolutely right. It's terrifying how easily you understand me. And the more patient you are, the more compelled I am to poke at you. We are so completely wrong for each other, Byron."

"Who's arguing?" He curled his fingers around her wrists, intent on pushing her hands aside.

"Take me to bed," she said simply, and slid her hands through his loosened grip to his shoulders. "Now."

CHAPTER 12

H E WASN'T EASILY shocked. But her simple demand rocked him back as efficiently as a short left jab. He'd been sure she was ending what had barely begun between them. He'd been prepared to be coldly furious, but to school himself into not giving a damn.

Because it was undoubtedly unwise to touch her, he kept his arms at his sides. "You want me to take you to bed, now, because it's a mistake, because you've theorized that I'm bad for you, and because we're completely wrong for each other."

"Yes. And because I want to see you naked."

He managed a laugh, and would have stepped back, but she locked her hands at the back of his neck. "I think I need a drink," he muttered.

"Byron, don't make me get rough with you." She moved in, her body bumping his, her arms tightening. "I've been working out. Sort of. I think I could take you if I had to."

Telling himself to be amused, he pinched her biceps gently. The tiny muscle gave like putty. "Yeah, you're a regular Amazon, honey."

"You want me." She nipped her way up his throat. "If you don't, I'll have to kill you."

The little blood left in his head shot straight to his loins. "I think my life's safe. Kate—" Her hands raced busily to the snap of his jeans. "Don't—Christ!" And tugged at his zipper. "Hell," he muttered, and gave in to the animal long enough to savage her mouth with his.

She made a sound in her throat like a cat purring over prey.

"Hold on." He grabbed her shoulders and pushed her back. "Just hold on one damn minute." He panted out a breath, then another. "You know the trouble with flings?"

"No, what's the trouble with them?"

"I'm trying to remember." He wanted to rub his hands over his face, but he didn't dare release her. "Okay, I've got it. However momentarily satisfying they are, you end up dissatisfied. That's not the way it's going to be here. This isn't going to be a fling. You're going to have to accept that."

What was wrong with him? she wondered. Men weren't supposed to complicate sex. "Fine, we'll call it something else."

"There are strings, Kate." His hands still on her shoulders, he began slowly backing her toward the house. He could already see her naked and gleaming. "Trust. Honesty. Affection. Once I touch you, no one touches you but me."

"They're not exactly lined up around the block waiting to get their hands on me." Her feet bumped into the steps. Automatically, she stepped up, back again. He was looking at her in that way that made her both nervous and eager. As if he were looking beyond, to what no one else had seen, even herself. "I don't sleep around."

"Neither do I. I consider intimacy a serious business. And I'll have intimacy from you, Kate, in bed and out. That's bottom line."

"Look—" Her throat was burning dry, her hormones bouncing. "This isn't a business contract."

"No." He backed her easily through the kitchen. "It's a personal one. That's much more involved, much more important. You put the deal on the table." He swept her into his arms. "I'm defining the terms."

"I— Maybe I have terms of my own."

"Better put them out here then. This deal's about to close."

"We need to keep this simple."

"Not an option." At the top of the stairs, he turned left, carried her through a doorway and into a room washed with the last vivid light of the western sky.

"We're healthy, unattached adults," she began, talking fast now. "This is a mutual physical relationship."

"There's more to sex than the physical." He smiled as he laid her on the bed. "I guess I'll have to show you."

He kissed her, a long, slow, lazy meeting of lips that lingered until every nerve in her body was vibrating like the strings of a plucked harp. Eager for more, she dragged him closer so that all the heat swirling through her seemed to center on their mouths.

He could have taken her in one greedy gulp. Knowing it, he eased back. "Honey, where I come from, we pace ourselves." He linked his fingers with hers so that she couldn't tear down his defenses with those narrow, nervous hands. "Now relax." He lowered his head to trail nibbling kisses along her jawline. "And enjoy." Down her throat. "We've got all the time in the world."

She thought he would kill her with patience, rip her to shreds with gentleness. His lips were soft, smooth, deliciously, devastatingly slow as they cruised over her face. Each time they met hers, he took the kiss just a degree deeper, just a whisper warmer. Her muscles went from hot wires to soft wax.

The change aroused him mercilessly. The sound of her breathing, low and deep and slow, the thrill when a breath ended on a moan, a sigh. Her quivering impatience slipped into mindless pliancy. When he unbuttoned her shirt, revealing the simple white camisole beneath, she did nothing more than murmur her pleasure.

Fascinated by the simplicity of her form, he traced his fingertips over the soft cotton, then up over softer flesh. The most subtle of curves, he mused as her breath began to quicken again at his feathering touch. Linking fingers again, he nuzzled the cotton aside, flicked his tongue over her nipple.

She arched in response, biting back a groan. So small, he thought, so firm. So sensitive. He swept his tongue under the cotton, moistening her other breast, and felt her quake beneath him.

So he suckled slowly, gently, darkly pleased with the way she writhed under him, with the quick, helpless whimpers that sounded in her throat as he increased pressure and speed.

When he felt as if he might die if he didn't plunge into her, when her hips were pistoning as if she would explode if he didn't fill her, he drew back and slipped out of bed.

"What? What?" Dazed, desperate, she sat up.

"The light's going," he said quietly. "I can't see you. I want to see you." There was the abrasive scratch of a match striking, the flare of light that softened as flame was touched to the wick of a candle, then a second, a third. And the room was suddenly rich and romantic with wavering light.

She pressed a hand to her breast, shocked to realize that the hot, quivering nerves inside belonged to her. What was he doing to her? She wanted to ask, but was afraid of the answer.

Then he tugged the T-shirt over his head, tossed it aside. She let out a breath of relief. Now—it would be now. And all these twisting sensations would smooth out into the understandable.

He stepped out of his shoes. She was only mildly surprised when he slipped hers off as well, slid his hand up her leg to just under the hem of her rucked-up skirt.

"Would you take your top off?"

All but hypnotized, she blinked at him. "What? Oh."

"Slowly," he said, laying a hand on hers before she could yank it free. "No rush."

She did as he asked because her limbs were so heavy. His gaze took a lazy journey from her face, down her torso and back again, before he took the thin cotton from her, set it aside. His eyes stayed on hers as he eased her back.

"You keep looking at me," she murmured. Her skin trembled when he slid his hands further under her skirt, when he curled his fingers around the waistband of her panty hose and began to draw them down. "I don't know what you expect."

"Neither do I. I thought we'd find out together." He lowered his head and pressed his lips to her inner thigh. "Now I know why you always walk as if you were ten minutes late for a five-minute appointment. It's all this leg. All this long leg."

"Byron." She was burning up. Good God, couldn't he feel it? "I can't take this."

But she would, he thought, and unhooked her skirt. "I haven't even started yet." He slipped the skirt off and quivered himself at the sight of that slim, angular body in his bed. Resting a bent knee on the bed, he cupped her. She bowed back, pressing desperately against him.

His eyes darkened dangerously as he watched her face, the play of sensations and light, the helpless trembling of lashes and lips. Then the utter surrender to self and to him when the orgasm rippled through her.

Wanting more as wildly as she, he closed his mouth over her breast and built her relentlessly toward peak again.

"I can't." Nearly terrified at what he'd pulled out of her, of what he seemed to create inside her, she dragged at his hair. "I'm not—"

"Sure you can." He gasped out the words before his mouth fused with hers. Heat was pouring out of her, all but pumping out of her pores. He'd never known a woman to be so responsive and so resistant at once. The need, the drive to show her he was the one, the only one who could bring that response and break that resistance made him hold off that final pleasure for the tortured maze of sensations between.

It seemed he owned her body. She had no control, and had lost the will to find any. His hands, his lips were everywhere, and each time she thought he would rush to finish it, he would cause her to erupt again, then move patiently on.

She was painfully aware of her body, and his, the melding and the contrasts, the race of pulses. Candlelight flickered over his face, those sleek, slick muscles, making it all almost too beautiful to bear. The taste of him was potent, like some dark, slow-acting drug that had already seeped into her blood to addict her.

He braced himself over her, waiting for her eyes to open and focus on his. "I didn't want you," he said in a voice strained to the edge of control. "Then I wanted nothing else. Understand that."

"For God's sake, Byron. Now!"

"Now," he echoed and plunged into her. "But not just now."

THE WARM RED haze over her mind cooled slowly. She became aware of the world outside of her own body. The candlelight continued to flicker against her closed lids in soft, surreal patterns. The night wind had risen, causing the curtains at the windows to whisper. She could hear the music again, the low throb of bass from the stereo downstairs, the answering wail of a tenor sax. The smell of hot, pooling wax, and sweat, and sex.

She had the taste of him in her mouth, and the good, solid feel of him beneath her. He'd rolled her over so that she lay sprawled across him. Concerned, she supposed, that he would crush her. Always the gentleman.

Just how did she play this? she wondered. How did she handle the aftermath of such wild, spectacular sex? Initiating it was one thing, participating was clearly, and fabulously, another. But she felt certain that these first few moments of the after would set the precedent for how they would go on.

"I can actually hear your mind clicking back in gear," he murmured. There was a hint of amusement in his voice as he smoothed down her messy cap of hair. "It's fascinating. I don't know that I've ever been quite so attracted to a woman's brain before." When she started to shift, he ran his hands down her back, gave her butt a friendly squeeze. "No, don't move yet. Your head's ahead of me."

She took a chance, raised her head to look at him. Those gorgeous green eyes of his were at half-mast. The mouth that had so recently sent her system into overdrive was softened with a faint smile. He was, she decided, the perfect picture of the fully satisfied male animal.

"Is this going to be awkward?" she wondered aloud.

"Doesn't have to be. It seems to me that we've been heading here since the first minute we met. Whether we knew it or not."

"Which poses the next question."

Ah, that tidy, practical, ordered mind, he thought. "Which is, what direction do we take from here? We'll have to talk about that." He rolled her over and, before she could speak again, took her mouth in a long, deep, mind-hazing kiss. "But first, the practicalities."

He scooped her off the bed, into his arms. Her system gave a fresh jerk. It was so odd, being carried this way, experiencing the arousing vulnerability of being physically outmatched. "I'm not sure I like the way you do this."

"Let me know when you make up your mind. Meanwhile, I vote for a shower and dinner. I'm starving."

No, IT WASN'T going to be awkward, she concluded. In fact, it was amazingly pleasant to be wearing one of his faded T-shirts, listening to Bob Seger's sandpaper vocals grinding out rock. Byron had trusted her to put a salad together while he grilled the steaks. She was finding the process enjoyable—the colors and textures of the vegetables he'd set out for her. The summer-garden scent of them. She couldn't remember being quite so aware of food before. She liked to eat, Kate thought, but taste had always been the main stimulus. Now she decided there was more to it than that. There was the feel of the food, the way different ingredients played off each other, harmonized or clashed.

The moist, feathery layers of an artichoke heart, the firm snap of a carrot, the subtle bite of cucumber, the delicacy of salad greens.

She set down the chef's knife and blinked. What the hell was she doing? Romanticizing a salad? Good God. Carefully, she poured herself half a glass of the wine he'd set on the counter to breathe. Though she hadn't had any recent flare-ups, she was still leery of alcohol. She sipped the wine gingerly.

She could see him through the glass doors, talking to the dogs as he turned the steaks. Flame and smoke billowed.

They were cooking together, she thought. She was wearing his shirt. Dogs were begging for scraps, and music was playing.

It was all so quietly domestic. Terrifying.

"Honey—" Byron slid open the doors. "You want to pour me a glass of that? These steaks are about done."

"Sure." Easy, girl, she warned herself. This was just a nice, pleasant evening between two consenting adults. Nothing to get jittery over.

"Thanks." Byron took the glass she brought to him, swirled the wine before drinking. "You want to eat out here? It's a nice night."

"Okay." And more romantic, she thought as they carried out the dinnerware. Why shouldn't she enjoy a little starlight and wine with the man who'd just become her lover? There was nothing wrong with that.

"You've got that line between your eyebrows," he commented, sampling and approving her mixed salad. "The one you get when you're trying to calculate your bottom line."

"I was calculating how much of this steak I can eat without exploding." Eyes on her plate, she cut another bite. "It's wonderful."

"While I find it surprisingly satisfying to feed you, the food isn't what's bouncing around in your mind like a pinball." He started to ask her to look at him, then took the more direct route. He laid a hand on her bare thigh and watched her gaze shoot to his. "Why don't I make it easy for you? I want you to stay with me tonight."

She picked up her wineglass, fiddled with the stem. "I don't have any clothes."

"So we'll get up early, give you enough time to swing by your place and change before work." He reached out, ran a fingertip down her throat. Such a long, slim throat. "I want to make love with you again. I want to sleep with you. Is that simple enough?"

Because it should have been, she nodded. "I'll stay, but I don't want any complaints when the alarm goes off at six."

He only smiled. It was a rare day for him not to be up already and jogging along the beach by six. "Whatever you say. Now, there's more. I said there were strings. I meant it."

That was what she'd been trying to keep neatly locked in the back of her mind. Wanting to choose her words with care, she continued to eat. "I'm not involved with anyone," she began.

"Yes, you are. You're involved with me."

A quick chill of warning ran down her spine. "I meant I'm not involved with anyone else. I don't intend to see anyone else while we're . . . involved. However it may seem by the way I came here tonight, sex isn't casual for me."

"Nothing's casual for you." He topped off his wine, then hers. "But sex is the easy part. It doesn't take a lot of thought, instinct kicks in, the body takes over."

His gaze rested on her face. Her eyes were wary, he noted, like those of a doe that had unexpectedly come across a stag in the woods. Or a hunter. "I have feelings for you."

Her heart bumped. She used knife and fork to cut meat as if the precise size and shape of it were paramount. "I think we've established that."

"Not just desires, Katherine. Feelings. I'd planned on sorting them out before we found ourselves at this stage. But . . ." He shrugged, ate, let her absorb the words. "I like maps."

Her already baffled brain clicked over into complete confusion. "Maps."

"Points of interest. Routes from one place to the next. I like plotting them out. One of the reasons I'm interested in hotels is because they're like a world. Self-contained, full of movement and places and people."

As he spoke, he cut the bone from what was left of his meal, then did the same with Kate's. He gave each of the wide-eyed dogs a feast.

"Hotels are never really stationary. Just the building is. But inside there are births, deaths, politics, passions, celebrations, and tragedies. Like any world, it runs more or less a certain way, along a certain route. But the detours, the surprises, the problems, are always there. You explore them, enjoy them, solve them. I fucking love it."

She pondered as he sat back, lit one of his cigars. She had no earthly idea how they had shifted from a discussion on their relationship to his work, but it was fine with her. Relaxed again, she picked up her wine.

"That's why you're so good at your job. My aunt and uncle consider you the best, and they're very picky."

"We generally do our best with something we enjoy." He watched her through a haze of smoke. "I enjoy you."

Her smile spread slowly as she edged toward him. "Well, then."

"You're a detour," he murmured, taking her hand before it could become too busy, bringing it to his lips. "When I map out the particular world I'm moving in, I always anticipate a few detours."

"I'm a detour." She was insulted enough to tug her hand free. "That's flattering."

"It was meant to be." He grinned at her. "While I'm on this intriguing and very attractive alternate route, I don't intend to worry how long it will take to navigate it."

"And I'm along for the ride? Is that it?"

"I'd prefer saying we're in this together. Where we end up depends on both of us. But I know this. I want you with me. I haven't completely figured out why, but I can't get past the wanting part. When I look at you, it's enough."

No one had ever made her feel more desired. He'd used no soft, alluring words, composed no odes to her eyes, and yet she felt vital and alive and very much wanted. "I'm not sure whether I'm confused or seduced, but it seems to be enough for me, too."

"Good." Most of the tension he'd been holding in seeped away as he brought her hand to his lips again. "Now that you're relaxed, why don't you tell me about this fascinating day of yours?"

"My day?" Absolutely blank, she stared at him. Then her eyes cleared, went bright. "Oh, Jesus, my day. I'd completely forgotten."

"I can't tell you how gratifying that is." He laid a hand on her thigh again, slid it slowly up. "If you'd like to forget about it for a while longer . . ."

"No." As she pushed his hand firmly away, she chuckled. "I was bursting to talk about it, and then I started thinking about getting you into bed, and it slipped down a couple of notches on the priority list."

"How about I let you get me in bed again, and we talk later?"

"Nope." She scooted out of reach. "I've already had you, pal. The encore can wait."

"That sound you hear is my ego deflating." He sat back with his cigar, his wine, gestured with the glass. "Okay, kid, spill it."

She wondered how it would feel to simply say it aloud. "In March I found out that my father had embezzled funds from the ad agency he worked for before he was killed." She let out a breath, pressed a hand to her stomach. "God."

It was, he thought, the piece he'd been sure was missing, falling into place. "In March," Byron repeated, studying her face. "You hadn't known about it before?"

"No, nothing. I keep expecting people to be shocked. Why aren't you shocked?"

"People make mistakes." And his voice softened when he calculated just how much she'd suffered. "Cut you off at the knees, didn't it?"

"I didn't cope very well. I thought I was. I thought I could bury it, just push it in. Didn't work."

"You didn't talk to anyone?"

"I couldn't. Margo found out she was pregnant, and Laura, she's handling so much and . . . I was ashamed. That's what it comes down to. I couldn't face it."

And had made herself ill, he thought, with worry and stress and guilt. "Then you got hit at Bittle."

"It didn't seem that it could really be happening. Some sort of cosmic joke. It paralyzed me, Byron. I've never been so afraid of anything, or felt so helpless. Ignoring it seemed the only solution. It would go away, somehow just go away. I'd just keep myself busy with other things, not think about it, not react, and it would get better."

"Some snap," he murmured, "some collapse, and some dig their trenches."

"And I pulled the covers over my head. Well, that's done." In a half-toast to herself, she lifted her glass. "I talked to my aunt and uncle. Instead of making it better, that made it worse. I hurt them. I was trying to explain why I was grateful to her and Uncle Tommy, and I said things wrong. Or I was wrong, and it came out badly. She was so angry with me. I don't remember her ever being that angry with me."

"She loves you, Kate. You'll square this with her."

"She's already forgiven me. Or mostly. But it made me realize I had to face it. All of it. I went to Bittle today."

"Now you're digging the trenches."

She let out a shaky breath at his response. "It's past time I did."

"Now are you going to beat yourself up because you weren't iron woman, because you needed time to pull your resources together?"

The corner of her mouth twitched. She'd been tempted to do just that. Apparently he knew her very, very well. "No, I'm going to concentrate on dealing with now."

"You didn't have to go to Bittle alone."

She looked down at the hand that had covered hers. What made him offer support so easily? she wondered. And what was making her count so heavily on the offer?

"No, I did have to go alone. To prove to myself and everyone at Bittle that I could. I used to play baseball, in school. I was a good clutch hitter. Two out, a run behind, put Kate in the box. I'd concentrate on the feel of the bat in my hands because my stomach would be churning and my knees shaking. If I concentrated on the feel of the ash solid in my hands and kept my eyes dead on the eyes of the pitcher, I'd still be terrified, but nobody would know it."

"Trust you to turn a game into life or death."

"Baseball is life or death, especially in the bottom of the ninth." She smiled a little. "That's how I felt when I walked into Bittle. Two out, bottom of the ninth, and they'd already winged two strikes past me while I stood there with the bat on my shoulder."

"So you figured if you were going to go down, you'd go down swinging."

"Yeah, now you get it."

"Honey, I was a starting pitcher all the way through college. Went All-State. I ate clutch hitters like you for breakfast."

When she laughed, some of his worry eased. She took a moment to sip her wine, study the star-strewn sky. "It felt good. It felt right. Even being scared felt right because I was doing something about it. I demanded a partners' meeting, and there I was, back in the conference room, just like the day they fired me. Only this time I fired back."

She took a deep breath before launching into a play-by-play of what had happened inside the conference room. He listened, admiring the way her voice strengthened, her eyes hardened. Perhaps her vulnerability pulled at him, but this confident, determined woman was no less appealing.

"And you're prepared to deal with the fallout if they press formal charges?"

"I'm prepared to fight and to face all the fallout. And I'm prepared to do some serious thinking about who set me up. Because somebody did. Either because they were focused on me or because I was convenient. But someone used me to cheat the firm and the clients, and they're not going to get away with it."

"I can help you." He held up a hand before she could object. "I've got a feel for people. And I've spent my entire adult life dealing with the intrigues and petty pilfering of a large organization. You're the expert with figures, I'm better with personalities, motivations."

He could see her turning it over in her mind, weighing the possibilities. He smiled. "Let's use baseball again. You're the batter, I'm the pitcher. You swing away. I finesse."

"You don't even know any of the people involved."

He would make it his business to, he thought grimly, but he kept his voice mild. "So, you'll tell me about them. You're practical enough to admit there's an advantage to a fresh viewpoint."

"I suppose it wouldn't hurt. Thanks."

"We can start working on the bios tomorrow. I can see why you were wired. You've had quite a day."

"It took some doing to bring myself down after the business at Bittle. Then I knew I had to face Aunt Susie. I took a breather at the cliffs, and—"

She jumped up from her chair. "Jesus, I forgot! I can't believe I actually forgot! God, what did I do with it?" Foolishly, she patted her hips, then remembered she was wearing nothing but an oversized T-shirt. "My pocket. I'll be right back. Stay here."

She streaked inside like a bullet, leaving Byron shaking his head after her. The woman was a mass of contradictions, he decided as he rose to clear the table. It was no use reminding himself that he preferred the quiet, soothing, and sophisticated type. The Laura type, he supposed. Well-mannered, well-read, well-bred.

Yet he'd never felt this bright, hot need with Laura. Or with anyone, for that matter.

Instead, it was Kate, this bumpy and often inconvenient detour, who continually fascinated him.

Just how would his complicated and turbulent Kate react if he told her he was beginning to believe he was falling in love with her?

"Hah!" Triumphant, she bolted back into the kitchen, prepared to bask in his astonishment. She smiled smugly as he stared at her, eyes dark and intense. "I found it."

She was flushed and rumpled. Her short hair stood in spikes, those long, slim legs pale gold beneath the hem of his shirt. She had no figure to speak of, was more bone than curve. The little mascara she'd bothered with was smudged under her eyes. Her nose was crooked. Had he noticed that before? The nose was just slightly off center, and her mouth was certainly too wide for that narrow face.

"You're not beautiful," he said in a quiet statement that made her brow knit. "Why do you look beautiful when you're not?"

"How much of that wine did you drink, De Witt?"

"Your face is wrong." As if to prove it to himself, he came around the counter for a closer look. "It's like whoever put it together used a couple of spare parts from someone else's."

"This is all very fascinating," she said impatiently. "But—"

"At first glance your body looks like it belongs to a teenage boy, all arms and legs."

"Thank you very much, Mr. Universe. Have you finished your unsolicited critique of my looks?"

"Almost." His lips curved a little as he skimmed a hand along her jaw. "I love the way you look. I can't figure out why, but I love the way you look, the way you move." He slipped his arms around her, drew her in. "The way you smell."

"This is a novel way to seduce me."

"The way you taste," he continued and skimmed his lips up her throat.

"And it's surprisingly effective," she managed between shivers. "But I really wanted you to look at this."

He plucked her up, set her down on the counter, then slid his hand around to cup her bare bottom. "I'm going to make love with you here." He closed his teeth over the nipple that strained against the thin cotton. "Is that all right with you?"

"Yes. Good." Her head fell back. "Wherever."

Satisfied with that, he rubbed his lips over hers. "What do you want me to see?"

"Nothing. Just this."

He caught the coin that slipped through her fingers and puzzled over it. "Spanish? A doubloon, I suppose. Isn't this Margo's?"

"No. Mine. I found it." She drew in a long, shuddering breath, let it out. "God, how do you do that? It's like turning off a switch in my head. I found it," she repeated, struggling to separate her sense from her senses.

"Today, on the cliffs. It was just lying there. Seraphina's dowry. You've heard the legend."

"Sure." Intrigued, he turned the coin over in his hand. "The star-crossed lovers. The young Spanish girl left behind in Monterey when the boy she loves goes off to fight the Americans. She hears he's been killed, and in despair she jumps off the cliffs."

He lifted his gaze from the gold to her eyes. "The cliffs, it's said, across from Templeton House."

"She had a dowry," Kate added.

"Right. A chest filled with her bride gift, bestowed by a loving, indulgent father. One variation says she hid it to protect it from the invaders until her lover returned. Another says she took it into the sea with her."

"Well." Kate picked the coin out of his palm. "I go with the first."

"Haven't you and Laura and Margo been combing those cliffs for months?"

"So? Margo found a coin last year, now I've found one."

"At this rate, you'll be rich beyond your wildest dreams about the middle of the next millennium. You believe in legends?"

"What of it?" Ready to pout, she shifted. "Seraphina existed. There's documentation, and—"

"No." He kissed her gently. "Don't spoil it. It's nice to know you can just believe. It's even nicer to know you want me to believe."

She studied his face. "Well, do you?"

He took the coin from her and set it down where it gleamed like a promise beside them. "Of course," he said simply.

CHAPTER 13

STORMS BLEW IN, pelting the coast with driving rain, sweeping it with raging winds. Relief that the dangerously dry season might be averted with the unrelenting wet warred with worry over flooding and mudslides.

Kate tried not to take the nasty weather personally. But there was no doubt that it prevented her from intensifying the treasure hunts. Even as the rains abated, the cliffs were too wet for safety.

So they would wait.

There was certainly enough to occupy her. Pretenses's summer season was in full swing. Tourists crammed Cannery Row, jammed the wharf, queued up for a trip through the aquarium. Arcades clattered with the sounds of games and jingling tokens, and families strolled the sidewalks licking ice cream from sugar cones.

The busy carnival atmosphere out in the streets meant business.

Some came to feed the gulls and watch the boats. Some came to gaze upon the street that Steinbeck had immortalized. Some came to bask in the eternal spring that Monterey offered, or take the sweeping drive along the coast.

Many, many were lured by Margo's clever display windows to come in and browse. And those who browsed often bought.

"I see dollar signs in your eyes again," Laura murmured.

"We're up ten percent from this period last year." Kate turned from her desk and looked at Laura. "By my calculations, Margo should be able to pay off all of her debts by the end of the next quarter. When the holiday shopping season hits, we're actually going to be in the black."

Eyes narrowed, Laura came farther into the room. "I thought we were already in the black."

"Not technically." As she spoke, she continued to crunch figures. "We take a minimum percentage in lieu of salary. We have our pool for resupplying. Then there's operating expenses."

She worked one-handed as she reached for her cup of tea—and tried to pretend it was coffee. "Initially the bulk of our stock was Margo's property, and she took the lion's share of those profits in order to square with her creditors. We're gradually moving into new stock, which is acquired by—"

"Kate, just skip all the details. Are we operating at a loss?"

"We have been, but—"

"I've been taking money every month."

"Of course you have. You have to live. We have to live," Kate amended quickly, seeing the guilt cloud Laura's eyes.

Seeing that it would be necessary to explain and reassure, she set the cup down, resisted the keyboard. "This is how it works, Laura. We take what we need—what we're entitled to, and plow the rest back into the business. Each of us has personal expenses in addition to the shop overhead. Once those are seen to, we reinvest the profit. If there is any."

"And if there isn't, we're in the red, and that means—"

"That means reality. There's nothing unusual in operating at a loss in a new business." Kate bit back a sigh and wondered why she hadn't begun the discussion a different way. "Forget all the ledgers for a minute. What I'm telling you is good news. We're going to end this calendar year not just eking out a minimal living and paying off old debts. We're going to make a profit. A real profit. That's rare in a business that's barely into its second year. By my projections, we'll have a net gain in the mid five figures."

"So we're okay?" Laura said cautiously.

"Yeah, we're okay." Smiling, Kate ran her fingers over the keys of her computer as if they were adored children. "If the charity auction goes as well as last year, we'll be cooking."

"That's what I came in to talk to you about." Laura hesitated, frowned at the figures on the screen. "We're really all right?"

"If you can't trust your accountant, who can you trust?"

"Right." She had to believe it. "Well, then, you won't have any problem cutting a few checks."

"You've come to the right place." Humming, Kate took the invoices from Laura, and then choked. "What the hell are these?"

"Refreshments." Laura offered a bright, hopeful smile. "Entertainment. Oh, and advertising. All auction-related."

"Christ, we're paying this for mind-numbing chamber music from a bunch of nerds? Why can't we just plug in a CD? I told Margo—"

"Kate, it's a matter of image. And this trio isn't a bunch of nerds. They're very talented." She patted Kate's shoulder, well aware why Margo had suggested that she be the one to pass along the bills. "It's union scale, just like the waitpeople."

Grumbling, Kate flipped open the checkbook. "Margo has to do everything in an ornate and showy fashion."

"That's why we love her. Just think how the cash register's going to sing the week after the auction. All those rich, materialistic customers with large disposable incomes."

"You're trying to sweet-talk me."

"Is it working?"

"Say 'large disposable incomes' again."

"Large disposable incomes."

"Okay, I feel better."

"Really? Good." Laura winced, held her breath. "About the fashion show we've set up for December? You agree that's still a good idea?"

"It's a great idea. A well-executed special event will more than pay for itself, and it has the potential of generating new clientele."

"Exactly my thought. Okay, here's my preliminary budget." She kept her eyes squeezed shut as she dropped the figures in Kate's lap. She heard the yelp, and when she opened her eyes, she saw Kate plucking at the back of her shirt.

"What are you doing?"

"I'm trying to pull out the knife you just stuck in my back. Jesus Christ, Laura, we've got the clothes, you've tapped your committees for the models. Why do you need all this money?"

"Decorations, advertising, refreshments. It's all listed. It's negotiable," she said, backing out. "Consider it a wish list. Gotta get back on the floor."

Making noises in her throat, Kate scowled at the door. The trouble was, she decided, both of her partners were too used to being rich to fully appreciate that they no longer were. Or that Pretenses wasn't, she corrected.

Margo had married for love, but she'd married a Templeton, and Templeton meant money.

Laura was a Templeton, and despite being hosed by her ex-husband, she would always have access to millions. She just wouldn't take it.

It was up to good old practical Kate, she decided, to keep things on an even keel.

When the door opened again, she didn't bother to turn around. "Don't hassle me, Laura. I swear I'll cut this wish list of yours down until you won't be able to serve anything but Popsicles and club soda."

"Kate." Laura's voice was quiet enough that Kate whipped around in her chair.

"What's wrong? What—"

She broke off at the sight of the man standing beside Laura. Fiftyish, she judged, with a hairline beyond what could legitimately be called receding. He had the beginnings of jowls, and bland brown eyes. His suit was neat and inexpensive. Somewhere along the line, he'd punched extra holes in his brown leather belt to accommodate his paunch.

But it was his shoes that tipped her off. She couldn't have said why those shiny black shoes with the double-knotted laces shouted cop.

"Kate, this is Detective Kusack. He wants to talk to you."

She wasn't certain how she managed to get to her feet when she'd stopped feeling her legs. But she was facing him, surprised somehow that their eyes were on a level. "Am I under arrest?"

"No, ma'am. I have a few questions regarding an incident at Bittle and Associates."

He had a voice like gravel bouncing on sandpaper. It reminded her foolishly of Bob Seger's gritty rock and roll. "I think I'd like to call my lawyer."

"Margo's already calling Josh." Laura moved to her side.

"That's your option, Ms. Powell." Kusack poked out his bottom lip as he considered her. "Maybe it would be best all round if he met us at the precinct. If you'll come along with me, I'll try not to take up too much of your time. I can see you're busy."

"It's all right." Kate put a hand on Laura's arm before Laura could step forward. "It's all right. Don't worry. I'll call you."

"I'm coming with you."

"No." With icy fingers, Kate picked up her purse. "I'll call you as soon as I can."

SHE WAS TAKEN to an interview room designed to intimidate. Intellectually, she knew that. The plain walls, the scarred center table and uncomfortable chairs, the wide mirror that was obviously two-way glass were all part of a setup to aid the police in getting information from suspects. No matter how Kate's practical side ordered her not to be affected, her skin crawled.

Because *she* was the suspect.

She had Josh beside her, looking particularly lawyerly in a tailored gray suit and muted striped tie. Kusack folded his hands on the table. Big hands, Kate noted distractedly, adorned with a single thin gold wedding band. He was a nail-biter, she thought, staring with dull fascination at his ragged, painfully short fingernails.

For the space of several heartbeats, there was nothing but humming silence, like the hushed anticipation just before the curtain rose on the first act of a major play. A bubble of hysterical laughter nearly fizzed out of her throat at the image.

Act one, scene one, and she had the starring role.

"Can I get you something, Ms. Powell?" Kusack watched her muscles jerk in reaction to his voice as her gaze flew from his hands to his face. "Coffee? A Coke?"

"No. Nothing."

"Detective Kusack, my client is here, at your request, in the spirit of co-operation." His cultured voice chilly and hard, Josh gave Kate's tense hand a comforting squeeze under the table. "No one wants this matter cleared up more. Ms. Powell is willing to make a statement."

"I appreciate that, Mr. Templeton. Ms. Powell, I'd like it if you'd answer a few questions, so I can get this all straight in my mind." He gave her a kindly, avuncular smile that made her insides quiver. "I'm going to read you your rights. Now that's just procedure, just the way we have to do things."

He recited the words that anyone who had ever watched an episode of a police drama from *Kojak* to *NYPD Blue* knew by rote. She stared at the tape recorder, silently documenting every word, every inflection.

"You understand these rights, Ms. Powell?"

She shifted her eyes, stared into his. The curtain was up, she thought. Damned if she was going to blow it. "Yes, I understand."

"You worked for the accounting firm of Bittle and Associates from . . ." He flipped pages in a small dog-eared notebook, read off dates.

"Yes, they hired me straight out of graduate school."

"Harvard, right? You got to have a lot of smarts to get into Harvard. I see you graduated as a Baker Scholar, too."

"I worked for it."

"Bet you did," he said easily. "What kind of stuff did you do at Bittle?"

"Tax preparation, financial and estate planning. Investment advice. I might work in tandem with a client's broker to build or enhance a portfolio."

Josh lifted a finger. "I want it on record that during my client's employment at this firm she increased business by bringing in accounts. Her record there was not only unblemished, it was superior."

"Uh-huh. How do you go about bringing in accounts, Ms. Powell?"

"Contacts, networking. Recommendations from current accounts."

He took her through the day-to-day business of her work, the questions slowly paced, quietly asked until she began to relax.

He scratched his head, shaking it. "Me, I can't make a damn bit of sense out of all those forms Uncle Sam wants us to fill out. Used to sit down with them every year, all spread out on the kitchen table. With a bottle of Jack to ease the pain." He grinned winningly. "The wife finally had enough of that. Now I take everything up to H & R Block in April and dump it on them."

"That makes you very typical, Detective Kusack."

"They're always changing the rules, aren't they?" He smiled again. "Somebody like you would have to understand rules. And how to get around them."

When Josh objected to the tone of the question, Kate shook her head. "No, I can respond to that. I understand the rules, Detective Kusack. It's my job to recognize what's black and white, and where the shades of gray are. A good accountant uses the system to circumvent the system when possible."

"It's kind of a game, isn't it?"

"Yes, in a way. But the game has rules, too. I wouldn't have lasted a month at a firm with Bittle's structure and reputation if I hadn't played by those rules. An accountant who doctors tax forms, or cheats the IRS endangers herself and her client. I wasn't raised to cheat."

"You were raised right here in Monterey, weren't you? You were the ward of Thomas and Susan Templeton."

"My parents were killed when I was eight. I—"

"Your father had a bit of a financial problem before his death," Kusack commented and watched Kate's face go sheet-white.

"Charges brought and never resolved concerning my client's father twenty years ago have no bearing here," Josh stated.

"Just background, counselor. And an interesting coincidence."

"I wasn't aware of my father's problems until recently," Kate managed. How had he found out so quickly? she wondered. Why had he looked? "As I said, both my parents were killed when I was a child. I grew up in Templeton House in the Big Sur area." She took a quiet breath. "The Templetons didn't consider or treat me as a ward but as a daughter."

"You know, I'd have figured they'd have taken you into the Templeton organization. A woman with your skills, and they've got all those hotels, the factories."

"I didn't choose to join the Templeton organization."

"Now why was that?"

"Because I didn't want to take anything else from them. I wanted to go out on my own. They respected my decision."

"And the door remained open," Josh put in. "Anytime Kate wanted to walk through. Detective, I don't see what this line of questioning has to do with the matter at hand."

"Just laying a foundation." Despite the recorder, he continued to make little notations in his tattered notebook. "Ms. Powell, what was your salary at Bittle at the time of your termination?"

"A base of fifty-two-five, plus bonus."

"Fifty-two thousand." Nodding, he flipped through his book as if checking facts. "That's quite a come-down for someone who had the run of a place like Templeton House."

"I earned it, and it was enough for my needs." She felt a line of cold sweat drip down her back. "I know how to make money from money. And in an average year, I would add twenty thousand to that base in bonuses."

"Last year you opened a business."

"With my sisters. With Margo and Laura Templeton," Kate qualified.

"It's risky, starting a business." Those bland eyes stayed on hers. "And expensive."

"I can give you all the statistics, all the figures."

"You like to gamble, Ms. Powell."

"No, I don't. Not in the standard sense of Vegas or the track. The odds always favor the house. But I appreciate an intelligent, and cautious, investment risk. And I consider Pretenses to be just that."

"Some businesses need to be fed a lot. Something like this shop of yours, keeping stock, all that overhead."

"My books are clean. You can—"

"Kate." Josh put a hand on her arm in warning.

"No." Furious now, she shook it off. "He's implying that I would take the easy way, because my father did. That I embezzled from Bittle to keep Pretenses afloat, and I'm not having it. We've worked too hard to make the shop run. Especially Margo. I'm not having it, Josh. He's not going to say that the shop's involved." She seared Kusack with one hot glare. "You pick up the books at the shop anytime. You go over them line by line."

"I appreciate the offer, Ms. Powell," Kusack said mildly. He opened a folder, slid papers out. "Do you recognize these forms?"

"Of course. That's the 1040 I completed for Sid Sun, and that other one is the altered duplicate."

"That's your signature?"

"Yes, on both copies. And no, I can't explain it."

"And these printouts for computer-generated withdrawals from Bittle's escrow accounts?"

"It's my name, my code."

"Who had access to your office computer?"

"Everyone."

"And to your security code?"

"No one but me, as far as I know."

"You gave it to no one?"

"No."

"You kept it in your head."

"Of course."

Kusack kept his eyes on hers as he leaned forward. "Must be some trick, keeping all kinds of numbers in your head."

"I'm good at it. Most people keep numbers in their heads. Social security, PIN numbers, telephone numbers, dates."

"Me, I have to write everything down. Otherwise I mix it all up. I guess you don't worry about that."

"I don't—"

"Kate." Josh interrupted again, met her impatient glance with a quiet look. "Where do you record the numbers?"

"In my head," she said wearily. "I don't forget. I haven't had to look up the security code in years."

Lips pursed, Kusack examined his ragged nails. "Where would you look it up, if you had to?"

"In my Filofax, but . . ." Her voice trailed off as the impact hit home. "In my Filofax," she repeated. "I have everything in it."

She grabbed her purse, fumbled through it, and took out the thick, leather-bound book. "For backup," she said, opening the book. "Backup's the first rule. Here." She located the page, nearly laughed. "My life in numbers."

Kusack scratched his chin. "You keep that with you."

"I just said it's my life. That's literally true. It's always in my bag."

"Where do you keep your bag—say, during office hours?"

"In my office."

"And you'd carry it around with you. I know my wife never takes two steps without her pocketbook."

"Only if I was leaving the building. Josh." She clutched his hand. "Only if I was leaving the building. Anybody in the firm could have taken the code. Christ, anybody at all." She squeezed her eyes tight. "I should have thought of it before. I just wasn't thinking at all."

"That's still your signature on the forms, Ms. Powell," Kusack reminded her.

"It's a forgery," she snapped and rose to her feet. "You listen to me. Do you think I'd risk everything I worked for, everything I was given, for a lousy seventy-five K? If money was what was important to me, I could have picked up the phone, called my aunt and uncle, called Josh, and they would have given me twice that without a single question. I'm not a thief, and if I were, I sure as hell would cover my tracks better than this. What idiot would use her own code, her own name, leave such a pathetically obvious paper trail?"

"You know, Ms. Powell"—Kusack folded his hands on the table again—"I asked myself that same question. I'll tell you what my take is. The person had to be one of three things: stupid, desperate, or very, very smart."

"I'm very smart."

"That you are, Ms. Powell," Kusack said with a slow nod. "That you are. You're smart enough to know that seventy-five large isn't peanuts. Smart enough to be able to hide it where it couldn't easily be found."

"Detective, my client denies any knowledge of the money in question. The evidence is not just circumstantial but highly questionable. We both know you can't make a case with this, and you've taken up enough of our time."

"I appreciate your cooperation." Kusack tidied the papers and put them back in his file. "Ms. Powell," he continued, as Josh led her to the door, "one more thing. How'd you break your nose?"

"Excuse me?"

"Your nose," he said with an easy smile. "How'd you break it?"

Baffled, she lifted a hand and rubbed it, felt the familiar angle. "Bottom of the ninth, stretching a double into a three-bagger in a bad imitation of Pete Rose. I cracked it against the fielder's knee."

His teeth flashed. "Safe or out?"

"Safe."

He watched her go, then flipped the file open again and studied the signatures on the forms. Stupid, desperate, or very, very smart, he thought.

CHAPTER 14

"HE DOESN'T BELIEVE me." Reaction set in the minute the door closed behind her. All the anger and righteousness jittered away into fear.

"I'm not so sure of that," Josh murmured and navigated her out of the interviewing area. He could feel her body vibrate through the hand he held to her back. "But what matters is they don't have a case. There isn't enough to take to the DA, and Kusack knows it."

"It does matter." She pressed a hand to her churning stomach. Not the ulcer this time, she hoped. But that was little comfort when the alternative diagnosis was shame and fear. "It matters what he thinks, what Bittle thinks, what everyone thinks. However much I don't want it to, it matters."

"Listen to me." He turned her in the corridor to face him, kept his hands on her shoulders. "You did fine in there. Better than fine. It might not have been the exact route I would have recommended as your attorney, but it was effective. The records in your Filofax open up a whole new area of investigation. Now consider who led you to that."

"You did." When he shook his head, she drew her brows together. Because Josh expected it, she ordered herself to think clearly. "He did. Kusack did. He wanted me to tell him I had the code written down somewhere."

"Somewhere where it could be accessed." Josh's hands gentled on her shoulders. "Now I want you to put this aside. I mean it, Kate," he continued even as she opened her mouth to protest. "Let Kusack do his job, let me do mine. You have people behind you. That's something I don't want you to forget again."

"I'm scared." She pressed her lips together, wanting her voice to be level even in the admission. "The only time I wasn't scared was when he made me mad. Now I'm scared all over again. Why did he bring up my father, Josh? How did he know about it? What reason would he have for looking that far into my background?"

"I don't know. I'm going to find out."

"They have to know at Bittle." Despair was a stone sinking in her gut.

"If Kusack knows, so do the partners. Maybe they knew about it before, and that's why—"

"Kate, stop."

"But what if they never find out who did it? If they don't find out, then I'm always going to—"

"I said stop. We will find out. That's a promise—not from your lawyer but from your big brother." He drew her close, kissed the top of her head, then spotted Byron striding down the hall. He recognized barely controlled fury when he saw it and decided it was just what Kate needed to take her mind off the interview.

"By, good timing. You'll run Kate home, won't you?"

She spun around, confused and embarrassed. "What are you doing here?"

"Laura tracked me down." He shot a look at Josh that clearly stated they would talk later and began to usher Kate down the hall. "Let's get out of here."

"I need to go back to the shop. Margo's alone."

"Margo can handle herself." He towed her down the steps, past the desk, and outside, where the sun was blinding bright. "Are you all right?"

"Yeah. A little turned around inside, but okay."

He'd driven his 'Vette, the sleek, streamlined two-seater in muscle-car black. Settling inside a thirty-year-old car only made the entire day all the more surreal.

"You didn't have to come all the way down here."

"Obviously." Despising the impotency, he gunned the engine viciously. "You'd have called if you'd wanted my help. Now you're stuck with it."

"There wasn't anything you could do," she began and winced at the molten look he shot her before he cruised out of the parking lot. "They didn't charge me with anything."

"Well, it's our lucky day, isn't it?" He wanted to drive. He wanted to drive fast to dissipate some of the bubbling anger before it boiled over and burned them both. To cancel any possibility of conversation, he flicked up the volume on the car stereo, and Eric Clapton's angry guitar licks scorched the air.

Perfect, Kate thought, and shut her eyes. Mean music, a muscle car and southern-fried temper. She told herself the migraine brewing and the highly possible visit by her old pal Mr. Ulcer were enough to worry about.

She found her sunglasses in her purse and put them on before dry-swallowing medication. Through the tinted lenses, the light seemed calmer, kinder. The wind whipped, cooling her hot cheeks. She had only to lay her head back, raise her face, to see the sky.

Byron said nothing, but sent the car slashing up Highway 1 like a bright black sword cleaving through sea and rock. It tore through a low-lying cloud, burst out of the thin vapor, and roared back into the flash of sun.

He'd been battling feelings of impotence and hot fury since Laura's call. *The police took Kate in for questioning. We don't know what they're going to do. A detective came to the shop, and he took her.*

The jingle of fear in Laura's usually calm voice had set off a violent chain reaction in him. The fear had been fueled by hurt. Kate hadn't called him.

He'd imagined her alone—it hadn't mattered that Laura had assured him Josh was with her. He'd envisioned her alone, frightened, at the mercy of accusations. His overworked imagination had pictured her handcuffed and led off in chains.

And there was nothing he could do but wait.

Now she was sitting beside him, her eyes shielded by dark glasses that made her skin all the more pale in contrast. Her hands were clasped in her lap, deceptively still until you noted the knuckles were white. And she had told him there was no need for him.

He didn't question the impulse, but swung to the side of the road. At the Templeton House cliffs where she had once wept on his shoulder.

She opened her eyes. It didn't surprise her in the least that he had stopped there, there at a spot of both peace and drama. Before she could reach for the door handle, he was leaning across her to jerk open the door himself.

An old habit, she decided. With all that temper swirling around in him, the gesture couldn't be considered courtly.

In silence they walked to the cliffs.

"Why didn't you call me?" He hadn't meant to ask that first, but it popped out of his mouth.

"I didn't think of it."

He whirled on her so quickly, so unexpectedly, that she stumbled back a step, crushed a scattering of tiny white wildflowers underfoot. "No, you wouldn't. Just where the hell am I on that agenda of yours, Katherine?"

"I don't know what you mean. I didn't think of it because—"

"Because you don't need anyone but Kate," he shot back. "Because you don't want to need anyone who might upset that profit-and-loss ledger in your head. I wouldn't have been of any practical use, so why bother?"

"That's not true."

How could she deal with an argument now? she wondered. How could she handle that brilliant fury in his eyes? She had a terrible urge to simply press her hands to her ears, squeeze her eyes shut so that she could neither see nor hear. So she could just be alone in the dark.

"I don't understand why you're so angry with me, but I just don't have the energy to fight with you now."

He gripped her arm before she could turn away. "Good. Then you can just listen. Try to imagine what it was like to be told by someone else that the police had taken you in. To visualize what might be happening to you, what you were going through, and to be powerless to change it."

"That's just it. There wasn't anything you could do."

"I could have been there." He shouted over the wind that raked through his hair like wild fingers. "I could have been there for you. You could have known there was someone who cared there for you. But you didn't even think of it."

"Damn it, Byron, I couldn't think at all." She jerked away, walked along the cliff path. Even a few steps would distance her from the upheaval of emotion, the avalanche, the flood of it, before she broke into pieces. "It was like being shut down, or frozen up. I was too scared to think. It wasn't personal."

"I take it very personally. We have a relationship, Kate." He waited while she slowly turned around, watching him through eyes guarded by dark glasses. With some effort, he drew in his temper and spoke with measured calm. "I thought I made it clear what that entails for me. If you can't accept the basic terms of a relationship with me, then we're wasting our time."

She hadn't thought anything could squeeze past the pain in her head, the ache in her stomach, the sizzle of shame in her blood. But she hadn't counted on despair. Somehow despair always made room for itself.

Her eyes burned as she looked at him, standing in the sun and wind. "Well, your dumping me certainly puts a cap on the day."

She started past him with some idea of running up to Templeton House, getting inside and shutting everything else out.

"Goddamn it." He spun her around, crushing his mouth to hers in a kiss that tasted of bitter frustration. "How can you be so hardheaded?" He shook her, then kissed her again until she wondered why her overtaxed brain didn't simply implode. "Can't you see anything unless it's in a straight line?"

"I'm tired." She hated, resented, the shakiness of her voice. "I'm humiliated. I'm scared. Just leave me alone."

"I'd like nothing better than to be able to leave you alone. Just walk away and chalk it up to a bad bet."

He pulled off her sunglasses, stuck them in his pocket. He'd wanted to see her eyes, and now he recognized swirling in them the same anger and hurt that twisted in him. "Do you think I need the turmoil and complications you've brought into my life? Do you actually think I'd tolerate all that because we're good in bed?"

"You don't have to tolerate it." She fisted her hands on his chest. "You don't have to tolerate any of it."

"Damn right I don't. But I am tolerating it because I think I'm in love with you."

She'd have been less surprised if he'd simply hauled her up and tossed her over the cliff. In an attempt to keep her reeling head in place, she pressed a hand to her temple.

"Hard to come up with a response?" His voice was as sharp and smooth as a newly oiled sword. "That's not surprising. Emotions don't add up in neat columns, do they?"

"I don't know what I'm supposed to say to you. This isn't fair."

"It's not about fair. And at the moment I don't like the situation any more than you do. You're a far cry from the girl of my dreams, Katherine."

That had her eyes clearing. "Now I know what to say. Go to hell."

"Unimaginative," he decided. "Now get this into that computer-chip brain of yours." He pulled her up onto her toes until their eyes were level. "I don't like to make mistakes any more than you do, so I'm going to take the time to figure out exactly how I feel about you. If I decide you're what I want, then you're what I'll have."

Her eyes narrowed, glinting with dangerous lights. "How incredibly romantic."

His lips curved in quick and genuine humor. "I'll give you romance, Kate, and plenty of it."

"You can take your warped concept of romance and—"

He cut her off with a soft, quiet kiss. "I was worried about you," he murmured. "I was afraid for you. And you hurt me because you didn't turn to me."

"I didn't mean to—" She snapped back before her bones could melt. "You're twisting this around. You're trying to confuse me." Surrendering to pain, she shut her eyes. "Oh, God, my head aches."

"I know. I can see it." As a parent might soothe a child, he touched his lips to her left temple, then her right. "Let's sit down." He eased her down onto a rock, then stood behind her to massage the tense muscles of her neck and shoulders. "I want to take care of you, Kate."

"I don't want to be taken care of."

"I know." Over her head he watched the sea gleam as the sun burned through a cloud and streamed down. She couldn't help that, he supposed, any more than he could help his own need to protect and defend. "We'll have to find an area of compromise there. You matter to me."

"I know. You matter to me, too, but—"

"That's a nice place to stop," he told her. "I'm asking you to think of me. And to accept that you can turn to me. For the little things—and for the big ones. Can you handle that much?"

"I can try." She wanted to believe it was the medication finally kicking in that was making the pain slide away. But a part of her, the part she'd long considered foolish, thought it was the sea and the cliffs. And him. "Byron, I didn't mean to hurt you. I hate hurting people I care about. It's the worst thing for me."

"I know." He pressed his thumbs to the base of her neck, searching out stubborn knots of tension. And smiled when she leaned back against him.

"When I saw you in the police station, I was embarrassed."

"I know that too."

"Well, it's nice to be so transparent."

"I know where to look in you. It seems to be some kind of innate skill. It's one of the reasons I think I may be in love with you." He felt the tension leap back into her muscles. "Relax," he suggested. "We may both learn to live with it."

"My life is, to put it mildly, in upheaval."

She stared straight ahead to the horizon. The sky always met the sea, she mused, no matter how distant. But people didn't always, couldn't always find that joining point.

"I also know my own limitations," she continued. "I'm not ready for that kind of leap."

"I'm not sure I am myself. But if I take it, I'm pulling you with me." He came around the rock to sit beside her. "I'm very good at handling complications, Kate. I'll handle you." When she opened her mouth, he pressed his fingers to it. "No you don't. You'll tense up again. You're just going to say you won't be handled, then I'll have to say something about how if you let someone take part of the control now and again you wouldn't have so many headaches. Then we'd just go around until one of us gets pissed off again."

She frowned at him. "I don't like the way you fight."

"It always drove my sisters crazy. Suellen used to say I used logic like a left jab."

"You've got a sister named Suellen?"

He raised an eyebrow. "From *Gone With the Wind*. My mother chose all our names from literature. Got a problem with that?"

"No." She plucked at a speck of lint on her skirt. "It just sounds so southern."

He chuckled, wondering if she realized she made the South sound like another planet. "Honey, we *are* southern. Suellen, Charlotte as in Brontë, Meg from *Little Women*."

"And Byron, as in Lord."

"Exactly."

"You don't have the poetic pallor or the clubfoot, but you do sort of have the dreamy good looks."

"Flattery." He kissed her lightly in response. "I guess you're feeling better."

"I guess I am."

"So." He draped an arm over her shoulders. "How was your day?"

With a weak laugh, she turned her face, nuzzled it against the curve of his neck. "It sucked. It really, really sucked."

"Want to talk about it?"

"Maybe." It wasn't really so hard to lean against a strong shoulder, she decided, if she just concentrated. "I should call Laura. I told her I would."

"Josh will tell her you're with me. She won't worry."

"She'll worry whether I call or not. Laura worries about everyone." Kate let the silence soothe a moment, then began with Kusack's appearance at the shop.

Byron didn't interrupt, but listened, assessed, and considered.

"I don't think he believed me. The way he kept watching me, with this kind of cat patience, you know? When he mentioned my father, my brain just froze up. I knew I should have been prepared for it. Right from the start of this I knew that would be the worst and I should have been prepared. But I wasn't."

"It hurt you," Byron murmured. "More than any of the rest."

"Yes." She reached back, gripped his hand, baffled and relieved that he would understand so easily. "It hurt that this stranger, this cop, should damage the man I'm trying to remember. The one who used to spin ridiculous dreams for me, who I'm trying to believe only wanted the best for me. And I can't defend him, Byron, because what he did is against everything I believe in."

"That doesn't mean you didn't love your father and aren't entitled to remember the best parts of him."

"I'm working on that," she murmured. "The problem is I have to stay focused on what's happening now. It's harder than I imagined. When Kusack brought out the forms, I couldn't explain why they both had my signature. But Josh seemed to think it went well, especially that business with the security code."

"Electronic thievery rolled in right along with the micro-chip. You said the siphoning off started about a year and a half ago. Who's had access to your computer during that time period?"

"Dozens of people." Isn't that why it's all so hopeless? she thought. "There's not a big turnover at Bittle. It's a good firm."

"So who needs money, who's smart, and who would point the finger at you?"

"Who doesn't need money?" she countered, irritated because her mind was refusing to travel a logical path. "Bittle hires smart, and I don't know anyone in the firm who has it in for me personally."

"Maybe it wasn't personal so much as convenient. A cautious amount of money," he murmured. "Like a test—or a way to offset small, annoying debts. And the timing, Kate, haven't you considered the timing?"

"I can't follow you."

"Why now, why you? Is it just a coincidence that you should find out about your father at essentially the same time this skimming was noticed?"

"What else could it be?"

"Maybe someone else found out and used it."

"I didn't tell anyone."

"What did you do? The day you found out, what did you do?"

"I sat there at my desk, reeling. I didn't want to believe it, so I checked." He would have banked on it. "How?"

"I accessed the library back in New Hampshire, ordered faxes of newspaper articles, contacted the lawyer who handled the details. I hired a detective."

He considered. Every one of those steps generated data. Phone records, computer records, paper trail. "And noted the data in your Filofax."

"Well, yes, the names and phone numbers, but—"

"And the transmissions to and from New Hampshire were on your computer?"

"I—" She began to see, began to feel ill all over again. "Yes. The records of faxes sent and received. If someone wanted to look. But still, they'd have to have my password, and—"

"Which is noted in your Filofax," he finished. "Who would be the last person questioned coming out of your office if you weren't there?"

"Any one of the partners, I suppose. One of the executive assistants." She shrugged, unsurprised to find that her shoulders were tightening up again. "Hell, any of the other accountants on that floor. No one would think twice about seeing an associate breeze out of another associate's office."

"Then we'll concentrate on those. The third Bittle you talked about. Who is it . . . Marty?"

"Marty wouldn't embezzle from his own company. That's ludicrous."

"We'll see. Meanwhile, how do you think he'd react if you asked him to get you copies of the forms in question?"

"I don't know."

"Why don't we find out?"

AN HOUR LATER, Kate hung up the phone in Byron's kitchen. "I should have known he'd come through. He'll make copies as soon as he's able to and bring them to you at the hotel." She worked up a smile. "It's like a little intrigue. I'm surprised he didn't ask for passwords. He's actually enjoying it."

"Our man on the inside."

"I should have thought of this angle right from the beginning. Now I can add feeling stupid to the rest of it."

"Emotions tend to cloud logic," he told her. "Otherwise I might have hit on it earlier myself."

"Well . . ." She wasn't sure she was ready to deal with that line of thought just now. "Anyway, Marty told me that they decided to turn it over to the police after my showdown the other day. His father's not happy about it, but the vote carried."

"Do you regret facing up to them?"

"No, but there's going to be gossip now. Plenty of it." Trying to keep it light, she smiled at him. "How do you feel about having an alleged embezzler of dubious lineage for a lover?"

"I think that requires a test." He gathered her close, skimming his hands up her back and into her hair in the way she'd come to anticipate.

Her mouth lifted to his, opened for his. "I guess this means you're not going back to work this afternoon."

"Good guess." His mouth stayed busy as he circled her out of the kitchen.

"Where are we going? Haven't I already mentioned all this floor you have around here?"

He chuckled against her throat. "I haven't shown you my new sofa."

"Oh." She let him ease her back on the generous cushions. "It's very nice," she murmured as his weight pressed her deeper into them. "Long." His fingers parted her blouse, exposing her as she arched to his touch. "Soft."

"We so rarely make it to the bedroom." He lowered his head, nipped lightly at her breasts. "I wanted something . . . accommodating . . . on the main level."

"Very considerate of you." She gasped when his mouth closed over her, sucked her in.

It was so easy to let the heat take her, to spin her mind away, to follow the demands of her own body. For pleasure. For sensation. For tastes and textures. She tugged his tie loose when his mouth sought hers again, loosened the buttons that prevented flesh from meeting flesh.

But he wouldn't let her hurry, and her impatience drained away until she was steeped and savoring.

Strong, broad shoulders, hair glorious gold at the tips, the subtle creases in his cheeks. That long, rippled torso. She luxuriated in the feel of those smooth hands gliding over her, lingering here, pressing there, then skillfully bringing her to a long, shimmering orgasm that poured through her system like warmed wine.

He thought it stunning to watch her, the flickers of pleasure and tension and release that played over her face. Arousal had blood rising to her cheeks, caused her eyes to darken and glow like rich, aged brandy. The body beneath his arched and flowed, quivered and grew erotically damp.

The taste of soap and salt between her breasts enchanted him. The feel of those narrow, restless hands enjoying his own flesh delighted him, darkly. The need to be in her, to join body to body and bury himself deep was overpowering.

He filled her, shuddering when those exotically female muscles clutched around him. Yet it wasn't enough.

He pulled her up until her arms were wrapped around his neck, her legs around his waist. With his mouth he swallowed each of the moans that trembled from her throat, then raced his lips over that long white column where a pulse beat like fury.

She panted out his name, blinded by the single primal urge to reach the summit. Her hips pumped, jackhammer quick, as the craving grew maddening, the pleasure unbearable. She was willing to beg, if only the words would come, but instead she sank her teeth into his shoulder.

It flashed through her like an overstoked furnace, hot and violent. Stunned and helpless, she clung, then felt the magic pulse between them as he poured himself into her.

THE PHONE AWAKENED her an hour later. Disoriented, Kate fumbled for the receiver before she remembered she wasn't home. "Yes, hello."

"Oh. I'm sorry. I must have the wrong number. I'm calling Byron De Witt's residence."

Dazed, Kate stared around the room. The antique oak chest of drawers, the warm green walls and white curtains, the clever watercolor seascapes. A thriving ornamental lemon tree in a glazed pot in front of the window. And the lulling, ceaseless sound of the sea.

Byron's bedroom.

"Ah . . ." She sat up, rubbing a hand over her face. Cool ivory sheets slipped down to her waist. "This is Mr. De Witt's residence."

"Oh, I didn't realize he'd gotten a housekeeper already. I expect he's at work. I was just going to leave a message on the machine for him. Tell him Lottie called, won't you, honey? He can reach me anytime this evening. He's got the number. 'Bye now."

Before Kate was fully awake, she was staring at the receiver and listening to the rude buzz of a dial tone.

Housekeeper? Lottie? He's got the number? Well, fuck.

She slammed down the phone and scrambled up. The scent of him was still on her skin, and he was getting calls from some bimbo named Lottie. Typical, she decided, and looked around for her clothes. Which were, she recalled, downstairs where he'd left them when he carried her up to bed. Ordered her to take a nap. And she'd been so softened by lovemaking that she meekly obeyed.

Hadn't she told herself from the start that men like him were all the same? The better-looking they were, the more charming they were, the bigger scum they were. Men who looked like Byron had women crawling all over them every day of the week.

And he'd said he thought he loved her. What a crock. Energized with righteous fury, she marched downstairs and snatched up her clothes. Scum. Swine. Slime. Ignoring her hose, she struggled into skirt and blouse, fumbling with her buttons as he came through the deck door with the dogs at his heels.

"Thought you'd still be sleeping."

She eyed him narrowly. "I bet you did."

"I took the dogs for a run on the beach. We should go down later. The storm's brought some nice shells in." He walked into the kitchen as he spoke. Swaggering like a gunslinger, she followed. "Want a beer?" He twisted the cap off one, guzzled. As he lowered the bottle, he caught the glint of steel in her eyes. "Problem?"

"Problem? No, no problem at all." Before she could stop herself she'd bunched up her fist and plowed it into his belly. It was like hitting rock. "Be sure when you see Lottie you tell her I'm not your goddamn housekeeper."

He rubbed his belly more in surprise than discomfort. "Huh?"

"Oh, brilliant. You always have such a sharp riposte, De Witt. How dare you? How dare you say the things you said to me, do the things you did, and have some . . . some tramp named Lottie on the side?"

It wasn't quite clear, but he thought he was starting to catch up. "Lottie called?" he ventured.

She made the same sound in her throat that he'd heard once or twice before. As much for her sake as his own, he held up a hand and backed off. "You're going to hurt yourself if you hit me again."

Her gaze shifted, lingered on the kitchen block filled with black-handled knives. He didn't believe it, not for an instant. But he stepped between her and the sharp implements.

"Now, I'm going to guess that the phone woke you up, and it was Lottie. And Lottie, by the way, is not a tramp."

"I say she is, and either way, you're still a lying, two-timing scum. How long did you expect to get away with telling her I was your housekeeper? And just what were you going to tell me she was?"

He studied his beer for a moment, tried to keep the gleam out of his eyes when they met hers. "My sister."

"Oh, very original. I'm out of here."

"Not so fast." It wasn't much of a challenge to grab her one-armed around the waist and haul her to a chair. She was kicking, swinging, but he managed it easily. "Lottie," he said as he shoved her in place again, "*is* my sister."

"You don't have a sister named Lottie," she fired back. "You idiot, you told me your sisters' names just a few hours ago. Suellen, Meg, and—"

"Charlotte," he finished, and didn't bother to conceal the smugness. "Lottie. She's a pediatrician, married, three kids. And she has just the kind of warped sense of humor that might make her appreciate having my lover call her a tramp." He watched the embarrassed blush stain Kate's cheek. "Want that beer now?"

"No." Voice strained, pride forfeited, she got to her feet. "I apologize. I don't normally jump to conclusions. It's been a difficult and emotional day."

"Uh-huh."

Damn him. "I was asleep when she called, and she never gave me a chance to say anything."

"That's Lottie."

"And I just assumed. I was asleep," she said, furious. "Disoriented. I was—"

"Jealous," he finished and backed her up against the refrigerator. "That's okay. I like it—to a point."

"I don't like it, to any point. I'm sorry I hit you."

"You're going to have to work on those arms if you want to have any impact." He put a hand under her chin to lift it. "You wouldn't have gone for the knives, would you?"

"Of course not." She slanted her gaze toward them, shrugged. "Probably not."

He let his hand drop, took another swig of beer. "Honey, you terrify me."

"I'm sorry, really. There's no excuse for behaving that way. It was knee-jerk." She pressed her hands together. Confession always hurt. "I was involved with someone a couple of years ago. I don't get involved easily, and he wasn't what you could term the faithful type."

"Did you love him?"

"No, but I trusted him."

He nodded, set the beer aside. "And trust is more fragile than love." He cupped her face in his hands. "You can trust me, Kate." He pressed his lips to her brow, then eased back with a grin on his face. "I would never risk having you slice off any important appendages with a chef's knife."

Feeling both soothed and foolish, she settled into his arms. "I would never have used it." Her lips curved against his. "Probably."

CHAPTER 15

"THIS IS SO incredibly dumb." Naked, Kate fidgeted and blew the bangs out of her eyes. "I feel like an idiot."

"Leave your hair alone," Margo ordered. "I worked too hard on it to have you screw it up. And stop gnawing on your lip."

"I hate wearing lipstick. Why won't you let me see my face?" Kate craned her neck, but Margo had draped the mirror in the wardrobe room. "I look like a clown, don't I? You made me look like a clown."

"Actually, it's more like a twenty-dollar hooker, but it's such a nice look for you. Hold still, damn it, so I can get you into this thing."

Suffering mightily, Kate lifted her arms as Margo hooked her into what seemed to be some instrument of medieval torture. "Why are you doing this to me, Margo? I cut the check for your dippy string trio, didn't I? I went along with the truffles—even though they're snuffed out by pigs and hideously expensive."

Her face set like a general leading troops into battle, Margo adjusted the bustier. "You agreed to follow my guidance for your image tonight. The Annual Reception and Charity Auction is Pretenses's most important event. Now stop bitching."

"Stop playing with my tits."

"Oh, but I love them so. There." Margo stepped back, then nodded in satisfaction. "I didn't have much to work with, but . . ."

"Keep it up, Miss D Cup," Kate grumbled, then looked down and goggled. "Jesus, where did they come from?"

"Amazing, isn't it? In the right harness, those puppies just rise."

"I have breasts." Stunned, Kate patted the swell rising above black satin and lace. "And cleavage."

"It's all a matter of proper positioning and making the most of what we have. Even when it's next to nothing."

"Shut up." Grinning, Kate slicked her hands down her torso. "Look, Ma. I'm a girl."

"You ain't seen nothing yet. Put this on." Margo tossed her a thin swatch of stretchy lace.

Kate studied the garter belt, tugged it, snorted. "You're kidding."

"I'm not putting it on for you." Margo patted the bulge under her sparkling silver tunic. "At seven months and counting, bending over isn't as easy as it used to be."

"I feel like I'm in dress rehearsal for a porn flick." But after a struggle, Kate snapped the garter belt into place. "It's a little hard to breathe."

"Hose," Margo ordered. "You'd better sit down to put them on." With her hands on her hips, Margo supervised the production. "Not so fast, you'll snag. Those aren't your industrial-strength panty hose."

Brows beetled, Kate flicked up a glance. "Do you have to watch me?"

"Yes. Where's Laura?" Margo wondered and began to pace. "She should be here. And if the musicians don't show up in the next ten minutes, they won't have time to set up before the guests start to arrive."

"Everything'll be fine." Stalling, Kate smoothed her hose up her legs. "You know, Margo, I really do think it would be best if I kept sort of a low profile tonight. With this cloud over my head, it makes things awkward."

"Chicken."

Kate's head shot up. "I am not a chicken. I'm a scandal."

"And last year I was the scandal." Margo shrugged her shoulders. "Maybe we can work something out so that Laura can fill the role next year."

"It's not funny."

"Nobody understands that better than I do." Margo laid a hand on Kate's flushed cheek. "Nobody understands how scared you are right now better than I do."

"I guess not." Comforted, Kate turned her face to Margo's palm. "It's just that it's dragging on for so long. I keep expecting that Kusack character to show up and cart me off in chains. It's not enough that they can't prove I did it if I can't prove I didn't."

"I'm not going to say you'll get through it. That's not enough either. But no one who knows you believes it. And didn't you say Byron had some sort of angle to work on?"

"He didn't really explain." She moved her shoulder, tugged at the elastic strap on the lacy belt. "Just mumbled the equivalent of me not worrying my pretty head over it. I really hate that."

"Men like to play white knight, Kate. It doesn't hurt to let them do that now and again."

"It's been weeks since Marty got the copies to us. I've gone over them all, line by line, but . . ." She trailed off. "Well, we've all been pretty busy, and I haven't been jolted out of sleep by the sound of bullhorns telling me they've got me surrounded."

"Don't worry. When that happens we won't let them take you alive. If they raid the shop tonight, we'll have Byron help you escape in one of his macho cars."

"If he makes it at all. He had to fly down to L.A. this morning. I thought I told you."

"He'll be back in time."

"He couldn't say for sure." And Kate refused to pout over it. "It doesn't matter."

"You're crazy about him."

"I am not. We have a very mature, mutually satisfying relationship." Distracted, she tugged on the strap again. "How do these silly things work?"

"God. Let me." Huffing, Margo knelt down and demonstrated how to hook the hose.

"I beg your pardon." Laura paused at the doorway, stuck her tongue in her cheek. "I seem to be *de trop*. Perhaps there's something you two would like to share with me."

"Another comedienne." Kate looked down at the top of Margo's head and giggled. "Christ, now here's a scandal. Pregnant former sex symbol and suspected embezzler celebrate their alternative lifestyle."

"Could I just go get my camera?" Laura asked.

"Done." Margo proclaimed, then held up a hand. "Stop snickering, Laura, and help me up."

"Sorry." As she hauled Margo to her feet, Laura's gaze fell on Kate. Her friend was sitting in an elegant Queen Anne chair wearing a black bustier with matching lacy garter belt and sheer black stockings. "Why, Kate, you look so . . . different."

"I have tits," she stated and rose. "Margo gave them to me."

"What are friends for? You might want to finish dressing, unless that's your outfit for this evening. The musicians pulled up behind me."

"Terrific. Laura, it's the off-the-shoulder floor-length bronze." Margo gestured vaguely as she started into the main showroom. "I'll be back."

"Why does she think I need to be dressed? I've been dressing myself for several years now."

"Let her fuss." Laura took down the gown Margo had chosen. "It helps keep her from being nervous about tonight. And . . ." Laura pursed her lips as she studied the dress. "She's got a hell of an eye. This is going to look great on you."

"I hate all this." Sighing lustily, Kate stepped into the gown. "I mean, it's okay for her, she loves it. And you—you'd look elegant in tinfoil. I'd never be able to wear what you've got on. What is that, anyway?"

"Ancient," Laura said, dismissing her smartly tailored copper-toned evening suit. "I'm getting one last wear out of it before I put it into stock. There, all hooked in. Stand back, let me see."

"I don't look stupid, do I? My arms aren't bad now. I mean, my biceps are sort of happening. I've been working on the delts, too. Bony shoulders aren't very attractive."

"You look beautiful."

"I don't really care, but I don't like looking stupid."

"Okay, we're right on schedule," Margo announced as she hurried back in. With one hand she supported her belly and tried to ignore the fact that the baby seemed determined to settle directly on her bladder. She tilted her head, took a long, narrowed-eyed study of her creation, and nodded. "Good, really good. Now a few finishing touches."

"Oh, listen."

"Oh, Mommy, do I have to wear that exquisite jeweled collar?" Margo whined as she lifted it from the box. "Oh, please, not those gorgeous earrings too."

Kate rolled her eyes as Margo decorated her. "Can you imagine what she's going to do to that kid? The minute it pops out she's going to have it swaddled in Armani and accessorized."

"Ungrateful brat." Margo took a purse atomizer out of her pocket and spritzed before Kate could evade.

"You know I hate that."

"Why else would I do it? Turn around and—drum roll, please." With a flourish, Margo tugged the draping off the mirror.

"Holy shit." Her mouth agape, Kate stared at the reflection. There was enough of Kate to recognize, she thought, dazed. But where had those exotic eyes come from, and that unquestionably erotic mouth? The figure, an actual figure, draped in shimmering bronze that made all that exposed skin seem polished.

She cleared her throat, turned, turned again. "I look good," she managed.

"A grilled cheese sandwich looks good," Margo corrected. "Baby, you look dangerous."

"I kind of do." Kate grinned and watched that siren's mouth move smugly. "Damn, I hope Byron gets here. Wait till he gets a load of me."

HE WAS DOING his best to get there. The trip to L.A. had been inconvenient but necessary. Under normal circumstances, he would have arranged to make a full swing of it, spot-checking the hotels and resorts in Santa Barbara, San Diego, San Francisco. It was important, he knew, for the staff at every Templeton hotel to feel that personal connection with the home base.

Josh handled the factories, the vineyards and orchards, the plants, and continued to spot-check the international branches. But California was Byron's responsibility. He never took responsibility lightly.

And there were still ruffled feathers to be smoothed from Peter Ridgeway's reign, which by all accounts had been as cold as it had been efficient.

He knew what was expected of him—the personal touch that Templeton was founded and thrived on. The memory for names and faces and details.

Even as he jetted back, Byron dictated a raft of memos to his assistant, fired off countless faxes, and completed one final meeting via air phone.

Now he was home, and late, but he'd anticipated that. With the finesse of long habit, he quickly fastened the studs on his tuxedo shirt. Maybe he should call Kate at the shop and tell her he was on his way. A glance at his watch told him the reception was into its second hour. She'd be busy.

Would she miss him?

He wanted her to. He wanted to imagine her looking toward the door whenever it opened. And hoping. He wanted her to be thinking of him, wishing he were there so they could share some comment or observation about the other guests. The way couples always did.

He looked forward to seeing that speculation in her eyes when she studied him. That look of hers that so clearly said, *What are you doing here, De Witt? What's going on between us? And why?*

She would continually march along looking for the practical answer, the rational one. And he would cruise on the emotional.

It made, he decided as he adjusted his black tie, for a good mix.

He was willing to wait for her to come to the same conclusion. At least for a little while. She needed to resolve this crisis, put the whole ugly business behind her. He intended to help her. And he could wait for that before looking toward the future.

When the phone beside the bed rang, he considered letting the machine take it. Family or work, he supposed, and either of those could do without him for a couple of hours. Then again, Suellen was expecting her first grandchild, and . . .

"Hell." He snapped up the phone. "De Witt."

He listened, questioned, verified. And with a grim smile on his face, hung up. It appeared he had a stop to make before the party.

KUSACK WAS STILL at his desk. It was his wife's bridge night and her turn to host the evening. He preferred the sloppy meatball sandwich and lukewarm cream soda at his desk to the tiny lady treats being served at Chez Kusack. He definitely preferred the smell of stale coffee, the headachy ringing of phones, and the incessant bickering and complaining of his colleagues to the cloying perfumes, the giggles and gossip of the ladies' bridge club.

There was always paperwork to see to. Though it would have earned him sneers to admit it, he enjoyed paperwork and plowed through it like a St. Bernard through a blizzard. Slow and steady.

He liked the tangibility of it, even the foolish convoluted policespeak so necessary to any official report. He'd made the adjustment to computers more smoothly than many cops his age. To Kusack a keyboard was a keyboard, and he had used what he called the Bible method of typing—seek and ye shall find—all of his professional life.

It never failed him.

He was tapping on keys, grinning to himself as the letters popped onto his screen when a man in a tuxedo interrupted him.

"Detective Kusack?"

"Yeah." Kusack sat back, skimmed his cop's eyes over the suit. No rental job, he deduced. Tailor-made and very pricey. "It ain't prom night, and you're too old anyhow. What can I do for you?"

"I'm Byron De Witt. I'm here regarding Katherine Powell."

Kusack grunted, picked up his can of soda. "I thought her lawyer's name was Templeton."

"I'm not her lawyer, I'm her . . . friend."

"Uh-huh. Well, friend, I can't discuss Ms. Powell's business with anybody who walks in here. No matter how nice they dress."

"Kate didn't mention how gracious you were. May I?"

"Make yourself at home," Kusack said sourly. He wanted the monotony of his paperwork, not chitchat with Prince Charming. "Underpaid public servants are always at your disposal."

"It won't take long. I have new evidence that I believe weighs in Ms. Powell's favor. Are you interested, Kusack, or shall I wait until you finish your dinner?"

Kusack ran his tongue around his teeth and eyed the second half of his meatball sub. "Information is always welcome, Mr. De Witt, and I'm here to serve." At least until the bridge club clears out. "What is it you think you have?"

"I obtained copies of the documents in question."

"Did you?" Kusack's bland eyes narrowed. "Did you really? And how did you do that?"

"Without breaking any laws, detective. Once the copies were in my possession, I did what it seems to me, in my muddled civilian capacity, should have been done at the outset. I sent them to a handwriting expert."

Leaning back, Kusack picked up what remained of his dinner, used his free hand to motion Byron to continue.

"I just received my expert's report, via phone. I had him fax it to me." Byron took the sheet out of his inside pocket, unfolded it, and laid it on Kusack's desk.

"Fitzgerald," Kusack said with his mouth full. "Good man. Considered tops in his field."

So Josh had said, Byron thought. "He's been used for over a decade by both prosecutors and defense attorneys."

"Mostly for the defense—rich defense," said Kusack. He caught the whiff of Templeton influence. "Costs a goddamn fortune."

And has a very full schedule, Byron thought. Hence the delay in the report. "Whatever his fee, detective, his reputation is unimpeachable. If you care to read his report, you'll see—"

"Don't have to. I know what it says." It was small of him, Kusack supposed, but it gave him a little lift to tweak a man who didn't appear to have an ounce of extra fat on his body and who could wear a monkey suit and not look like a fool.

Byron folded his hands. Patience was, and always had been, his best weapon. "Then you've been in contact with Mr. Fitzgerald on this matter."

"Nope." Kusack dug out a napkin, wiped his mouth. "Got our own handwriting analysts. Got their final take in a couple weeks ago." Politely, he stifled a belch. "The signatures on the altered forms are an exact match. Too exact," he added before Byron could snarl. "Nobody writes their name the exact and precise same way every time. All the doctored forms have the same precise signature, stroke for stroke, loop for loop. Copies. Likely tracings of Ms. Powell's signature on the one 1040."

"If you know that, why are you sitting here? This is hell for her."

"Yeah, I figured that. Trouble is I gotta cross all my t's, dot all my i's. That's the way things work around here. We've got a few lines of inquiry going here."

"That may be, Detective, but Ms. Powell has a right to know the status of your investigation."

"As it happens, Mr. De Witt, I'm finishing up my report on the progress of this investigation right now. I'll see Mr. Bittle first thing in the morning, and continue my investigation."

"You certainly don't believe Kate copied her own signature."

"You know, I believe she's smart enough to have done something just that clever." He balled up the napkin and two-pointed it into an overflowing wastebasket. "But . . . I don't think she's stupid enough or greedy enough to have risked her job and her freedom for a piddly seventy-five large." He rolled his shoulders, which had grown stiff after hours at his desk. "I don't believe she'd have risked it for any amount of money."

"Then you believe she's innocent."

"I know she's innocent." Kusack sighed a little and adjusted his girth. "Look, De Witt, I've been doing this job a long time. I know how to look into people's backgrounds, their habits, their weaknesses. My take is that Ms. Powell's weakness, if you want to call it that, was making a big splash at Bittle. Now why is she going to jeopardize something she wants that much for a little playing-around money? She doesn't gamble, she doesn't do drugs, doesn't sleep with the boss. If she needs flash, she's got the Templeton pool to play in. But she doesn't. She puts in sixty-hour weeks at Bittle and builds up her client list. That tells me she's hardworking and ambitious."

"You might have indicated to her that you believed her."

"It's not my job to soothe anxious souls. And I've got my reasons for keeping her on the hot seat. Hard evidence is what makes or breaks a case in the real world. And gathering hard evidence takes time. Now, I appreciate you coming by with this." He handed Byron the expert's report. "If it helps, you can tell Ms. Powell that the department has no plans to charge her with anything."

"That's not enough," Byron said as he rose.

"It's a start. I've got seventy-five thousand to track down, Mr. De Witt. Then we'll finish it."

It seemed he would have to be satisfied with that. Byron slipped the report back in his pocket, then eyed Kusack. "You never believed she was guilty."

"I go into an investigation with an open mind. Maybe she did it, maybe she didn't. After I took her statement, I knew she didn't. It's the nose."

Byron smiled curiously. "She didn't smell guilty?"

Laughing, Kusack stood, stretched. "There's that. You could say I've got a nose for guilt. I meant *her* nose."

"I'm sorry." Byron shook his head. "You've lost me."

"Anybody who dives headfirst into third and busts their nose to stretch a double has guts. And style. Somebody who wants to win that bad doesn't steal. Stealing's too easy, and this kind of stealing's too ordinary."

"Sliding into third," Byron murmured, grinning foolishly. "So that's how she did it. I never asked her." Because Kusack was grinning back, Byron offered a hand. "Thanks for your time, Detective."

The crowd was thinning out by the time Byron arrived at Pretenses. Three hours late, he thought with a wince. The auction was obviously over, and only those lingering over their drinks or conversations were left. The fragrance of night jasmine blooming on the veranda mixed with the scents of perfume and wine.

He spotted Margo first, flirting with her husband. Even as he hurried toward her, he was scanning for Kate. "Margo, I'm sorry I'm so late."

"You should be." She touched pouty lips to his. "You completely missed the bidding. Now you'll have to come in next week and buy something very, very expensive."

"It's the least I can do. Still, you look successful."

When you bother to look at me, she thought, smothering a grin at the way he kept searching the room. "We raised just over fifteen thousand for Wednesday's Child. Nothing makes me happier than raising money to help handicapped children."

Josh wrapped his arms around her from the back, placed their joint hands protectively over her belly. It rippled under them, thrillingly. "She's trying not to look too gleeful over the number of requests to hold merchandise."

"It's a charity event," she said primly, then laughed. "And boy, are we going to clean up next week. In fact, Kate's in the office logging in all the holds."

"I'll go let her know I'm here. Actually, I—" He broke off, torn. Josh was her lawyer, after all. "No, I have to tell her first. Don't go anywhere."

He started across the room just as Kate swung through the office door. "There you are." She beamed at him. "I thought you must have gotten stuck in L.A. You didn't have to—" She stopped because he was staring at her as if he'd had a lobotomy on the trip home. "What is it?"

He managed to close his mouth, get his lungs working again. "Okay, who are you and what have you done with Katherine Powell?"

"Boy, a guy doesn't see you for a few hours, and—oh!" Her face lit up and she tried a sophisticated turn. "I forgot. Margo did it. What do you think?"

He turned first to Margo. "God bless you," he said fervently, then took Kate's hand. "What do I think? I think my heart stopped." He kissed her fingers, then, wanting more, her mouth.

"Wow." A little surprised by the dizzying depth of the kiss, she took a cautious step back. "Look what a little goop on the face and a push-up bra gets you."

His gaze shifted down. "Is that what's under there?"

"You're not going to believe what's under here."

"How long is it going to take for me to find out?"

Amused by his reaction, she toyed with his tie. "Well, big guy, if you play your cards right, we can—"

"Damn." He grabbed her hands. "It's amazing how a sexy woman can shut a man's mind down. I have news for you."

"Fine. If you'd rather discuss current events than my underwear."

"Don't distract me. I've just come from seeing Detective Kusack. It's why I'm so late."

"You went to see him?" The excited flush drained out of her cheeks. "He called you in? I'm sorry, Byron. There's no reason for you to be involved."

"No." He gave her a little shake. "Be quiet. I went to see him because I finally got the report I've been waiting for. I had the documents Marty Bittle gave me sent to a handwriting expert that Josh recommended."

"Handwriting expert? But you never told me. Josh never said anything."

Before her eyes could heat, he hurried on. "We wanted to wait until we had some results. And now we do. They were forgeries, Kate. Copies of your signature."

"Copies." Her hands began to tremble in his. "He can prove it?"

"He's one of the most respected people in his field in the country. But we didn't need him. Kusack had already verified the signatures. He knows they're forgeries. He doesn't consider you a suspect, Kate. Apparently he never really did."

"He believed me."

"He got his expert's report shortly before I got mine. He's going to take the information and his progress report to Bittle in the morning."

"I—can't take it in."

"That's all right." He pressed his lips to her brow. "Take your time."

"You believed me," she said shakily. "From the first day, on the cliffs. You didn't even know me, but you believed me."

"Yes, I did." He kissed her again and smiled. "It must be that nose."

"Whose nose?"

"I'll explain later. Come on, we have to fill Josh in."

"Okay. Byron—" She squeezed his arm. "You went to see Kusack before you came here. Was that what you'd call a white knight sort of thing?"

Sounds like a trick question, he thought. "It could be construed in that manner."

"I thought so. Listen, I wouldn't want you to make it a habit, but thanks." Grateful and touched, she pressed her lips to his. "Thank you very much."

"You're welcome." Because he didn't want her eyes swimming, but laughing, he traced a fingertip over her beautifully bared shoulder. "Does that mean I get to see your underwear?"

CHAPTER 16

KATE HAD A long-standing concept of what Sunday mornings were for. They were for sleep. Throughout college she had used them for extra study time, or to finish up papers and projects. But once she entered the real world, she designated that time for indulgence.

Byron had a different agenda.

"You've got to resist both ways," he told her. "Mentally isolate the muscle you're working on. Right here." He pressed his fingers to her triceps as she lifted and lowered the five-pound weight, over her head, behind her back. "Don't flop your arm," he ordered. "You're pulling it up and pushing it down through mud."

"Mud. Right." She tried to envision a pool of thick, oozing mud instead of a nice soft bed with cool sheets. "And why am I doing this?"

"Because it's good for you."

"Good for me," she muttered, and watched herself in the mirror. She had thought she would feel ridiculous in the little sports bra and snug bike pants. But it wasn't really so bad. Besides, she got to look at him, too. A well-built man in a tank top and sweat shorts wasn't hard on the eyes at all.

"Now stretch. Don't forget the stretch. Go to the set of concentration curls. Remember?"

"Yeah, yeah, yeah."

She sat on the bench, frowned at the weight she lifted and lowered and tried to imagine her biceps growing. Good-bye, one-hundred-and-two-pound weakling, she thought. Hello, buff.

"And when we're finished here, you're going to make French toast, right?"

"That was the deal."

"I've got me a personal trainer and a chef." She flashed him a smile. "Pretty cool."

"You're a lucky woman, Katherine. Other arm now. Concentrate."

He moved her through flys and dead lifts, hammer lifts and extensions. Though he'd completed his Sunday routine before hauling her out of bed, they'd both worked up a nice sweat by the time he proclaimed her finished.

"So, I'm going to be buff, huh?"

He grinned, rubbing her shoulders, massaging his way down her arms. "Sure you are, kid. We'll put you in one of those little bikinis, oil you up, and shoot you into competition."

"In your dreams."

"Not my dreams," he said sincerely. "Believe me. I've discovered this latent desire for skinny women. In fact, it's starting to stir right now."

"Is that so?" She didn't object when his hands moved around her back and down to cup her bottom.

"I'm afraid it is. Hmm." His fingers roamed, clutched. "This reminds me. Tomorrow we work on the lower body."

"I hate those squats."

"That's because you don't have my vantage point." His gaze shifted to the mirror behind her, and he watched his hands take possession, watched her move against him, saw her shiver when he lowered his mouth to that wonderful curve of neck and shoulder.

It was almost ridiculous the way he wanted her, the way the need would rise up time after time, again and again. Like breathing, he thought, nibbling his way up to her ear. Like life.

"I think we should finish off your morning routine with a little aerobics."

She managed a sound between a groan and a sigh. "Not the Nordic-Track, Byron. I'm begging you."

"I had something else in mind." His busy mouth skimmed over her cheek. "I think you'll like it."

"Oh." She got the idea when his hand moved up to palm her breast. "You did say that for overall training, aerobics is essential."

"Just put yourself in my hands."

"I was hoping you'd say that."

She gave so easily, he thought. So eagerly. The way her mouth moved on his, the mating of tongues, the press of bodies. All of his old fantasies about the woman of his dreams had faded and shifted and reemerged as her. Only her.

An image of her flickered into his mind. The way she'd looked the night before in that slim, shoulder-baring dress. All that smooth skin, those surprising curves. That wide, wet mouth.

And beneath the dress had been a wanton fantasy of black lace. The sight of her had been staggering, and so unexpected, so impractical for his practical Kate. It was a side of her he had loved exploring. Knowing she had been exploring it as well had been brutally erotic.

She was just as appealing to him now, in damp workout gear that he could hastily peel off.

Both of them were naked to the waist when they tumbled to the mat.

She laughed, rolling with him as they tugged at those last barriers. It was wonderful, wasn't it, to feel so . . . unbound. So completely liberated. She'd stopped questioning how it was he knew just where, just how to touch her. As if he'd always known. And his body was so strong, so hard. It was like making love with a dream. Rolling on top of him, she poured the sheer joy of it into a kiss.

Yes, touch me, she thought. And taste. Here. And here. Let me. Again. Always again, she thought as her heart pounded and her blood swam. Over and over, moment to moment, he could fill her with so many clashing sensations. The wave of heat, the chill of anticipation, a shiver of greed, the warmth of giving.

She wanted to hold him forever, to steep herself in him. Lose herself. And so she took him inside here, trembling to a gasp at that bright instant of joining. She arched back, savoring, tormenting herself with the power, groaning at the texture of his hands that slicked up her to torture her aching breasts.

She held them there, her tensed fingers gripping as she began to move.

It staggered him, the look of her. The dark cap of hair framed her glowing face. Breath heaved and hitched through her parted lips. That long swan's neck was bowed back, the doe's eyes closed. Sunlight poured in over her, so bright, so full, they might have been outdoors in some verdant meadow. He could see her there, a hot-blooded Titania, lusty and sleek.

He wanted her to feed herself, feed herself to satiation. But she increased her rhythm, driving him with her. Her moans and cries swarmed into his blood until they were thrust for desperate thrust.

He exploded beneath her, into her. With one long, glorying sigh, she slid down and crushed her mouth to his.

* * *

S<small>HE SANG IN</small> the shower. This was unusual even when she was alone. Kate was well aware that she did not have a voice like a bell. As they lathered and soaped he joined in for a miserably off-key, if heartfelt, version of "Proud Mary."

"Ike and Tina had nothing on us," she decided as she toweled her hair.

"Not a thing. Except maybe talent." Byron wrapped a towel around his hips, rubbed his face, and prepared to shave. "You're the first woman I've showered with who sings as badly as I do."

She straightened, watched him lather up. "Oh, really? Just how many women might that be?"

"The mind boggles." He grinned at her, enjoying the laser gleam in her eyes. "And a true gentleman never keeps score."

She watched him swipe the razor through lather, leaving a smooth, clean path. It occurred to her she'd never actually watched a man shave before. Unless she included Josh, and a brother didn't count. But she refused to be distracted by the interesting male ritual. Instead she smiled sweetly and looked over his shoulder into the foggy mirror.

"Why don't you let me do that for you, darling?"

He lifted an eyebrow. "Do I look stupid enough to put a sharp instrument in your hands?" He rinsed the blade. "I don't think so."

"Coward."

"You betcha."

She snorted, nipped his shoulder with her teeth, then headed toward the bedroom to dress.

"Kate." He waited until she'd turned, aimed that smug look in his direction. "There's only one woman now." He watched her quick, almost shy smile spread before she slipped out the door.

Thoughtfully, Byron stroked off lather and stubble. The room was full of mist and heat, and their mixed scents. She'd hung her towel neatly and efficiently to dry. The little jar she used to moisturize her face sat on the counter. She'd forgotten to use it. She hadn't forgotten to put her workout clothes in the hamper or to replace the cap on the toothpaste. No, she would never overlook any practical detail.

It was the extras she forgot, particularly when they applied to herself. She wouldn't let herself browse through a shop, dreaming, and buy something foolish for herself. She wouldn't forget to turn off the lights or to give a faucet an extra twist to prevent a drip.

Her bills would always be paid on time, but stopping to eat lunch would slip her mind when it was crowded with other details.

She didn't have a clue that she needed him. Byron smiled as he lowered his head to rinse off the excess lather. Nor did she know what he'd just discovered. He no longer thought he might be falling in love with her. He knew that she, with all her contrasts and complexities, her strengths and weaknesses, was the only woman he would ever love.

He dried his face, slapped on aftershave, and decided this might be the perfect time to tell her. He stepped into the bedroom. She was standing beside the bed in black leggings and an old Yankees sweatshirt.

"See this?" she demanded, shaking a mangled rawhide bone at him.

"Yes, I do."

"It was in my shoe. How my shoe escaped the same treatment, I'm not sure." She tossed the bone to Byron, then scooped her hands through her hair to check for dryness. "It was Nip, that I am sure of. Tuck has much better manners. Last week it was that fish head he found on the beach. He has to be disciplined, Byron. He's very unruly."

"Now, Kate, is that any way to talk about our child?"

She sighed, put her hands on her hips, and waited.

"I'll talk to him. But I'm sure if you considered the psychology of it, you'd agree that he puts things in your shoe as a token of his great affection."

"And that includes the time he peed in it."

"Well, I'm sure that was just a mistake." He rubbed a hand over his mouth, too wise to let the grin show. "And it was outside. You took them off to walk on the beach, and . . . you're not buying it."

"I don't think you'd find it so amusing if he was using your shoes for his depository." As if on cue, there came the sound of frantic barking, of growing canine bodies thudding. "I'll deal with them," Kate stated. "You're too soft."

"Yeah, and who bought them collars with their names on them?" he muttered.

"What?"

"Nothing." Retreating, Byron opened his drawer for underwear. "I'll be down in a minute."

"To make French toast," she reminded him and rushed down to quiet the dogs. "Okay, guys, kill the racket. Keep it up and there's not going to be any walk on the beach. And nobody's going to play sock with either of you."

They rushed up and bumped against her, two alarmingly growing masses of fur and feet. Even as she started to ruffle them, they raced toward the front door and set up a fresh din.

"You know you go out the back way," she began, then the idiotic door chimes sounded. It seemed Byron had decided they were whimsical and had kept them. "Oh." Ridiculously pleased, she beamed at the dogs.

"Pretty cool, guys. You were sounding the alarm. Listen, if it's anybody selling anything I want you to do this. Look, look—bare your teeth."

She demonstrated, but they only thumped each other with their wagging tails and offered canine grins.

"We'll work on it," she decided and opened the door.

Her bright mood plummeted. "Mr. Bittle." Automatically she grabbed collars to prevent the dogs from leaping joyfully on the new humans. "Detective."

"I'm sorry to disturb you on Sunday, Kate." Bittle eyed the dogs warily. "Detective Kusack indicated that he intended to speak with you today, and I asked to come along."

"Your lawyer said I would find you here," Kusack put in. "You're free to call him, of course, if you want him here."

"I thought—I was told I was no longer a suspect."

"I'm here to apologize." Bittle kept his solemn eyes on hers. "May we come in?"

"Yes, of course. Nip, Tuck, no jumping."

"Nice dogs." Kusack held out a beefy hand, and it was duly sniffed and licked. "Got me an old Heinz 57 hound. She's getting up in years now."

"Please, sit down. I'll just put them out." That task gave her time to compose herself. When the dogs were racing maniacally over the yard, she turned back. "Would you like some coffee?"

"There's no need for you to trouble," Bittle began, but Kusack leaned back in the ancient recliner and said, "If you're making it anyway."

"I'll make it," Byron volunteered as he came down the stairs.

"Oh, Byron." Relief rippled through her. "You know Detective Kusack."

"Detective."

"Mr. De Witt."

"And this is Lawrence Bittle."

"Of Bittle and Associates," Byron said coolly. "How do you do?"

"I'll say I've done better." Bittle accepted the formal handshake. "Tommy's mentioned you. We had an early round of golf this morning."

"I'll put the coffee on." He sent a look to Kusack that said as clearly as words that anything of import would wait until he came back.

"Nice place here," Kusack said casually. Kate stood where she was, twisting her fingers together.

"It's coming along. Byron takes his time. He just settled on it a couple of months ago. He's, ah, having some things sent out from Atlanta. That's where he's from. Atlanta." Stop babbling, Kate, she ordered herself. Couldn't. "And he's looking for things out here. Furniture and things."

"Hell of a spot." Kusack settled into the recliner, thinking it was a chair that knew how to welcome a man. "House just down the road has a putting green right on the front lawn." He shook his head. "Guy can walk right out his front door and sink a few. Used to drive the kids down here. They got a kick out of the seals."

"Yes, they're wonderful." Gnawing her lip, she glanced toward the kitchen. "Sometimes you can hear them barking. Detective Kusack, are you here to question me?"

"I've got some questions." He sniffed the air. "Nothing like the smell of coffee brewing, is there? Even the poison down at the station house smells like heaven before you taste it. Why don't you sit down, Ms. Powell? I'll tell you again you can lawyer yourself up, but you're not going to need Mr. Templeton for what we have to talk about."

"All right." But she'd reserve judgment on calling Josh. She was not going to be lulled by small talk and paternal smiles. "What do you want?"

"Mr. De Witt showed you the report from his handwriting expert?"

"Yes. Last night." She sat on the arm of the couch. It was the best she could do. "It said the signatures were copies. Someone duplicated my signature on the altered forms. Used my signature, my clients, my reputation." She rose again when Byron came in with a tray. "I'm sorry," she said quickly. "For the trouble, here."

"Don't be ridiculous." He slid easily into the well-mannered host. "How do you take your coffee, Mr. Bittle?"

"Just cream, thank you."

"Detective."

"The way it comes out of the pot." He sampled the brew Byron offered him. "Now we're talking coffee. I was about to go over the progress of the investigation with Ms. Powell. I'm explaining that our conclusions jibe with those of your independent expert. At this point, indications are that she was set up to take the heat if the discrepancies were discovered. We're looking into other areas."

"You mean other people," Kate said, struggling not to clatter her cup in her saucer.

"I'm saying my investigation is moving along. I'd like to ask you if you have any idea who would focus on you as a scapegoat. There are a lot of accounts in the firm. Only those under your hand were touched."

"If someone did this to damage me, I don't have a clue."

"Maybe you were just convenient. The charges against your father made you prime, maybe gave someone an idea."

"No one knew. I only found out myself shortly before the suspension."

"Interesting. And how did you find out?"

Absently, she rubbed a finger over her temple as she explained.

"You have words with anybody? A tiff? A personality clash, maybe?"

"I didn't have a fight with anyone. Not everyone at the firm is a close friend and confidant, but we work well together."

"No grudge matches, petty grievances?"

"Nothing out of the ordinary." She set her coffee aside, nearly untasted. "Nancy in Billing and I squared off over a misplaced invoice during the April crunch. Tempers are high then. I think I snapped at Bill Feinstein for taking half my computer paper instead of going into stock himself." She smiled a little. "He stuck three cases of it in my office to get back at me for that. Ms. Newman doesn't like me, but she doesn't like anyone but Mr. Bittle Senior."

Bittle stared into his coffee. "Ms. Newman is efficient and a bit territorial." He winced as Kusack busily made notes. "She's worked for me for twenty years."

"I didn't mean she would do something like this." Horrified, Kate sprang up. "I didn't mean that at all! I wouldn't accuse anyone. You might as well say Amanda Devin did it. She guards her lone female partner status like a hawk watching for vultures. Or—or Mike Lloyd in the mail room because he can't afford to go to college full time. Or Stu Cominsky because I wouldn't go out with him. Roger Thornhill because I did."

"Lloyd and Cominsky and Thornhill," Kusack muttered as he wrote, and Kate stopped her pacing.

"You write whatever you want to write in that little book of yours, but I'm not going to go around casting blame." She lifted her chin, set it. "I know how it feels."

"Ms. Powell." Watching her, Kusack tapped his stubby pencil against his knee. "This is a police investigation. You're involved. Every member of your former firm is going to be considered. It's a long process. With your cooperation it can be shortened."

"I don't know anything," she said stubbornly. "I don't know anyone who needed money that badly, or who would choose to implicate me in a crime. I do know I've already paid all I intend to pay for something I didn't do. If you want to ruin someone else's life, Detective, you'll have to do it without me."

"I appreciate your position, Ms. Powell. You're insulted, and I can't blame you. You do your job, do what's expected of you, and go the extra mile. You see what you've been aiming for swing just into reach, then you get kicked in the teeth."

"That's a nice and very accurate summary. If I knew who did the kicking, I'd be the first to tell you. But I'm not going to put someone whose only crime was to irritate me into the position I've been in."

"Think about it," he suggested. "You've got a good brain. Once you set your mind to figuring it out, I have a hunch you'll come up with something."

The detective rose, and Bittle followed his lead saying, "Before we go, Kate, I'd like another moment of your time. In private, if there's no objection."

"All right. I—" She glanced at Byron.

"Perhaps you'd like to see the view, Detective." Byron gestured, then led the way to the deck doors. "Did I hear you say you had a dog?"

"Old Sadie. Ugly as homemade sin, but sweet as they come." His voice faded away as Byron closed the doors.

"An apology isn't enough," Bittle began without preamble. "Is far from enough."

"I'm trying to be fair and understand the position you were in, Mr. Bittle. It's difficult. You watched me grow up. You know my family. You should have known me."

"You're quite right." He looked very old. Very old and very tired. "I've damaged my friendship with your uncle, a friendship that is very important to me."

"Uncle Tommy doesn't hold grudges."

"No, but I hurt one of his children, and that isn't easy for either of us to forget. I can tell you, for what it's worth, that none of us initially believed you would do anything criminal. We needed an explanation, and your reaction to the questions was, well, damning. Understandable now, under the circumstances, but then . . ."

"You didn't know about my father then, did you?"

"No. We learned about it later. There was a copy of a newspaper article in your office."

"Oh." As simple as that, she thought, and as stupid. She must have missed one when she'd stuffed them into her briefcase. "I see. That made it all look worse."

"It clouded the issue. I should tell you that when Detective Kusack contacted me, I was immensely relieved, and not terribly surprised. I could never reconcile the woman I knew with one who would cheat."

"But you reconciled it enough to suspend me," she said, and heard the brittleness of her own voice.

"Yes. However much I regretted it, and however much I regret it now, I had no choice. I have called each of the partners and relayed this new information. We're meeting in an hour to discuss it. And to discuss the fact that we have an embezzler in our employ."

He paused a moment, gathering his thoughts. "You're very young. It would be difficult for you to understand the dreams of a lifetime, and the way they change. At my age, you have to be very careful, very selective about dreams. You begin to become aware that each one may be your last. The firm has been mine for most of my life. I've nurtured it, sweated over it, brought my children into it." He smiled a little. "An accounting firm doesn't seem like something anyone would dream over."

"I understand." She wanted to touch his arm, but couldn't.

"I thought you might. Its reputation is my reputation. Having it damaged in this way makes me realize how fragile even such a prosaic dream can be."

She couldn't help but bend. "It's a good firm, Mr. Bittle. You made something solid there. The people who work for you work for you because you treat them well, because you make them part of the whole. That isn't really prosaic."

"I'd like you to consider coming back. I realize that you may feel uncomfortable doing so until after this matter is fully resolved. However, Bittle and Associates would be very fortunate to have you back on board. As a full partner."

When she didn't speak, he took a step toward her. "Kate, I don't know whether this will make matters worse or better between us, but I want you to know that this offer had already been discussed and voted on prior to this . . . this nightmare. You were unanimously approved."

She had to ease herself back down on the arm of the chair. "You were going to make me a partner."

"Marty nominated you. I hope you're aware that you always had his complete trust and support. Amanda seconded your nomination. Ah, I believe that was why she was so harsh when she believed you had taken the money from escrow. You'd earned the offer, Kate. I hope, once you've had time to think it over, you'll accept it."

It was difficult to deal with despair and elation at once. Not long before she would have leapt at such an offer, seized it, hugged it to her. She opened her mouth, certain that acceptance would pop out.

"I do need some time." She heard her own words with a kind of vague surprise. "I have to think it through."

"Of course you do. Please, before you consider going elsewhere, give us a chance to negotiate."

"Yes, I will." She held out a hand, just as Byron and the detective returned. "Thank you for coming to see me."

She was still dazed when she led Bittle and Detective Kusak out, said her good-byes. In silence she walked back into the house with Byron, stood staring at nothing.

"Well?" he prompted.

"He offered me a partnership." She said each word slowly, unsure whether she was savoring them or weighing them. "Not just to make up for all this. They'd already voted on it before everything got screwed up. He's willing to negotiate my terms."

Byron angled his head. "Why aren't you smiling?"

"Huh?" She blinked, stared at him, then burst into laughter. "A partnership!" She threw her arms around his neck and let him swing her. "Byron, I can't tell you what this means to me. I'm too dazzled to tell myself. It's like—it's like being cut from the minors, then being signed to bat cleanup for the Yankees."

"The Braves," he corrected, home team loyal to the last. "Congratulations. I think we should have mimosas with that French toast."

"Let's." She kissed him hard. "And go light on the OJ."

"A dollop for color," he assured her, as they walked into the kitchen arm in arm. He released her to get champagne out of the refrigerator. "Well, aren't you going to pick up the phone?"

She opened the glass-fronted cabinet that held his wine glasses. "The phone?"

"To call your family?"

"Uh-uh. This is too big for the phone. As soon as we eat"—she grinned foolishly at the pop of the cork—"I'm going to Templeton House. This requires the personal touch. It's the perfect way to send Aunt Susie and Uncle Tommy back to France." The minute he'd finished pouring she lifted her glass. "Here's to the IRS."

He hissed through his teeth. "Do we have to?"

"Okay, what the hell. Here's to me." She drank, twirled once, then drank again. "You'll come with me, won't you? We'll get Mrs. Williamson to make one of her incredible dinners. We'll take the dogs, too. We can— What are you looking at?"

"You. I like seeing you happy."

"Get that French toast going and you'll see me ecstatic. I'm starving."

"Give the master room, please." He took out eggs and milk. "Why don't we swing by your apartment and pick up a few more of your things? We can extend our celebration by having you stay another night."

"Okay." She was too high to think of objecting, though it broke her unspoken rule of staying more than two nights running. "I'll get it," she said when the phone rang. "You keep cooking. And use lots of cinnamon. Hello? Laura, hi. I was just thinking about you." Grinning, she swung over to nip at Byron's ear as he whisked. "We were going to come over later and invite ourselves to dinner. I have some news that I—What?"

She fell into silence and the hand she'd lifted to mess with Byron's hair dropped back to her side. "When? At the—yes. Oh, God. Oh, God. Okay, we'll be right there. We're on our way. It's Margo," she said, fumbling to disconnect the portable phone. "Josh took her to the hospital."

"The baby?"

"I don't know. I just don't know. It's too early for the baby. She had pain, and some bleeding. Oh, God, Byron."

"Come on." He clasped the hand that reached for his. "Let's go."

CHAPTER 17

SHE WAS GRATEFUL that it was Byron behind the wheel. No matter how she ordered herself to be calm, she knew her hands would have trembled. Flashes of Margo ran through her head.

There were images of them as children, sitting on the cliffs, tossing flowers out to the sea and Seraphina. Margo parading around the bedroom in her first bra, smug and curvy while Kate and Laura looked on in flat-chested envy. Margo curling Kate's hair for the junior prom, then slipping a condom into Kate's bag—just in case.

Margo on her first visit home after running off to Hollywood to become a star. So polished and beautiful. Margo in Paris after she'd nagged Kate to come over and see the world as it was meant to be.

Margo at Templeton House—always back to Templeton House.

In despair after her world had crumbled, in fury when one of her friends was hurt. The determination and glassy bravado as she'd fought to rebuild her life.

As a bride walking down the aisle to Josh, so outrageously lovely in miles of white satin and French lace. Weeping as she rushed into the shop to announce she didn't have the flu but was pregnant. Weeping again when she felt the baby quicken. And cooing over the tiny clothes her mother was already sewing. Showing off her bulging belly, beaming when it rippled with a kick.

Margo, always so passionate, so impulsive, and so thrilled with the idea of having a baby.

The baby. Kate squeezed her eyes tight. Oh, God, the baby.

"She doesn't want to know if it's a girl or a boy," Kate murmured. "She said they want to be surprised. They have names picked out. Suzanna if it's a girl, for Aunt Susie and Annie, and John Thomas if it's a boy, for Margo's father and Uncle Tommy. Oh, Byron, what if—"

"Don't think about 'what ifs.' Just hold on." He took his hand off the gearshift long enough to squeeze hers.

"I'm trying." Just as she tried to block the shudder when he pulled into the parking lot in front of the tall white building. "Let's hurry."

She was quaking when they reached the door. Byron pulled her back, studied her face. "I can go and find out what's going on. You don't have to go in."

"Yes, I do. I can handle it."

"I know you can." He linked his fingers with hers.

Margo was in the maternity wing. As she hurried down the corridor, Kate blocked out the sounds and smells of hospital. At least this wing had familiar and good memories. Laura's babies. The rush and thrill of being a part of those births soothed away the worst edge of panic, urged Kate to remember what it was like to watch life fight its way into existence.

And to tell herself that this place was one of birth, not death.

The first face she saw was Laura's.

"I've been watching for you." Laura wrapped her arms around Kate in relief. "Everybody's here, in the waiting room. Josh is with Margo."

"What's going on? Is she all right? The baby?"

"Everything's all right as far as we know." Laura led her toward the waiting area and struggled to maintain the pretense of calm. "Apparently she went into premature labor, and she was hemorrhaging."

"Oh, my God."

"They've stopped the bleeding. They've stopped it." Laura took a slow breath to steady herself, but her eyes mirrored her inner fears. "Annie was just in to see her. She says Margo's holding her own. They're trying to stabilize her, stop the labor."

"It's too early, isn't it? She's only in her seventh month." Kate stepped into the waiting area, saw worried faces, and ruthlessly smothered her own fears. "Annie." Kate caught both the woman's hands in hers. "She'll be all right. You know how strong and stubborn she is."

"She looked so small in the bed in there." Ann's voice broke. "Like a little girl. She's too pale. They should do something for her. She's too pale."

"Annie, we need coffee." Susan slid an arm around her shoulders. "Why don't you help me get some?" After stroking a hand down Kate's arm, she led Annie away.

"Susie will take care of her," Thomas murmured. He often thought there was too little for a man to do at such a time, and too much for him to imagine. "Now sit down, Katie girl. You're too pale yourself."

"I want to see her." The walls were closing in already, thick with the scent of fear that meant hospital to her. "Uncle Tommy, you'll make them let me see her."

"Of course I will." He kissed her cheek, then shook his head at his daughter. "No, you stay here. I'll check on the girls while I'm at it. Though you should know they'll be fine down in day care."

"They're worried. Ali especially. She adores Margo."

"I'll tend to them. I'm leaving all my women in your hands, Byron."

"I'll take care of them. Sit down," he murmured and nudged both of them to a couch. "I'll help your mother and Ann with the coffee." He saw their hands link before he turned away.

"Can you tell me what happened?" Kate asked.

"Josh called from his car phone. He didn't want to take time to call an ambulance. He was trying to sound calm, but I could tell he was panicked. He said she'd been feeling tired and a little achy after last night. When they got up this morning, she wasn't feeling well, complained of back pain."

"She's been working too hard. All that prep for the auction. We should have postponed it this year." *I should have pulled more weight*, Kate thought.

"Everything was fine at her last checkup," Laura put in, rubbing her brow. "But you may be right. She said she was going to take a shower, then she started shouting for him. She was bleeding and having contractions. By the time we got here, they'd admitted her. I haven't seen her yet."

"They'll let us see her."

"Damn right they will." Laura took the coffee Byron offered, remembering to thank him.

"The waiting's hell." He sat beside Kate. "It always is. My sister Meg had a bad time with her first. Thirty-hour labor, which translates to the rest of your life when you're pacing."

Just talk, he ordered himself. *Just talk and give them something else to focus on.* "Abigail was a hefty nine pounds, and Meg swore she'd never have another. Went on to have two more."

"It was so easy for me," Laura murmured. "Nine hours for Ali, only five for Kayla. They just sort of slid out."

"Selective memory," Kate corrected. "I distinctly remember you breaking all the bones in my hand while we were in the birthing room. That was Ali. And with Kayla, you—"

She sprang to her feet when a nurse stopped in the doorway. She stepped over the coffee table, prepped for battle. "We want to see Margo Templeton. Now."

"So I've been informed," the nurse said dryly. "Mrs. Templeton would like to see you. You'll have to keep it short. This way, please."

She led the way down a wide corridor. Kate blocked out the hospital sound of crepe-soled shoes slapping on linoleum. There were so many doors, she thought. White doors, all closed. So many people inside them. Beds with curtains around them. Machines beeped and hissed inside. Tubes and needles. Doctors with sad, tired eyes who came to tell you your parents had died, gone away. Left you alone.

"Kate." Laura soothed the hand that gripped hers.

"I'm okay." She ordered herself to stay in the now and relaxed her grip. "Don't worry."

The nurse opened the door, and there was the room. It was designed to be comforting, cheerful. A room to welcome new life. A rocking chair, warm ivory walls with dark trim, thriving plants and the quiet strains of a Chopin sonata were all pieces of the serene whole.

But the machine was there, beeping, and the rolling stool that doctors used, and the bed with its guarded sides and stiff white sheets.

Margo lay in it, glassily pale, her glorious hair pulled back. A few loose tendrils curled damply around her face. The bag hanging from the IV stand beside the bed dripped clear liquid down a tube and into her. She had one hand pressed protectively to her belly, the other in Josh's.

"There you are." Margo's lips curved as she gave her husband's hand a reassuring squeeze. "Take a break, Josh. Go ahead." She rubbed their joined hands over her cheek. "This is girl talk."

He hesitated, obviously torn between doing what she wanted and being more than a step away from her. "I'll be right outside." He lowered his head to kiss her, and his hand brushed over the bulge of her belly. "Don't forget your breathing."

"I've been breathing for years. I've almost got it down pat now. Go on out and pace like an expectant father."

"We'll make her behave," Laura assured him. She sat on the edge of the bed and patted his thigh.

"I'll be right outside," he repeated, and waited until he was in the hall to rub unsteady hands over his face.

"He's scared," Margo murmured. "You hardly ever see Josh scared. But it's going to be all right."

"Of course it is," Laura agreed and glanced at the fetal monitor that beeped away the baby's heartbeats.

"No, I mean it. I'm not messing this up. My timing's off, that's all." She looked at Kate. "I guess this is the first time in my life I've been early for anything."

"Oh, I don't know." Striving for the same light tone, Kate eased down on the side of the bed opposite from Laura. "You developed early."

Margo snorted. "True. Oh, here comes one," she said in a shaky voice and began to breathe slowly through the contraction. Instinctively Kate took her hand and breathed through it with her.

"They're very mild," Margo managed. "There's something in there that's supposed to be slowing them down." She flicked a glance toward the IV. "They'd hoped to stop them altogether, but it looks like the kid wants out. Seven weeks too early. Oh, God." She squeezed her eyes shut. Fear circled back no matter how hard she focused on willing it away. "I should have taken more naps. I should have stayed off my feet more. I—"

"Stop that," Kate snapped. "This is no time to feel sorry for yourself."

"Actually, labor's the perfect time for self-pity." Remembering her own, Laura stroked Margo's belly to bring comfort. "But not for blame. You've taken good care of yourself and the baby."

"Milked it for all it was worth." Kate arched a brow. "How many times did I have to run up and down the stairs at the shop because you were pregnant and I wasn't?" She wanted to weep, promised herself a nice long crying jag later. "And those cravings in the afternoons so I had to go over to Fisherman's Wharf and get you frozen strawberry yogurt with chocolate sauce? Do you think I bought that?"

"You bought the yogurt," Margo pointed out. "Actually, I wouldn't mind having some now."

"Forget it. You can chew your chipped ice."

"I'm going to do this right." Margo took a deep breath. "I know the doctor's worried. Josh is worried. And Mum. But I'm going to do this right. You know I can."

"Of course you can," Laura murmured. "This hospital has one of the best birthing wings in the country. They take marvelous care of preemies. I was on the committee that helped raise funds for new equipment, remember?"

"Who can remember all the committees you were on?" Kate commented. "You'll do fine, Margo. Nobody focuses on what they want and how to get it better than you."

"I want this baby. I thought I could will the labor away, but well, apparently the kid takes after me already. It's going to be today." Her lips trembled again. "It's so small."

"And tough," Kate added.

"Yeah." Margo managed a genuine smile. "Tough. The doctor's still hoping they can stop the labor, but it's not going to happen. I know it's today. You understand?" she asked Laura.

"Absolutely."

"And he's being snotty about delivery. Just Josh. I wanted you to be there. Both of you. I just had this image of a big, noisy, bawdy event."

"We'll have one after." Kate leaned down to kiss her cheek. "That's a promise."

"Okay. Okay." Margo closed her eyes and dealt with the next contraction.

"She's strong," Laura said to Kate as they walked back down the corridor.

"I know. But I don't like to see her scared."

"If the drip doesn't stop labor, she'll be too busy to be scared much longer. All we can do is wait."

Wait they did, as one hour passed into two. Restless, Kate paced the room, walked out to badger the nurses, drank too much coffee.

"Eat," Byron ordered and handed her a sandwich.

"What is it?"

"Any time a sandwich comes out of a vending machine, you don't ask what it is, you just eat it."

"Okay." She took a bite, thought it might have something to do with chicken salad. "It's taking so long."

"Barely three hours," he corrected. "Miracles take time."

"I guess." Considering it necessary fuel, she took another bite of the sandwich. "We should be in there with her. It would be better if we were with her."

"It's hard to wait. Harder for some." He combed his fingers through her hair. "We could take a walk outside, get you out of here for a while."

"No, I'm okay." She damn well would be. "It's easier concentrating on Margo than thinking about where I am. Phobias are so . . ."

"Human?"

"Dumb," she decided. "It was a horrible night in my life. The worst I'll ever have to go through, I imagine. But it was twenty years ago." It was yesterday if she let her mind drift. "Anyway, I handled the hospital both times Laura had kids. Maybe that was easier because I was in on it, and labor really keeps you busy. But this is the same thing. I want to be here."

Linking his fingers with hers, he tugged her into the moment. "You pulling for a boy or a girl?"

"I hadn't thought of it. How—how big does a baby have to be to have a good shot?"

"It'll be beautiful," he said, sliding over her question. "Think of the gene pool it's coming from. A lot of times you think a baby could get lucky and get the best features of his parents. You know, his mother's eyes, his father's chin. Whatever. This one strikes gold anywhere he turns. Going to end up being spoiled rotten."

"Are you kidding? You should see the nursery Margo and Josh put together. I'd like to live there." She laughed and barely noticed he'd handed her tea rather than coffee. "They bought this incredible antique cradle, and this old-fashioned English pram they found in Bath. We were going to have the baby shower next week at Templeton House. All that loot . . ." She trailed off.

"You'll have to make it an after-the-birth shower. What did you get?"

"It's silly." She turned the cup around and around in her hands, trying not to cry or scream or simply bolt up and break into the birthing room. "Margo's got this thing for Italian designers. Especially Armani. They have this junior line. It's ridiculous."

"You bought the baby an Armani?" He burst out laughing, roaring all the harder when she flushed.

"It's a joke," she insisted. "Just a joke." But she found herself smiling. "I guess the first time the kid spits up on it, the joke's on me."

"You're incredibly sweet." He cupped her face in his hands and kissed her. "Incredibly."

"It's only money."

Comforted, she leaned her head against his shoulder and watched her family. Laura had come back from checking on the girls and was sitting with Ann. Her aunt and uncle were standing at the window. Uncle Tommy's arm was around her aunt's shoulders. There was a television bolted to the wall. The Sunday news on CNN rolled by, reporting on a world that had nothing to do with the room where people waited.

Others came and went, bringing with them frissons of worry, anticipation, excitement. She heard the hollow echoes of the PA system, the brisk, efficient footsteps of nurses, and occasional laughter.

She saw a young man leading his enormously pregnant wife down the hall, rubbing her back with intense concentration as she took slow, measured steps.

"Laura always liked to walk during labor," Kate murmured.

"Hmm?"

"Margo and I would take turns walking with her, rubbing her back, breathing with her."

"What about her husband?"

"Right." Kate made a derisive sound, eyed Laura to make certain she was out of earshot. "He didn't have time for the Lamaze route. Didn't consider it necessary. I was her coach for both girls, with Margo pinch-hitting."

"I thought Margo was living in Europe during those years."

"Yeah, but she came back for the births. Kayla was a few days early, and Margo was on assignment. The plan had been for her to spend the last week with Laura at Templeton House, but when she called from the plane, Laura had just gone into labor. Margo ended up coming to the hospital straight from the airport. We were with her," she said fiercely. "Right there with her."

"And Ridgeway?"

"Breezed in after everyone was all cleaned up and tidy. Made what I'm sure he considered a manful attempt to conceal his disappointment that the babies didn't have penises, then gave Laura some elaborate gift and left. Creep."

"I've never met him," Byron mused. "I can't say I'd formed a favorable opinion of him from reports. Normally I prefer to form my own opinion on a firsthand basis." He was silent for a moment. "But I think I can make an exception in this case and just despise him."

"Good call. She's well rid of him. As soon as she stops feeling guilty for being glad she's rid of him, she'll be fine. Oh, God, why is it taking so long? I can't stand it." She sprang to her feet. "They've got to tell us something. We can't just sit here."

A nurse in green scrubs stepped into the doorway. "Then perhaps you'd all like to take a little walk."

"Margo," Ann choked out as she got to her feet.

"Mrs. Templeton is doing just fine. And Mr. Templeton is floating somewhere in the vicinity of Cloud Nine. As for Baby Templeton, I think you'd like to see for yourselves. Come with me, please."

"The baby." Ann reached out, found Susan's hand. "She's had the baby. Do you think it's all right? Do you think it's healthy?"

"Let's go see. Come on, Grandma," Susan murmured as she walked Ann out.

"I'm scared." Trembling as she followed, Kate gripped Byron's hand. "The nurse was smiling, wasn't she? She wouldn't have been smiling if something was really wrong. You can tell by their eyes. You can tell if you look in their eyes. She said Margo was fine. Didn't she say Margo was fine?"

"That's exactly what she said. They'll let you see for yourself soon. And look at this."

They approached a glass door. Behind it, Josh stood, the grin on his face breaking records. In his arms was a small bundle with a golden sprinkle of hair topped with a bright blue bow.

"It's a boy." Thomas's voice broke as he pressed a hand to the glass. "Look at our grandson, Susie."

"Five pounds," Josh mouthed, gingerly tilting his son for his family to view. "Five full pounds. Ten fingers. Ten toes. Five full pounds." He lowered his head to touch his lips to the baby's cheek.

"He's so tiny." With her eyes swimming, Kate wrapped her arms around Laura. "He's so beautiful."

"John Thomas Templeton." Laura let her own tears fall. "Welcome home."

They cooed at him, objecting noisily when a nurse came to take him away. When Josh came through the door they fell on him as villagers might fall on a conquering hero.

"Five pounds," he said again, burrowing his face in his mother's hair. "Did you hear that? He's five pounds even. They said that was really good. He has all the right working parts. They're going to check him out some more because he didn't cook enough, but—"

"He looked done to me," Byron put in. "Have a cigar, Daddy."

"Jesus." Josh stared at the cigar Byron handed him. "Daddy. Oh. I'm supposed to be passing out the cigars."

"Handling details is part of my job description. Grandma." Byron handed one to Ann, who delighted everyone by popping it into her mouth.

"Margo, Josh." Laura took his hand. "How is she?"

"Amazing. She's the most amazing woman. He came out wailing. Did I tell you?" Laughing, he lifted Laura off her feet, kissed her. He couldn't seem to get the words out fast enough. "Just howling. And the minute he did, Margo started to laugh. She was exhausted, and we were both scared bloodless. Then he just slid out."

Baffled, he clasped his hands together and stared at them. "It's the most incredible thing. You can't imagine. Well, you can, but you had to be there. He's crying and Margo's laughing, and the doctors says, 'Well, it looks like there's nothing wrong with his pipes.' Nothing wrong with his pipes," Josh repeated, his voice hitching. "Nothing wrong with him."

"Of course not." Thomas closed Josh in a bear hug. "He's a Templeton."

"Not that we're not glad to see you." Kate brushed the hair back from Josh's face. "But when are they going to let us in to see Margo?"

"I don't know. In a minute, I guess. She had the nurse get her purse." His grin broke out fresh. "She wanted to fix her makeup."

"Typical." Kate turned and threw her arms around Byron. "That's just typical."

CHAPTER 18

THE WEEK FOLLOWING the appearance of J. T. Templeton was hectic and complicated. Laura's schedule didn't allow for more than a few hours at the shop. With Margo involved with her new son, Kate was left to deal with the results of a successful reception. Early delivery had thrown their vague plans for interviewing and hiring a part-time clerk out the window.

Kate was on her own.

She opened the shop every day, learned to control her impulses to hurry browsers along. Though she would never understand the appeal of dawdling in a store, she told herself to appreciate that others enjoyed it.

She studied the inventory lists and tried to recognize the more esoteric items in Pretenses's stock. But why anyone would feel the need to own a designer pillbox with pearl inlay remained beyond her.

Simple honesty was sometimes taken for a credit, sometimes an insult. For every woman who appreciated being told an outfit didn't suit her, there were two who bristled at the information.

She persevered by remembering that for at least one hour every day she could close herself in the back office and be alone, blissfully alone, with her ledgers.

They didn't talk back.

"The customer is always right," Kate muttered to herself. "The customer is always right—even when the customer is an asshole." She marched out of the wardrobe room where one particular customer had just informed her that the Donna Karan was mislabeled. It couldn't possibly be a size ten, as it was too snug at the hips.

"Too snug at the hips, my butt. The old bat couldn't get one thigh in a size ten if she greased it with motor oil."

"Miss, oh, miss." Another customer snapped her fingers, like a diner signaling a particularly slow waitress to bring more wine. Kate gritted her teeth into a smile.

"Yes, ma'am. Can I help you?"

"I want to see this bracelet. The Victorian slide. No, no. I said the Victorian slide, not the gold cuff."

"Sorry." Kate tried again, following the direction of the woman's pointing finger. "It's charming, isn't it?" Fussy and foolish. "Would you like to try it on?"

"How much is it?"

There's a tag right on it, isn't there? Still smiling, Kate turned the tag around, read off the price.

"And what are those stones?"

Oh, shit. She'd studied, hadn't she? "I believe there's garnet and . . . carnelian and . . ." What was that yellow one? Topaz? Amber? Citrine? "Citrine," she hazarded, because it sounded more Victorian to her.

As the customer studied the bracelet, Kate scanned the shop. Just her luck, she thought. It was packed, and Laura was gone for the day. She had three hours to go, and in three hours she judged that what was left of her mind would resemble a mass of cold rice.

The sound of the door jangling made her want to whimper. When she saw who breezed in she wanted to scream.

Candy Litchfield. Her long-standing enemy. Candy Litchfield, whose bouncy stride and perky looks, tumbling red hair and perfect nose hid the heart of a spider.

And she'd brought pals, Kate noted as her heart sank. Perfectly groomed, canny-eyed society matrons in Italian shoes.

"I never find anything I like in here," Candy announced in her bright and far-reaching voice. "But Millicent told me she'd noticed a perfume atomizer that might fit in with my collection. Of course, they overprice everything."

She strolled through, envy packed solidly in ill will.

"Can I show you something else?" Kate said to the customer, who was now studying Candy as carefully as the bracelet.

"No." She hesitated, but avarice won over and she took out her credit card. "Would you gift wrap it, please? It's for my daughter's birthday."

"Of course."

She boxed and wrapped, rang up and bagged, all the while keeping a weather eye on Candy's progress. Two customers left without a purchase, but Kate refused to give Candy's viciously criticizing tongue credit for it.

Feeling like Gary Cooper at the end of *High Noon*, she stepped out from behind the counter to face them alone. "What do you want, Candy?"

"I'm browsing in a public retail facility." She smiled thinly, and exuded a not-so-subtle whiff of Opium. "I believe you're supposed to offer me a glass of rather inferior champagne. Isn't that store policy?"

"Help yourself."

"I was told by a friend there was a perfume bottle that I might like to have." Candy cast an eye over the displays. Her gaze latched on to a gorgeous design in the shape of a woman's body, beautifully fashioned in frosted rose glass.

She would have revealed her own age before she would have shown a flicker of interest.

"I can't imagine what she was thinking of," she drawled.

"She probably mistook your taste." Kate smiled. "That is, she mistook you for having any. How's the pool boy these days?"

Candy, who had a reputation for enjoying very young men in between husbands, bristled. "How does it feel to be a shop clerk? I heard you were fired. Stealing clients' funds, Kate. How . . . ordinary."

"Someone must have pruned your grapevine prematurely, Candy Cane. You're way behind."

"Am I?" She filled a glass to the rim with champagne. "Am I really? Everyone knows that with the Templeton influence behind you, all your petty crimes will be brushed aside. Like your father's were." Her smile sharpened when she saw that shaft strike home. "But then, only fools would have you handling their accounts now." She sipped delicately. "Where there's smoke, after all. You're so lucky to have rich friends who'll throw you crumbs. But then, you always were."

"Always wanted to be a Templeton, didn't you?" Kate said sweetly. "But Josh never looked twice in your direction. We used to laugh about it. Margo and Laura and I. Why don't you finish your champagne and go diddle your pool boy, Candy? You're really wasting your time here."

Candy's skin darkened, but she kept her voice even. Her approach had been to divide and conquer. She'd never been able to score any real points when Kate had Margo or Laura around. But alone . . . And this time she had more ammunition.

"I've heard you're seeing quite a bit of Byron De Witt. And that he's seeing quite a bit of you."

"I'm so flattered you've taken an interest in my sex life, Candy. I'll let you know when we release the video."

"A smart, ambitious man like Byron would be very aware of the advantages of developing a relationship with the Templeton ward. Imagine how high up he can climb using you as a springboard."

Kate's face went blank, pleasing Candy enormously. Candy sipped more wine, her eyes alive with malice as she studied Kate over the rim. The malice blurred into shock as Kate threw back her head and laughed.

"God, you really are an idiot." Weak with laughter, Kate took a few steps to the side so she could support herself against the counter. "To think we just thought you were a mean little snake. All this time you've just been stupid. Do you actually believe a man like Byron needs to use anybody?" Because her ribs were beginning to ache, she took several deep breaths. Something in Candy's eyes tipped her off. "Oh, I get it. I get it. He didn't look twice at you either, did he?"

"You bitch," Candy hissed. She slammed down her glass before stalking over to Kate. "You couldn't get a man on your own if you danced naked in front of a Marine band. Everyone knows why he's sleeping with you."

"Everyone can think what they want. I'll just enjoy it."

"Peter says he's an ambitious corporate shill."

Now Kate's interest piqued. "Peter does, does he?"

"The Templetons booted Peter out because Laura whined about the divorce. They were so concerned with protecting their darling daughter they ignored the fact that Peter is an excellent hotelier. All the years he worked for them, helped build the Templeton chain into what it is today."

"Oh, please. Peter never built anything but his own ego."

"He'll use his talents to open his own hotel soon."

"With Templeton money," Kate commented, thinking about Laura and the girls. "How . . . ironic."

"Laura wanted the divorce. Peter was entitled to financial compensation."

"You'd know all about making a profit out of marriage terminations." Kate decided Candy's visit wasn't such a pain in the butt after all—not when it brought along such interesting news. "Going to use some of your alimony to invest in Ridgeway's hotel?"

"My accountant, who isn't a thief, considers it a smart investment." Her lips curved again. "I believe I'll enjoy being in the hotel business."

"Well, you've spent a lot of time in them, on the hourly plan."

"How droll you are. Hold on to that sense of humor, Kate. You'll need it." Candy's smile was still there, but her teeth were set. "Byron De Witt will make use of you until he achieves the position he wants. Then he won't need you anymore."

"Then I guess I'd better enjoy the ride." She angled her head. "So you've set your sights on Peter Ridgeway. That's just fascinating."

"We've run into each other in Palm Springs a number of times and have discovered many mutual interests." She smoothed her hair. "Be sure to tell Laura he's looking extremely well. Extremely."

"I'll do that," Kate said as Candy headed for the door. "And I'll give Byron your best. No, on second thought, I'll give him mine."

She snickered, turning when the customer nearest the counter cleared her throat. The woman's eyes darted from the door to Kate, bright and wary as a bird's. "Ah, show me these evening bags. If you don't mind?"

"Sure." Kate beamed at her. For some reason Candy's visit had brightened her mood. "I'd love to. Have you shopped with us before?"

"Yes, actually, I have."

Kate took three ridiculously fussy jeweled bags from the shelf. "We value your business. Aren't these just fabulous?"

"AND THEN SHE said how lucky I was to have rich friends throwing me crumbs." Kate stuffed a home-baked chocolate chip cookie into her mouth. "So thanks, since I suppose you're one of my rich friends."

"What an ass." From her position on the patio chaise Margo stretched up her arms.

"She hit me with the business about my father."

Margo lowered her arms again, slowly. "I'm sorry. Damn it, Kate."

"I knew I'd get smacked with it sooner or later. I just hate that it was her, of all people. I hate more that she could see she'd jabbed me. I wish it didn't matter, Margo."

"Everything about the people we love matters. I'm sorry I wasn't there." Her eyes narrowed in thought. "I'm really overdue for a manicure. I think Candy's day for the salon is Wednesday. Won't it be fun to bump into her?"

Well able to picture the event, and the outcome, Kate chuckled. "Give yourself a couple weeks to get back in shape, champ, then you can take her on. I knew I'd feel better if I came here to wallow."

"Remember that the next time you've got something eating away at your insides."

"Never going to let me forget that, are you?" Kate muttered. "I said I was wrong not to tell you and Laura. I was stupid."

"After you've said it at regular intervals for the next year or two, we'll forget all about it."

"I have such understanding friends. Christ, these are criminal," Kate mumbled through another cookie. "It must be great having Annie here baking and fussing."

"It really is. I never would have believed we could live under the same roof again, even for the short term. It was awfully sweet of Laura to insist that Mum stay here for a couple of weeks."

"Speaking of Laura." Kate had made a point of dropping by Margo's after work, knowing that Laura would be too busy for an early-evening visit. "Candy mentioned Peter."

"So?"

"It was the way she mentioned him. First she was on me and Byron."

"Excuse me." Margo indulged in a cookie herself. "In what way?"

"Well, she said how he's a corporate shill, and he's using me to earn points with the Templetons. You know, like he brings me to orgasm, and they give him another promotion."

"That's pathetic." She narrowed her eyes at Kate's face. "You didn't buy that?"

"No." She shook her head quickly. "No. I might have if it had been anyone other than Byron. It was a pretty clever chain to pull. But he's just not made that way. I laughed at her."

"Good for you. What does that have to do with Peter?"

"Apparently that's where she got the idea. At least partially. It sounds to me as if they've gotten . . . close."

"Jesus. What a frightening thought." She shuddered dramatically. "Two creeps in a pod."

"She wanted to make sure I mentioned it to Laura. I don't know if I should."

"Let it alone," Margo said immediately. "Laura doesn't need that. If she hears it, she hears it. Besides, with Candy's track record, it's probably already fizzled."

"I was leaning that way." Kate toyed with the rest of her cappuccino, studied the view. "It's so beautiful here. I never really told you what a terrific job you've done putting the place together. Making it like home."

"It is home. It was, straight off." Margo smiled. "I owe that to you. You're the one who told me about the place."

"It seemed right for you—you and Josh. Do you think you can tell sometimes if a place is where you want to be?"

"I know it. It was Templeton House for me. I was too young to remember anything before we came there, but it was home, always. My flat in Milan."

When Margo broke off, Kate shifted uncomfortably. "I'm sorry. Didn't mean to stir up old memories."

"It's all right. I loved that flat. Everything about it. I was home there, too. It was right for me at the time." She shrugged her shoulders. "If things had stayed as they were, it would be right for me still. But they didn't. I didn't. Then there was the shop." She smiled and sat up straighter. "Remember how I was so dazzled by that big, empty building while you and Laura rolled your eyes and wondered if you should cart me off?"

"It smelled of stale marijuana and spiderwebs."

"And I loved it. I knew I could make something there. And I did." Her eyes glowed as she looked out to the cliffs. "Maybe childbirth has made me philosophical, but it's not hard for me to say I needed to make something there. And I wouldn't have without you and Laura. Let me be sappy for a minute," she ordered when Kate grimaced. "I'm entitled. I've started to think that things move in a circle, if you let them. We're together on this, through varying circumstances. But we're together. We always have been. It matters."

"Yes. It matters." Kate rose, wandered to the edge of the patio where the ground spread green and bloomed with colorful blossoms. The autumn sky was still brilliantly blue, ranging out to the rocking sea and beyond.

This was a home, she thought. Not hers, though she felt at home here as she did at Templeton House. It worried her that she'd fallen in love with the bent cyprus, the blooming vines and wood and glass of a house on Seventeen Mile that wasn't her own.

"It was always Templeton House for me," she said, putting an image of the towers and stone over the image of multilevel decks and wide windows. "The view from my bedroom, the way it smelled after the floors were polished. I never felt that way about my apartment in town. It was just a convenient place to stay."

"Are you going to keep it?"

Puzzled, Kate turned back. "Of course. Why wouldn't I?"

"I thought since you were staying at Byron's—"

"I'm not staying there," Kate said quickly. "Not living there. I just . . . sleep over sometimes. That's entirely different."

"If you want it to be." Margo tilted her head. "What worries you about him, Kate?"

"Nothing. Exactly." Blowing out a breath, she came back and sat. "I was going to ask you—figuring you'd be the expert on such matters."

Margo waited, tapped her fingers on the arms of the chaise. "Well?"

"Okay, I'm working up to it." She braced, looked Margo dead in the eye so that she could detect any flicker. "Can you become addicted to sex?"

"Damn straight you can," Margo said without a single flicker. "If you do it right." The corners of her lips turned up. "I'd bet Byron does it very right."

"Rake in your winnings," Kate said dryly.

"And you're complaining."

"No, not complaining. I'm asking. I've just never . . . Look, it's not like I haven't had sex before. I just never had such an appetite for it as I seem to now. With him." She rolled her own eyes, chuckled at herself. "Christ, Margo, five minutes with him and I want to bite him."

"And since the taste suits you, what's the problem?"

"Because I wondered if you could get too dependent on certain aspects."

"On great sex?"

"Yeah, all right. On really great sex. Then people change, and move on."

"Sometimes they do." She thought of herself, and of Josh. Smiled. "Sometimes they don't."

"Sometimes they do," Kate repeated. "Candy got me thinking—"

"Oh, please. Damn it, Kate, you said you didn't buy that shit she was spewing."

"About him using me? Absolutely not. It just made me think about our relationship. If it is a relationship. We don't have anything in common really but, well, sex."

With a long sigh, Margo leaned back, helped herself to another cookie. "What do you do when you're not busy pounding each other into puddles of passion?"

"Very funny. We do stuff."

"Such as?"

"I don't know. Listen to music."

"You like the same music?"

"Sure. Who doesn't like rock and roll? Sometimes we watch movies. He's got this incredible collection of old black and whites."

"Oh, you mean the old movies you like."

"Hmm." She shrugged. "We walk on the beach, or he whips me through a workout. He's tough about that." More than pleased, she flexed her biceps. "I've got definition."

"Hmm. I guess you never talk, though."

"Sure, we talk. About work, family, food. He's got this thing about nutrition."

"Always serious, huh?"

"No, I mean we have a good time. We laugh a lot. And we play with the dogs, or he works on one of his cars and I watch. You know—stuff."

"Let me see if I have this straight. You like the same music, the same kind of movies, which translates into being entertained together. You enjoy walking on the beach, pumping iron, share an affection for a pair of mongrel dogs." Margo shook her head. "I can see the problem. Other than sex, you might as well be a couple of strangers. Dump him now, Kate, before it gets ugly."

"I should have known you'd make a joke out of it."

"You're the joke. Listen to yourself. You've got a terrific man, a wonderful, satisfying relationship that includes great sex and mutual interests, and you're sitting there looking for hitches."

"Well, if you find them before they happen, you can work around them."

"It isn't an audit, Kate, it's a love affair. Relax and enjoy it."

"I am. Mostly. Nearly." She shrugged again. "I've just got a lot on my mind." And, she thought, it might be time to bring up the fact that she'd been offered a partnership at Bittle. "There's some, ah, adjustments coming up," she began, but was interrupted as Ann came out, carrying the baby.

"The little man woke up hungry. I've changed him," Ann said, cooing as she carried him toward Margo's open arms. "Yes, I did. Changed him and put on one of his fancy suits. There's a lad. There's a darling."

"Oh, isn't he gorgeous?" Margo cuddled him, and smelling mother, J. T. sent up a call for dinner. "He's more beautiful every time I look at him. Just like a man, can't wait for a woman to open her blouse. There you are, sweetie."

He settled happily at her breast, his small fists kneading, his newborn blue eyes intent on hers.

"He's gained four ounces," she told Kate.

"At the rate he's going, he'll be ready for heavyweight status in another week." Charmed, Kate shifted to the edge of the chaise to stroke his downy head. "He has your eyes and Josh's ears. God, he smells so good." She drew in the powdery, milky scent of baby and decided to talk business another time. "I get to hold him when you're done."

"You'll stay for dinner, Miss Kate." Ann put her hands behind her back to end her struggle not to adjust the way Margo was holding the precious boy. "Mr. Josh has a late meeting at the hotel, and you'll keep us company. Then you can hold our baby as long as you want."

"Well . . ." Kate traced a fingertip over the curve of J. T.'s cheek. "Since you've twisted my arm."

THE BAY SUITE of Templeton Monterey was elegantly appointed. Black-lacquered tables held huge porcelain urns filled with exotic blooms. A curved settee in icy blue brocade was sprinkled with pillows that picked up the tones of a floor-spanning Oriental rug. The drapes on both sets of wide glass doors were open to invite in the glorious bleeding colors as the sun slowly sank into the sea.

The table in the dining area was conference size, graced with high-backed, ornately carved chairs with tapestried seats. Dinner was served on bone-white china, accented with a Fumé Blanc from the Templeton vineyards.

The meeting might have been held at Templeton House, but both Thomas and Susan considered that to be Laura's home. This, as pleasant as it was, was business.

"If there's a weakness in the Beverly Hills location, it's in room service." Byron glanced at the notes beside his plate. "The complaints run to the usual—the amount of time for delivery, mix-up in orders. The kitchen runs well as a whole. Your chef there is . . ."

"Temperamental," Susan suggested with a smile.

"Actually I was going to say frightening. I know he scared me. Maybe it was being ordered out by a very large man with a thick Brooklyn accent and a cleaver, but there was a moment."

"Did you leave?" Thomas wanted to know.

"I reasoned with him. From a safe distance. And told him, quite sincerely, that he made the best coquilles St. Jacques it had ever been my privilege to taste."

"That goes a long way with Max," Josh commented. "As I recall, the line chefs there work like machines."

"They appear to. They're terrified of him." Grinning, Byron sampled his tarragon chicken. "The problem doesn't seem to be in the preparation, but in the servers. Naturally there are certain hours when both the kitchen and the servers are backed up, but the room service staff has become undeniably lax."

"Suggestions?"

"I'd recommend transferring Helen Pringle to the Beverly Hills location, if she's agreeable, in a managerial position. She's experienced and efficient. We'd miss her here, of course, but I believe she would eliminate the problem in L.A. And she'd certainly be my first choice for a promotion."

"Josh?" Thomas turned to his son for verification.

"Agreed. She has an excellent record as an assistant manager."

"Make her the offer." Susan picked up her wine. "With the appropriate increase in salary and benefits."

"Fine. I think that closes Beverly Hills." Byron skimmed down his notes. San Francisco had been dealt with and tabled. San Diego required a personal spot check but posed no immediate need for discussion. "Ah, there is a little matter here at the flagship." Byron scratched his cheek. "Maintenance would like new vending machines."

Thomas raised a brow as he finished off his salmon. "Maintenance came to you about vending machines?"

"There was a problem with the plumbing on the sixth floor. Sabotage by a toddler who decided to drown his Power Rangers in the toilet. Hell of a mess. I went down to soothe the parents."

And ended up sending them down to the pool while he helped the mechanic stem the flood. But that was beside the point.

"I supervised the disgorging, so to speak, and the matter of vending machines came up. They want their junk food back. It seems candy bars and chips were ditched a couple of years ago and replaced with apples and fat-free cookies. Believe me, I got an earful about corporate interference in personal choice."

"That would be Ridgeway," Josh decided.

Susan made a dismissive sound, but held a napkin to her lips to disguise her grin. She had an image of Byron, elegant in a suit and polished shoes, wading through water and listening to a mechanic's gripes about snacks. "Recommendation?"

"Keep them happy." Byron shrugged. "Let them eat Milky Ways."

"Agreed," Thomas said. "And is that the biggest staff problem here at Templeton Monterey?"

"Just the usual hitches, nothing that isn't typical day-to-day. There was the dead woman in 803."

Josh grimaced. "I hate when that happens."

"Heart attack, died in her sleep. She was eighty-five, led a full life. Gave the maid a hell of a start."

"How long did it take you to calm her down?" Susan asked.

"After we caught her? She went screaming down the hall. About an hour."

Thomas topped off the wine, lifted his glass. "It's a relief for Susie and me to know that California is in good hands. Some people believe that running a hotel means sitting up in the fancy office and pushing paper— and people—around."

"Now, Tommy." Susan patted his arm. "Peter's no longer our problem. We can hate him for strictly personal reasons now." She beamed at Byron. "But I agree. We'll go back to France at the end of the week knowing things here are well looked after." She tilted her head. "Professionally, and personally."

"I appreciate that."

"Our Kate's looking very happy," Thomas began. "Very healthy and fit. Are you making plans?"

"Uh-oh, here it comes." With a grin, Josh leaned back, shook his head. "Sorry, By, I'm just going to sit here and watch you twist in the wind."

"It's a reasonable question," Thomas insisted. "I know what the man's prospects are, obviously. I want to know what his intentions are."

"Tommy," Susan said patiently, "Kate's a grown woman."

"She's my girl." His face clouded as he pushed his plate aside. "I let Laura rush off her own way and look what that got her."

"I'm not going to hurt her," Byron said. He wasn't as offended as some might have expected by the probing. After all, he'd been raised in the old school, where family interest and interference went hand in hand. "She's very important to me."

"Important?" Thomas tossed back. "A good night's sleep is important."

Susan sighed. "Eat your dessert, Thomas, You know how you love tiramisu. Working for Templeton doesn't require you to answer personal questions, Byron. Just ignore him."

"I'm not asking as his employer. I'm asking as Kate's father."

"Then I'll answer you in that spirit," Byron agreed. "She's become a major part of my life, and my intentions are to marry her." Since he hadn't fully understood that himself until this moment, Byron fell silent and frowned into his glass.

"Well, then." Pleased, Thomas slapped his palm on the table.

"It'll be news to her," Byron muttered, then let out a breath. "I'd appreciate it if you'd let me deal with your Kate in my own way. I haven't quite worked it out."

"I'll have him out of your way in a few days," Susan assured Byron. "Six thousand miles."

Thomas forked up creamy cake. "But I'll be back," he warned and shot Byron a wide grin.

HE WAS A detail man, after all, Byron reminded himself when he let himself into his house. He knew how to handle sensitive problems. Surely he could handle something as basic as a proposal of marriage to the woman he loved.

She wouldn't want anything flowery, he decided. Kate wouldn't go for the down-on-one-knee routine. Thank God. She'd prefer the direct, the simple. It was all in the approach, he concluded and tugged off his tie.

He wouldn't put it as a question. Phrasing something as "will you" opened up too much leeway for the answer to be no. Better to make it a statement, being certain to keep it short of a demand. Because it was Kate, after all. And it would be wise, because it was Kate, to have at the ready a list of rational reasons why it would be sensible.

He only wished he could think of a single one.

He'd pulled off his shoes before he realized something was wrong. It took him another minute to pinpoint it. It was the quiet. The dogs always set up a greeting din when he pulled into the drive. But there was no barking. When he raced to the deck door, wrenched it open in panic, he saw that there were no dogs.

He called, whistled, hurried down the steps to check the fence that kept them safely in the backyard. His frantic mind whirled with the possibility of dognappers, newspaper articles about stolen pets sold for experiments.

The first happy bark weakened his knees. They'd gotten through the safety gate, he thought as he strode toward the beach steps. That was all. Somehow they'd gotten through and gone for a run on their own. He'd have to give them a good talking-to.

They topped the stairs at a run, tails waving flags of devoted joy. They leapt on him, licking and wriggling with the trembling delight they displayed whether he'd been gone for hours or had simply run to the store for milk.

"You're grounded," he informed them. "Both of you. Haven't I told you to stay in the yard? Well, you can just forget gnawing on those ham bones I got from the hotel kitchen. No, don't try to make up," he said, laughing when they held up paws for shaking. "You guys are in the doghouse—for real."

"Well, that'll teach them." Kate climbed the last step and stood smiling at him in the moonlight. "But I have to take the heat on this one. I asked them to escort me down to the beach, and being well-bred gentlemen, they could hardly refuse."

"I was worried about them," he managed. He couldn't seem to stop staring at her. She was standing there, windblown, slightly breathless from the climb. Just there, as if he'd wished it.

"I'm sorry. We should have left you a note."

"I didn't expect to see you tonight."

"I know." Feeling awkward now, as she always did after following an impulse, she tucked her hands in her pockets. "I went by Margo's after I closed the shop, had dinner and played with the baby. He's gained four ounces."

"I know. Josh told me. He has pictures. About six dozen."

"I got to see videos. I loved it. Anyway, I started to head back to my apartment." Her apartment, she thought. Dull, empty, meaningless. "And I ended up here instead. I hope you don't mind."

"Do I mind?"

He wrapped his arms around her, slowly. Drew her close against him, gradually. For three humming heartbeats his eyes stayed on hers. His mouth brushed hers, retreated. Brushed again, shifted angles. Then his lips covered hers, heated hers, parted hers. Soft and deep and welcoming, the kiss shimmered through her. Her hands stayed in her pockets, too limp to move. The muscles in her thighs went lax, her knees weak. When he drew away she could have sworn she saw stars dazzling her own eyes.

"Well," she began, but he was kissing her again, in that same drugging, devastating, delicious way. It was as if they had forever to simply be there, caught in soft sea breezes and quiet passion.

She gulped in air when his mouth lifted. His eyes were so close, so clear, she could see herself trapped in them. It jolted her back a step, made her fumble for a casual smile.

"I'd have to say, at a guess, you don't mind."

"I want you here." He took her hands, brought her palms, one at a time to his lips. And watched her. "I want you."

He could see that she was struggling to recover, to plant her feet back on the ground. He didn't intend to let her. "Come inside," he murmured, drawing her with him. "I'll show you."

CHAPTER 19

DAYS LATER, SHE was still there.

Byron's idea of a break from weight training was a three-mile jog on the beach. It was difficult for a woman whose idea of a morning start had always been two very hot, very strong cups of coffee to adjust to the concept of running at dawn.

Kate told herself it was the experience that mattered. And, more important, the waffles he'd promised her if she stuck it out.

"So you, like," she puffed, huffed, and tried to concentrate on her pace, "really enjoy this."

"It's addictive," Byron assured her. He was going at a snail's pace to bring her along gradually, and admiring the way her legs looked in baggy shorts. "You'll see."

"No way. Only sinful stuff is addictive. Coffee, cigarettes, chocolate. Sex. Good stuff never becomes addictive."

"Sex is good stuff."

"It's good but sinful—sinful in a good way." She watched the dogs race into the surf and shake themselves so that little bullets of water flew and sparkled in the strengthening sun.

She supposed there was something to be said for dawn, after all. The light was achingly beautiful, and the smells so fresh, so renewed, they seemed unreal. The air was just cool enough to be bracing.

She had to admit her muscles felt loose. Oiled, in a way, as if her body was becoming a well-tuned machine. It made her feel foolish to realize she'd accepted feeling unwell for so long simply because she'd found it too much trouble to change.

"Where did you run in Atlanta? No beaches there."

"We've got parks. Indoor tracks when the weather's bad."

"Do you miss it?"

"Bits and pieces. Magnolia trees. The sound of slow voices. My family."

"I've never lived anywhere but here. Never wanted to. I liked going to school back east. Seeing snow, frost on the windows. The way the leaves look in New England in October. But I always wanted to be here."

She saw the beach steps in the distance. Her aching calves all but applauded. "Margo's lived lots of places, and Laura's done much more traveling than I have."

"Someplace you'd like to see?"

"No, not really. Well . . . Bora Bora."

"Bora Bora?"

"I did this report on it in high school. You know, a geography report. It seemed so cool. One of those places I told myself I'd go when I took a real vacation. Just a hang-out-and-do-nothing vacation. Oh, thank goodness," she breathed and sank to the sand in front of the beach steps. "I made it."

"And you're going to cramp up if you don't keep moving." Unsympathetically, he hauled her to her feet. "Just walk. You've got to cool down. Why haven't you gone to Bora Bora?"

She walked, for three paces, then bent over at the waist and breathed. "Come on, Byron, real people don't just go to Bora Bora. It's one of those daydreams. Do you think jogging can dislocate internal organs?"

"No."

"I was pretty sure I could hear my ovaries rattling."

He paled a bit. "Please." He handed her the bottle of water he'd screwed into the sand at the base of the stairs. He whistled for the dogs before starting up the steps with her.

"Normally, I'd just be getting up now, stumbling into the kitchen, where my timed coffee machine would be finishing up its last few drips. Leave the house at eight twenty-five, hit the office at eight forty-five. Have the coffee machine there brewing away and be at my desk with the first cup by eight fifty-five."

"Eat the first roll of antacids by nine fifty-five."

"It wasn't quite that bad." She fell silent as they crossed from steps to lawn toward the house. The dogs winged through the gate, streaking toward their bowls in anticipation of breakfast. "I haven't had a chance to tell Margo and Laura about going back to Bittle."

Byron hefted the twenty-five-pound bag of dog food out of the pantry. "Haven't had a chance?"

"All right—haven't found the right way." She shifted as the nuggets clattered into plastic. "I feel like I'm letting them down. I know that's not right. I know they won't feel that way. They'd understand this is right for me."

Byron replaced the bag, signaling the dogs to chow down. "Is it?"

"Of course it is." She brushed back her hair. "What a thing to say. It's what I studied for, worked for. It's what I've always wanted."

"All right, then." He gave her a friendly pat on the rump and headed in.

"What do you mean by that? 'All right, then'?" She rushed in behind him, scowling. "It's a partnership, with all the bells and whistles. I've earned it."

"Absolutely." As a matter of habit, he started upstairs toward the shower. Kate followed at his heels.

"Well, I have. That whole business about the altered documents is just about cleared up. In any case, I'm clear. The rest is Detective Kusack's problem. And the firm's problem. I'll have more control over what's done after I'm a partner."

"Are you worried about it?"

"About what?"

He tugged off his short-sleeved sweatshirt, flung it toward the hamper. "About clearing up the escrow discrepancies."

"Of course I am."

"Why haven't you pursued it?"

"Well, I—" She broke off as he flicked on the shower and stepped inside. "I've been busy. There's not a hell of a lot I could do, in any case, and with Margo being pregnant, and the auction, and Laura tossing me all these details about this holiday fashion show she wants, I haven't had time."

"Okay," he said agreeably.

"That doesn't mean it doesn't matter." Disgusted, she stripped and joined him under the spray. "It just means I've had other priorities. It all came to a head a couple of weeks ago. The forgeries, the offer, the baby. It didn't seem fair to tell Margo and Laura I'd have to cut back at the shop just when Margo had to cut back herself. And until I do, and I'm back at Bittle, I don't see what I can do about finding out who tried to screw me and the firm. But once I'm there, you can bet your ass I'm going to find out who set me up."

"That makes sense."

"Of course it makes sense." Irritated for no reason she could name, she stuck her head under the spray. "Just like it makes sense for me to accept the offer. It's the most practical course."

"You're right. It's definitely the most practical. Pretenses is an investment. Bittle is your career."

"That's right." Instead of being soothed by his agreement, she bristled. "So what are we arguing about?"

"I don't have a clue." He gave her an absent kiss on the shoulder and stepped out to dry off. "I'll get breakfast going," he announced, and chuck-led his way down the stairs.

She was, he thought, as easy to see through as a chain-link fence.

KATE WORKED WITH Laura shoulder to shoulder throughout the morning. She told herself the minute they had a real break in traffic, she would sit Laura down and explain about her plans. She would, of course, continue to take care of the books. A few evenings a week, the occasional Sunday—that would be enough for her to run Pretenses's finances. Naturally, she would be very busy as a partner at Bittle, but she would also be in a posi-tion to delegate a great deal of the grunt work that she had been accus-tomed to handling herself.

She would have more leeway, more freedom. And, of course, more clout. Her schedule would be crammed, but she was used to that. Working at the shop had certainly kept her busy, but it had also given her large chunks of free time that weren't necessary.

She told herself she would be glad to have her hours prioritized again. That was her way.

And she would be thrilled not to have to chitchat with strangers. Not to be asked to give fashion opinions or have a say in gift-giving decisions. What a relief it would be to settle back at her computer and not have to speak to a soul for hours on end.

"My sister's going to be thrilled with that," a customer said, as Kate carefully removed the tag from a coral cashmere tunic.

"I hope she is."

"Oh, she will be. This is her favorite shop. And mine, too." The woman beamed at the varied selections she'd placed on the counter. "I don't know how I managed before you opened up. Look at the wonderful dent I've made in my Christmas shopping."

"Getting an early start," Kate commented and blinked herself back into focus. "I'd say everyone's going to be happy."

"My mother would never buy herself something as frivolous as this." The woman trailed a finger over the delicate lines of a crystal Pegasus. "That's what gifts are for. And where else but here could I find an antique pocket watch for my father, cashmere for my sister, sapphire studs for my daughter, a crystal flying horse for my mother, and a pair of navy suede Ferragamo pumps for me?"

"Only at Pretenses," Kate said, her own spirits lifted by the woman's ex-uberant good nature.

The customer laughed and stepped back. "You have the most wonderful place here. If you could gift-box everything but the shoes? I think I'll take one more turn around in case I missed something I have to have."

"Take your time." Smiling to herself, Kate began to box the selections. She caught herself humming as she settled the pocket watch in a bed of cotton. Well, what was wrong with humming? There was nothing wrong with enjoying your work, even though it wasn't your chosen field. Being temporary, it was like playing at a job.

She glanced up as Laura came down the winding stairs from the second floor, chatting with a customer. "I know Margo picked this up on a buying trip to London last year, Mrs. Quint."

"Oh, call me Patsy, please. I shop here so often I feel like we're old friends. And this is just what I was looking for." She gloated over the cherry slant-top writing box Laura set on the counter. "But then, I always find what I'm looking for here. That's why I'm here so often." She laughed at herself, then caught sight of the crystal horse. "Oh, how wonderful! How charming. Someone beat me to it."

"I did." The first customer straightened from her survey of jeweled compacts and smiled. "He's beautiful, isn't he?"

"Gorgeous. Tell me you have something else like him," she begged Laura.

"I think we have a winged dragon—Baccarat, that we haven't shelved yet. Kate?"

"In inventory, priced but not tagged. In the storeroom. I'll find it as soon as I'm done here."

"No, I'll find it. I hope. If you don't mind waiting a minute."

"Not at all. You know, even my husband likes to shop here," Patsy confided to Kate when Laura slipped into the back. "No small accomplishment that, since getting him to stop for a can of peas is a major feat. Of course, I think he likes to come in and look at the pretty girls."

"We're here to serve." Kate affixed a gold seal to the tissue she'd wrapped over the cashmere.

"This compact here." The first customer tapped on the glass. "The heart-shaped one. I think my sister-in-law would love it."

"Just let me get it out for you."

While the two customers chatted about the compact, Kate boxed the horse. A fresh discussion broke out when Laura brought out the dragon. When the door opened, everyone sighed.

"Oh, what a gorgeous baby!" Patsy pressed her hands together under her chin. "Why, he's an absolute angel."

"He is, isn't he?" Margo shifted the baby carrier to show off her son. "He's seventeen days old."

Business ground to a halt, as it was necessary to admire his fingers, his nose, to comment on how bright and alert his eyes were. By the time Kate brought the cradle out of the back room and John Thomas was settled in it, the women had bonded over the baby.

"You should have called me if you wanted to get out for a little while," Laura scolded. "I'd have picked you up."

"Mum dropped me off. She had some marketing she wanted to do. I think her plan is to stock my kitchen so that if we're locked in for a year, we'll have provisions." Margo settled in a chair with the cradle at her side. "God, I've missed this place. So, how's business?"

"The pair who just left?" Kate began, pouring tea.

"On their way to lunch, yes."

"They became fast friends about fifteen minutes ago over mythical glass animals. It was kind of fun to watch."

"This is the first time the shop's been empty since we opened this morning," Laura added. "We're getting a lot of those people who always have their holiday shopping done by Thanksgiving."

"And to think how I used to hate them." Margo sighed. "I checked with my doctor. He says if I keep it to mostly sitting behind the counter, I can start coming in a few hours a day starting next week."

"There's no need to rush," Kate objected. "We're handling it."

"I don't like you handling it without me. I can bring J. T. with me. Babies mist shoppers' brains."

"I thought you were going to interview nannies."

"We are." Pouting a little, Margo bent over her son, adjusted his blanket. "Soon."

"She doesn't want to share," Laura murmured. "I know how it feels. When Ali was born, I—" She broke off as a trio of fresh customers came in.

"I'll take them," Kate volunteered. "You two indulge yourself in mommy talk."

For the next twenty minutes, she showed one customer every diamond earring in stock while the second poked through the bric-a-brac and the third cooed over a napping J. T.

She helped serve tea, saved a frantic husband with a last-minute anniversary gift, and rehung the castoffs left in the wardrobe room.

Shaking her head at the way some people treated silk, she stepped out again. New customers were browsing amid a hum of female voices. Someone had switched on an Art Deco lamp to test the effect, and smooth golden light shimmered in the corner. Margo was laughing with a customer, Laura was stretching on her toes to reach a box for a purchase. And the baby slept.

It was a wonderful place, she thought suddenly. It was a magical little treasure chest filled with the sublime and the foolish. Crafted, she realized, by the three of them. From desperation, from practicality, and most of all from friendship.

How odd that she had ever considered it a business to be measured in profit and loss, overhead and expenditure. And odder still that she hadn't realized until this moment how happy she was to be a part of something so risky, so ridiculous, so entertaining.

She walked to Laura. "I have an appointment I'd forgotten about," she said quickly. "Can you handle things here until I get back? It should only take an hour or so."

"Sure. But—"

"I won't be long." She grabbed her purse from behind the counter before Laura could ask any questions. "See you later," she called out, and bolted.

"Where's she going?" Margo demanded.

"I don't know. Just out for a little while." Concerned, Laura stared through the glass after Kate. "I hope she's all right."

SHE WASN'T SURE that she was. It was a test, Kate told herself. Going back to Bittle, gauging her feelings. Her reaction would be a test.

The lobby was familiar, even comforting, with its quiet colors and no-nonsense furniture. Chrome and leather, efficient and easily cleaned, made up the small sitting area where stacks of *Money, Time,* and *Newsweek* were handy for the clients' perusal.

The main receptionist offered Kate a quick and slightly embarrassed smile. She took the steps, as was her habit and passed through the first floor. No nonsense here either, she mused. Clerks and computer operators went about their business, busy as bees and just as focused on the task at hand. One of the mailroom clerks pushed his cart along, passing out the afternoon deliveries. Someone's fax was clicking.

On the second floor, the hum of business continued. Account executives plowed through the daily routine in their own offices. The phones were active, reminding her that it was, after all, the middle of the last quarter of the year. Clients were beginning to call for advice on how to squeeze in more deductions, how to defer income until the next tax year, how much they might need to contribute to their Keoghs or IRAs.

Of course, she thought, twice as many would wait until the last week of December and call in a panic. It kept accounting interesting.

She stopped at her old office. No one had claimed it, she mused. Her computer and phone sat on the desk, but otherwise it was bare. The fax machine was silent, but she could remember the way it had beeped and clicked along.

The blinds were closed on the window behind the desk. She'd often left them that way herself, she realized. Working in artificial light, never taking notice of the view.

The shelf was a handy stretch away from the desk and would have held her research books, tax manuals, supplies. No tchotchkes, she thought. No distractions. And, she decided with an inner sigh, no style. Just another bee in the hive.

Good God, she was boring.

"Kate."

She turned, shaking off the moment of self-pity. "Hello, Roger."

"What are you doing?"

"Taking a good look in the mirror." She gestured toward her empty office. "No one's using it."

"No." His smile was a little weak as he glanced in. "There's talk about hiring a new associate. There's a lot of talk," he added, looking back at her face.

"Is there," she said coolly. "And?"

"I'm just surprised to see you here. That cop's been around a lot."

"That doesn't worry me, Roger. I didn't do anything to be worried about."

"No, of course you didn't. I never believed it. I know you too well." He glanced over his shoulder, the movement jerky and ripe with nerves. "Bittle Senior called a full staff meeting last week, made the announcement that you'd been cleared of any implication. Now everybody's looking at everybody else. Wondering."

"That's not surprising, is it?" Curious, she studied his face. "Still, only one person should be worrying as well as wondering. Don't you think, Roger?"

"The finger pointed at you," he said. "Who knows who it might point to next?"

"I think Detective Kusack knows how to do his job. Then there's the FBI."

"What do you mean, the FBI?"

"Tampering with tax forms is a federal offense."

"Nobody tampered with the forms filed with the IRS. Nobody fucked with the government."

"Just with me, and a few clients. You bastard."

His head snapped back as if she'd slapped him. "What the hell are you talking about?"

"You're sweating. You know, I don't believe I've ever seen you sweat before. Not in bed. Not when you told me one of my top accounts was transferring to you. But you're sweating now."

When she started to pass him, he grabbed her arm. "Don't be ridiculous. Are you actually accusing me of doctoring files?"

"You son of a bitch. You knew where I kept all my records. You knew just how to pull it off and point the finger at me. You found out about my father, too, didn't you?" Fury was pouring through her hot blood. "And you had the nerve to come on to me again after what you'd done. I couldn't figure out why you were suddenly interested in me again. Just another way to cover your ass."

"You don't know what you're talking about."

Yeah, he was sweating, she noted. Scared. Scared as a fucking rabbit caught in oncoming headlights. She hoped to God he suffered. "Take your hand off me, Roger. And do it now."

He only tightened his grip, leaned closer. "No way you can prove any of this. If you try to put this off on me, you're going to look like a fool. I dumped you. I got that account because I'm better, I'm more innovative. I work harder."

"You got that account because you slept with a lonely, vulnerable woman."

"Like you never slept with a client," he said in a furious undertone.

"No, I never did. And you took the money because you were greedy, because it was easy, and you'd found a way to set me up."

"I'm warning you, Kate, if you go to Bittle and try to put me on the hot seat, I'll—"

"What?" she tossed back, her eyes alight with eager challenge. "Exactly what?"

"Is there a problem here?" Newman glided down the hall in her eerily silent way. Her mouth was pursed, as usual, in disapproval.

Kate sent her a feral smile. "I don't believe there is." She jerked her arm out of his loosened grip. "Is there, Roger? I believe Mr. Bittle's expecting me, Ms. Newman. I called in on the car phone."

"He'll see you now. Your phone's ringing, Mr. Thornhill. If you'll come with me, Ms. Powell." Newman glanced over her shoulder once, measuring Roger as he stood grim-faced in the hall, then looked down when Kate rubbed her aching arm. "Are you all right?"

"I'm fine." She drew in a breath as Newman opened the door to Bittle's office. "Thank you."

"Kate." Bittle rose from behind his desk, held out a hand in welcome. "I'm very glad you called." He closed both hands around hers. "Very glad."

"Thank you for seeing me."

"Please, sit. What can we get you?"

"Nothing. I'm fine."

"Ms. Newman, inform the partners that Kate is here."

"No, please, that's not necessary. I'd like to speak just with you."

"As you wish. That'll be all, Ms. Newman." He took the chair beside Kate rather than the one behind his desk. "I wish I could tell you about the progress on the investigation. But Detective Kusack asks more questions than he answers."

"I'm not here about that." She thought of Roger. No, she wouldn't point the finger, not yet. She would let him stew, and sweat, and she would find a way to prove what he'd done. Then she'd watch him fry. "I came about your offer."

"Good." Pleased, he sat back, folded his hands. "We're very anxious to have you back. We're all agreed that the partners could use some fresh young blood. It's too easy for a firm such as this to become stodgy."

"It isn't stodgy, Mr. Bittle. This is a good firm. I've just started to realize how much I benefited from my years here."

Without any idea of what she was going to say, she, too, folded her hands in her lap. "First, I want to say that I've thought about what happened a great deal and come to the conclusion that under the circumstances you did what you had to do. What I would have done in your position."

"I appreciate that, Kate, very much appreciate it."

"My mistake was in not facing it, and maybe I'm starting to give myself a break about that, too. I can't always handle things by myself. I don't always have all the answers." She let out a little breath. That was a tough one to admit.

"Mr. Bittle, I had one goal when I got my M.B.A. That was to work my way up in this firm to a partnership. Working for you was one of the best experiences of my life. I knew that if I made it here, if I met your standards and became a partner, it meant I was the best. It was very important to me to be the best."

"This firm has never had an associate with a finer work ethic. While I realize the timing of our offer might worry you, I'll assure you again that our regret for your involvement in this police matter has nothing whatever to do with the terms of partnership."

"I know that. It means a great deal to me to know that." She opened her mouth, acceptance hovering on her tongue. Then shook her head. "I'm sorry, Mr. Bittle, I can't come back here."

"Kate." He reached out to take her hand again. "Believe me when I say I understand your discomfort. I expect that you'd be reluctant to accept until this matter is completely cleared up. We're certainly willing to give you time."

"It's not a matter of time. Or maybe it is. I've had time to readjust, reevaluate. For the past few months I've deviated from the path I set for myself when I was still in high school. I like it, Mr. Bittle. No one's more surprised than I am that I'm happy running a secondhand shop on Cannery Row. But I am, and I'm not willing to give it up."

He sat back, tapping his fingertips together as he did when he faced a knotty problem. "Let me talk to you a moment as an old friend, someone who's known you most of your life."

"Of course."

"You're goal-oriented, Kate. You've put all your time and effort into achieving success in your chosen field. A field, I might add, that you're eminently suited for. Now perhaps you've needed a break. We all do from time to time." He spread his fingers, tapped them together again. "But to lose sight of that goal, to settle in a position you're not only overqualified for, but unsuited for, is a waste of time and talent. Any adequate bookkeeper could handle the daily finances of a shop, and a high-school girl can ring up sales."

"You're right." Delighted to hear it all put into logical, unemotional terms, she smiled at him. "You're completely right, Mr. Bittle."

"Well, then, Kate, if you'd like a few more days to sort out your thoughts—"

"No, I've got them sorted. I've told myself basically the same thing you've just said to me. What I'm doing makes absolutely no sense. It's illogical, irrational and emotional. It's probably a mistake, too, but I have to make it. You see, it's our shop. Margo's and Laura's and mine. It's our dream."

CHAPTER 20

S HE COPPED A bottle of champagne from the shop, then decided to go one better and attempt to cook a meal. She had a tacit agreement with Byron that he would cook and she would wash up, as he was light-years ahead of her in culinary skills. But since this was to be a celebration of a new stage of her life, she wanted to give it a shot.

She'd always considered cooking a kind of mathematical skill. She could handle the formulas, like calculus, calculate the answer, but she didn't particularly enjoy the process.

Wrapped in a bib apron, her sleeves rolled up past the elbows, she lined up her ingredients like elements in a physics lab.

First the antipasto, she decided, and warily eyed the mushrooms she'd washed. It couldn't be easy to stuff them with cheese, but the recipe claimed it could be done. She removed the stems and chopped them fine, as directed. Following the steps she cooked them with the green onions and garlic and found herself smiling at the scent.

By the time she'd finished with the bread crumbs and cheese and spices, she was enthralled with herself.

It wasn't long before she was happily smearing the stuffing mixture into the caps, then popping them into the oven.

There were cucumbers to marinate, peppers to slice, tomatoes to deal with. Oh, right—and the olives. She fought with the lid on a jar of plump black olives, cursing it as the oven timer beeped. Out came the mushrooms.

She was in control, she told herself as she sucked on the thumb she'd brushed against the hot baking dish. It was just a matter of efficiency. What the hell came next?

She sliced cheese, struggled over the perfect consistency for the basil and olive oil she wanted for the bread she intended to serve.

An emergency call to Mrs. Williamson, the cook at Templeton House, calmed her down enough that she could arrange the antipasto meticulously on a platter.

Where the hell was Byron? she wondered and nibbled her nails over the recipe for pasta con pesto. "Coarsely chopped basil leaves," she read. What the devil did "coarsely chopped" mean, exactly? And why the hell did you have to grate Parmesan when anybody with half a brain could buy a nice can of it in the market? And where was she going to find pine nuts?

She found them in a labeled canister in his cupboard. She should have known he would have them. The man had everything that had to do with eating, preparing to eat, and serving eats. The carefully measured ingredients went into the blender. Deciding that a little prayer couldn't hurt, she closed one eye, sent it up, and hit the switch.

Everything whirled satisfactorily.

Smug now, Kate put water on to boil for the pasta and set the table.

"Excuse me," Byron said from the kitchen doorway. "I seem to have walked into the wrong house."

"Very funny."

The dogs, who had been keeping her company, and keeping an eye out for scraps, dashed to greet him. Since he'd followed his nose and his curiosity straight into the kitchen, he still had his briefcase with him. He set it aside now to pet the dogs and grin foolishly at Kate.

"You don't cook."

"'Don't' doesn't mean 'can't.'" Anxious for feedback, she took a mushroom off the platter and popped it into his mouth. "Well?"

"It's good."

"Good?" She arched a brow. "Just good?"

"Surprisingly good?" he ventured. "You're wearing an apron."

"Of course I'm wearing an apron. I'm not getting splatters all over me."

"You look so . . . domestic." He slid his hands over her shoulders, kissed her hello. "I like it."

"Don't get used to it. This is pretty much a one-shot deal." She went to the refrigerator to take out the champagne. "I remember when Josh went through this phase and wanted to marry Donna Reed."

"Donna Reed." After opening the door to let the dogs streak out, Byron settled on a stool. "Well, she did look pretty hot in those aprons, now that I think about it."

"He got over it and decided he'd rather go for Miss February." With a quick, efficient twist, she popped the cork. "Of course, he always wanted Margo anyway. Donna and Miss 42-D Cup were just distractions."

She took flutes out of the cabinet and turned back with a wicked grin. "Now, if I have the line right, I say, 'And how was your day, dear?'"

"It was good. This is better." He took the glass she'd filled for him, toasted her. "What's the occasion?"

"I'm glad you realize there has to be one for me to go through this mess." She blew out a breath as she looked around the kitchen. No matter that she'd tried to be careful, there was a hell of a cleanup in store. "Why do you do it? You know, cook."

"I enjoy it."

"You're a sick man, Byron."

"Your water's boiling, Donna."

"Oh, right." She picked up the clear canister of pasta, frowned at it. "You take this stuff out of the box and put it in here. Okay for aesthetics, I guess, but how am I supposed to know how much is ten ounces?"

"Estimate. I know that goes against the grain for you, but we all have to live dangerously now and again."

He watched her worry over it, started to tell her she was putting in too much, then shrugged. It was her dinner, after all. In any case, he found himself easily distracted by the way the neat bow of the apron strings accented her tidy little butt.

Just how would it look if she was naked under that sturdy white apron?

At his laugh, she glanced around. "What?"

"Nothing." He drank more wine. "Just an unexpected and slightly embarrassing fantasy. It passed. Mostly. Why don't you tell me what happened to set you off on this domestic campaign?"

"I'll tell you. I was—Shit, I forgot the bread." Her brow furrowed as she slid the pan into the oven, adjusted the heat and timer. "There's no way you can hold a conversation and deal with all the details of a meal in progress. Why don't you put on some music, light the candles. Do that kind of stuff while I finish this."

"All right." He rose, started out, turned back. "Katherine, about that little fantasy . . ." Amused at himself, he shook his head. "Maybe we'll try it later."

Too preoccupied to pay attention, she waved him away and got back to business.

She thought she'd managed very well when they were settled at the table, scents wafting, candles flickering, and Otis Redding crooning on the stereo. "I could handle doing this," she decided after she'd sampled and approved the pasta. "About once a year."

"It's fabulous, really. And very much appreciated. It's quite a feeling coming home to a pretty woman and a home-cooked meal."

"I had some excess energy." She broke bread, offered him half. "I thought about just dragging you up to the bedroom when you walked in, then I figured that could wait until after dinner. Anyway, I was hungry. My appetite's definitely improved in the last few months."

"So has your stress level," he commented. "You've stopped popping aspirin and antacids like candy."

It was true, she admitted. She had. And she certainly felt better than she remembered feeling in years. "Well, I've done something today that is going to either keep me on that same route or send me back to the pharmacy." She took a hard look at the bubbles in her wine, swallowed some. "I turned down the partnership."

"Did you?" He laid a hand over hers, toyed with her fingers. "Are you okay with that?"

"I think so." Out of curiosity she said, "You don't sound very surprised. I didn't know I was going to turn it down until I was sitting in Mr. Bittle's office."

"Maybe your head didn't know it, but your gut did. Or your heart. You've wrapped yourself up in Pretenses, Kate. It's yours. Why would you give it up to be a part of something someone else had built?"

"Because it's what I've always wanted, always aimed for." A bit unsure of him, she shrugged her shoulders. "It turned out it was enough just to know I was good enough. It's a little scary, changing directions this way."

"It's not that radical a change," he corrected. "You're partners in a business, in charge of accounts."

"My degree, all that education—"

"You don't really believe that's wasted, do you? It's part of who you are, Kate. You're just using it in a different way."

"I just couldn't go back to that office, to that—life," she decided. "It all seemed so rigid. Margo was in the shop today with the baby. People were fussing over him, and Margo was sitting there with the cradle beside her, and Laura had to look for this winged dragon, and I boxed a pocket watch and put away shoes . . ." Embarrassed, she trailed off. "I'm babbling. I never babble."

"It's all right. I get the drift. You're having fun working there, being part of it. You're enjoying the surprises of something you helped create."

"I never liked surprises. I always wanted to know the when, where, and how, so I could be prepared. You make mistakes if you aren't prepared, and I hate making mistakes."

"Are you doing something that feels right to you?"

"It looks that way."

"Well, then." He lifted his glass, touched it to hers. "Go for it."

"Wait until I tell Margo and Laura." The idea of it made her laugh. "Margo was gone when I got back, and Laura had to run pick up the girls, so I didn't have the chance. Of course, we're going to have to make some changes. It's ridiculous not to have a regular posted schedule of our work hours. And the pricing system needs to be completely overhauled. The new software I've just installed will completely streamline our—" She caught herself and found him grinning at her. "You can't change overnight."

"You shouldn't change at all. That's the kind of thing they need you for. Play to your strengths, kid. Which apparently include Italian cooking. This pesto is terrific."

"Really?" She sampled more herself. "It is kind of good. Well, maybe I could throw something together. On special occasions."

"You won't get an argument from me." Thoughtfully, he twirled pasta on his fork. "Speaking of special occasions, now that you're going to continue to be self-employed, you should be able to flex your schedule a bit. For a variety of reasons, I'm not going to be able to get back to Atlanta for Christmas, so I'm making plans to take a few days for the trip over Thanksgiving."

"That's nice." She refused to acknowledge the thud of disappointment. "I'm sure your family will be happy to have you, even for a few days."

"I'd like you to come with me."

"What?" Her fork paused halfway to her mouth.

"I'd like you to come to Atlanta with me for Thanksgiving and meet my family."

"I—I can't. I can't just fly across the country like that. There's not enough time to—"

"You have the best part of a month to arrange your schedule. Atlanta's not Bora Bora, Kate. It's Georgia."

"I know where Atlanta is," she said testily. "Look, besides the time factor, Thanksgiving's a family holiday. You don't just bring someone and dump them on your family on Thanksgiving."

"You're not someone," he said quietly. Oh, it was panic in her eyes, all right. He could read it perfectly. Though it irritated him, he determined to follow through. "It's traditional where I come from to invite the woman who's important to you to meet your family, to have them meet her. Particularly if it's the woman you're in love with and want to marry."

She jerked back as if scalded, nearly knocking over the chair as she sprang to her feet. "Wait a minute. Hold it. Whoa. Where did that come from? I cook one stupid meal and you get delusions of grandeur."

"I love you, Kate. I want to marry you. It would mean a great deal to me if you'd spend a few days with my family. I'm sure Margo and Laura would be willing to adjust the work schedule to accommodate a short trip over the holiday."

It took several tries before the sounds coming out of her mouth could be fashioned into words. "How can you sit there like that and calmly talk about scheduling in the same breath as marriage? Have you gone insane?"

"I thought you'd appreciate the practicality." Not sure who was irritating him more, himself or Kate, he topped off his wine.

"Well, I don't. So just stop it. I don't know where you got this brainstorm about marriage, but—"

"I wouldn't call it a brainstorm," he said, contemplating his glass. "I've given it quite a bit of thought."

"Oh, have you? Have you really?" Temper began to bubble beneath panic. Preferring it, Kate let it spew. "That's how you work, isn't it? That's how Byron De Witt works, in his quiet, thoughtful, *patient* way. I see it all now," she fumed, storming around the center island. "I can't believe I didn't see it all along. How clever you are, Byron. How canny. How fucking devious. You've just been reeling me in, haven't you? Taking over, step by little step."

"You're going to need to explain that for me. What have I taken over exactly?"

"Me! And don't think I can't see it all perfectly now. First it was sex. It's hard to think rationally when you're nothing more than one big throbbing gland."

He might have laughed, but instead carefully chose an olive. "As I recall, the sex was as much your idea as mine. More, actually, in the beginning."

"Don't try to confuse the issue," she spat out, slamming her hands on the counter.

"Far be it from me to confuse the issue with facts. Keep going."

"Then it was the let's-get-Kate-healthy campaign. Hospitals, damn doctors, medicine."

"I suppose it would be confusing the issue again to point out that you had an ulcer."

"I was handling it. I could have gotten myself to the doctor just fine on my own. Then you're cooking and feeding me all this healthy stuff. 'You've got to have a decent breakfast, Kate. You really should cut back on the coffee a little.' And before I know it I'm eating regular meals and exercising."

Byron ran his tongue around his teeth, stared down at his plate. "I'm so ashamed. Setting this diabolical trap for you. It's unforgivable."

"Don't you get glib with me, buster. You bought puppies. You tuned up my car."

He rubbed his hands over his face before he rose. "Now I got the dogs and fixed your car in order to blind you to my evil plot. Kate, you're making a fool of yourself."

"I am not. I know perfectly well when I'm making a fool of myself, and I'm not. You set everything up in clever little stages until I'm practically living here."

"Honey," he said with a mix of affection and exasperation, "you *are* living here."

"See?" She threw up her hands. "I'm living with you, without even realizing it. I'm cooking meals, for God's sake. I've never cooked for a man in my entire life."

"Haven't you?" Touched, he moved forward, reached for her.

"Don't you do that." Still blazing, she retreated behind the island. "You've got a hell of a nerve confusing things like this. I told you you weren't my type, that it wasn't going to work."

His patience straining, he rocked back on his heels. "The hell with types. It has been working, and you're perfectly aware of just how well it works with us. I love you, and if you weren't so damn pigheaded you'd admit that you love me."

"Don't you assume my feelings, De Witt."

"Fine. Then I'm in love with you. Deal with it."

"I don't have to deal with it. *You* have to deal with it. And as far as your half-assed proposal of marriage—"

"I didn't propose marriage," he said coolly. "I told you I want you to marry me. I didn't ask you. Just what are you afraid of, Kate? That I'm a replay of that jerk Thornhill who used you until something more appetizing came along?"

She went cold. "Just how do you know about Roger? You've been poking around in my business, haven't you? And why am I not surprised?"

It was no use biting his tongue now. Better, he thought, to play it out. "When someone is as important to me as you are, her business is important to me. Her welfare is important to me. So I made it my business to find out. You mentioned his name to Kusack, I've kept in touch with Kusack."

"You've kept in touch with Kusack," she repeated. "You know it was Roger who set me up."

He nodded. "And apparently so do you."

"I just figured it out this afternoon. But at a guess I'd say you've known a bit longer and didn't find it necessary to mention it to me."

"The trail led back to him. A personal clash between the two of you, access to your office. He made phone calls to New Hampshire around the time you were told about your father."

"How do you know about the phone calls?"

"Josh's investigator accessed the information."

"Josh's investigator," she repeated. "So Josh knows, too. But still no one thought it necessary to pass any of this handy information along to me."

"It wasn't passed to you because you'd have stormed right up into Thornhill's face and blasted him." The way, Byron admitted, he'd wanted to take Thornhill's face apart with his fists. "We didn't want him tipped off before the investigation is complete."

"You didn't want," she shot back. "Too bad, because I've already blasted him and ruined your neat plans. You had no right to work around me, to take over my life."

"I have every right to do whatever I can to protect you, and to help you. And that's what I've done. That's what I'm going to continue to do."

"Whether I like it or not."

"Essentially. I'm not Roger Thornhill. I'm not, and I've never used you for anything."

"No, you're not a user, Byron. Do you know what you are? You're a handler. That's what you do, you handle people. It's what makes you so good at your job—that patience, that charm, that skill at easing people onto your side of an issue without them ever really seeing they've been maneuvered. Well, here's a flash for you. I will not be handled. I sure as hell won't be maneuvered into marriage."

"Just a damn minute."

He shifted to block her path before she could storm out. When he closed his fingers around her arm, she yelped. Afraid that he'd misjudged his strength in temper, he jerked back holding her arm much more gently. But the bruises he saw on her arm were already formed. The haze that smothered his brain was dark and ugly.

"What the hell is this?" he demanded.

Her heart thudded hard into her throat as his eyes snapped to hers. "Let go of me."

"Who put these marks on you?"

Her chin angled in defense. The fury hardening his eyes was as lethal as the slice of a well-honed sword. "I've seen your white knight routine already, Byron. I'm not interested in a reprise."

"Who touched you?" he said, spacing each word carefully.

"Someone else who couldn't take no for an answer," she snapped. She regretted the words, bitterly, before they were fully formed. But it was too late. His eyes went carefully blank. Smoothly, he stepped out of her path.

"You're mistaken." His voice was cool and calm and deliberate. "I can take no for an answer. And since that seems to be the case, we don't seem to have anything left to discuss."

"I'll apologize for that." She felt the heat of shame burning her cheeks. "It was uncalled for. But I don't appreciate your interference in my business, or your assumption that I'd just fall into your plans."

"Understood." Hurt was a rusty ball of heat in his gut. "As I said, that seems to end it. It's clear you were right from the beginning. We want different things, and this isn't going to work." He walked over to the table, more to distance himself from her than because he wanted the wine he picked up and drank. "You can get your things now or at your convenience."

"I—" She stared at him, stunned that he could close the door between them so neatly. "I don't—I can't—I'm going," she managed and fled.

He listened for the slam of the door, then sat, as carefully as an old man. He put his head back, closed his eyes. It was a wonder, he thought, that she could assume he was such a brilliant strategist when a blind man on a galloping horse could see just how badly he'd bungled it.

SHE WENT HOME, of course. Where else did you go when you were wounded? The scene she burst in on in the parlor was so cheerful, so familial, so much what she had just been offered and refused, that she wanted to scream.

Josh sat in the wing chair near the fire, the pretty lights from the flickering flames playing over him and his sleeping son. Laura, her younger daughter at her feet, poured coffee into pretty china cups. Margo snuggled on the end of the couch with Ali so they could pore over a fashion magazine together.

"Kate." Laura glanced up with a welcoming smile. "You're just in time for coffee. I bribed Josh to bring the baby over with one of Mrs. Williamson's honey-glazed hams."

"He might have left a few scraps," Margo added. "If you're hungry."

"I only had seconds."

"You had seconds twice, Uncle Josh," Kayla pointed out, and got up, as she had every few minutes, to peek at the baby.

"Stool pigeon." He tweaked her nose.

"Aunt Kate's mad." Ali straightened up on the couch in anticipation. "You're mad at somebody, aren't you, Aunt Kate? Your face is red."

"So it is," Margo drawled when she took a closer look. "And I think I hear her teeth grinding."

"Out." Kate pointed a finger at Josh. "You and I, we're going to go round later, but right now, go away and take your testosterone with you."

"I never go anywhere without it," he said easily. "And I'm comfortable right here."

"I don't want to see a man. If I do see a man in the next sixty seconds, I'll have to kill him with my bare hands."

He sniffed, feigning insult. But he rose. "I'm taking J. T. into the library for port and cigars. We're going to talk about sports and power tools."

"Can I come, Uncle Josh?"

"Of course." He gave Kayla his free hand. "I'm no sexist."

"Bedtime in thirty minutes, Kayla," Laura called out. "Ali, why don't you go keep Uncle Josh company until bedtime?"

"I want to stay here." She poked out her bottom lip and folded her arms over her chest. "I don't have to leave just because Aunt Kate's going to shout and swear. I'm not a baby."

"Let her stay." Kate made a grand, sweeping gesture with her arms. "She can't learn too early what men are really like."

"Yes, she can," Laura corrected. "Allison, go into the library with your uncle or go upstairs and have your bath."

"I always have to do what you say. I hate it." Ali stormed out, stomping up the stairs to sulk alone.

"Well, that was pleasant," Laura murmured, and wondered yet again what had happened to her sweet, compliant Ali. "What cheerful note would you like to add to that, Kate?"

"Men are pigs." She grabbed a cup of coffee and downed it like whiskey.

CHAPTER 21

"AND YOUR POINT is?" Margo said after a long moment.

"What do we need them for, anyway? What possible purpose do they have other than procreation, and with advances in technology we'll be taking care of that in a lab soon."

"Very pleasant," Laura decided and poured another cup. "Perhaps we don't need them for sex, but I still depend on them for large-insect disposal."

"Speak for yourself," Margo put it. "I'd rather kill spiders than give up sex. What crime did Byron commit, Kate, or do we get to guess?"

"The sneak, the conniving son of a bitch. I can't believe I was idiot enough to fall into a relationship with a man like that. You never really know a person, do you, never really know what's behind their beady little eyes?"

"Kate, what did he do? Whatever it is, I'm sure it's not as bad as you think." As Kate tore off her coat, Laura's gaze settled on the bruises. She was on her feet in a blink. "Dear God, Kate, did he hit you?"

"What? Oh." She dismissed the bruises with a wave of the hand. "No, of course he didn't hit me. I got this bumping into something warped at Bittle. Byron wouldn't hit a woman. It's too direct an approach for someone like him."

"Well, what for Christ's sake did he do?" Margo demanded.

"I'll tell you what he did. I'll tell you what he did," she repeated as she stormed around the room. "He asked me to marry him." When this was met with silence, she whirled. "Did you hear what I said? He asked me to marry him."

Laura considered. "And he has, what, a closet full of the heads of his former wives?"

"You are not listening to me. You are not getting it." Struggling for calm, Kate breathed deep, pushed at her hair. "Okay, he cooks, pushes vitamins on me, gets me working out. He gets my juices all stirred up so I'm ready to fall onto any handy surface and have incredible sex. He goes to see Kusack, he's been working with Josh behind my back, tries to get all the worry out of my life. He sees to it that I have a closet so that I can just start leaving my clothes over there. Of course, he's bought that house," she continued, pacing. "And those damn dogs that anyone with half a heart would fall for. My car hasn't run better since the day I drove it off the lot. And regularly, so you hardly notice, he brings flowers home."

"Not flowers." Margo pressed a hand to her breast. "Good God, the man is a fiend. He must be stopped."

"Just shut up, Margo. I know you're not on my side. You're never on my side." Certain of Laura's loyalty, Kate dropped down on her knees in front of her, clutched her hands. "He asked me to go with him to Atlanta over Thanksgiving and meet his parents. He says he loves me and wants me to marry him."

"Darling." All sympathy, Laura pressed Kate's hands. "I can see that you've been through an ordeal tonight. Obviously the man is deranged. I'm sure Josh can arrange to have him committed."

Stunned, Kate yanked her hands away. "You have to be on my side," she insisted.

"You want me to feel sorry for you?" The flash of anger in Laura's eyes had Kate blinking.

"No—yes. I—no. I just want you to understand."

"I'll tell you what I understand. You have a man who loves you. A good, considerate, thoughtful man who's willing to share the burdens of living as well as the pleasures with you. Who wants you, who cares enough to make an effort to make you happy, to make your life run a little more smoothly. One who wants you in bed and out. One who cares enough to want you to meet his family because he loves them and wants to show you off to them. And that's not good enough for you?"

"No, I didn't say that. It's just . . ." She got to her feet, staggered by the heat. "I didn't plan—"

"That's your problem." Laura—small, delicate-boned, and furious—rose as well. "It has to be in tidy order in Kate's plan. Well, life's messy."

"I know. I meant—"

Riding on a fury and frustration she herself hadn't guessed at, Laura barreled over Kate's protest. "And if you don't think yours is adequate, try mine. Try having nothing." And her voice was bitter. "An empty marriage, a man who wanted your name more than you and didn't even pretend otherwise after he had you. Try coming home every night knowing there's not going to be anyone there to hold you, that all the problems that need fixing come to you, that you have no one to lean on. And having your daughter blame you for not being good enough to keep her father under the same roof."

She stalked over to stare at the crackling flames of the fire while her friends watched in silence. "Try feeling unloved, unwanted, and crawling into bed every night wondering how you're going to make it work, how you can possibly make it right again, then come crying to me."

"I'm sorry," Kate murmured. "Laura, I'm so sorry."

"No." Exhausted and ashamed, Laura moved away from Kate's comforting hand and sat again. "No, I'm sorry. I don't know where that came from." She leaned her head back against the cushion a moment, her eyes shut as the last of the temper drained away. "Yes, I do. Maybe I'm jealous." She opened her eyes again and managed a smile. "Or maybe I just think you're stupid."

"I should have moved back in here after Peter left," Kate began. "I should have realized how much you were dealing with alone."

"Oh, stop. It's not about me. I'm just a little raw." Laura rubbed her aching temples. "That wasn't the first go-round Ali and I had today. It makes me edgy."

"I can move in now." Kate sat down beside Laura.

"Not that you're not welcome," Laura told her, "but you're not moving in."

"Blocked that escape route," Margo murmured.

"I'm not looking for escape." Kate struggled to get a grip on her tumbling emotions. "I could help with the girls, share the expenses."

"No. This is my life." Laura grimaced. "Such as it is. You have your own. If you don't love Byron, that's one thing. You can't tailor your feelings to suit him."

"Are you kidding?" Margo reached for the coffeepot. "She's been cross-eyed over him for months."

"So what? Emotions aren't any guarantee when it comes to something as big as marriage. They weren't enough for Laura." Kate sighed, shrugged. "I'm sorry, but they weren't."

"No, they weren't. If you want guarantees, send in your warranty card when you buy a toaster."

"Okay, you're right, but that's not the whole point. Can't you see he was playing me? He's been handling me all through this relationship."

Margo made a low feline sound. "Being handled by a strong, gorgeous man. Poor you."

"You know very well what I mean. You'd never let Josh push all the buttons, make all the moves. I'm telling you that Byron has a way of undermining things so that I'm sliding along in the direction he's chosen before I realize it."

"So change directions if you don't like the destination," Margo suggested.

"He called me a detour once." Remembering, Kate scowled. "He said he liked taking long, interesting detours. I actually thought it was sort of charming."

"Why don't you go back and talk this out with him instead of arguing?" Laura tilted her head, well able to imagine the scene that had taken place in Byron's kitchen. "He's probably feeling just as unhappy and frustrated as you are."

"I can't." Kate shook her head. "He told me to pick up my things at my convenience."

"Ouch." Margo looked at Kate with genuine sympathy now. "In that polite, mannerly tone of his?"

"Exactly. It's the worst. Besides, I don't know what I'd say to him. I don't know what I want." At a loss, she buried her face in her hands. "I keep thinking I know what I want, then it shifts on me. I'm tired. It's too hard to think rationally when I'm tired."

"Then talk to him tomorrow. You'll stay here tonight." Laura rose. "I have to put the girls to bed."

"She's made me so ashamed," Kate murmured when she was alone with Margo.

"I know." Margo slid closer. "At least all she made me feel was like killing Peter Ridgeway if he ever shows his sorry face around here."

"I didn't realize she was still so hurt, so unhappy."

"She'll be all right." Margo patted Kate's knee. "We'll see to it."

"I'm, ah, not going to go into another accounting firm."

"Of course you're not."

"Everybody seems to know what I'm going to do before I do," Kate griped. "Bittle offered me a partnership."

"Congratulations."

"I turned him down this afternoon."

"My, my." Margo's million-dollar smile flashed. "Haven't we had a busy day!"

"And Roger Thornhill is the embezzler."

"What?" Margo's cup clinked into its saucer. "That slimy weasel who two-timed you with your own client?"

"The very same." It pleased Kate to see that she could say something that got a rise out of Margo. "It was the way he acted when I ran into him at Bittle today. He's smart enough to have figured out how to siphon funds, and I was his main competition for the partner slot. He gets a little playing money and screws me at the same time."

"You've been to Kusack with this?"

"No, apparently Byron, the cop, and your husband, whom I will deal with shortly, already knew."

"And left you in the dark." Understanding perfectly, Margo pulled Kate to her feet. "Occasionally men have to be reminded that they are no longer hunting out of caves, fighting dragons, or blazing trails west while we huddle around the fire. I'll help you remind Josh."

AT NINE FORTY-FIVE the next morning, Kate opened the till at Pretenses. She would run the shop alone that morning. She took some pride in her competence. Laura was at her office at the hotel, and Margo remained on maternity leave. She decided to relish these last few minutes before she unlocked the door, turned the sign to Open.

She'd brought her own CD's. Margo preferred classical. Kate preferred the classics. The Beatles, the Stones, Cream. After putting the music on, she went into the powder room, filled the copper watering can. She was going to enjoy the pleasant little duties of nurturing an elegant business, she told herself.

She was not going to think about Byron De Witt.

He was in the penthouse suite by now. Probably in some meeting or on a conference call. He might be glancing over an itinerary for a trip to San Francisco. Didn't he say he had to fly up?

Didn't matter, she reminded herself, and stepped out on the veranda to water the tubs of pansies and impatiens. He could fly anywhere he wanted—to the moon, for that matter. Her interest in his affairs was over. Finished. A closed book.

She had her life to worry about, didn't she? After all, she was beginning a whole new phase. A new career with a new goal to aim for. She had dozens of ideas to improve and expand the shop floating around in her head. Once Margo was back in gear, they would have a meeting. An efficiency meeting. Then there was the fashion show right around the corner. The advertising had to be placed. They needed to discuss other promotions for the holidays.

What they needed was a regular weekly brainstorming and progress meeting. She would set it up, fix it into the schedule. You couldn't run a successful business without regular structured meetings. You couldn't run a life without structure, without specific plans and goals.

Why the hell couldn't he see that she had specific plans and goals? How could he have thrown marriage at her, knocking down all of her carefully placed pins?

You didn't marry someone you'd known barely a full year. There were stages to a relationship, careful, cautious, and sensible stages. Maybe, just maybe, after two years, after you'd worked out the kinks in the relationship, after you fully understood each other's faults and foibles and had learned to accept them or compromise on them, you began to *discuss* the possibility of marriage.

You had to outline what you wanted out of marriage, assign roles and duties. Who handled the marketing, who paid the bills, who took out the trash, for God's sake. Marriage was a business, a partnership, a full-scale commitment. Sensible people didn't just jump into it without first fine-tuning the details.

And what about children? It was obvious who had the children—if there were going to be children—but what about assignment of responsibilities? Diapers and laundry, feedings and doctors' appointments. If you didn't nail down the details of responsibilities, you had nothing but chaos—and a baby needing to be taken care of by a responsible adult.

A baby. Oh, God, what would it be like to have a baby? She didn't know anything about having a baby. Think of all the books she would have to read, all the mistakes she was bound to make. There were so many . . . things you had to have for a baby. Strollers and car seats and cribs.

And all those adorable little clothes, she thought dreamily.

"You're drowning those pansies, Ms. Powell."

She jerked back, slopping water on her shoes. She stared blankly at Kusack while her mind whirled. She had just all but named a baby she hadn't conceived with a man she didn't intend to conceive it with.

"Daydreaming?" His lips curved in that now familiar paternal fashion.

"No, I—" She wasn't a daydreamer. She was a thinker. A doer. "I've got a lot on my mind."

"Bet you do. Thought I'd catch you before you opened up. Do you mind if we go inside?"

"No, of course not." Still fumbling, she set the watering can down and opened the door. "It's just me today. My partners are—aren't here."

"I wanted to talk to you alone. I didn't mean to spook you, Ms. Powell."

"No, that's all right." Her speeding heart seemed to have settled back to a reasonable rate. "What can I do for you, Detective?"

"Actually, I just came by to catch you up on the progress of the investigation. I figured after the trouble you went through, you deserve to know how it panned out."

"Well, that makes one of you," she murmured.

"Your boyfriend nudged me toward Roger Thornhill."

"He's not my boyfriend," Kate said quickly, then set her teeth. "If you're referring to Mr. De Witt."

"I am." He smiled a bit sheepishly and tugged on his ear. "I never know how to refer to these kinds of things. Anyway, Mr. De Witt nudged me toward Thornhill. Fact is, I was already looking in that direction. You don't look shocked speechless by the news," he commented.

"I figured it out yesterday." She shrugged her shoulders, discovering it simply didn't matter any longer.

"Thought you would. Thornhill's got a little gambling problem. Gambling's one of the best reasons to need quick money."

"Roger gambles?" That did shock her. "You mean he bets on horse races, that sort of thing?"

"He bets on Wall Street, Ms. Powell. And he's been losing steady for the past couple of years. Overplayed his hand, so to speak, and lost his ante. Then there was his personal relationship with you. Then add in the information about your father and the fact that he was the one who found the newspaper article in your office and passed it to Bittle."

"Really." She nodded. "I didn't know that."

"A little too pat, to my way of thinking. Connections usually aren't coincidences in my line of work. You had a little run-in with him yesterday at Bittle."

"And how do you know about that?"

"Ms. Newman. She's got good eyes and ears, and a sharp nose." He grinned. "I asked her to report any unusual incident, officewise. She's another who didn't like the way Thornhill smelled, so to speak. And she stood by you from the start."

"Excuse me?" Kate tapped her ear as though her hearing had gone suddenly off. "Newman stood by me?"

"First interview I had with her on this business, she said if I was looking in your direction I was looking in the wrong one. She said Katherine Powell wouldn't steal so much as a paper clip."

"I see. I always thought she disliked me."

"I don't know whether she likes you or not, but she respects you."

"Are you going to bring Roger in for questioning, then?"

"Already have. I had to move a little quicker after I learned you'd had a face-off with him. So I paid him a little visit last night. He was already packed and on his way to the airport."

"You're kidding."

"No, ma'am. Had reservations for a flight to Rio. He's been living on the edge since you were cleared. Whatever you said to him at the office yesterday broke his nerve. He lawyered himself pretty quick, but we figure to cut a deal by the end of the day. They call this sort of thing a victimless crime. I guess that's a misnomer this time around."

"I don't feel like a victim," Kate murmured. "I don't know what I feel."

"Well, I'd feel right pissed—if you'll pardon my French. But . . ." He shrugged his shoulders. "His career's in the toilet, and he's going to be paying off fines and his lawyer for a long time to come. And the federal government is going to have him as their guest for a while."

"He'll go to prison." As her father would have gone to prison, she thought. For a mistake, an error in judgment. A moment of greed.

"Like I said, we're cutting a deal, but I don't see him walking away without doing some time. You know, the way things work today, you could sue him yourself. Defamation of character, emotional pain and suffering, all that. Your lawyer would tell you."

"I'm not interested in suing Roger. I'm interested in turning the page."

"I figured that." He smiled at her again. "You're a nice woman, Ms. Powell. It's been a pleasure meeting you, even under the circumstances."

She thought about it. "I suppose I have to say the same, Detective Kusack. Even under the circumstances."

He stepped toward the door, stopped. "It's about opening time, isn't it?"

She glanced at her watch. "Just about."

"I wonder . . ." He tugged on his ear again. "My wife's got this birthday coming up. Tomorrow, actually."

"Detective Kusack," she beamed at him, "you've come to the right place."

KATE TOLD HERSELF she felt wonderful, revived. All of her troubles were behind her. She was starting the next phase of her life.

There was no reason to be nervous about going to Byron's. It was the middle of the day—lunchtime. He wouldn't be home. She would simply pick up her things, as he'd requested, and thereby close that chapter cleanly.

She would not regret. It was fun while it lasted, nothing lasted forever, all good things came to an end.

And if another cliché popped into her mind, she would scream.

She pulled into his driveway. The key she had meticulously removed from her own ring was in her pocket. But when she reached in to pull it out, she found herself holding Seraphina's coin. Baffled, she stared at it. She would have sworn she'd put that in the top drawer of her jewelry box.

She turned it in her hand. The sun caught the edge and shot out dazzling light. That was why her eyes watered, she told herself. It was the reflection off the gold, and she'd taken off her sunglasses. It wasn't because she felt a sudden, wrenching connection to that young girl, standing on the cliff, ready to throw her life away.

Kate Powell was not throwing her life away, she told herself firmly. She was facing it. Only the weak tossed away hope. She had years of happiness left in her life. Years. And she was not going to stand here and cry over some old coin and a misty legend.

This was reality. She blinked back tears. Her reality, and she knew exactly what she was doing.

She found the key, replaced the coin in her pocket. But it was harder than she'd imagined to use the key, knowing it would be the last time.

It was just a house, she thought. There was no reason for her to love it, no reason to feel this aching sense of welcome when she opened the door. There was no reason at all for her to walk to the glass doors and want to weep because the pups were napping in the sunshine.

And geraniums were blooming in gray stone pots. Wind chimes of copper and brass sang in the breeze from the sea. Shells that she had gathered with Byron from the beach were arranged in a wide-mouthed glass bowl on the redwood table.

It was so perfect, she realized, so simply perfect. That was why she wanted to weep.

When the dogs' heads popped up in unison, and they scrambled up to bark and race, she realized she hadn't heard the car. But they had. They reacted just that way whenever they recognized the sound of Byron's return home.

Jolted with panic, she turned around and faced the door as he came in.

"I'm sorry," she said immediately. "I didn't realize you'd be home early."

"I don't suppose you did." But he'd known, thanks to Laura's call, that she would be there.

"I came to get my things. I . . . I thought it best to come by when you were at work. So it would be less awkward."

"It's awkward now." He stepped toward her, eyes narrowed. "You've been crying."

"No, not really. It was . . ." Her fingers slid into her pocket, touched the coin. "It was something else entirely. And then I guess it was the dogs. They looked so sweet sleeping in the yard." They were at the door now, tails waving furiously. "I'll miss them."

"Sit down."

"No, I really can't. I want to get back to the shop, and . . . and I do want to apologize, Byron, for shouting at you the way I did. I really am sorry for that, and I'd hate to think we couldn't at least be civil." She closed her eyes on her own absurdity. "This is very awkward."

He wanted to touch her, badly wanted to touch her. But he knew his own limitations. If he so much as brushed his hand over that short cap of hair, he would want to touch more, have to touch more until he was holding her against him and begging.

"Then let's try being civil. If you won't sit, we'll stand. There are a few things I'd like to say." He watched her open her eyes, saw the wariness in them. What the hell did she see when she looked at him? he wondered. Why couldn't he tell?

"I'm going to apologize as well. I handled things badly last night. And at the risk of getting kicked in the teeth again, I admit that you weren't that far off the mark in some of your, let's call them . . . observations about my character."

He walked to the doors, jingling the change in his pocket. The dogs, still hopeful, sat sentry on the other side of the glass. "I do plan things out. We have that in common. I admit I eased you into living here. It seemed to me that it would help both of us get used to it. Because I wanted you here."

When he turned back to her, she struggled for a reply, but found none.

"I wanted to take care of you. You see vulnerability as a weakness. I see it as a soft, appealing side of a strong, intelligent, and resilient woman. It's in my nature to protect, to fix—or at least try to fix—what's wrong. I can't change that for you."

"I don't want you to change, Byron. But I can't change either. I'm always going to resist being guided along, however well intentioned it might be."

"And when I see someone I love stressed out to the point of illness, taken advantage of, hurt, I'm going to do whatever it takes to turn it around. And when I want something, when I know it's right, I'm going to work toward making it happen. I love you, Kate."

Her heart swam into her eyes, filled them. "I don't know how to handle this. I don't know what to do. I can't figure it out."

"I've figured it out. You know, every once in a while it doesn't hurt to let someone else figure it out."

"Maybe. I don't know. But there were points in all of this I had to come to myself. I didn't even realize some of them. They've arrested Roger."

"I know."

"Of course you do." She tried to laugh, then turned away. "When Kusack came by and told me, I wasn't sure how I felt at first. Relieved, vindicated—but there was more. I thought of my father. He'd have gone to jail, just as Roger will go. It's the same crime, the same punishment. They're both thieves."

"Kate—"

"No, let me finish. It's taken me so long to get here. My father made a mistake, a criminal mistake. As much as it hurts me to know that, I also know that he never tried to shift the blame, implicate anyone else. He wasn't like Roger. He would have faced what he'd done, and he would have paid for it. I realized today that that made all the difference. I can live with that, and forgive, and remember what he was to me for the first eight years of my life. He was my father, and he loved me."

"You're a beautiful woman, Katherine."

She shook her head, brushed away tears. "I had to get that out. It seems I can always pull out what's inside me and hand it to you. It worries me how easy it is to do that."

"You worry too much. Let's see if I can help there. We'll try a simple logic test. I'm thirty-five years old. I've never been married, never been engaged, never formally lived with a woman before. Why?"

"I don't know." She dragged her hands through her hair, fighting to use intellect over emotion as she turned back to him. "There could be a dozen reasons. You resisted commitment, you were too busy sampling southern delights, you were too focused on your career."

"It could have been any of those," he agreed. "But I'll tell you what it comes down to. I don't like to make mistakes any more than you do. I'm sure there are other women I could be happy with, build a decent life with. But that isn't enough. I waited, because I had this image, this dream about the woman I'd share my life with."

"You're not going to tell me I was that image because I know very well I wasn't." She stared blankly at the handkerchief he offered. "What?"

"You're crying again." When she snatched it away and mopped at her face, he continued. "Some of us are more flexible in our dreams and can even enjoy when they take a different shape. Look at me, Kate," he said gently and drew her gaze to his. "I've been waiting for you."

"That's not fair." She pressed crossed hands to her swelling heart as she backed away. "It's not fair to say things like that to me."

"We said civil. We didn't say anything about fair."

"I don't want to feel this way. I don't want to hurt this way. Why won't you just let me think?"

"Think about this." He did touch her now, drawing her in until their faces were close. "I love you." And kissed her. "I want to spend my life with you. I want to take care of you and be taken care of."

"I'm not the kind of woman people say those things to." She thumped her hand on his chest. "Why can't you see that?"

He'd have to make sure she got used to hearing those things, coming from him. His lips curved as he ran his hands up her back.

"No. I see it." She jerked back out of reach. "I can actually see that look come into your eyes. Kate needs to be soothed and stroked and eased into it. Well, it's not going to work. It's just not going to work. I've just got things sorted out," she fumed, stalking around the room. "I've got the shop. Isn't it enough of a shock to deal with that I love being there? How am I supposed to suddenly adjust to all of this? There aren't any rules to being in love. Oh, I figured that out all right, tossing and turning all night because you'd told me to pick up my things at my convenience." She spun back and seared him with a look. "Oh, that was low."

"Yes, it was." He grinned at her now, delighted with the image of her spending as miserable a night as he had. "I'm pleased to see it hit the mark. You hurt me last night."

"See? That's just what happens when you get tangled up in love. You hurt each other. I didn't ask to be in love with you, did I? I didn't plan it. And now I can't bear the idea of being without you, of not sitting at the table in the morning watching you cook breakfast, or listening to you tell me to concentrate when you've got me lifting those damn weights. Walking on the beach with you and those mangy dogs. And I want a baby."

Stunned, he waited a beat. "Now?"

"You see? You see what you've done?" She sank onto the couch and buried her face in her hands. "Listen to what I'm saying. I'm a mess. I'm insane. I'm in love with you."

"I know all that, Kate." He sat beside her, pulled her into his lap. "It suits me just fine."

"What if it doesn't suit me? I could really screw this up."

"That's okay." He kissed her cheek, nuzzled her head on his shoulder. "I'm good at fixing things. Why don't we look at the big picture and work on the details as we go along?"

She sighed, closed her eyes, and felt blissfully at home. "Maybe you'll be the one to screw it up."

"Then you'll be there to put everything back in place. I depend on you."

"You—" Those words, the look in his eyes that showed he meant them, were more powerful to her than any declaration of love. "I want you to. I need to know you do, and will. But marriage—"

"Is a practical, logical step," he finished and made her smile.

"It is not. And besides, you never asked me."

"I know." He smiled back at her. "If I asked you, there's a possibility you would say no. I'm not going to let you say no."

"You're just going to ease me into it until it's a done deal."

"That's the idea."

"It's pretty smart," she murmured, feeling the beat of his heart under her palm. Fast and not quite steady, she realized. Maybe he was just as nervous as she was. "I guess since most of my stuff's here already anyway, and I love you so much and I've gotten used to your cooking, it isn't such a bad idea. Being married, I mean. To you. So, it looks like your idea worked."

"Thank God." He pressed her hand to his lips. "I have been waiting for you, Kate, all my life."

"I know. I've been waiting right back."

He tilted her head back and smiled into her eyes. "Welcome home."

FINDING THE DREAM

PROLOGUE

*I*T WAS A *long way for a man to travel. Not only the miles from San Diego to the cliffs outside of Monterey, Felipe thought, but the years. So many years.*

Once, he had been young enough to walk confidently along the rocks, to climb, even to race. Defying the fates, celebrating the rush of wind, the crash of waves, the dizzying heights. The rocks had bloomed for him in spring once. There had been flowers to pick for Seraphina then, and he could remember, with the clear vision of age looking back to youth, how she had laughed and clutched the tough little wildflowers to her breast as if they were precious roses plucked from a well-tended bush.

His eyes were weak now, and his limbs were frail. But not his memory. A strong, vital memory in an old body was his penance. Whatever joy he had found in his life had been tainted, always, with the sound of Seraphina's laughter, with the trust in her dark eyes. With her young, uncompromising love.

In the more than forty years since he had lost her, and the part of himself that was innocence, he had learned to accept his own failings. He had been a coward, running from battle rather than facing the horrors of war, hiding among the dead rather than lifting a sword.

But he had been young, and such things had to be forgiven in the young.

He had allowed his friends and family to believe him dead, slain like a warrior—even a hero. It had been shame, and pride, that caused him to do so. Small things, pride and shame. Life was made up of so many small blocks. But he could never forget that it was that shame and that pride that cost Seraphina her life.

Weary, he sat on a rock to listen. To listen to the roar of water battling rock far below, to listen to the piercing cry of gulls, the rush of wind through winter grass. And the air was chilled as he closed his eyes and opened his heart.

To listen for Seraphina.

She would always be young, a lovely dark-eyed girl who had never had the chance to grow old, as he was old now. She hadn't waited, but in despair and grief had thrown herself into the sea. For love of him, he thought now. For reckless youth that hadn't lived long enough to know that nothing lasts forever.

Believing him dead, she had died, hurling herself and her future onto the rocks.

He had mourned her, God knew he had mourned her. But he hadn't been able to follow her into the sea. Instead, he had traveled south, given up his name and his home, and made new ones.

He had found love again. Not the sweet first blush of love that he had had with Seraphina, but something solid and strong, built on those small blocks of trust and understanding and on needs both quiet and violent.

And he had done his best.

He had children, and grandchildren. He had a life with all the joys and sorrows that make a man. He had survived to love a woman, to raise a family, to plant gardens. He was content with what had grown from him.

But he had never forgotten the girl he had loved. And killed. He had never forgotten their dream of a future or the sweet, innocent way she had given herself to him. When they had loved in secret, both of them so young, so fresh, they dreamed of the life they would have together, the home they would build with her dowry, the children they would make.

But war came, and he left her to prove himself a man. And proved himself a coward instead.

She had hidden her bride gift, the symbol of hope that a young girl treasures, to keep it out of American hands. Felipe had no doubt where she had hidden it. He had understood his Seraphina—her logic, her sentiment, her strengths and weaknesses. Though it had meant that he was penniless when he left Monterey, he had not taken the gold and jewels Seraphina had secreted.

Now, with the dreams of age that had turned his hair to silver, that had dimmed his eyes and lived in his aching bones, he prayed that it would be found one day by lovers. Or dreamers. If God was just, He would allow Seraphina to choose. Whatever the Church preached, Felipe refused to believe God would condemn a grieving child for the sin of suicide.

No, she would be as he had left her more than forty years ago on these very cliffs. Forever young and beautiful and full of hope.

He knew he would not return to this place. His time of penance was almost at an end. He hoped when he saw his Seraphina again, she would smile at him and forgive a young man's foolish pride.

He rose, bending in the wind, leaning on his cane to keep his feet under him. And left the cliffs to Seraphina.

THERE WAS A storm brewing, marching across the sea. A summer storm, full of power and light and wild wind. In that eerie luminescent light, Laura Templeton sat content on the rock. Summer storms were the best.

They would have to go in soon, back to Templeton House, but for now, she and her two closest friends would wait and watch. She was sixteen, a delicately built girl with quiet gray eyes and bright blond hair. And as full of energy as any storm.

"I wish we could get in the car and drive right into it," Margo Sullivan laughed. The wind was fitful and growing stronger. "Right into it."

"Not with you behind the wheel," Kate Powell sneered. "You've only had your license a week, and you already have a rep as a lunatic."

"You're just jealous because it'll be months before you can drive."

Because it was true, Kate shrugged. Her short black hair fluttered in the wind. She took a deep gulp of air, loving the way it thickened and churned. "At least I'm saving up for a car, instead of cutting out pictures of Ferraris and Jaguars."

"If you're going to dream," Margo said, frowning at a minute chip in the coral polish on her nails, "dream big. I'll have a Ferrari one day, or a Porsche, or whatever I want." Her summer-blue eyes narrowed with determination. "I won't settle for some secondhand junker like you would."

Laura let them argue. She could have defused the sniping, but she understood it was simply part of the friendship. And she didn't care about cars. Not that she didn't enjoy the spiffy little convertible her parents had given her for her sixteenth birthday. But one car was the same as another to her.

She realized it was easier, in her position. She was the daughter of Thomas and Susan Templeton, of the Templeton hotel empire. Her home loomed on the hill behind her, stunning under the churning gray sky. It was more than the stone and wood and glass that composed it. More than the turrets and balconies and lush gardens. More than the fleet of servants who kept it shining.

It was home.

But she had been raised to understand the responsibilities of privilege. Within her was a great love of beauty and symmetry, and a kindness. Aligned with that was a need to live up to Templeton standards, to deserve all she'd been given by birthright. Not only the wealth, which even at sixteen she understood, but also the love of her family, her friends.

She knew Margo always fretted at limitations. Though they had grown up together at Templeton House, as close as sisters, Margo was the daughter of the housekeeper.

Kate had come to Templeton House when her parents had been killed. An eight-year-old orphan. She was cherished, absorbed into the family, as much a part of the Templetons as Laura and her older brother, Josh.

Laura and Margo and Kate were as close as—perhaps closer than—sisters who shared blood. But Laura never forgot that the Templeton responsibility was hers.

And one day, she thought, she would fall in love, marry, and have children. She would carry on the Templeton tradition. The man who came for her, who swept her up in his arms, who made her belong to him, would be everything she'd ever wanted. Together they would build a life, create a home, carve out a future as polished and perfect as Templeton House.

As she pictured it, dreams budded in her heart. Delicate color bloomed on her cheeks while the wind tossed her blond curls around them.

"Laura's dreaming again," Margo commented. Her grin flashed, transforming her striking face to stunning.

"Got Seraphina on the brain again?" Kate asked.

"Hmm?" No, she hadn't been thinking of Seraphina, but she did now. "I wonder how often she came here, dreaming of the life she wanted with Felipe."

"She died in a storm like the one that's coming. I know she did." Margo lifted her face to the sky. "With lightning flashing, the wind howling."

"Suicide's drama enough by itself." Kate plucked a wildflower, twirled the stubby stem between her fingers. "If it had been a perfect day, with blue skies and sunshine, the results would have been the same."

"I wonder what it is to feel that lost," Laura murmured. "If we ever find her dowry, we should build a shrine or something to remember her by."

"I'm spending my share on clothes, jewelry, and travel." Margo stretched her arms up, tucked them behind her head.

"And it'll be gone in a year. Less," Kate predicted. "I'm going to invest mine in blue chips."

"Boring, predictable Kate." Margo turned her head, smiled at Laura. "What about you? What will you do when we find it? And we will find it one day."

"I don't know." What would her mother do? she wondered. Her father? "I don't know," she repeated. "I'll have to wait and see." She looked back toward the sea, where the curtain of rain was inching closer. "That's what Seraphina didn't do. She didn't wait and see."

And the sound of the rising wind was like a woman weeping.

Lightning jagged, a flashing pitchfork of brilliant white through the heavy sky. The blasting boom of answering thunder shook the air. Laura threw back her head and smiled. Here it comes, she thought. The power, the danger, the glory.

She wanted it. Deep inside her most secret heart, she wanted it all.

Then came the squeal of brakes, the angry pulse of gritty rock and roll. And an impatient shout.

"Jesus Christ, are you all nuts?" Joshua Templeton leaned out of his car window, scowling at the trio. "Get the hell in the car."

"It's not raining yet." Laura stood. She eyed Josh first. He was her senior by four years, and at the moment he looked so much like their father at his crankiest that she wanted to laugh. But she'd seen who was in the car with him.

She wasn't certain how she knew that Michael Fury was as dangerous as any summer storm, but she was sure of it. It was more than Ann Sullivan's mutterings about hoods and troublemakers—though, to be sure, Margo's mother had definite opinions on this particular friend of Josh's.

Maybe it was because his dark hair was just a little too long and too wild, or because of the little white scar just above his left eyebrow, which Josh said Michael had gotten in a fight. Maybe it was his looks, for they were dark and dangerous, and just a little mean. Like a greedy angel's, she thought as her heart fluttered uncomfortably. Grinning all the way to hell.

But she thought it was his eyes. So startlingly blue they were in that face. So intense and direct and intrusive when he looked at her.

No, she didn't like the way he looked at her.

"Get in the damn car." Impatience shimmered around Josh in waves. "Mom had a fit when she realized you were out here. One of you gets hit by lightning, it'll be my ass."

"And it's such a cute one," Margo added, always ready to flirt. Hoping to make Josh jealous, she opened the door on Michael's side. "It'll be a tight fit. Mind if I sit on your lap, Michael?"

His gaze shifted from Laura. He grinned at Margo, a quick flash of teeth in a tanned, hollow-cheeked face. "Make yourself at home, sugar." His voice was deep, a little rough, and he accepted the weight of a willing female with practiced ease.

"I didn't know you were back, Michael." Kate slipped into the backseat, where, she thought sourly, there was plenty of room for three.

"On leave." He flicked a glance at her, then looked back at Laura, who still hesitated at the car door. "I ship out again in a couple days."

"The merchant marine." Margo toyed with his hair. "It sounds so . . . dangerous. And exciting. Do you have a woman in every port?"

"I'm working on it." As the first fat drops of rain splatted the windshield, he raised a brow at Laura. "Want to sit on my lap, too, sugar?"

Dignity was something else she'd learned at an early age. Not sparing him a reply, Laura got into the backseat with Kate.

The minute the door was closed, Josh sent the car streaking across the road and up the hill toward home. When her eyes met Michael's in the rearview mirror, Laura deliberately looked away, then back. Back toward the cliffs, and her place of comfortable dreams.

CHAPTER 1

ON THE DAY of her eighteenth birthday, Laura was in love. She knew she was lucky to be so certain of her feelings, and her future, and the man who would share them both with her.

His name was Peter Ridgeway, and he was everything she had ever dreamed of. He was tall and handsome, with golden good looks and a charming smile. He was a man who understood beauty and music, and the responsibilities of career.

Since he had been promoted in the Templeton organization and transferred to the California branch, he had courted her in a fashion designed to win her romantic heart.

There had been roses delivered in glossy white boxes, quiet dinners at restaurants with flickering candlelight. Endless conversations about art and literature—and silent looks that said so much more than words.

They had taken walks in the garden in the moonlight, long drives along the coast.

Her fall into love had not taken long, yet it had been a gentle tumble with no scrapes or bruises. Very much, she thought, like sliding slowly down a silk-lined tunnel into waiting arms.

Perhaps, at twenty-seven, he was a bit older than her parents might have liked, and she a bit younger. But he was so flawless, so perfect, Laura couldn't see how the years could matter. No boy of her own age had Peter Ridgeway's polish, his knowledge, or his quiet patience.

And she was so much in love.

He had hinted at marriage, gently. She understood that this was to give her time to consider. If only she knew how to let him know she had already considered, already decided he was the man she would spend her life with.

But a man like Peter, Laura thought, needed to be the one to make the moves, the decisions.

There was time, she assured herself. All the time in the world. And tonight, at the party to celebrate her eighteenth birthday, he would be there. She would dance with him. And in the pale blue dress she'd chosen because it matched his eyes, she would feel like a princess. More, she would feel like a woman.

She dressed slowly, wanting to savor every moment of preparation. It was all going to be different now, she thought. Her room had been the same when she'd opened her eyes that morning. The walls were still papered with those tiny pink rosebuds that had grown there for so many years. The winter sunlight still tilted through her windows, filtering through lacy curtains as it had done on so many other January mornings.

But everything was different. Because she was different.

She studied her room with a woman's eyes now. She appreciated the elegant lines of the mahogany bureau, the glossy Chippendale that had been her grandmother's. She touched the pretty silver grooming set, a birthday gift from Margo, studied the colorful, frivolous perfume bottles she'd begun to collect in adolescence.

There was the bed she had slept in, dreamed in, since childhood—the high four-poster, again Chippendale, with its fanciful canopy of Breton lace. The terrace doors that led to her balcony were open, to invite the sounds and scents of evening inside. The window seat where she could curl up and dream about the cliffs was cozy with pillows.

A fire burned sedately in the hearth of rose-grained marble. Atop the mantel were silver-framed photos, the delicate silver candlesticks with the slim white tapers she loved to burn at night. And the Dresden bud vase that held the single white rose Peter had sent that morning.

There was the desk where she had studied all the way through high school, where she would continue to study through what was left of her senior year.

Odd, she mused, tracing a hand over it, she didn't feel like a high school student. She felt so much older than her contemporaries. So much wiser, so much more sure of where she was going.

This was the room of her childhood, she thought, of her youth and of her heart. As Templeton House was the home of her heart. Though she knew she would never love any place as much, she was prepared, even eager to build a new home with the man she loved.

At last, she turned and looked at herself in the cheval glass. And smiled. She'd been right about the dress, she decided. Simple, clean lines suited her small frame. The scoop neckline, the long, tapered sleeves, the straight column that skimmed down to flirt with her ankles—the effect was classic, dignified, and perfect for a woman who met Peter Ridgeway's standards.

She might have preferred that her hair be straight and flowing, but since it insisted on curling frivolously, she'd swept it up. It added maturity, she thought.

She would never be bold and sexy like Margo, or casually intriguing like Kate. So she would settle for mature and dignified. After all, those were qualities that Peter found appealing.

She so badly wanted to be perfect for him. Tonight—especially tonight.

Reverently she picked up the earrings that had been her parents' birthday gift. The diamonds and sapphires winked flirtatiously back at her. She was smiling at them when her door burst open.

"I am not putting that crap all over my face." Flushed and flustered, Kate continued her argument with Margo as both of them strode inside. "You have enough on yours for both of us."

"You said Laura would be the judge," Margo reminded her, then stopped. With an expert's eye she studied her friend. "You look fabulous. Dignified sex."

"Really? Are you sure?" The idea of being sexy was so thrilling, Laura turned back to the mirror. All she saw was herself, a small young woman with anxious gray eyes and hair that wouldn't quite stay in place.

"Absolutely. Every guy at the party is going to want you, and be afraid to ask."

Kate snorted and plopped onto Laura's bed. "They won't be afraid to ask you, pal. You're a prime example of truth in advertising."

Margo merely smirked and ran a hand over her hip. The lipstick-red dress dipped teasingly low at the bodice and clung to every generous curve. "If you've got it—which you don't—flaunt it. Which is why you need the blusher, the eye shadow, the mascara, the—"

"Oh, Christ."

"She looks lovely, Margo." Always the peacemaker, Laura stepped between them. She smiled at Kate, spread out on the bed, her angular frame intriguing in thin white wool that covered her from throat to ankle. "Like a wood nymph." She laughed when Kate groaned. "But you could use a little more color."

"See?" Triumphant, Margo whipped out her makeup bag. "Sit up and let a master do her work."

"I was counting on you." Complaining all the way, Kate suffered the indignity of Margo's brushes and tubes. "I'm only doing this because it's your birthday."

"And I appreciate it."

"It's going to be a clear night." Margo busily defined Kate's cheekbones. "The band's already setting up, and the kitchen's in chaos. Mum's rushing around fussing with the floral arrangements as though it's a royal reception."

"I should go help," Laura began.

"You're the guest of honor." Kate kept her eyes closed in self-defense as Margo dusted shadow on her lids. "Aunt Susie has everything under control—including Uncle Tommy. He's outside playing the sax."

Laughing, Laura sat on the bed beside Kate. "He always said his secret fantasy was to play tenor sax in some smoky club."

"He'd have played for a while," Margo said as she carefully smudged liner under Kate's big doe eyes. "Then the Templeton would have come out, and he'd have bought the club."

"Ladies." Josh loitered in the doorway, a small florist's box in his hands. "I don't mean to interrupt a female ritual, but as everyone's slightly insane, I'm playing delivery boy."

The way he looked in his tux shot heat straight through Margo's loins. She sent him a sultry look. "What's your usual tip?"

"Never draw to an inside straight." He struggled not to let his gaze dip to her cleavage and cursed every man who would be offered a glimpse of those milky white curves. "Looks like more flowers for the birthday girl."

"Thanks." Laura rose to take the box, and kissed him. "That's my tip."

"You look wonderful." He caught her hand. "Grown up. I'm starting to miss my annoying little sister."

"I'll do my best to annoy you, as often as possible." She opened the box, sighed, and forgot everything else. "From Peter," she murmured.

Josh set his teeth. It wouldn't be fair to say that she was already annoying him in her choice of men. "Some guys think single roses are classy."

"I'd rather have dozens," Margo stated. And her eyes met Josh's in perfect agreement and understanding.

"It's lovely," Laura murmured as she slipped it into the vase with its mate. "Just like the one he sent this morning."

BY NINE, TEMPLETON House was overflowing with people and sound. Groups of guests spilled out of brightly lit rooms onto heated terraces. Others wandered the gardens, strolling down bricked paths to admire the blooms and the fountains, all lit by the white ball of a winter's moon and the charm of fairy lights.

Margo had been right. The night was clear, a black sky stabbed by countless diamond-bright stars. Under it Templeton House stood awash in lights.

The music pulsed, inviting couples to dance. Huge tables elegantly clad in white linen groaned under the weight of food prepared by a fleet of caterers. Waiters trained by Templeton Hotels standards wandered discreetly among the guests, carrying silver trays filled with flutes of champagne and tiny delicacies for sampling. Half a dozen open bars were set up to serve mixed or soft drinks.

Steam rose off the swimming pool in misty fingers, while dozens of white water lilies floated on the surface. On terraces, under silky awnings, over the lawns, dozens of tables were draped in white linen, centered with a trio of white tapers ringed by glossy gardenias.

Indoors, there were more waiters, more food, more music, more flowers for those who wanted the warmth and relative quiet. Two uniformed maids upstairs stood ready to assist any lady who might wish to freshen up or fix a hem.

No reception ever held at any Templeton hotel around the world was more carefully planned or executed than the celebration of Laura Templeton's eighteenth birthday.

She would never forget that night, the way the lights flashed and glowed, the way the music seemed to fill the air, mating with the scent of flowers. She knew her duties, and she chatted and danced with friends of her parents and with her contemporaries. Though she wanted only Peter, she mixed and mingled as was expected of her.

When she danced with her father, she pressed her cheek against his. "It's a wonderful party. Thank you."

He sighed, realizing she smelled like a woman—soft, elegant. "Part of me wishes you were still three years old, bouncing on my knee."

Thomas drew her back to smile at her. He was a striking man, his bronzed hair lightly touched with silver, the eyes he had passed on to both of his children crinkled at the corners with life and laughter.

"You've grown up on me, Laura."

"I couldn't help it." She smiled back at him.

"No, I suppose you couldn't. Now I'm standing here aware that a dozen young men are aiming arrows at my back, hoping I'll keel over so they can dance with you."

"I'd rather dance with you than anyone."

But when Peter glided by with Susan Templeton, Thomas saw his daughter's eyes go soft and dreamy. How could he have predicted, he thought, when he brought the man out to California, that Ridgeway would take his little girl away?

When the music ended, Thomas had to admire the smooth skill with which Peter changed partners and circled away with Laura.

"You shouldn't look at the man as though you'd like to flog him, Tommy," Susan murmured.

"She's just a girl."

"She knows what she wants. She's always seemed to know." She sighed herself. "Apparently it's Peter Ridgeway."

Thomas looked into his wife's eyes. They were wise, always had been wise. She might be small and delicate-framed like her daughter, and perhaps she gave the illusion of fragility. But he knew just how strong she was.

"What do you think of him?"

"He's competent," she said slowly. "He's well-bred, well-mannered.

God knows, he's attractive." Her soft mouth hardened. "And I wish he was a thousand miles away from her. That's a mother talking," she admitted. "One who's afraid she's losing her little girl."

"We could transfer him to Europe." He warmed to the idea. "No—Tokyo, or Sydney."

Laughing, she patted her husband's cheek. "The way Laura looks at him, she'd follow him. Better to keep him close." Struggling to accept, she shrugged her shoulders. "She could have fallen for one of Josh's wilder friends, or a gigolo, a fortune hunter, an ex-con."

He laughed himself. "Laura? Never."

Susan merely raised an eyebrow. A man wouldn't understand, she knew. Romantic natures like Laura's most usually were drawn to the wild. "Well, Tommy, we'll just have to see where it goes. And be there for her."

"ARen't you going to dance with me?" Margo slid into Josh's arms, fit there, before he had a chance to agree or evade. "Or would you rather just stand there brooding?"

"I wasn't brooding. I was thinking."

"You're worried about Laura." Even as her fingers skimmed flirtatiously up the nape of his neck, Margo shot a concerned glance toward Laura. "She's mad for him. And bound and determined to marry him."

"She's too young to be thinking of marriage."

"She's been thinking of marriage since she was four," Margo muttered. "Now she's found what she thinks is the man of her dreams. No one's going to stop her."

"I could kill him," Josh considered. "Then we could hide the body."

She chuckled, smiled into his eyes. "Kate and I would be happy to help you toss his lifeless corpse off the cliffs. But hell, Josh, maybe he's right for her. He's attentive, intelligent, apparently patient in certain hormonal areas."

"Don't start that." Josh's eyes went dark. "I don't want to think about it."

"Rest assured your little sister will walk down the aisle, when the time comes, in blushing-bride white." She blew out a breath, wondering why any woman would consider marrying a man before she knew if he was her mate in bed. "They have a lot in common, really. And who are two jaded cynics like us to judge?"

"We love her," Josh said simply.

"Yeah, we do. But things change, and before much longer we're all going to be moving in our own directions. You've already started," she pointed out. "Mister Harvard Law. And Kate's chafing at the bit for college, Laura for marriage."

"What are you chafing for, duchess?"

"Everything, and then some." Her smile turned sultry. She might have pushed the flirtation a bit further, but Kate swung up and pried them apart.

"Sexual rituals later," she muttered. "Look, they're going off." She scowled in Laura's direction, watching her walk away hand in hand with Peter. "Maybe we should go after them. Do something."

"Such as?" But understanding, Margo draped an arm over Kate's narrow shoulders. "Whatever, it won't make any difference."

"I'm not going to stand around and watch, then." Disgusted, Kate peered up at Josh. "Let's go sit in the south garden for a while. Josh can steal us some champagne."

"You're underage," he said primly.

"Right, like you've never done it before." She smiled winningly. "Just a glass each. To toast Laura. Maybe it'll bring her luck, and what she wants."

"One glass, then."

Margo frowned, noting the way he scanned the crowd. "Looking for cops?"

"No, I thought Michael might show after all."

"Mick?" Kate angled her head. "I thought he was down in Central America or somewhere, playing soldier of fortune."

"He is—was," Josh corrected. "He's back, at least for a while. I was hoping he'd take me up on the invitation." Then he shrugged. "He's not much for this kind of thing. One glass," he repeated, tapping a finger on Kate's nose. "And you didn't get it from me."

"Of course not." After tucking her arm through Margo's, Kate wandered toward the gaily lighted gardens. "We might as well drink to her if we can't stop her."

"We'll drink to her," Margo agreed. "And we'll be there, whatever happens."

"SO MANY STARS," Laura breathed in the night as she and Peter walked across the gently sloping lawn. "I can't imagine a more perfect evening."

"Much more perfect now that I have a moment alone with you."

Flushing, she smiled at him. "I'm sorry. I've been so busy, I've hardly had a moment to talk with you." Be alone with you.

"You have duties. I understand. A Templeton would never neglect her guests."

"Not ordinarily, no. But it is my birthday." Her hand felt so warm and sheltered in his. She wished they could walk forever, down to the cliffs, so she could share that most intimate place with him. "I should have some leeway."

"Then let's take advantage of that." He guided her toward the fanciful white shape of the gazebo.

From there the sounds of the party became muted background, and the moonlight filtered through the latticelike lace. Scents from the flowers perfumed the air. It was precisely the setting he'd wanted.

Old-fashioned and romantic, like the woman he intended to have.

Drawing her into his arms, he kissed her. She came so willingly, he thought. So innocently. That lovely mouth parting for his, those delicate arms winding around him. It stirred him, this youth combined with dignity, eagerness flushed with innocence.

He could have her, he knew. He had the skill and the experience. But he was a man who prided himself on control, and he drew her gently back. He wouldn't soil the perfection, or rush into the physical. He wanted his wife untouched, even by himself.

"I haven't told you enough how lovely you look tonight."

"Thank you." She treasured those warm, liquid pulls of anticipation. "I wanted to. For you."

He smiled and held her tenderly, letting her head rest against his heart. She was so perfect for him, he thought. Young, lovely, well-bred. Malleable. Through the slats he spotted Margo, flashy in her clinging red dress, laughing bawdily at some joke.

Even though his glands stirred, his sensibilities were offended. The housekeeper's daughter. Every man's wet dream.

His gaze shifted to Kate. The prickly ward, with more brains than style. It amazed him that Laura felt this childish attachment for those two. But he was sure it would fade in time. She was, after all, sensible, with a dignity admirable in one so young. Once she fully understood her place in society— and her place with him—she could be gently weaned from inappropriate attachments.

He had no doubt she was in love with him. She had so little experience in coyness or deception. Her parents might not completely approve, but he was confident that their devotion to their daughter would sway them in his favor.

They would find no fault with him personally or professionally, he was certain. He did his job, and did it well. He would make a suitable son-in-law. With Laura beside him, with the Templeton name, he would have everything he wanted. Everything he deserved. The proper wife, the unshakable position in society, sons. Wealth and success.

"We haven't known each other long," he began.

"It feels like forever."

Over her head, he smiled. She was so sweetly romantic. "Only a few months, Laura. And I'm nearly ten years older than you are."

She only pressed closer. "What does it matter?"

"I should give you more time. God, you're still in high school."

"Only for a few more months." Her heart beat wildly with anticipation as she lifted her head. "I'm not a child, Peter."

"No, you're not."

"I know what I want. I've always known."

He believed her. And he, also, knew what he wanted. Had always known. That, too, he mused, they had in common.

"Still, I told myself I would wait." He brought her hands to his lips, watched her eyes. "Another year, at least."

She knew this was what she had dreamed of, had waited for. "I don't want you to wait," she whispered. "I love you, Peter."

"I love you, Laura. Too much to wait even another hour, much less another year."

He eased her down onto the padded bench. Her hands trembled. With all her heart she absorbed every aspect of the moment. The sound of music in the distance that carried over the clear night air in quiet notes. The scent of night-blooming jasmine and hints of the sea. The way the shadows and lights played through the sheltering lattice.

He got down on one knee, as she'd known he would. His face was so beautiful in the delicate, dreamy light, it broke her heart. Her eyes were swimming with tears when he took a small black-velvet box from his pocket, opened it. The tears made the light that glinted off the diamond refract into rainbows.

"Will you marry me, Laura?"

She knew what every woman felt at this one shining moment of her life. And held out her hand. "Yes."

CHAPTER 2

Twelve years later

WHEN A WOMAN turned thirty, Laura supposed, it was a time for reflection, for taking stock, for not only shuddering because middle age was certainly creeping closer and closer around that blind corner, but for looking back over her accomplishments.

She was trying to.

But the fact was, when she awoke that morning in January on her thirtieth birthday to gray skies and unrelenting rain, the weather perfectly mirrored her mood.

She was thirty years old and divorced. She had lost the lion's share of her personal wealth through her own naïveté and was struggling mightily to fulfill her responsibilities to her family home, raise two daughters alone, hold down two part-time jobs—neither of which she had prepared herself for—and still be a Templeton.

Crowding the minus side was the failure to hold her marriage together, the personal and somewhat embarrassing fact that she had slept with only one man in her life, worry that her children were being penalized by her lack, and fear that the house of cards she was rebuilding so carefully would tumble at the first brisk wind.

Her life—the unrelenting reality of it—bore little resemblance to the one she had dreamed of. Was it any wonder she wanted to huddle in bed and pull the covers over her head?

Instead, she prepared to do what she always did. Get up, face the day, and try to somehow get through the complicated mess she'd made out of her life. There were people depending on her.

Before she could toss the covers aside, there was a soft knock at the door. Ann Sullivan poked her head in first, then smiled. "Happy birthday, Miss Laura."

The Templetons' longtime housekeeper stepped inside the room, carrying a fully loaded breakfast tray accented with a vase of Michaelmas daisies.

"Breakfast in bed!" Scrambling to reorganize her schedule, which had room for a quick cup of coffee at best, Laura sat back. "I feel like a queen."

"It isn't every day a woman turns thirty."

Laura's attempt at a smile wobbled. "Tell me about it."

"Now don't you start that nonsense."

Brisk and efficient, Ann settled the tray over Laura's lap. She'd seen thirty herself—and forty, and Lord help her, she'd just run smack into fifty. And because she understood just how those decades affected a woman, she brushed Laura's sigh aside.

She had been fretting after this girl, as well as her own and Miss Kate besides, for more than twenty years. She knew just how to handle them.

Ann went to rekindle the fire in the hearth not only to chase away the January chill but to add light and cheer. "You're a beautiful young woman with the best of her life ahead of her."

"And thirty years of it behind her."

Ann methodically pushed the right buttons. "And nothing to show for it but two beautiful children, a thriving business, a lovely home, and family and friends who adore you."

Ouch, Laura thought. "I'm feeling sorry for myself." She tried the smile again. "Pathetic and typical. Thank you, Annie. This is lovely."

"Drink some coffee." As the fire caught, crackling briskly, Ann poured the coffee herself, then patted Laura's hand. "You know what you need? A day off. A full day just for yourself, to do exactly as you choose."

It was a fine fantasy, and one that not so many years before she would have been able to indulge. But now, she had the girls to ready for school, a morning in her office at Templeton Monterey, and an afternoon at Pretenses, the shop she and Margo and Kate had started together.

Then it was a quick dash to take the girls to their dance class, time out to go over the bills and to pay them. Then there was homework to oversee, as well as dealing with any and all of the myriad problems her daughters might have encountered during the day.

And she needed to carve out time to check on old Joe, the gardener. She was worried about him but didn't want him to know it.

"You're not listening, Miss Laura."

At the faintly censorious tone, Laura pulled herself back. "I'm sorry. The girls need to get up for school."

"They're up. As a matter of fact . . ." Pleased with her surprise, Ann walked to the door. At the signal, the room filled with people and noise.

"Mama." The girls came first, rushing in to jump on the bed and rattle plates on the tray. At seven and ten they weren't babies any longer, but she cuddled them just the same. Kayla, the younger, was always ready for a hug, but Allison had been growing distant. Laura knew the extended embrace from her elder daughter was one of the best gifts she would receive that day.

"Annie said we could all come and start your birthday off right." Kayla bounced, her smoky gray eyes bright with excitement. "And everybody's here."

"So they are." With an arm around each girl, Laura grinned at the crowd. Margo was already passing her three-month-old son to his grandmother so she could supervise as Josh opened a bottle of champagne. Kate slipped away from her husband to help herself to one of the croissants on Laura's tray.

"So how does it feel, champ?" Kate asked with her mouth full. "The big three-oh?"

"It was feeling lousy until a minute ago. Mimosas?" She raised a brow at Margo.

"You betcha. And, no," she said, anticipating Ali, "straight o.j. for you and your sister."

"It's a special occasion," Ali complained.

"So, you're going to drink your o.j. in a champagne flute." With a flourish, she passed juice to the girls. "For a toast," she added, then hooked an arm through her husband's. "Right, Josh?"

"To Laura Templeton," he began, "a woman of many talents—which includes looking pretty great for a kid sister on the morning of her thirtieth birthday."

"And if anyone brought a camera in here," Laura said, pushing back her tumbled hair, "I'll kill them."

"I knew I forgot something." Kate shook her head, then shrugged. "Well—let's get to the first gift. Byron?"

Byron De Witt, Kate's husband of six weeks and the executive director of Templeton California, stepped forward. He touched his glass lightly to Laura's and grinned. "Ms. Templeton, if I see you anywhere on hotel property before midnight tonight, I'll be forced to pull rank and fire you."

"But I have two accounts I have to—"

"Not today you don't. Consider your office closed. Somehow Conventions and Special Events will have to limp along without you for twenty-four hours."

"I appreciate the thought, Byron, but—"

"All right." He sighed. "If you insist on going over my head. Mr. Templeton?"

Enjoying himself, Josh joined ranks with Byron. "As executive vice president, Templeton, I'm ordering you to take the day off. And if you've got some idea about going over my head, I've already talked to Mom and Dad. They'll be calling you later."

"Fine." When she discovered she was getting ready to pout, she shrugged instead. "It'll give me a chance to—"

"Nope." Reading Laura well, Kate shook her head. "You're not setting foot in the shop today."

"Oh, come on. This is just silly. I can—"

"Lie in bed," Margo continued, "walk the cliffs, read a book, get a facial." Over the sheets, she grabbed Laura's foot, waggled it. "Pick up a sailor and . . ." Remembering the girls, she backtracked. "Go for a sail. Mrs. Williamson is planning an elaborate birthday feast for you tonight, to which we have all invited ourselves. At that time, if you've been a good girl, you'll get the rest of your presents."

"I have something for you, Mama. I have something and so does Ali.

Annie helped us pick them out. You have to be good so you can open them tonight."

"Outnumbered." Laura took a contemplative sip of her mimosa. "All right, I'll be lazy. And if I do something foolish, it'll be your fault. All of you."

"Always willing to take the credit." Margo took J. T. back as he began to fuss. "He's wet," she discovered and, laughing, handed him to his father. "And it's your turn, Josh. We'll be back at seven sharp. Oh, and if you decide on that sailor, I'll want to hear every detail."

"Gotta go," Kate announced. "See you tonight."

They went out as quickly and as noisily as they had come in, leaving Laura alone with a bottle of champagne and a cooling breakfast.

She was so lucky, she thought, as she settled back against the pillows. She had family and friends who loved her. She had two beautiful daughters, and a home she had always called her own.

Then why, she wondered as her eyes swam with sudden tears, did she feel so useless?

THE TROUBLE WITH having free time, Laura decided, was that it reminded her of the days when most of her free time had been eaten up by committees. Some she had joined because she enjoyed them—the people, the projects, the causes. Others, she knew, she'd involved herself with because of pressure from Peter.

She had, for too many years, found it easier to bend than to stand.

And when she had rediscovered her backbone, she had also discovered that the man she had married didn't love her, or the children. It had been the Templeton name he had married; he had never wanted the life she dreamed of.

Sometime between Ali's birth and Kayla's, he dropped even the pretense of loving her. Still, she stuck with it, maintained the illusion of marriage and family. And the pretense was all hers.

Until the day she walked in on that most pathetic of clichés: her husband in bed with another woman.

Thinking of it now, Laura crossed the beautifully tended lawn, strolled through the south gardens and into the grove beside the old stables. The rain had subsided to a mist that merged with the swirl of fog crawling along the ground. It was, she thought, like walking through a cool, thin river.

She rarely walked here, rarely had time. Yet she had always loved the play of sunlight or shadow through the trees, the scent of the forest, the rustling of small animals. There had been times during her youth when she imagined it was a fairy-tale woods and she was the enchanted princess, searching for the one true love who would rescue her from the spell cast upon her.

A harmless fantasy, she thought now, for a young girl. But perhaps she had wanted that fairy-tale ending too badly, believed in it too strongly. As she had believed in Peter.

He had crushed her. Quite literally he had crushed her heart with simple neglect, with casual disinterest. Then he had scattered the pieces that were left with betrayal. At last, he had eradicated even the dust when he had taken not only her money but the children's too.

For that, she would never forgive or forget.

And that, Laura thought as she wandered a path under an arch of lazily dripping branches, made her bitter.

She wanted to swallow the taste of that bitterness once and for all, to get beyond it, fully, and move ahead. Perhaps, she decided, her thirtieth birthday was the time to really begin.

It made sense, didn't it? Peter had proposed to her on her birthday twelve years before. On a starry night, she remembered, raising her face to the misting rain. She'd been so sure then, so positive that she knew what she wanted, what she needed. Now was the time to reevaluate.

Her marriage was over, but her life wasn't. In the past two years she'd taken quite a few steps to prove that.

Did she mind the work she'd taken on to rebuild her life and her personal finances? Not the work itself, she decided, stepping over a fallen log and going deeper into the forest. Her position with Templeton Hotels was a responsibility, a legacy, that she'd neglected too long. She would damn well earn her keep.

And the shop. She smiled to herself as her boots squished on the soggy path. She loved Pretenses, loved working with Margo and Kate. She enjoyed the customers, the stock, and the sense of accomplishment. The three of them had built something there, for themselves, for each other.

How could she resent the hours and the effort that she put into raising her girls, seeing that they had a happy, healthy life? They were her heart. Whatever it took to make up for the loss of the home she had somehow helped break, she would try to do.

Kayla, she thought, her little Kayla. So resilient, so easy to please. A loving, happy child was Kayla.

But Allison. Poor Ali had needed her father's love so desperately. The divorce was hardest on her, and nothing Laura did seemed to help her adjust. She was doing better now, Laura thought, better than she had been during those first months, even the first year. But she had pulled in, and back, and was only rarely spontaneous with her affections, as she had been.

And wary of her mother, Laura thought with a sigh. Still blaming her mother for a father who had no interest in his daughters.

Laura sat on a stump, closed her eyes, let the faint breeze that was the music of the forest surround her. She would handle it, she promised herself. She would handle all of it—the work, the rush, the worry, the children. No one was more surprised than she herself that she was handling it well.

But how, she wondered, how in God's name would she continue to handle the loneliness?

LATER, SHE SNIPPED deadheads out of the garden, did some pruning, hauled away the debris. Old Joe simply couldn't keep up any longer. And young Joe, his grandson, couldn't afford more than a few hours a week in between his college courses to add his help. Since it would cut too much into her budget, and old Joe's pride, to hire an assistant, Laura had convinced Joe that she wanted to take on some of the gardening tasks.

It was partially true. She had always loved the gardens of Templeton House—the flowers, the shrubs, the vines. As a child she had often dogged Joe, nagging him to teach her, to show her. And he would pull a pack of cherry Life Savers out of his pocket, thumb one out for her, and demonstrate the proper way to train a creeper, to deal with aphids, to prune a tea rose.

She had adored him—his weathered face, old even then, his slow, thoughtful voice, his big, patient hands. He had come to work in the gardens of Templeton House as a boy, in her grandparents' day. After sixty years of service, he had a right to his pension, to spend his days tending his own garden, to a life sitting in the sunshine.

And, Laura understood, it would break his heart if she offered it.

So she picked up the slack under the guise of wanting a hobby. When her schedule allowed, and often when it didn't, she would stand with Joe and discuss perennials and bonemeal and mulch.

Today, as afternoon faded to dusk, she took stock. The gardens of Templeton House looked as they should in winter: quiet, waiting, the hardiest blooms splashes of defiant color. Her parents had given the house into her hands for tending, and for cherishing. Laura did both.

She stepped out onto the skirt of the pool, nodded in approval. She maintained the pool herself. It was, after all, her indulgence. Whatever the weather, if she could squeeze in a few laps, she did so. She'd taught her children to swim in that pool, as her father had taught her. The water sparkled, a delicate blue, thanks to some of her recent dickering with the pump and filter.

The mermaid lived beneath, a mosaic fantasy of flowing red hair and glossy green tail. Her girls loved to dive down and touch that smiling, serene face, even as she had.

Out of habit, she checked the glass tables for smudges, the cushions of the chairs and lounges for dampness or dust. Ann would have already done so, but Laura didn't turn toward the house until she was certain everything was perfect.

Satisfied, she walked down the stone path and chose the kitchen door. Scents assaulted her, made her taste buds yearn. Mrs. Williamson, ample of hip and bosom, stood at the stove, as she had done for all of Laura's memory.

"Leg of lamb," Laura said and sighed. "Apple chutney. Curried potatoes."

Turning, Mrs. Williamson smiled smugly. She was well into her seventies. Her hair was the hard glossy black of a bowling ball and approximately the same shape. But her face was soft, full of folds and wrinkles and as sweet as her own cream centers.

"Your nose is as good as ever, Miss Laura—or your memory is. It's what you always want for your birthday."

"No one roasts a lamb like you, Mrs. Williamson." Because she knew the game, Laura wandered the spacious kitchen, making her poking about obvious. "I don't see a cake."

"Maybe I forgot to bake one."

Laura expressed the expected dismay. "Oh, Mrs. Williamson!"

"And maybe I didn't." She chuckled, gestured with her wooden spoon. "Now off you go. I can't have you around pestering me while I'm cooking. Get yourself cleaned up—you're carrying garden dirt."

"Yes, ma'am." At the kitchen door, Laura turned back. "It wouldn't be a Black Forest cake, would it? Double chocolate?"

"Just you wait and see. Scat!"

Laura waited until she was well down the hallway before she chuckled. It would be a Black Forest cake. Mrs. Williamson might be a tad forgetful these days, and her hearing wasn't what it had been. But vital matters such as Laura's traditional birthday meal would be remembered in every detail.

She hummed to herself as she climbed the stairs to bathe and change for dinner. Her mood had lifted, but it plummeted quickly when she heard the sounds of a sibling argument in full swing.

"Because you're stupid, that's why." Ali's voice was shrill and bitter. "Because you don't understand anything, and I hate you."

"I am not stupid." There were tears trembling on the surface of Kayla's retort. "And I hate you more."

"Well, this is pleasant." Determined to lose neither her temper nor her perspective, Laura paused in the doorway of Ali's room.

The tableau seemed innocent enough. In a girl's pretty mint-and-white room, dolls from around the world wearing their countries' traditional dress ringed the shelves that flanked the wide window. Books, ranging from *Sweet Valley High* to *Jane Eyre*, filled a case. A jewelry box with a twirling ballerina stood open on the dresser.

Her daughters faced each other from either side of the canopy bed like mortal enemies over embattled soil.

"I don't want her in my room." Her fists clenched, Ali whirled to face her mother. "This is my room and I don't want her in it."

"I just came in to show her the picture I drew." With trembling lips, Kayla held it out. It was a clever crayon sketch of a fire-breathing dragon and a young, silver-clad knight with a raised sword. The natural youthful talent in it reminded Laura that she needed to arrange for Kayla to have drawing lessons.

"It's wonderful, Kayla."

"She said it was ugly." Never ashamed of tears, Kayla let them fall. "She said it was ugly and stupid and that I had to knock before I came into her room."

"Ali?"

"Dragons aren't real, and they're ugly." Ali thrust her chin out, challenging. "And she can't just come into my room if I don't want her."

"You're entitled to your privacy," Laura said carefully, "but you're not entitled to be mean to your sister. Kayla—" Laura crouched down, brushed tears off her daughter's cheeks. "It's a wonderful picture. We can frame it if you like."

Tears dried up. "We can?"

"Absolutely, and we can hang it in your room. Unless you'd let me hang it in mine."

The smile bloomed, brilliantly. "You can have it."

"I'd like that very much. Why don't you go back to your room and sign it for me, just like a real artist. And Kayla . . ." Laura rose, kept a hand on Kayla's shoulder. "If Ali wants you to knock on her door, then that's what you'll do."

Mutiny flared briefly. "Then she has to knock on mine, too."

"That's fair. Go on now. I want to talk to Ali."

After sending her sister a smug look, Kayla sailed out.

"She wouldn't leave when I told her to," Ali began. "She's always running in here whenever she wants."

"And you're older," Laura said quietly, trying to understand. "There are privileges that go along with that, Ali, but there are also responsibilities. I don't expect the two of you never to fight. Josh and I fought, Margo and Kate and I fought. But you hurt her."

"I just wanted her to go away. I wanted to be alone. I don't care about her stupid picture of a stupid dragon."

There's more going on here, Laura thought, studying her daughter's miserable face, than sibling sniping. She sat on the edge of the bed so that her eyes were level with Ali's. "Tell me what's wrong, honey."

"You always take her side."

Laura bit back a sigh. "That's not true." Determined, she took Ali's hand, pulled her closer. "And that's not what's bothering you."

There was a war going on inside this little girl, Laura realized as she watched Ali's eyes swim. With all her heart, Laura wanted to find the right way to make peace.

"It doesn't matter. It won't make any difference." Tears came closer to the surface. "You won't do anything about it."

It hurt, but then, this recent distrust from Ali always hurt. "Why don't you tell me, then we'll see. I can't do anything about it if I don't know what it is."

"They're going to have a father-daughter dinner at school." The words burst out, full of anger and pain. "They're all going to bring their dads."

"Oh." No peace here, Laura admitted and touched her daughter's cheek. "I'm sorry, Ali. That's hard. Uncle Josh will go with you."

"It's not the same."

"No, it's not the same."

"I want it to be the same," Ali said in a furious whisper. "Why can't you make it be the same?"

"I can't." There was relief when Ali went unresisting into her arms. And there was grief.

"Why don't you make him come back? Why don't you do something to make him come back?"

Now there was guilt to layer on top of grief. "There's nothing I can do."

"You don't want him to come back." With her eyes bright and hot, Ali jerked back. "You told him to go away, and you don't want him to come back."

This was a thin and shaky line to travel. "Your father and I are divorced, Ali. That's not going to change. The fact that we can't, and don't want to, live together anymore doesn't have anything to do with you and Kayla."

"Then why doesn't he ever come?" Tears poured out again, but they were hot now, and angry. "Other kids have parents that don't live together, but their dads come and they go places together."

The line got shakier. "Your father's very busy, and he's living in Palm Springs now." Lies, Laura thought. Pitiful lies. "I'm sure once he's more settled, he'll spend more time with you." When did he ever?

"He doesn't come because he doesn't want to see you." Ali turned away. "It's because of you."

Laura closed her eyes. What good would it be to deny it, to defend herself and leave her child vulnerable? "If it is, I'll do what I can to make it easier for him, and for you." On legs that weren't quite steady, Laura rose. "There are things I can't change, I can't fix. And I can't stop you from blaming me for it."

Fighting to control both grief and temper, Laura took a slow breath. "I don't want you to be unhappy, Ali. I love you. I love you and Kayla more than anything in the world."

Ali's shoulders slumped. "Will you ask him if he could come to the dinner? It's next month, on a Saturday."

"Yes, I'll ask."

Shame eked through the anger and misery. She didn't have to look at her mother's face to know she would see hurt. "I'm sorry, Mama."

"So am I."

"I'll tell Kayla I'm sorry, too. She draws really good. And I . . . I can't."

"You have other talents." Gently Laura turned Ali around, cupped her shoulders. "You dance so beautifully. And you play the piano so much better than I did at your age. Better than I do now."

"You never play anymore."

There were a lot of things she didn't do anymore. "How about a duet tonight? We'll play. Kayla can sing."

"She sounds like a bullfrog."

"I know."

And when Ali looked up, they grinned at each other.

ANOTHER CRISIS AVERTED, Laura decided, as she settled down with her family after dinner. There was a cheery fire blazing in the hearth and rich, creamy cake to be devoured. The curtains in the parlor were opened to a starry night. And the lights inside glowed warm.

Birthday presents had been unwrapped, opened, and admired. The baby was sleeping upstairs. Josh and Byron were puffing on cigars, and her daughters, fences mended for the moment, were at the piano. Kayla's booming frog of a voice competed with Ali's skillful playing.

"Then she went for the Chanel bag," Margo was saying, comfortably curled on the sofa as she talked shop. "It took her more than an hour, and she just kept piling up stock. Three suits, an evening gown—your white Dior, Laura—four pairs of shoes. Count them, four. Six blouses, three sweaters, two silk slacks. And that was before she started on the jewelry."

"It was a red-letter day." Kate propped her bare feet on the Louis XIV coffee table. "I had a hunch when the woman pulled up in a white stretch limo. She'd come up from L.A. because a friend of hers had told her about Pretenses."

Kate sipped herbal tea, hardly missing the punch of coffee. "I'm telling you," she went on, "this woman was a pro. She said she's buying a country home and she's going to come back and choose some of the furnishings and whatnots from the shop. Turns out she's the wife of some hotshot producer. And she's going to tell all her friends about this clever little secondhand shop in Monterey."

"That's wonderful." So wonderful, Laura could almost accept not being in on the kill.

"It's making me wonder if we shouldn't think about expanding sooner. Maybe in L.A. rather than Carmel."

"Hold it, hotshot." Kate eyed Margo narrowly. "We're not talking seriously about another branch until we've been in business two full years. Then I run some figures, do some projections."

"Always the accountant," Margo muttered.

"You bet your ass. So, what did you do with your day off, Laura?"

"Oh, a little gardening." A little bill paying, closet cleaning, moping.

"Is that J.T.?" With a mother's superhearing, Margo tuned in to the sounds whispering out of the baby monitor beside her. "I'd better check on him."

"No, let me." Laura rose quickly. "Please. You get to have him all the time. I want to play."

"Sure. But if he's . . ." Margo trailed off, glancing toward the two young girls at the piano. "I guess you know what to do."

"I think I have a pretty good idea." Aware that Margo might change her mind, Laura hurried out.

It was amazing and gratifying to see the way her impulsive, glamorous friend had taken to motherhood. Even two short years before, no one would have believed Margo Sullivan, supermodel, the rage of Europe, would be settled down in her hometown, running a secondhand shop and raising a family. Margo certainly wouldn't have believed it herself, Laura mused.

But fate had dealt her a tough hand. Rather than fold and run, she'd stuck. And, with determination and flair, had turned fate on its ear.

Now she had Josh, and John Thomas, and a thriving business. She had a home she loved.

Laura hoped that somehow, someday, she could deal fate the same blow.

"There he is," Laura cooed as she approached the antique crib that she and Ann had hauled out of storage. "There's the darling. Oh, what a handsome boy you are, John Thomas Templeton."

Truer words were never spoken. He'd had a rich gene pool to choose from, and he'd chosen well. Golden hair grew thick around a glorious little face. Round with babyhood it was, with his mother's stunning blue eyes, his father's well-sculpted mouth.

His fretful whimpering stopped the moment she lifted him. And the feeling, one that perhaps only a woman understands, soared through her. Here was baby, beginnings, beauty.

"There, sweetheart, were you lonely?" She walked him, as much to pleasure herself as to soothe. She'd wanted more children. She knew it was selfish when she had two such beautiful daughters. But, oh, she'd wanted more children.

Now she had a nephew to spoil. And she intended to do so, lavishly. Kate and Byron would have children, Laura mused as she laid J. T. on the changing table. There would be more babies to cuddle.

She changed him, powdered him, tickled him to make him giggle and kick his legs. He grinned at her, wrapped a fist around a curl and tugged. Laura went with the pull to nuzzle his neck.

"Bring back memories?" Josh asked as he stepped inside the nursery.

"Does it ever! When Annie and I were putting this room together for his visits, we wallowed in memories." She lifted J. T. high over her head, where he could gurgle in delight. "Both my babies slept in that crib."

"So did you and I." He ran a hand over the curved rungs before moving to his son. Josh's fingers itched to hold him, but he held back, allowed Laura to cuddle the baby.

"Everyone who's been there says it, but I can't stop myself. The years go so fast, Josh. Treasure every second of it."

"You did." He touched her hair. "You are, and have been, the most incredible mother. I've admired you for that."

"You're going to make me sloppy," she murmured, and buried her face in the sweet curve of J. T.'s neck.

"I figure you and I had the best possible examples to follow. We've been lucky, Laura, to have people like Mom and Dad for parents."

"Don't I know it. I know they're in the middle of negotiating the construction of the new hotel on Bimini, but they called today just to wish me happy birthday."

"And Dad told the story of how he drove Mom through the worst winter storm in the history of central California when she went into labor with you."

"Of course." She lifted her head and grinned. "He loves telling that story. Rain, floods, mud slides, lightning. All but an appearance of the Angel of Doom and the seven plagues of Egypt."

"'But I got her there,'" Josh quoted his father. "'With forty-five minutes to spare.'" He stroked his son's hair. "Not everybody's as lucky. Do you remember Michael Fury?"

Images of a dark, dangerous man with hot eyes. Who could forget Michael Fury? "Yes, you used to hang around with him and look for girls and trouble. He went into the merchant marine or something."

"He went into a lot of things. There were some problems at home—an unpleasant divorce. Well, two actually. His mother got married for the third time when he was about twenty-five. This one seems to have stuck. Anyway, he came back to the area a few weeks ago."

"Oh, really? I didn't know."

"You and Michael never ran in the same circles," Josh said dryly. "The thing is, he took over the old place, where he grew up. His mother and stepfather relocated in Boca, and he bought the property from them. He's raising horses now."

"Horses. Hmm." Not terribly interested, she began to walk the baby again. Josh would get to his point eventually, she knew. Sometimes he was such a lawyer, caging the meaning with words.

"Those storms we had a couple weeks ago?"

"Oh, bad ones," she remembered. "Almost as bad as the fateful night of Laura Templeton's birth."

"Yeah, more mud slides. One of them destroyed Michael's place."

"Oh, I'm sorry." She stopped walking and tuned in. "I'm really sorry. Was he hurt?"

"No. He managed to get himself and his stock out. But the house is a loss. It's going to take some time to rebuild, if that's what he wants to do. Meanwhile, he'll need temporary lodgings for himself and his horses. Something he could rent, you know, for the short term. And I was thinking, the stables and the groom's apartment above them aren't being used."

Alarm came first. "Josh."

"Just hear me out. I know Mom and Dad were always a little, well, wary of him."

"To say the least."

"He's an old friend," Josh returned. "And a good one. He's also handy. No one's done any maintenance or repairs on that building in years, not since—" He broke off, cleared his throat.

"Not since I sold off the horses," Laura finished. "Because Peter didn't care for them, or the amount of time I put in with them."

"The point is, the building should be looked after. Right now it's just sitting there empty. You could use the rent, since you refuse to dip into Templeton capital to run this place."

"I'm not going over that ground again."

"Fine." He recognized that set to her mouth and didn't bother. "The rent from a building you're not using would help you out. Right?"

"Yes, but—"

He held up a hand. He would cut through the logic and practicalities first. "You could use someone around here, in the short term, to do some heavy work, to put the stables back in shape. That's something you simply can't do yourself."

"That's true, but—"

Now, Josh thought, for the clincher. "And I have an old friend whose home has been washed out from under him. I'd consider it a personal favor."

"Low blow," she muttered.

"They're always the most effective." Knowing he'd scored, he gave her hair a quick, affectionate tug. "Look, it should work out for everyone, but give it a couple of weeks. If it's not working, I'll find an alternative."

"All right. But if he starts having drunken poker parties or orgies—"

"We'll try to keep them discreet," Josh finished and grinned. "Thanks." He kissed her and took the baby. "He's a good man, Laura. One you can count on in tight squeezes."

Laura wrinkled her nose at his back as he carried J. T. out of the room. "I don't intend to count on Michael Fury, particularly in a tight squeeze."

CHAPTER 3

THE LAST PLACE Michael Fury had expected to take up residence, however temporarily, was on the great Templeton estate. Oh, he'd visited there often enough in the past, under the subtly watchful eyes of Thomas and Susan Templeton and the not so subtly watchful eye of Ann Sullivan.

He was well aware that the Templeton housekeeper had considered him a mongrel let loose among her purebreds. And he assumed that she'd been worried about his intentions toward her daughter.

She could have rested easy there. As lip smackingly gorgeous as Margo was, and always had been, she and Michael had never been more than casual friends.

Maybe he'd kissed her a couple of times. How was a red-blooded man supposed to resist that mouth? But that had been the beginning and end of it. She'd been for Josh. Even that long ago and despite the shortsightedness of youth, he'd realized that.

Michael Fury didn't poach on a pal.

Despite their different backgrounds, they had been friends. Real friends. Michael didn't consider many people real friends. He would, and had, gone to the wall for Josh, and he knew he could depend on the same.

Still, he would never have asked for the favor and would likely have refused it but for his horses. He didn't want them boarded any longer than necessary in a public facility. He'd gotten sentimental over them, and he wasn't ashamed of it. In the last few years they'd been one of the few constants in his life.

He'd tried a number of things. He'd drifted. He liked to drift. Joining the merchant marine had been an escape; he'd reveled in it. He'd seen a lot of the world, and he liked some of it.

It had been cars for a time. He still had an affection for them, liked to drive full out. He'd had some success on the race circuit in Europe, but it hadn't satisfied him in the long term.

In between the sea and the cars, there had been a brief stint as a mercenary, during which he'd learned too much about killing and warring for profit. And maybe he'd been afraid he was too good at it, afraid it would satisfy him too well. It had fattened his wallet but scarred his heart.

He'd been married once also, only briefly, and could claim no success from that experience either.

It was during his stuntman stage that he fell for horses. He'd learned that craft, gained a reputation, broken several bones. He jumped out of buildings, rioted in staged bar fights, was shot off roofs, set on fire. And he tumbled off of countless horses.

Michael Fury knew how to take a fall. But he wasn't able to roll when he fell in love with horses.

So he bought them, and bred them, and trained them. He had put down a sick horse and labored through the birth of a foal.

Though he knew the odds were long, he thought he'd found what he'd been looking for.

It seemed like fate when his stepfather called, telling Michael that he and Michael's mother were going to sell the property in the hills. Though he had no sentiment for it, Michael heard himself offering to buy it.

It was good horse country.

So, he'd come back, and nature had delivered a hard backhanded slap in welcome. He didn't give a good damn about the house. But his horses—he would have died saving them, and he'd come dangerously close as those acres of mud tumbled down.

There he was, filthy, exhausted, alone, looking at what had been his next start. The oozing rubble of it.

There had been a time when he would have simply cut his losses and moved on. But this time he was sticking.

Now Josh had offered him a hand, and weighing his pride against his horses, Michael had accepted.

As he swung up the drive toward Templeton House, he hoped he wasn't gambling on the wrong roll of the dice. He'd always admired the place. You couldn't help it. So he stopped in the middle of the drive, got out, and took a long look.

He stood in the mild winter air, a rangy man with an athlete's disciplined body, a brawler's ready stance. He was dressed in black, his most usual attire, because it saved him from thinking when he reached for clothes. The snug black jeans and sweater under a scarred leather bomber jacket gave him the look of a desperado.

He would have said it wasn't far from the truth.

His black hair danced in the breeze. It was longer than practical, sleek and thick by nature. When he was working, he often pulled it back in a stubby ponytail. He hated the barber and would have suffered torments of hell going to what they called a stylist.

He'd forgotten to shave—he'd meant to, but he got involved with the horses. The stubble only added to the dangerous appeal of a rawboned face. His mouth was surprisingly soft. Many women could testify to its skill and generosity. But whatever softness was there was often overlooked when the observer was pinned by hard eyes the color of ball lightning.

Over them, his brows were arched, the left one marred by a faint white scar.

He had others on his body, from car wrecks, fights, his stunt work. He'd learned to live with them, just as he lived with the scars inside.

As he studied the glinting stone, the spearing towers, and glinting glass of Templeton House, he smiled. Christ, what a place, he thought. A castle for modern royalty.

Here comes Michael Fury, he thought. And what the hell are you going to do about it?

He chuckled to himself as he drove up the winding lane, cutting through rolling lawns accented by stately old trees, shrubs waiting to burst into bloom. He didn't imagine that the reigning princess was too happy about his impending stay. Josh must have done some fast talking to persuade his proper society sister to open even the stables for the likes of Michael Fury.

They'd both get used to it, he imagined. It wasn't for long, and he was sure they could manage to stay out of each other's way. Just as they had in the past.

FOR LAURA, CARVING out this hour in the middle of the day was problematic but necessary. She had sent the maid Jenny to do what she could about cleaning the groom's apartment above the stables. God knew it was a mess of dust and debris and spiderwebs. Mice, Laura thought, shuddering as she hauled up a bucket of soapy water.

She couldn't expect the girl to perform miracles. And there just hadn't been enough time. It hadn't been possible to ask Ann's help. At the mere mention of Michael Fury's name, the housekeeper had sniffed and gone stone-faced.

So, Laura had decided the final work fell to her. She wasn't about to welcome anyone into her home, or a part thereof, and not have it spic and span.

An extended lunch hour away from her duties at Pretenses, a quick change of clothes, and now, she thought, a great deal of elbow grease. The state of the bathroom in the apartment had shocked young Jenny speechless.

Small wonder. With her hair pulled back, her sleeves rolled up, Laura climbed into the tub and began to attack the worst of the grime. When her guest—tenant—whatever the hell he was—arrived the following day, at least he wouldn't find scum on the tiles.

As far as the stables themselves went, she'd decided after one look that they fell into Michael Fury's territory.

While she worked, she rattled through her head for the rest of her day's schedule. She could get back to Pretenses by three. Close out by six-thirty. A quick dash to pick up the girls from piano lessons.

Damn it, she'd forgotten to look into finding a good drawing instructor for Kayla.

Dinner at seven-thirty. A check to make certain both girls were prepared for whatever tests and assignments were coming up.

Was it spelling for Kayla tomorrow or math for Ali? Was it both? Good God, she hated going back to school. Fractions were killing her.

Puffing a bit as her muscles sang, she swiped soap and grit over her cheek.

She really did have to go over that report on the cosmeticians' convention next month. She could do that in bed, once the girls were down. And Ali needed new ballet shoes. They would see to that tomorrow.

"Well, that's quite a sight." Michael stepped into the narrow doorway and was treated to the appealing view of a pretty female butt straining against faded denim. A butt that he assumed belonged to some nubile Templeton maid. "If this is among the amenities, I should be paying a hell of a lot more rent."

Yelping, Laura sprang up, rapped her head on the shower nozzle, and slopped filthy water over her feet. It was a toss-up as to who was more surprised.

Michael hadn't realized until that moment that he'd carried an image of Laura in his head. Perfect. Perfectly lovely, gold and rose and white, like a glossy picture of a princess in a book of fairy tales.

But the woman facing him now, eyes huge and darkly gray, had wet dirt smeared on her cheeks, her hair was a mess, and her tea-serving hands held a scrub brush.

He recovered first. A man who'd lived on the edge had to have quick reflexes. And he grinned widely as he leaned on the doorjamb. "Laura Templeton. That is you in there, isn't it?"

"I wasn't—we weren't expecting you until tomorrow."

Ah, yes, he thought. The voice hadn't changed. Cool, cultured, quietly sexy. "I always like to get the lay of the land. The front door was wide open."

"I was airing the apartment."

"Well, then. It's nice to see you again, Laura. I don't know when I've had someone quite so attractive scrub out my john."

Humiliated, knowing her cheeks were hot, she nodded. "As Josh probably told you, we haven't been using the building. I wasn't able to spare the staff to put things to rights so quickly."

It surprised him that she knew which end of a scrub brush was which. "You don't have to bother for me. I can handle it myself."

Now that he took a close look, he could also see for himself that she was just as lovely underneath the grime as ever. Delicate features, soft mouth, the aristocratic hint of cheekbone, and those dreamy storm-colored eyes.

Had he forgotten how small she was? Five two, maybe three, and slim as a fairy, with hair the color of gold in dim sunlight. Subtle again, with the richness but not the flash.

She remembered he had often stared, just as he was doing now, saying nothing, just looking, looking until she wanted to squirm.

"I'm sorry about your home."

"Hmm?" He lifted a brow, the scarred one, drawing her eyes to his. "Oh, it was just a house. I can always build another. I appreciate you providing a place for me and my horses."

When he offered a hand, she took it automatically. His was hard, rough with calluses, and held on to hers even when she tried to slip away.

His lips curved again. "You going to stay standing in the tub, sugar?"

"No." She cleared her throat, allowed him to help her out. "I'll show you around," she began, then her eyes went cool when he remained where he was. "I'll show you around," she repeated.

"Thanks." He shifted, enjoyed the waft of scent, again subtle, that she carried with her.

"Josh would have told you this was the groom's apartment." Her voice was clear again, the polite hostess. "It's self-sufficient, I think. Full kitchen." She gestured toward an alcove off the main room, where Jenny had dutifully cleaned the white stove, the stainless steel sink, the simple white countertops.

"That's fine. I don't do a lot of cooking."

"Josh mentioned that you'd lost your furniture, so we brought over a few things."

She waited, hands folded at her waist as he wandered about the room. The sofa had been in the attic and could have used re-covering. But it was a good solid Duncan Phyfe. Some Templeton or guest in the past had scarred the Sheridan coffee table with a careless cigarette, but it was functional.

She'd added lamps, simple brass ones that she felt suited a masculine taste, an easy chair, other occasional tables, even a vase of winter windflowers. She was too much the innkeeper's daughter not to have put thought and effort into her temporary inn.

"You've gone to some trouble." Which surprised and humbled him. "I figured on roughing it for a few months."

"It's not exactly Templeton Paris." She unbent enough to smile. "The bedroom's through there." She gestured toward a short corridor. "It's not terribly large, but I went with instinct on the bed. I know Josh likes room to, ah . . ." She trailed off when Michael grinned. "Room," she finished. "So we stuffed a queen size in there. We had the iron head- and footboards in storage. I've always liked them. There's not much of a closet, but—"

"I don't have much."

"Well, then." At a loss, she wandered toward the front window. "The view," she said and left it at that.

"Yeah." He joined her, intrigued by the way her head fit neatly below his chin. He could see the cliffs, the azure sea beyond, the splits of rock islands, and the fuming water that charged them. "You used to spend a lot of time out there."

"I still do."

"Still looking for treasure?"

"Of course."

"What was the name of the girl who tossed herself off the cliff?"

"Seraphina."

"Right. Seraphina. A romantic little tale."

"A sad one."

"Same thing. Josh used to laugh about you and Margo and Kate haunting those cliffs and looking for Seraphina's lost dowry. But, I figured he secretly wanted to find it himself."

"We look every Sunday now. Margo and Kate and I, and my daughters."

That brought him up short. He'd forgotten for a moment that this small, delicate woman had given birth to two children. "You've got kids of your own. Girls."

"Yes." Chin lifted, she turned back. "Daughters. My daughters."

Something here, he mused, and wondered which button he'd pushed. "How old are they?"

She hadn't expected him to ask, even out of politeness. And she softened all over again. "Ali's ten. Kayla's seven."

"You got started early. Girls that age usually go for horses. They can come by and see mine whenever they like."

More of the unexpected. "That's kind of you, Michael. I don't want them to get in your way."

"I like kids."

He said it so simply that she believed him. "Then I'll warn you, they're both eager to see them. And I suppose you're eager to see the stables." Out of habit she glanced at her watch, and winced.

"Got an appointment?"

"Actually, yes, I do. If you don't mind taking the rest of the tour on your own, I really have to change."

To get her hair done, he imagined, or her nails. Or to make her fifty-minute hour with some society shrink. "Sure."

"I left the keys in the kitchen," she continued, juggling details. "There isn't a phone. I didn't know if you wanted one. There's a jack. Somewhere. If you need anything, you—"

"I'll be fine." He slipped a check out of his pocket and handed it to her. "Rent."

"Oh." She slipped it into her own pocket, sorry that she couldn't welcome one of her brother's old friends as a guest. But the rent would go a long way toward new ballet shoes and drawing lessons. "Thank you. Welcome to Templeton House, Michael."

She went to the door and down the steps. He walked to the side window and watched her cross the rolling lawn toward Templeton House.

"AND THERE I was," Laura muttered, "standing in the bathtub." She sighed, grateful for a lull in the customer flow in Pretenses so that she could vent to her friends. "Wearing rags. Holding a scrub brush. Stop laughing."

"In a minute," Kate promised, holding a hand to her aching stomach. "I'm perfecting the image in my mind first. The elegant Laura Templeton caught fighting pesky bathtub ring."

"Ring, hell. It's more like bathtub plague. And maybe I'll think it's funny in a year. Or two. But right now it's mortifying. He just stood there grinning at me."

"Mmm." Margo touched her tongue to her top lip. "And if memory serves, Michael Fury had one hell of a grin. Is he as wickedly, dangerously handsome as ever?"

"I didn't notice." Laura sniffed and gave her attention to rubbing a fingerprint off the glass display case.

"Liar." Margo leaned closer. "Come on, Laura. Tell."

"I suppose he looked a bit like a twentieth-century version of Heathcliff. Dark, brooding, potentially violent, and rough around the edges." Her shoulders shrugged again. "If that sort of thing appeals to you."

"It wouldn't make me look the other way," Margo decided. "Josh said he was a mercenary for a while."

"A mercenary?" She'd forgotten that and remembering now, nodded, "Figures."

"And I ran into him once in France when he was racing. Cars." Margo tilted her head as she brought the memory back. "We had an interesting evening together."

Laura lifted a brow. "Oh, really?"

"Interesting," Margo repeated and left it at that. "Then it was stunt work in Hollywood. And now it's horses. I wonder if he'll stick around this time. I know Josh hopes he does."

"At least the situation has pushed me into getting the stables in shape." Wanting busy work, Laura moved to the shelves and began to tidy glassware. "I've neglected them too long. In fact, I may think about getting a horse myself once I can manage it. The girls might like that."

"So what kind of horses does he raise? Breed. Own. Whatever," Kate wondered.

"I didn't ask. I just showed him around the apartment, gave him the keys. I suppose he's competent. Josh seems to think so. And if his rent check doesn't bounce, I'll assume he's reliable. I can't imagine I'd want any more out of a tenant. Horses take a lot of time and work." Which meant, Laura thought, she couldn't even consider having them again for at least a decade. "He'll be busy. I doubt we'll see much of him."

The door opened for a pair of customers. Recognizing them as regulars, Laura smiled, stepped forward. "I'll take them," she murmured to her partners. "Good to see you, Mrs. Myers, Mrs. Lomax. What can I show you today?"

As Laura led the customers into the wardrobe room, Margo considered. "She's trying not to be interested."

"Hmm?"

"Laura. She had the look of a woman who's been intrigued by a man and is trying not to be." After a moment's thought, Margo smiled broadly. "Good."

"And why would that be good?"

"It's time she had a little distraction in her life. A little male distraction."

"And do you ever think of any other kind of distraction?"

"Kate—" Amused, Margo patted her friend's hand. "From a woman newly married to a certified hunk, that's a very stupid question. Laura's never let herself cut loose when it comes to men. I think Michael Fury might just be the perfect thirtieth birthday present."

"He's a man, Margo, not a pair of earrings."

"Oh, but darling, I think he might look wonderful on her. So to speak."

"And I don't suppose it occurs to you that they might not be interested in each other, in a sexual way. Wait." Kate held up a hand. "I forgot who I was talking to."

"Don't be snide." Margo tapped her fingers on the counter. "You've got a man and a woman, both unattached as far as we know, both attractive. Josh has put them in close proximity. Though I doubt it was his intention, he's created a very interesting situation."

"When you put it like that." Concerned, Kate glanced toward the wardrobe room. "Look, I always liked Mick, but he was a wild child. We could have a lamb and wolf situation here."

"I certainly hope you're right. Every woman needs at least one close encounter with a wolf. But . . ." They were talking about Laura, after all. "I'll have to invite Michael over for dinner. Check him out myself."

"And I suppose we'll have to bow to your greater judgment and experience."

"Naturally." The door jangled open again. "Back to work, partner."

IN THE WARDROBE room Laura was patiently showing their selection of cashmere sweaters. If she had been aware of the direction her friends were taking she would have been both amused and appalled.

Men in general simply weren't of interest to her. She didn't hate them. Her experience with Peter hadn't turned her into a shrew, made her frigid, or narrowed her vision so that she considered men the enemy. Too many good men had touched her life for that. She had her father as a prime example. Her brother was another. And over the past months, she had come to love Byron De Witt.

Family was one thing. Intimate, even casual, relationships were another. She didn't have the time, inclination, or energy for one. In the two years since she had ended her marriage, she had been struggling to rebuild her life on all levels. Her children, her home, her work for Templeton. And Pretenses.

While her customers debated their selections, she eased back to give them room, musing on the events that had led to starting the shop. It had been an impulse, a step she'd taken for Margo as much as for herself.

Margo's career and finances had been in ruins when she returned to Monterey from Europe. The idea of liquidating her possessions and creating an intriguing space in which to sell them had been a risk, but it had paid off from the first moment.

Not just in dollars, Laura thought, as she wandered back into the main showroom. In pride, in confidence. In friendship and fun.

When they bought the building, it was an empty space, dusty, scarred, smelly. Their vision, their effort had turned it into the remarkable. Now the glass of the wide display window sparkled in the sunlight and teased passersby with clever hints of what was offered inside.

A sassy cocktail dress in emerald, with the nostalgic touch of peacock feathers at the shoulder, was draped over the elegant chair of a woman's vanity. Colorful bottles stood on the glossy surface, along with a jeweled collar. One of the drawers was open so that glittery rhinestones and shimmering silks spilled out. There was a lamp shaped like a swan, a single crystal flute beside an empty bottle of champagne. A man's cuff links and carelessly tossed formal black tie mingled with the woman's trinkets. A pair of red spike heels was artfully positioned to give the impression that their owner had just stepped out of them.

The little vignettes in the display were usually Margo's domain, but Laura had designed this one. And was proud of it. As she was of the shop as a whole. Throughout the spacious showroom was scattered the unique, the fanciful. The warm rose walls complemented glass shelves filled with treasures. Porcelain boxes, silver services, gold-ringed stemware. A velvet settee—the third they'd had to stock—provided customers a chance to sit, enjoy a cup of tea, a glass of champagne.

Gilded tightwinder stairs spiraled up toward the open balcony that ringed the room and led to the boudoir where negligees, peignoirs, and other night apparel were displayed in a gorgeous rosewood armoire. Everything was for sale, from the rococo bed to the smallest silver trinket box. And nothing was duplicated.

The shop had quite literally saved all three of them. And though she wouldn't have thought it possible, it had brought them even closer together.

As she hovered outside the wardrobe room, she watched Margo show a customer a sapphire bracelet from the display. Kate discussed the origins of an Art Nouveau lamp with another. A new customer studied an opal snuff bottle while her companion perused the selection of evening bags.

Mozart was playing on the stereo, softly. Through the window, Laura caught glimpses of the busy traffic on Cannery Row. Cars chugged or streamed or jockeyed for position. People strolled by on the sidewalk. A man passed with a young boy giggling from his perch on Daddy's shoulders. A couple, arm in arm, stopped to admire the display—and moments later came inside.

"Ms. Templeton?"

Pulling herself back from her reverie, Laura turned to the wardrobe room. "Yes, Mrs. Myers, did you find something you like?"

The woman smiled, held out her choice. "I never leave Pretenses disappointed."

The glow of pride was swift and satisfying. Laura accepted the cashmere. "We're here to see that you never do."

CHAPTER 4

"PRETTY GOOD DIGS, right, boy?" Michael groomed Max, his pride and joy while the enormous buff-colored Tennessee walker snorted in agreement.

The Templeton horse palace was a far cry from the simple working stables that Michael had built in the hills, then watched collapse under walls of mud. Not that it had looked much like a palace when he stepped inside that first afternoon, when he ran into Laura. Then it bore more than a slight resemblance to some fairy-tale cottage long under a wicked spell, deserted by all who had once inhabited it.

He had to grin at the thought, and at the fact that everything about the Templeton estate made him think of fairy tales with golden edges.

What he found in the stables was dust, disuse, and disrepair.

It had taken him the best part of a week to ready the building. No easy task for one man and a single pair of hands, but he wasn't willing to move his horses in until their temporary home had been cleaned and organized to his specifications.

On the other hand, for that week he'd had to endure the public stables, the painfully high fee for boarding, and the fact that his own lodgings were miles away from his stock. But the results were well worth the investment of a few sixteen-hour, muscle-aching days.

It was a good, solid building, with the stylish touches that the Templetons were known for. The loose boxes had plenty of space and light and air, a more important feature to Michael than the intricately laid brick flooring, the decorative tiles around the mangers, or the ornate ironwork above them, with its center stylized T in polished brass.

Though he did consider the fancy work a nice touch.

The layout was practical, with the tack room at one end of the block, the feed room at the other. Though he was baffled by the obvious neglect and disuse, he put his back into it and dug in to correct the situation. He hauled and hammered, swept and scrubbed until every stall met his stringent standards for his babies.

He thought of them as such, secretly.

He'd had fresh hay and straw delivered that morning and had been grateful that the boy who delivered it had been willing to make a few extra dollars by helping Michael store the bales.

Now each stall was deeply bedded with wheat straw—expensive and difficult to come by, but these were his babies, after all. Some tools and some ingenuity had put the automatic drinking bowls back in working order. He oiled hinges on stall doors, replaced hooks that had rusted away.

Since he'd lost all of his supplies in the mud, he had to restock grain, electrolytes, vitamins, medicines. He'd managed to salvage some tack, some tools. Every piece had been cleaned and polished, and what couldn't be saved had been, or would shortly be, replaced.

His fifteen horses were housed as royally as he could manage, but as yet, he hadn't done more than sleep in the upstairs apartment.

"You've come up in the world, Max. You might not know it, but you are now a tenant of the Templeton estate. That is one big fucking deal, pal, take my word for it."

He slapped the horse affectionately on the flank and pulled a carrot out of the pouch tied at his waist. "I've already started designing your new place. Don't worry. Maybe we'll add a few of the fancier touches ourselves this time around. But in the meantime, you can't do much better than this."

Max took the carrot politely, and the dark eye he turned to Michael was filled with patience, wisdom, and, Michael liked to think, affection as well.

He stepped out of the stall, latched the bottom half of the door with its foot bolt, then moved down the block. The floor might have been fancy enough for a garden party, but it sloped perfectly. His boot heels clicked. In anticipation, a chestnut head poked over the adjoining stall door.

"Looking for me, baby?" This was his sweetheart, as kind and gentle a mare as he had ever worked with. He'd bought her as a foal, and now she was heavily pregnant and had been assigned to the foaling stall. He called her Darling.

"How's it going today? You're going to be happy here." He stepped inside and ran his hands over her enormous sides. Like an expectant father, he was filled with anticipation and concern. She was small, barely fourteen hands, and he worried about how she would fare when her time came.

Darling liked to have her belly rubbed, and she blew appreciatively when Michael obliged her. "So beautiful." He cupped her face in his hands as a man might hold the face of a cherished woman. "You're the most beautiful thing I've ever owned."

Pleased with the attention, she blew again, then lowered her head to nibble at his pouch. Chuckling, he took out an apple—she preferred them to carrots. "Here you go, Darling. You're eating for two."

He heard the voices—young, excited, almost piping—and stepped out of the stall.

"Mama said we're not supposed to bother him."

"We're not going to bother him. We'll just look. Come on, Kayla. Don't you want to see the horses?"

"Yeah, but . . . What if he's in there? What if he yells at us?"

"Then we'll just run away, but we'll get to see the horses first."

Amused, wondering if Laura had painted him as an ogre or a recluse, Michael stepped out of the shadows of the stables and into the sunlight. If he'd been a poetic man, he would have said he'd encountered two angels.

They thought they were looking into the face of the devil himself. He was all in black, with shadows behind him. The hard, handsome face was unsmiling and dark with stubble. His hair reached almost to his shoulders, and he had a black bandanna tied around his forehead, like a wild Indian, or a pirate.

He seemed big, huge, dangerous.

Her heart jittering, Ali put a hand on Kayla's shoulder, both to protect her sister and to steady herself. "We live here," she stammered. "We can be here."

He couldn't resist playing it out a little. "Is that so? Well, I live here. And I don't look kindly on trespassers. You wouldn't be horse thieves, would you? We have to hang horse thieves."

Shocked, appalled, terrified, Ali could only shake her head vigorously. But Kayla stepped forward, fascinated.

"You have pretty eyes," she said, dimpling into a smile. "Are you really a troublemaking hoodlum? Annie said so."

All Ali could do was whisper her sister's name in mortification and fear.

Ah, he thought, Ann Sullivan, sowing his youthful reputation ahead of him. "I used to be. I gave it up." Christ, the kid was a picture, he thought. A heart melter. "Your name's Kayla, and you have your mother's eyes."

"Uh-huh, and that's Ali. She's ten. I'm seven and a half, and I lost a tooth." She grinned widely to show him the accomplishment.

"Cool. Have you looked for it?"

She giggled. "No, the Tooth Fairy has it. She took it up into the sky to make a star out of it. Do you have all your teeth?"

"Last time I checked."

"You're Mr. Fury. Mama says we have to call you that. I like your name, it's like a storybook person."

"A villain?"

"Maybe." She twinkled at him. "Can we see your horses, Mr. Fury? We won't steal them or hurt them or anything."

"I think they'd like to see you." He offered a hand, which Kayla took without hesitation. "Come on, Ali," he said casually. "I won't yell at you unless you deserve it."

Biting her lip, Ali followed them into the stables. "Oh!" She jolted back, then giggled at herself when Max stuck his huge head over the stall door. "He's so big. He's so pretty." She started to reach out, then stuck her hand behind her back.

"You can pet him," Michael told her. The older girl was a little shy, he decided, and pretty as a picture in a book. "He doesn't bite. Unless you deserve it." To demonstrate, he hauled Kayla up on his hip. "Go ahead, meet Max. He's a Southern gentleman."

"Our uncle is a Southern gentleman," Kayla announced. "But he doesn't look like Max." Delighted, she stroked the soft cheek. "Smooth," she murmured. "Hello, Max. Hello."

Not one to be outmatched by her kid sister, Ali stepped forward again and touched Max's other cheek. "Does he let you ride him and everything?"

"Yep. Max and I have fought wild Indians together, been wild Indians together, robbed stagecoaches, jumped ravines." Looking down into two pairs of wide eyes, he grinned. "Max is a Hollywood star."

"Really?" Enchanted, Kayla touched one velvet ear, giggling when it flicked under her fingers.

"Really. I'll show you his press clippings later. Come meet Darling. She's going to have a baby soon."

"Aunt Margo just had one." Kayla chattered gaily as they made the new acquaintance. "His name is John Thomas, but we call him J. T. Do horses have babies the same way people have them?"

"Pretty much," Michael murmured and skirted the issue by distracting the girls with the mare.

They met Jack, the dignified gelding, and Lulu, a frisky mare. Then Zip, the fastest horse—so Michael claimed—in the West.

"Why do you have so many?" Suspicion of the man couldn't hold out against delight with horses. With shyness outmatched by curiosity, Ali dogged Michael's every move and peppered him with questions.

"I train them. I buy them, sell them."

"Sell them?" The very idea had Kayla's lip poking out.

"All but Max and Darling. I won't sell them, ever. But the others will go to people who'll appreciate their talents and take good care of them. They all have a destiny. Now Jack here, he's going to make someone a good saddle horse. He'll ride forever if you ask him. And Flash, he'll be a hell of a stunt pony when I'm finished with him."

"You mean he'll do tricks?"

"Yeah." Michael grinned at Kayla. "He's already got a few up his sleeve. But Max—now Max knows them all. Want a show?"

"Really, can we?"

"It'll cost you."

"How much?" Kayla demanded. "I have money in my bank."

"Not money," Michael said as he led them back to Max. "If you like the show, you have to come back and work it off."

"What kind of work?" Ali wanted to know.

"We'll talk about it. Come on, Max." Michael took a bridle and slipped it on. "You've got a couple of ladies to impress here."

At five, Max was a veteran performer. He high-stepped it outside, pleased to have an audience. Michael led him to the small paddock beside the building. "You girls stay at the fence there. This could get hairy. Take your bows, Max."

Max gracefully bent his front legs and lowered himself. When the girls erupted with applause, Michael could have sworn that Max grinned.

"Up," he ordered.

Using voice and hand signals, Michael took Max through his routine. The big horse reared, pawed the air, let out a high whinny. He pranced, sidestepped, danced, circled. Then when Michael swung up onto his bare back, he repeated the routine with variations.

"Now here's his 'we've been walking in the desert for three days without water routine.'" At the signal, Max drooped, his head fell limply, and he plodded along as though each step would be his last. "Now, look out, rattlesnake." Max leapt back, bunched up, cowered. "God almighty, the posse shot my horse right out from under me. Dead horse, Max."

For his finale Max wheeled, cantered to the left, and dropped to the ground. Michael tumbled off, rolled. As he got to his feet, he caught sight of Laura, racing in skinny little heels across the yard.

"Oh, God, are you all right? How did it happen? Oh, your horse!"

Though he started to speak, Michael found himself too involved in watching that nifty length of bare leg as she vaulted the fence in her neat little lady's suit.

Max lay dead, hardly flicking an eye when Laura knelt at his head. "Poor thing, poor thing! Is it his leg? Who's your vet?"

At the sight of the horse lying with his big head nestled in the lap of Laura's pretty blue skirt, Michael tucked his tongue in his cheek. "Looks like it's curtains for old Max."

"Don't say that," Laura snapped back. "He might have just bruised something." But what if he hadn't? She pushed back the hair that curled flirtatiously at her jaw. "Girls, go back to the house now."

"But, Mama—"

"Don't argue." She couldn't bear the idea of either of them witnessing what might have to be done.

"Laura," Michael began.

"Why are you just standing there?" Worry and temper warred in her eyes. "Why aren't you doing something? The poor thing is suffering, and you're just standing there. Don't you care about your own horse?"

"Yes, ma'am, I do. Max, cut."

On cue, and to Laura's astonishment, the big horse rolled again, then got to his feet.

"It was a trick, Mama." Kayla laughed gaily at the shared joke while Michael pulled Laura up. "Max does tricks. He was playing dead. Like a dog does. Isn't he wonderful? Isn't he smart?"

"Yes." Under a ragged cloak of dignity, Laura brushed off her skirt. "He's certainly talented."

"Sorry." A wise man knew when to smother a grin. Michael rarely chose to be wise. "I'd have warned you if I'd seen you coming. Then you were off and running." He scratched his cheek. "Seemed a lot more worried about my horse than about me. I could have broken my neck."

"The horse was down," Laura said primly. "You weren't." But everything faded into admiration as Max bent his head to her. "Oh, he is beautiful. Aren't you gorgeous? Aren't you clever?"

"Max has been in lots of movies." Ali moved closer. "So has Mr. Fury."

"Oh?"

"Stunts," Michael explained. He took a carrot out of his pouch, handed it to Laura. "Give him that, he's your slave for life."

"Who could resist?" As she offered the treat, she spoke slowly. "Didn't I tell you girls not to pester Mr. Fury?"

"Yes, but he said we weren't." Kayla smiled hopefully up at Michael. Standing on the rail of the fence, she lifted her arms, confident.

"Because you weren't." He hauled her up, fit her so naturally on his hip that Laura frowned. "I like the company," he said to Laura. "So do the horses. They get tired of looking at me all day. The kids are welcome to come by anytime. If they're in my way, I'll tell them."

To Kayla's delight, and Laura's momentary horror, he plunked Kayla onto Max's wide back.

"It's high. Look how high up I am."

"I'm trying not to," Laura said, her hand automatically going to the bridle. "He's a stunt horse, not a saddle pony."

"Gentle as a lamb," Michael assured her, then lifted Ali over the fence and put her behind her sister. "He'll carry the three of you if you want. He's also strong as a bull."

"No, thank you." Her heart settled as she looked into Max's eyes. They were indeed gentle. "I'm not exactly dressed for it."

"So I noticed. You look good, Ms. Templeton. And you looked damned good climbing over the fence."

She looked back, into Michael's eyes. Gentle? No, indeed, she thought. But just as compelling. "I imagine I made quite a picture."

"You don't know the half of it, sugar."

She stepped back. "Okay, girls, party's over. You need to wash up for dinner."

Ali started to complain, stopped herself. She didn't want to risk being told she couldn't come back. "Can Mr. Fury come to dinner?"

"Oh." Discomfort and manners. Manners always won. "Of course Michael, you're welcome to come."

And if he'd ever received a cooler and less enthusiastic invitation, he couldn't remember. "Thanks, but I have plans. I'm heading over to Josh's to meet his son."

"Well, then." She reached up, lifted Kayla, then Ali to the ground. "We'll get out of your way."

"There were a couple of things I wanted to run by you. If you've got a minute."

"Of course." Her feet were killing her. All she wanted was to take off those damn heels and sit down. "Girls, tell Annie I'll be in shortly."

"Thank you, Mr. Fury." Her mother's daughter to the core, Ali offered a hand.

"You're welcome."

"Thanks, Mr. Fury, for showing us the horses, and the tricks and everything. I want to tell Annie." Kayla started to race off but stopped at the fence. "Mr. Fury?"

"Yes, ma'am?"

She giggled at that, then sobered. "Can you teach dogs, too? If you had a puppy, or somebody did, could you teach him tricks like Max?"

"I expect I could, if he was a good dog."

She smiled again, wistfully, then hurried away behind her sister.

"She wants a dog," Laura murmured. "I didn't know. She never said. She asked years ago, but Peter. . . . Damn it. I should have realized."

Intrigued, Michael watched the varied emotions play over her face. And the weightiest was guilt. "Do you always beat yourself up this way?"

"I should have known. She's my child. I should have known she wanted a puppy." Suddenly tired, she dragged her hands through her hair.

"So get her one."

Her chin set. "I will. I'm sorry." Shaking off the guilt, she looked back at Michael. "What did you need?"

"Oh, I need a lot of things." Casually, he draped an arm around Max's neck. "A hot meal, a fast car, the love of a good woman—but what we both need is a couple of mousers."

"Excuse me?"

"You need some barn cats, Laura. You got rodents."

"Oh, God." She shuddered once, blew out a breath. "I should have realized that, too. We used to keep some when we had horses, but Peter—" She broke off, shut her eyes. No, she was not traveling down that road again. "I'll be making a trip to the pound, it seems. I'll get a couple of cats."

"You're going to get your kid a dog from the pound?"

"And why not?"

"No reason." He led Max toward the fence. "Figured you for the pure-bred type, that's all. That's the way some people are about horses. They want Arabians, Thoroughbreds. I've got me one of the prettiest fillies you could want in that stable. She's smart as a whip and quick as a snake. She's what you'd call a mongrel, though. Always liked mongrels myself."

"I prefer character above lineage."

"Good for you." In an absentminded movement, he bent down, plucked a struggling buttercup out of its patch of grass, and handed it to her. "I'd say you've got both in those girls of yours. They're beauties. Heartbreakers. The little one's already wrapped her fist around mine. And she knows it."

"You surprise me." She stared down at the sunny yellow flower in her hand, baffled. Despite fatigue and aching feet, she followed him into the stables. "You don't strike me as a man who'd take to children. Little girls."

"Mongrels are full of surprises."

"I didn't mean—"

"I know you didn't." He settled Max in his stall, latched the door. "The little one's got your eyes, smoke and storms. Ali's got your mouth, soft and wanting to be stubborn." He grinned then. "You breed good, Laura."

"I suppose I should thank you, though no one's ever put it quite that way before. And I appreciate your entertaining them, but I don't want you to feel obligated."

"I don't. I said I like them. I meant it. Besides, they owe me for the show. Me and Max don't work for free. I could use some help around here."

"Help?"

"Mucking out, hauling hay. Unless you've got a problem with your progeny shoveling manure."

She'd shoved plenty herself in her day. "No. It'll be good for them." Automatically, she lifted a hand to stroke Max's nose. "You've worked a minor miracle here," she noted, glancing down the spotless building.

"I've got a strong back and plenty of ambition."

"For?"

"Making something out of this. Saddle horses, trick ponies, jumpers. I've got a way with them."

"If Max is any example, I'd say you've got a major way with them. Were you really a mercenary?"

"Among other things, including the troublemaking hoodlum Mrs. Sullivan claims I am."

"Oh." She rolled her eyes at Max, cleared her throat. "I expect Annie's remembering the boy who gave Josh his first cigarette."

"One of my lesser crimes. I quit six months ago myself. Easier than worrying about setting fire to the hay."

"Or dying of lung cancer."

"You gotta die of something."

She turned just as he reached up to slip the bridle off Max. Their bodies bumped. As much out of curiosity as to steady her, he took her arms.

Soft. Fragile as he'd imagined. And as he shifted, just a little, the gentle swell of her breasts pressed against him. Her eyes had whipped to his at first contact. They stayed there as her heart hammered.

"I always wondered what kind of handful you'd be." He smiled, let his hands run up and down those pretty arms. "Never had the opportunity to find out before. Of course, you were too young for me back then. You've caught up close enough now."

"Excuse me." That was her voice, calm and cool. She was able to manage that, though everything inside her was hot and unsteady.

"You're not in my way." Easily, he lifted a hand to toy with a curl that flirted with her cheek.

"Then you're in mine." She didn't know how to handle men. Had never had to, really. But she was smart enough to know that now she needed a crash course. "I'm not interested in flirtations."

"Me either."

She borrowed a page from Margo's book, made her eyes bored.

"Michael, I'm sure scores of women would be flattered. If I had the time, I might be flattered myself. But I don't have the time. My children are waiting to have their dinner."

"You've got that down," he acknowledged. "Lady of the manor. You were born for it." He stepped back. "If you find yourself with time on your hands, you know where to find me."

"Give my best to Josh and Margo," she said as she set out on watery legs for the house.

"Sure. Hey, sugar?"

Bristling only a little at the term, she looked back. "The mousers. Don't come bringing me some furry little kittens. I want big hungry toms."

"I'll see what I can do."

"I'm sure you will," he murmured as she walked away. "Christ, what a package," he said to Max. Amused at himself, Michael rubbed the heel of his hand against his heart. It had yet to settle down for him. "She's the type that makes a man feel like a big hungry tom. And clumsy with it."

Shaking his head, Michael headed upstairs to wash off the stable dirt.

"So, MARGO'S A mommy." Michael grinned at his hostess, who failed to look the least bit maternal in a peach-toned jumpsuit that clung glamorously to every curve.

"I'm a great mommy." She kissed both his cheeks, European fashion. "I love being a mommy." Drawing back, she took a long look and wasn't disappointed. "What's it been, Michael? Six years, seven?"

"Longer. I was trying to tear up the European circuit, and you were taking the Continent by storm."

"Those were the days," she said lightly and, tucking her arm through his, led him inside.

"Great place." He wasn't surprised by the elegance of the California Spanish, but he was by its coziness.

"Kate turned us on to it. You remember Kate Powell."

"Sure." They strolled out of the tiled foyer into a spacious room with a blazing fire and twin sofas in deep maroon. "How's she doing? I heard she's married now."

"Still a newlywed. You'd like Byron, I think. We'll have to have a party when you're settled. Introduce you around."

"I'm not much of a partier these days."

"A small one, then. What can I get you to drink?" She glided behind a deeply carved bar. "Josh will be right down. He had a meeting run over."

"Got a beer?"

"I think we can manage that." From the small cold box under the bar she chose a bottle. "So it's horses now."

"It seems to be."

He watched her open the bottle, pour beer smoothly into a pilsner. On the third finger of her left hand diamonds and gold flashed. Her hair was more gold, soft, flowing waves of it. And there were more diamonds at her ears. Still, he saw that it was her eyes that shined the brightest.

"You look good, Margo. Happy. It's nice to see you happy."

A little surprised, she glanced up. "Really?"

"You never seemed to be really quite there."

"Apparently you were right." She set the glass on the bar and pried the silver wine saver off a bottle of champagne. "But I've gotten there."

"A wife, a mommy, and a shopkeeper." He lifted his glass in a toast. "Who'd have thought it?"

"And doing a marvelous job at all three." After pouring herself a flute of champagne, she toasted herself in turn. "You'll have to come by Pretenses, Michael. We're on Cannery Row."

"I'll come see your shop, you come see my horses."

"That's a deal. I'm sorry about your house."

He shrugged his shoulders. "No big deal. I didn't like it anyway. I was more pissed off about the stables. I'd barely gotten them finished when I lost them. Still, it's just wood and nails. I can buy more."

"It must have been horrible. I've seen film of mud slides and the aftermath of some. I can't imagine being in the middle of it."

"You don't want to."

He still had moments when the image of driving rain, thundering earth, and wicked winds flashed into his mind. And the panic that came with the flash that he wouldn't be quick enough, strong enough, smart enough to save what mattered to him.

"Anyway, I'm working on the plans for rebuilding, got a contractor lined up. It's mostly just time and money."

"I'm sure you'll be comfortable at Templeton House until you've rebuilt."

"It's hard not to be. I met Laura's kids today. Beautiful kids. The older one's reserving judgment on me, but Kayla—" He chuckled. "She just moves right in."

"They're wonderful girls. Laura's done a terrific job there."

"She hasn't changed much."

"More than you might think. The divorce was hard on her. Terribly hard. But she's got that strong Templeton core. You never met Peter Ridgeway, did you?"

"Nope."

"Trust me," Margo said and drank deeply. "He's a bastard."

"Sugar, you hate him, I'll hate him, too."

Laughing, she took his hand. "It's good to have you back, Michael."

"Moving in on my wife already, Fury?" Josh came in, an owl-eyed baby on his hip. "My kid and I'll fight you for her."

"I think he could take me." Curious, Michael set his beer aside and walked over to study J. T. The baby studied him right back, then reached out and grabbed a handful of Michael's hair. "Come here, slugger."

Even as Margo opened her mouth, dozens of maternal warnings on her tongue, Michael nipped J. T. neatly out of Josh's arms and settled him on his own hip. The natural move made Margo's eyes blink in surprise, then narrow with speculation.

Enjoying the stranger, J. T. gurgled.

"Great job, Harvard." Michael gave J. T. a quick nuzzle. "Congratulations."

"Thanks." Josh grinned at his wife. "I had a little help."

CHAPTER 5

LAURA DID BRING home a fuzzy little kitten. In fact, she brought home two. And a pair of lean, sharp-eyed toms. And a big-footed puppy with a spotted coat and an eager tongue.

The small zoo in her car caused her a bit of trouble but gave her a great deal of pleasure. She drove home with cats meowing bitterly in their boxes, kittens sleeping on the car mat, and an adoring puppy sprawled in her lap.

"Wait until the girls get a load of you." Already in love, she stroked the puppy's head. "And I guess if they fight over you, I'll just have to go back and pick up a brother or sister for you."

Laughing, she turned into the drive at Templeton House. So foolish, she realized, not to have done this before. Old habits, she mused. Peter hadn't wanted pets, so there had been no pets. But Peter had been gone nearly two years. And that was two years too long not to have made some simple adjustments.

After parking the car, she glanced around at her menagerie and blew out a breath. "How the hell am I going to manage to get you all inside?"

She had a leash for the pup, which she attached to his brand-new collar. She held out no hope that he would understand the purpose. For a brief moment, she considered laying on the horn until someone came out to give her a hand. Which, she assumed, would send her new petting zoo into a frenzy.

So she'd deal with it herself. "You first," she decided, and opened the door. The puppy cowered, sniffed at the empty space on the other side of her lap. Then, gathering his courage, he jumped. If she hadn't been laughing so hard, she would have held on to the leash. But the pup landed in a sprawl and looked so surprised that she roared with laughter and the leather slid out of her hands.

He was off and running.

"Oh, damn it." Still laughing, she sprang out of the car. "Come back here, you idiot."

Instead, he raced in circles, then cut through old Joe's pampered bed of narcissus, yapping joyously all the way.

"Oh, that's going to be a problem," she realized. Wincing, she walked around the car to retrieve the sleepy kittens. In the back, the toms continued to complain at the top of their lungs. "All right, all right. Give me a minute here."

Inspired, she tucked a kitten in each of her jacket pockets, then hauled out the cat boxes. "You two are Michael's problem." Following the excited barks, she headed toward the stables.

The sight that greeted her when she stepped through the arbor of wisteria was worth every moment of annoyance. In the far yard, her daughters were kneeling on the ground embracing and being embraced by a wildly enthusiastic spotted mutt.

She took the picture in her mind, slipped it into her heart.

"Look, Mama!" Kayla was already shouting as Laura started toward them. "Come quick and look at the little puppy. He must be lost."

"He doesn't look lost to me."

"He has a leash." Ali giggled—a sound Laura could never hear often enough—as he scrambled into her lap. "Maybe he ran away from home."

"I don't think so. He is home. He's ours."

Ali simply stared. "But we can't have pets."

With a smile, Laura adjusted her boxes. "He doesn't seem to agree with you."

"Do you mean it?" Kayla rose. The expression of stunned joy on her face carved itself into Laura's heart. "Do you mean he can be our puppy and we can keep him? Forever?"

"That's exactly what I mean."

"Mama!" In one leap, Kayla had her arms wrapped around her mother's waist. She clung hard, fierce. "Mama, thank you. I'll take such good care of him. You'll see."

"I know you will, honey." She looked over at Ali, who remained still, staring. "We all will. He needs a good home and lots of love. We'll give him that, won't we, Ali?"

Inner conflict held her back. Her father had said pets were a nuisance, messy. They shed hair all over the rug. But the puppy was sniffing at her leg, wagging his tail and trying to jump into her arms.

"We'll take good care of him," she said solemnly. She started to step forward, stopped. Her mouth went lax in shock. "Mama, your pockets are moving."

"Oh." With a laugh, Laura set her boxes down, reached in and plucked out two furry balls, one silken gray and the other sassy orange, from her pockets. "What have we here?"

"Kittens?" Kayla squealed, grabbed. "Kittens. We have kittens, too! Look, Ali, we have everything."

"They're so tiny." Gently, cautiously, Ali took the mewling gray. "Mama, they're so tiny."

"They're just babies. Just over six weeks old." Every bit as much in love as her daughters were, Laura stroked a fingertip down the sleepy gray. "They needed a home too."

"It's really all right?" Half afraid to hope, Ali looked up into her mother's eyes. "It's really all right for us to keep them all?"

"It's really all right."

"More!" Tuning in to the sounds coming from the cardboard boxes, Kayla pounced.

"No, those aren't ours. Those are barn cats, for Michael."

"I'll take them to him." Desperate to share her fabulous news with anyone who would listen, Kayla handed her kitten to Ali and hefted both boxes by the straps. Grunting a little, she headed toward the stables. "Come on, cats. Come on, I'll take you home."

"Do they have names?"

"Hmm." Absently Laura stroked her daughter's hair, then made herself look away from the comical picture of Kayla, bobbling along with two boxes full of impatient felines and a puppy racing around her legs in clumsy, big-footed circles. "They will have, when we pick them out."

"Can I name one myself? Pick out the name all by myself? For the little gray kitten?" Ali lifted it to her cheek.

"Of course you can. What name would you like?"

"Is it a boy or a girl?"

"It's—I don't know," Laura realized. "I forgot to ask. It's probably on one of the papers I filled out." With one arm around Ali's shoulders, she walked after Kayla. "The puppy's a boy, and both big cats are boys because that's what Michael wanted."

"Because he likes boys better?"

Uh-oh. "No, honey. I guess he figured tomcats would be meaner, and he wanted mousers."

Her eyes went huge. "He's going to let them eat mice?"

"Baby, I'm afraid that's what cats do."

Ali pressed the little ball of fluff to her cheek. "Mine won't."

Kayla's voice was already echoing in high, excited chirps, accented by the yaps of the pup, who had raced inside the stables with her. When Laura stepped in and her eyes adjusted to the dim light, she saw Michael and Kayla crouched together on the brick floor, taking stock of Templeton House's new mutt.

"Looks like a good dog to me," Michael stated, giving the pup an energetic scratch between the ears.

"So you can teach him tricks, right, Mr. Fury? How to sit and play dead and shake?"

"I expect."

The pup sniffed curiously at one of the cat boxes and was rewarded with a spitting hiss. Yelping, he streaked away and cringed behind Laura's legs.

"He's already learned something." With a grin, Michael opened the first box. "Don't mess with a cornered tom. No, honey." Michael took Kayla's hand before she could reach in to pet the cat. "I doubt he's in a friendly mood at the moment. Don't like being cooped up there, do you, big guy? Let's get you and your pal out."

He opened the other box, then drew Kayla back. "We'll just let them get the lay of the land. Once they've catted around some, they'll settle in." His eyes skimmed over Laura, lingered, then moved on. "Whatcha got there, Ali?"

"Kittens." Ali's hands and heart were full of them already. "Mama brought us kittens too."

"Fuzzy little kitties." As he walked to them, he ran his tongue around his teeth. "Cute."

"Mama said I could name the gray one myself."

"Then I get to name the orange one." Staking her claim, Kayla took the orange kitten out of Ali's hand and nuzzled it against her cheek. "Don't I, Mama?"

"Fair enough. We'll have a naming marathon after dinner. We'll just get out of Mr. Fury's way—"

"Can't we show the kittens to Max? Can't we?"

"Sure you can." Michael winked at Kayla. "He's a real softie." When the girls raced off, the pup at their heels, Michael shook his head. "What the hell have you done, Laura?"

"Made my girls very happy." She pushed back her hair. "And saved five lives in the bargain. Do you have a problem with kittens and puppies?"

"Nope." The cats had leaped out of their boxes and were slinking around, growling softly. Michael reached over and stroked the nose of his sober gelding. "You ever do anything halfway?"

"I've been known to." She unbent enough to smile. "I couldn't stop myself. If you'd seen the girls' faces when I told them that silly little dog was theirs . . . I'll never forget it."

With the same absent affection he'd shown the gelding, Michael stroked her cheek. He didn't know if he was amused or annoyed when she jerked like a spring. "You need some training yourself."

"Excuse me?"

"You shy easy. I appreciate you picking up the cats for me," he said before she could think of a response.

"No trouble. The whole lot of them need to go to the vet. Shots. Neutering."

"Ouch!" In a knee-jerk male reaction, he winced. "Yeah, I guess that's the deal."

"It's the responsible choice—and it's required when you adopt from the shelter. I have all the paperwork. Except I—"

"What?"

"Well, I didn't think to ask about the sex of the kittens. I don't know if they told me. It started to get complicated and confusing, and I think I've heard that it's difficult to tell with young kittens."

It took an effort, but he kept his eyes solemn. "I've always heard you shake 'em. If they don't rattle, they're female."

It took her a moment. Then she broke into easy, appreciative laughter. "I'll be sure to try it. When the girls aren't around."

"There you are. I don't suppose I've heard you laugh like that more than a half a dozen times since I've known you. You were always being too dignified when I was around."

"I'm sure you're mistaken."

"Sugar, I don't make many mistakes when it comes to women."

"No, I don't imagine you would." To give herself a moment to make her retreat—yes, damn it, a dignified retreat—she turned to the gelding. "This is a handsome horse."

"He's smart. Quiet-natured. Jack?"

give me his name, and I'll talk to him. I don't have to go to some lame dance. And I'm the last person your sister wants taking her to some lame dance."

"It's not like a date." So Margo had said when she'd drilled the request into his head. "It's just that Laura's feeling like a third wheel at these things. I didn't realize it myself, but Margo pointed it out."

And, Josh thought as he watched Michael divvy up grains, had made him feel like a lower form of life. "Then I realized how often Laura either skips going to events, or cuts out early. It would be nice for her to have an escort, that's all."

"A woman like your sister ought to have a platoon of likely escorts lined up and waiting." And all with the proper pedigree, Michael thought.

"Yeah, well, she doesn't seem interested in swimming with the sharks in the dating pool." Was he supposed to do something about that, too? Josh wondered and nearly shuddered. "She knows you, Mick. She'd be comfortable with you. And it would give you the chance to make some contacts. Everybody's happy."

"I'm not happy when I have to wear a tie." He glanced over his shoulder and grinned. "Not like you, Harvard, in your fancy Italian suit. Get the hell out of my barn."

"Come on, Mick. It's just one night out of your fascinating and fun-filled life. We'll hit the game room, play some billiards, tell some lies."

There was that, Michael considered. And the alternative was a sandwich and an evening hunkered over his drawings for his projected house. "I can still bury your ass at pool."

"I'll lend you a tie."

"Fuck you." One of the cats streaked by, pounced in a blur of black. There was a short squeal.

"Christ, that's disgusting."

"That's life, Harvard." Michael moved back to deal with Darling's meal, measuring the additives necessary for her condition.

"You really know what you're doing around here, don't you?"

"Apparently we all have our niche."

Josh mused over how many niches Michael had already found and rejected. Yet he had a feeling this one was different. They'd known each other too long and too well for Josh to miss the easy contentment in his friend's moves. A contentment, he thought, that had never quite been there before.

"This is the one, isn't it?"

Michael glanced over. He didn't need to explain, not to Josh. He only needed to say one word. "Yeah."

At his name the horse pricked his ears. Soberly, he turned his head to Michael. "How old are you, Jack?"

In response, the horse stomped a foot four times.

"What do you think of the lady here?"

Jack rolled his eyes toward Laura and let out a quiet and undeniably roguish whinny.

Charmed, Laura laughed again. "How do you get him to do that?"

"Jack? He understands every word you say. Want to take the lady for a ride, Jack?" The response was a decisive nod. "See?" Michael turned his own swift—and undeniably roguish grin—on Laura. "Want a ride, lady?"

"I—" God, she would love one, love to feel a horse beneath her again, let it have its head. Let herself lose hers. "I'd enjoy that, but I don't have the time." She offered Michael a polite, distant smile. "I'll take a rain check."

"Cash it in whenever you like." Too used to Thoroughbreds, he assumed, and shrugged. He'd take Jack over some finicky purebred any day.

"Thank you. I'd better get my motley crew inside. That is, if Annie lets us inside."

"She's a tough nut, Mrs. Sullivan."

"She's family," Laura corrected. "But I should have warned her before I started a small zoo."

"That small zoo is going to keep you up most of the night."

"I'll manage."

SHE MANAGED, BUT it wasn't a walk in the park. The puppy whimpered and whined and, despite Kayla's lavish love, was satisfied with nothing less than Laura's bed. She knew it was a mistake, but she couldn't bring herself to banish him when he cuddled so hopefully against her side.

The kittens mewed, fretted, cried, and eventually were comforted by each other, and the hot water bottle that an already doting Annie provided.

As a result, Laura was gritty-eyed and foggy-brained the next morning.

She fumbled at the keyboard in her office at the hotel, cursed herself, then focused on the file for an upcoming writers' convention. Twelve hundred people checking in at approximately the same time, certainly on the same day, were going to present a challenge. Then there were the hospitality suites, banquet and seminar rooms, audio equipment, pitchers of water, requests for coffee services, catering demands.

Cartons of books were already arriving by the truckload. She appreciated the spirit of the planned book signing for literacy, as well as the headaches it was going to cause her and her staff.

Composing a memo one-handed, she picked up her ringing phone. At the sound of the conference coordinator's voice, she struggled not to wince. "Yes, Melissa, it's Laura Templeton. How can I help you today?"

And tomorrow, and for the rest of my natural life, she thought as the woman requested more additions, more changes, just a few more little adjustments.

"Naturally, if the weather's inclement and we're unable to hold your welcoming party at poolside, we'll provide you with an alternate space. The Garden Ballroom is lovely. We often hold wedding receptions there. It's still available for that date."

She listened, rubbed fingers against her temple. "No, I'm not able to do that, Melissa, but if we do book the ballroom, we'll provide another alternate. I realize we're talking more than a thousand people. We'll accommodate you."

She continued to listen, made notes that somehow became mindless doodles. "Yes, I'm looking forward to seeing you again, too. I'll be in touch."

Taking one breath, one moment to clear her mind again, she got back to her memo.

"Laura."

She didn't groan, but she wanted to. "Byron, did we have a meeting?"

"No." He stepped in, seemed to fill her small office with his size. "Aren't you taking lunch?"

"Lunch? It can't be noon."

"No, it can't," he said mildly as she looked at her watch. "It's half past noon."

"The morning got away from me. I'm due at the shop in an hour. I have to finish this. Is there something urgent?"

Eyeing her, he closed the door at his back. "Take a break."

"I really can't. I need—"

"Take a break," he repeated. "That's an order." To ensure that she obeyed it, he sat down. "Now, Ms. Templeton, let's talk about delegating."

"Byron, I do delegate. It's just that Fitz is running ragged over the Milhouse-Drury wedding reception, and Robyn's swamped. The pharmaceutical convention and a kid with chicken pox. And—"

"And it all comes down to you," he finished. "You look exhausted, honey."

She pouted. "Are you speaking as my brother-in-law or as executive director?"

"Both. If you're not going to take care of yourself—"

"I am taking care of myself." She smothered a smile. Byron's stand on

health and fitness was well known. "I just didn't get much sleep last night. I went to the pound yesterday."

He brightened, as she'd known he would. He'd adopted two dogs the year before. "Yeah? What did you get?"

"A puppy and two kittens. The girls are in ecstasy. And this morning, I caught Annie carrying the pup like he was a newborn baby, and telling him that good dogs mustn't piddle on the Bokhara rug."

"Start stocking up on newspaper. We'll have to come over and check out your new additions."

"Come by tonight."

He raised an eyebrow. "Before or after the country club dance?"

"The Valentine's Day dance." She shut her eyes. "I forgot."

"No getting out of it, Laura. You're a Templeton. You're expected."

"I know, I know." There went the long, indulgent bath-and-early-to-bed night she'd been fantasizing about. "I'll be there. I would have remembered."

"If you hadn't, Kate and Margo would have reminded you. Look, why don't you let your partners handle the shop this afternoon? Go take a nap."

"J. T. is having his checkup this afternoon. I can't leave Kate on her own. We're inundated with the Valentine's Day sale."

"Which reminds me . . ."

Understanding, she smiled. "It's only the tenth, Byron. You still have time to pick up that well-thought-out, loving gift. And no matter what Kate says, don't buy her computer software. Flowers always work for me."

And no one had sent her flowers, she thought, in too long to remember. When her mind drifted to a tiny yellow wildflower, she pulled it back, and called herself an idiot.

"She's not getting that new calculator she's been hinting for, either." He rose. "Do you want a lift to the club tonight?"

So went the life of a single woman, Laura mused. Always tagging along with couples. "No, thanks. I'll see you there."

"I'M NOT THE country club type, Josh." As if someone had already forced him into a suit, Michael rolled his shoulders.

"I'd consider it a favor."

Scowling, Michael measured out grain. "I hate it when you do that."

"And I'd be able to introduce you to a lot of potential horse owners. I happen to know someone who has an impressive stud. You did say you have a mare ready to breed."

"Yeah, she's ready." And he wanted the right sire for her. "So, you'll

"If I know you, you want to make something big out of it."

He yearned to. "In my own time."

Josh took his, waiting while Michael fed the expectant mother, checked her hay-net, babied her. "Monterey Riding Academy? The owners are friends of the family."

"So?"

"They'll be at the club tonight. Kate was their accountant when she was with Bittle and Associates. They do a lot of buying and selling. So do their students."

Ambition, Michael admitted, was always a trap. "You're a slick son of a bitch, Harvard. You always were."

Josh merely grinned. "We all have our niche."

"Laura might not go for this little arrangement of yours."

"I can handle Laura," Josh said confidently, and checked his watch. "I've got enough time to slip by the shop and do just that before my last meeting today. The dance is at nine. I'll tell her you'll pick her up at eight-thirty—wearing a tie."

"If you don't make this worth my while, pal, I'll have to kick your ass." He brushed grain dust from his hands. "I won't enjoy it, but I'll have to do it."

"Understood." Satisfied with the outcome of his mission, Josh headed for the door. "Ah, you do know the way to the club, don't you?"

Appreciating the sarcasm, Michael tilted his head. "Maybe I will enjoy it after all."

SHE WAS FURIOUS, livid. And trapped. They'd ganged up on her, Laura fumed as she yanked the pearl gray Miska cocktail dress out of her closet. Josh and Margo and Kate, cornering her at Pretenses and all but presenting her with a fait accompli.

Michael Fury was escorting her to the country club dance. The arrangement would suit everyone. They wouldn't have to worry about her driving there and back alone or about her feeling awkward at an event designed for couples. Michael would gain an entrée and make contacts in the horse world.

Oh, yeah, it suited everyone just fine. Everyone but herself.

It was humiliating, she thought as she jerked the zipper up. A thirty-year-old woman being fixed up by her big brother. Worse, now Michael knew that she was the pathetic divorcée who couldn't get her own date. As if she wanted one in the first place, or the last place, or any place at all, for that matter.

"Which I don't," she told the dog, who had come into her room to watch her every move with adoring eyes. "I don't even want to go to the damn country club tonight. I'm tired."

Sympathetically he wiggled his butt as she stormed over to the closet for shoes and a beaded jacket. She didn't need to hang on to a man's arm to feel complete. She didn't need to hang on to anything, anyone. Why couldn't she just crawl into bed and read a book, she wondered. Eat popcorn and watch an old movie on TV until she fell asleep with the set still on.

Why did she have to dress up, go out in public, and be Laura Templeton?

She stopped, sighed. Because she *was* Laura Templeton. That was something she couldn't forget. Laura Templeton had responsibilities, she had an image to maintain.

So, she told herself as she picked up her lipstick and applied it skillfully, she would maintain it. She would get through the evening, say the right things to the right people. She would be as polite and friendly to Michael as necessary. And when the whole blasted thing was over, she would fall facedown on her bed and forget it. Until the next time.

She checked her hair. God, she needed a trim. And when was she going to fit that in? She turned for her bag and watched in mild horror as the pup wet on her Aubusson.

"Oh, Bongo!"

He grinned up at her and sat in his own pee.

IT WAS ONLY a small rebellion, but Michael didn't wear a tie. He figured that with Laura Templeton at his side they wouldn't boot him out for wearing a black turtleneck under his jacket.

He parked between the island of spring bulbs and the grand front entrance. And if he'd been wearing a tie, he would have tugged at it.

Nerves. They amazed him, disgusted him. But no matter how much he wanted to deny it, he felt like some pimply-faced teenager on a first date.

Ignoring the sky dusted with icy stars, the sheen of silvering moonlight, the scent of sea and flowers, he walked to the door like a man taking his last mile in shackles.

How the hell had he let himself get talked into this?

He'd never used the front door at Templeton House. As a boy, if he came by for Josh, or came along with him, he used the side or rear. The entrance was so damned imposing, grandly tall, recessed, and framed in tile. The knocker was a huge brass affair in the shape of a stylized T. Over his head hung an antique carriage light.

It didn't make him feel welcome.

Nor did Ann Sullivan when she opened the door to his knock. She stood, tight-lipped, in her starched black dress. He noted first that the years sat lightly on her. She was a lovely woman, if you looked past the jaundiced eye. Margo had come by her looks naturally.

"Mr. Fury." The faint hint of Ireland in her voice might have been charming if it hadn't been so damning.

Because for reasons he couldn't name he'd always wanted her approval, she put his back up. His smile was insolent. His voice matched it. "Mrs. Sullivan. It's been a while."

"It has," she returned, clearly telling him it hadn't been nearly long enough. "You're to come in."

He accepted the grudging invitation and stepped into the soaring foyer. The ivory and peacock-blue tiles were the same, he noted. As was the gorgeously ornate chandelier that sprinkled light. The place was welcoming, even if its doyenne wasn't. It was full of cozy scents, rich color, warming light.

"I'll tell Miss Laura you're here."

But as she turned to do so, Laura came down the wide, curving steps. Though Michael would tell himself later that he was a fool, his heart stopped.

The lights caught the fussy beads of her jacket and shot color. Beneath was a simple dress the color of moondust. There were jewels at her ears, sapphires and diamonds, framing the face that her swept-back hair accented.

She looked so perfect, so lovely, with one ringless hand trailing along the glossy banister. She might have stepped out of a painting.

"I'm sorry to keep you waiting." Her voice was cool, betraying none of her panic at the way those eyes of his bored into her, or her fluster at having to mop up after the dog.

"Just got here," he said, equally cool. Then some of the absurdity struck him. Here he was, Michael Fury, holding out a hand for a princess. "I wasn't supposed to bring, like, a corsage or something, was I?"

She managed a small smile of her own. "It's not the prom."

"Amen to that."

"You be careful, Miss Laura." Ann shot a warning look at Michael. "And you drive responsibly, boy-o. It isn't one of your races."

"Annie, the dog's in with the girls, but—"

"Don't you worry." She gestured toward the door, thinking philosophically that the sooner they were gone, the sooner she'd have her girl back. "I'll take care of him, and them. Try to enjoy yourself."

"And I'll try to bring her back in one piece," Michael added, for the hell of it, as he opened the door.

"See that you do," Ann muttered and began to worry the moment the door closed.

"It's nice of you to drive me to the club." She would put things on the proper footing, Laura determined. And keep them there. "You don't have to feel obliged to entertain me once we're there."

He'd been planning to say pretty much the same thing himself, but he resented her saying it first. He opened her door, leaned on it. "Who are you pissed off at, Laura? Me, or the world in general?"

"I'm not angry with you or anyone." Gracefully, she slipped into the passenger seat of his Porsche. "I'm simply explaining matters so that we get through the evening comfortably."

"And here you said you liked mongrels."

She blinked. "I don't know what you mean."

"Right." He resisted—barely—slamming the door. The evening, he thought as he rounded the hood, was off to a flying start.

CHAPTER 6

IT COULD HAVE been worse, Michael supposed. He could have been back in some Central American jungle sweating bullets and dodging them. He could have had his skull bashed in, as he had once when a stunt gag went wrong.

Instead he was standing in a room with people he didn't know and didn't care to know.

He'd rather have had his skull bashed in.

He thought the room itself was overly cute, with its glossy red hearts hanging from swatches of paper lace. The flowers were nice, he supposed. He didn't have any objection to flowers. But he thought they carried the obsessive red and white theme too far.

All of the pink-draped tables were centered with a grouping of white tapers ringed by a halo of fluffy red and white carnations. At least he thought they were carnations. And the music. He decided it represented the widest culture clash, with its mild strings and discreet piano, all played by middle-aged men in white suits.

Give him blues or honest rock any day.

But there was a spiffy view of the coastline through a wall of windows. The drama of it, the war of fretful waves against mean-edged rocks, provided an interesting contrast to the quiet, undeniably stuffy group inside the polished, overheated club.

The women had decked themselves out, absolutely dripping bangles and beads and other jewelry, he noted. They wore layers of perfumes and silks and lace. Overdone, in his estimation, like the decor. He preferred Laura's simple and feminine choice. It was class, he supposed, that set her apart. Simple class that came straight through the blood and bone. He might have mentioned it to her, but she had drifted away quickly, making, as he termed it, her Templeton rounds.

Most of the men were in tuxes. A little fact that Josh had conveniently neglected to mention. Not that Michael minded. He wouldn't have worn one anyway. If he'd had one to wear.

Still it gave him another bone to pick with his old friend. If the slippery son of a bitch ever showed up.

On the bright side, he had a cold beer in his hand. The finger food spread out artistically on buffet tables looked delicate, but it tasted fine. He'd already enjoyed a mild flirtation with a woman who mistook him for some Hollywood young gun. Michael hadn't bothered to disabuse her.

He was considering wandering about, maybe taking a turn outside in the fresh air or checking out one of the other rooms. He might find that pool table and a few suckers to fleece. Then Laura moved back to him.

"I'm sorry. There were a few people I needed to speak with." In a gesture that was both absentminded and automatic, she accepted a glass of champagne from a roving waiter, murmured her thanks.

"No problem."

But it was, she thought, her problem. She'd had some time to think about it. "I am sorry, Michael. I was annoyed with Josh for maneuvering me into this evening and I took it out on you." When he didn't respond, she drummed up a smile. "So, what were you and Kitty Bennett talking about?"

"Who? Oh, the ditzy brunette with all the teeth."

Laura choked on her champagne. She'd never heard the chair of the Monterey Arts Council described just that way. Or quite that accurately. "Yes."

"She dug my last flick."

"Did she?"

He decided to be friendly, smiled. "Not *Braveheart,* though I had a couple of nice stunts in it. She thought I was the director of some art house film. Something about foot fetishes."

"Mm-hmm. And you discussed the metaphoric twists on our sex-obsessed society, along with the multiple layers of symbolism representing moral decay."

He started to feel better. "Something like that. She thinks I'm brilliant, and underrated. I think I might be getting a grant."

"Congratulations."

"Of course, she really only wanted my body."

"Well, an artist must make sacrifices. Ah, there's Byron and Kate."

Michael glanced over. His brows rose in surprise as he saw the streamlined brunette in slinky black. The gamine face, all sloe-colored eyes, and the close-cropped dark hair tipped him off, though the girl he remembered had been skinny, coltish—a borderline nerd.

"That's Kate? Kate Powell?"

"She works out now," Laura muttered. "She's gotten obsessive about it, so don't get her started."

"That her trainer?" Michael muttered back, measuring the broad-shouldered, long-limbed man beside her.

"And husband. He's also my boss. Byron." She held out a hand as the couple maneuvered through the crowd toward them. A quick kiss and she turned to Kate. "Margo was right, as usual. The Karan suits you. Byron De Witt, Michael Fury."

"Nice to meet you. Kate's been telling me stories."

"And I didn't even need to exaggerate." Grinning, she stepped forward and gave Michael a quick, friendly hug.

Her arms might have been lean, Michael noted, but they were tough. Enjoying her, he drew her back. "Katie Powell. Looking good."

Because she'd always enjoyed him as well, she wiggled her brows. "Same goes, Mick."

"Can I get drinks for anyone?" Byron asked in a voice that reminded Michael of mint juleps and magnolia.

"I'll have what Laura's having," Kate decided.

"Michael?"

"Bass ale."

"That ought to go down just fine," Byron decided. "I think I'll join you. Excuse me a minute."

"It's the Southern," Kate said, watching him walk toward the bar with a proprietary and satisfied gleam in her eye. "He's just a gentleman."

"It doesn't look like it's just the dress that suits you," Michael commented.

"It's not." Kate turned back, smiled warmly. "And unlike the dress, which goes back into stock tomorrow, he's all mine. So, how the hell are you, Michael Fury, and when do we get to see your horses?"

It was so easy for Kate, Laura thought as she listened, to make the appropriate comments. She'd fallen right into casual conversation with

Michael. Didn't she feel any of those . . . oh, she hated to use the term "vibes," but it was the only word that came to her. Dark, restless, dangerous vibes. It made her jittery to stand next to him, to encounter a brush of his arm against hers, to catch that gleam in his hot blue eyes.

It helped when Josh and Margo arrived. There was more conversation, and laughter. Byron fell into an easy discussion of horses with Michael. Apparently Byron's family owned several. Before the topic switched to cars—another interest the men shared—Byron had arranged to take a look at Michael's stock.

It wasn't difficult to ease away again and draw Margo with her. "So," Margo began, "are you enjoying yourself? You and Michael are getting some speculative looks."

Nothing could have been better designed to set Laura off. She could see it now, perfectly, and wondered how she'd missed the master plan.

Her temper hitched, but she controlled it.

"Is that part of your little plot? To give the country club set an eyeful of poor Laura and her escort?"

"When the escort looks like Michael." Margo waved an impatient hand. "Oh, lighten up, Laura. It's only one evening out of your life, and why shouldn't you spend part of it with a good-looking man? God knows, you've been hiding out long enough."

"Hiding out." There was that hitch again. "Is that what you call it?"

"Don't." Regretting her choice of words, Margo put a hand on Laura's arm. "I just meant that you've been so focused on work and responsibility, you haven't let yourself have much fun. So have some. Ask him to dance, take a walk, whatever, before he and Byron bond like Siamese twins over engine talk."

"I don't want to dance, or take a walk with Michael," Laura said evenly. Now she felt pathetic. The homely younger sister, the neglected wallflower, the pitiable ex-wife. "And I'm relieved that he's found something to salvage his evening. He's been miserably bored."

"Then you haven't been doing your job, have you?" Irritated herself, Margo inclined her head. "It wouldn't hurt you to be friendly to the man, Laura. In fact, it would be good for you and everyone in close proximity to you if you had a nice hot bout of sex with him and popped your own frustration cork."

Laura's calm gray eyes turned to steel. "Oh, really? I hadn't realized that those in close proximity were so affected by my lifestyle."

"Hey." Recognizing the signs of a battle in progress, Kate sidled up. "Are we fighting?"

"Laura's peeved because we made her come here with Michael tonight."

"I like Mick." Kate chose an olive from her tiny plate and popped it into her mouth. "What's the problem?"

"I'm peeved," Laura returned, emphasizing the word, "because Margo apparently thinks I should jump into bed with him so that she and my other friends don't have to put up with my sexual frustration."

Kate glanced around to where Michael and Byron and Josh stood. "Couldn't hurt," she said with a shrug. "If I wasn't a happily married woman I'd consider it myself."

"That's nice for you, isn't it? For both of you happily married women. Christ, I hope I wasn't ever so smug." Training overcame temper just enough that she managed to walk away instead of stalking.

"Wrong buttons," Kate muttered. "We definitely pushed the wrong buttons."

"It's past time some of them were pushed." But Margo sighed before sipping her wine. "I don't mind making her angry, but I didn't mean to make her unhappy. I just hoped that she'd enjoy herself, let Michael entertain her. And eventually screw her brains out."

Kate chuckled. "You're a considerate friend, Margo. Hell, are we smug?"

"I'm afraid so."

A FEW MINUTES in the ladies' lounge cooled Laura off. She sat on one of the dainty padded stools at the long, mirrored counter and meticulously reapplied her lipstick.

Was she frustrated? Was she becoming difficult to be around? She didn't like to think so. What she was was busy, focused, committed to her family and work.

What was so wrong with that? Then she sighed, propped her elbows on the counter, her head in the vee of her hands. No, it was she who had blown a simple evening out of proportion, she admitted. Because she hadn't had a simple evening in too long.

And because, she could admit privately, she didn't know how to behave with a man, especially one like Michael Fury.

She'd been seventeen when she fell in love with Peter. Eighteen when she married him. Her dating record beforehand had been brief and uncomplicated.

She'd been married for ten years and had indulged in no flirtations, much less affairs. The men she knew were relatives or old family friends.

They were casual acquaintances, the husbands of women she knew, or business contacts.

She was thirty years old, she thought miserably, and she didn't know how to date. Even when it wasn't a bona fide date.

When the door to the lounge opened, she straightened quickly and took out her comb.

"Hi, Laura."

"Judy." Her smile warmed. Judy Prentice was a friend and a regular customer at Pretenses. "It's good to see you. You look wonderful."

"Holding my own." Always ready for a chat or a quick gossip, Judy sat down beside her. "Did you see Maddie Greene? She had a boob job last month."

She simply couldn't be overly dignified with Judy. "It was a little hard to miss her with those twin soldiers."

"Well, watch yourself. I made the polite comment when she brought it up. I think I said something about them looking very perky." She grinned when Laura snorted. "Next thing I knew, she'd dragged me in here and stripped to the waist to show them off. Up close, my dear, and much too personal."

"Oh, God, thanks for the warning."

"I have to admit, they're beauties. Speaking of which." Judy set down her jeweled compact. "I didn't recognize that incredibly gorgeous specimen you're with tonight. Is he from around here?"

"He's an old friend."

Judy rolled her eyes. "We should all have such old friends."

"He's just moved back to the area." A little thought leaked through. "Your daughter takes riding lessons, doesn't she, Judy?"

"She's horse crazy. I went through the same stage, but it seems to be sticking with Mandy."

"Michael raises horses, trains them. He's working out of Templeton House for the moment until he can rebuild. His property was destroyed in those mud slides."

"Oh, God, weren't they horrible? Another friend of mine watched her house slide down a cliff. Just going, going, gone. Heartbreaking." Judy dabbed perfume at her wrists. "Why do we live in California?"

"I hear it's the weather," Laura said dryly. "In any case, you might want to contact Michael if you decide to get Mandy a mount of her own."

"Actually, we are considering it. Her birthday's coming up, and there's nothing she'd like better than her own horse." Lips pursed in thought,

Judy replaced her perfume. "Thanks for the tip. I'll talk to my husband about it. Meanwhile, good luck with your old friend."

Laura left the lounge in better spirits. The evening was wearing on, she was getting through it. The least she could do was make an effort to enjoy what was left of it.

"Cooled off?"

She jumped a little, muffled an oath. Must the man sneak up behind her? "I'm sorry."

"You looked ready to chew steel when you marched off to the ladies' room." Michael handed her a fresh glass of champagne.

"Maybe it was indigestion. I ran into a friend in there."

"You women have little summit meetings in the john, don't you? Isn't that why you usually go inside in packs?"

"Actually, we play poker and smoke cigars, but my point is, this friend of mine has a daughter and she's very keen on riding. They're considering buying her a horse. I gave Judy your name. I hope you don't mind."

"Hey, anytime you want to toss business my way, feel free. I like your brother-in-law."

"It showed. I expected the two of you to have a secret handshake by now."

"Is that a subtle way of telling me I was ignoring you?"

"No." She said it too quickly, and then tried to backtrack. "Not at all. I'm glad you and Byron hit it off." She spotted him on the dance floor with Kate. And her eyes warmed. "They're so happy together. They've only been married a couple of months, but with some people you can just tell that the way they look at each other isn't going to change."

"Your romantic side's showing."

She didn't take offense. "I'm allowed to have one."

"Then I guess I should ask you to dance."

She looked up at him. What the hell, she decided. "Then I guess I should accept."

Before he could take her hand, he saw her smile fade and freeze, her color drain to white. The hand that had lifted to take his fell to her side.

"What's the problem?"

She only took a quiet, shaky breath. "Hello, Peter. Candy."

"Laura."

Michael shifted, his hand instinctively moving to the small of Laura's back to support her. This must be the ex, he realized, with the perky, cat-eyed redhead clinging to his arm.

He supposed this would be Laura's type. Tall and golden, distinguished, perfectly presented in a tailored tux, diamonds winking discreetly at his cuffs.

"I didn't realize you were in town," Laura managed. She knew, though conversations continued, that attention was focusing on the little tableau. "When I spoke to you about Allison's school supper, you indicated you'd be away."

"My plans changed a bit, but I'm still not able to attend." He said it formally, as if declining an invitation to a polo match.

"It's very important to her, Peter. Just a few hours—"

"And my plans are important to me." His gaze flicked to Michael, lingered in speculation. "I don't believe I know your escort."

"Michael Fury." And Michael didn't offer a hand.

"Of course. I thought I recognized you." Candy Litchfield's voice bubbled up. "Michael is an old friend of Josh Templeton's, darling. You ran away to sea or something, didn't you?"

"Or something," Michael said, sparing her a glance. Her type had always grated on him. Overly bright, overly vicious. "I don't remember you."

The statement had been calculated to deflate and annoy. He usually hit his mark. She bristled a little, then purred. "Well, after all, we didn't run in the same circles, did we? Your mother was a waitress, wasn't she?"

"That's right. At Templeton Resort. And my father ran off with a redhead. I don't think she was related to you."

"I shouldn't think so." After sneering down her nose, she looked back at Laura. "Now don't nag Peter, Laura. We've been so incredibly pressed. We've hardly had time to catch our breath since we got in this morning. We've been in St. Thomas."

"How lovely for you, but the fact is that these pesky domestic details do require some communication. If you'd . . ."

She trailed off as her gaze lighted on the ring Candy was displaying on the hand she deliberately fluttered against Peter's chest. The stone was as big as a hen's egg, sitting atop a platinum Tiffany setting.

Satisfied that she'd finally shifted Laura's attention where she wanted it, Candy giggled. "Oh, dear, you've found us out. Peter and I want to make the announcement quietly, but I'm sure I can trust you to be discreet." And miserable, she hoped. She'd detested Laura for more years than she cared to count, and now she savored her moment of triumph.

Every muscle in her stomach twisted as Laura looked into Peter's eyes. Oh, they were amused. Coolly amused. "Congratulations. I'm sure you'll be very happy together."

"I have no doubt of it." Candace was perfect for him, he thought. Perfect for this new stage of his life, just as Laura had been perfect for another stage. "We're planning a small ceremony in May in Palm Springs."

"Not too small." Candy pouted prettily, but her eyes were gleaming as they stayed locked on Laura's face. "May's such a lovely month for a wedding, don't you think? Something charming and alfresco would be nice. But not too small or informal. After all, a bride needs to show off a bit."

"And you'd know all about that." Laura's hands were threatening to tremble. It couldn't be permitted. "Are you planning on telling the girls about your marriage, Peter, or is that up to me?"

"I'll leave that to you."

"I'm sure they'll be delighted," Candy purred, as she slid a glass off the tray of a nearby waiter. "Mine are. Little Charles is very fond of Peter, and Adrianna is thrilled with the prospect of a wedding."

"How nice for you," Laura said stiffly. "But then, Charles and Adrianna must be used to your weddings by now."

"Don't be snide, Laura." Peter's voice was cool and mild. "It never suited you. You'll have to excuse us now. We need to mingle."

"Steady," Michael murmured as they slipped away.

"That bitch! How am I going to tolerate that bitch being stepmother to my babies? How am I going to stand it?"

It surprised him that that would be her first thought. Then he realized it shouldn't have. "They're bright girls, Laura, and she doesn't strike me as the maternal type."

"I can't stay here."

Before she could dash, he took a firm hold on her arm. The way he drew her to him made it seem as if they were sharing secrets. "You run out now, it's going to look like retreat. That's not what you want."

"I can't stay here." There was panic swirling inside her, along with a bubbling brew of fury. "How could he do this? How could he do this to them?"

Odd, he thought, that she couldn't see that both Peter and Candy had done it to her. Very deliberately, and very well. "If I'm any judge, everybody in this room is wondering just how Laura Templeton is going to handle this little meeting with her ex and his Kewpie doll. I think we should have that dance."

He was right, of course. He was exactly, pathetically right. However hurt, however shocked, there was still pride. She wouldn't allow Candy to snicker over her retreat.

"Okay."

She walked with him to the dance floor as if she wanted nothing more than a quiet turn. The music was soft, some moody number from the forties. It was designed to be romantic, she thought. Instead it rang in her ears like a battle cry.

"She's not going to get her pinching little fingers on my babies," Laura said between her teeth.

"I don't imagine she'd get past you to pinch anyone, if that was her goal. It wouldn't hurt if you looked at me." He slipped his arms around her, found they fit well. Discovered her steps matched his smoothly. "Maybe even smiled."

"They only came here to slap at me. Neither one of them gave a single thought to the children. She's a mother herself, Michael. How can she not care about the children?"

"Too much in love with herself. Stop worrying about it. She isn't going to make time in her social calendar to play stepmama. Smile," he murmured, touching a hand lightly to her cheek. "You can make everybody believe you're only thinking about me and what we're going to do when we leave here. That'll burn their ass."

He was right again, and she made her lips curve. "I'm sorry you got caught in the cross fire."

"Hell, it's just a flesh wound." He was rewarded by a quick, honest laugh.

"You're nicer than I remembered, Michael. And I'm a mess."

"You look pretty neat and tidy to me. You always did. We've got them wondering now." He bent his head so that his cheek brushed hers, his mouth close to her ear. "Just who is that guy Laura Templeton's wrapped around? How long has this been going on?"

She was beginning to wonder the same thing herself. "Not everyone's that interested in my business."

His breath blew warm against her ear. "Come on, sugar. You fascinate them. Cool, composed Laura."

"It's been poor Laura for a little too long now." Her voice was tight again. "Poor Laura, whose husband cheated on her with his secretary. Poor Laura, who'll have to hold her head up now that her ex is marrying her former co-chair of the Garden Club."

"Jesus, you played with that irritating little redhead?" He shook his head. "I'm disappointed in you. Tell you what, now that they're wondering, why don't we give them something to talk about over brunch tomorrow?"

His mouth slid around, grazed her cheek. Before she could jolt from the shock of that, it was fixed warmly on hers. The kiss was long and slow. Her head reeled once, and the hand on his shoulder flexed open and dug in.

He eased back, barely an inch so that the only thing she could see was his eyes. "Let's try that again," he said softly. "I think you'll get the hang of it."

She would have protested. She wasn't the kind of woman who indulged in smoldering kisses in public. Or in smoldering kisses in private, for that matter. But his mouth was on hers again, clever, persuasive. Hot. And she was swept along.

The rich male taste, the firm, knowing lips, the confident exploration of tongue and rough scrape of teeth. No one had kissed her like that before, as if her mouth was the source of all pleasure. Something hummed in her throat that might have been shock but was more likely wonder.

As he had wondered. What would she taste like, feel like, be like? What he found was a banquet of contrasts. Heat filtered through cool armor. Shyness fluttering under composure. She was trembling, erotic little shivers that shot need straight to his loins.

And that reminded him that no matter how much he might enjoy the experiment, they weren't alone in a place where they could analyze the results.

"That ought to do it," he murmured. "It sure as hell convinced me."

She could do nothing but stare up at him. Somehow they were still dancing. She knew her feet, however disassociated they seemed from the rest of her, were moving.

"Sugar." Struggling to keep it light when he would have been happier devouring her in a couple of quick bites, he lifted her hand, nipped at the knuckles. "You keep looking at me that way, they're going to have more to talk about than a couple of kisses."

She tore her gaze away, stared determinedly over his shoulder. "You caught me off guard."

"That makes two of us. We can leave now, if you want. Nobody's going to think it's a retreat."

"Yes." She kept her back stiff, fighting to ignore the familiar and enticing way his hand continued to stroke it. "I'd like to go home."

She didn't speak again until they stood on the wide veranda of the entrance to the clubhouse. One of the eager valets rushed off to fetch Michael's car, and they remained there, sheltered, with the lights and music behind them and the night, moonswept and shadowed, in front.

"Should I thank you?"

"Jesus." He rammed his hands into his pockets. She was about as approachable now as polished marble. "Did it seem like I was making a sacrifice? I've given some thought to kissing you, and if you want to step off that goddamn pedestal again for a minute, you'll admit you knew I'd given some thought to it."

"I'm not trying to make you angry."

"Just a happy accident, then. Laura—" he turned to her, not completely sure of his next move, then swore as the valet zipped his car up to the base of the stairs.

"That's a beauty, sir," the boy said, then beamed at the tip Michael all but threw at him. "Thank you, sir. Drive safely."

Calmer once he had the car racing away from the club, Michael took a breath. "Look, sugar, you took a hard knock in there. I'm sorry for it. If you ask me, that jerk you made the mistake of marrying isn't worth a minute of your time."

She wasn't asking him, was she? Laura thought nastily. "I'm not concerned about me. It's the girls."

"Parents get divorced. It's a fact of life. Fathers take off and ignore their kids. Another fact."

"That's very easy to say when you don't have children to concern you."

A shadow crossed his face. "No, I don't have any children. I've been one who lived through divorce and neglect, though. You get through it."

She shut her eyes. She'd forgotten that his father had left him and his mother. "I'm sorry, but that doesn't make it right. Allison needs his attention, and his disinterest hurts her."

"What about you? Are you still in love with him?"

"No. God, no. Candy's welcome to him. She's just not welcome to my girls."

"I don't see them giving her more than the patented Templeton dismissal. That small, polite smile."

"We don't do that."

"Oh, sugar, yes, you do."

She shifted and aimed a steady glance at him. "Do you know why you call women 'sugar,' Michael? That way, when you roll off one in the middle of the night, you don't have to remember annoying little details like her name."

His mouth twitched into something between a grimace and a smile. "Close enough. I guarantee I'll remember yours . . . Laura. If you're considering letting me roll off of you tonight."

She wasn't sure if she was shocked, outraged, or amused. But she did know that most of the sting from Peter had faded. "That's an incredibly flattering offer, Michael. I don't know when I've had one quite so—"

"Honest," he suggested.

"Crude," she finished. "I'm afraid I'll have to decline."

"Up to you. How about a walk on the cliffs instead?" On impulse, he swung the car to the shoulder.

They speared, magnetic, moon-kissed, and entirely too romantic. Because she could envision herself walking them with him, their hands clasped, she shook her head. "I'm not wearing the right shoes for cliff walking."

"Then we'll just sit here a minute."

"I don't think—"

"I have something to say to you."

Nerves began to hum again. She clasped her hands in her lap. She was parked on a dark road in the moonlight. Something she hadn't done in too many years to count. "All right."

"You're a beautiful, desirable woman." When her head snapped around and he saw her eyes wide and confused, he nearly laughed. "I guess that's something you hear all the time."

It certainly wasn't, which left her at a loss as to how to respond. "I'm flattered you think so."

"I want you."

Now there was panic, fizzing up like champagne in a shaken bottle. "I don't—What do you expect me to say to that? God!" Despite the shoes, she wrenched open the door and stepped out into the night.

"I didn't ask you to say anything. I'm telling you." He came up beside her and turned her to face him. "It's probably a mistake, but I'm telling you anyway. I have memories of you. I didn't realize how many until I saw you again and they just popped out of my head. I used to think about you. Damned inconvenient, and embarrassing to be thinking about you the way I was when you were the kid sister of my best friend. Josh would have kicked my ass for what I was thinking, and I'd have had to let him."

"I'm no good at this." She moved back, retreating quickly. "I'm no good at this sort of thing. You'll have to stop."

"Not till I'm finished. I never stop until I'm finished. Keep backing up that way, sugar—Laura," he corrected himself as he grabbed her arm, "you're going to break an ankle. I don't mind you being afraid of me. I'd be surprised if you weren't." His grin flashed. "Hell, I'd be insulted. Just hold still a minute."

He held both of her hands at her sides and moved in. "I'm not going to hurt you," he murmured as his mouth lowered. "This time."

It didn't hurt. Devastation came too quickly for pain. He simply undid her with one soft, lazy kiss. Then with another, harder, impatient, until that reckless, relentless mouth against hers chipped away at the wall of restraint.

And she knew that marriage hadn't prepared her for this kind of desire—

the kind that curled like raw, ragged fists in the gut and twisted in angry frustration.

When she gave, he wanted more. He wanted her there, atop the windy cliff with the moon spotlighting them and the violent thrust of the waves matching the way he imagined thrusting into her. And he knew greed could be his undoing.

"I want you to think about it," he told her. "The horses taught me patience, so I've got a small store where you're concerned. It seems only fair to let you know that I want you. It doesn't have anything to do with saving your face in front of the country club set, or with making your idiot ex-husband steam a little. It has to do with you and me. And it's unlikely when it's done that you'll have to ask whether you should thank me."

"I have children."

Laughter, he discovered, could relieve even a great amount of tension. "Christ Almighty. You've got great children, Laura. But this is between you and me."

"I—let go of me and let me breathe, will you?"

She jerked away, rubbing her hands through hair that the wind had tossed into curling confusion. However shaken she was, she felt the simplest way out was honesty.

"I don't have any experience with affairs." Her voice was composed again, but her hands continued to twist together. "I was married for ten years, and I was faithful."

"You've been divorced how long?"

When she didn't respond, he stared. Then he began to see what she was telling him. There'd only been one man—which made her former husband even more of a fool, in Michael's opinion.

"Is that supposed to make me less attracted to you? You know what it makes me, Laura? It makes me want to toss you over my shoulder and find out if I still know how to pleasure a woman in a parked car."

He saw her glance toward his Porsche, and for a moment he was sure there was speculation in her eyes. "Sugar, I'd be willing to give it a shot."

When he stepped forward, she risked a wrenched ankle and evaded him. "Don't. Just don't."

She turned and stared out over the sea where waves slashed white against speared fingers of rocks. It was a long fall, she thought. Reckless jumps were always followed by long falls.

And she had never taken one.

"I don't know how I'm going to react to this. I don't know what I'm going to want to do about it."

"Think about it," he suggested. "I'm going to be around for quite a while. You want to neck in the car, or do you want me to take you home?"

Now she smiled. How could she help it? "Another of those intriguing offers of yours. I'll take the ride home, thanks."

"Your loss, sugar."

CHAPTER 7

"AND THEN MRS. Hannah said that everyone who'd finished all their assignments could have extra time on the computer. I picked the Art Studio so I got to draw a picture and print it out and everything. Then she put it on the board because she said it was excellent."

While Kayla chattered about her school day, Michael continued to water brush his mare's mane. Kayla had fallen into the habit of visiting him, and he'd discovered that if a day passed without her poking her head into the stables, he felt deprived.

Her mother, on the other hand, was keeping her distance. He hadn't seen her in three days, since the night of the country club dance.

"Mama's going to get me drawing lessons, and that'll be fun because I like to draw pictures. I can draw you one if you want."

"I'd like that." He sent her a quick smile. "What would you draw for me?"

"A surprise." She beamed at him. Big people didn't always really listen, Kayla knew. Mr. Fury always listened, even when he was busy. "Do you have time to teach Bongo a trick?"

"I might." Michael tapped the dampened water brush in his palm as he studied the pup, who was currently sprawled on the brick eyeing one of the cats. "I've got to put this lady through her paces first, though. Got somebody coming by to look at her."

Kayla's bottom lip poked out as she reached up to smooth the mare's glossy flank. "To buy her?"

"Maybe." Understanding, he crouched down. "She needs a good home. Like Bongo did."

"You're a good home."

He didn't think this called for an explanation of business, the profit-and-loss ledgers that often made him cross-eyed. So he kept it simple. "I can't keep them all, honey. What I do is take good care of them while they're here and look for people who'll take care of them when they're not. And your mom's the one who found these people. You know Mrs. Prentice?"

"She's nice." Kayla gnawed on her lip as she considered. She did like Mrs. Prentice—she had a fun laugh. "Her daughter rides horses. Mandy's fourteen and has a boyfriend."

"Does she?" Amused, Michael tousled Kayla's hair. "If they like the lady here, and she likes them, she'll be their horse. Do you think Mandy would take good care of her?"

"I guess so."

"Let's take her out to the paddock, you and me."

"I'll get her blanket. I'll get it."

While Kayla raced off, he made a final check of his lady. She was a pretty chestnut hack, her coat gleaming now from his meticulous work with brush and currycomb. Her eyes were clear, intelligent, her heart strong, her hooves healthy and smartly presented, with a coating of oil. At fifteen hands she was a good size, well lined, a cooperative, well-behaved animal who would bring him a good profit on his investment.

He was, he knew as he stroked her neck, going to miss the hell out of her.

Together, he and Kayla saddled the mare, with Kayla watching every move carefully. She hoped that one day Mr. Fury would let her hook the cinches, but she didn't want to ask. Yet.

"Where's Ali today?"

"Oh, she's in her room. She has to clean it and finish all her homework. She can't come outside today because she's being punished."

"What did she do?"

"She had another fight with Mama." With the dog at her heels, Kayla skipped along beside Michael as he led the mare out. "She's mad because our dad's marrying Mrs. Litchfield and he's not going to go to the father-daughter supper at school. She says it's Mama's fault."

"How does she figure that?"

"I don't know." Kayla shrugged her shoulders. "She's silly. Uncle Josh is going to the supper, and he's more fun anyway. Our dad doesn't like us."

The careless tone caused Michael to stop, glance down. "Doesn't he?"

"No, but that's okay because . . ." She trailed off, bit her lip. "It's bad."

"What is, darling?"

She looked behind her toward the house, then back into Michael's eyes. "I don't like him, either. I'm glad he went away and that he's not coming back. But don't tell Mama."

Now there was alarm, and beneath it a silvery rush of defense. "Honey." He crouched down, taking her little shoulders carefully in his hands. "He didn't hurt you, did he? He didn't hit you or your sister?" Even the thought of it churned in his gut like acid. "Or your mom?"

"No." She seemed so baffled by the idea. Michael relaxed again. "But he never listens and he never plays and he made Mama cry, so I don't like him. But don't tell."

"I won't." Michael made an X over his heart, then touched the finger to her lips. How anyone, particularly a father, could not adore this fascinating child was beyond him. "How about a ride?"

Her eyes went huge, hopeful. "Can I? Can I really?"

"Well, let's see." He picked her up, set her on the saddle. "We have to see if the lady likes girls, right?" he said as he adjusted the stirrups. "This here's an English saddle because that's what Mandy uses. Take a rein in each hand. No, like this, sugar," he said and adjusted her grip. "That's the way."

Patiently he explained the proper way to guide the mare while Kayla listened in solemn-eyed concentration. "Now, heels down. Good. Knees in. Back straight." With a hand on the bridle he led the mare into a sedate walk. "How's it feel up there, Miss Ridgeway?"

She giggled, bounced. "I'm riding the horse."

"Now draw back on the left rein, easy now, the way I showed you. See how nice she turns. She's a good girl."

He had work to do, calls to make. And he forgot all of it. For the next twenty minutes he indulged himself, teaching Kayla the basics, hopping up behind her once to take the mare into a quick, circling canter that had the child shrieking with delight.

The day might have been overcast, more rain threatening. But here was sunshine.

When he plucked her off and her arms wound tight around his neck in a hug, he felt, for the first time in his life, like a hero.

"Can I do it again sometime, Mr. Fury?"

"Sure you can."

With easy affection and trust, she wrapped her legs around his waist, grinning at him. "When Mama gets home she'll be so surprised. I rode the horse all by myself and steered her and everything."

"You sure did. And now we know she likes girls."

"She'll like Mandy, so she'll be happy. I'm going to tell Annie right now how I rode the horse. Thanks, Mr. Fury."

She wiggled down and raced off, the pup scrambling after. Michael watched her, stroking the mare's neck. "You've done it now, Fury," he murmured. "Gone and fallen in love with that pretty little blonde." He looked into his mare's eyes, kissed her. Sighed. "Not supposed to fall for what you can't keep."

*   *   *

TWO HOURS LATER, he repeated the warning to himself. The Prentices had fallen for the mare at first sight, had barely bothered to dicker over his asking price. Now he had a check in his pocket and the lady was no longer his.

With mixed feelings, he approached Templeton House. He'd made a sale, and that was part of his business. The mare, he had no doubt, was going to be pampered and adored for the rest of her life. And it was a sure bet that the Prentices would spread the word that Michael Fury had good stock for sale.

He had Laura to thank for it, and he intended to do so.

The duty call would give him the opportunity to see her again, to gauge how she reacted to him. Out of habit, and a little fear instilled by the thought of encountering Ann Sullivan, he wiped his feet outside the kitchen door. His knock was answered by a harried call to come in. When he did, fear turned to pleasure.

Mrs. Williamson was exactly as he remembered. Broad back to the room, big, capable hands stirring something wonderful on the huge six-burner stove. The bowl of black hair atop her head wouldn't have stirred in an earthquake.

The room smelled of spices and flowers and the mouthwatering aroma of whatever she had in the oven.

"Got any cookies around this place?"

She turned, wooden spoon in one hand. Her wide face creased into a huge welcoming smile. She'd always had a soft spot for lost boys. And bad ones.

"Well, if it isn't Michael Fury himself. I wondered when you'd come knocking on my door."

"Ready to marry me now?"

"I might just be." She sent him a saucy wink. "You've grown up handsome enough."

Because with her he'd always felt at home, he crossed the room, took one of her big hands in his, and brought it to his lips. "Name the time and place."

"Oh, you're a one." From anyone else, the sound that bubbled out would have been called a giggle. "Sit down there, boy, and tell me all about your adventures." As she always had, always would, when one of her children came to visit, she took cookies out of the bin, arranged them on a plate. "Selling horses now, are we?"

"Yes, ma'am. Just did." He patted his pocket while she poured his coffee.

"That's fine, then. And you haven't found a woman to suit you in all your travels?"

"I've been holding out for you." He bit into a cookie, rolled his eyes dramatically. "Nobody bakes like you, Mrs. Williamson. Why should I set-tle for less than the best?"

She laughed again and gave him a vigorous slap on the back that nearly sent him headfirst into his coffee. "Oh, you're a bad one, Michael."

"So they always said. You still do those apple pies? The ones that bring tears of joy to a man's eyes?"

"If you behave yourself I might just send you one over." She went back to her stove and her stirring. "Our little Kayla's been spending a lot of time down at the stables lately."

"I'm going to marry her if you keep turning me down."

"She's an angel, isn't she?" She let loose a windy sigh. "Allison, too. Darling girl, sweet as you please and bright as buttons on a new suit. Miss Laura's done a fine job there. And by herself, too. *He* never paid any mind to them."

When you want information, Michael mused as he took another cookie, go to the source. Mrs. Williamson was a fount of inside information. "*He* isn't very popular around here, I take it."

She sniffed loudly. "And why should he be, I'd like to know? Fussy, stiff-necked, too good to say how do you do? Never gave a minute of his valuable time to those beautiful girls, either. And fooling around with his secretary, and God knows who else, on the side." She pressed a hand to her heart as it swelled with outrage. "I shouldn't speak of it. Not my place."

But he knew she'd speak of it plenty with a little prompting. "So, Ridgeway wouldn't make father of the year?"

"Hah! He wouldn't make father of the minute. And as for husband, well, he treated our Miss Laura more like an accessory than a wife. Prissy about the staff, too, with his highfalutin ideas."

Michael ran his tongue around his teeth. "Laura stayed married to him for a long time."

"She takes her promises and her duties seriously. That girl was raised right. Near to broke her heart when she filed for divorce, not that it wasn't the proper thing to do or that any of us regretted it for a blink. Good riddance, I say, and I said so straight out to Mrs. Sullivan. Now he's going to be marrying that redheaded cat. Well, they deserve each other, I say."

To emphasize her sentiments, she rapped her spoon on the edge of the pan, letting the sound ring.

"I bet Ridgeway never got any cookies in your kitchen."

"Hah! As if he'd have lowered himself to come inside the room. Master of the house, my eye. My hearing may not be what it was, but I hear what I need to hear, so don't think I didn't know he tried to make Miss Laura pension me off so he could hire himself some fancy Frenchman to cook his meals. But she wouldn't do it."

Her face softened as she turned back. "Our Miss Laura knows about loyalty, and about what's right. She's a Templeton, and so are her girls, whatever their name might be legal."

She stopped, narrowed her eyes. "There you've done it. Got me blabbing and haven't told me a thing. You haven't changed there, Michael Fury."

"Nothing much to tell." She still brewed the best coffee in central California, he thought as he sipped. And the Templeton kitchen, despite its grandeur and shine, was still one of the coziest spots on earth. "Been there, done that. Now I'm back."

She could just imagine where he'd been, and what he'd done. Still, she saw in him what she'd always seen: a dark, broody-eyed boy brimming with potential.

"Back where you belong, you ask me. Been out gallivanting long enough."

"Seems like," he agreed and took another cookie.

"Going to make your mark this time around, are you?"

"That's the plan. You come on down to the stables while I'm here, Mrs. Williamson." He grinned wickedly. "I'll give you a ride."

She threw back her head, exploding with laughter just as the door swung open. Ann Sullivan stepped inside. The instant she spotted Michael, lounging at the table with cookies and coffee, her mouth tightened.

"I see you're entertaining, Mrs. Williamson."

"The boy just dropped in to visit." They'd worked together too long for Mrs. Williamson to miss the icy disapproval. Or to pay any heed to it. "Coffee, Mrs. Sullivan?"

"No, thank you. Miss Laura is in the solarium and would like some."

The door burst open behind her, and Kayla rushed in. "Mama said to— Hi!" Instantly distracted, she ran toward Michael, jumped in his lap. "Did you come to see us?"

"I came to talk Mrs. Williamson out of some cookies. And I needed to see your mom for a minute."

"She's in the solarium. You can go see her. I drew your picture. Do you want to see?"

"You bet I do." He kissed the tip of her nose, grinned. "What is it?"

"A surprise." Eager, she scrambled down. "I'm going to go get it. I'm going to tell Ali you came. Don't go away."

Ann stood where she was as Kayla bolted out. If she'd been blind, she would have been able to recognize the easy affection between man and girl.

A considering look came into her eye. She was far from ready to soften, but she would consider.

"You can go on to the solarium if you remember the way," she said stiffly. "I'll bring the coffee."

"Fine. Thanks." He rose, equally stiff, until he turned to Mrs. Williamson. "Thanks for the cookies. And that offer still holds."

"Get on with you."

He got on. He remembered the way to the solarium. The fact was, he realized, he remembered everything about Templeton House. Walking down the polished hallway, glancing into elegant rooms, was like stepping back in time. His time. His youth.

This was a constant, he thought. The soaring ceilings and ornate moldings, the carefully selected and lovingly tended furnishings. The sweep of the stairway in the main hall, the bowl of flowers set just so on a credenza. Candlesticks with their tapers burned down to varying heights.

In the parlor he noticed the quiet fire sizzling. The hearth was lapis, he remembered. Josh had told him that, had explained to him about the deep blue stone. There was a large crystal compote on the piano, a floor-spanning faded rug over the waxed wood.

Flowers everywhere, he observed, fresh and dewy from garden or greenhouse. Not just hothouse roses but simple daisies, sunny tulips. Their scents were subtle, an elemental part of the air.

He knew the Templetons had entertained with lavish parties in this house—he had even been permitted to attend a few. People as glamorous as gods had wandered through the rooms, under the arching doorways, spilled out onto flower-decked terraces.

The house he had grown up in could fit into a single wing of this one with room to spare. But it hadn't been the space that awed him. Or not as much, not nearly as much as the beauty of it. The way it stood looking out over cliffs and hills and banks of flowers. The way the tower speared up into the sky and the windows gleamed with light, day or night. And the rooms inside, streaming into other rooms, with an openness, a welcoming that he'd never been able to analyze.

Of permanence. A statement that he'd always understood said family mattered. At least to the Templetons. Despite its grandeur, Templeton House was a home. And that he had never had.

Shaking himself, he moved through the short breezeway that led to the solarium. There would be lush greenery there, flowers in profusion, padded chairs and lounges, glass tables, colorful mats. The rain that had just started to mist would patter on the glass walls, and you would see the fog rise over the cliffs.

It was exactly as he remembered. The glass walls swirled with fog and rain, lending the room a magical kind of intimacy. A single lamp was lit, casting a soft gold light. Music, something with weeping violins that he didn't recognize, spilled like tears from hidden speakers.

And there was Laura, curled on the pastel cushions of a high-backed wicker lounge. Sleeping.

Perhaps it was the atmosphere, the light, the fog, the music, the flowers, that made him feel as though he were stepping into a spellbound bower. He was rarely a fanciful man, but the sight of her sleeping there made him think of enchanted princesses, castles, and the magic of a kiss.

He bent over her, brushed the hair from her cheek, and laid his lips on hers.

She woke slowly, as an enchanted princess should. Her lashes fluttered, a faint flush rose to her cheeks. The sound that sighed through her lips to his was soft, lovely.

"Doesn't seem like a hundred years," he murmured.

Her eyes stayed on his, heavy, clouded, unfocused. "Michael?"

"Now either we live happily ever after or I turn into a frog. I can never keep the stories straight."

She lifted a hand to his face. Real, she thought. She wasn't dreaming. As reality began to seep in, her color deepened and she hastened to sit up. "I fell asleep."

"I figured that one out." And there were shadows under her eyes. He hated knowing that worry over her daughter gave her restless nights. "Long day?"

"Yes." Concern for Allison had given her some bad moments at three A.M. But so had the man who was studying her now. Then there had been her convention duties at the hotel, a glitch in a shipment at the shop, and a headachy session of sentence diagramming in the homework division. "I'm sorry—"

The words slid down her throat as his mouth cruised over hers again. "You made me think of fairy tales when I walked in here. Beauty sleeping."

"That's Sleeping Beauty."

"I know." His lips curved. "I didn't have a close acquaintance with fairy tales, but I think I caught the Disney version somewhere. Let's see if I've got it right."

When he would have kissed her again, she sprang to her feet. "I'm awake." Too awake, she thought as her heart hummed in her throat. Too alive. Too needy.

"I guess that's the best we can do, for the moment. I was in the kitchen charming Mrs. Williamson out of her cookies. I actually came by to see you, but I'm weak."

"No one can hold fast against her cookies." Well aware that she must look rumpled, she tried to smooth her hair.

"Don't. I like it mussed. You never seem to be mussed."

"You ought to catch me after convincing the girls it really is bedtime now." But she made herself stop fussing. "Kayla said that Judy Prentice was coming by this evening."

"She did, with her husband and her daughter. Who, by the way, is quite a horsewoman. They bought a good mare. I think they'll work out well together."

Pleased for him, she said, "Oh, that's wonderful, Michael. Congratulations."

He plucked a creamy white hibiscus from the bush beside the lounge and handed it to her. "I came by to thank you."

Absurdly touched, violently nervous, she stared at the blossom. "I didn't do anything but mention your name, but you're welcome. Judy knows a lot of the horse set. I'm sure she'll pass your name along."

"I'm counting on it. I'd like to take you to dinner."

She shifted away a full inch. "What?"

"I'm flush," he said, patting his pocket. "And I owe you."

"No, you don't. It was just—"

"I'd like to take you to dinner, Laura. I'd like to take you, period, but I think we'll have to do this along more conventional lines. You've been avoiding me."

"No, I haven't. Really." Or hardly at all. "I've been busy."

He imagined her social calendar was full enough. Committees, ladies' luncheons, the jobs she'd taken to fill her time. "I wouldn't imagine a Templeton would scare off so easy."

It was exactly the right switch to pull. "It isn't a matter of scaring off. I have a great deal to do."

"Then take another rain check. You let me know when you can squeeze me in."

When he started to rise, she touched his hand. "I don't mean to sound ungracious."

"You?" He smiled thinly. "Never."

"I wasn't expecting you to . . ."

"Move on you?" he suggested. "Last time I checked, I still had blood in my veins. If you're not interested, just say so. I can probably take a no."

"I don't know what I am, but it's not disinterested." She resisted, barely, tracing the hibiscus along her cheek. "And I don't think I'm prepared to deal with that gleam you just got in your eye. In fact, I know I'm not. I'm going to change the subject."

She drew a deep breath, willing to accept the embarrassment of having him grin at her. "Kayla told me you've been teaching her to ride."

"Is there a problem with that? I guess I should have asked you."

"No." She dragged her hand through her hair again. "No, there's no problem. I'm very grateful that you'd take the time and trouble. I don't want her pestering you, Michael."

"She doesn't pester me. In fact, I'm thinking about giving it ten or fifteen years and asking her to marry me."

Her smile came fast and warm. "She's so easy to fall for. She's so open and loving. She's full of you. Mr. Fury this, and Mr. Fury that. She's certain you're going to turn Bongo into some sort of dog genius."

"I'll have to work on that."

"That's what I wanted to discuss with you. I'd like to compensate you for your time, with Kayla. I—"

"Stop." He said it quietly, the steel of temper a sharp edge beneath. "I'm not a servant."

"I didn't mean that." Horrified that she'd insulted him, she rose again. "I only meant that if you're going to be taking so much of your time to—"

"It's my time, and I'll use it as I please. I don't want your damn money. I'm not for hire as a friend for your kids or as a temporary father substitute or whatever the hell you have in mind."

Now she went pale, very pale. "Of course not. I'm sorry."

"Christ, don't give me that wounded look. You make me feel as though I kicked a puppy." Frustrated, he jammed his hands in his pockets. Compensate him, for Christ's sake. The way you compensate a waiter for good service. He should have expected it. "Just leave it alone."

He spun away to stare out at the swirling fog. Keeping her face blank, Ann stepped inside with the coffee tray. Not by a flicker of the eye did she reveal she'd heard a great deal of that last exchange.

"Your coffee, Miss Laura. The girls are on their way down." If they hadn't been, Ann might have smothered conscience and eavesdropped a bit longer.

"Oh, thank you, Annie." She put a smile on her face, kept it there as her children came in. "I believe Kayla has something for you, Michael."

Kayla held the picture behind her back as she approached. "If you like it, you can hang it on your wall."

"Well, let's see." He took the heavy drawing paper from her, stared. "Damn."

Kayla's face dropped comically. Automatically, Laura put a hand on her shoulder to comfort.

"You don't like it." Kayla's head drooped. "I shouldn't have drawn it so fast, but I wanted to do it while I remembered everything."

"No, it's great." When he looked up from the drawing, his smile was huge. "I was surprised, just like you said I'd be. It looks just like the lady, Kayla. Just exactly like her."

"Really?" With her tongue caught between her teeth, Kayla peeked over to critique her own work. "Usually I draw things I see in books, or that are right there. But I thought if you had to sell her, you could have a picture so you'd always remember her."

"It's beautiful." And nothing like the childish drawing he'd expected. She'd captured the mare's springy gait in the movement, the proud head. He supposed a trained eye could find room for improvement, things like perspective and range that he knew nothing of. All he knew was that he was impressed, and touched. "It's my first original Templeton."

If anyone noticed he hadn't used her legal name, there was no comment. Kayla merely preened and slipped a hand into his. "I'll draw you more if you want."

"I'd like that a lot." He scooted her onto his knee and looked at Allison. The older girl stared down at her feet, obviously miserable. "You finish cleaning your room, Blondie?"

Her head came up, and so did her color. She eyed her sister, and her sister's big mouth with disdain. "Yes, sir."

"Good. I figured once you were off the bread-and-water routine, you might want to catch up with Kayla here on the riding lessons."

Her mouth fell open before she remembered her manners. "I'd like to learn to ride." Though it cost her, she turned to her mother. "May I?"

"I think that would be a wonderful idea. I may have to brush up myself before the two of you get ahead of me." She laid a hand on Ali's shoulder. The stiffness faded reluctantly, but it faded. "Thank you, Michael. We'll see what we can do to meld our schedules."

"Mine's flexible." After a quick bounce, he set Kayla on her feet and rose. "But right now I've got to get back."

"Your coffee," Laura began.

"I'll take a rain check." His smile spread slowly. "You know about redeeming rain checks, don't you, Laura?"

"Yes." How did a mother handle sexual flutters with her two daughters looking on? Laura didn't have a clue. "Thank you for coming by."

"My pleasure."

"I'll see you out," Ali said with great dignity.

To his credit, Michael nodded gravely. "Thank you."

"I'll go, too. Mr. Fury, do you think you can teach Bongo to shake? Uncle Byron's dogs can shake."

Alone, Laura sat again as her daughter's bright voice echoed away. Experimentally, she pressed a hand to her stomach. Yes, it was churning. And to her heart. Yes, it was pounding.

How did a woman with absolutely no point of reference go about redeeming a rain check for an affair?

She had absolutely no clue about that, either.

CHAPTER 8

THE SUN TORE away the clouds and fog and the chill of coastal winter. While reports of a Midwest ice storm hit the news, Monterey enjoyed soft blue skies and a breeze that held teasing hints of spring.

On the cliffs, the wind was rougher, whipped in from the sea and tasting, as Laura always thought, of adventure and romance.

The winter grass rustled, and the waves roared, fuming water like froth from a bottle of champagne. Once a young girl had died there, through her own will. An old man had grieved there, through his own memories. And somewhere, gold hidden for more than a century waited to be found.

Laura enjoyed the company and the leisure as much as the search. Nearly every Sunday, she and her friends and her daughters came here with the shadow of Templeton House behind them to look for Seraphina's dowry.

"We could buy a horse when we find it, couldn't we?" Kayla looked up from her enthusiastic scraping with a garden spade. "From Mr. Fury. I know how to take care of a horse now. He showed us. You have to feed them and water them, and brush them and clean out their feet—"

"Hooves," Ali put in, feeling superior. "You pick out their hooves. And you have to exercise them, too. And muck out their stalls."

"Have you been mucking out, Ali?"

Ali shrugged her shoulders, hoping the new earrings in her pierced ears showed off to their best advantage. "Mr. Fury says it's part of the job. You don't just get on and ride, you have to take care of them."

"Yes, you do." The father-daughter supper was behind them, and Ali had survived it. Laura touched Ali's hair. "When I was a girl and we had horses, I mucked out my share of stalls. I never minded."

"Couldn't we have some?" She'd tried not to ask. Ali wasn't quite willing to forgive her mother for letting her father go away and marry some other woman. "Mr. Fury's going to build his own stables and house. When he goes away, he'll take the horses."

"We'll talk about it."

"You say that when you mean no." Ali rose from her crouch.

"I say that," Laura returned, praying for patience, "when I mean we'll talk about it. Right now Mr. Fury's renting the stables and there isn't really time for another horse."

"He'd sell us one of his if you wanted. If you really wanted." Ali turned her back and went over to where Margo and Kate ran the metal detector.

"She's still mad because he's getting married soon," Kayla said.

"Hmm?"

"You know, Mama. He's marrying Mrs. Litchfield."

"I'll talk to her again." Though she could think of nothing left to say on the matter. "Are you mad, baby?"

"No, I don't care if he marries her. I don't know why he wants to when she has that mean smile. And when she laughs it hurts my ears."

With an effort, Laura muffled a laugh of her own. Leave it to Kayla, she thought, to sum up Candy in such accurate terms. "People get married because they love each other." Or so she'd once believed, Laura mused as she looked out to sea. So she'd once dreamed.

"Are you going to be in love with someone and get married?"

"I don't know." Dreams change, Laura reminded herself. "You can't plan these things."

"I heard Mrs. Williamson tell Annie that Mrs. Litchfield planned to catch Dad in her trap, and how he deserved it."

"Ah." She cleared her throat. "She just meant that they were going to be happy together."

"I guess." Kayla thought no such thing but was wise enough to let it pass. "I'm going to get some lemonade from the thermos. Do you want some?"

"That would be nice." Laura rose as well and wandered over to her friends.

"I'm not skimming, damn it." Blowing hair out of her face, Margo continued to run the detector. "I'm doing it the way I always do."

"Half-assed." Kate rolled her eyes as Ali giggled. "Sorry."

"She's been hanging around the gym too much," Margo told Ali. "Picking up bad language along with locker room sweat."

"You've got too much jewelry on," Kate complained. "You're going to send the thing into convulsions."

"Bitch and moan." Margo winced herself. "Sorry, Ali. Here, why don't you wear my bracelet a while?"

"Can I?" Thrilled, Ali watched her glamorous aunt transfer the heavy gold links, then held up her arm, watching the sun bounce off them. "It's so beautiful. It glitters."

"What's the point in wearing it if it doesn't glitter?" She winked and flicked a finger at Ali's earlobe. "Those are pretty."

"Mama got them for me. I got an A on my science report." She glanced toward her mother, and her smile bloomed hesitantly. "She said I worked hard and deserved a reward."

"You did—and you did," Laura confirmed. "Would you mind helping Kayla get lemonade? I think we're all dry."

"All right." She took a step, stopped. "Would you like a sandwich?"

It was an apology, Laura realized, and though she wasn't hungry, she smiled. "That would be terrific. Why don't you and Kayla spread out the blanket and we'll take a break for lunch?" Laura murmured as her daughter picked her way around rocks, "She's trying. It's hard for her to accept."

"If I had the prospect of Candy Cane as my stepmother, I'd find it more than hard," Kate muttered.

Margo merely lifted one elegant shoulder. "Candy's too much in love with Candy to give them the time of day. And the girls are smart enough not to give her any more than that back."

"I suppose it would be easier if they liked her—a little." Then Laura sighed and gave in. "And it's probably selfish of me to be glad they don't. But I'm glad they don't."

"Anyone want to take bets on how long the Peter and Candy show runs? My take is—" A little dizzy, Kate sat down abruptly on a rock. "There it goes again."

"Are you all right?" Kate had a history of ulcers, and now Laura leapt to her side. "Is it a flare-up?"

"No." Kate took easy breaths, waiting for the world to settle. Yes, there was the sky, nicely blue and back in its proper place. "You know what? I think I'm pregnant."

"Pregnant?" With a thud, Margo set the detector aside and crouched in front of Kate. "How late are you? Have you taken a test?"

"Late enough." Kate closed her eyes, tried to analyze what she was feeling. "I bought one of those instant things at the drugstore. I haven't used it because I'm afraid it'll say I'm not."

"You're using it first thing tomorrow," Margo ordered, and she cupped Kate's face in her hand to take a long look. "Morning sickness?"

"Not really. A little queasy when I first get up, but it passes." She shifted her eyes. "The two of you stop looking at me with those smug, knowing grins."

"Not a chance." Laura sat beside her. "What does Byron say?"

"I haven't mentioned it. In case I'm wrong. I don't want to be wrong," she said shakily. "I know we've only been married a few months and we have all the time in the world, but I don't want to be wrong."

"Another sure sign," Laura declared. "Unstable and heightened emotions."

Then she heard a voice, slow, deep, and male, and admitted that pregnancy wasn't the only cause of unstable and heightened emotions. Lust was definitely right up there in the running.

With her hand still on Kate's shoulder, she got to her feet.

"Is this club for women only?"

"Depends." Margo went to automatic purr. "On the man. Want to help us look for treasure, Michael?"

"You all would be pretty ticked if I got lucky and found it first shot, after all the time you've put in."

"He has a point." Kate reached up to pat Laura's hand, signaling that she was fine now. "Anyway, men just don't get Seraphina's dowry. Do they, Mick?"

"Seems to me if she'd had one, she'd have been better off doing something with it instead of burying it somewhere and taking a header off a cliff."

"See?" Her point made, Kate rose. "I'm going to check out lunch. Rumor is Mrs. Williamson made potato salad."

"I'll give you a hand." Enjoying the tension that had leapt into the air, Margo decided to let it hum. She sent Michael a quick wink before following Kate.

"I'd gone upstairs to make some calls," Michael began before Laura could retreat. "Looked out the window and saw five pretty girls scattered over the cliffs. It was hard to think about going back to work without getting a closer look."

"We try to spend a few hours out here every Sunday. So far we've found two coins. Or rather Margo found one and Kate found one. The girls and I are batting zero."

"Is it important to you? Finding gold?"

"The hunt's important. And the mood." She shifted her gaze to the sea. "The possibilities. I imagine her there, that young girl standing on the edge of the cliff thinking she had nothing left to live for."

"There's always something to live for."

"Yes, there is." She did retreat, the few bare steps the rocks allowed, when he lifted a hand to her face. "I should help with lunch. You're welcome to have some if you like."

"I wanted to talk to you about the girls, if you have a minute."

"Oh." The wariness in her eyes became concern. "If they're getting in your way—"

"Laura," he said patiently. "Do you really think you're the only one who can appreciate their company?"

"No, of course not." Annoyed with herself, logic hampered by rampaging emotions, she dropped her hands to her sides. "What is it?"

"I've been giving them a few pointers in the saddle. Kayla . . ." He glanced back, grinning as he watched the little blond head bob. "She's a pistol. She'd be doing bareback jumps if I let her."

"Please." Laura shuddered. "My heart."

"Kid wants to gallop full out in the worst way. Wants everything full out. You gotta admire that. But she listens. She learns. I'm crazy about her."

Laura blinked against surprise and sunlight. "She . . . she's full of Mr. Fury and his horses every time she comes back from the stables." Determined to relax, she sat on the rock, and barely jolted when he joined her. "She's starting to lose interest in her dance lessons."

"I don't want to mess with your plans."

"No." Smiling now, Laura shook her head. "She only wanted them because Ali had them. That's Kayla, always determined to keep up."

There were tiny blue flowers fighting out of a crack in the rock toward the sun. In an absentminded move, Michael plucked one and offered it. "Did you get her that drawing instructor?"

Surprise again flitted into her eyes. How odd that he should remember those little family details. "As a matter of fact I did find someone." She glanced down at the bloom in her hand, wishing she could take those habitual offer of flowers as casually as he did. "She'll start next week."

"Kid's got real talent. Me, the only way I can draw is with a ruler. About Ali."

"She's going through a difficult time. She's not as flexible as Kayla, or as resilient. She's so easily bruised."

"She'll come around." He took her hand, playing with her fingers. "The riding lessons. I don't know how far you want me to push it."

With a sigh, Laura studied her older girl, sitting so ladylike on the ground beside Margo. "If she isn't cooperating, there's no reason for you to push anything."

"Laura, she's a natural."

"Excuse me?"

"The kid sits a horse like she's been doing it all her life. She's got this kind of baffling grace. And she listens to me as if what I'm saying is etched in stone. It's scary. If you want to pursue this for her, you might want to look for someone with more experience in teaching than I have."

Staggered, Laura stared at him. "She never says anything. Kayla comes back talking a mile a minute, and Ali just shrugs and says it was fine."

"Kayla's a bullet. Ali's a song. She'll sing when she's ready."

How could he know her children so well? she wondered. How could he see inside and understand their hearts so well, so quickly?

"She trusts you," Laura said slowly. "Trust isn't easy for Ali these days. If you don't mind, I'd like you to stick with it. She needs something so badly right now, and I don't seem to have whatever it is."

Annoyed, he cupped a hand under her chin and turned her face to his. "You're wrong. You have exactly what it is. She's only blaming you because she knows you'll take it. You'll be there."

He dropped his hand, resisted getting up to pace. He wasn't a damn shrink, but anyone with eyes could see the woman needed something. "I went through a period when I blamed my mother for a lot of things. But I never said it to her. Because I didn't know if she'd take it. I didn't know if she'd be there."

Perhaps that was how he saw, she mused. How he understood. "Maybe it's easier for you to understand her. I never had anyone let me down. My mother and father were—are—as steady as this rock. Never faltered, never wavered. Never failed."

And she had done all of those, Laura thought. Faltered. Wavered. Failed. It wasn't a simple matter to regain balance after you'd been rocked.

"Then again," he said, watching her face, "maybe she blames you because you blame you. Get a grip, Laura."

"You've never been married," she shot back.

"Yeah, I was. Six months." He lifted a brow as he rose. "And I didn't fuck it up alone. I'll keep working with the kids," he continued when she said nothing. "But I've got a condition."

He'd been married? Her mind swung there, back, tried to keep up. "All right. What is it?"

"Stop hiding in the house. Come down and see what they're doing." Amused at both of them, he took the flower from her, tucked it in her hair. "I'm not going to jump you in front of your children."

"I haven't been hiding, and I never assumed your behavior in front of them would be inappropriate."

"Christ, it's fascinating to watch you click into that lady-of-the-manor mode. I don't know whether to pull my forelock or jump you after all."

Cool as snowmelt, she inclined her head. "I'd prefer you do neither. Now that we've spoken, I certainly will come down and check on the girls' progress. I appreciate your bringing me up to date."

"Yes, ma'am, Ms. Templeton."

"Sarcasm suits you, Michael."

He grabbed her arm before she could stride past him. "So do you." He said it softly, his face close to hers. "By Christ, so do you. You want to be careful playing princess to peasant with me, Laura. Puts my back up. Makes me want to prove something."

"You don't have anything to prove to me. Now let go of my arm."

"When I'm finished." He preferred her like this, the challenge of her, encased in ice. The wounded woman made him feel weak and clumsy and eager to soothe.

"Let me remind you who you're dealing with, in case you've forgotten," he continued. "I like to break rules, and if someone puts up a barrier I like to step over it, just for the hell of it. When I'm pushed, I push back. Harder. And meaner."

She didn't doubt it, any of it. The man who faced her now looked capable of anything—sins, crimes, atrocities. When she had time to think, she would analyze what warped part of her was attracted to just that facet of him. For now, escape would have to substitute for valor.

"I appreciate the reminder. Don't let me keep you from your work."

"You won't." In a rapid shift of mood that left her baffled, he brought her clenched fist to his lips. Watching her, he pried it open, pressed his mouth to the palm. "Don't forget, sugar, you're still holding that rain check."

He strolled off, pausing long enough at the picnic blanket to steal a sandwich and make the girls giggle. When there was enough distance, and she was sure the heat had died from her cheeks, she went over to join her family.

"Mr. Fury kissed your hand, Mama," Kayla announced. "Just like in the movies."

"He was just being funny." Laura took a glass of lemonade to ease her dry throat. "He was telling me how well both of you are doing with the riding lessons." Though her stomach was still jumping, she casually chose a slice of apple. "I think he's enjoying them as much as you are."

"They're all right." Though she pretended disinterest, Ali studied her mother from under her lashes. The hand kiss hadn't looked at all funny to her. And her mother had a flower in her hair.

"Michael seems to think both of you are doing more than just all right."

"You ought to get back into riding yourself, Laura." Delighted with the progress, Margo nibbled on a cube of cheese. No, that palm buss hadn't looked funny. It had looked perfect.

"I'll think about it." Because she wanted to watch Michael climb the hill back to Templeton House, she looked deliberately west, out to sea.

SHE COULDN'T SLEEP. Being bone-tired didn't seem to make any difference. Laura wanted to believe that it was because the night was so clear, so full of stars, that it would be a shame to waste it. But she knew it was the dreams that kept her from bed.

She had begun to dream of him, and the content, the detail of the content, both shocked and amazed her.

She could, with concentration, control her thoughts during the day. But how could she control what snuck into her dreams?

They were so . . . sexual. "Erotic" was too tame, too formal a word for what went on in her head during sleep.

She should have been able to accept them, laugh at them, even share them with her friends. But she could do none of those things. Quite simply, she mused as she wandered the silent garden, because she had done none of those *things* that her subconscious created.

That rough, sweaty, elemental sex was a far cry from the dreams of her girlhood—except for those few scattered and shocking dreams she'd had about Michael as a girl. Those had been hormonal aberrations, Laura assured herself, not wishes. And they were best forgotten. In any case, most of her dreams had been soft, lovely, when she'd imagined love in all its forms to be tender and sweet. There'd been no ripping of fabric, no bruising hands or frantic cries of release in her innocent fantasies.

And none, she thought with a grimace, in the reality of her marriage.

Peter had never torn her clothes, dragged her to the ground, driven her to screams. He had, long ago, been tender, almost sweet. Then he had been disinterested. She would take the blame for that, for being too inhibited, too naive, too rigid perhaps to inspire in him unthinking lust. It was easier to accept, and perhaps to start to forgive, his faithlessness now that she understood those darker needs.

Now that those darker needs had been awakened in her.

But dreaming of wild sex and acting on such dreams were still two different matters. She slipped her hands into the pockets of her jacket, breathed in the night, and hoped to cool her thoughts before bed.

She would not go to Michael. Whether it was cowardice or wisdom, she would not go to him. He was beyond her scope, she decided as she walked through the arbor and studied the dark stables with the swirl of fog at their base. He was both too dangerous and too unpredictable for a woman with her responsibilities.

And despite the years he had been Josh's friend, she didn't know him. Certainly didn't understand him. Couldn't risk him.

So she would be what she had been raised to be: a strong woman who understood and met her obligations. She would fill her life with what she had been so fortunate to be given. Children, home, family, friends, work.

She needed nothing else. Not even in dreams.

She saw the lights flash on in the apartment above the stables. Like a voyeur caught spying, she slipped back into the shadows. Did he dream too? she wondered. Of her? Did those dreams make him restless and achy and confused?

Even as she wondered, she saw him come bursting out of the door, hair flying. His boots echoed hard on the steps as he raced down them and into the stables.

She stood where she was a moment longer, unsure. But something was wrong. A man like Michael Fury didn't run in a panic for nothing. He was a tenant of Templeton House, she reminded herself. And she was a Templeton.

Self-preservation could never hold out against duty. Laura ran across the lawn with the moonlight chasing her.

There were lights on inside the stable now. Laura shielded her eyes against the glare, but she didn't see him. She hesitated again, wondering if she should leave. Then she heard his voice, the words low and unintelligible. But the concern in them was clear. She walked down the wide brick aisle and looked into the open foaling stall.

He was kneeling beside a horse, his hair falling forward like a black wing to curtain his face. His dark T-shirt was rumpled and revealed arms toughly muscled and the faint shine of a thin scar above his left elbow. She saw his hands, wide, tanned, gently stroking the bulge of the mare's heaving sides.

She had a moment to think that no woman on the brink of childbirth could ever want for more loving comfort, then she was inside, kneeling with him.

"She's going to foal. There, sweetheart." Instinctively, she went to the mare's head. "It's all right."

"Always in the middle of the night." Michael blew his hair out of his eyes. "I heard her upstairs. Guess I've been listening for her."

"Have you called the vet?"

"Shouldn't need him. Last time he checked her out, he said it should go smooth." In an impatient move, he tugged a bandanna out of his back pocket. "What are you doing here?"

"I was in the garden. It's all right, baby," she murmured, shifting the mare's head onto her lap. "I saw your lights go on, and then you ran down here. I was afraid something was wrong."

"She'll be fine." But it was Darling's first, and he was as nervous as an expectant daddy pacing a waiting room. "Go on to bed. This sort of thing isn't usually complicated, but it's plenty messy."

She lifted both brows, and the amusement in the eyes under them was clear and bright. "Really? I wouldn't know anything about that, as I've only been through childbirth twice myself. And when the stork arrived, he was very neat and polite."

Her attention shot back to the mare as a new contraction began. "All right now, all right. We'll get through this, honey. He doesn't know anything, does he?" she murmured, as the mare rolled pain-filled eyes toward Laura's. "He's just a man. Let him try it, yeah, let him try it once, then we'll see what he has to say."

"Guess I've been told." Torn between worry and laughter, Michael rubbed his chin. "Should I go outside and pace? Boil water, buy cigars?"

"You could go make some coffee. This could take a while."

"I can handle this, Laura. I've done it before. You don't have to stay."

"I'm staying," she said simply. "And I'd like some coffee."

"Okay."

When he rose, she noted that he'd taken the time to zip his jeans, but not to button them. With twelve hundred pounds of horse in labor between them, it was no time to have her mouth watering. She looked back, a little blindly, at the mare.

"I take mine black. Please."

"I'll be right back." He paused at the stall door. "Thanks. I can use the help, and the company. She's . . . special."

"I know." Her lips softened into a smile as she looked up at him. "I can see that. Don't worry, Papa, you'll be handing out cigars by morning. Oh, Michael, what's her name?"

"Darling." Embarrassment didn't suit him, but he shrugged. "She's Darling."

"Yes, she is." Laura continued to smile as his boot heels clicked on the bricks. "And so," she murmured, "much to my surprise, are you."

CHAPTER 9

I
T WASN'T PRECISELY the way he'd imagined spending the night with her. When he allowed himself to think of it, and he allowed himself often, the circumstances were quite different.

Yet here they were, sweaty, exhausted, and united.

She had more stamina than he'd given her credit for. They'd been at it nearly four hours, the mare rising to pace, lying down again, sweating as she moved from the first to the second stage of her labor.

Laura hadn't wilted. And while the coffee was beginning to jangle his nerves, Laura was calm as a lake.

"Why don't you take a walk?" she suggested. She sat comfortably on the hay, her arms circling her knees, her gaze on the mother-to-be.

"I'm fine." His brow creased as he wiped down the mare. Since he'd tied his hair back, Laura could see his eyes perfectly.

"You're a wreck, Fury."

Okay, okay, he knew it. He didn't care to have it pointed out to him though. His eyes darkened moodily when they shifted to Laura. "I've done this dozens of times."

"Not with her you haven't. She's holding up better than you are."

Hell with it, he decided, and eased back a moment to stretch his back. "I'll never understand why something this basic takes so damn long. How do you stand it?"

"A woman in this position doesn't have much choice," Laura said dryly. "And you just focus everything on what's happening to your body. Inside your body. Nothing else exists. Wars, famines, earthquakes. Hell, they're nothing compared to this."

"Guess not." He struggled to relax, to remind himself that Nature generally knew what she was doing. "First time I went through a foaling, I thought of my mother. Figured I should have cut her more slack. I'd rather have my tongue pulled out than go through this."

"Actually, it's more like having your bottom lip pulled out and over your head until it reaches the nape of your neck." She laughed as he went white.

"Thanks for the visual."

It would do him good to talk, she decided. And until the mare's water broke, they had time. "Your mother moved to Florida, didn't she?"

"Yeah, her and Frank. That's the guy she married about ten years ago."

"You like him?"

"It's hard not to like Frank. He just goes with the flow and manages to turn the current in his direction without making waves. They're good for each other. Up to him her taste in men sucked."

"The divorce was hard on you?"

"No, it was hard on her." Idly, he picked up a shaft of hay, spun it through his fingers. Then, to Laura's amusement, he handed it to her as he had the flowers.

"I don't suppose it's ever easy. Divorce."

"I don't see why. Something doesn't work, it doesn't work. My father cheated on her from the get-go, never troubled to hide it. She just wouldn't let go. Never could figure that either."

"There's nothing mysterious about wanting to hold a marriage together."

"There is when it's a sham. He wouldn't come home a couple nights running, then he'd show up. She'd rant and throw things, and he'd just shrug and plop down in front of the TV. Then one day he didn't come back at all."

"Ever?"

"We never saw him again."

"Michael, I'm sorry. I didn't realize." Though her hands continued to soothe the mare, her attention was on him.

"Didn't matter to me. Or not much." He shrugged. "But she was miserable, and pissed, and that made it hard to be around her. I didn't spend much time at home for a couple of years. Hung out with Josh, drove Mrs. Sullivan crazy thinking I was going to corrupt him."

She remembered him. Remembered well, now that she allowed herself to, those brooding, dangerous eyes. And her reaction to them. "My parents always liked you."

"They were cool. It was an eye-opener, watching them, you, what went on in Templeton House. Whole different world for a cliff rat like me."

And the world he was describing was different for her. "Your mother married again."

"She hooked up with Lado when I was about sixteen. I hated the son of a bitch. I always figured she picked him because he was the opposite of the old man. He was sloppy and mean and jealous. Gave her lots of attention," Michael muttered, and his eyes were dark with memory. "Lots of it. He used to knock her around."

"God! He hit her?"

"She always denied it. I'd come home and she'd have a black eye or a split lip and make up some lame excuse about tripping or walking into a door. I let it go."

"You were just a child."

"No, I wasn't." His eyes, stormy now, latched on to hers. "I was never a child. By the time I was sixteen, I'd already seen and done more than you will in your lifetime, sugar. It suited me fine."

"Did it?" She kept her eyes level. "Or did it keep you from feeling helpless?"

He nodded. "Maybe both. But the fact is, Mrs. Sullivan always had the right idea. I was a bad companion, and if Josh hadn't been who and what he was, we both would have ended up in juvie. Or worse. Fact is, he's the reason I didn't."

"I'm sure he'd appreciate the testimony, but I'd think you had something to do with that yourself."

For the first time in months he had a strong, nagging urge for tobacco, even patted his pocket before remembering that that part of his life was over. "You know why I took the hitch with the merchant marine?"

"No."

"Well, I'll tell you. One night I came home. Been drinking a little, me and Josh and a couple of others down at the cliffs. We were eighteen and stupid, and I'd copped a six-pack from Lado. So I walked into the house, feeling a nice comfy buzz, and there he was, that big fat bastard, using his fists on my mother because she hadn't kept his supper warm or some such shit. I wasn't going to let him get away with it, figured it was my job to look out for her. So I took him on."

Absently, he brushed a finger over the scar above his eye. Laura's glance flickered at the movement, then held steady.

"He outweighed me, but I was young and fast, and I'd already had my share of dirty fights. I beat the hell out of him. And I kept beating the hell out of him even when he was down and bleeding and unconscious and I couldn't feel my own hands pounding into his face. I'd have killed him, Laura, that's a fact. I'd have beat him until he was dead and I wouldn't have looked back."

She couldn't envision it, wasn't equipped to. But she thought she could understand it. "You were protecting your mother."

"Started out that way, but then I just wanted him dead. I wanted to make him dead. That was inside me. I would have finished him if she hadn't stopped me. And while I was kneeling over him, while she was holding a hand to her face where it was bleeding and bruised, she told me to get out."

"Michael."

"She told me I had no right to interfere. She said a lot of things along those lines, so I got out and left her with him."

"She didn't mean it." How could a mother, any mother, turn on her own child? It was impossible to absorb. "She was upset and afraid and hurt."

"She did mean it, Laura. At that moment she meant every word. Later, she changed her mind. She got rid of him and pulled herself together. She got together with Frank. But by then, I was gone, and I've never really been back. Do you know where I went that night I left home?"

"No."

"I went to Templeton House. I don't know why. It was just there. Mrs. Williamson was in the kitchen. She fussed over me, cleaned me up. She talked to me, and she listened to me. She fed me cookies." On a long breath he rubbed his hands over his face. He hadn't realized so much of that night was still inside him. "She probably saved my life. I don't know what I would have done if she hadn't been there. She told me I had to make something out of myself. Not that I had a choice, or that here were my options, just 'Boy, you've got to make something out of yourself.'"

"She's always had a soft spot for you, Michael." And he deserved one, she thought now. He deserved comfort and care and understanding. Poor, lost boy.

"She was the first woman I ever loved." He plucked up another shaft of hay, and to kill the urge for a cigarette, chewed the tip. If he'd had a glimmer of Laura's description of him, he wouldn't have been amused. He'd have been appalled.

"Maybe the last woman," he added. "She told me to go over to the stables, and she went up and got Josh. He and I sat in this place and talked all night. All fucking night. Every time I talked about doing something crazy, he'd steer me back with that cool lawyer logic of his. The next day I signed up. I stayed here in the stables until I shipped out."

"Here? You stayed here? Josh never said anything about it."

"Maybe he understood client confidentiality even then. He always understood friendship. Mrs. Williamson brought me food. She and Josh were the only ones I ever wrote to while I was gone. She was the one who sent me word that my mother had kicked Lado out. I guess Mrs. Williamson went to see her. I never asked."

He shook it off, grinned. "You know, her cookies were my claim to fame on ship. Once a month this box would come, full of them. Once I was losing my shirt in a poker game and anted up her—what do you call them—snickerdoodles. I walked away flush."

"She'd like hearing that." Taking the chance, she reached over the mare's neck and touched his hand. "Anyone Mrs. Williamson takes under her wing deserves it. She recognizes fools, and she doesn't suffer them. You're a good man, Michael."

He studied her, saw his advantage in her eyes. "I could let you think that and get you into bed quicker." Then he smiled. "I'm not a good man, Laura, but I'm an honest one. I told you what I've only told two other people in my life because I figure you ought to know what you're getting into."

"I've already decided, for a variety of reasons, that I'm not getting into anything."

"You'll change your mind." He shifted, winked cockily. "They all do."

And the horse's water broke in a gush that soaked the bedding. "Zero hour," he snapped, nerves jangled. "Keep to her head."

Laura jolted back. The fatigue, the almost dreamlike state she'd drifted into while he was talking now burst into an adrenaline rush.

The first flood of fluid didn't alarm her. It was a natural process, just as the mare's plaintive whinnies were part of the whole. A process she had shared in, and one, though the mare's eyes rolled in fear and pain, that Laura knew she longed to experience again.

Laura buckled down to the task at hand, following Michael's terse orders without question and issuing some of her own.

"Here it comes. Hold steady, Darling. Almost over." He knelt in blood and birth fluid, laboring as hard as his mare, and those long, thin forelegs appeared. "I've got to give her a hand here, turn it some." Where was the damn head? "You got her?"

"Yes, I've got her." Sweat dripped into her eyes. "Do it. She's exhausted."

"It's coming." He got a grip on the slippery, gleaming limbs and reached inside the birth canal to rotate and ease. There, lying along the forelegs, was the head. "Come on, Darling, just a little more. Just a little more."

"Oh, God." Now there were tears mixed with the sweat on Laura's face as the foal slid out. "There he is."

Once the foal's shoulders were clear, Michael cleaned the membrane away from the nose. The foal was wet, still attached by the umbilical cord. Though Michael wanted to pull it clear, see for himself, he waited with Laura as the foal struggled free of the birth sac, and the cord broke as nature intended.

For a while, there was no sound in the stall but the mare's steadying breathing and her first soft, delighted whinny as she understood she had a child.

"He's beautiful," Laura murmured. "Just beautiful."

"She." Grinning, Michael swiped at the sweat on his face. "We got ourselves a girl here, Laura. A beautiful girl. God bless you, Darling, look what you did."

She looked, and with a mother's instinct climbed to her feet and began to clean her baby.

"It's lovely every time," Laura murmured, easing back so as not to interfere with the bonding. "You're not disappointed?" she asked Michael. "No stud?"

"She's got four legs and a tail, doesn't she? And her mother's coloring."

"Apparently you're not." She laughed, delighted with the look of stunned joy on his face, and held out a formal hand. "Congratulations, Papa."

"The hell with that." Riding high, he yanked her into his lap and crushed his mouth to hers.

Instantly breathless. And dizzy. And weak. They were covered with sweat and blood, punchy from a night without sleep. The hay beneath them was filthy, the air thick and ripe.

And they were locked together like hope and glory.

He'd meant it only to share with her that heady exuberance, to thank her, in his way, for being a part of the moment. But he sank into her, into the need, into the heat, into those silky limbs that clung as though she were suspended over a cliff and he was her only salvation.

He was murmuring something, a jumble of the wild and reckless thoughts that jammed into his head. His hand streaked up her hip, closed possessively over her breast. She bucked, arched, moaned.

"Steady." He used the same patient, soothing tone he had with the laboring mare. But his teeth nipped at her jaw, scraped over the rampaging pulse in her throat and made the quiet order impossible.

"I can't." Can't breathe. Can't think. Can't let go. "Michael." Dazed, she pressed her face against his throat. "I can't."

He could, he thought as the ache spread viciously. He could, and more. But he'd chosen his time and place poorly. She'd stood by him through the night, he reminded himself. Taking advantage of her now, as he was, only proved that even an honest man could lack integrity.

"I wasn't angling for a roll in the hay." He kept it light, whatever it cost him. "Relax." Careful to keep his hands gentle, he shifted her. "Look, our little girl's growing up already."

The hands Laura clenched in her lap slowly loosened as she watched the foal struggle to her feet. After a few comical spills, she gained them.

"Have you . . ." Laura wiped her palms hard on the knees of her slacks to ease the tingling. "Have you chosen a name for her?"

"No." He tortured himself a little by sniffing her hair. "Why don't you?"

"She's yours, Michael."

"The three of us brought her into the world together. What do you want to call her?"

She leaned back against him and smiled. The foal had already learned how to suckle. "I had a mare when I was a girl. Her name was Lulu."

"Lulu?" He chuckled and buried his face in her hair.

Her eyes closed as he nuzzled, and her heart tilted. "I rode her over the hills and into dreams."

"Lulu it is." He got to his feet, pulled Laura to hers. "You're pale." He brushed a thumb over her cheek, almost expecting it to pass through like a mist. "The closer it got toward morning, the more fragile you looked. And the more I wanted to touch you."

"I'm not going to be able to give you what you want."

"You haven't got a clue what I want. If you did, you wouldn't have let me within a mile of Templeton House. But since both of us are too tired for me to explain it now, you'd better go get some sleep."

"I'll help you clean up."

"No, I can handle it. I'm not that tired, Laura, and you're too damn tempting. Go away."

"All right, then." She stepped out of the stall and looked back. He stretched, a long, lean male wearing black with snug jeans unbuttoned at the waist. Everything that was female in her stirred. And yearned. "Michael?"

"Yeah?"

His eyes were heavy, she noted. Exhausted. But they still focused on her in a way that made her blood tingle. "No one's ever wanted me the way you seem to. I don't know how I feel or what to do about that."

Those exhausted eyes went hot. "That's not the kind of statement designed to make me want you less." Quick as a snake, and deadly, he reached out and snagged her by the shirt front. His free hand circled her throat, squeezed lightly as his mouth came down hard on hers. When he let her go, she stumbled back, her eyes clouded with arousal and panic.

"Go away, Laura," he repeated. "You're not safe here."

She walked blindly out of the stables, into the white flash of morning. Her bones felt bruised, her mind battered. Lifting an unsteady hand, she brushed her fingertips over her swollen mouth. Felt him there. Tasted him there.

Even as she walked toward Templeton House, she looked back over her shoulder and wondered if she wanted to be safe after all. She always had been, hadn't she, and her life hadn't been a rousing success so far. Then again, she had the unsettling feeling that she was thinking with her glands, not with her head. God knew that's what she felt like now, one enormous pulsating gland.

That was a new experience, and she wasn't sure if she wanted to explore it further.

Before she could decide she stepped into the kitchen and all hell broke loose.

"Miss Laura. My God!" Ann leapt at her. While Laura goggled in shock, she was embraced fiercely, yanked back, patted down, and shoved into a chair at the kitchen table. "What did he do to you? That monster, that spawn of the devil. Where are you hurt, my baby?" Eyes wild, Ann smoothed Laura's tousled hair, patted her pale cheeks. "I knew there'd be trouble with the likes of him around, but never did I imagine . . . I'll kill him, kill him with my bare hands. See if I don't."

"What? Who?"

"She's in shock, Mrs. Williamson. The poor lamb. Fetch the brandy."

"Now, Mrs. Sullivan, calm yourself."

"Calm myself? Calm myself? Would you look at what he's done to our Miss Laura?"

After wiping her hands on her apron, the cook bustled over from the stove. "What happened, darling?"

"I was just—"

"I'll tell you what happened," Ann interrupted, the light of vengeance sword-bright in her eyes. "That man happened, that's what. Anyone can see she tried to fight him off. Oh, he'll pay, he will. When I get through with Michael Fury there won't be anything left to scrape off the bottom of a shoe."

"Michael?" Maybe it was fatigue, Laura thought hazily. Hadn't she just left Michael? "What did he do?"

Her lips in a thin, grim line, Ann sat, took Laura's hands in hers. "Now don't be ashamed, and don't worry. None of it was your fault."

"All right," Laura said slowly. "What wasn't my fault?"

"Sweetheart." Obviously the poor girl was trying to block out the horror of it, Ann thought. "Let's get your clothes off and see how bad things are. I'm praying that's his blood on your clothes."

"Blood?" Laura glanced down, looked at the mess of her cotton shirt and slacks. "Oh, Lord." And it began to come clear. "Oh, Lord," she said again and let out a long, wild laugh.

"The brandy, Mrs. Williamson. Fetch the brandy."

"No, no, no." Fighting for control, Laura grabbed Ann before the housekeeper could spring up to exact revenge. "It's not my blood, Annie, or Michael's either. The foal." She hiccuped, managed to get a grip on herself. "I helped Michael birth a foal last night."

"Well, then." Satisfied, Mrs. Williamson went back to her cooking.

"A foal?" Suspicion still gleamed in Ann's eyes. "You were down at the stables birthing a foal?"

"Yes, a filly. A beauty." She sighed and was tempted to lay her head on the table and drift off. Every drop of adrenaline had drained, leaving only floaty exhaustion. "It's a messy job, Annie. I suppose Michael and I both look like we've been in some sort of bar fight."

"Oh." Shaken, and mortified, Ann rose. "I'll get you some coffee, then."

"I've had about all the coffee my system can take for the next couple of years." She sobered then, took Ann's hands again. "Annie, I'm surprised at you. Michael wouldn't hurt me."

"I've told her the boy's got gold in him," Mrs. Williamson put in. "But will she listen?"

"I know a rogue when I see one."

"This rogue," Laura said quietly, "spent the night worrying over a horse. He's taking his own time to teach my children to ride. He's kind to them, and attentive. And from what I've seen of the stables and his stock, he works harder than two men."

Ann remembered the way little Kayla had run to him, and his easy response. But she set her jaw. She knew what she knew. "A leopard doesn't change his spots, I say."

"Maybe not. But a man can remake himself. If he's given the chance. However you feel about him, he is, for the moment, part of Templeton House." Dragging herself to her feet, Laura rubbed her hands over her gritty eyes. "Now I need a shower and a little—" When she dropped her hands her gaze fell on the clock over the stove. "Oh, my God, seven-thirty? How can it be seven-thirty? I've got a nine o'clock meeting. The girls, are they up?"

"Don't you worry about the girls," Ann told her. "I'll see that they're dressed and taken to school this morning. You just cancel that meeting, Miss Laura, and go to bed."

"Can't. It's important. I'll make sure they're getting dressed and grab a quick shower. I can drop them at school on my way to work. See that they have their breakfast, please, Annie."

"And yours, Missy?"

But Laura was already at a dash. "Just coffee, thanks. I don't have time."

"Taken on too much," Mrs. Williamson clucked as she whipped up batter for waffles. "Keeps this up, she's going to drop flat on her face before much longer. You mark my words."

And she wouldn't mind it if a certain young rogue caught her when she did. She wouldn't mind it one little bit.

"Shouldn't have been up all night worrying over someone else's business."

"Mrs. Sullivan, you're a fine woman, but you're as stubborn as six mules when it comes to certain matters. And while you mark my words, I'll wager a month's pay you'll be eating your own soon enough."

"We'll see about that, won't we?" Miffed, Ann poured coffee for Laura and prepared to take it upstairs. "That boy is trouble."

"If he is," Mrs. Williamson said placidly, "it's the kind of trouble a smart girl dreams of having. Wish I'd had more of that sort of trouble in my life."

As Ann sailed out, streaming dignity behind her, Mrs. Williamson hummed a bright tune.

IT WASN'T THAT she didn't believe there'd been a foal born in the night. It was simply that Ann Sullivan preferred to see with her own eyes. She marched to the stables, grudgingly carrying the basket of muffins Mrs. Williamson had pressed on her. If she had her way, Michael Fury wouldn't be eating from the Templeton House kitchen for long.

She looked up at the apartment first, frowning a bit as she noticed the fresh paint on the trim. Just trying to ingratiate himself, that was all, she thought. Making himself handy and agreeable until he could wreak havoc. Well, he could pull the wool over everyone's eyes but hers.

She strode into the stables, something she had avoided doing since Michael's arrival. Surprise came first. The place was tidy as a drawing room and smelled not at all unpleasant, of hay and horses. She jolted when Max poked his head out and bumped her shoulder in greeting.

"Lord save us, you're big as a house." But his mild eyes made her smile, and checking over her shoulder first to make certain she was unobserved, she stroked his silky nose. "What a pretty boy you are. Are you the one who does all the tricks the girls are forever talking about?"

"He's one of them." When Michael stepped out of the foaling stall down the block, Ann dropped her hand and cursed herself for not looking around more carefully. "Want to try him out?"

"Thank you, no." Stiff as a lance, she moved forward. "Mrs. Williamson sent you some muffins."

"Yeah?" He took the basket, chose one. Steam poured out when he bit in. He could have whimpered in gratitude. "The woman is a goddess," he said with his mouth full. "I don't think you're playing Red Riding Hood, delivering goodies to the wolf, Mrs. Sullivan."

"A lot you know about fairy tales. She was waylaid by the wolf, an innocent girl on her way to her grandmother's."

"I stand corrected." Because she put his back up every bit as much as he put up hers, he went back into the stall to finish medicating the lactating mare and her foal.

"That's a fine-looking horse."

"She is. They are. Had a long night, didn't you, Darling?"

The stall didn't look like the site of a long, messy birth. The straw was clean as a whistle, and both mother and child were well groomed. Since it had been only an hour since Laura had stumbled into the kitchen, it seemed the boy hadn't been wasting his time.

"You've had one as well, Mr. Fury, from what I'm told. I'm surprised you're not snoring in your bed."

"I hope to be as soon as I finish up here. The horses need to be fed and watered first." Because he knew it would annoy her, he grinned over his shoulder. "Want to give me a hand?"

"I have my own duties to see to. You'll keep your own house." And he was apparently keeping it well, she admitted. Tidy habits earned Ann's respect. But . . . "Apparently you had no problem imposing on Miss Laura and keeping her up through the night."

Satisfied that mother and child were settled, he moved out, skirted around Ann's rigid form and began to deal with the feed. "No, I didn't."

"The girl needs her sleep."

"Well, she's getting it now."

"She's on her way to Monterey."

The scoop paused, grain dribbled as he turned back to her. "That's ridiculous. She was up all night."

"She had an appointment this morning."

"She was exhausted."

"I know it." She was surprised that he did and that he seemed so annoyed.

"Stupid." He thrust the scoop back into the grain bin. "She could get her hair or her nails done later."

"Get her hair done, her nails?" Disgusted, Ann slapped her hands on her hips. "If that's what you think Miss Laura is about, you're stupid. And I've never thought otherwise. She's gone to work, you baboon, at the hotel. And this afternoon she's going to work at the shop. Then, if she's able to stand after you kept her up all night with your horse, she'll tend her children, then she'll—"

"She owns the damn hotel," he shot back. "And the damn shop. And I imagine both could stand if she took a lousy day off."

"She takes her obligations seriously. And she's got children to raise, doesn't she? Tuition to pay for, clothes and food to buy, bills to pay."

"Templetons don't work for paychecks."

"Laura Templeton does. Do you think she'd live off her family? Do you think that even after that heartless bastard took all her money she'd go crying to her parents?"

"What are you talking about, took all her money?"

"As if you didn't know." Now she sneered. "As if all of Big Sur and Monterey and down to Carmel don't know that that man all but emptied all their bank accounts, and the stocks and bonds and properties before the divorce."

"Ridgeway." His eyes flashed, dark, sharp, swords tilted for battle. "Why isn't he dead?"

Ann sucked in a breath. On this, at least, she could agree even with a rogue. But she had said more than she'd intended. "It isn't my place to gossip with a stablehand."

"I'm not a stablehand, and you've never let your place stop you when it comes to me. Why did they let Ridgeway get away with it? Josh could have stopped it, the Templetons could have crucified him."

"It's Miss Laura's business, and her choice." Ann folded her hands and closed her lips.

"It doesn't add up." He took the grain to Max, who was waiting patiently. "She's got to have family money to wade in. She's got that house, and servants. Nobody lives like that and worries about pennies."

Ann made a derisive sound. "Miss Laura's financial business is none of yours, Michael Fury. But if you've been thinking to soften her into letting loose of some of her money in your direction, you'll have to look elsewhere."

She recognized black fury in a man when she saw it, and also the rigid control that prevented it from spewing out. She'd expected the first, but never the second.

"So warned," he said and went back to feeding his horses.

She started to speak again. Had that been hurt beneath the boiling temper? No, she refused to believe it of a man like him. Still, she bit her lip, wondering how her words would taste if she was wrong and did indeed have to eat them.

"I'll leave you to your business."

When she left, he continued to measure grain, precisely. Then the scoop flew out of his hands, smashed against the stable wall with enough force to snap its handle off. In the stalls several of the horses stirred nervously. Max stopped eating long enough to look out and study his master.

"Fuck me," Michael murmured and rubbed his hands over his face. "I've got enough to do. Goddamn woman should be in bed." He picked up the scoop, threw it again. Then went to find a new one.

CHAPTER 10

BY TWO IN the afternoon, Laura had entered a new phase of exhaustion. It was almost pleasant, the way she seemed to float just an inch or so off the ground and the way the air around her seemed rather soft and fluid.

She'd handled her meeting with the conference chair for the writers' convention, had briefed her staff one last time for the influx of guests that would be arriving over the following two days, and had checked and rechecked the details with the banquet manager, maintenance and shipping, catering, room service, and housekeeping.

At one, she'd fueled herself with coffee and a candy bar and headed out to Pretenses. The one bright spot in the day had been Kate's semi-hysterical call just as Laura was racing out of the shower that morning.

"It's pink! It turned pink. I'm pregnant. Byron, put me down. Did you hear, Laura? I'm going to have a baby!"

She'd heard, and they'd laughed together, wept a little. Now Kate was wandering in a dream state around the shop.

"How about Guinevere if it's a girl?" Kate wondered. "Byron's family has this tradition of choosing names from literature."

"Guinevere was a weak-moraled round heel," Margo commented. "She boffed her husband's best friend. But if that's the kind of thing you want—"

"I've always liked Ariel," Laura put in. "From *The Tempest*."

"Ariel De Witt." Kate took a notebook out of her pocket and jotted it down. Names were a serious matter, she thought, and had to be considered from all angles. Had to sound right, look right. Feel right. "Hmmm." This one definitely had potential. "Not bad." She pocketed her reading glasses as she looked at Laura. "Laura's nodding off again."

"I'm not." Caught, she jerked her lolling head up, struggled to focus. What the hell had they been talking about? "Names," she said quickly, as though it were a pop quiz. "Girl names for the baby out of literature. Hester, Juliet, Delilah."

"And your prize for the correct answer is a complete home entertainment center." Kate arched a brow. "Would you like to move on to round two and try for the trip to Honolulu?"

"Very funny." Laura resisted rubbing at her eyes like a cranky child. "I rather like Juliet."

"We'll put it before our distinguished panel of judges. Laura, take five before you fall on your face."

"And if anyone knows the consequences of overextending herself," Margo put in, "it's our pregnant pal with the dopey look in her eyes. Why don't you go in the back and catch a quick nap?" As she studied Laura, Margo polished glassware. "Spending the night with Michael's bound to sap a woman's energy."

Laura winced and looked around to see if there were any customers within hearing distance. "I told you we were birthing a foal, not tearing up the sheets."

"Which only proves you've got your priorities skewed. Kate, I think that customer's ready for a little push." Margo nodded toward a man contemplating snuffboxes. "He's got his eye on you," she added when Kate walked away.

"The customer?"

"Michael, Laura. Michael. If you don't have yours right back on him, you need to visit your optometrist."

"I don't have time for . . . all right, maybe I've looked."

Margo set down a Waterford water glass and turned away. Progress, she thought, at long last. "And are you ready for a little push?"

Laura blew out a breath. "He wants to— He wants me."

"Surprise, surprise."

"No, I mean, he said it. Just like that. How do you respond to something like that?"

"There are a variety of ways. Let's see, I believe I've tried them all." Margo tapped a finger on her cheek. "Which of Margo's ploys would you prefer?"

"I'm not looking for a ploy." Because her knees kept disappearing on her, Laura sat down on the stool behind the counter. "Margo, I've slept with one man in my life. I was married to him for ten years. I don't have any ploys, or ways, or answers."

"No ploys, maybe, and good for you. But every woman has ways, and I think you have answers. Try this question. Are you attracted to him?"

"Yes, but—"

"The answer is yes," Margo interrupted, and kept one eye on a pair of customers contemplating the jewelry in the display along the side wall.

"You are a responsible, unattached adult female, who is attracted to an attractive unattached adult male."

"That works fine if you're a rabbit."

"It can work fine for people, too. Laura, there aren't any guarantees. You certainly know that. Yes, you could be hurt. You could also be happy. Or you could just get your oil checked."

Snorting, Laura shook her head. "Sex has always been easier for you than me."

"I won't argue that, but I'm not particularly proud of it."

"I didn't mean—"

"I know you didn't. I've slept with more than one man. Some of them were married to someone else. Sometimes it meant something, sometimes it didn't." She could shrug it off now, without regret or recriminations, because she understood that everything she'd ever done had carried her toward where she was now. "Josh is the only one who really mattered."

"Because you love each other," Laura said quietly. "We're not talking about love between Michael and me. It's just plain lust."

"And what's wrong with that?"

"I can usually figure out what's wrong with it, until he puts his hands on me, or kisses me."

As far as Margo could see, that was an excellent sign. "And then?"

"Then I just want, and I've never wanted like that. Everything's too hot, too fast." She shifted uneasily—even thinking about it stirred something inside her. "It's not comfortable."

"Hallelujah!" With a chuckle, Margo leaned closer. "Surprise yourself, Laura, go down to the stables some night and jump him."

"Right. That's just what I planned. Really, Margo, I could use some sensible advice here."

"Sensible's for retirement plans."

"Miss." One of the customers signaled. "Could I see this pin, please?"

"Of course." Taking up the keys, Margo moved away. "Oh, don't you adore Art Deco? That's a fabulous piece. I found it at an estate sale in Los Angeles. They said it once belonged to Marlene Dietrich."

Laura scanned the shop, stifled a yawn. They were busy, she noted, but not overwhelmed. Maybe she could sneak in a quick catnap. She slid off the stool, wandered toward a customer to ask if she needed help. Prayed the answer would be no. And then the door opened.

"Peter." She stopped in her tracks.

"I called your office at the hotel. They indicated I would find you here."

"Yes, this is one of my regular afternoons at Pretenses."

"Interesting." He hadn't been in before, had purposely stifled his curiosity about his ex-wife's little venture into shopkeeping. Now that he was here, he took a slow, measuring study.

Candy's description of the shop as a jumble of secondhand junk hadn't been quite accurate. Then again, understanding his fiancée's feelings toward Laura and her partners, he hadn't expected it to be.

Still, neither had he expected to find the place charming, peopled with well-to-do clientele as well as the tourist trade. He hadn't expected to be intrigued by the displays and more than a little envious of the merchandise.

"Well?" She recognized the appraisal. "What do you think?"

"It's different, isn't it? Certainly a change of pace for you." He looked at her again. Still cool and lovely, he mused. Odd, he'd never have believed Laura or either of her friends had the brains, the wherewithal or the imagination to create something so appealing, so successful.

"It's not a change of pace any longer." She refused to allow the way he studied her, and hers, to upset her. "It is the pace."

"I suppose you're enjoying the distraction."

"It's a business, Peter, not a distraction." Why should she expect him to understand Pretenses? He'd never understood his wife. Perhaps, she thought, he would deal much more comfortably with the new wife he'd chosen. "I doubt you came in to pick up a gift for Candy. She doesn't care for our stock as a rule."

"No, I came to speak with you."

He looked around again, noted the twisting staircase, the open balcony. Then he spotted Margo, watching him with a cold look of calculated dislike. He certainly didn't have to tolerate silent abuse from the daughter of a servant.

"Do you have an office, a private office we can use?"

"We use most of our space for merchandise." There was an office, of course, but she wasn't willing to speak with him in the shop. It was hers; it was not to be soiled with personal problems. "Why don't we take a walk outside? Margo, I'll be back shortly."

"If that's what you want." Margo smiled thinly at Peter. "Be sure to give our best to your fiancée, Peter. Kate and I were just saying how delighted we are you've found your match."

"I'm sure Candace will find your sentiments . . . entertaining."

Laura merely shook her head at Margo, to forestall another, pithier comment. "I won't be long." She opened the door herself, waited for Peter to step through onto the veranda.

He didn't care for Cannery Row or what he considered its carnival atmosphere. It was crowded, noisy, inconvenient. "This is hardly private, Laura."

She smiled at the people strolling on the sidewalk, the busy families, the snarled traffic.

"Nothing's so private as a crowd." Without asking him what he preferred, she moved to the curb to wait for a break in traffic. "We find the location quite a plus. We lure in a lot of browsers who come to the Wharf, or wander down after a tour of the aquarium."

Idly brushing her hair back as the breeze teased it, she started across the street, wanting to be closer to the sea. "And, of course, it's pleasant being able to take a break now and again and come out to watch the water, feed the gulls."

"You'll hardly keep a business afloat by daydreaming over the sea."

"We're managing." She leaned on an iron rail, skimmed her glance over waves and boats. Gulls fluttered and sent a young girl into excited laughter when they landed one by one on her knee as she sat with a bag of crackers. "What do you want, Peter?"

"To discuss Allison and Kayla."

"All right." She turned to him, leaned back. "Allison is doing very well in school. Her grades are exceptional. I'm sure you'd approve. Kayla's having a little trouble with math, but we're working on it."

"That's hardly what I—"

"Excuse me, I'm not finished." She knew he wasn't interested, but she was revved. "Ali played Clara in the *Nutcracker* production put on by her ballet class last December. She was beautiful, and she cried afterward because her father hadn't come as he'd told her he would."

"I explained that I had a conflict."

"Yes, you did. Kayla played one of the mice, and she didn't care particularly whether you were there or not. I believe Ali will continue the dance lessons, and should be *en pointe* in another year. Kayla's losing interest, but her drawing is improving every day. They're also taking riding lessons now from Michael Fury. He's very impressed with both of them. Kayla had the sniffles a few weeks ago, but they didn't slow her down for long. Oh, and I've gotten them a puppy and two kittens."

He waited a beat. "Are you done?"

"There's quite a bit more, actually. They're active, growing children. But that should cover the high points for now."

"I came here hoping to have a calm and civilized discussion, not to be treated to one of your diatribes, Laura."

"That wasn't even close to a diatribe, Peter, but I can oblige you."

He shifted, irritated when someone bumped his shoulder. "Candy and I are to be married in just over eight weeks in Palm Springs. Allison and Kayla should attend."

"Is this a demand or an invitation?"

"People will expect the children to be there. Candy is making arrangements for her children to attend. Her au pair will bring them down the day before the ceremony. Allison and Kayla can travel with them."

How civilized, she thought. And how cold. "You want them delivered by Candy's au pair, and returned the same way, I suppose."

"It's sensible, and it's convenient."

"And it won't infringe on your time at all." She held up a hand before he could speak. "I'm sorry. I'm tired and apparently short-tempered. I'm sure the girls would appreciate being included. If you'd call tonight—"

"I have plans. I hardly see the necessity of running through the details again."

She turned away, looked once more out to sea. She could and would bury her own resentments and try, once again, to give her daughter what she needed. "Peter, Ali is very hurt, very confused, and very afraid. You so rarely come to see them or call. She feels abandoned."

"We've been over this before, Laura." And he considered himself infinitely patient for listening to it all again. "You wanted the divorce. Now it's done, settled, there's been adequate time for her to adjust. I have my own life to think about."

"And do you ever think of the children?"

He sighed, checked his Rolex. He could spare ten minutes more, and no longer. "You always expected more than I found manageable in that area."

"They're not an area, they're children."

She whirled around, stopped herself from spewing out all the resentment, the bitterness. And simply looked at his face. So handsome, she thought. So cool, so composed. So perfect.

"You don't love them, do you, Peter? You never did."

"Simply because I refuse to dote on them, to spoil them as you've chosen to do doesn't mean I don't understand my responsibilities."

"That's not what I asked." Surprised at herself, she laid a hand on his arm. "Peter, it's just the two of us here. We've neither of us anything to lose at this point, so let's be honest. Let's put this in its place so that we can stop going over the same ground again and again and accomplishing nothing."

"It's you who insists on going over the same ground," he reminded her.

"All right, I keep going over it." Arguments were useless and, she admitted, just too tiring. "I want to understand. I need to. It's no longer a matter of what you did or didn't feel for me, or I for you. They're children. Our children. Help me understand why you don't want them."

For a moment, he stared down at the hand on his arm. Delicate. He'd always found that delicacy appealing. The fact that there was steel under it had been both disconcerting and disappointing.

And perhaps if they cleared up this matter, she would stop her constant requests that he flex his schedule to meet her expectations.

"I'm not father material, Laura. I don't consider that a flaw, simply a fact."

"All right." Though her heart ached, she nodded. "I'll accept that. But, Peter, you are a father."

"Your definition of that term and mine are essentially different. My responsibilities are met," he said stiffly. "You receive the child support payments every month."

And they were banked, she thought, into the college funds that he had emptied before the divorce. "Is that it? A financial burden, an obligation. That's all there is for you?"

"I'm not a doting parent, and never have been. I thought once that I would do better with sons. That I wanted them." He spread his elegant hands. "The simple truth is that it doesn't matter now. We didn't have sons, and I don't want more children. Candy's are well tended, polite, and don't require my attention. I don't believe Allison and Kayla require it either. They're being raised well and comfortably in a good home."

Like poodles, she thought, as pity stirred. "The answer is, you don't love them."

"I don't feel the connection you'd like me to." He angled his head to look down at her. "Let's both be honest, Laura. They're more Templeton than Ridgeway. More yours than mine. That's always been true."

"It didn't have to be," she murmured. "They're so beautiful. Miracles. I'm so sorry you can't take what they would give you."

"And I would say that all of us are better off the way things stand. I was angry initially when you insisted on divorce. Angry that it cost me the position I had earned at Templeton. But over the past few months I've come to see that it was inevitable. I enjoy the challenge of running my own hotel, and frankly, Candace is more the kind of woman who suits my needs and my nature."

"Then I hope you're happy. Really." She shuddered out a breath. "Do you really want the girls at the wedding, Peter, or is it for form?"

"If they choose not to attend, it's a simple matter to make the proper excuses."

"All right. I'll talk to them, leave it up to them."

"I'll expect to hear from you by the end of the week. If we're done, I have an appointment shortly." He glanced back across the street. With the air somewhat cleared between them, he chose to be magnanimous. "Your shop is very impressive, Laura. I hope it's successful for you."

"Thank you. Peter," she said when he turned to leave her. People milled around them, but they didn't matter. She remembered a magical night, with moonglow drifting through the gazebo and the scent of flowers and the promise of a dream. "Did you ever love me? I have to know. I also have my life to think about."

He looked at her, standing with the sea at her back, the sun glinting off her hair, her skin pale and fragile. Until the words were out of his mouth he'd had no plans to tell her the truth.

"No. No, I didn't love you. But I wanted you."

A heart could break again, she realized as she nodded and turned back to the sea. It could break again, and again, and again.

THE MINUTE SHE walked back into the shop, Kate pounced. "Upstairs."

"What?" Dizzy with fatigue and grief, Laura let herself be hauled up the winding steps.

"Upstairs and into bed."

"But we're open. The boudoir—"

"Is closed for the rest of the day." In the boudoir, Kate pushed her onto the slippery satin quilt on the big bed and knelt to pry off her shoes. "You get in, turn it off. I don't want you thinking about anything. Anything. Especially whatever that creep said to upset you."

Odd, Laura mused, her vision was all gray at the edges, like a screen narrowing. "He never loved them, Kate. He told me. He never loved my babies. He never loved me."

"Don't think about it." In sympathy, Kate's eyes began to swim. "Don't worry. Go to sleep."

"I feel so sorry for him. So sorry for all of us. I'm so tired."

"I know. I know, honey. Lie down." Fussy as a mother hen over a sick chick, she smoothed the covers over her friend. "Sleep." She sat on the side of the bed, took Laura's hand.

"I used to dream about the way things would be. So perfect. So lovely."

"Shh," Kate murmured even as Laura's voice trailed off. "Dream about something else. Find a new dream."

"Is she out?" Margo said from the doorway.

"Yeah." Kate sniffled and wiped her cheek. And thought of the child inside her. Of the man she'd loved and married, who already cherished it, and her. "I hate Peter fucking Ridgeway."

"Stand in line." Margo stepped in to lay a hand on Kate's shoulder. "When she walked back in, she looked so . . . broken. I could kill him for putting that look in her eyes."

"Stand in line," Kate echoed. "She'll be all right. We'll make sure of it."

LAURA'S MIND WAS still fuzzy with fatigue when she returned home. She thought briefly about a long, steaming bath, cool, smooth sheets, and oblivion. But she needed her children, and needed them badly.

She found them, as she'd expected to, at the stables. Bongo greeted her first, racing forward with his tongue lolling out in a grin. He skidded to a halt at her feet, promptly sat his rump down, and lifted a paw.

"What's this?" Charmed, she crouched down to shake. "Trick dog. Michael's been playing with you. What else can you do, huh? Can you lie down?"

He flopped down into the prone position instantly, looking up for approval, and the expected biscuit.

"Can you roll over? Play dead?"

"We're still working on that." Michael strolled over and to Bongo's relief offered him a biscuit. "You've always got to pay for the show," he said to Laura.

"The girls must be thrilled."

"They're teaching him the rollover. He's making progress." But his eyes were on Laura's, and the shadows under them. "You just getting back?"

"Um. I came down to see the girls and to get a look at the foal. How's she doing?"

"She's doing great, which is more than I can say for you." The frustration and annoyance he'd pent up all day spewed out in rough words. "Are you crazy, going to work a full day on no sleep? You might have nodded off behind the wheel and killed yourself on Highway 1."

"I had meetings."

"That's bullshit, Laura. Just bullshit. What's going on around here? What's this crap about you letting Ridgeway walk with your money and you holding down two jobs to pay the bills?"

"Be quiet." She glanced anxiously over his shoulder, relieved that the girls weren't in sight or earshot. "I don't know who you've been talking to, but it's none of their business or yours. I don't want the girls hearing any of this."

"It's my business when you lose a night's sleep helping me out, then come out here looking as though I could knock you over with a careless breath." He yanked her to her feet. "I figured you were out playing all day at the shop, diddling at an office, and getting your hair done."

"Well, you were wrong, weren't you? And it isn't your concern one way or the other. Now, where are the girls?"

He vibrated with impotence, with the rage of not being able to help or hinder. With a shrug, he turned on his heel. "In the paddock."

"Alone?" Visions of calamities raced through her head even as she dashed toward the stables. When she saw them in the paddock, fear turned to shock.

Her daughters were happily riding in circles on a pair of patient quarter horses.

"I haven't got them jumping through flaming hoops yet or doing flips," Michael said dryly. The woman, he thought, was an open book. "That's next week."

"Aren't they great?" Annoyance with him vanished as she gripped his arm and watched. "Ali's trotting. She posts so well already."

"I told you she was a natural. Kayla," he called out, "heels down."

Her little boots adjusted immediately and, like the pup, she looked over for approval. "Mama! Look, Mama, I can ride!"

"You sure can!" Thrilled, Laura moved to the fence, hooked one foot on the bottom rung. "You both look fabulous."

Her head high, Ali trotted over and drew her mount to a polite stop. "This is Tess. She's three. Mr. Fury says she's a very good jumper, and that he'll teach me."

"She's beautiful, Ali. You look beautiful on her."

"That's why I want her. I can buy her with my own money. I can take it out of my savings." Her eyes tilted down in challenge. "It's my money."

Had been, Laura thought wearily. Peter had taken it, along with the college fund. And she hadn't nearly begun to replace the loss. "A horse is a very big responsibility, Ali. It's not just the buying, it's the keeping."

"We have the stables." She'd thought about this, dreamed about this for days. "I can feed her, and pay for the hay with my allowance. Please, Mama."

Now a headache brewed nastily in the fog of fatigue. "Ali, I can't think about this right now. Let's wait and—"

"Then I'll ask my father." Ali jerked her chin up even as her lips trembled. "I'll call him and ask him."

"You can certainly call him, but he doesn't have anything to do with this."

"You had a horse when you were a girl. You had anything you wanted, but you always tell me to wait. You never understand when something's important. You never understand."

"Fine. All right. I'm not going to fight with you now." Because she was going to break, could already feel the first fissures forming, Laura turned and walked away.

"Get off the horse, Ali." When her stormy eyes came to his, Michael reached over for the bridle. "Dismount. Now."

"I haven't finished my lesson."

"Yeah, you have. Now you're going to get another one." The minute she hit the ground, he wrapped the reins around the fence rail, then plucked the girl up and sat her beside them so his gaze was level with hers. "Do you think you have the right to talk to your mother that way?"

"She doesn't listen—"

"No—you don't listen, and you don't see. But I listened, and you want to know what I heard?" He jerked her chin up when it drooped. "I heard a spoiled, ungrateful brat sassing her mother."

Her teary eyes went wide with shock. "I'm not a brat."

"You just gave a damned good imitation. You think you can snap your fingers and get whatever you want or have a tantrum if it doesn't happen, or doesn't happen quick enough to suit you?"

"It's my money," Ali said hotly. "She doesn't have any right to—"

"Wrong. She's got all the rights. Your mother just came home from working her butt off so that you can have a nice home and food on the table. So you can have your lessons and your fancy school."

"I've always lived here. She doesn't have to work. She just goes away every day."

"Open your eyes." Something, he admitted, he should have done himself. "You're old enough and smart enough to see what she's going through."

Tears began to leak now. "She divorced him. She made him go away."

"I guess she did that just to make you miserable."

"You don't understand. Nobody understands."

"Bull. I understand just fine, which is why I'm not tanning your hide."

"You can't spank me."

He leaned closer. "Wanna bet?"

The very idea was so shocking, so unbelievable, that she closed her mouth tight. "Good choice," he said and nodded. "This horse isn't for sale to you."

"But, Mr. Fury—"

"And you're not welcome in the stables until you've apologized to your mother. If I ever see you sass her again, you will get your hide tanned." He lifted her off the fence and set her down.

On her feet again, Ali fisted her hands at her sides. "You can't make me do anything. You're just a tenant."

"Who's bigger?" Placidly, he stepped over the fence to tend the waiting horse. "And right now, Ms. Ridgeway, you're standing on my property."

"I hate you." It came out on a choked sob, but was nonetheless passionate. "I hate everyone."

She streaked away while Michael stroked the mare. "Yeah, I know how that feels too."

"You yelled at her."

Wincing, he looked over to see Kayla still astride, her eyes huge and fascinated. He'd forgotten he had an audience.

"Nobody ever yells at her. Mama has a couple of times, but she always says she's sorry after."

"I'm not sorry. She deserved it."

"Would you really spank her?" Gray eyes glittered. "Would you spank me if I was bad?"

There was such a poignant wistfulness to the question that Michael gave up. He plucked her out of the saddle, held her hard. "I'd whale the tar out of you." He gave her bottom a light pat. "You wouldn't sit down for a week."

She squeezed harder. "I love you, Mr. Fury."

Hell, what had he done? "I love you too." Which was, he realized with some amusement, the first time he'd said those words to a female in all of his life. "I was pretty hard on her," he murmured, as the picture of Ali's unhappy face swam into his mind. And guilt seeped into his heart.

"I know where she'll go. She always goes there when she's mad."

He should leave bad enough alone, he told himself. He should stay out of it. He should . . . shit. "Let's go see."

CHAPTER 11

WITH ANGER AND shame snapping at her heart, Ali raced over the lawn, through the arbor of wisteria. Nobody understood her, nobody cared. Those thoughts drummed a miserable beat in her head as she whipped down the stone path through banks of hibiscus and night-blooming jasmine.

She didn't care either, she didn't care about anything or anyone. Nothing could make her care. She burst through arching yews into a sun-dappled alcove with marble benches and a central fountain shaped like spearing calla lilies.

Her headlong rush halted with a skid of her boots on brick. And with shock.

It was her spot, where she came when she needed to be alone. To think, to plan, to sulk. She hadn't known her mother came here too. The cliffs were her mother's special place. Yet her mother was here, sitting on a marble bench. Weeping.

She'd never seen her mother cry, not like this. Not with her hands covering her face, her shoulders heaving. Not such violent, helpless, hopeless tears.

Staggered, she stared, watching the woman she had always believed invincible sobbing as though the well of grief would never run dry.

Because of me, Ali thought as her own breath hitched. Because of me. "Mama."

Laura's head shot up. She sprang off the bench, fought for control. Lost. Breaking, she sank down again, too tired, too bruised, too shattered to fight.

"I don't know what to do anymore. I just don't know what to do. I can't take any more."

Panic, shame, emotions she didn't understand spurted so high so fast that Ali was across the bricks and wrapped around her mother before she'd thought to move. "I'm sorry, Mama. I'm sorry. I'm sorry."

Under the arch, Kayla gripped Michael's hand. "Mama's crying. Mama's crying so hard."

"I know." It destroyed him to see it, to hear it, to know there was nothing he could do to stop it. "It'll be all right, baby." He lifted Kayla up, let her press her face into his shoulder. "They just need to get it out, that's all. Let's leave them alone."

"I don't want her to cry." Kayla sniffled against him as he carried her away.

"Neither do I, but sometimes it helps."

She leaned back, sure that he would hold her. "Do you ever cry sometimes?"

"I do stupid man things instead. Say bad words, break things."

"Does it make you feel better?"

"Mostly."

"Can we go break something now?"

He grinned at her. Lord, what a character. "Sure. Let's go find something good to break. But I get to say all the bad words."

In the alcove, Laura held her daughter close, rocked her. Comforting, as always, brought comfort. "It's all right, Ali. It's all right."

"Don't hate me."

"I could never hate you. No matter what." She tilted her daughter's tear-streaked face up. Her baby, she thought, swamped with love and guilt and sorrow. Her firstborn. Her treasure. "I love you. Allison, I love you so much, and nothing could ever change that."

"You stopped loving Daddy."

Laura's heart shuddered again. Why did it have to be so hard? "Yes, I did. But that's different, Ali. I know it's hard to understand, but it's so very different."

"I know why he went away." Ali struggled to steady her jaw. She had made her mother cry, and nothing, she knew, nothing she had ever done could be worse. "It was my fault."

"No." With firm hands, Laura cupped Ali's face. "No, it was not your fault."

"It was. He didn't like me. I tried to be good. I wanted to be. I wanted him to stay and to love us, but he didn't want me, so he went away."

Why hadn't she seen this? Laura wondered. Why hadn't the family counselor? Why hadn't anyone seen it? "Ali, that's not true. People get divorced. It's sad and it's sorry, but it happens. Your father and I got divorced because of him and because of me. You know I don't lie to you, Ali."

"Yes, you do."

Stunned, Laura jerked back. "Ali?"

"You don't lie, exactly, but you make excuses, and that's the same." She bit her lip, terrified that her mother would cry again. But she had to say it. "You always made excuses for him. You'd say he wanted to come to the recital, but he had an important meeting. He wanted to go with us to the movies, or the zoo, or anyplace, but he had work. But it wasn't true. He didn't want to go. He didn't want to go with me."

Oh, dear God, how could protecting your child cause so much damage? "It wasn't because of you. Not because of you, Ali, or because of Kayla. I promise you that's not true."

"He doesn't love me."

How could she answer? What was right? Praying that whatever words she chose would be best, she stroked Ali's tumbled hair. "It might be hard for you to understand this, but some people aren't cut out to be parents. Maybe they'd like to be, or they want to be, but they just can't. Your father never meant to hurt you or Kayla."

Ali shook her head slowly. "He doesn't love me." She said it quietly. "Or Kayla. Or you."

"If he doesn't love you in the way you wish he did, it isn't your fault. It's nothing you did. Nothing you are or aren't. It's not his fault either, because—"

"You're making excuses again."

Laura drew back, shut her eyes. "All right, Allison. No excuses."

"Are you sorry you had me?"

Laura's eyes flashed open. "What? Sorry? Oh, Allison." This part, at least, was easy as breathing. "Do you know, when I was a girl, hardly older than you, I used to dream that I would fall in love one day, and get married. I'd have a home, and beautiful children to fill it. I'd watch them grow."

Her lips curved now as she stroked the hair away from her daughter's damp cheeks. "Not all of that dream worked out the way I thought it would, but the best part did. The best part of the dream, and the best part of my life, is you, and it's Kayla. Nothing in the world could be truer than that."

Ali knuckled a tear from her cheek. "I didn't mean those things I said."

"I know."

"I said them because I knew you would never go away. No matter what, you'd never go away."

"That's right." Smiling, Laura flicked a finger down Ali's cheek. "You're stuck with me."

"I felt bad, and I wanted it to be your fault." She had to swallow before she could speak again. "Did he go to bed with another woman?"

Just when you thought it was safe, Laura thought with a jolt. "Where did you hear a thing like that?"

"At school." The flush rose up into Ali's cheeks, but she kept her eyes steady. "Some of the older girls talked about it."

"That's nothing you—or the older girls—should be talking about."

Ali's mouth firmed. "He did." She nodded and, leaving a small, lovely part of her childhood on the bench, rose. "That was wrong. He hurt you, and you made him go away."

"There were a lot of reasons I asked for a divorce, Ali." Tread carefully, Laura warned herself, even as her heart was breaking to see that too-adult look in her baby's eyes. "None of them is appropriate for you or your friends to discuss."

"I'm talking to you, Mama," Ali said so simply that Laura had no response. "It wasn't my fault," she continued. "It wasn't your fault, either. It was his fault."

"No, it wasn't your fault. But two people make a marriage, Ali. And two people break it."

No, Ali thought, studying her mother. Not always. "Did you go to bed with another man?"

"No, of course not—" Laura stopped herself, appalled that she was discussing her sex life with a ten-year-old. "Allison, that question is completely inappropriate."

"Cheating is inappropriate, too."

Weary again, Laura rubbed her brow. "You're too young to judge, Ali."

"Does that mean it's all right to cheat sometimes?"

Trapped. Trapped by the unbending logic and admirable values of a ten-year-old girl. "All right—no, it's not."

"He took our money, too, didn't he?"

"Oh, good God." Laura rose. "Gossip isn't attractive, and it's irrelevant."

She understood now, Ali thought, understood the titters from other girls, the murmured conversations of adults. And all the pitying glances. "That's why you had to go to work."

"Money is not an issue here." She refused to let it be. "I went to work because I wanted to. I opened the shop because I wanted to. Templeton Hotels has always been part of my life. So have Margo and Kate. Working is sometimes hard, and it's sometimes tiring. But it makes me feel good, and I'm good at it."

She took a breath, struggled for the right angle. "You know how you're tired after a long rehearsal for a recital? But you love it, and when you've done well, when you know you've done well, you feel strong and happy."

"That's not an excuse?"

"No." Laura's lips curved again. "It's not an excuse. Fact is, I'm seriously considering asking my boss at the hotel for a raise. I'm damned good."

"Granddad would give you one."

"Templetons don't pull rank."

"Can I come with you to the hotel one day and watch you work? I like going to the shop, but I've never gone to your other office."

"I'd like that." She stepped forward, brushed a hand over Ali's hair. "It's never too soon to start training the next generation in the Templeton organization."

Settled again, Ali rested her head on her mother's breast. "I love you, Mama."

It had been, Laura thought, much too long since she'd heard those words. There were birds singing in the garden, she realized. And the little fountain was playing musically. The air was soft, and her child was in her arms.

Everything would be all right.

"I love you, Ali."

"I won't sass you anymore, or be a brat or say things to make you cry."

Of course you will, Laura thought, settling herself. You're growing up. "And I'll try not to make excuses."

Smiling, Ali lifted her head. "But I'm still not going to like Mrs. Litchfield, and I'm never, ever going to call her mama."

"Oh, I think I can live with that." Eyes gleaming wickedly, Laura bent down. Woman to woman. "I'll tell you something, just between you and me. I don't like her either." She traced her finger over Ali's lips when they bowed up. "Are we better now?"

"Uh-huh. Mama, everyone said our home was broken, but they were wrong. It's not broken at all."

Laura tucked her daughter under her arm and looked across the gardens to Templeton House. "No, it's not. We're not. We're just fine, Ali."

It wasn't an easy thing for a young girl with a great deal of pride to take the first step. Though it had troubled her, and kept her awake a long time during the night, Ali hadn't told her mother what Michael had said to her. Or how it had made her feel.

She wasn't sure what her mother would have done, or said, but she did know when you'd done something wrong, you were supposed to fix it.

She'd gotten up early and dressed for school, then slipped out the side door to avoid any questions. Old Joe was here this morning, humming to his azaleas. Ali cautiously skirted that section of the garden and made her way toward the stables.

She had her speech all worked out, and she was very proud of it. She thought it was mature, dignified, and clever. She was certain that Mr. Fury would nod wisely, impressed, after she was done.

She stopped for a moment to watch the horses he'd let out into the paddock. He would be cleaning the stalls, then. She tried not to pout as she watched Tess and thought about what it was like to ride her and brush her and feed her apples.

Her mother might have evaded the subject of money, but Ali knew, with her new wisdom, that buying and keeping a horse would strain the budget.

Besides, she didn't intend to ask Mr. Fury for anything.

He had yelled at her, scolded her, threatened to spank her. That was simply not permitted.

Head high, she walked into the stables. All the smells she'd begun to love were there. Hay and grain and horse and leather. She remembered the way he'd shown her to saddlesoap the tack, how to curry a horse. How he had put her in the saddle for the first time. And praised her.

She bit her lip. None of that mattered. He'd insulted her.

She heard the sounds of the shovel, and she walked to the end of the row, where Michael was filling a wheelbarrow with soiled straw and manure.

"Excuse me, Mr. Fury." Her voice had a royal ring that she would have been surprised to know closely echoed her mother's.

He looked behind him, took in the slight young girl in the tidy blue dress and trendy Italian sneakers. "You're out early." Thoughtful, he leaned on his shovel. "No school today?"

"I don't have to leave for a little while." She glanced at her watch, folded her hands. The gestures were so like Laura's he had to fight back a smile.

"Something you want to say?"

"Yes, sir. I want to apologize for being rude, and for causing a family scene in front of you."

Little Miss Dignity, he thought, your chin's trembling. "Apology accepted," he said simply and bent to his work.

He was supposed to apologize now. It was, after all, the proper way to close a misunderstanding. When he didn't, her brows drew together. "I think you were also rude."

"I don't." He dumped the last load, propped up his shovel, then gripped the handles of the wheelbarrow. "Better move aside. You'll get your dress dirty."

"You raised your voice, you called me names."

He cocked his head. "And your point is?"

"You're supposed to say you're sorry."

He released the handles, brushed his hands over his jeans. "I'm not sorry. You deserved it."

"I'm not a brat." All her dignity crumbled, as did her face. "I didn't mean the things I said. I didn't mean to make her cry. She understands. She doesn't hate me."

"I know she understands. She loves you. A kid who has a mother like that in her corner's got everything. Pushing it away's pretty stupid."

"I'll never do it again. I know better now. I know lots of things better now." She knuckled a tear away. "You can spank me if you want, and I won't tell. I don't want you to hate me."

Michael crouched down, gave her a long, steady look. "Come here."

Trembling, terrified at her images of humiliation and pain, she stepped forward. When he grabbed her, she muffled a cry of alarm, then was dazzled to find herself being hugged.

"You're a stand-up gal, Blondie."

He smelled of the horses. "I am?"

"Swallowing pride's hell. I know. You did a good job."

Full of wonder, she held on tight. It was like Granddad, or Uncle Josh, or Uncle Byron. But different, just a little different. "You're not mad at me anymore?"

"No. You mad at me?"

She shook her head, and let the words tumble out. "I want to ride the horses, please. I want to come back and help you and feed them and brush them. I told Mama I was sorry, and I won't sass her anymore. Don't make me stay away."

"How am I supposed to get things done around here without you? And Tess has already been missing you."

She sniffed, eased back. "Has she? Really?"

"Maybe you've got time to say hi to her before you take off for school. But you want to get rid of these."

He took out a bandanna. Ali, experiencing the thrill of having her tears dried by a man for the first time, fell headlong in love.

"Will you still give me riding lessons and teach me how to jump?"

"I'm counting on it." He held out a hand. "Friends?"

"Yes, sir."

"Michael. My friends call me Michael."

HE'D NEVER BEEN inside Templeton Monterey. Though Michael had grown up just up the coast, it wasn't so odd. He'd never had a need for a hotel in the area, and if he had, Templeton would have been beyond his touch.

He'd been to the resort. After all, his mother had worked there. So he knew what to expect. Then again, he mused as he passed the uniformed doorman, you usually got more than you expected from Templeton.

The lobby was enormous, sprawling, with conversation and waiting areas tucked away behind potted palms and greenery to offer the cozy and the private. The bar, long and wide with generous chairs and gleaming tables, was up a short flight of stairs and separated by a trio of brass rails.

Those who wanted a little lift could enjoy their cocktail and watch the people come and go.

There were plenty of them, Michael noted.

They were six deep at check-in, flooding the long mahogany counter while clerks hustled to assign rooms. Two waitresses worked the waiting crowd and passed out glasses of fizzing water.

The noise was huge.

Wherever they stood, sat, or wandered, they talked. Primarily women, he observed, some of them dressed for business, others drooping from travel. And all, he thought, studying the heaped luggage carts, with enough suitcases for a six-month stay.

As he maneuvered out of the way, two women streaked toward each other over the shining tile and met with squeals and embraces. Several others were eyeing him. Not that he particularly minded being ogled, but being so completely outnumbered, he chose discretion as the better part of valor and contemplated retreat.

Then he saw her, and there might not have been another woman in the room. She carried a clipboard tucked atop a fat file. Her hair was pinned up, smoothed somehow into a neat, professional twist. She wore a simple black suit that even one with a fashion-impaired eye could see was painfully expensive.

For his own pleasure, he let his gaze wander down to her legs. And gave thanks to whatever sadist had convinced women to wear those skinny high heels.

Though she was deep in conversation with the conference chair and frantically sorting out details in her head, Laura felt a flush of heat, a tingle at her back.

She shifted, struggled to ignore it, and at last glanced over her shoulder.

In the midst of all those women—many of whom where rolling their eyes behind his back—he stood with his thumbs tucked in the front pocket of his jeans. Smiling at her.

"Ms. Templeton? Laura?"

"Hmm? Oh, yes, Melissa, I'm going to check on that right away."

The conference chair was as busy, as harried, as Laura. She was also as human, and she felt a quick tug as she looked across the room. "My, my." Grinning, she blew out a breath. "You sure do grow them fine in Monterey."

"Apparently. If you'll excuse me a minute." Tucking her clipboard under her arm, she hurried toward Michael. "Welcome to bedlam. Did you come by to see Byron?"

"I had no idea corporate executives were so sexy." He lifted a hand, flicked it over a glittering heart pin on her lapel. "Cute."

"All the staff are wearing them. It's a romance writers' convention."

"No kidding?" Intrigued, he surveyed the crowd, met several pairs of equally intrigued female eyes. "These women write those books with all that steam?"

"Romance novels are an enormous industry that accounts for more than

forty percent of the paperback market and provides enjoyment and entertainment for millions while focusing on love, commitment, and hope."

She reached around to rub the back of her neck. "Don't get me started.
I used to read because I liked a story. Now I've become an advocate. Byron's in the penthouse. The elevators—"

"I didn't come to see Byron, though I might swing by. I came to see
you."

"Oh." She turned her wrist to glance at her watch. "I'm awfully pressed
just now. Is it important?"

"I went by your shop first. Quite a place." It had impressed him, as the
hotel impressed him with its style and charm. "You had a crowd there too."

"Yes, we're doing well." She tried to imagine him taking a turn around
Pretenses. Not quite the bull in the china shop, she decided. More like the
wolf among the lambs. "Did anything catch your eye?"

"The dress in the front window had its points." His eyes slid down her.
"Would have had more with a woman in it. I don't know much about doodads and glitters. Kate fast-talked me into some blue horse."

"Ah, the aquamarine mare. It's lovely."

He jerked a shoulder. "I don't know what the hell I'm supposed to do
with it, or how she managed to con me out of three bills for that little
statue."

Laura laughed. "She's good. But I'm sorry you had to run around looking for me. And now I've—"

"I like looking at you." He eased forward.

"Michael." She backed up, bumped into a shamelessly eavesdropping
guest. "I really have to get into my office."

"Fine. I'll go with you."

"No, it's this way," she began when he took her arm. "I really don't have
time."

"I do. I'm meeting another breeder in a couple hours." He saw the glass
door with "Executive Offices" printed on it. "Is it always so noisy around
here?"

"No. Check-in for a convention livens things up considerably."

It wasn't much more sedate behind the desk. Phones were ringing,
boxes were stacked, people whizzed by. Laura turned into a small office
with a central desk piled with tidy stacks of paper. The fax machine was
humming away, spitting out an enormous stream.

"Christ, how do you work in here?" Feeling immediately hemmed in, he
rolled his shoulders. "How do you breathe in here?"

"It's more than adequate, and the limited space demands efficiency."

She tore off the fax and skimmed it as she picked up her phone. "Sit down if you like. I'm sorry, I have to finish this."

After punching in numbers, she cradled the phone between her neck and shoulder to keep her hands free. "Karen, yes, I've got it right here. It looks fine. They need to set up their registration desk an hour earlier. Yes, I know, but they've had to readjust their estimate on walk-ins. Yes, I know Mark's handling that, but he doesn't answer his page. No, I don't think he's gone over the wall."

Chuckling, she set the fax aside and picked up a memo. "Uh-huh. That's on my list, don't worry. If you could just . . .   My life for you. No, I'll buy the bottle when it's over. Thanks. I want to— Hell! I've got another call coming through. I'll check with you later."

Michael took his seat, rested his ankle on his knee, and watched her work. Who would have thought it, he mused, the cool, pampered princess, up to her elbows in details. Swinging from phone to computer and back like a veteran soldier flanking the enemy.

Depending on the topic, her voice was warm, chilly, brisk, or persuasive. And she never missed a beat.

Actually, her heart missed quite a few—every time she looked over and saw him sitting there. Black denim and worn boots and dark windblown hair. Eyes that watched everything.

"Michael, you don't—"

Before she could finish, even begin to nudge him along, a skinny man with a quick smile poked his head in the door. "Sorry. Laura?"

"Mark, I've been paging you for an hour."

"I know. I was trapped, I swear it. I'm on my way to deal with conference registration setup. But there's a small crisis in the Gold Ballroom. They want you."

"Of course they do." She rose. "Michael, I need to see what this is about."

"Let's go."

"Don't you have something to do?" He made her nervous, matching her pace as she strode back into the lobby.

"I'm having fun watching you. A guy's entitled to an hour off now and again."

As they climbed a flight of wide carpeted steps, he looked around curiously. "I've never been in here before. Hell of a place."

"I didn't realize. I wish I could show you around, but . . ." She shrugged her shoulders. "You can take a tour on your own, but I wouldn't recommend using the elevators. We've got about eight hundred checking in today and they'll be jammed."

"Jammed into an elevator with women who write romance." He shook his head. "I can think of worse things."

The second-floor meeting-room level was as spacious as the lobby, as elegantly appointed, and nearly as crowded. Enormous chandeliers were brilliantly lit, shooting light onto brass and silver, dripping it on pots of flowering begonias in snowy white and bloodred. Along one wall, heavy drapes were open to a spectacular view of the bay.

Laura marched toward a bank of six doors topped with an ornate brass plate identifying the Gold Ballroom.

"You have to admire the Templetons."

"What?"

"They know how to build a hotel."

Because she appreciated the statement, she stopped for a moment. "It is wonderful, isn't it? It's one of my favorites, though I can't think of any that don't have some special aspect. The one in Rome rising above the Spanish steps. There are views from the windows that break your heart. Templeton New York has this lovely courtyard. You never expect to find something that quiet in the middle of Manhattan. You take a step off Madison Avenue, and the world changes. There are fairy lights in the trees, a little fountain. And in London . . ." She trailed off, shook her head. "That's something else you shouldn't get me started on."

"I always figured you'd take it for granted. Misconceptions," he murmured as they walked toward the ballroom again. "There's a lot more I don't know about you than I do."

"Templetons don't take anything for granted." And because she didn't, she stepped inside the ballroom prepared for anything.

It was chaos. Half the tables for the evening's mass literacy signing were set up, half were still stacked and waiting. Mountains of boxes lined the walls. Even the thought of what it would take to unpack them and distribute the books to the right spot made her eyes cross. That, at least, was not her job.

"Laura." It was Melissa again, her wire-framed glasses sliding down her nose as she all but leapt across the carpet and into Laura's arms. "I'm so glad you're here. We still haven't been able to locate shipments for six authors, and an entire shipment from one of the publishers is lost somewhere in the bowels of the hotel."

"I'll put a trace on them. Don't worry."

"Yes, but—"

"And I'll go down to shipping and receiving myself." Her smile was meant to be reassuring and not weary. "If necessary, I'll brave the bowels personally and find the books."

"I can't tell you what that means to me. You have no idea what it's like to have to tell an author she doesn't have any books to sign. It doesn't matter if it was flood, pestilence, or Armageddon, she's going to jump you."

"Then we'll see that they're here, even if we have to send someone out to raid the bookstores."

Melissa blew the hair out of her eyes. "I've worked four nationals and six regional conferences. You're the best I've ever worked with. And I'm not saying that just because my life is in your hands."

Relieved, she shifted her gaze to Michael, smiled winningly. "Hello. I'm Melissa Manning when I'm not insane."

"Michael. Are you a writer?"

"Yes, I am, even—maybe particularly—when I'm insane."

"Got a book I can buy?"

She blinked, her eyes lighting with delight behind the lenses of her glasses. "As a matter of fact, I happen to have one in my briefcase, which you can have. Would you like me to sign it for you?"

"That'd be great."

"Just give me a minute."

"That was very sweet," Laura murmured when Melissa dashed off for her briefcase.

"I like to read, and I might learn something." He shifted, slid a hand down her arm until it linked with his. "How about dinner tonight, maybe a drive, maybe some wild, unbridled sex?"

"As usual, an interesting offer." It was humiliating to have to clear her throat, but she had no choice. "I'm working here tonight."

"Now that's insane." Amused, Melissa strolled back and handed Michael her book. "You're a stronger woman than I, Laura, choosing work over hot, unbridled sex."

Michael grinned. "I'm going to like your book."

"I hope you will."

"Count on it. Excuse me a minute."

He tugged Laura into his arms, lowered his head and kissed her until every ounce of blood in her head drained to her feet and tingled. He let her go and nipped lightly at her chin.

"You're still holding the rain check, sugar. Nice to meet you, Melissa."

"Yeah." Staring after him, Melissa rubbed a hand over her heart. "I believe in quality, descriptive, and well-crafted writing," she began. "And all I can think of to say now is, Wow." She blew out a breath. "Wow."

"Yeah." Laura made an effort to find the top of her head. It had to be spinning somewhere close by. "I, um . . ."

"It's okay. Take a minute."

"I'm going to book on those checks for you right away."

Melissa tucked her tongue in her cheek. "Appreciate it."

"Excuse me."

As Laura struggled not to stagger to the door, Melissa indulged in a long sigh. "God, I love this business."

CHAPTER 12

I T WAS AFTER ten when Laura turned up the drive to Templeton House. She had the good, solid tired of accomplishing a job well. The kind of tired, she realized as she let herself in the house, that didn't yearn for sleep.

Still, she reminded herself, she had another full day coming up starting in just over nine hours. What she needed was a nice hot bath and bed.

After checking in on her daughters and finding them both deeply asleep, she drew that bath, filled it lavishly with fragrant salts and bubbles, and sank in with a long sigh.

She stretched out, gazed up through the tiny skylight over the tub, and dreamed over the stars. Her life was clicking back into gear, she thought. She had her daughter back. There were bound to be some bumps along the way, and she would negotiate them. But everything had been so blissfully normal that morning on the drive to school.

Her family was in order—her parents busily enjoying their lives and their work, Josh and Margo doting on their new baby, Kate and Byron anticipating theirs.

Her job at the hotel was fulfilling, and made her feel part of the Templeton team again. And the shop . . . she smiled and smoothed frothy bubbles down her leg. The shop was an exciting, unexpected fantasy that brought so much pleasure, so many surprises. As busy as she'd been throughout the day, she'd missed swinging in, ringing up sales, talking to customers. Just being with Kate and Margo.

She would manage a few hours the next afternoon, barring any calamity. Then again, she'd begun to enjoy, even to anticipate, certain kinds of calamity. They offered her the challenge of finding the right answer, the satisfaction of knowing that she could find the solution, inside herself.

Like a book, she mused, a whole new chapter of her life was opening up. She was going to enjoy it.

She let the water drain, stepped out of the deep, oversized tub, toweled off slowly, and creamed her skin dreamily. After removing the pins from her hair and placing them in the little silver box where she kept them, she brushed until the curls bounced and shone.

It wasn't until she was dressing again and caught herself humming that she fully realized she wasn't going to bed. Or not alone.

Shocked, she stared at the reflection in the mirror. The woman there, simply dressed in silk slacks and blouse, stared back. She'd been preparing for a man, she realized. The bath, the lotions, the scents. She'd been preparing for Michael.

But now she was thinking again, and she wasn't sure she could go through with it.

He wanted her, but he didn't know her. He didn't know what she wanted, needed. She wasn't certain herself, so how could he be? She didn't know how to offer herself to a man. Not in reality. In dreams, perhaps, where everything was slow and misty, but in the clear dark where there were movements and consequences, she wasn't sure.

Once she had offered herself to another man, in another life. And it hadn't been enough. To do so again, and fail again, would destroy her.

Coward, she thought, closing her eyes. Was she going to remain alone and celibate for the rest of her life because she hadn't succeeded as a wife, and therefore as a lover?

If he wanted her, she wanted to be taken. Tonight. She wanted him to give her no choice tonight.

She rushed downstairs quickly before she could change her mind.

And the night was thrilling, windswept, full of sound and scent. She ran through it as women had for centuries. Toward fate, toward a man.

And lost her nerve at the base of the steps.

His lights were on. She had only to climb up that one short flight of wooden stairs and knock on the door. He would know, and would take. She would, she promised herself as she crossed her hands over her speeding heart. As soon as she had composed herself, as soon as the giddiness faded a little.

She went into the stables instead, moving down the line of drowsy horses. She hadn't seen the foal since its birth, she reminded herself. She only wanted to look, to admire. Then she would go up and knock.

At the stall door, she studied the mother and child. The foal lay curled on the hay, the mare standing slack-legged beside her.

"I miss having a baby who needs me," she murmured. "They trust you to take care of them. It's the most incredible feeling, isn't it? Knowing that came from you."

She indulged herself another moment, stroking the mare's head when it was offered. Then she turned, and he was there. All in black, he was like a shadow that became real in a blink. She stepped back.

"I was—I hadn't seen the foal since—I didn't mean to disturb you."

"You've been disturbing me for a long time. Longer than I realized." His gaze holding hers, he stepped forward. "I saw you, running across the lawn. In the starlight. You looked like something out of a dream. But you're not, are you?"

"No." She retreated again, nerves shattered. "I should go, I—" She couldn't take her eyes off his as he came closer, boxed her against the stall door. "I should go."

"Pretty Laura Templeton," he murmured. "You always look so polished, so perfect. Nothing out of place." He skimmed a finger over the soft lapel of her blouse, dipped a finger in the vee and watched her eyes go dark. "Makes a man like me want to muss you up, get right under that polish and find out just who the hell you are."

He closed his hands over her breasts, calloused hands over thin silk. Felt her shudder. "Who the hell are you, Laura? Why are you here?"

Her heart was pounding against his palm, so violently that she wondered it didn't simply leap out into his hand. "I came to see the foal."

"Liar." He pressed her back against the wood, and when the door gave, she would have stumbled if he hadn't held her. "I bet he never mussed you up, did he? Always polite, always the gentleman. You won't get that from me."

"I—" She was panicked now, thrilled, terrified. Her gaze darted from his as hay crackled under her feet. The stall was empty but for them. She was alone with him. Trapped. "I don't know how to do this."

"I do. I can make you stay, or I can make you run. I wonder which it'll be. But you came to me, so it'll be my way."

He fisted his hands on the opening of her blouse, shredded it in one quick, shocking yank. "Stay or run."

His eyes were dark, demanding, focused on hers. Cool air shivered over her bare skin. "If you stay, you're mine. My way. Stay or run." He gripped her hair, yanked her head back, and watched her, waited.

"Stay," he murmured, then crushed his mouth to hers and ravished.

Speed and desperation. She was pummeled by both as he dragged her down into the hay and branded her lips, her throat, her breasts. She cried out when his teeth closed over her, lancing heat from breast to loins until her body was a bucking, writhing mass of sensation.

The asking was over, she knew. The choice was made. Now he would take, as he had in the dreams that haunted her at night. Rough and fast and mercilessly.

And she wanted that, the painful spin out of control, the hard, tough, impatient hands scraping her skin, the relentless, almost brutal mouth feeding on her.

She found his flesh—hot, smooth. The hay beneath her was prickly, abrading her skin and adding one more reeling sensation. The sound of her clothes tearing under his frantic hands, hands that streaked back to squeeze and probe and possess, was unreasonably erotic.

She could hear herself cry out, hear her own short, harsh panting, each gasp of shock and pleasure. Helpless as a raft on a storm-tossed sea, she rolled, thrashed, and gave herself over to fate.

Every time her hands gripped him, those neat lady's nails biting in, his blood swam. Each time she whimpered, moaned, his pulses whipped. The first time her body convulsed and his name—his name—burst like a sob through her lips, his head reeled.

He could see every fresh shock in her eyes, those clouded gray storms that widened, unfocused, closed on a throaty moan. No one had given her this, of that he could be sure. No one had taken her where he would take her. Of all the things she'd been given, all the places she'd traveled in her privileged life, this was new. Though some part of him, deeply buried, hurt that this was all he could offer, he would make it enough for tonight.

For tonight, and as long as it lasted, he would and could be to her what no one had ever been.

He could feel every dark flash of new pleasure sing through her body and explode inside his own. He could hear her shocked gasps, and swallow them. He could take more, still more, and make her arch violently against him in desperate greed. And that delicate ivory skin, so smooth, so fragrant, dewed with the clean sweat of good sex.

His hands, so strong, so quick, so powerful. They cupped her, bruised, destroyed. Her own were lost in his hair, dragging him down until his mouth found hers again, until she could answer that hard, vicious kiss with one of her own.

His body was so tight, so relentlessly male, muscles bunching under her hands, ridges of old scars sliding under her questing fingers. His skin was hot, burning, and bloomed damp when she bit desperately at his shoulder.

The air was ripe, thick, and tasted of him on each gulping breath she took. Whatever he did to her, she welcomed; whatever he demanded, she gave.

He lifted her hips, high, and his eyes burned into hers. With one violent thrust, he was inside her, hilt deep. The hands she'd gripped on his arms slid limply to the hay as her body simply erupted.

"Stay with me, Laura." His fingers dug into her flesh, and he began to move. "Stay with me."

What choice did she have? She was locked, trapped, steeped. Her breathing was slow now, shallow, her vision misted at the edges, but she moved with him. Stroke now for stroke.

He shuddered when she came, when she closed around him like a damp fist, and he fought a vicious war with himself not to follow. Not yet. There was more. Even as the blood roared like the sea in his head, he wanted more.

And so he dragged her up until her legs locked around him, until her body flowed back so fluidly it might have been made of water. Worked her until her new frenzy was met, matched, until her head dropped on his shoulder.

Then, and then only, he buried his face in her hair and let himself fall.

His weight pinned her to the floor. It was an odd and drugging feeling, having a man's full weight on her again. And it was a triumphant feeling to know that he was incapable of moving, that he was as dazed, as sated, as she.

She didn't have to doubt it. She'd seen his eyes, felt his hands, heard the gritty groan sound in his throat. He had been caught, trembling, on that stunning moment when he had lost himself and come inside her.

There, in the darkened stables with the sweet smell of hay and horses, her clothes in tatters and her blood singing, she felt like a woman again. Not like a mother, a friend, a responsible member of society. Like a woman.

She didn't want to fumble now, to begin stuttering out foolish truths. That it had never been this way before, that she hadn't known it could be. Better, she thought, for both of them, to keep it light.

So she smiled, found the strength to lift her hand and stroke his hair. "Looks like I redeemed that rain check."

His chuckle tickled her throat. "What was your name again, sugar?"

Gathering his reserves, he rolled lazily over, pulling her with him until she was sprawled on his chest. Her smile was both smug and sleepy. There was hay in her hair.

"God, you're pretty. Such a pretty little thing. The proper Laura Templeton with the surprising, and flexible, steam engine of a body. Who'd have thought it?"

She certainly hadn't, and she raised a brow. "I can't say that I or it has ever been described quite that way before." Her lips quirked. "I think I like it."

"Since you're in such a good mood, why don't you tell me now why you came here tonight."

"To see the foal." Fastidiously, she picked hay out of his hair, then shifted her gaze back to his. "On the way to you. You knew I'd come."

"I was counting on it. If you hadn't I'd have had to breach the castle walls and drag you out. I don't know how much longer I could have done without you."

"Michael." Moved, she laid her hand on his cheek. "Would you have ravished me?"

"Sugar, I *did* ravish you."

"It's the first time anyone has." She waited a beat, watched her own finger trace down his throat. "I hope it won't be the last."

"I wasn't looking for one quick romp in the hay."

Satisfied with that, she nodded, smoothed his hair again. "Then I'll come back." She lowered her mouth to his, lingered over it. "I should go now."

He merely shifted their positions, pinned her again. "Laura, you don't really think I'm going to turn you loose tonight."

She felt the quick, hitching thrill of being overpowered. "You aren't?"

"No." That rough-palmed hand slid up, closed over her breast, and his mouth became busy at her throat.

She arched under him, shuddered out a sigh. "Good."

STILL, SHE HADN'T meant to stay until morning. Hadn't meant to fall into twilight sleep in a pile of hay with her body curled around his. Hadn't realized she would awake fully aroused with his mouth on hers, and his hands . . . his hands.

"Michael." And when her eyes fluttered open, he slid slow and deep inside her. Moved inside her with long, lazy strokes that had dreams misting over reality.

He watched her face, that lovely flush from sleep and sex that warmed her cheeks. The eyes smoky and dazed. The mouth, swollen from his, that trembled on each breath.

They would look at each other now in the light, see as they took each other up with a rhythm soft and silky.

Hay motes fluttered in the fragile light of morning, danced in the quiet air. Night birds gave way to the lark. In the stables, horses began to stir, cats stretched and hunted up sunbeams.

And her hands reached for him, cupped his face, guided his mouth once again to hers as they gently slid over.

"Michael," she said again.

"I can't keep my hands off you."

"I don't want you to."

But he'd seen bruises on that delicate skin as she'd slept. "I was rough with you last night."

"Did I forget to thank you for it?"

He lifted his head, grinned. "I guess screaming my name ten or twelve times was thanks enough."

"Well, then." She pushed his hair back from his face, and her eyes were sober. "I don't ever want to be treated like some fragile piece of glass. Not ever again."

"So if I want to break out the cuffs and whips, you're game?"

Her mouth fell open in speechless shock. "I—I—"

"I'm kidding." Christ, what a package she was, he thought on a roar of laughter. And all his. On a spurt of delight, he got to his feet and picked her up. "At least until we've established trust."

"You don't really—I mean, I don't think I could, or would like . . ." When he laughed so hard he nearly dropped her, she lifted her chin. "I don't care to be the butt of your sick joke."

"It wasn't that sick, and, sugar, you've got a first-class butt." He planted a loud, smacking kiss on her mouth. "But since I doubt you want to stroll back to the house showing it off, let's go get you some clothes."

"I'd appreciate it if you would—what are you doing?" She all but squeaked it as he carried her out of the stall.

"Taking you upstairs to get you something to put on."

"You can't just cart me outside this way. I'm naked. We're naked. Michael, I mean it— Oh, my God." Sunlight and cool morning air slapped her as he stepped through the stable door.

"It's early," he said easily. "No one's around yet."

"We're naked." It was all she could say as he started up the stairs. "We're standing outside naked."

"Looks like it's going to be a hell of a day, too. You got anything on for tonight?"

"I—" Didn't he understand that they were standing on his little porch in the full light of day, buck naked? "Get me inside."

"Chilly? I'm working on it." He shifted her and managed the doorknob.

The insult, she fumed. The insensitivity. The outrageousness of it. "Put me down."

"Sure." He set her obligingly on her feet and waited for the show to begin. She didn't disappoint him.

"Are you out of your mind? What if one of the girls had looked out the window and seen us?"

"It's not even six in the morning. Do they usually stare out the window at dawn, with binoculars?"

Of course not. "That's hardly the point. I won't be hauled around that way because you, in your warped brain, find it amusing. Now get me a shirt."

He ran his tongue around his teeth as he considered her. Even with hay in her hair, and flushed head to toe with embarrassment and temper, she managed to be dignified. It was . . . fascinating.

"Sugar, you're getting me stirred up again, and I don't think we have time for another round."

"You—"

"Peasant? Barbarian?"

With an effort, she reined in. It was impossible to have a reasonable argument under the circumstances. "I'd like to borrow some clothes, please."

"What the hell. It'll only take a few minutes."

"Michael." She jerked back, stunned, when she saw the intention in his eyes. "Michael, I will not be—"

Dragged to the floor, kissed into mindless submission, driven to bone-splitting climax.

"Oh, God." She fisted her hands on the rug and let herself be ravished.

IT TOOK MORE than a few minutes, so that Laura found herself sneaking like a thief into her own house. If she could just get upstairs, she thought, easing open a side door and creeping into the parlor. Into her room.

Her children would be waking for school any minute. Her children. Wincing, carrying her shoes, she tiptoed into the hall. Was she out of her mind? How could she possibly explain herself if—

"Miss Laura!"

If the worst happened, Laura thought fatalistically and turned to face a shocked Ann Sullivan.

"Annie. I was just, ah, out . . . early. Walking."

Very slowly, Ann continued down the stairs. She had been widowed for more than twenty-five years, but she knew the look of a woman who'd spent the night in a man's arms.

"You're wearing a man's shirt," she said stiffly. "And there's hay in your hair."

"Ah." Clearing her throat, Laura reached up and plucked out a bent shaft. "Yes, that's true. I was . . . out, as I said, and . . ."

"You've never been able to lie your way out of an open door." Ann stopped at the base of the stairs, facing down her quarry very much like a mother about to lecture a reckless child. With a mixture of amusement and apprehension, Laura recognized the signs.

"Annie—"

"You've been down at the stables rolling around in the hay with that sharp-eyed, womanizing Michael Fury."

"Yes, I've been down at the stables," Laura said shrugging on her cloak of dignity. "Yes, I've been with Michael. And I'm a grown woman."

"With the sense of a peanut. What were you thinking of?" Ann continued, poking out a finger. "A woman like you wrestling in a hayloft with the likes of him."

Because where she loved, she had patience, Laura's voice was calm. "I imagine you know very well what I was thinking of. Whatever you think of him, or of my sense, the fact remains that I'm thirty years old, Annie. He wanted me. I wanted him. And in all of my life—all of it—no one has ever, ever made me feel the way he did."

"A moment's pleasure for—"

"A moment's pleasure." Laura nodded. If that was all it amounted to, she swore she would go to her grave grateful. "I was married ten years and never knew what it was like to be pleasured or, I hope, to pleasure a man like that. And I'm sorry you disapprove."

Ann's face pokered up. "It's not my place to disapprove."

"Oh, don't give me that dignified-housekeeper-to-mistress routine, Annie. It's years too late." With a sigh, she laid a hand over the rigid one with which Ann gripped the newel post. "I know how much you care. I know that everything you say you say out of concern and love, but even that can't change the way I feel. Or what I need."

"And you think you need Michael Fury?"

"No. I know I do. I haven't decided what to do about it, or where I want to go from here, but I do know that I fully intend to have a great many moments of pleasure."

"Whatever the cost?"

"Yes. For once in my life, the hell with the cost. I need to shower." She started up the stairs, paused, turned. "I don't want you going down there badgering Michael over this, Annie. That is not your place, or anyone else's."

Ann inclined her head, kept it lowered until she heard Laura close the door to her room. Perhaps it wasn't her place to speak to Michael Fury. But she knew her duty, and she would do it.

Without hesitation, she walked down the hall and into the library. The call to France wouldn't take long. Then they would see, she thought, brooding out the window. They would see.

"I'd like to speak with Mr. or Mrs. Templeton, if you please. It's Ann Sullivan, the housekeeper of Templeton House."

"IN THE STABLES. In the hay. All night?" In the second-floor kitchen of Pretenses, Kate swiveled on the stool and gaped. The ten-minute afternoon break was a great deal more interesting than she'd expected. "You?"

"Why is that so shocking?" Ignoring her tea, Laura drummed her fingers on the counter. "I'm human, aren't I? Not some sort of windup doll."

"Pal, it sounds like you were pretty wound up to me. And I'm not shocked, exactly. I mean, I wouldn't have imagined bouncing on the hay was your style, but hey, whatever works." She grinned and sampled one of the cookies Laura had picked up at the bakery. "And I take it that it worked just fine."

Mollified, Laura took a cookie herself. "I," she said smugly, "was an animal."

With a snort, Kate raised one of Laura's arms over their heads. "Way to go, champ. So, now—about the details."

"I can't. Well, maybe. No." The gleam in her eye matched Kate's. "No."

"Come on, just one detail, then. One little detail of Laura's Wild Night."

She laughed, shook her head, nibbled on her lip. God knew, she could tell Kate, or Margo, anything. And it had been so rare lately for her to be able to share something so wonderful and reckless. Fastidiously, she brushed crumbs off the counter.

"He ripped my clothes off."

"Metaphorically or literally?"

"Literally. Just tore them to shreds. Just . . ." She pressed a hand to her stomach. "God."

"God," Kate echoed, fanning a hand in front of her face.

"That's it." Laura scooted off the stool and dumped her cold tea into the sink. "I can't do this. It feels like high school."

"Pal, you've graduated and your cap and gown are in tatters. Congratulations." She cocked her head as Laura rinsed out her cup. She knew the woman who carefully washed out china as well as she knew herself. "Are you in love with him?"

Laura watched the water run and drain. "I don't know. Love, this kind of love, isn't as simple as I once thought it was. I'm afraid I could be, and I don't want to complicate everything."

"You once told me that love just happened, couldn't be planned," Kate pointed out. "I found out you were right."

With care, she set the cup to drain. She'd already given Kate's question a great deal of thought, knowing it would be asked by those who cared the most. "If it does happen, I'll deal with it. There's so much more to him than I ever imagined. And every time I see one of those pieces I didn't know was there fall into place, I'm more involved."

Laura dried her hands and turned back to Kate. "I'm not going to get dreamy-eyed this time around, or want more than someone's capable of giving. I'm just going to enjoy it."

"Is that going to work for you?"

"The way I feel this afternoon, it's working perfectly." Feeling loose, she stretched her arms high. "Absolutely perfectly."

"Glad to see you two are enjoying yourselves." Margo stepped into the doorway and scowled. "One of you was supposed to relieve me, remember? I, unlike my feckless partners, haven't had a break in four hours."

"Sorry." Laura dropped her arms. "I'll go."

"No, I'll go." Kate hopped off the stool. "It'll give you a chance to fill Margo in."

"Fill me in on what?"

"Michael screwed Laura's brains out last night in a horse stall."

Gracefully, Margo fluffed her hair while Laura flushed. "Really?"

"Ripped her clothes off," Kate added as she headed out the door. "I'll leave Laura to fill in the details."

On a long hum, Margo settled herself on one of the padded ice cream chairs, crossed her long, shapely legs. "Pour me some tea, would you, Laura? I'm whipped."

Automatically Laura poured a cup, brought it to the table. "Want a cookie?"

"Don't mind if I do." Margo debated them, selected, nibbled. "Now, sit your butt down and start filling in those details. And don't worry about being too specific."

CHAPTER 13

WHISTLING BETWEEN HIS teeth, Michael sent Zip into a raging gallop, bursting out of the woods into the sun like a flaming fire. The little demon could run, Michael thought. He'd be sorry to lose him, but the offer that had come in that morning closed the deal.

In a matter of hours, the speedy little colt would be on his way to Utah.

"Going to have some fun with the fillies up there, kid. And breed some champs."

And the asking price meant that Michael could close the deal he'd been negotiating for a particularly fine-looking Palomino mare and her doe-eyed foal.

The mare was ornery, he mused, had twice tried to kick him and her handler during the inspection. Michael liked her the better for it, and for the fact that she'd bred such a tough little foal. A foal he was already planning to raise for stud.

Couple more years, Michael thought, the new colt would cover twenty mares, and at four his full complement of sixty.

They'd do fine together, he decided. That snippy Palomino mare and the energetic little buckskin she'd birthed would help him start a new phase of his business.

Within two years, he projected, Fury Ranch was going to mean something—something more than livelihood and survival. It was going to mean quality. And that, Michael thought as Zip tore around the stables, was something he'd lived most of his life without.

It would have been impossible and, worse, embarrassing, for him to explain to anyone that he had always wanted quality. Not just for what he had, or what he built, but for what he was. He'd always wanted to come from something. To be something.

And he had come from nothing. That he'd had to face, couldn't be changed. Nor could he change the fact that it left a sore spot inside him that was never really eased.

He'd gone years telling himself it didn't matter what his parents had been, how he'd grown up, or how he'd lived. But it did matter; now more than ever, he knew it mattered. There was a woman in his life who shouldn't have been there.

Sooner or later, he had no doubt, she'd see that for herself. The insult of it, and the inevitability, made him push the colt for more speed. Not for a minute would he have admitted that he was racing away rather than toward. Nor would he admit, even to himself, that his emotions had been in turmoil from the moment he'd stepped inside the stables last night and found her.

As if she was meant to be there, with him. For him. As if he could take, and hold, maybe even deserve something as lovely and fine and vital as Laura. And be for her what she could be for him.

The hell with that, Michael told himself, squinting into the sunlight as the colt flew over the ground. No way he was going to start fashioning pretty little dreams about a life with Laura. If he was one thing, he was a realist. His time with her was temporary, and he would damn well pack as much into it as he could while it lasted.

He was already into the run, the colt bunched for the leap when Michael spotted the figure loitering at the paddock. They sailed over the fence, spewed up dirt and dust.

"That's a hell of a horse," Byron called out as Michael trotted to him.

"He is." Bending, Michael slapped Zip's neck, then dismounted. "Sold him today. Guy in Utah." After uncinching the saddle, Michael hung it over the fence. "Wants to breed for speed."

"He'll get it." Byron leaned over, patted the colt's sleek throat. "Isn't even winded."

"Nope. He'll tire his rider out first."

"I'm surprised you're not using him for stud yourself. He's prime."

"Yeah, he's prime. But I have more foundation to build before I add a stud." Couple more years, he thought, picturing the foal again, and we'll both be ready. "Right now it's horse trading and building on the investment."

"You've got a good start. That walker there." Byron gestured. "What are you asking?"

"Max?" Michael glanced around, watched the horse swish his tail. "I'd sell my own mother first." He held up his hand, and Max walked over. "Glad to see me, Max?"

Max peeled back his lips so his teeth showed and split the air with a horsey laugh. "Give us a kiss, then."

Max nibbled affectionately on Michael's chin, and being nobody's fool, sniffed at his pockets. "True love is never enough. Want one?"

"A kiss from your horse or a carrot?"

"Whichever."

"I'll pass on both, thanks." But he stroked Max's mane as the horse crunched the carrot. "You got some fine-looking stock here."

"You in the market?"

"I told myself I wasn't, especially with the baby coming." He looked longingly at the mare nursing her foal. "Shit, this takes me back."

Michael picked up a dandy brush and began to groom Zip. "What are you, about two-ten?"

"Twelve," Byron said absently. "Two-twelve."

"That bay gelding with the two front socks? He'd carry you."

Byron studied the bay, noted the lines, the flashy white blaze. "Handsome bastard, isn't he?"

"Good saddle horse, well mannered but no pussy. Needs a firm hand.

The right hand." Michael tucked his tongue in his cheek as he continued to work. "Make you a good deal, seeing as you're related to Josh and married to one of my favorite people."

"I didn't come by to horse-trade."

"No?" Placidly, Michael leaned against Zip, lifted a hoof to pick it out. "Why, then?"

"I was in the neighborhood, more or less, and thought you might want to come by on Saturday night. Poker."

"I'm usually up for a game." Then he paused, narrowed his eyes. "This isn't going to be one of those enlightened evenings with women asking if a straight beats a flush."

"Kate would knock you on your ass for that comment." But Byron grinned. "No, it's purely sexist, men only."

"Then I'm in, thanks."

"Maybe I'll win that bay from you."

"Keep dreaming, De Witt."

"Good heart room," he murmured. "About sixteen hands, isn't he?"

Michael smothered a grin, continued to clean his mount's hooves. "About. Just turned four. His sire was a walker, his dam a dark-eyed floozy from Baton Rouge."

"Shit." He was sunk. "You stable?"

"Yep. Here, for now. Then at my place when it's finished. Should be ready to start construction in a couple weeks."

"Let's take a closer look." In his Saville Row suit and Magli shoes, Byron climbed into the paddock.

"I've heard you Southern boys are cardsharps and horse thieves," Michael commented as they strolled companionably toward the bay.

"You heard right."

How long was she going to make him wait? Michael paced the floor, contemplated the bottle of wine on the counter. It made him scratch his head. He'd actually gone out and bought wine. Not his usual style, but he'd figured sex in a horse stall wasn't Laura's usual either. The least he could do was offer her a civilized drink. Before he jumped her again.

Which was just what he wanted to do.

If she ever got there.

Of course she was coming. He'd reminded himself of that half a dozen times over the last hour. The way it had been between them the night before, she had to be just as eager for a repeat performance. She'd have thought of him during the day, countless times, the way he'd thought of her.

The way he would have sworn he'd smelled her every time he took a breath. The way he'd caught himself going off into some brainless trance because he could see her face in his head, or hear her voice, or . . .

Want her. Just want her.

When had he ever wanted anything like this? Once he'd wanted escape, and he'd gotten it. He'd wanted danger and risk and reckless adventure. And he'd gotten that, too. And when he'd wanted peace, a life he could look at with some measure of pride, he'd gone out and gotten that as well.

But did he have Laura? Was she going to slip silkily through his fingers before he'd gotten a good grip, or before he'd figured out what the hell to do with her? About her?

She was out of his league, and knowing it pissed him off. Made him determined to drag her to equal ground. Sex was a great equalizer, and he had her there. For now.

Furious with himself for niggling at what shouldn't have been a problem, he poured a glass of the wine. He sniffed it, shrugged, downed it.

"When in Rome, Fury."

But he set the glass aside and began to pace again, prowling back and forth across the length of the room like a cat prowling the confines of a cage.

He'd caught a glimpse of Ann that afternoon, when he supervised the transfer of the colt. From the bullets she shot out of her eyes, he had the feeling that Laura hadn't managed to get past her that morning.

It made him grin to think of it, the elegant lady of the house sneaking in at dawn in a baggy shirt and jeans, caught by the ever-present, cold-eyed housekeeper.

Maybe Sullivan had locked Laura in. His grin vanished as the idea popped into his head. Maybe she had Laura trapped inside, refusing to let her out. Maybe she was . . .

And maybe he should get a grip on himself, he decided.

The hell with it. He headed for the door. He was going after her.

When he yanked it open, Laura jumped back a full step, pressed a hand to her throat. "You scared the life out of me."

"Sorry. I was about to rescue you from the dungeon."

"Oh?" She smiled, puzzled. "Were you?"

"But you seemed to have managed it on your own."

"I couldn't come any sooner. We've been having a little chaos. My parents have decided to come out for a quick visit. They'll be here in a couple of days, and the girls were so excited, I had a hard time getting them to bed. Then we had to—"

"You don't have to explain to me. Just come here." He pulled her close and released a portion of frustrated need in one rough kiss. Pressing her back against the doorjamb, he fisted his hands in her hair and released more.

The same, she thought, wrapping herself around him. The same heat, the same rush, the same wonder. When she could breathe again, she kept her clenched hands on his shirt.

"I thought . . ."

"What?"

But she shook her head. "Nothing." Smiling, she lifted her hands to frame his face. "Hello, Michael."

"Hello, Laura." He circled her inside, closed the door with his boot. "I was going to offer you some wine."

"Oh, thank you. That would be nice."

"But it's going to have to wait." He swung her into his arms.

"Oh. That's even nicer."

HE DID BRING her a glass when she was sitting on his rumpled bed wearing his shirt. Not having what he considered her misplaced sense of modesty, he sat across from her naked, knee to knee.

"I'm kind of celebrating," he told her, and tapped the glasses together.

She felt so loose she was certain she could slide right into the sheets. "What are you kind of celebrating?"

"I sold two horses today. One to your brother-in-law."

"Byron?" Surprised, she sipped, recognized the rich tang of a good Templeton Chardonnay. "Funny, Kate never mentioned that they were buying a horse."

"I guess he hadn't told her yet."

"Oh . . . uh-oh."

"Does Kate have a problem with horses?"

"No, but it's quite a commitment. I'm surprised they didn't discuss it first. I'm sure she will be, too."

"I'd say he can handle her."

"It's not a matter of handling, one way or the other. Marriage is a partnership, and decisions require discussion and mutual agreement. And what are you grinning at?"

"You look cute, sitting there all mussed up from sex and lecturing me on relationship ethics."

"I wasn't lecturing." She took a small, cool sip from her glass. "I was simply stating. Don't you believe in relationship ethics?"

"Yep." His hand wandered up her thigh. "But I figure like in any partnership, sometimes one end makes a decision on its own, and ethics get bent a little. I like this little birthmark way up here." His fingers skimmed high on her thigh over a small crescent shape. "Looks like a moon. Sexier than a tattoo."

"You're trying to distract me."

"Doesn't take much effort." But he trailed his finger back down to her knee. "I don't want to see the guy get popped by his wife. He fell for the horse, and maybe I gave him a little push." He moved his shoulders. "If Kate has a problem, we can lose the deal."

Laura tilted her head. "And then, in your opinion, Kate would be a shrew, and Byron a Milquetoast."

"I was thinking wuss actually." Amused, he straightened her leg so that he could lift her knee and kiss it. "Did you always talk everything over, nice and civilized with Ridgeway?"

"No, that was part of the problem. I did what I was told and behaved like a proper, dutiful, and spineless wife."

"Sorry." Annoyed with himself for the need to pry open that door to her life, he gave her knee a quick squeeze. "Bad question."

"No, it wasn't." She shifted a little, leaning back on the pillows propped on the iron headboard. "I learned from it. I learned I won't ever be spineless again, or ineffectual, or quietly desperate."

She tapped her fingers against the glass as she put into words what had been in her heart. "What he did, I let him do, which makes it as much my fault as his. I'm only sorry it took finding him in bed with another woman to force me to fix my life."

"You're happy now?"

"Yes, and grateful." She smiled again. "Grateful to you, too."

His thumb skimmed around to rub the back of her knee. "For?"

"For helping me realize I have a sex drive."

Appreciating her, he leaned up, nipping her lips with his as he set his glass on the table beside the bed. "You had problems with that?"

"I'm not having them now."

"Maybe I should check, just to be sure." But before she could circle him into her arms, he slipped back. "I think I'll start down here," he murmured, and lifted her foot.

"You're not going to . . . Oh." Her head fell back as his teeth and tongue went to work. "They do reflexology in the spa at the resort," she murmured as he bombarded all manner of tiny, sensitive nerves. "It never felt like this."

"You're not going to start fantasizing that I'm Viktor the massage boy, are you?"

She laughed, moaned, shuddered. "No. The reality's just—Jesus!" She dropped her glass, splattering wine over herself and the sheets. "Oh, I'm sorry. Let me—"

"No, you don't." He gave her a gentle shove that sent her weakly back onto the pillows. "Just stay where you are until I finish." He scraped his teeth over her ankle. "Things were a little rushed before. I think I skimmed over some of the finer points."

He pressed the heel of his hand lightly against her, had her hips rising. "I suggest you hang on, sugar. I'm going to take you for a long, hard ride."

It was like being assaulted on all sides. Inside and out, mind and body. She could do nothing but absorb, react, experience. He worked his way up, as if she were a meal to be savored, course by course.

The lights he left burning blazed too bright, burned her eyes even when she closed them. The air, breezy through the open windows, was suddenly too thick, so that each breath she took was a gasp. Her skin, no longer cool, pulsed with the beat of blood beneath and with the skim of hands and mouth.

The long muscles in her thighs quivered as he cruised over them, and the sheets rustled at the bunch and flex of her hands.

She'd never been tasted this way, touched this way, as if she were everything, and all things.

And his mouth closed over her, suddenly greedy, rough and focused on that core of wet heat until she flew up like an arrow with the sharp edge of her own pleasure stabbing her.

He was mad for her now, wild to see her pinned on the jagged peak of her own ecstasy. Her head was flung back, her eyes blind, her hands wrapped around the iron posts of the bed as if only that desperate grip kept her anchored.

And he was mad to drive her further.

He used his hands until she bucked against him in frantic, pleading rhythm. Watched her, watched her, until his name sobbed out of her, until her hands lost their grip, until her body went pliant as pooled wax.

She lay still, wrecked, unable to do more than moan when he lifted her enough to slip the shirt away from her shoulders.

"You're beautiful, Ms. Templeton. Gold." He touched his hand to her hair. "Rose." And her breast. She trembled under his touch.

"Michael." She opened heavy eyes, saw the room spin. "I can't."

"Can't you?" Gently now, he lowered his head, flicked his tongue over her nipple. "I wonder."

"I know you didn't—you haven't—" She reached for him, knowing she would find him hard and ready. "Let me."

"Some other time." He smiled, though his blood had leaped when her fingers closed around him. "I'll take a rain check. Let's just see if we can finish this the old-fashioned way."

This time he closed his mouth over her breast and sent the ache echoing down.

"You do things inside me." Her breath began to hitch again. That curl of new need began to spread and ache and throb. "You have no idea what you do inside me."

It was building again, impossibly strong. She could have wept. He feasted on her breasts, teeth and tongue hungry for the flavor of her, that fragile and floral taste he'd come to crave. He took her hands, wrapping them around the posts again, keeping his clamped over hers.

The thought ran through her reeling head that they were both trapped, both locked in, both prisoners of this.

Accepting, she lifted her mouth to his, linking there as well, and met his fast, desperate thrust.

Then it was only blind speed, blazing heat, gasps and the animal's song of flesh against flesh. Harder, deeper, until he was buried in her. Until, still linked, hands, mouths, sex, they plunged.

LATER, WHEN BLOOD had cooled and the air was quiet again, she shifted. His arm curled around her, held.

"I thought you were asleep," she murmured.

"Was."

"I have to go. I can't sneak in the house at dawn every morning carrying my shoes."

"Little while more." He was still half asleep, and his voice was thick with it. "I wanna hold you."

Her heart melted. Gently, she brushed the hair back from his face. Wild, untamed hair, she thought. Devil's hair, dark and seductive. "Only a little while."

She rested her head on his shoulder, her hand on his heart. But he was already asleep again. So she lay there, for a little while, feeling his heart beat.

MRS. WILLIAMSON SLID a stack of pancakes under Michael's nose. It seemed the least he could do was eat them. She watched him take the first bite, her arms folded over her breasts.

"The best," he said. "When I get my place back together, I'm going to miss sneaking over here and having you feed me. Sure you don't want to marry me and come along?"

"You keep asking, you might get surprised." She topped off his coffee. The boy had always had a raging appetite, she reflected. For all manner of things. "Did you finish up that casserole I sent down?"

"I ate it, bowl and all." Absently, he reached down to scratch the kitten that wound hopefully through his legs. "And the pie, and those cookies." He grabbed her hand, nibbling on it while she clucked at him. "If you were to see your way to making one of those chocolate cakes. The one with the cream and the cherries?"

"Black Forest. Miss Laura's favorite."

"It is?" Apparently they shared the same taste out of bed as well. "She probably wouldn't miss a piece, or two, of it."

"We'll see about it." She skimmed her hand through his hair, tugged on the ponytail. "You need a decent haircut. Man your age wearing your hair like a hippie."

"The last hippie emigrated to Greenland in 1979. There's a small commune there where they still make love beads."

"Oh, you're a smart one, you are. Eat your breakfast. I've got to see that those children are fed before they go off to school. And Miss Laura," she continued, bustling back to the stove. "Eats like a sparrow. Never takes the time to sit down and start the day with a decent meal. 'Just coffee,' she tells me. Well, you can't fuel a body on coffee."

Laura's body seemed fueled fine to him, but he didn't think it wise to mention it. Mrs. Williamson might be fond of him, but he didn't imagine she'd approve of him luring the mistress into hot, sweaty bouts of sex.

"She's going to make herself sick, like Miss Katie did last year."

Michael stopped brooding, looked up. "Kate was sick?"

"An ulcer." Even the idea of it insulted her. Mrs. Williamson stopped flipping pancakes to turn around to him. "Can you imagine that? Overdoing, undereating, overworrying until she was flat on her back. Well, we took care of that right enough."

"She's okay now? She looks great."

"Fit and fine. And expecting, too."

"Kate's pregnant?" The grin split Michael's face. "No shit?" He winced when she sent him a narrowed look. He remembered she didn't care for such language in her kitchen. "Sorry."

"We'll overlook it, this time. She's got herself healthy and happy, our Kate. That man she married won't let her get away with that kind of nonsense. There's a sensible man, one who knows how to take care of a woman."

"They look good together." Classy, Michael thought, frowning down at his plate. But then, Byron had grown up in Southern comfort, and Kate was, in every way that mattered, a Templeton. "They fit," he added.

"That they do. It's a good feeling to see Miss Kate happy, and Miss Margo so nice and settled. And what's Miss Laura got but those two angels to raise on her own?" She gestured with her spatula, stopped for a breath. "It's a good thing her parents are coming back for a time. There's no one in the world straightens out a tangle like Mr. and Mrs. T."

When the door opened, she closed her mouth, not wanting to be taken for gossiping.

"Mrs. Williamson, I—oh, hello, Michael."

Laura looked as fresh as a rosebud in her neat pale yellow suit. Not at all like the woman who had sobbed out his name the night before. Unless you looked at the eyes.

"Hello, Laura. Mrs. Williamson took pity on a starving man."

"Blueberry pancakes. The girls will be in heaven."

"Sit down, Miss Laura, and have a plate now."

"No, I can't. Just coffee, please. I was looking for Annie." She accepted the cup Mrs. Williamson handed her. "I've got to go in early. There's a problem at the office." She looked at her watch. "I should be in the car already. I can't find Annie, and I need to see if she can run the girls to school."

"She's gone. It's her day for the farmers' market."

"Oh." Laura pressed her fingers to her eyes. "I forgot. Then I'll have to—"

"I'll run them in."

Busily rearranging her schedule, Laura blinked at him. "What?"

"I'll run them to school."

"I couldn't impose, but—"

"It's no problem, and I don't think you have time to argue about it. Go on to work. I think I can get two girls to school without permanent damage."

"I didn't mean—" He was right, she admitted with another glance at her watch. She didn't have time to argue. "I appreciate it. Thanks. It's Hornbecker Academy. If you take 1 South to—"

"I know where it is," he interrupted. "Same place you went."

"Yes." She'd had no idea he'd known where she went to school, much less remembered it. "I really appreciate this, Michael. I'm so late." She set the coffee aside, then stood, flustered, when he took her hand.

"Relax. The hotel's not going to collapse if you're late for a meeting."

"No, but my department might. Ali has to turn in her English composition this morning. She has it; I checked. But you might want to remind her. And Kayla should go over her spelling words on the drive in. She has a test. Ali can help her."

"I said I'll handle it."

"Yes, but, if you'd make sure they take umbrellas. I've set them out. It may rain."

"Now." He rose and, forgetting he had an audience, took her face in his hands and kissed her. "Go away."

"I—" She glanced over to where Mrs. Williamson was by all appearances busy humming over her pancakes. "I'm going. But they need to be reminded to feed the dog. Sometimes—"

"Out." Because she apparently needed a boost, he pulled her to the door. "Go nag somebody else."

When she opened her mouth again, he gave her a friendly slap on the butt to send her along. "How does anyone start a morning like that?" he wondered, then turned and found Mrs. Williamson eyeing him soberly.

He cursed, but was wise enough to do it only mentally. "Is it like that around here every day?"

Ignoring his question, she stepped forward, walked around him. He thought he had a pretty good idea of what she was seeing. A man who came in the back door because he didn't belong at the front one.

She stopped, faced him, pursed her lips. "I wondered if you had your eye on anything else around here besides my cooking."

Because she had a way of making him want to shuffle his feet, he tucked his hands in his pockets. "So?"

"So—good." She gave his cheek a brisk pat, and was amused by the surprise on his face. The boy, she thought, had never had a clue of his own worth. "So—good for both of you, and about time, I say. First time in her life that girl's had a real man."

Humbled speechless, he shook his head. When he found his voice again, he took her hands. "Mrs. Williamson, you slay me."

"I will if you break her heart. But in the meantime, you should be good for each other. Now sit down and finish your breakfast before it's cold. If you're going to handle those girls yourself this morning, you need your fuel."

"I love you. I really do."

Her face creased in a wide smile. "I know that, boy. I love you right back. Now sit down and eat. They'll be down in a minute and chattering like magpies."

CHAPTER 14

MICHAEL FURY HAD jumped off buildings, fought in jungles, weathered a typhoon at sea, raced cars at high speed and, at one time or another, broken several major bones in his body.

He'd been in bar fights, spent the night in a cell where the artwork on the walls ran to anatomically exaggerated etchings of female organs. He had killed men and loved women.

And he had, he realized, led a sheltered life.

He had never faced the perils and predicaments of getting two girls out of the house on a school day.

"What do you mean you can't wear those shoes?"

"They don't go with my outfit."

His eyes narrowed as he studied Ali's floral skirt and pink sweater. Hadn't she been wearing some green thing a minute ago? "That's what you said the last time. And it looks fine to me. They're just shoes."

In the way of every female since Eve strapped on a fig leaf, Ali rolled her eyes. "They're the wrong shoes. I have to change them."

"Well, hurry up. Jesus," he muttered as she dashed back upstairs, leaving Kayla tugging on his hand.

"I forgot how to spell 'bedlam.'"

"A-l-l-i-s-o-n."

She giggled at that. "No, really. Is it l-a-m or l-e-m?"

"A." He was pretty sure. Spelling homework wasn't exactly his strong point. And if they didn't get moving, he was going to be late meeting his contractor. The backup with building permits had already put him behind. Now Allison and her shoes . . . "Allison, I'm walking out the door with or without you in ten seconds."

"Sometimes Mama says that, too," Kayla informed him. "But she never does."

"I will. Come on." He tugged Kayla to the door.

"You can't go without her." Eyes wide, Kayla trotted beside him to his car. "Mama's going to be mad if you do."

"We're going. In the car, come on."

"How will Ali get to school?"

"She can walk," Michael said grimly. "In whatever shoes she's picked out this time."

He'd solved the crisis of Kayla's broken barrette, hadn't he? And her hair looked okay to him tied back with the rubber band he'd pulled out of his own hair. He hadn't panicked when Ali claimed to have misplaced her book bag but had found it himself, under the kitchen table, where she'd dumped it during her breakfast.

He'd remained the calm mediator when the two girls had fallen into a minor catfight over whose turn it was to feed the pets. And he had not faltered when Bongo had expressed his sorrow that his young mistresses were leaving him by peeing in the foyer.

No, he had stood strong through all of that, Michael thought as he gunned the engine. But he knew when he was being dicked around, and he wasn't taking it.

Impatience turned to smugness when he saw Ali flying out of the house. Indignation flashed in her eyes as she pulled open the car door. "You were going without me."

"That's right, Blondie. Get in."

Not wanting him to see, under the circumstances, that the nickname delighted her, she angled her chin. "There's only two seats. Where am I supposed to sit?"

"Beside your sister."

"But—"

"In. Now."

At the snapped order, she moved fast, squeezing beside Kayla. Pouting dramatically when Michael reached over to tug the seat belt around both of them, she announced, "I don't think this is legal."

It was her best lady-of-the-manor voice, Michael realized. Her mother's voice. "Call a cop," he muttered and started down the drive.

For the next fifteen minutes, he was treated to a run of complaints. "She's pushing me." "She's taking all the room." "She's sitting on my skirt."

The muscle behind his eye began to twitch. How did anyone—*anyone*—tolerate this every morning of their life?

"I need to go over my words," Kayla wailed. "I'm having a test. Michael, Ali's pushing her elbow in me again."

"Ali, get a grip." He blew away the hair that, thanks to his gift to Kayla, danced in his eyes.

"There's not enough room," Ali informed him loftily. "She's taking up the whole seat."

"I am not."

"You are too."

"I am—"

At the snarl issuing from the man beside them, both girls lapsed into momentary silence.

Satisfied, Michael took a calming breath. "What are the spelling words?"

"I can't remember. I have them written down in my notebook." The wail inched back into her voice. "If I don't get a hundred, I don't get to play on the computer at free time."

"So get the notebook out."

This, as he should have known, caused more complaints.

"You're stepping all over my shoes. You're getting them dirty. Kayla, I'm going to—"

"I don't want to hear about those shoes, Blondie." The twitch was back, double time. "Not a word about the shoes."

"Here are my words." Triumphant, Kayla waved the notebook, conking him on the head in her enthusiasm.

"Well, study them or something."

"No, Ali reads them, and I spell them. And I have to use each one in a sentence."

"I don't want to read them."

Michael sent Ali a narrow look. "Want to walk?"

"Oh, all right." With little grace, she snatched the notebook. "They're just baby words."

"They are not. You're just mad because Tod likes Marcie better than you."

"He does not. And I don't care anyway. And you didn't learn your words because you were too busy drawing dumb pictures."

"They are not dumb. You're dumb because—"

"Cut it out. Right now. If I have to stop this car . . ." Appalled, he trailed off. Had he just said what he thought he'd said? Dear Christ. He was forced to take several calming breaths. "Allison, just read the words."

"I'm going to." She sniffed, peered down her nose at Kayla's carefully written list. "Committed."

"C-o-m-m-i-t-t-e-d." She parroted the letters, then bit her lip. She fumbled for the sentence, looked hopefully at Michael.

"Michael Fury, innocently volunteering to drive two young girls to school, has now been committed to an institution for the permanently insane."

It made Ali laugh. "He's just being silly."

"Don't bet on it, kid." But he racked his brain to come up with an alternative. "The witness pointed accusingly at the man who had committed the crime. How's that?"

"Okay."

They ran through the rest, with Michael nearly cross-eyed by the time he pulled through the gates of the academy. His ancient Porsche merged with shining Mercedes, sedate Lincolns, and snappy four-wheel-drives.

"Scram," he said, unhooking the seat belt. "I'm late."

"You're supposed to say 'Have a good day,'" Kayla reminded him.

"Yeah? Well, have one, then. Later."

"Michael." She rolled her eyes. "Now kiss us good-bye." She pursed her lips, planted one on him.

Amused, he peered over at Ali. "Ali doesn't want to kiss me. She's still mad at me."

"I am not." She sniffed, then graciously leaned over Kayla and touched her lips to his cheek. "Thank you for driving us to school."

"It was my . . . education," he told her, then watched them scurry up the granite steps with hordes of other children.

"Jesus, Laura." He rested his aching head on the steering wheel. "How do you get through that every day without drinking heavy?"

SHE COULD HAVE told him it was all a matter of planning, discipline, and priorities. And prayers for patience. At the end of this particular day, because the first three had crumbled in her hands, she was doing a lot of praying.

Could she have anticipated that two women from rival romance magazines would start a fistfight in the lobby? She didn't think so. Could she have guessed that after their efforts to dispel the hair-pulling, teeth-snapping, name-calling furor, two of her bell people would require stitches? She doubted it.

She could have, after the event, predicted the arrival of the press, the cameras, the questions, and the necessity for her to answer questions. But she didn't have to like it.

Things hadn't gone that much more smoothly when she'd arrived, late, at Pretenses to find Kate in an uproar because Margo had delved into her sacrosanct spreadsheets.

Then there had been the customer who instead of watching the three children she'd herded into the shop with her, loitered in the wardrobe room while they ran rampant.

The result was a broken vase, finger-smudged counters, and frazzled nerves. The woman left in a huff after being asked to watch her children and pay for the damages.

Life was no more simple when she returned home, ready to whimper, and found herself faced with an upcoming science project, the request to volunteer to chaperone a field trip to the aquarium, and that parental terror, long division.

It didn't perk up her mood to discover that Bongo had expressed his adoration for her by burrowing into her closet and chewing three shoes—each from a different pair.

And her parents were arriving the next day.

All right. Laura scrubbed her hands over her face after she'd changed into slacks. She would handle it. Homework was done, Bongo chastised, and it was unlikely that Templeton would be sued because a couple of women went ballistic in the lobby.

Still, she needed some air, which would give her an opportunity to make certain that old Joe had the garden up to speed, that the paths had been swept. And since she'd forgotten to ask Ann to see that the pool was vacuumed and readied for her mother's visit, she would see to that herself.

Rolling up her sleeves as she went, she passed Ali's room. She stopped a moment and smiled. She heard both of her daughters inside, chattering away over some recent movie heartthrob who wasn't yet old enough to shave. They were giggling.

Nothing could be really wrong with the world when her daughters were giggling.

She slipped out the side door, knowing that Ann would lecture her to leave the landscaping and pool to old Joe and his grandson. But Laura knew that young Joe was cramming for his final exams. And it would take her ten—well, twenty—minutes to put things right. Besides, she enjoyed the mindless task of manually vacuuming the pool.

It gave her a chance to dream in the garden, which, she noted with pleasure, was blooming beautifully. Old Joe's bursitis must have been behaving itself. He'd put in new beds of annuals, filling in among the perennials with splashes of color and sweeps of shape.

The paths were swept clean, the mulch damp from watering and raked smooth. "Looks like we're in business," she said to the pup, who trotted along with her. She'd had to forgive him for the shoe incident when he looked so ashamed and contritely licked her face. "Now you sit and behave yourself."

Willing to make amends, Bongo plopped on the skirt of the pool, watching her over his shaggy paws out of eyes dazed with love.

Of course, Laura thought, if she'd remembered to pick up a new droid, the pool would be cleaned automatically. All she had to do was remember to write it down when she went back in the house. Otherwise, she was going to have to break down and buy one of those electronic pads like Kate kept in her pocket at all times.

But it wasn't a problem to unwind the hoses from their tidy box in the pool shed, or slip the attachments together. She went about it mechanically, daydreaming. She would settle the kids for the night. It was so good to have Ali smile and mean it at their good-night hug.

Perhaps Ali was disillusioned about her father, but she felt better about herself. That was what mattered most.

Then she would go over the household accounts with Annie, Laura mused. Things were looking up there as well. Her dual incomes and the interest on the investments Kate had made for her were holding them above water. By Laura's calculations, in another six months or so, they might actually be able to swim a few laps.

So, she wouldn't sell any more of her jewelry unless absolutely necessary. She wouldn't have to duck and dodge questions from her parents, or Josh.

And maybe, just maybe, she'd be able to juggle funds to buy that horse for Ali after all. She'd take a close look at her own books later. Or tomorrow, she mused, thinking of Michael.

She wanted to go to him again tonight, to forget everything but being. Feeling. He did that for her, made her feel like the center of the universe when he made love to her.

She'd always dreamed of a man who would think of nothing but her when she was in his arms. Who would lose himself in her as she lost herself in him. Of knowing that he was so focused on her when he touched her that there was room for nothing else in his mind or heart.

Oh, she did wish she knew his heart.

That was her problem, she admitted, running the pole smoothly through the water. She wanted that foolishly romantic love she'd dreamed of as a girl.

Seraphina's love, she thought with a quiet laugh. The kind a woman would die for.

Well, she couldn't afford to be dewy-eyed enough to hurl herself off a cliff for anyone. She had children to raise, a house to run, and a career—a surprisingly interesting career—to maintain.

So she would happily settle for whatever she and Michael had between them, and be grateful for it. More than grateful, she thought, tonight, in bed, when he put his hands on her again. Those impatient, rough-palmed hands that took whatever they wanted and made her wild with need.

The way he murmured her name, softly, deeply, when he slid into her to mate.

"What the hell are you doing?"

The pole nearly slipped out of her hands at the sharp tone. Her head jerked up, and there was her lover, scowling, standing spread-legged, hands in his pockets, with his hair loose and flowing.

Fighting against a reckless urge to leap on him and tear in, she tilted her head. "Why, I'm mixing a souffle. What does it look like?"

"Why the hell are you doing that yourself?" He was beside her in two angry strides, pulling the pole away. "Don't you have servants to do this?"

"Actually, no. I let the pool boy go a couple of years ago when I learned that Candy was using him for her personal maintenance as well as her pool. I found it . . . awkward."

He wasn't going to smile, or even smirk. Coming across her like this, seeing her laboring over some ridiculous menial chore after putting in a full day burned him.

"Then hire another one."

"I'm afraid it doesn't fit into the scheme of things just now. In any case, I'm perfectly capable of doing it myself." Taking a closer look, she brushed at his hair. "You seem a little frazzled, Michael. Rough day?"

He'd been in a pisser of a mood since his contractor had estimated it would be six months before the rebuilding was completed. There had been a lot of blah-blah about permits, inspections, zoning, but the upshot was that he was going to be Laura's tenant for a great deal longer than he'd anticipated.

He didn't want to be her tenant, to hand over a rent check every month. It wasn't the money, he thought, fuming. It was the . . . It was awkward.

"I've had better." He nudged her aside and began to run the vacuum himself. "But we're not talking about me. You can't raise two kids, hold down two jobs, and deal with this sort of nonsense too. Why don't you just close the damn pool?"

"Because I enjoy swimming, and there are a lot of women who do a great deal more than I do and manage very well."

"They're not you." Which said it all in his mind.

"No, they don't have a beautiful home that no one would ever take from them, and they don't necessarily have a job that they're in no danger of jeopardizing if they need to flex their schedule."

Insulted, she fought with him over the pole. "I am not the pampered princess you seem to think. I'm a"—she hissed, tugged—"capable, intelligent woman who can run her life very well. I'm sick and tired of people patting me on the head and saying 'poor Laura' behind my back." She yanked, swore. "I am not poor Laura and I can clean my own goddamn pool. Give me back the stupid pole."

"No." It had calmed him considerably to see her temper flare. It wasn't much of one, as far as he could see, but there was potential in those stormy eyes, flushed cheeks, gritted teeth. "Keep messing with me, sugar, and I'll toss you in. It's a little cool for a dip this evening."

"Fine. Do it yourself. You're a man, after all, and men are so much more capable of doing mindless chores. But I didn't ask for your help, nor do I need it. Nor do I need your sterling advice or your unsolicited criticism on how I handle my life."

"That's telling me," he said equably. "My hands are starting to shake."

Her eyes narrowed into slits. "You, too, could be taking a dip."

Interesting, he thought. Did she actually have a physical temper in there? "Is that so? You want to try to take me down?"

"If I did you'd be treading water in—oh, no! Bongo, no!" Insults paled when she caught sight of the pup busily digging up the newly planted pansies. "Stop that! Stop that right now!" She dashed across the pool skirt, snatched up the pup, and frowned at his dirt- and mulch-smeared nose. "How could you? Didn't I tell you no? It's bad. You're not to dig in the flowers."

When she set him down to survey the damage, Bongo cheerfully leaped into the mess and began digging again.

"I said no. Stop it. Why don't you listen to me?"

"Because he knows you're a pushover. Bongo." At Michael's voice, the pup lifted his head and grinned sheepishly. Michael could almost hear the sentiment: "Well, gee, Mick, just having a little fun here." Michael snapped his finger, pointed, and Bongo padded out, shook himself, and sat politely.

Torn between disgust and admiration, Laura hissed between her teeth, "How do you get him to do that?"

"It's a gift."

"That's just great." Disgust won. She dragged her hands through her hair. "I can't control a five-pound puppy."

"Just takes practice, and patience."

"Well, I don't have time to practice now." She was down on her knees in a flash, salvaging bedding plants. "And I'm out of patience. Old Joe is going to kill me for this."

"Laura." Though it seemed obvious to point it out, Michael crouched and pointed it out anyway. "He works for you."

"A lot you know," she muttered, desperately smoothing upturned mulch with her bare hands. "If I so much as sniff an undesignated rose in his garden, he—" she broke off, scowling. "Don't just sit there. Help me."

"I thought you didn't need any help."

"Shut up, Michael." She brushed a hand over her cheek, smeared it with garden dirt. "Just shut up and save these pansies before Bongo and I both end up in the pound."

"Since you ask so nice." He shoved roots back into soil and heard her let out a long, keening moan.

"Not like that. For Lord's sake, you're not planting redwoods. Have a little delicacy."

"Sorry. It's my first day on the job." He shook his head as she shifted and knelt in the dirt in a way that was sure to send her trim pastel slacks into the rag heap. And all, he thought, to save the sensibilities of an ancient gardener.

"You run scared of the rest of your staff, too?"

"Damn right. Most of them have been here longer than I have. This could work." Her hands, coated now with black soil, smoothed and patted. "You'll hardly be able to tell when I'm done here. But who am I fooling? He can tell if you pluck a spray of crabgrass, which is fine, as long as you've asked first."

"It's looking fine to me."

"Like you'd know a pansy from a geranium," she muttered.

"Now you're getting nasty. You've got something . . ." Casually, he swiped his hand over her cheek, adding a fresh layer of dirt. "There. And here, you need a little to even out the look."

"I suppose you think that's funny." Struggling for dignity, she brushed at her face and only succeeded in making it worse.

"No." He picked up a handful of damp pine mulch and dropped it onto her hair. "That's funny."

"A pity I don't have your raucous sense of humor. But let me try." She rubbed both of her filthy hands over his shirt. "There. I'm dying from laughter now."

He glanced down at his shirt. He'd just washed the damn thing. "Now you've done it," he said quietly.

The tone warned her not to inch back, not to bother with reason and excuses. But to run. She sprang to her feet, sending the dog into frantically joyful barks. She managed two sprinting yards before he snagged her around the waist and lifted her off her feet.

"You started it," she managed between choked laughs.

"Uh-huh. So I'm obliged to finish it."

"I'll have your shirt cleaned. Whoops." She watched the world revolve as he flipped her over into his arms. "Why, Mr. Fury, you're so . . . masterful, so strong, so—what are you doing?" Amusement turned to panic as she caught a glimpse of his direction and realized his intention. "Michael, this isn't funny now."

"Just my raucous sense of humor again," he told her as he strode toward the edge of the pool.

"Don't. Now I mean it, Michael." In self-defense, she locked her arms around his neck. "I'm covered with dirt, and it's chilly, and I've just cleaned the pool."

"Just look at the way it sparkles, too." Controlling her frantic wiggling, he toed off his shoes. "Looks so pretty in the twilight, doesn't it?"

"I will make you pay," she vowed. "I swear I will make you pay if you dare—"

"Hold your breath," he suggested and jumped in.

But she was shrieking when she hit the water, swallowed it, came up choking. "You fool. You idiot. You—" She swallowed more when he pushed her head under.

What he hadn't counted on was that Laura Templeton had been captain of her swim team, had won a drawer full of medals, and had more than once successfully defended herself against a big brother's bullying.

While he treaded water and roared with laughter, she nipped fluidly between his legs, grabbed hold where a man was most vulnerable, and squeezed. She could hear the muffled echo of his yelp, smiled grimly, and yanked downward.

Streaking away, she broke the surface and waited smugly for him to wheeze out breaths and flail toward the side.

"Now that," she said, slicking back her dripping hair, "was funny."

He had his breath back, mostly, and eyed her narrowly. "Want to fight dirty, sugar?"

"This is my element, Michael. You're in over your head."

"Think so?" He'd done more than a few water stunts in his day. He pushed off the side and pursued.

She was faster than he'd given her credit for, and slicker. He knew when he was being taunted—the way she nipped just out of reach in a dive for the bottom. The fluidity with which she changed direction and dodged.

They surfaced again, watching each other over the lapping water. "Wet jeans are constricting."

She cocked her head. "If you need an excuse." She snagged one of her shoes as it floated by, sighed. "Four pair in one day. Has to be a record." Philosophically, she planted her feet and stood.

The water streamed off her, glued the thin material of her blouse to the high, full curve of breast, to the narrow torso and subtle flare of hip. In the shadowed light her dripping hair curled wildly and glowed like wet gold.

"Now you are playing dirty," he murmured.

Pouring the water out of her shoe, she looked over at him. Her hand remained aloft, her eyes on his as he slowly skimmed through the water toward her. As he stood, he slid his hands over her thighs, hips, sides, and left them molded to her breasts.

"Michael." The shoe dropped out of her hand and plopped into the water. "We can't."

"I'm just going to kiss you." His hands slipped wetly to her back, down to cup her bottom as he eased back until they were floating again. "And touch you. And drive us both a little crazy."

"Oh." Her head was already spinning as his teeth caught her lip, tugged. "Well, if that's all."

She wrapped herself around him, let him take her through the cool water. It was her mouth that grew hungrier, more avid, seeking his over and over again, going deeper with tongues tangling, breath clashing.

Need pounded through him with anvil shocks. She was destroying him, her legs gripped hard so that her tight little body molded to his, her hips moving seductively so that sex rubbed sex.

"Laura—"

But she answered with an impatient moan, tunneling her hands through his hair, savaging his throat. His loins began to throb like a wound.

"Hold on a minute."

"I want you." Her voice was thick, the words hot against his skin. "I want you. I want you."

"We can't do this here." Could they? His mind went blank when her mouth fit to his again. He sank with her so that the water surrounded them. Her hair floated out, like the mermaid who watched them from the bottom.

He wanted to keep sinking, sinking, just like this with his mouth hard on hers. Sink into a world where air didn't matter, light didn't matter. Where there was nothing but her and this churning, sweet ache of need.

When they surfaced again, he shook his head, trying to clear it. Then kicked once to keep them afloat. "No." It wasn't a word he'd expected to say to a woman under the circumstances. And it came out weak as he pressed her head onto his shoulder. "You'd better give me a minute."

She floated with him, dizzy with desire, dazed with triumph. "I seduced you."

"Sugar, you damn near killed me."

She threw her head back and laughed. "I seduced you," she repeated, her face glowing. "I didn't know I could. It's . . . liberating."

"You come on over to my place tonight and you can be as liberated as you want. Right now, keep your hands off me."

She linked her hands behind his neck, easing back so that she could see his face in the falling light. "You wanted to tear my clothes off again."

"I'm still thinking about it, so behave yourself."

"I wanted to tear yours off, too. I wonder what that would feel like, to just rip away at your clothes, and . . . bite you. Sometimes I just want to sink my teeth into your—"

"Shut up." In defense, he cupped her head and pulled it to his shoulder again. "I think I've created a monster."

"I don't know about that, but you sure hit the switch. I like it." She laughed again and arched back so that she was floating from the waist up. "Let's come back here tonight when everyone's asleep and go skinny-dipping and make love in the water. Then we'll go for a walk on the cliffs and make love there, just like Seraphina and Felipe."

She rose up again, water streaming from her. "Let's do something crazy."

He was about to do something crazy just then, when he caught the sound of footsteps on the path, and movement. Subtly, he hoped, he changed his grip, hoping he wasn't holding any inappropriate part of the daughter of the house.

"Laura?" Susan Templeton's brows shot up into her spiky bangs. She didn't consider herself to be a woman who was easily surprised, but it certainly rocked her to see her daughter clinging to a man in the pool with the look of a woman who had recently been thoroughly aroused still on her face.

"Mom?" Shock came first, then the heat in her cheeks from embarrassment. She wiggled, but Michael held firm. Neither of them knew if it was out of stubbornness or habit. "You're here."

"Yes. I am."

"But you were supposed to be here tomorrow."

"We finished up our business a little early." She spoke smoothly. But then, she was a smooth woman. Small and delicately built like her daughter, she looked young and chic in her Valentino traveling suit, her dark blond hair capped gamine style around a sharp, interested face.

"We thought," she said with a faint edge of amusement, "that we'd surprise you. I think we succeeded."

"Yes. I was just—we were . . . How was the trip?" Laura ended lamely.

"Fine." Manners polished to a high sheen, Susan stepped forward, smiled. "It's Michael, isn't it? Michael Fury?"

"Yeah." With a jerk of his head he tossed his wet hair back. "Nice to see you again, Mrs. Templeton."

CHAPTER 15

"IF I'D KNOWN you were coming in this evening, I'd have held dinner, called the rest of the family." Composed now, and dry, Laura sat beside her father in the parlor.

"We ate on the plane." Thomas patted her hand. He was, thanks to his wife's discretion, blissfully unaware of what his daughter had been doing in the pool an hour earlier. "And we'll see everyone tomorrow. I swear, those girls have grown a foot since Christmas."

"It seems like." Laura sipped brandy. Her mother was upstairs putting the girls to bed, at her insistence. It postponed the questions, Laura knew. Didn't eliminate them. "They're so excited that you're here. We didn't think you'd be back until summer."

"Got to see our Katie girl," he told her. Only one of the reasons, he mused. But it would do well enough. "Imagine, our little Kate having a baby."

"She's glowing. I know it's a cliché, but she really is. She and Byron go around beaming all the time. Oh, and wait until you see J. T. Oh, Dad, he's so perfect. He's sitting up now, and he laughs all the time. Those wonderful belly laughs. I could just eat him up." She curled her legs up, studied him over the rim of her snifter. "And how are you?"

"Fit and fine."

It was no less than true. He was a handsome man, one who didn't take his health for granted and disciplined himself with exercise and interests. He wasn't one who took his business or his success for granted; he watched over things with a shrewd and focused eye. Nor did he take his family for granted—he kept them close in heart and mind.

The result was a firm body, still lanky in his fifties, a face that had lived well and accepted the lines and dents of time with gratitude. His eyes were smoke, like his daughter's, and the silver in his hair glinted richly in the lamplight.

"You don't look fit and fine," she said and smiled when his brow knit. "You look dashing."

"And you look happy."

It relieved him, but he worried at the cause. Was it, as Annie had prophesied darkly, a transitory state attributable to Michael Fury? Or was his little girl finally finding her feet again?

"You're taking some time for yourself again?"

"I'm enjoying myself." It wasn't quite the answer, but it was truth. "Ali and I have resolved some things. She's happier, so I'm happier. I love my work. My sisters keep giving me new babies to play with." With a sigh, she leaned her head on his shoulder. "I haven't felt quite so content in a long time."

"Your mother and I worry about you."

"I know. And I won't bother to tell you not to, but I will tell you I'm fine. Better than fine."

"We heard that Peter's to be married again." Her teeth went on edge. "To Candace Litchfield."

"Word travels," Laura murmured.

"People are more than pleased to spread that sort of news. Are you all right with it?"

"I was upset initially," she admitted, remembering that hammer blow to the midsection when they'd made the announcement that night at the club. "A knee-jerk reaction, really. It was mostly the idea of Candy being stepmother to my babies and worry about how the girls would handle it."

"And?" he said quietly, his hand over hers.

"And now that it's all settled in, it just doesn't matter." She turned her hand under his, squeezed. "Really doesn't matter at all. The girls have adjusted. They'll go to the wedding in May because it's the right thing for them to do. They don't particularly care for Candy, but they'll be polite. Then they'll come home," she added, "and we'll get on with our lives."

"They're good girls," Thomas agreed. "Good, sharp girls. I know it's not easy for them, but they have you. So it's you I'm concerned with."

"There's no need. In fact, I've come to the conclusion that Peter and Candy are perfectly suited. I couldn't be more happy for them."

He waited a beat, ran his tongue around his teeth. "That's nasty."

"Yes." She sighed lavishly. "It is. I like it."

"That's my girl."

"Now, let's talk about something much more interesting." She sat back again, grinning. "Let me tell you about the impromptu boxing match in the lobby today."

WHEN SUSAN CAME back in, it was to the roar of her husband's laughter and the rich undertone of her daughter's. She stood for a minute, enjoying the scene. She could count every week, every month, that had passed since she had seen her little girl laugh that freely.

Gnawing her lip, she considered. If Michael Fury had anything to do with it, she owed him. Whatever Annie might think. As a woman, she understood and appreciated the need of another woman to have, at least once, at least briefly, a dangerous man in her life.

As a mother . . . well, they would see.

"Tommy, your granddaughters want a kiss good night."

He was up like a shot. "I'll have to give them one, then."

"And no more than one story," Susan murmured to him as he passed. "No matter how much you want to play."

He pinched her cheek, winked, and walked on.

"That should keep him busy for an hour." Susan glided over to the liquor cabinet, poured herself a brandy. "And will give you time to tell me about Michael Fury."

Her mother, Laura thought, rarely circled around a point if she could zero right in. "Josh must have told you about the mud slides, how Michael lost his house."

"Yes, I know the background, Laura." Her daughter, Susan thought, could evade like a champ. "He's raising horses now and renting the stables for a time."

"He's got wonderful horses." Laura leapt on the ploy. "You'll have to see for yourself. Several are trained for stunts. It's fascinating. He's teaching the girls to ride, you know. They're crazy about him."

"And are you? Crazy about him?"

"It's been good for the girls to be around a man who pays attention to them."

Patient, Susan reached down to pet Bongo. Only one of the changes, she mused as the dog vibrated with pleasure under her hand. "I was asking about you, Laura. How you feel about him."

"I'm very fond of him. He's been helpful and kind. Are you sure you don't want me to get you something to eat? Some fruit and cheese?"

"No, I don't want fruit and cheese." Susan reached over to still her daughter's nervous hand. "Are you in love with him?"

"I don't know." Laura leveled her breath and met her mother's gaze. "I'm sleeping with him. I'm sorry if you disapprove."

"It's not for me to disapprove over something that personal at this point in your life." But there was a pang. "You're being careful?"

"Of course."

"He's very attractive."

"Yes, he is."

"And nothing like Peter."

"No," Laura agreed. "Nothing at all like Peter."

"Is that why you're attracted to him? Because he's the antithesis of your ex-husband?"

"I'm not using Peter as a yardstick." Restless, she rose. "Maybe I was, to some extent. It's difficult not to compare when you've only been with two men. I'm not sleeping with Michael to prove anything to anyone, but because it's—he makes me . . . I want him. And he wants me."

"Will that be enough for you, Laura?"

"I don't know. It's enough for now." She turned away, paced to the fire. It was quiet tonight, just a warm glow and a subtle hiss. "I failed before. I wanted it to be perfect. I wanted to be perfect. Maybe I wanted to be you."

"Oh, honey."

"It's not your fault," Laura said quickly when her mother got to her feet. "Please don't think I mean that. It's only that I grew up seeing you, how you were, how you are. So competent and wise and flawless."

"I'm not flawless, Laura. No one is."

"You were to me. You are. You never faltered, never stumbled, never let me down."

"I stumbled." She crossed the room, took her daughter's hands. "Countless times. I had your father to help me get my balance."

"And he had you to help him. That's what I always wanted, dreamed of. The kind of marriage and life and family you made. And I'm not foolish enough to think it didn't take effort and mistakes and sleepless nights to make it. But you did. I didn't."

"You make me angry when you blame yourself."

Laura shook her head. "I don't, completely. But I know I'm not blameless either. I set my sights impossibly high. Every time I had to readjust them, lower them, it was harder. I don't ever want to do that again."

"If you set your sights too low, you can miss a great deal."

"Maybe. But I'm not pushing for more here than what I have. Part of me will always want what you and Dad have. Not only for myself but for my children. But if it's not in the cards, I'm through crying over it. I'm going to give them the best life I can, and make the best one for myself too. Right now, Michael's an important part of it."

"Does he know how important?"

Laura shrugged her shoulders. "It's often difficult to tell how much Michael knows. But I know this. Peter didn't love me, not ever."

"Laura—"

"No, it's true, and I can live with that." In fact, she discovered it was easier to live with than she had imagined. "But I loved him, and I married him, and stayed with him for ten years. Both of us, and certainly the children, would have been better off if I hadn't been so determined to make it work. If I had just accepted the failure and let go."

"I think you're wrong," Susan said quietly. "By doing everything you could do to hold your marriage and your family together, you can look back and know you did your best."

"Maybe." And perhaps one day she would look back. "With Michael I don't have to carry the burden of making something work, or of living with the illusion that I have a man who loves me and wants what I want. And I'm happier than I've been in too long to remember."

"Then I'm happy for you." And will keep my own counsel, Susan thought, for now. "Let's go rescue your father," she said, tucking her arm through Laura's. "Before those girls have him wrapped around their fingers so tight he bounces."

THE YEAR THOMAS Templeton married Susan Conroy, he added the tower suite as his innovation for Templeton House. The house had already stood a hundred years, with nearly every generation of his family toying with or expanding the original design.

He had built it out of fancy, and a love for the romantic. He had made love with his wife there countless nights, conceived both of their children within the charming rounded walls, in the big rococo bed. Although Susan often said Josh had been made on the Bokhara rug in front of the fire.

He never disputed her on such matters.

Now with flames simmering in the Adams fireplace, a bottle of Templeton champagne chilled in a silver bucket and moonlight filtering in through the high windows, he curled with his wife of thirty-six years on that same rug.

"I think you're trying to seduce me."

He offered her a glass brimming with frothy wine. "You're such a sharp woman, Susie."

"And smart enough to let you." Smiling, she touched a hand to his face. "Tommy. How could so many years have gone by?"

"You look the same." He pressed his lips to her palm. "Just as lovely, just as fresh."

"Now it takes me hours to maintain the illusion."

"It's no illusion." He nestled her head on his shoulder, watched the fire leap as a log gave way to the heat. "Do you remember the first night we slept here?"

"You carried me up the steps. Up every single one. And when you brought me in here, you had flowers everywhere, gardens of them, roses strewn over the bed. Wine chilling, the candles lighted."

"You cried."

"You overwhelmed me. You often did, and do still." She tilted her face up, brushed her lips over his jaw. "I knew I was the luckiest woman in the world to have you, to be loved the way you loved me. And to be wanted the way you wanted me." She shut her eyes, turned her face against his throat. "Oh, Tommy."

"Tell me what's troubling you. It's Laura, isn't it?"

"I can't bear to see her hurt. I can stand anything but that. Even though I know that children have to go their own way, fight their own battles, it breaks my heart. I can still remember the day she was born, the way she curled into my arms. So small and precious."

"And you think Michael Fury is going to break her heart?"

"I don't know. I wish I did." She rose, walked to the window that looked out over the cliffs. Cliffs, she knew, that Laura had haunted since childhood. "It's knowing she's already had it broken that kills me inside. I spoke with her tonight when you were up with the girls. And I realized as she talked to me, that as hard as she's worked to rebuild her life, part of her is still so vulnerable, so raw. So . . . exposed. She believes she's failed, Tommy."

"Failed, my ass." Incensed, he sprang up. "Peter Ridgeway failed, in every way possible."

"And did we fail, by not preventing?"

"Could we have stopped her?" It was a question he'd asked himself dozens of times over the last few years. "Could we have?"

"No," Susan said after a long moment. "We might have postponed it, we might have persuaded her to wait. A few months, a year. But she was in love. She wanted what we have. That's what she said to me tonight, Tommy. She wanted what we have."

When he laid a hand on her shoulder, she reached back, gripped tight. "I hate that she couldn't have it. That she was denied the security and excitement and beauty of it. Now she doesn't believe she ever will have it."

"She's a young woman, Susie. A lovely and loving young woman. She'll fall in love again."

"She already has. She's in love with Michael, Tommy. She hasn't admitted it to herself yet; she protects herself by thinking of it as sex."

"Please." He winced. "It's not easy to think of my little girl that way."

It made her laugh and turn to him. "Your little girl is in the middle of a hot affair with Josh's rebellious young friend."

"Should I get the gun?"

So she laughed again, embraced him. "Oh, Tommy, here we are, with no way to stop it again. Nothing to do but wait and hope."

"I could have a . . . little talk with him."

"You could. I could. But nothing we say is going to change Laura's mind, or her heart. He's gorgeous."

Intrigued, Thomas eased her back, frowned into her eyes. "Is that so?"

"Absolutely devastatingly, dangerously gorgeous. Sexy as sin." Her lips trembled at the corners as his frown deepened. "And he still has that the-hell-with-it look in his eye, the one that makes every woman still breathing think she's the one person on earth who could make him care."

"Is that what you think?"

Flattered, she patted his cheek. "I think I admire her taste and, as a woman, her luck. As a mother—I'm terrified of him."

"Maybe I will have a chat with him. Soon." Then he blew out a breath. "Damn it, Susie, I've always liked the boy."

"So have I. There was always something rawly honest about him. And whatever Annie thinks, he wasn't, and isn't, a hoodlum. What he is, is basic."

"And do we want our daughter involved with a basic man who ran off to sea at eighteen and has done any number of things not discussed in polite company?"

She winced. The same thought had passed through her head. "That sounds so snobbish."

"It sounds like parental concern to me. It doesn't matter if she's three or thirty, it's still our job to worry about her."

"And men like Michael come and go on their own whim," she murmured. "They aren't looking for roots. Laura would wither without them. And from what she said, the girls are attached to him. How will it affect them to have another man walk out of their lives?" She burrowed against him. "There's nothing we can do but be there for them."

"Then that's what we'll do. We watched Margo and Kate find the way through their problems. Laura will get through."

"And they have each other." She shifted so that they could look out toward the cliffs together. "The three of them are always there for each other. That shop of theirs has worked magic for them. Whatever happens, Laura has them, and the pride in what they've built together. But I'm greedy, Tommy."

She took his hand, laid it on her heart. "I want her to have her dream. I want her to have what we have. I want to believe that she'll stand at the window, look toward the sea, with a man's arms around her. A man who loves her and will stand by her. A man who can make her feel the way you make me feel."

She cupped his face in her hands. "So I'm going to believe it. And if she's got any of me inside her, she'll fight for what she wants. The way I fought for you."

"You ignored me," he reminded her. "Wouldn't give me the time of day."

Her smile bloomed slowly. "And it worked, didn't it? Perfectly. Then one day I let you find me, by calculated accident, alone in the rose garden at the club. And I let you kiss me, like this." She lifted her mouth, drew the kiss out, warm and slow. "And Tommy Templeton, never seeing the punch, went down for the count."

"You always were sneaky, Susie." He swung her up into his arms and made her laugh.

"And I got exactly what I wanted. Just," she murmured as he lowered her to the rug, "the way I'm going to get exactly what I want right now."

LAURA SAW THE lights in the tower room as she walked toward the cliffs. And for a moment she stood watching the silhouette of her parents embracing. It was a lovely sight, stirred her heart. And her envy.

They fit so perfectly together, she thought, turning back toward the song of the sea. Their rhythms, their styles, their goals, their needs.

She'd learned, the hard way, that what her parents had, what they worked for and preserved, wasn't a given but a rarity to be celebrated.

Her new perspective only brought her more admiration for them.

She walked the cliffs alone, something she hadn't done for weeks. She wanted Michael. The low hum of desire was constant and thrilling, but she wouldn't go to him tonight. Nor, she believed, did he expect her.

They had parted awkwardly. She, undeniably embarrassed at having been caught frolicking in the pool by her own mother. He, obviously uncomfortable. She thought they both would need time to adjust.

The light was strong, glowing, with the clouds chased away to clear skies by a stiff westerly wind. As familiar with the cliffs as with her own parlor, Laura picked her way down, easily negotiating rocks and a path slippery with pebbles until she came to a favored ledge.

There she sat, letting the wind whip at her face and the sea thunder in her ears. And there, listening for the whisper of ghosts, thinking of lost love, she was content.

FROM HIS WINDOW, Michael watched her go down the slope, the long, loose jacket she wore streaming out behind her like a cloak. Romantic, mysterious. He pressed his hand to the glass as if he could touch her. Then drew it back, irritated with himself.

She wasn't coming to him. Small wonder, he thought, hooking his thumbs in his pockets as he watched her climb down rocks as gracefully as a fawn. Her parents were back, and with them, he expected, came a reminder of the difference in their positions.

Laura Templeton may have been working for a living, she may have scrubbed a few bathtubs, but she was still Laura Templeton. And he was still Michael Fury, from the wrong side of the hill.

She'd be busy now, he supposed. Entertaining, scheduling dinner parties during her parents' stay. Those fancy, flower-bedecked, exclusive affairs that Templeton House was renowned for.

There would be lunch at the club, quick rounds of tennis, erudite conversations over coffee and brandy.

The ritual was more foreign to him than Greek.

And he had no desire to learn either.

So, if she was going to brush him off, what was the difference? With a shrug, he turned away from the window and stripped off his shirt. He could lure her back into the sack another time or two if he wanted. Sex was nothing more than a weakness. He could exploit hers to satisfy his own.

He heaved the shirt aside, frustrated that it wasn't something hard and breakable. Goddamn it, he wanted her. Now. Here. With him.

Who the hell did she think she was?

Who the hell did he think he was?

Eyes grim, he pulled off his boots and threw them both against the wall, where they at least made a satisfying thud.

He knew exactly who he was, and so, he thought, did she. Laura Templeton was going to find herself hard-pressed to shake him loose until he was damn good and ready. He wasn't finished with her yet, not by a long shot.

She could have tonight, he thought, stripping off his jeans. He'd let her have tonight all quiet and safe. Because her nights weren't going to stay quiet, and they weren't going to stay safe.

He dropped naked to the bed and glared at the ceiling. And he would have her right back where he wanted her. The hell with her parents, her fancy friends, and her perfect pedigree.

She'd taken on a mongrel. Now she'd have to deal with him.

FROM HER PERCH on the ledge, Laura stretched her arms up. Cool, damp air caressed her skin where the sleeves of her jacket fell down to her elbows. She thought of how Michael caressed that skin. Rough and demanding one moment, then the next with surprising and devastating tenderness.

He had so many moods, she thought, so many needs. He had in such a short time awakened so many moods, so many needs in her. No, she was no Sleeping Beauty, she reflected, but she felt as though she'd been sleeping for decades. Waiting for him to find her.

And he had, she realized. They'd found each other. So why was she sitting here alone, trying to reorganize her schedule for the next day, and the day after that? Tomorrow would come anyway. She could be with him right now. She'd go to him. Laura closed her eyes tight, wished. If his lights were still on when she stood and looked back, she would go to him. And he would be there waiting, wanting.

She stood, holding her breath, and turned. And let it out again as she saw nothing but night and the deeper silhouettes of darkened buildings.

He hadn't waited.

She brushed the chill from her arms, calling it foolish. It wasn't rejection, it only meant he was tired and had gone to bed. And she should do that herself. There were dozens of things that needed to be done the next day that would be done better after a good night's sleep.

And they weren't bound to spend every night together. There'd been no promises between them. None at all, she thought, furious that her eyes stung as she turned back to the sea. No promises, no plans, no soft words.

Was that what she wanted, still? After she should have known better? What weakness was this in her that craved those words, those promises, those plans? Couldn't she be content with what was and not always dream about what could be?

It didn't matter what she'd told herself, she realized, as she sat down again. It didn't matter what she'd told her mother, or Margo or Kate. Or what she'd told Michael. It had all been lies. She, who was famous for being a pathetically poor liar, had pulled this one off beautifully.

She was in love with him. She was so stupidly in love with him, and no one had a clue. Part of her had already seen them together, tomorrow, a year from tomorrow, ten years. Lovers, partners, family. More children, a home, a life.

She'd lied to him, to everyone, including herself. And now, as it was with lies, she would have to continue to spin them, and live them, to make the first of them hold.

It wouldn't be fair to him otherwise. For he hadn't lied. He had wanted her, and she had no doubt that he cared for her. He cared for her children, was willing to offer a hand to help. He gave her his body, had awakened hers, and had offered her a friendship that she valued.

And still she wasn't satisfied.

Selfish, she wondered, or just foolish? It hardly mattered. She had created the illusion and would continue it. Or lose him.

When it was over, whenever it ended, she wouldn't regret it or curse God. She'd go on, because life was long and precious and deserved the best she could give it. When the time came and she had no choice but to live without him, she'd remember what it had been like to feel again, and to love. And she'd be grateful.

Steadier now, she braced a hand on the ground to push herself up. Her fingers closed over the disk as if they'd known it was there, waiting for her. With her heart drumming, loud as the waves below, she lifted it up, turned it under the stream of the moonlight.

It glinted dully, the single gold coin. Untouched, she thought with a shiver, unseen, for a hundred and fifty years. Since a young girl, desperate, had hidden it away to save for her lover. This, the symbol of the dream, the promise and the loss, lay cool in the center of her palm.

"Seraphina," she murmured. And her breath caught as she closed her fingers over the coin, as she felt the wild need of a reckless young girl.

Laura curled into a ball on the ledge, high over the violent waves. And wept.

CHAPTER 16

THE SORREL COLT was bright, pretty, and stubborn as a flea-bitten mule. Michael was working hard to prove that he was even more stubborn.

"By God, you'll do it, you little bastard. You know how."

As if to say that was hardly the point, the colt tossed his head, rolled his eyes in Michael's direction, and stood firm. They'd been dealing with each other for just over six months, and both of them wanted to be in charge.

"You think you've got these fancy digs and three squares to stand around posing?" Michael slapped the bat in his hand, and the colt's ears flickered. "You even think about kicking me again and you'll be eating dirt."

He stepped forward, the colt danced back. Michael's eyes narrowed dangerously. "Hold!"

Vibrating, the colt did so, pawing the ground in challenge as Michael approached.

"You and me," Michael said, gripping the bridle as the colt began to swing around to get a good shot with his back leg, "we're going to go a round."

"Don't you dare strike that animal."

Both Michael and the colt looked up in annoyance at the sharp order and saw the trim form swinging through the paddock gate.

"You should be ashamed of yourself." Fired up, Susan grabbed the colt's bridle and stepped between the horse and the bat. "I don't care if he belongs to you or not. I won't have an animal mistreated on my property."

As if realizing that sympathy was on his side, the colt lowered his head and nuzzled Susan's shoulder.

"Suck up," Michael muttered. "Look, Mrs. Templeton, I—"

"Is this the way you treat your horses? Clubbing them when they don't behave as you'd like? You brute." Color flashed into her cheeks, reminding Michael of Laura. "If you dare to raise a hand to one of these animals while I'm around, I'll personally kick your butt off Templeton property and halfway to hell."

Yes, he could see now where Laura got those licks of temper he'd caught a few glimpses of. And he could have sworn the colt was smirking at him. "Mrs. Templeton—"

"Then I'll have you arrested," she barreled on. "There are laws against cruelty to animals. Laws created to deal with insensitive brutes like you. And if you ever dare to mistreat this sweet horse—"

"There's not a sweet bone in his body," Michael interrupted, resisting the urge to rub the thigh that still sang from its rude encounter with a hoof. "And I wasn't going to use this to beat sense into his hard head, though it's tempting."

She'd seen the look in his eye, and the bat in his hand. Threw up her chin. "I suppose you were going to play baseball with him."

"No, ma'am." It might be funny, years later, when he didn't ache everywhere. "We're not playing at anything here. And if you want to take a good look, you'll see the only one with bruises on him in this paddock is me."

She did look, noted that although the coat was gleaming with a healthy layer of sweat, the horse was unharmed. In fact, he was magnificent. And the look in his eye wasn't fear, she realized. It was, if such a thing were possible, humor.

Michael, on the other hand, was filthy, and there was the telltale outline of a hoofprint on the leg of his jeans.

"If you threaten him with a bat, his only recourse is to strike out. I would think you'd—"

"Mrs. Templeton." Patience was wearing thin and going ragged around the edges. "Does this little bastard look threatened to you? Right now all he's doing is gloating."

It appeared that he was, Susan admitted, making another close study of the colt's eyes.

"Then explain why—"

"If you'd just let loose of him before he sees I can be slapped around by a woman half my weight and I completely lose the upper hand here, along with six months' work, I'd appreciate it."

She did loosen her grip on the bridle, but warily. "I'm warning you, Michael. If you dare to hurt him, I'll do more than slap you around."

"I believe it," Michael muttered as she took a single step back. "Would you move back to the fence, please? Bastard still has a problem with control."

"Charming name." With her arms folded, Susan took a few more steps in retreat. And stayed poised, ready to leap.

"You've got me in it now, haven't you?" With a firm hand, Michael took the bridle, pulled the colt's head down until their eyes were level. "Make me look like an idiot, pal, and I might just mistake your face for a Spalding. Got that?"

The colt snorted, then jerked his head clear when Michael released it. Michael shifted his grip on the bat, curling fingers around tip and base, then lifted it. After a humming war of wills, the colt reared up, pawed the air.

"Up." Heedless of striking hooves, Michael stepped under them. "Stay up there, Bastard. Nobody'll feed you if you kill me." Shifting the bat again, he grabbed a handful of mane and swung up onto the nearly vertical back.

At the quick and easy grace of the move, the fluidity with which man and horse merged, Susan sighed in admiration. And again when Michael turned the mount in a half circle.

The pressure of Michael's knees brought the horse down. "Stay back," Michael ordered Susan, without looking at her. "This is the part we're having trouble with."

He brought Bastard into a rear again, rolled off and under the dancing hooves. "Don't you step on me," Michael muttered, as he felt the ground shake. "Don't you step on me, you son of a—shit!"

A hoof caught him in the hip. Just a graze, but it was the principle of the thing. He was on his feet again, staring the horse down. "You did that on purpose. You're going to do it again till you get it right."

Limping only a little, Michael picked up the discarded bat and went through the entire routine again. And again.

When they were both winded and he'd managed to complete the drill without breaking anything, Michael, limping a bit more, went over to the bag he'd slung over the fence and took out an apple.

The colt followed him, pushed his head against Michael's back. "Don't try to make up. I'm only giving you this because I'm not on my way to the hospital."

The colt nudged him again, then tried to eat Michael's hair.

"Cut it out. You are such an ass kisser. Here." The apple he offered was taken eagerly. "And you have revolting manners," he added when bits of apple flew.

"I owe you an apology."

Michael stopped rubbing his bruised butt and looked at Susan. In his concentration, he'd forgotten she was still there. "No problem. Maybe I was thinking about bashing him one."

"No, you weren't." She stepped over, ran a hand over the colt's smooth neck. "You're in love with him."

"I hate the bastard. Don't know why I ever took him on."

"Um-hmm." She smiled, absently brushed some of the paddock dirt off the sleeve of Michael's shirt. "He certainly looks ill-kept, ill-used. Ill-fed too."

Embarrassed now, Michael shrugged. "He's an investment. A good stunt horse earns good money."

"I'm sure." She simply couldn't stand it—now she broke into excited questions. "How in the world did you teach him to do that? How do you keep him from trampling you? Aren't you worried? How long have you been working with him?"

Rolling his aching shoulders, Michael settled on the last question. "Not long enough. He's smart, but he's got some rough edges." Then he grinned. "You had me quaking, Mrs. Templeton. I figured you were going to grab the bat out of my hands and go to work on me with it."

"I might have." She caressed the colt. "I can't stand to see something abused."

"Can't say I care for it myself. There was this wrangler on a set a while back. He had this terrific horse, sweet-natured, generous. But the wrangler was never satisfied, always pushing for more, working that horse to exhaustion and never giving anything back. It was bad enough to see him breaking that horse's heart, and his spirit, but then he started using a whip, and his fists, and whatever else came in handy."

Michael paused to shovel the hair out of his eyes, squint at the sun. "He got himself a bad rep. Nobody wanted to hire him or work with him any-more. They all said it was too damn bad, 'cause that horse was a rare one."

"Why wasn't something done?"

"There's politics, the network—the wrangler'd been in the game a long time. I was pretty new at it then, and I never did care much for politics. I talked him into selling me that horse. Made a pretty decent stake working with him."

"You talked the wrangler into selling?"

Michael looked back at her. "More or less."

"Did you use the whip, or just your fists?"

"I don't care for whips. And Max, the walker I bought, he can't stand the sight of them." He nipped the bag away before the colt could investi-gate the contents. "You out for a walk this morning, Mrs. Templeton?"

"I could use that for an excuse. But I imagine we both know I wanted to speak with you."

"Yeah, I figured you or your husband would come down." And he'd prepped himself for it. "You're going to have to talk while I work. My stock need some exercise."

"All right." She went with him as he walked out of the paddock and into the stables. "Laura tells me you're giving the girls riding lessons."

"Just a few basics. I've got some quiet saddle ponies."

"I was treated to a dissertation on Mr. Fury and his horses over break-fast this morning. You've made quite an impression on my granddaugh-ters. Let me help you," she said, taking the bridle of one of the horses he'd begun to lead out. "And you've made an impression on my daughter as well."

"She's a beautiful woman."

"Yes, she is. And she's been through hell. In many ways it's made her stronger. But she's vulnerable, Michael, and more easily bruised than ei-ther you or she might realize."

"You want me to promise not to hurt her." He stepped back as the horses trotted into the paddock. "I can't do that."

"No, you wouldn't do that. As I recall, even as a boy you were careful not to make promises."

"You don't make, you don't break," he said simply and went back to the stables.

"You had a difficult childhood," she began, then broke off, raising her eyebrows, when his head whipped around.

"I don't believe in blaming what is on what was. I imagine you had a dandy childhood. Is that responsible for everything you are?"

She nodded slowly as he led out the next horses. "Well put," she murmured. "No, I wouldn't like to think so, but it did give me a solid foundation to build on."

"And mine's shaky." Though he'd told himself he wouldn't allow it, the bitterness came through. "You don't have to tell me where I come from, Mrs. Templeton. I know."

She stopped him by reaching up, closing her hand over his. "That wasn't a criticism. I'm not blind, Michael, and I don't like to think I'm narrow-minded either. I can see you're building something here. And I know why you left your childhood behind before anyone should have to."

When he said nothing, she smiled and let him go. "I know what goes on in my own house, Michael, and I know what goes on in the lives of my children's friends. If your back needs to go up because I felt sorry for that boy, then so be it. My heart broke for you."

"You wasted your sympathy."

"I don't think so, but as you said, that's what was. Now is what is. You never cross the wire in the marathon of parenthood, Michael. You never finish the race and take a victory lap. Laura is a grown woman, free to make her own choices and live her own life, but that doesn't stop me from worrying or wondering or hoping she chooses well."

He knew what she was telling him, had expected it. "And you've got to wonder, considering things, if she's choosing well this time."

She nodded slowly. "Yes. I won't say that sex doesn't last. It can and does if you're lucky. But it isn't enough by itself."

He'd expected to be warned away, but he wasn't ready to be pushed. "If you've come down here to ask me to stay away from her, you're wasting your time. I won't do it."

She measured him. "I'd be disappointed in you if you would. What I'm asking you to do is be kind." She looked away to where the horses pranced. "Just be kind."

"You want a promise, I'll give you one. I'll never treat her the way Ridgeway did. I won't cheat or lie or take anything from her she doesn't want to give me. And I won't leave her feeling like a failure."

Susan's gaze came back and sharpened. It was the words, yes, but more the edgy anger behind them that had her reevaluating. "You understand better than I gave you credit for."

"I understand failure just fine." And he knew that compared to a woman like Susan Templeton, he might not be a failure, but he could hardly be considered a success. "If that's all, I've got work to do."

"Michael." Remembering that he'd always been easily roused and prone to impatience, she kept her hand firm and her eyes level with the storm in his. "It's nice to have you at Templeton House again. Now will you show me the horse you told me about? Is it that walker over there watching you as if he'd die if you asked him to?"

Michael blew out a breath and wondered how a man was supposed to understand any of the Templeton females. "Yeah, that's Max. He's just hoping for a handout."

"Why don't you introduce me?"

"I ACTUALLY TOLD her I was sleeping with him." Laura kept her voice low as she slipped clothes back onto hangers in the wardrobe room. "I can't believe I stood there and told my own mother I was having sex with Michael."

"Odds are, she'd figured it out for herself." Margo slipped discarded shoes back into their slots. "And probably wasn't all that shocked, as it's likely she knew you'd had sex before. Seeing as you have two children."

"You know what I'm talking about," Laura mumbled. "It's weird."

"How'd she take it?"

"Well enough. Poor Dad is tiptoeing around the subject as though if he wakes it up it would start an orgy."

"Well, you could hardly pretend nothing was going on when Mrs. T. caught you and Michael playing lifeguard in the pool." She chuckled, checked her hair in the mirror. "God, I wish I'd seen that one."

"I'm sure it was illuminating for all parties. It felt like that time Annie caught us necking with Biff and Mark on the cliffs. The cliffs!" she exclaimed before Margo could comment. "Lord, my mind is a sieve today! Wait."

She dashed out, nearly bumping into a customer and causing Kate to eye her curiously. In the back office, Laura dug her purse out of a drawer and the coin out of the small zippered compartment.

"What's the problem?" Kate demanded, slipping in. "Did Margo forget to order boxes again? We'll be out by Monday if she hasn't—what have you got there?"

"The cliffs." Laura pressed a hand to her heart. "Last night. I forgot."

"You found one!" In a leap, Kate snatched it from Laura's hand. Excitement and triumph spurted straight up into her heart. "You found another one! Seraphina's dowry. And you forgot to tell us?"

"This morning was such a zoo. I didn't know I would be in until Dad insisted he'd cover for me at the hotel, and then Kayla and Ali were begging to stay home from school to spend time with Mom, and—oh, never mind," she finished with a wave of her hand. "Yes, I forgot."

Margo opened the door behind them. "Would the two of you mind terribly if we attempted to run the business today? We have customers who—what have you got?"

"Laura found it. And forgot."

"When?" Letting the door close smartly at her back, Margo took the coin from Kate. "Where?"

"Last night. On the cliffs. On that ledge where I like to sit sometimes. I was just sitting there, thinking, and when I started to go back, I saw it. Well, felt it," Laura corrected. "I put my hand down right on it. I'd been sitting right beside it."

"Just like the other times," Margo murmured. "When one was just there for me and one was just there for Kate. It's a sign."

"There she goes." Kate rolled her eyes and eased a hip onto the desk.

"Well, what would you call it?" Margo snapped back. "We search like maniacs, have been on and off since we were kids. Nothing. We've all but groomed those cliffs with tweezers. Nothing," she said again, gesturing wildly. "Then each one of us goes there, at some turning point in her life, and there it is. A coin. One for each. Which means . . ."

She stopped, looked up from the gold glinting in her hand, and stared at Laura. "Which means," she said slowly, "you're in love with Michael Fury."

"What in the world does one have to do with the other?" To buy time, Laura took the coin back, set it in the middle of the desk blotter.

"The day I went there and found mine, I was thinking about Josh and what I was going to do about being in love with him. And Kate—" She looked over at her friend, who was frowning in thought. "She went, thinking about Byron. You were in love with him, weren't you?"

"Yeah, but . . ." Kate trailed off. "Look, this is a little too *Twilight Zone* for me."

"Open that accountant's mind for a minute." Impatient, Margo turned back to Laura and took her by the shoulders. "Are you in love with Michael?"

"That isn't—"

"I asked a direct question, Laura, and I'll know if you lie."

"All right, yes, but it doesn't—"

"Love matters," Margo said quietly. "We matter. Maybe that's the whole point." She released Laura and reached into her pocket, where she habitually carried her coin. "This matters." She placed it beside Laura's and looked at Kate, who rose and took her own out of her purse.

"It matters," Kate agreed when the three coins sat side by side. "We're still in it together. Have you told Mick, Laura?"

"No. And no, I don't know if I'm going to, or how I'll handle it. I can't plan things out like you, Kate, or run on instinct the way you do, Margo. I have to do it my way. Which means, I suppose, maintaining illusions and waiting to see what comes. And my emotions are my responsibility."

Then she smiled, traced a fingertip over all three coins. "A sign from Seraphina. Well, maybe it is. Maybe she's telling me not to put all my dreams into one man's hands this time."

"Or she might be telling you that you can find that dream if you know where to look." Margo draped an arm over Laura's shoulders. "Either way, you can't stop looking. It's the same as jumping off a cliff."

"I haven't stopped looking." She patted Margo's hand before reaching for her coin. "And I think this calls for a celebration. Why don't we get together tonight and open some champagne?"

"Talked me into it." Kate pocketed her own coin. "I was coming over anyway. Poker night at the De Witts'."

"That's right." Laura grinned. "Dad's already rubbing his palms together. So, Margo, are you up for it?"

"I'll be there." Margo picked up her coin but held it. She hoped Laura wouldn't put hers—or her dreams—away too quickly. "Maybe we can get Mum and Mrs. T. a little drunk and play some poker ourselves."

"I'm game. Why don't we—" Kate broke off at the brisk knock on the office door. The customer who poked her head in seemed annoyed and impatient.

"Excuse me, but is anyone working here?"

"I'm so sorry." All conciliatory smiles, Laura stepped over. "We had a small problem. What can I help you with?"

MICHAEL HAD NEVER been driven to a poker game in a limo, and he wasn't sure how he felt about it. Not that he hadn't ever ridden in one before. After all, he'd worked in Hollywood for five years.

But to a poker game? It felt, well, pretentious.

Then again, as Josh had said when he came to the stables to fetch him, no one would have to worry about how many beers they knocked back.

Obviously at home in the plush surroundings, Thomas leaned back and tapped his finger on his knee in time with the aria playing on the stereo.

All Michael could think was that big limos, opera, and poker didn't mix. And he began to worry just what the hell he'd gotten himself into.

"I'm feeling lucky." Thomas wiggled his eyebrows. "I hope you two boys brought plenty of money."

Which made Michael realize that his idea of plenty of money and

Thomas Templeton of Templeton Hotels' idea of plenty of money were unlikely to be in the same ballpark.

Jesus, he could lose his shirt, and his ego, in one fun-filled evening.

"My wife fell in love with a Tennessee walker you have down at the stables, Michael." Thomas crossed his legs at the ankles and decided to see how much of a rise he could get out of young Michael Fury. "Maybe I'll win him from you before we're done tonight."

"I don't bet my horses," Michael said easily, "or my friends. Nice watch, Mr. Templeton." He flicked a glance over Thomas's slim gold Rolex. "I could use a new watch."

Thomas let out a bark of laughter and slapped Michael on the knee. "A boy needs his dreams. I ever tell you about the time I played seven-card stud for thirty-six hours? That was in Chicago in '55. Now we—"

"Not the 'thirty-six hours in Chicago' story," Josh moaned. "I'm begging you."

"Shut up, Harvard." Almost comfortable, Michael stretched out his legs. "Some of us haven't heard it."

Pleased, Thomas grinned at Michael. "Then I'll tell you, and you can be afraid."

IT WASN'T SUCH a bad ride after all. And things looked up when they pulled into the driveway of the multi-decked house on Seventeen Mile and the uniformed driver unloaded two cases of Blue Moose beer—a Templeton product—from the limo's trunk.

"Now that's a hell of a beer," Michael said, then hooked his thumbs in his pockets and studied the wood and glass, the decks and gardens of the De Witt homestead. "And that's a hell of a house."

"Easy access to the beach, too," Josh added. "Kate recommended the property to Byron before they got together."

"Good call. It looks like her," Michael decided. "Streamlined, classy, unique. Man, oh, man! '65 Mustang. And it's cherry too." He walked over to the car, ran a loving hand over the fender. "What a beaut. And that 'Vette. First-round Sting Ray. Mmm, sweetheart, let me pop your hood."

"We going to play poker or are you going to make love to inanimate objects all night?"

He shot a look at Josh. "Inanimate, my ass. Honeys like this have more personality and sex appeal than half the women you dated."

"Shows that you haven't met the women I've dated."

"I dated some of them myself." Michael strolled toward the front door, glancing over his shoulder at the cars, then at Josh. "Including your wife."

Josh's grin faltered and so did his feet. "You never dated Margo."

"Didn't I?" Enjoying himself, Michael climbed the short flight of wooden steps. "I seem to recall a couple of interesting evenings in France."

"You're just trying to psych me out."

And it was working. "Ask her," Michael said mildly.

Damned if he wouldn't. His head reeling with visions he didn't want, Josh reached around and opened the door. Two big yellow dogs raced forward and flung themselves at the newcomers.

"Nip, Tuck, sit." Byron called out the order as he stepped into the wide living area. The dogs sat, butt to butt, and continued to vibrate. "You can put the beer in the kitchen. Thanks." He motioned the driver toward the kitchen. "Think you brought enough?"

"We run out," Josh said, "we send for more. Got food?"

"I whipped up a few things."

Unable to resist two lolling tongues and two pairs of adoring eyes, Michael crouched and made friends with the dogs. "You cook?"

"How do you think he got me to marry him?" Kate stepped out, smiled thinly.

"You still here?" Josh moved over to tug her hair. "Go play with your own kind."

She elbowed him away. "I was just leaving. But I want to say that the concept of the all-male poker game is a Neanderthal practice that I find insulting, particularly when it's taking place in my own house."

Being a wise man, Byron limited himself to rolling his eyes behind her back. But Michael didn't have to live with her. He straightened, grinned.

"Yeah, yeah, tell it to Gloria Steinem and get lost."

"I have no desire to stay and listen to a bunch of fools belch, snort, and tell lies about the women they've had." Chin lifted, she snatched her purse from a chair.

"And I was going to tell Byron all about that night I picked you up on Fisherman's Wharf and we—"

"Shut up, Mick." Her brows drew together, her color rose. "I'm leaving."

"Wait a minute." Her husband made a grab, missed. "What night?"

"It was nothing." She seared Michael with a look. "It was *nothing*."

"Aw, sugar," Michael murmured. "Now you've hurt my feelings."

"Men are pigs," she tossed back as she slammed the door behind her.

"Well, that got rid of her," Michael decided. "Where are the cards?"

"Margo *and* Kate?" Josh eyed him narrowly.

"Can't fault my taste, can you?" Michael tucked his hands in his pockets. "Like I said, where are the cards?"

MEN DESERVE THEIR little rituals." Susan stretched out on the long arm of the conversation pit in the family room. "Just as we deserve ours."

"I don't mind." Snuggled back against a mountain of pillows, Margo nibbled from a bowl of popcorn. "Kate gets huffy."

"Where is Kate?" Wandering to the window, Laura looked out. "She should be here by now."

"Oh, she'd have waited to yank their chains before she left." Margo shrugged and reached for the champagne. "She'll be along. God knows this is better than poker and beer and a bunch of cigar smoke, but she's got to make her point. Ready for a glass, Mum?"

Ann paused in her perusal of the videotapes chosen for the marathon viewing. "Well . . . maybe just a little one."

They had champagne, popcorn, a platter of crudités, fresh fruit, three choices of dip, including white chocolate, and a stack of movies. The baby was sleeping in the nursery and her favorite women were here. Margo judged it the perfect girls' night out.

"I'm going to do your nails."

"I don't want the fussing."

Margo smiled at her mother. "It's fun, Mum. I've got the perfect shade for you. Red Hot Lover."

Ann snorted into her wine. "I won't wear any such thing. As if I'd be painting my fingernails anyway."

"Men go for it." To tease, Margo leaned closer. "And Bob the butcher's had his eye on you for years."

"He certainly has not." Her face flaming, Ann fumbled with the stack of tapes. "That's nonsense. We have a good customer relationship. Nothing more."

"He saves the leanest cuts for Miss Annie." Margo fluttered her lashes, then laughed. "You should give him a break one of these days. Oh, Laura, stop worrying about Kate. She'll be here."

"I'm not worrying, just watching." And thinking of Michael, she admitted. What was he doing? Why was it their paths hadn't crossed once since the night before? But she made herself come away from the window and pour a glass of champagne. "What are we going to watch first? I vote for *To Have and Have Not*."

"'You know how to whistle, don't you, Steve?'" Susan sighed, dipped a moist red strawberry into creamy white chocolate. "The world's champion come-on."

"World's best brush-off," Margo said, continuing the theme. "Bette Davis. 'I'd love to kiss you, but I just washed my hair.'"

"Best wrenching good-bye." Laura said, getting into the swing. "Bogart to Bergman. 'We'll always have Paris.'"

When Kate came in ten minutes later, they were in a heated debate over the ten most dangerous men in cinema history.

"Newman," Margo insisted. "It's the eyes. Cold or hot and incredibly blue. You watch *The Long, Hot Summer*, *Hud*, or—"

"Grant." Susan sat up to make her point. "Dangerous because it's unexpected. The charm undermines a woman's defenses, and he has her."

"Bogart," Laura disagreed. "In anything. Raw, dangerous, elemental, a hero despite his instincts."

"I can't believe you're discussing men." Disgusted, Kate plopped down. "I just left those four baboons. Is that white chocolate?" She reared up again and used her finger to dip in. "And," she continued, licking it, "they were already smug, superior, and sarcastic. Mick's the worst. I can't believe he brought up that time I ran into him on the wharf and we . . ."

"We?" Laura came to attention. "We what?"

"Nothing." She should have filled her mouth, Kate decided, and began to do so. "It was nothing. He was home on leave and he looked sort of . . . interesting. We went for a drive, that's all."

"You went for a drive?" Laura repeated. "With Michael? That's all?"

"Well, yeah, mostly." Done it now, Kate thought, as every eye in the room focused on her. "Well, okay, so maybe I experimented a little, for a minute. Who's in charge of the VCR?"

Before she could pop up to take charge herself, Laura clamped a hand on her shoulder. "Define 'experimented.'"

"I let him kiss me . . . a couple of times. That's it. Just that. Do we have *Bringing Up Baby*? I could use a laugh."

"You and Michael necked in his car?"

"Not necked, exactly. I wouldn't call it necking. Margo—" She appealed to her friend for help.

"No, a couple of kisses does not constitute necking. I necked with him, so I know this to be true."

"You—" Laura choked, grabbed the champagne bottle. "You—"

"I give him a ten on both technique and style. And since that was a number of years ago, I can only assume he's improved even that." She laughed, got up to pop a movie in. "Now Mrs. T. is trying to figure out if she should make a comment or a statement of any kind, and Mum is sitting there steaming over the idea that the disreputable Michael Fury has had his very tasty lips clamped on all three of her girls."

"That's just the kind of talk I expect from you," Ann said with a sniff.

"And I'd hate to disappoint you. He's one of the dangerous men, all right." She leaned back and patted her mother's knee affectionately. "Thank God for them."

CHAPTER 17

H E WASN'T FEELING particularly dangerous with the trash Byron had dealt him. He'd held fairly steady in the first hour of the game, keeping his bets conservative, even predictable, while he studied each of his opponents for their tells.

They were good, he admitted, all three of them. This wasn't any sucker's game. They may have been the classy high rollers who normally gambled in palaces, but he had learned his skills aboard ship, where boredom could tempt a man to toss a month's pay into the pot just to break the monotony.

At a card table, any card table, Michael knew a wise man studied his quarries, and his foes.

Josh flicked a thumb over his jaw when he had a solid hand, and his eyes went blank and cool when he was bluffing. De Witt tended to reach for his beer when he had a winner. And Templeton, well, Templeton was a cagey dog, but as the second hour got under way, Michael noted that the man puffed harder on his cigar when he prepared to rake in the chips.

Calculating, Michael discarded, drew into a pitiful pair of treys. He had a choice, considered the practicalities, and decided it was time to shake things up.

"There's your ten," he told Josh, flipping in his chips. "Raise it ten."

"Twenty to me." Absently Byron reached down to scratch one of his dogs. A sign, Michael thought smugly, that he had nothing. "I'm in."

"Twenty." Tommy knocked into the pot. "And ten more."

"Out." Josh tossed his cards down and rose to help himself to one of the fat sandwiches on the counter.

"I'll see your raise and bump it twenty."

"And you two can fight this hand out." Byron pushed back, gulped his beer.

The boy had been bumping the pot since the deal, Thomas mused, and studied the pretty trio of ladies in his hand. Well, they would have to see what he was made of. "Your twenty, and fifty more."

Michael's eyes met Thomas's over the cards, held steady as he pushed chips into the pot. "Fifty. And fifty back. Call or fold."

Thomas studied his opponent, then wheezed out a breath between his teeth. "I'll give you this one," he decided and tossed his cards down. Well?" he demanded when Michael scooped back the chips. "What did you have?"

When Michael merely smiled and began to stack his chips, Thomas hissed out another breath. "You bluffed me. I can see it. You didn't have shit."

"A man has to pay to see, Mr. Templeton."

Eyes narrowed, Thomas leaned back. "Tommy," he said. "When a man bluffs me cold, he ought to call me by name."

"My deal." Michael gathered the cards, shuffled. "Stud. Seven-card." He grinned. "You in, Tommy?"

"I'm in, and I'll still be in when you're writhing on the floor and begging for mercy."

Michael flipped in his ante. "A boy needs his dreams."

Thomas let loose a laugh, then reached into his pocket. "Damned if I don't like you, Fury. Have a cigar. A real one, not one of those girl smokes Byron puffs on."

"Thanks, but I quit." Still, he sniffed longingly at the clouds of smoke. "Anyway, those Cubans look too much like a dick."

Josh choked on smoke, pulled his cigar out of his mouth. "Thanks, Mick. I'm really going to enjoy this now."

Howling with laughter, Thomas slapped his hand on the table. "Deal the cards—and prepare to lose your shirt."

DURING HOUR THREE, Michael took a pass and walked outside. He peed companionably with the dogs and watched the night-drenched sea.

"Hell of a spot, isn't it?"

Michael looked back over his shoulder as Byron approached. "You sure picked one."

"I was thinking I could put up a small stable there, at the edge of the cypress grove. Simple. Two stalls."

"Two?"

"I figure solo's lonely, even for a horse. I liked the look of that pinto mare."

"She's a sweetheart." He tucked his tongue in his cheek. "You clear it with your wife?"

Byron's eyes were mild and amused. "I know all kinds of ways around my wife. More, I assume than you do even after picking her up on Fisherman's Wharf."

"I was just rattling her cage. And yours." He lifted his hands, palms out. "Never laid my hands on her. Hardly."

Byron chuckled, shook his head. "I think we'll just leave that particular door closed, but if you want to ride Josh about Margo, I'd find it entertaining."

"I don't want to have to fight him. He's tougher than he looks. Loosened three of my teeth when we were twelve." Michael checked them with his tongue. "And his old man's liable to take bets on the outcome."

"That's the Templetons. They'll bet on anything. Look at the way Kate, Margo, and Laura bet on the shop."

"I keep meaning to go by there again. I'm not much on fancy-lady shops, but I'm wondering how Laura handles clerking."

"I think you'll be surprised, and impressed. I have been. It's given them something solid and special."

"Gives them a living."

"It gives them more than that. It gives them unity, and a goal and love." Either the beer or the women were making him sentimental, but Byron went with it. "I wasn't around when they conceived it, put it together, took the chance. Margo selling off almost everything she owned, my conservative accountant pooling her investments to make her share. And Laura selling her wedding ring."

"She sold her wedding ring to build that shop?"

"Yeah. It was right after they found out Ridgeway had pretty much cleaned out their joint accounts. She wouldn't take Templeton money for the shop, so she hocked her wedding and engagement rings to make the down payment on the building. What women they are!"

"Yeah." Michael frowned out to sea. "The socialite, the model, and the accountant."

"They sweated over it. They cleaned and sanded and painted. And figured out how to make it work. It knocks me out to walk in there and see how they are together, how they are together anywhere. You see them out on the cliffs, rooting around in the rocks and dirt for Seraphina's dowry. All these years they're still together, still looking. Kate was wild tonight when she told me Laura had found another coin."

He was trying to see it all, to settle all these facets into an image in his head. He blinked. "Laura? She found a coin? When?"

"Last night. Took a walk down on the cliffs. Kate says she does that from time to time when she needs to clear her head or just be alone. She found one, a gold doubloon just like Margo did, and Kate did. Oddest fucking thing. Each one of them finding a coin, months apart, by accident rather than design. Their treasure hunts turn up nothing, then boom, one of them just picks up a gold piece off the ground as if it had been there all along. Makes you wonder."

The back door slammed open and Thomas's voice boomed out. "Is this a poker game or a damn church social? Cards are getting cold."

"Then deal 'em," Byron called back. "Coming?" he asked Michael.

"Yeah. Laura walks on the cliffs at night?"

"Now and again." Byron waded through the dogs, who ran circles around him.

"And last night she just reached down and picked up a gold coin?"

"Spanish, 1844."

"Son of a bitch. That's weird."

"I'll tell you what's weirder. I'm beginning to believe they're going to find the whole thing. That they're the only ones who will."

"Never believed it existed."

"Ask Laura to show you her coin," Byron suggested. "You might change your mind."

"I might do that," Michael murmured, then walked back into the comforting arena of cigar smoke and beer.

WHEN HE DRAGGED himself up the stairs at three A.M., he still had his shirt, his horses, and his ego. He would have counted himself lucky for that. The fact that he was also eight hundred dollars richer was just icing.

He thought he might put it toward buying a pretty yearling Quarter Horse he'd had his eye on.

He stepped through his front door and stumbled over the warm bundle stretched out there.

"Jesus Christ!" As he hit the floor, the dog yelped, shuddered, then licked humbly at Michael's face. "Bongo, what the hell are you—Jesus, get your tongue out of my mouth!" Michael swiped a hand over his face, shifted and ended up with wriggling puppy on his lap. "Yeah, yeah, you're sorry. How the hell'd you get in here? Learn how to pick locks now?"

"He came with me." Laura stepped out of the bedroom. "He loves me. He didn't want to sleep in my bed all alone. Me either."

Maybe it was the beer, or his abrupt meeting with the floor, but his voice seemed to have been lost somewhere along the way.

She was standing in the lamplight, smiling. And wearing nothing but one of his shirts. Her hair was tousled, her skin flushed. And when he managed to clear his vision, he noted that her eyes were bright, if a bit unfocused.

She was in simple words, beautiful, sexy, and drunk.

"Did you come for the rent?"

Her laugh was low and frothy. "It's after business hours. I came for you. Thought you'd never get here. How was the poker game?"

"Profitable. How was the movie marathon?"

"Illuminating. Did you ever watch, really watch, the way people kiss in black and white? It's . . ." She sighed, ran a hand down her breasts until he had to roll his tongue back into his mouth. "Wonderful," she decided. "Just wonderful. Come and kiss me, Michael. In black and white."

"Sugar . . ." He had very few rules and was struggling to remember this one as he set the dog aside and rose. "You're plowed."

"I am, indeed." She shook back her hair, leaned against the doorway for balance. "D'you know, Michael, I have never been drunk in my life. A little tipsy, I will admit to having been, on occasion a little tipsy. But drunk, never. Not done, not acceptable for a woman of my standing in the community."

"Your secret's safe with me. Bongo and I will walk you home."

"I'm not going home." She straightened, steadied herself, enjoying the liberating way the room tilted as she stepped toward him. "Until I've had you. Then you can tell me if I kiss as good as Kate and Margo."

"Shit," he muttered under his breath. "Word travels fast around here."

"You can even rip my clothes off again." She linked her arms around his neck. "It's your shirt anyway. I like wearing your clothes. It's almost like having your hands on me. Are you going to put your hands on me, Michael?"

"I'm debating."

"I'll tell you a secret." She pressed against him, put her mouth on his ear. "Wanna know my secret?"

She was going to be sorry come sunrise, but—he skimmed his hands under the shirt—what the hell. "Yeah, tell me a secret."

"I have dreams about you. I used to have them before, too. Long time ago, when you would come around with Josh, I had dreams about you. But I never told anybody, because—"

"It wouldn't be appropriate for a woman of your standing."

She chuckled, nipped his earlobe and sent his blood pressure through the roof. "'Xactly. You know what I'd dream about you? I'll tell you. You'd find me. I'd be on the cliffs or in my room or in the forest, and you'd find me. And my heart would start to pound, so hard, so fast."

She took his hand, pressed it against her heart. To show him. "I couldn't move or breathe, or even think," she continued, and her hand laid over his on her breast. "You'd come toward me, not saying anything, just looking at me, looking until my knees were weak, until the blood was rushing in my head. You'd kiss me, so rough, so hot. The way no one else ever would. No one else would dare to touch me the way you touched me."

"No." It was like drowning, he thought. Staring into those deep gray eyes was like drowning. "No one would."

"You'd rip my clothes, rip them off, and take me right there, wherever we were. Just the way you did that night, just like in my dreams. I must have always known you would one day."

She circled away, arms lifted like a dancer on point while he stood where he was, aching. Viciously aching.

"That's my secret. I dreamed of you. Oh, my head's spinning." She laughed, pressed a hand to it. "Being drunk feels just like it feels having you on top of me, inside me, pounding in me. God, God, I love it."

She combed her hair back from her face, grinned at him. "Look at you, standing there, watching me. Never expected to hear such talk from Laura Templeton, did you?"

He knew, standing there, watching her, that if he'd been dying of thirst he would have begged for her rather than a single sip of water. "No. And if you don't remember this in the morning, I'm going to be damn sorry."

"I'm just full of surprises tonight." She lifted her arms, hooked them behind her head and stretched. "I watched all those movies, drank all that wine. Ate chocolate and laughed. And cried, and sighed. All those things women do."

Laura lowered her hands again and turned a slow, fluid pirouette that made his shirt flow up, out.

"I watched Margo talk Annie into having her nails painted, and Kate dozing off with her head on my mother's lap. Margo nursing the baby when he woke. I loved it all so much, loved being with them. My life is them and my babies, but through it all, you were in the back of my mind. Where is Michael? Does he still want me? And I thought, we'll see. I'll be there when he comes home, and we'll see if he does. If I can make him want me. Do you?"

He didn't speak, couldn't have. Simply crossed to her, dragged her against him and plundered. Joy and need and pleasure burst through her in one sizzling ball of heat. Her laugh was smoke, like her eyes as he pulled her to the floor.

"No, no." Giddy now, and brave enough, she rolled on top of him. "Let me. This time. I want to see if I can."

He was ripe to explode and pulled her down again. "Laura, for Christ's sake—"

"Me." She jerked back, shook her reeling head. "I want to do things to you, things that might be considered inappropriate for a woman of my station."

He struggled to clamp down on hurry when she straddled him. "Want to use me, do you?"

Her lips quirked at the gleam in his eyes. "That's right. Look, we scared Bongo. He's curled up in the corner."

"He'll get over it. What do you want to do to me?"

"I have to figure it out." She blew out a breath, toyed with the buttons of his shirt. "I've got another secret."

"If it's anything like the last one, it'll probably kill me."

"It's not a good one." Now her lips pouted. "Well, maybe since it turned out this way it is. Peter never ripped my clothes off."

"Christ. Forget it, and him."

But when he reached up, she evaded him. "I want to tell you so you'll know. It's kind of funny, really. We always had very appropriate sex. Not like with you." She traced the vee above the button with a fingertip. "Always proper sex, except when we didn't have sex at all, which was most of the time and all through the last year we were married. And you know what?" She placed her hands on either side of his head and leaned down, a heavy-eyed, more-than-tipsy woman.

"What?"

She hummed in her throat as he stroked her breasts. "You can do that," she murmured. "I don't mind at all. But I was saying. We had a system. No, he had a system, I was just there. He would put on classical music. Chopin, always the same sonata. I sometimes still get a tick in my eye when I hear it. He would close the door, lock it, lest a wandering servant be shocked by the goings-on, though the staff would hardly have business in there at ten forty-five in the evening. It was mostly always at ten forty-five."

"So he was a creature of habit." Michael flipped open buttons and found her flesh.

"Umm. No, you don't." She sat up again. "You're trying to distract me. He would turn off the lights, get into bed. He would kiss me three times. Not two, not four, but three times. Then he would—"

"I don't think I want a play-by-play here of Ridgeway's style in the sack."

"In the marital bed, please. Well, we'll just skip right along, then, since it isn't very interesting anyway. At eleven-oh-five, he would wish me a pleasant night and go to sleep."

"The twenty-minute special, huh?"

"You could set your clock by it. Oh, Michael." She stretched her arms up, giving him tempting glimpses of soft white swells. "I thought it was me. I thought that was just the way it was, had to be. But it isn't, it wasn't, it doesn't."

She cupped her breasts in her hands, let her eyes close. "It's never predictable with you. I never know what you'll do, where you'll touch me next, or how. And it's never proper. It's so wonderfully improper. The things you do with your hands, with your mouth on me." She dropped her hands to his chest. "Do you have any idea what it's like to discover, at thirty, that you have a sex drive?"

"No." He couldn't help but smile at her. She was so beautifully drunk. "I found mine at sixteen and never lost sight of it."

She laughed, flinging her head back and making his teeth ache with the need to bite into that slim white throat. "Oh, but this is better. Has to be. It's like finding Seraphina's dowry. Somehow you know it's there, somewhere, or hope it is. And then when you find it, after all that time, all that wondering, it's so sweet."

"Since you found that elusive sex drive"—his hands slid up her torso— "why don't we put it to use?"

"I'm going to make you sweat." She eased down again, scraped her teeth over his jaw. "You might even beg."

"Now you're getting cocky."

"I take that as a challenge." To demonstrate, she shoved up her sleeves, which fell right back down again. "Are you man enough to agree not to touch me until I say you can?"

He lifted a brow, wondering just what the lady had in mind. "Your loss, sugar."

"I don't think so, ultimately. No hands," she murmured and pressed his to his sides. "Except mine."

She lowered her lips to his, brushed, teased, nibbled. "Margo said you had a very tasty mouth." She smiled when he winced. "She was right. I think I'll stay right here a while."

She lingered on his mouth, changing the angle, the depth, the tone of the kiss. Light one moment, intense and urgent the next, then sultry, smoky.

His fingers, aching, curled into the carpet. "Not bad for a beginner," he managed in a voice rusty with need.

"And I learn fast. Your heart's pounding, Michael." She nipped at the pulse in his throat, cruised over dampening flesh. Then she gripped his shirt at the shoulder, pulled. When the seam stayed fast, he chuckled from both humor and frustration.

"Want me to do that for you?"

"I can handle it." She eased back, kept her eyes on his as she yanked hard. The seam ripped, exposing muscle and skin. She pounced on it like a starving cat. "Oh, your body," she whispered, then crossed her hands, taking hold of his shirt and sending cloth and buttons flying. "You have such a body. Tough and scarred and tight. I want it."

Her mouth streaked down his shoulder, over his chest. Quick, greedy bites and sucks, feathering openmouthed kisses and flicks of tongue. But when his hands came up to grip her hips, she shoved them away with a single word.

"Mine."

Rising up, she shrugged off the shirt, then once more bent to her task.

She was destroying him in a way he hadn't known he could be destroyed. Slowly, inevitably. She was taking him in a way he hadn't known he could be taken. Greedily, intently. His breath thickened, caught, released on a groan when she laved her tongue low on his belly. Every muscle quivered, taut wires close to snapping.

Thoughts filled and emptied from his mind so rapidly that he couldn't gain hold. Sensation rammed violently into sensation like two clenched fists. The scent of her, elegant as royalty, the sheen of her skin, glossy as a damp rose, and the stroke of her hands, restless as lust.

Giddy on her own power, she tugged open the button of his jeans, felt his body tense like a runner on the mark. She lowered her mouth, tasting there, just there where denim and flesh met. And heard him choke out her name.

She could do this to him, she thought as she dipped her tongue under the denim to tease. She could create this desperation, and weakness, this violent need in a strong, vital man. She could make him want her to the point of madness, and she could take whatever she wanted from him.

She nudged the material down, closed her teeth over his hip. And heard the breath explode out of his lungs. He was helpless, she knew, lost in her. And she could make him ache.

She took him into her mouth, clamped him in a wet velvet vise and shot his system into chaos.

His hands fisted in her hair as his body bucked under her. When her mouth cruised up to his belly again, over quaking muscle, he was ready to kill to have her.

Still gripping her hair, he yanked her head back, reared up. She felt one shocking jolt at the dark burn of his eyes, then his mouth was clamped on hers.

"I didn't say you could touch me." She panted it out as his lips branded her throat, her shoulders, her breasts. "You didn't beg."

"I need you." He found her with his hand, shoved her over the peak he was still clinging to. "Now. Goddamn it, take me in."

Triumphant, she threw her head back, and her laugh was rich and wild. Locking her legs around his waist, she arched back, "Yes." Bowed like a bridge when he drove himself into her.

She cried out, no longer surprised but shuddering nonetheless over the speed and violence of the orgasm. She arrowed up again, her body locked to his, her hips pumping.

"More," she demanded, tearing nails down his back. "Michael. More."

Blind with greed, she shoved him back, dug her hands into his waist, and took more.

The storm raged through him, whipping toward peak, but he could see her. Rising and falling over him, her eyes closed to heated slits, her head back in abandon. The animal inside him mated with hers until she'd ridden both to exhaustion.

Through hazy vision he saw her melt down on him. And felt the quakes of the aftershocks rush through her. His own body felt bruised, numbed, weightless so that he wasn't even aware that his arms were locked tight around her, like a man holding everything that mattered.

"Told you I could do it," she murmured, turning her lips to his throat.

"Yeah, you sure showed me." He pressed his lips to her hair, wallowed there. "Laura." He said her name quietly, almost to himself. Then closed his eyes and tried, for both their sakes, not to hear the rest of it. *I love you. Love you.*

"You wanted me."

"Yes. I wanted you." Her hair smelled like sunlight, weakened him all over again.

"Will you do something for me, Michael?"

"Yeah." Anything. Terrifying thought. Anything.

"Will you carry me to bed? I'm still drunk."

"Sure, baby. Just hold on." He rose with her, a feat that even in her impaired state made her heart flutter.

"And one more thing." Her head dropped limply against his shoulder, and when she moaned he had panicked visions of finding a basin to shove under her face before she was sick.

"Okay, don't worry. I'll take care of you. It'll be fine."

"All right." Warm and soft and trusting, she curled into him, then blinked against sudden hard light. "What? What?" Her head cocked curiously. "Why are we in the bathroom?"

"It's the handiest place to be sick. Go ahead and toss up that wine, sugar, you'll feel better."

"I'm not going to toss up perfectly good champagne." She wrapped her arms tighter when he tried to set her down. "I'm not going to be sick." Then she flopped back, dead weight, like a woman in a faint and laughed until it echoed off the walls. "Oh, that's so sweet. You were going to hold my head while I vomited. God, Michael." She raised up again, kissed him sloppily. "You're the cutest thing. Just so cute and sweet I could eat you right up. My hero."

Embarrassed, he narrowed his eyes. "Maybe I'll just stick your head in the toilet anyway. If you're not going to lose the champagne and chocolate, what do you want?"

"I told you to carry me to bed. I would think it would be obvious." Smiling, she traced a finger down his chest. "I want you to want me again. If it wouldn't be an imposition."

He glanced down at her, warm, rosy, naked female. His female. "I guess I could manage that."

"Good, and do you think you could, well . . ." She leaned over and whispered something in his ear that made his blood take a quick trip to his loins.

"That's pretty inappropriate behavior, but . . ." He made a beeline for the bed. "Under the circumstances . . ."

CHAPTER 18

EXPERIENCING A FIRST hangover, Laura discovered, wasn't nearly as much fun as experiencing a first drunk. Instead of having a head filled with light and color and gloriously rambling ideas, she had one crammed with noise—along the lines of a poorly directed high school band, with the percussion section banging away gleefully at her left temple.

Her system didn't feel free and floaty, but clogged, the way her mouth seemed clogged with enough dirt to make half a dozen mud pies.

She was grateful that Michael had left her alone rather than witness the humiliation.

She wouldn't think about the fact that she'd spent the night in his bed and now would have to stagger into the house, where her family and the staff would shoot her questioning looks.

She tried to drown those unmerciful drummers under the shower, then bit down on her lip when she realized the new sound she heard was her own whimpering.

Under normal circumstances she would never have gone through any of Michael's things, but she finished up a fumbling search through the mirrored medicine cabinet and bathroom drawers and nearly wept when she found a bottle of aspirin.

She took four, another break in tradition; then, deciding she couldn't be much more intrusive, used his toothbrush.

She didn't look in the mirror until she'd dressed, and even then it was a mistake. Her face was deathly pale, her eyes smudged and swollen. And as she didn't have so much as a tube of lipstick with her, there was nothing she could do about it.

Knowing she had to get it over with, she stepped outside and moaned quietly as the sunlight sent hot little spears into her eyes. Her head didn't feel like the practice field for a marching band now; now it felt like glass. Very thin, very fragile glass. And it was balanced precariously on her neck.

"How's it going, sugar?"

She winced, jerked. Her head fell off, smashed on the steps at her feet. Thank God she had another one. She turned it, struggled to smile as Michael dusted his hands on his hips and walked toward her.

"Good morning. I'm sorry I didn't hear you get up."

"The way you were sawing them off, I figured you'd sleep till noon."

The insult of the headache faded. Snore? She certainly did not snore. She wouldn't dignify such a lie with a comment. "I have to be at the shop in a couple of hours."

"You're working today?" She didn't look to be in any shape for it to him. "Give yourself a break, Laura, and go crawl back into bed."

"Saturdays are our busiest day."

He shrugged his shoulders. Her choice. "How's the head?"

"Which one?" Now she did smile, a little. Certainly a man like Michael would understand hangovers. "It's bad, but no longer unbearable."

"Next time you go on a bender, chug plenty of water and pop a couple aspirin before you pass out. It usually helps take the edge off the morning after."

"I don't intend to have a next time, but thanks."

"Now that might be a shame." He trailed a finger over the back of her hand. "You make a very inventive drunk. How's the memory?"

Her blood must have been moving still, for she felt it rise up to sting her cheeks. "It's good. A little too good. I certainly wouldn't have—I can't believe that I—" She shut up, closed her eyes. "You can stop me anytime from making a total fool of myself."

"I kinda like it. Come here." He drew her against him, cradling her aching head on his shoulder. "Ice water," he murmured. "Stick your face right into a bowl of ice water, try to get some food in your system, then you just have to tough out the rest of it."

"Okay." She'd have preferred just staying there for the rest of her life. "I have to go. I shouldn't have slept here last night." With her face pressed against him she didn't see the disappointment and the hurt shadow his. "I can't imagine what everyone will think."

"Right." His eyes were impassive again when he drew her away. "You go on and shore up the damage to the Templeton name."

"I didn't mean—"

"Forget it." He wasn't going to let it touch him. "Forget it," he repeated. "Why don't you go riding with me tomorrow?"

"Tomorrow?" She pressed her fingers to her eyes. If she didn't get them out of the sun soon they were going to implode. "We have the treasure hunt."

"We'll go in the morning. You'll be back for Seraphina."

Riding. It had been years since she'd ridden in the hills, through the forest. "All right. I'd love it. Can we go about eight? That way I can—"

"Sure, eight." He gave her a quick pat on the cheek before walking away. "Don't forget the ice water."

"No, I—" But he had already disappeared around the side of the building. Baffled by his rapid shift of mood, she considered following him. Then she looked at her watch and accepted the reality that her obligations for the day didn't allow time to puzzle out the enigma of Michael Fury.

NO ONE ASKED questions, demanded answers, or voiced disapproval. When Laura tucked her children into bed that night, she realized she had gotten through the entire day without having anyone question her absence from her own bed.

Oh, there'd been vibes in the air. Worry, curiosity, but she'd dodged even those. She'd survived a hangover as well, and the world had not come to an end.

Maybe, just maybe, Laura Templeton did not have to be perfect after all.

She left her daughters and crossed the hall to her own room. There she freshened her lipstick, brushed her hair. She needed to go and join her parents and the old friends who had come for dinner. She needed to make certain everyone was comfortable and entertained.

And, oh, she needed to stretch out for five minutes. Just five, she promised herself as she lay down crosswise on the bed. A quick catnap would set her up, help her get through the rest of the evening.

The minute she closed her eyes, she was dead to the world.

*   *   *

"SOMETHING HAS TO be done, Mrs. T." Hands gripped tight at her waist, Ann stood in Susan's quiet sitting room in the tower suite. "It has to be."

"All right, Annie, sit down." It had been a long evening, and though she'd been pleased to see old friends, Susan had hoped for a few moments of solitude before bed. The look on Ann's face warned her she wouldn't get it. "Now what's the trouble?"

"You know what the trouble is, Mrs. T." Too fretful to sit, Ann wandered the room, fussing with curtains, realigning candlesticks, fluffing pillows. "You saw how pale and tired Miss Laura was today. You had to see for yourself."

"Yes, I did see. And I've been pale and tired myself the day after I've overindulged in champagne."

"Oh, as if that was all of it. And that's something she's never done before him, either."

Perhaps she should have, Susan thought. She sighed. "Annie, stop tidying the room and sit down."

"She spent the night with him. The whole of it. Over there with him above the horses."

Because her lips wanted to twitch, Susan glanced down at her own hands as Ann sat across from her. "Yes, Annie. I'm aware of that."

"Well, it can't go on." And that, Ann felt, was that.

"Just how do you expect to prevent a grown woman from doing as she chooses? The fact is, Laura is very attracted to Michael, perhaps more than attracted. She's been lonely and unhappy, and now she isn't."

"He's taking advantage of that. He's a bad influence. Why, she didn't even come down and say good night to her guests. She's never shirked her duties that way."

"She was tired, Annie, and the Greenbelts are my and Tommy's friends. Which isn't the point at all, really. You can't worry yourself so about all of this."

"You're her mother, but you know I love her, just as you love my girl. When Margo had troubles, you worried yourself for her."

"Yes." Understanding, Susan laid a hand over Ann's. "They're our children, and that's as it's always been. But children grow and go their own way no matter how we worry. That's how it's always been, too."

"She'd listen to you, Mrs. T. I've been thinking on it." The words came out fast now and seemed so logical to her. "Miss Laura, she hasn't gone away with the girls for such a long time. She's been working hard and hasn't had a holiday. The spring vacation's coming up for Ali and Kayla. They could go away for a while. You know how the girls love to go to Disneyland. If you put the notion in Miss Laura's head, she'd take them.

And it would give her time, and distance. She'd have a clearer eye about what she's doing."

"I think Laura and the girls deserve a break, but a week in Disneyland isn't going to change her feelings for Michael, Annie."

"She's just caught up right now. If she had some time without him clouding her mind, she'd see that man for just what he is."

At a loss, Susan threw up her hands, let them slap down on the arms on her chair in a show of impatience. "For God's sake, Annie, what is he? Why do you dislike him so intensely?"

"He's a brute is what he is. A brute and a user and probably a fortune hunter as well. He'll hurt her in more ways than one, and I'm not having it." She pressed her lips tight together. "I'm not."

To clear her own temper, Susan took a long breath. "I want you to explain to me what he's done."

"You know very well that when he was no more than twelve he was sneaking around this house."

"He was Josh's friend."

"And giving Mister Josh stolen cigarettes, daring him into all manner of foolishness."

"Boys do foolish things at twelve. Christ, Annie, I taught my best friend how to smoke when we were fourteen. It's stupid, but it's children."

"And was it a child's foolishness that sent him to jail?"

"What's this?" Susan's face paled a bit. "Michael was in jail? How do you know?"

"I hear things. He was locked up for fighting. In a bar. Oh, they didn't keep him but overnight, but they locked him up right enough. The man likes to use his fists."

"Oh, for heaven's sakes, I thought he'd robbed a bank or killed someone. I may not approve, but I can't condemn a man for sleeping in a cell overnight because he punched someone in a bar. You don't even know who started it, or why, or—"

"How can you make excuses?" Suddenly furious, Ann sprang up. "How can you? The man is with your daughter night after night. He'll use them on her eventually. She'll do or say something and he'll use his fists on her the way he did on his own mother."

"What are you saying?" A jiggle of fear settled low in her stomach.

"A man who will strike his own mother, bloody her mouth and blacken her eye, won't think twice about doing the same to another woman. She's so small and delicate, Mrs. T. I can't bear the thought of what he could do to her."

"You believe Michael Fury beat his own mother?" Susan said slowly.

"She told me so herself. Came looking for him here with her poor face all black and blue. I took her into my room and did what I could for her, and she told me Michael had come home the night before, drunk, and had hurt her, had driven her husband off, then left her there alone. I wanted to go to the police, but she wouldn't have it."

She whirled away, emotions choking her. "Ah, he belonged in a cell. He belonged in a cage. If you had only seen her face. If that man raises a finger to Miss Laura, I—"

"Annie, I did see Michael's mother." Susan rose. "I did speak with her."

"Then you know. He ran off to sea just after that rather than face what he'd done. Mrs. T, we have to make him go away from here. We can't have a man who's capable of what he is near Miss Laura and her babies."

"I'll tell you what she told me, Annie, after she came to shout at me for keeping Michael here after that night."

"Here?" Ann had to press a hand to her outraged heart to keep it in place. "That man was here? You let him stay here in this house after—"

"He slept in the stables until he shipped out. He never laid a hand on that woman."

"You saw her. She told me—"

"She blamed him. She couldn't blame herself, not then. But I had the truth out of her. It was her husband who beat her, and who had done so before. She had come to work with black eyes before, and Michael didn't put them there."

"But she said—"

"I don't care what she said," Susan shouted. The memory of it still made her blood burn. A mother blaming a child for her own failings. "That boy came home and saw his stepfather beating his mother. And he protected her. The thanks he got for giving that beast what he deserved was having his own mother kick him out of the house, tell him he had no right to interfere, that he was to blame."

She stopped for a moment, struggled to calm herself. "And when Michael was gone, when she knew she'd lost him, she sat right here in this room and broke down. She told me everything."

"But she told me . . . I believed . . ." Ann sank down in a chair. "Oh, sweet God."

"She begged me to help her find him, to persuade him to come back. She was alone, you see, and Michael's mother was a woman who didn't know how to be alone. I want to believe that somewhere inside, she regretted what she'd done, what she'd said to him, and she loved him. But all

I saw was a miserable, selfish woman who was afraid to be without a man, even if the man was the son she'd driven away."

"Oh, Mrs. T." Ann pressed her hand against her mouth. The tears that swam in her eyes were tears of guilt and pity. "You're sure of this?"

"Annie, forget what she told you, even what I've just said, and tell me, honestly, what you see when you look at him. As if you knew nothing more about him than what you've seen since he came here."

"He works hard." She sniffled and tugged a tissue from her pocket. "He's good with children and his animals. He's kind to them. He's got the devil in his eye, and something hard comes into it. He doesn't watch his language as he should around the children, and I don't think . . ." She trailed off, wiped her eyes. "He's good to them. And he's been good for them. I can't deny it. And I'm ashamed."

"There's no shame in worrying over the ones you love. I'm sorry you were living with the fear that Laura had gotten herself involved with the kind of man you thought he was."

"I've hardly slept since he's been here. I kept waiting for him to— Oh, the poor boy. What a terrible thing to go through. And him barely old enough to shave regular."

"You'll sleep better now," Susan murmured.

"But I'm still keeping my eye on him." She managed a weak smile. "Men who look that way, they're not to be trusted around a woman."

"We'll both worry." Susan squeezed Annie's hand. "We know our Laura, don't we? She needs home, family, love. When everything else is brushed aside, that's what she is. I don't know if she'll find that with Michael, or what it will do to her if she doesn't."

SHE'D FOUND SOMETHING else. The thrill of streaking over the hills, of racing through low-lying fog that hugged the ground like a river. Of hearing the thunder of hooves and feeling the strong, sleek mount beneath her gather itself to jump.

She sailed over a fallen log and burst into a clearing where the sun flashed white.

"Oh, God, it's wonderful!" After reining in, she leaned low over the horse's neck. "I'll never be able to do without this again. You're a clever man, Michael Fury." She straightened and turned to study him as he sat easily on Max. "How could I buy a horse for myself and not buy that mare for Ali?"

"I'll give you a hell of a deal on three. The little bay gelding fits Kayla like a glove. You ride like a demon, Laura." He reached down to pat the neck of the mare Laura rode. "And Fancy here suits you. I figured she would."

"Apparently you know your horses, and your women."

His eyes flicked up to hers. His woman. For the moment. "Apparently. You look . . ." Stunning, vital. "Rested."

"I slept like the dead last night. Nearly ten hours." Trying her hand at flirting, she sent him a sidelong look under her lashes. "Did you miss me?"

He'd reached for her half a dozen times during the night. "Nah." When her face fell, he laughed. Grabbing her by the shirt, he tugged her sideways just enough to meet her lips. "What do you think?" He dismounted. "Let's give them a rest. We've been riding them hard."

He tossed the reins over a branch as she slid agilely to the ground. "Did you find any more coins yesterday?"

"Nothing. Not even a bottle cap. I can't— Oh, I didn't tell you, did I? The other night—"

"I heard." For reasons he couldn't pin down, it had annoyed him that she hadn't come running to him with her coin. "Good for you."

"It was the oddest thing." She stretched muscles unused to riding. "I put my hand right on it. Just the way you would if you'd dropped a quarter and reached down to . . ."

She blinked, lost her train of thought. He was standing there, just standing there with the sun at his back and his eyes focused on her face. "What is it?"

"You said you'd dreamed of me. Now, and years ago. On the cliffs, in your room, in the forest. You'd turn and I'd be there."

"Yes." Wasn't it foolish to have her heart lodged in her throat? To feel both fear and anticipation prickle hot on her skin. "Michael."

"And I'd touch you." He floated a palm over the curve of her breast, felt the quiver. There were parts of her life that were barred to him, parts of his that he would keep barred from her. But here . . . here was equal ground. "And taste you." Laid his mouth over hers, felt the heat. "And take you." Swept her into his arms, felt the ache. "And I will."

SHE LAY BESIDE him, naked in the sunlight, with birds singing in the trees. He hadn't torn her clothes. It amazed her that she wouldn't have stopped him from doing so even if she'd had to ride back to Templeton House bare as Lady Godiva.

Instead, he had been so gentle, so tender that even now she could have wept.

"I've never made love outside," she murmured. "I didn't know it could be so lovely." She sat up, stretched. "So many firsts. I don't suppose there are many firsts I can give you." She smiled down at him. "Bad Michael Fury's already done them all."

"And then some," he said with his eyes closed.

"There's so much you don't talk about." Knowing it was all too typical to pry into a man's past when you were in love didn't stop her. She traced a finger down his chest. "So many secrets inside."

"You told me a couple of yours last night. Quid pro quo?"

"No, of course not."

He opened his eyes. "You want to know something about me, ask."

She shook her head and started to shift, but he reached up and held her still. "Afraid of the answer?"

"No," she said steadily, "I'm not. And I'm surprised you'd think I would be."

"Fine. Ask."

"I—" she hesitated still, then gave in. "All right. You said you were married before, but you never mentioned her or what happened."

"Her name was Yvonne. We got divorced."

"All right." Miffed by the terse response, she reached for her shirt. "We should be getting back."

"Shit." He rubbed his hands over his face and sat up as she shrugged into the soft—and now wrinkled—broadcloth. "Okay, you want to know. I met her when I was racing. She liked to party with drivers."

"And you fell in love with her?"

"Christ, you're a child in so many ways." He stood and dragged on his jeans. "I fell into bed with her. We liked each other, we had good sex. So we kept falling into bed, and we kept having good sex. Then she got pregnant."

"Oh." She rose slowly and kept her eyes on her trousers as she slipped them on. "You said you didn't have children. I assumed—"

"Do you want to hear this or not?"

She looked up, surprised by the bitterness in his voice. "Not if you don't want to tell me."

"If I'd wanted to talk about it, I probably would have." He swore again, then took her arm as she bent to retrieve her boots. "Sit down. Just sit, goddamn it. Nobody uses that wounded look the way you do."

He pressed his fingers to his eyes and struggled for control. Once he'd opened up this part of his life, he would have to open others. She would ask more questions, he would give her the answers.

He accepted it there, in the sun-washed woods, with his body still warm from hers, that this was the beginning of the end.

"Okay, she got pregnant. So we talked about it. The best thing for everybody was to go for the abortion. Simple, quick, done. So we made the arrangements."

"I'm sorry. That's a difficult decision. You—you never questioned that you'd been the one who—"

"That I'd gotten her pregnant? Yvonne wasn't a liar or a cheat. She said the kid was mine, it was mine. We were friends, Laura."

"I'm sorry. It was hard for both of you."

"We figured we were doing the smart thing. I was trying to make a name for myself on the circuit, she had just started a new job. A baby didn't fit. Hell, neither of us knew anything about kids, about parenthood. We were what we were." He looked her in the eye. "Scrabblers, looking for a good time."

She kept her gaze level. "Are you telling me it was easy? A casual shrug. An oops?"

"No." His eyes shifted, stared off into the trees, into the shadows. "No, it wasn't easy. It just made sense. We agreed it was the best solution. But the night before we were to go in for it, we figured out something else. We both wanted it. We both wanted the baby. It didn't make any sense, we didn't know what we were doing, but we both wanted the baby."

"She didn't have the abortion."

"No. We got married. We figured what the hell, let's do it, let's have a baby. She tried to knit things." A smile ghosted around his mouth. "She didn't have a clue. We read books. Went in for one of those sonogram things. Jesus Christ, it was just . . . beautiful. We argued about names and did all the things I guess everybody does."

The smile went away and, she thought as she watched his eyes, so did he.

"Middle of the night, she was about four months along, she started bleeding, bad. She was in pain and scared. We were both so scared. I got her to the hospital, but it was already pretty much over by then. We lost the baby."

"I'm sorry." She rose again, but didn't touch him. "I'm so sorry, Michael. There's nothing more painful than losing a child."

"No, there's nothing. The doctors said she was young and healthy and we could try again in a little while. We pretended we would. Tried to keep it together. But we started fighting, sniping at each other. I'd slam out, leave her alone. She'd slam out, leave me alone. One night I came home and she was waiting for me. She'd figured it out before I had. She was a smart woman. We'd stopped being friends. All we'd had to keep us married was the baby, and the baby was gone. Now we were stuck, and we didn't have to be stuck. She was right. So we decided to start being friends again and stop being married. End of story."

She touched him now, took his face in her hands, felt the tension. "There's nothing I can say to ease that kind of grief, the kind you carry with you forever, no matter what."

He shut his eyes, let his brow rest on hers. "I wanted the baby."

"I know." She eased her arms around him. "You loved it already. I understand. I'm sorry, Michael." Gently, she stroked his back. "I'm sorry I made you tell me."

"It was almost ten years ago. It's done." He drew back, then swore at the tears on her cheek. "Don't do that. Hell, you should have asked me something else." Uneasy, he brushed the tears away. "Like about how I used to stunt double for Mel Gibson."

She sniffled, struggled to give him the smile he wanted. "Did you? Really?"

"You women always go for Mel. Maybe you should come down to Hollywood with me. I could introduce you." He twined a blond curl around his finger. "Me and Max, we have to go down tomorrow."

"Tomorrow?" She shook her head. "You're going to L.A.? You didn't mention it."

"Just got a call Saturday." With a shrug, he sat down to tug on his boots. "Action western with your pal Mel. He wants me and Max. So we got to do some meetings, some test shots. See if we can give them what they're looking for."

"That's wonderful. I'd think you'd be more excited."

"It's a job. I don't suppose you're interested in tagging along."

"I'd love to, but I can't leave the girls, and work. How—" How long will you be gone? She bit the question back. "They'll be so impressed when I tell them."

"I've got a guy coming in for a few days to see to the stock while I'm gone. I should be back by Friday."

"Oh." Only a few days. She smiled again. "If you are, I have this opening I have to go to on Friday night. Would you like to go?"

"An opening of what?"

"It's an exhibit at the art gallery. Expressionists."

To his credit, he didn't snort. "You want me to go look at paintings and make all sorts of idiotic comments on brushstrokes and underlying meanings." His cocked his head. "Do I look like a guy who's going to stand around sipping espresso and talking about the use of color on canvas?"

"No." He was sitting on a stump, bare to the waist, with faint purpling bruises on his ribs. His hair was wild and tousled. "No, you don't."

No more, he thought, than she looked like a woman who would toss aside responsibility and run off to L.A. with her lover for a week.

What the hell is she doing with me? he wondered as he rose. And to me? If this goes on much longer, what will we do to each other?

"We'd better get back." He shrugged into his shirt. "You don't want to keep Seraphina waiting."

"Michael." She laid a hand on his chest. "I'll miss you."

"Good." He lifted her into the saddle.

CHAPTER 19

HE WASN'T GONE a few days, but nearly two weeks. Laura reminded herself every night that he was under no obligation to call her, to tell her what was delaying him. Or just so that she could hear his voice.

She reminded herself that they had an adult relationship in which each party was free to come and go as he or she pleased. It was because she'd never had a relationship like it before, she told herself, that she was fretting. Worrying. Feeling hurt.

She certainly had plenty to keep her busy. And she had learned the hard way never to allow a man to be responsible for providing her with a fulfilling life. That was her job, one she intended never to neglect again.

With her work, her children, her family and friends, she had a full, contented life. Perhaps she wanted to share it with Michael and to be a part of his life, but she wasn't a lovestruck teenager who sat by the phone hour by hour waiting for it to ring.

Though she did try to will it to ring a time or two.

At the moment, though, she wasn't worried about the phone. She had other problems on her hands. Ali's spring dance recital would begin in less than two hours. Not only was no one ready but one of the kittens had coughed up a hairball in the middle of Kayla's bed, causing much dismay and more female disgust—and one of the barn cats had gone exploring, seducing Bongo into giving mad chase through the herb garden, which resulted in bad news for the chamomile and tansy and earned Bongo a bloody nose.

Nothing Laura did could lure the insulted, hissing cat down from the cypress tree where he had taken shelter. And Bongo continued to whimper pitifully under her bed.

Despite all of that, her biggest problem was Ali herself. The girl was moody, uncooperative, and whiny. Her hair was terrible, she claimed. Her stomach was upset. She didn't want to go to the recital. She hated recitals. She hated everything.

Her patience strained, Laura tried one more time to style Ali's hair to the child's specifications.

"Honey, if you're nervous about tonight, it's all right. You'll be wonderful. You always are."

"I'm not nervous." Ali pouted into the mirror. "I never get nervous before I dance. I just don't want to go."

"People are depending on you—your instructors, the other girls in your troupe. The family. You know how excited Grandma and Granddad were when they left for Uncle Josh's. Everyone's looking forward to tonight."

"I can't depend on anybody, can I? I have to do what I say I'll do, but nobody else does."

Around the circuit again, Laura thought. "I'm sorry you're disappointed your father won't be there. He's—"

"I don't care about him." In a bad-tempered move, Ali shrugged and scooted out from under her mother's hands. "He never comes anyway. It doesn't matter."

"Then what's the problem?"

"Nothing. I'll go. I'll do it because I keep my promises. My hair looks much better now," she said with dignity. "Thank you."

"Honey, if you'd—"

"I have to finish getting dressed." She pressed her lips together, a small girl, pretty in her tights and ballet skirt. "It's not your fault, Mama. I didn't mean it to sound that way. I'm not angry with you."

"Then what—"

"Mama!" Kaya's wail bounced down the hallway. "I can't find my red shoes. I want to wear my red ones."

"You can go help her," Ali said and tried to smile. "I'll be downstairs in a minute. Thanks for doing my hair over."

"It's all right." Because she could see the sorrow haunting Ali's eyes, she leaned down and kissed her on both cheeks. "I love playing with your hair. And I suppose if you wanted to put just a little of that lip gloss on, it would be all right."

"You mean before we go, not just for onstage?"

"Just for tonight." Laura tapped her fingers against Ali's lips. "You're not growing up on me any faster than I can help it."

"Maaamaaa, my shoes."

"And neither is she," Laura murmured. "I'm coming. Downstairs, Ali, ten minutes tops."

She found the shoes. Who would have expected to find them right there on the shoe shelf in the closet? After pulling a brush through her own hair, Laura herded her girls toward the door.

"Come on, troops, get a move on. This train leaves in five minutes. I'll get it, Annie," she called out when the doorbell rang. "Could you check on Bongo before you leave? He's under my bed and—"

She broke off as she pulled the door open and found Michael standing on the other side.

"Michael! You're home."

"It looks that way."

If she had leapt into his arms, right there in her own home, there in front of her children, he doubted he could have stuck with the decision he'd made. But she didn't. She only smiled at him, held out a hand.

It was Kayla who leapt. "Did you bring Max back?" With the simplicity of childhood, she hugged his waist and lifted her mouth for a kiss. "Did he come home too?"

"Sure. Max and I travel together. Where'd you get the red shoes, kid? Pretty snappy."

"Mama bought them. They're my favorites."

"You came."

Michael halted his admiring study of Kayla's red shoes and lifted his gaze to Ali's face. She looked, he thought, so much like her mother just then, with that stunned wonder on her face and the emotion swimming in her eyes.

"I told you I would."

"I thought you'd forgotten. I thought you were too busy."

"Forget an invitation from a beautiful ballerina to watch her dance?" He shook his head as he straightened. "Boy, that wouldn't say much about my memory." Head cocked, he held out the bouquet of pink baby roses. "We do have a date, right? You didn't go call some other guy to take my place?"

"No. Are these for me?" Mouth open in a litle O of confused delight, she stared at the roses. "For me?"

"Who else?"

"For me." She breathed it, taking the flowers in her hands. "Thank you. Mama, Michael brought me flowers."

"I see." And her eyes stung a bit. "They're lovely."

"We'll use the Waterford." Annie stood a few steps back in the hall, her hands folded, her eyes on Michael's face. "When a girl receives her first flowers from a man, they should be treated as something very special."

"I want to put them in the vase myself."

"And so you should. It will only take a moment, Miss Laura."

"Yes, all right. Thank you, Annie."

"I'll help." Kayla raced down the hall. "Let me smell them, Ali."

"Her first flowers," Laura murmured.

"Man, why do females always get wet-eyed over a bunch of posies?"

Which reminded him that he'd never given Laura flowers. Never real ones, just something plucked carelessly out of the ground. He'd never thought of it. Had never, he realized, given her anything but good, hot sex.

"Flowers are symbolic." And she remembered the pretty little wildflowers he'd given her. So sweet, so simple. So right.

"Everything is to women."

"You could be right." She turned back, beaming at him. "It was so thoughtful of you to bring them. And to come. I didn't realize she'd asked you. Had no idea she was counting on it."

"She asked me a couple of weeks ago." He dipped his hands in his pockets. Laura hadn't asked him, he remembered. Hadn't mentioned it. "I've managed to avoid ballet for thirty-four years. This ought to be an experience."

"I think you'll find it painless." She started toward him now, and he took his hand out of his pocket to take hers before she could touch him.

"So how are you?" he asked.

"Fine." Was he just tired, she wondered, or was this distance she felt? "Did things go well in L.A.?"

"Yeah, it went. They'll start shooting in about three weeks. We'll get a couple months' work out of it. Maybe more."

"You'll stay in L.A. during the filming," she said slowly as a weight sank in her stomach.

He shrugged. It wasn't the time to get into all of this, and he was spared when Ali marched back down the hall, bearing her vase of baby roses like a trophy.

"Don't they look beautiful, Mama? Annie's going to put them in my room."

"They're perfect. We really need to go. Performers have to be there thirty minutes before curtain."

"I'll take those now, sweetheart." Annie slipped the vase from Ali's hand. "And I'll be there to see you dance." She inclined her head toward Michael in what, from anyone else, he would have taken as a friendly smile. "We all will."

IT WASN'T IMPOSSIBLE to put everything out of his mind for a couple of hours. The kid was so cute. All of them were. But it was hard to sit beside Laura, in the middle of all those people—the families, the partners, the couples—and not be miserable.

But he'd had time, and he'd had the distance to allow himself to take a good hard look at what was going on. And what was happening to him. He'd fallen for her, all the way.

It would never work.

He'd seen himself in the dingy little bar in south L.A., drinking beer and swapping stories with wranglers. Going back to his hotel room after a long day, sweaty, dirty, smelling of horse. And he'd seen himself growing up in a house that had breathed neglect and violence and tension.

He'd seen himself for what he was. A man who had chased all the wrong things most of his life and had found plenty of them. A cliff rat, son of a waitress and a wastrel, who would in time and with effort be able to make a decent living.

And he'd seen Laura, the Templeton heiress, sitting in her plush country club drinking tea, dressed in her tidy suit, running a fancy boutique, strolling through a grand hotel that she owned.

He didn't doubt that he'd given her something. Or that under different circumstances, they could give each other more. But it would be only a matter of time before the haze of lust cleared from her eyes and she saw what she was doing. Having an affair with a horse trainer.

They were both better off that he'd seen it first. Knowing her, he doubted she would be able to break it off clean. She was too soft, too kind, to walk without guilt. Worse, she might continue the relationship long after she'd realized her mistake because of that sterling sense of obligation.

He was no good for her. He knew it. The people who knew both of them understood it. Eventually she would know it. And it would kill him.

Maybe if he hadn't run into that old buddy of his in L.A., the old merchant marine stevedore he'd shipped with, drunk with, raised hell with. One of the men who had gone to war with him for profit after the sea lost its lure.

But they had run into each other. And the stories were rehashed, the memories swam back. And for one harsh, illuminating moment, he had looked into the surly, bitter, used-up face of the man across from him. And had seen himself.

Michael Fury was a man he never wanted to touch Laura, a man he never wanted her to know. If such a man tried to touch her, to know her, she would cringe in shock.

Before either of them had to cope with that, he would do her a favor and slip out of her life.

As Ali twirled on stage, Laura laid a hand over his and squeezed. And broke his heart.

* * *

"DON'T THEY LOOK wonderful?" Margo murmured.

Beside her, Josh tapped his foot absently to the music and continued to watch his niece. "They're all great, but Ali's the best."

"Naturally." She chuckled a little, leaned closer to his ear. "But I was talking about Laura and Michael."

"Hmm?" Distracted, he shifted and glanced at the couple one row in front of them. "Laura and Michael what?"

"They're wonderful together."

"Yeah, I guess . . ." He trailed off, stunned as the meaning seeped in. "What do you mean 'together'?"

"Ssh." She shushed him, fighting back another laugh. "Together, together. What, are you blind?"

His throat went dry and tight. "They're not seeing each other. They're not dating."

"Dating." She had to clamp a hand over her mouth. "For God's sake, Josh, they've been sleeping together for weeks. How could you not know?"

"Sleeping—" Shock, rage, disbelief all slammed together against the words. "How the hell do you know that?"

"Because Laura told me," she hissed into his ear. "And because, if she hadn't, I have eyes in my head. Ssh," she ordered when he opened his mouth. "You're annoying people. And here's Ali's solo."

He shut his mouth, but not his mind. He had a great deal to think about. And as far as he was concerned, his old pal Michael Fury had a great deal to answer for.

THERE'D BEEN NOTHING he could do about it that night but go home and grill his wife. Then argue with her over the situation. Josh put her attitude down to female hormones. Women found Michael romantic—which had always been his good luck and was the crux of the current problem.

Josh found him in the paddock, working a yearling on the lounge line. "I need to talk to you, Fury."

Michael recognized the tone. Something was stuck in Josh's craw. He wasn't in the mood for it, not when he was still thinking about the baffled hurt on Laura's face the night before when he'd given her a quick pat on the head and told her he was beat.

In other words, I'm going to bed, sugar, and you're not invited.

Still, he released the yearling and walked to the fence where Josh waited. "So talk."

"Are you sleeping with my sister?"

Ah, well, the time had come. "We don't sleep much," Michael said easily and braced when Josh's hand whipped out and gripped his shirt. "Watch it, Harvard."

"What the fuck do you think you're doing? Who the hell do you think you are? I asked her to rent this place to you. Do you a favor, and you just jump right in."

"I didn't jump alone." Damned if he'd take the rap for that. "She's a big girl, Josh. I didn't lure her into the stables promising her candy. I didn't force her."

The idea of it curdled his blood, then shamed him. "You wouldn't have to," he shot back. "You forget who you're talking to. I know you, Mick. I know your style. Christ, we cruised together often enough."

"Yeah, we did." Eyes level, Michael pried Josh's fingers off his shirt. "But that was all right, the two of us going out sniffing out babes."

"This is my sister."

"I know who she is."

"If you knew, if you had any idea what she's been through the past few years, how easily bruised she is, you'd stay the hell away from her. The women you played with always knew the rules, went in for the game. That's not Laura."

"And because she's your sister, because she's a Templeton, she's not entitled to play." Bitterness rose like bile. "Certainly not with me."

"I trusted you," Josh said quietly. "I always trusted you. It's one thing for you to hit on Kate, and on Margo, but I'm damned if I'm going to stand back and watch you make it three for three."

His eyes went very cold, very hard. At his side his fist clenched, and in his mind he saw it strike out, fast. It took all of his will and a lifetime of friendship not to follow through.

"Get the fuck away from me. Now."

"You want to take a swing, you take one. We've gone around before."

Not like this, Michael thought as his system revved toward violence. Now they were men, and the stakes were higher. And if he had any family, any that really mattered, this was it, standing here right now, prepared to break his neck.

"Why don't we try this instead—I'll be out by the end of the week. I've already started making the arrangements."

Torn now between friendship and family, Josh narrowed his eyes. "What arrangements? You barely have your foundation up on the new construction."

"I'll probably sell it as is once I've relocated to L.A. Is that far enough away from your sister, Harvard? Or do I have to go to hell?"

"When did this come up?"

"Do I have to check that with you too? Go away, Josh. I'm busy here and you've made your point."

"I'm not sure I have." And as he watched his oldest friend walk away, Josh was no longer sure what the point was.

HE KNEW SHE would come. There was no way to avoid or prevent it. They hadn't been together in two weeks, and she would expect him to want her. Of course he did, pitifully.

But he wouldn't touch her. It was only worse now. He'd nearly talked himself out of his earlier decision, had told himself he could find a way to make it work between then. The visit from Josh had snapped things back into reality.

He would make it clean, he would make it quick.

She would be hurt, a little. There was no way to avoid or prevent that either. But she would get over it.

Still, though he'd known she would come, he hadn't expected her so soon, hadn't expected himself to be so unprepared when he saw her standing in his doorway with the sun in her hair and her eyes so pure, so gray, so warm.

"I took off from the shop a little early," she began. She knew she was talking quickly, bubbling over with nerves. Something was wrong. She could have been deaf and blind and still have sensed it. "I thought since my parents were taking the girls into Carmel for dinner, I'd see if you'd like me to fix yours."

"Women like you don't cook, sugar. They have cooks."

"You'd be surprised." She came in, not waiting for the invitation, and swung past him into the kitchen. "Mrs. Williamson taught us all, including Josh, at least the basics. I make an exceptional fettuccine Alfredo. I thought I'd see what you had before I brought over ingredients."

Seeing her poking around the kitchen as if she belonged there, as if he could come home after a hard day and find her cheerfully waiting for him, tore him apart. So his voice was cool and careless.

"I'm not much on fancy sauces, sugar."

"Well, we'll try something else." Why wouldn't he say her name? she wondered, fighting panic. He hadn't once said her name since he'd come home. She turned to him and couldn't prevent herself from leading with her heart. "Oh, I missed you, Michael. So much."

She was halfway across the room, reaching for him. He could all but feel the way her soft, delicate arms would wrap around his neck. He stepped back, lifted both hands to ward her off.

"I'm filthy. I haven't had a chance to jump in the shower. You wouldn't want to mess up a nice silk blouse."

Why should it matter? He'd once torn one off her. He hadn't held her in days. Yet he stood there now with—was it boredom in his eyes?

"What is it, Michael?" Her stomach jittered, echoed in her voice. "Are you angry with me?"

Deliberately he tilted his head. "Why do you do that? Why do you always assume that whatever's going on around you is your fault or your responsibility? That's a real problem you've got there," he added as he walked past her to get a beer out of the refrigerator.

He twisted off the top, drank deep. "Do I look mad to you?"

"No." She folded her hands, gathered her composure. "No, you don't. You look vaguely annoyed that I'm in your way. I assumed you'd want me to come, that you'd want to be with me tonight."

"It's a nice thought, but don't you think this has run its course?"

"This?"

"You and me, sugar. We've taken this about as far as it's going to go." He tipped the beer back again, wiped his mouth with the back of his hand. "Listen, you're a hell of a woman. I like you. I like your style, in bed and out. But we both know we've got to move on eventually."

She would breathe, she told herself. However tight the fist was around her heart, she would breathe, slow and easy. "I take that to mean you've decided to move on now."

"Some things came up when I was in L.A. Changed my plans. I like to be fair with a woman I've slept with, so I figured I should let you know I'm moving down there next week."

"You're moving to L.A.? But your house—"

"Never meant a damn to me." He jerked his shoulder. "Just a place. One's the same as the other."

One's the same as the other, she thought dully. One house. One woman. "Why did you come back at all?"

"I left my horses." He forced his lips into a grin.

"You went to Ali's recital. You brought her flowers."

"I told the kid I'd go. I don't make many promises, so I don't break the ones I do make." In this at least, he didn't have to improvise. "You've got terrific kids, Laura. I've liked getting to know them. And I wouldn't have let her down last night."

"If you go, they'll be devastated. They'll—"

"Get over it," he said, his voice roughening. "I'm just a guy who passed through."

"You can't believe that." She stepped toward him. "You can't believe you mean so little to them. They love you, Michael. I—"

"I'm not their father. Don't lay that guilt trip on me. I've got my own life to worry about."

"And that's it." She drew in another breath, but it wasn't slow, it wasn't easy. " 'See you around, it's been fun?' We meant nothing to you."

"Sure you did. Look, sugar, life's long. A lot of people walk through it. Both of us gave each other what we were looking for at the time."

"Just sex."

"Great sex." He smiled again. Then, because his reflexes were good, dodged by inches the bottle she picked up and heaved at him. Before he could recover from the shock of that, she was using her hands. Both of them shoved hard enough against his chest to knock him back two full steps. "Hey."

"How dare you! How dare you lower what we have, what I felt, to some animal urge? You son of a bitch, you think you can brush me off like an inconvenient speck of lint, then walk away?"

A lamp went next, and he could only watch, speechless, and duck, fast, when she threw whatever came to her hand at his head.

"You didn't think I'd cause a scene, did you?" She picked up an end table, toppled it. "Wrong. Finished with me, are you? Just like that." She snapped her fingers under his nose. "And I'm supposed to meekly walk away, sob into my pillow and say nothing?"

He backed up. "Something like that." So it wasn't going to be quick and clean, he decided, but messy. Nonetheless, it had to be done. "Break the place up if it makes you feel better. It's your stuff. I expect even royalty has to have its tantrums."

"Don't you speak to me that way, as if I were some interesting toy that's suddenly run amok. You came into my life, you exploded into my life and changed everything. Now you're just finished?"

"We've got nothing here and we both know it. It's just one of those times I saw it first."

She snatched up a bowl and sent it crashing through his kitchen window. Another time he might have been impressed with the force and velocity. And her aim. But at the moment he could only suffer.

"I ain't paying for the damages, sugar. And I never made you any promises, told you any lies. You knew yourself what you were getting when you came looking for me. You wanted me to take the choice out of your hands. You wanted me to take you so you wouldn't have to say it. That's fact."

"I didn't know how to say it," she shot at him.

"Well, I did, and that was fine with both of us. You haven't got a choice here either. It's just done."

Her breath was heaving, shuddering as she tried to calm it. Temper— her temper—she knew, was horrible when unlocked. And when the key was turned with pain, so much the worse. "That's cruel, and it's cold."

Where the temper had missed its mark, the quiet words arrowed straight into his heart. "That's life."

"Just done." She let the tears come, they hardly mattered. "So that's how this sort of thing is accomplished. You say it's just done, and it is. So much less complicated than divorce, which is the only way I've ended a relationship."

"I didn't cheat on you." He couldn't bear having her think that of him, or herself. "I never thought of another woman when I was with you. This has nothing to do with you. I've just got places to go."

"Nothing to do with me." She closed her eyes. The temper was gone now, quickly as always. Drained to exhaustion. "I never would have said you were a stupid man, Michael, or a shallow one. But if you can say that, you're both."

She lifted her hands, rubbed away the tears. She wanted to see him clearly, since it would be the last time. He was rough, wild, moody. He was, she thought, everything.

"I wonder that you don't even know what you're throwing away, what I would have given you. What you could have had with me, and Ali and Kayla."

"They're your kids." This was another hurt, just as deep, just as bloody. "Templetons. You wouldn't have given them to me."

"You're wrong, pathetically wrong. I already had." She walked to the door, opened it. "You do what you have to do and go where you have to go. But don't ever think it was just sex for me. I loved you. And the only thing more pitiful than that is that even as you turn me away like this, so carelessly, I still do."

CHAPTER 20

MICHAEL TOOK A step forward, then stopped himself. She didn't know what she was saying. Couldn't know.

He forced himself to step back from the door, then turned and watched her walk away across the lawn. Continued to watch when she changed directions, broke into a run.

She'd go to the cliffs, he realized. She was angry and hurt, so she would go to the cliffs to finish crying. When she was finished she would think. She would stay angry and hurt for a while, and hate him longer than that, but he knew that eventually she would see it was for the best.

She wasn't in love with him. He scrubbed his hands over his face. It already felt raw and battered. Maybe she thought she was, or had talked herself into it, he decided. It was a knee-jerk female reaction, that was all. It fit a woman like Laura—sex and love, need and emotion. She wasn't seeing the big picture.

But he could.

Men who had lived as he had lived didn't end up happy ever after with women of her class, her breeding. Sooner or later she'd have come to the same conclusion, found herself drawn back to the country club style. Maybe she would never forgive him for seeing it first, but that couldn't be helped.

It would kill him to be with her and wait. To know that when the passion had dimmed she would still stay with him. She'd be kind. She couldn't be otherwise. But he would know when he had become just another obligation.

He was doing them both a favor by getting out of her life.

Josh was right. And no one knew him better.

But he continued to stand, staring out at the cliffs and the lone figure who stood there twisting the knife in his own heart. Finally he turned away and left the room that was as disrupted as his life to go down to his horses.

SHE HADN'T KNOWN how completely a heart could shatter. She'd thought she knew. When her marriage had ended, Laura had been certain she would never grieve in quite the same way again.

She'd been right, she thought now and pressed both hands to the ache in her heart. This was different. This was worse.

Her feelings for Peter had eroded so slowly over the years that there had barely been any left by the time it was over. But this . . . she squeezed her eyes tight, and though the air was still and warm, she shuddered.

She'd never loved anyone the way she loved Michael. Wildly, outrageously. Brutally. And all those feelings were so fresh. So bright and new. She had treasured them. She'd treasured discovering that she could feel again, realizing she could want and be wanted as a woman. She'd admired what he was, what he'd made himself, and she had fallen as much in love with the rough and dangerous man as the kind and gentle one within.

Now he wanted it over, and there was nothing she could do. Crying didn't help, and her tears were already dry. Temper changed nothing, and she was already ashamed of the way she had snapped in front of him. He'd think her pitiful now, but that couldn't be helped either.

She stepped closer to the edge to watch the waves beat against rock. She felt that way, she mused. Battered by forces that were beyond her control, trapped in a violent, endless war with no choice but to stand.

It didn't help, it simply didn't help, to tell herself she wasn't alone. That she had her family, her children, her home, her work. Because she felt alone, completely alone, there on the edge of the world with only the thunder of the sea for company.

Even the birds were gone. No gulls cried today, none wheeled white toward the hard blue sky or dipped toward the spewing waves. She could see nothing but the rolling of the endless sea.

How could she accept it that she would never love this way again? Why was she expected to go on, to do everything that needed to be done, alone, always alone, and know that she would never turn in the night and find someone there who loved her?

Why had she been given this glimpse into what she could have and feel and want if it was only going to be taken away? And why was the one thing she had dreamed of all of her life always, always, just out of her reach?

She imagined that this was what Seraphina had felt as she stood here so many years before grieving the loss of her lover. Laura looked down, pictured that dizzying, somehow liberating plunge into space and the fierce, furious heart that had taken it.

Had she screamed as the rocks rushed up, Laura wondered, or had she strained to meet them?

Trembling, Laura took a step back. Seraphina had found nothing but an end, she thought, a horribly easy end to pain. Her own wouldn't be easy, because she would have to live with it. Live without Michael. And finally accept that she would live without her dream.

She barely noticed the rumble, took it at first for the sea's thrashing. The ground seemed to jitter under her feet. Blank for a moment, she stared down, watched pebbles dance. Then the roar filled her ears, and she knew.

Panicked, she tried to stumble back, away from the edge. The ground rolled, unbalancing her as she grabbed frantically for a rock. The wave of earth lifted her up and pushed her hard over the rim of the world.

THE HORSES SENSED it first. Eyes wheeling white, panicked whinnies. Michael reached up to calm the mare he was grooming. Then he felt it. The ground shuddered under him. He swore as the noise grew and horses plunged. Above his head came the sound of crashing glass, straining wood.

The freight train roar deafened him as he fought to keep his balance. Tack leapt off the walls and fell jangling on the shuddering brick.

He yanked stall doors open, focused on getting his horses out. In the wild confusion of the moment, one thought pierced like a lance.

Laura. My God. Laura.

He stumbled forward, fighting free when the earth tried to heave him back. He raced into the brilliant sunlight, ignoring the violent undulations of the tidy green lawn. When he was knocked flat, he clawed his way back up, skidded down the slope. No one would have heard him screaming her name as he ran toward the cliffs. He didn't hear it himself.

It lasted no more than two minutes, that stretch and shift of the earth. All was still, preternaturally still, when he reached the cliffs.

She'd gone home, he told himself. She'd gone back to the house, was safe, secure. A little shaken perhaps, but a native Californian didn't panic at every trembler. He'd go check on things himself as soon as he . . . as soon as he made sure.

When he looked over the edge and saw her, his legs buckled. On a ledge fifteen feet below, inches away from oblivion, she lay white as death. One of her arms was flung out so that her hand dangled over that narrow bed of rock into space.

He wouldn't remember the climb down to her, the sharp bite of rock into his hands, the small, nasty avalanches of dirt and pebbles where his feet slid, the stinging slices as roots and rock tore viciously at his clothes and flesh.

Blind terror and instinct took him down fast where a single misstep, one incautious grip, would have sent him plunging. Cold sweat dripped into his eyes, skidded along his skin. He thought—was sure—she was dead.

But when he reached her he fought back the panic and fear and placed a trembling finger on the pulse in her throat. And it beat.

"Okay, okay." His hands trembled still as he brushed the hair from her cheeks. "It's all right, you're all right." He wanted to drag her up, hold her, rock her to him until this greasy sickness in his gut passed.

He knew better than to move her, even with thoughts of aftershocks spinning in his head. He knew he had to check the extent of her injuries before he risked shifting her.

Concussion, broken bones, internal injuries. Christ, paralysis. He couldn't get his breath and had to squeeze his eyes shut for a moment and force air in and out until he was calm. He made himself move slowly, carefully. Lifting her eyelids to check the pupils, gently moving his hands over her head, gritting his teeth at the blood that smeared on his fingers.

Her shoulder—she'd dislocated it, he realized as he probed. It would be screamingly painful when she woke. Dear God, he wanted her to open her eyes. His breath came fast and harsh as he continued to check her. No breaks—a lot of bruises and some bad cuts and scrapes, but nothing was broken.

He agonized over her back and neck, knew he had to leave her to call for an ambulance. And the thought of leaving her alone there on that ledge, knowing that if she woke it would be to terror and pain, ripped him.

"It's going to be all right." He took her hand, squeezed gently. "Trust me. I won't be long. I'll be back."

When her fingers flexed in his, relief burned through him in cold fire.

"Laura, can you hear me? Don't move, baby. Open your eyes if you can hear me, but I don't want you to move."

Her world was white and thick and cold, so cold. Then there were shadows, shifting, receding, voices whispering under a brilliant roar. Then his face, close to hers, dark eyes so blue they burned.

"Michael?"

"Yeah." He had to swallow, couldn't. Fear had dried up every bit of the saliva in his mouth. "Yeah. You're going to be all right. You just took a little fall. I want you to—"

"Michael," she said again, then her white world flashed red. Pain sliced through her, long, ragged blades of it that had her crying out, rearing against his hands.

"Stop. I know it hurts, but I don't know how bad it is. You have to lie still. Lie still." But the way she'd already twisted terrified him. "Look at me. Look at me. Tell me if you can feel this."

He put a hand on her thigh, pressed. When she nodded, he pressed her other leg. "Move your feet for me, Laura. Okay, good." Part of his throat opened again when he saw her feet move and flex. "You're a little banged up, that's all." And in shock, he noted, studying her pupils. And in pain. "I'm going to get you up."

"My shoulder." She tried to reach for it, fought off a wave of nausea. Black and boiling nausea. The pain was unspeakable, and even breathing threatened to make her retch. "Did I break it?"

"No, just knocked it out of joint." His hands were clammy when he closed them over hers. Blood oozed from a dozen gashes he didn't even feel. "Done it myself a couple times. Hurts like hell. I'm going to be right back, okay? Just a couple minutes."

"No, don't—" The wrenching pain slammed into her. She tried to move away, escape it. Sweat pearled on her face and her eyes went glassy.

"Okay, hold on." He couldn't leave her like this, in shock and pain. Simply couldn't leave her here, suffering. He could fix it—though the thought of what it would take out of both of them churned like acid in his stomach. "I can pop it back in. I'll hurt you, but it'll give you relief. You're better off with a doctor, though. Just hanging on until I can get—"

"Please." She closed her eyes. Agony was an icy white knife digging into muscle and bone. "I can't think. I can't think over it."

He shifted, braced himself beside her. He wiped a hand over his mouth, smearing blood. "Don't think. I want you to scream. Let out one long, loud scream."

"What?"

"Scream, goddamn it." He held her down with one hand, took a firm grip on her arm, hissing when her eyes opened wide and stared into his. "Now."

She felt the jerk, the sick roll of it echoing in her stomach. And white again, white-hot. Then nothing.

His hands were slick with sweat and blood, slippery enough that he nearly lost hold. His stomach churned as he watched her eyes roll back, felt her go limp under him. Gritting his teeth, he snapped the joint into place. Then his breath whooshed out and he lowered his brow to hers.

"Oh, baby, I'm sorry. I'm sorry." He did lift her now, cradling her in his arms, rocking them both. He lost track—ten seconds, ten minutes, he had no sense of time passing until she stirred again.

"It's all done, don't worry." He pressed his lips to her hair, buried his face there until he managed a greasy grip on control. "It's better now."

"Yes." She was floating. Pain was everywhere, but it was dull now, throbbing almost gently in her limbs. "It's better. I can't remember—what happened? An earthquake?"

"It knocked you off, onto the ledge." Gently, he checked her head. The bleeding had stopped, but he worried over the lump and the broken skin. "You're going to have some champion bruises."

"Knocked me off—my God." She turned her face into his chest, shivered. Off the cliff, nearly into the sea, she thought. Onto the rocks below. Like Seraphina. "How bad? The house—the horses? Oh, Michael, the girls."

"It's fine. Everything's fine. It wasn't a big one. I don't want you to worry." He'd do that for both of them.

Now that he was calmer, he was taking stock. The quake had shifted rock and earth. There was nothing left of the rough path leading back up. He'd have to leave her, climb back up and get ropes.

"Let me look at you." He studied her face. Too pale, he thought, and her pupils were still dilated. "How's your vision? Blurry?"

"No, it's fine. I have to see if the girls are all right."

"They're fine. They're with your parents, remember? In Carmel." She was lucid, he told himself. Her pulse was rapid but strong. "How many fingers?"

"Two," she said and gripped the hand he'd held up. "Annie, the house—"

"I said everything's fine. Trust me."

"All right." She closed her eyes again and let herself float. "I fell off the cliff."

"That's about it." He pressed her hand to his lips, held it there until he could speak again. "Now, listen—I'm going to have to leave you here for a couple minutes. Then I'm coming back and I'll get you up."

"You have to leave me."

"You can't make the climb. I want you to lie right here, stay still. Promise me. Laura, open your eyes and look at me. Promise me you won't move until I come back."

She looked at him. "I won't move until you get back. It's cold."

"Here." He stripped off his denim jacket, laid it over her. "That'll help a little. Just relax now. Relax and wait for me."

"I'll wait for you," she murmured.

The world seemed to revolve in slow motion. She watched him rise, turn. Confused, she saw him scale the cliff, his hands and feet finding purchase, showering down little cascades of dirt. She smiled dreamily, thinking he looked like a hero scaling castle walls.

Was he saving her from the tower? Climbing up, so high, to kiss her awake? No, no, he was leaving her, she remembered. He was leaving her, she thought dully, and watched, too buffered by shock to feel alarm as he slid five full feet down the cliff face. She watched as he swung a hand up, dug in with bare fingers, and fought his way up the rough, unforgiving wall.

He was going away, she thought, but he would come back for her. He'd come back, then he would leave again.

When he reached the top, he stared down at her. His eyes seemed oddly close again, as if she could reach up and touch his face. Then he was gone, and she was alone.

He'd left her. He didn't want to be part of her life any longer. Or to allow her to be part of his. He would come back, she didn't doubt that he would come back and do as he'd promised. But she would still be alone.

And she would survive, Laura thought. Because there really was no other choice. She hadn't leapt from the cliff. She hadn't tossed her life aside. Fate had pushed her, but she would survive that as well. And go on.

Poor Seraphina. Drifting a little, Laura turned her head. She hadn't fought for life, hadn't survived. And had lost all of her dreams.

A tear trickled down her cheek, in sympathy, in sorrow, and as she turned to brush it away, her gaze fell on the small, dark hole in the wall of the cliff.

A cave? she thought hazily. There was no cave on this ledge. The rocks had moved, she realized, and sighed a little. Everything had moved. She inched her way toward the opening. A secret place, she thought. A hiding place. A lovers' place. She was smiling as she pushed herself up, sat, smelled—surely she smelled the faint scent of a young girl's perfume.

"Seraphina," she murmured even as she reached her hand inside the opening and laid it on the polished wood of a chest. "I've found you. Poor Seraphina, lost for so long."

She continued to speak, and if the words were incoherent, there was no one to hear. She knelt, waited for her head to stop spinning, and tried to drag the chest into the light.

"Laura, goddamn it."

Her smile soft, her eyes vague, she lifted her face and saw him atop the cliff. "Seraphina. We've found her. Michael, come and see."

"Stay put. Stay just where you are."

It was the hit on the head, he thought, and worked rapidly to secure the rope to the horn of Max's saddle. She was disoriented, confused. His heart drummed in his throat at the idea that she might try to stand. She might fall before he could get back to her.

"Hold steady," he ordered Max, then played out the rope. He went over the edge with more speed than caution, the rope burning his wounded hands and the cliff striking out to punish him.

His ankles sang when he landed, and his breath came fast. But he had her again, hard against him. Safe.

"You promised not to move."

"Seraphina. In the cave. I can't get it by myself. It's too heavy. I need Margo and Kate."

"In a minute. Let's get this on you." Working fast, he looped the rope around her. "You're not going to have to do anything but hold on to me. Max and I will get you up."

"All right." She didn't question it. It was all so simple, after all. "Could you get it out for me? Just out here in the light. It's been in the dark so long."

"Sure. Now I'm going to lift you up. You look at me, nothing but me."

"I will—but the chest."

"What chest?"

"In the cave."

"Don't worry about it. I'll—" But he glanced over at the gesture of her hand. And saw the dull gleam of brass against wood, the shadow of shape. "Jesus Christ!"

"Seraphina's dowry. Would you pull it out into the light?"

It was small, no more than two feet long, a domed box of cedar fitted with brass hinges. And no more than twenty pounds, he judged as he hefted it out. A simple box, uncarved, yet he could have sworn he felt something as his hands closed over it. Heat where there should have been none, a faint vibration that tickled his fingertips. It lasted only a moment, no more than two heartbeats, then it was just a small chest fashioned out of smooth wood and brass.

"All of her dreams locked away," Laura said softly. "All locked away because the one she wanted most was over."

"The quake shifted the rocks." Frowning, Michael studied the cave, cut so neatly in the wall. "I'd say another one some time ago covered it up."

"She wanted us to find it. She's been leading us here all our lives."

"Now you have it." However intriguing the find, he had priorities. "I want you to put your arms around my neck and hold on. Can you do that? How's the shoulder?"

"It's sore, but I can manage. How are we going to—"

"Let me worry about it." He helped her to her feet, kept himself between her and the edge. "Just keep looking at me," he continued, pulling her arms up until they linked around him. It's a good strong rope. You've got nothing to worry about."

"Did you climb up the cliff? I thought I saw you climbing up."

"Nothing to it," he said, aware that her mind was drifting. "Fell off a few, too, on film." He continued to talk as he tested the rope. "Hold tight now, we're going up. Max! Back. Back." The rope went taut. With one arm firmly around Laura's waist, Michael let his feet leave the ground and put himself in the walker's hands.

Rocks scraped painfully against his back. He used his heels to aid the ascent while sweat ran down his face and the muscles of his arms screamed.

"Almost there," he told her.

"We didn't get Seraphina. We have to get her."

"I'll go back and get her. Just hold on. Look at me."

She snapped back into focus, stared into his eyes. "You came back for me."

"Sure. Hold on." For an instant his heart stopped. They were inches from the edge, dangling between sky and sea. If any one of them faltered, they would lose. "Reach up. Just one hand now. Reach up, Laura, and grab hold."

She did as he asked, watched her own hand grip the edge of rock and dirt, slip away, grip again.

"That's it! Pull."

Ignoring his tortured muscles, he levered her up, dragging himself behind her as his horse strained to pull them the last foot. Michael bellied up to level ground, then simply lay there, his body sheltering hers, his face buried in her hair.

"Laura. God. Laura."

His mouth sought hers, and for a moment he sank out of terror and into oblivion.

"We'll get you home. We'll get you home now." He drew back. "Pain?"

"My head. It's all right."

"Lie still, let me take care of you." He released the rope, let it dangle and gathered her into his arms.

"Max?"

"He'll come. Don't worry, he'll come." He carried her away from the cliffs and up the long slope to Templeton House, with Max following placidly behind.

His legs didn't begin to shake until Ann burst out of the front door.

"Oh, sweet Lord, I've been looking for her everywhere. What happened? My poor lamb."

"She took a fall." He continued moving through Ann's fluttering hands. "She needs to get inside."

"In the parlor." Sprinting ahead, Ann called desperately up the stairs. "Mrs. Williamson, Jenny! I've found her." Then, to Michael, "How bad is she? Everyone's on the way. I called when I couldn't find her. Lay her down here on the sofa and let me see. Oh, sweetheart, your head."

"What in the world—" Mrs. Williamson stopped, out of breath, in the doorway.

"She's had a fall," Ann snapped out. "We need hot water, bandages."

"I fell off the cliff," Laura said as her head settled back into place.

"Oh, my dear God. Where does it hurt? Let me look at you."

She broke off when she heard the sound of cars speeding up the drive, doors slamming. "Everyone's here." Ann pressed a kiss to Laura's brow. "Everything's all right now."

Susan burst through the doorway first, stopped, braced herself as her heart tilted. "Well," she managed calmly enough, "what's all this?"

"I fell off a cliff," Laura told her. "Michael got me up. I hit my head."

That was all she got out before the room filled with people and hands that wanted to touch and voices that babbled questions.

"Quiet." Thomas took his daughter's hand, shot the order out to the group at large. "Josh, call the doctor, tell him we're bringing Laura in—"

"No." Rousing herself, Laura sat up and patted Kayla's head as her daughter laid it in her mother's lap. "I don't need the doctor. I've just hit my head."

"It's a nasty bump," Mrs. Williamson tutted as she continued to clean the blood and dirt from Laura's head. "Wouldn't be surprised if you have a concussion here, little girl. Michael?"

He didn't notice all the eyes that focused on him. All he could do was stare down at Laura. "I don't know how long she was out. Five, six minutes. But she's been lucid, her vision's not blurred. There's nothing broken." He wiped a hand over his mouth. "She had a dislocated shoulder. She probably fell on her left side. It'll be sore, but she's got good rotation."

"I don't want to go to the hospital. The ER will be packed with people after a tremor. I don't want to be one of them. I need to be home."

"Then you should stay home." Margo crouched beside her. "We can take care of you. You gave us a scare."

"Gave myself one." Murmuring, she wrapped her arm around Ali as the girl burrowed into her side. "I'm fine. Just a few bumps and bruises. It was quite an adventure."

"Try scuba diving the next time you want an adventure." Reaching over the back of the couch, Kate laid a hand on Laura's shoulder. "My heart can't take this."

"We found Seraphina's dowry."

"What?" Kate's fingers gripped. "What?"

"It's there, on the ledge where I fell. There was a cave, and it was there. Wasn't it, Michael? I didn't imagine it, did I?"

"It's there. I'll get it for you."

"You'll be getting nothing," Mrs. Williamson said, lifting her voice over the fresh spurt of questions. "Sit down before you fall down, boy, and let me see to your hands. You've made a fine mess of yourself."

"Oh, good Lord." Focusing on someone other than her daughter for the first time, Susan snagged Michael's wrist. His hands were coated with dirt and blood, the knuckles mangled. "You've cut them to pieces." Her eyes lifted to his, swam, overflowed as she realized what he'd done. "Michael."

"They're fine. I'm fine." He jerked away. Abruptly, he couldn't breathe, wasn't certain how much longer he could stand. "I've got to see to my horses."

When he staggered out, Susan took a step after him. "Mom." Josh put a hand on her arm. "Let me. Please."

"Bring him back here, Josh. He needs tending to."

"He won't come," Josh said to himself as he went after his friend. "Michael." He hurried across the terrace, over the yard, feeling like a fool for chasing a man who walked like a drunk beside a clopping horse. "God-damn it, Michael, wait." He caught Michael by the shoulder, spun him around, and stepped back involuntarily at the molten fury that spurted out.

"Get away from me. I'm done here."

"I'm not. You listen—"

"Don't fuck with me now." Ignoring the pain in his hands, Michael shoved Josh back. "I'm in the mood to hurt somebody, and it might as well be you."

"Fine. Take a shot. The shape you're in, I could blow on you and knock you down. You idiot, you stupid son of a bitch, why didn't you tell me you were in love with her?"

"What the hell difference does it make?"

"Only all. You stood there and let me dump a pile of shit on you and did nothing. All you had to do was open your mouth and say it. I thought you were using her."

"I did use her, didn't I? I used her, then I tossed her aside just like you said I would. Ask her."

"I know what it's like to be in love with a woman and be scared boneless you won't make it work. And I know what it's like to want it so much you screw it up. Now I know what it's like to be a part of making two people I care about miserable. And I don't like it."

"This isn't about you. I'd figured out it was time to move on before you had your say. I've got other plans. I've got things . . ."

He trailed off, turned to press his face into Max's warm throat. "I thought she was dead." His shoulders shuddered, and he didn't have the will or the energy to shrug off Josh's hand. "I looked down and saw her ly-ing there and thought she was dead. I can't remember anything else until I was down there and put my hand on her throat. Felt her pulse beating."

"She's going to be all right. Both of you are."

"She wouldn't have been down there if I hadn't told her it was done. If I hadn't hurt her." He drew back, rubbed his hands over his face, smearing blood. "She's being taken care of, so that's fine. I've got no place here."

"You're wrong. No one's shutting you out but you. Christ, Mick, you're a mess." He took a good look at the battered hands, the torn and bloody clothes. He didn't want to think, quite yet, of how close his sister and his friend had come to dying. "Come back inside, let Mrs. Williamson fuss over you. You look like you could use a drink, too."

"I'll get one when I'm done."

"Done with what?"

"I told her I'd get the damn chest, didn't I? I'm going to get it."

Josh opened his mouth as Michael started away again. Arguments, he decided, were fruitless. "Hold up. I'll get Byron. We'll do it together."

CHAPTER 21

AN HOUR LATER, dirty and a little sore, Josh and Byron brought the small chest into the parlor. There'd been a couple of dicey moments during an aftershock when the three of them had been caught crouching on the ledge, wondering if they'd lost their minds. Fortunately it had passed, and now the chest, still unopened, sat on the coffee table. Waiting.

"I can't believe it," Margo murmured. She brushed the wood with her fingertips. "It's real. After all this time." She smiled over at Laura. "You found it."

"We found it," she corrected. "We were always meant to." Her head throbbed dully as she reached for Kate's hand. "Where's Michael?"

"He didn't—" Josh bit back an oath. "He needed to check on his horses."

"I'll get him for you," Byron offered.

"No." It was his choice, Laura reminded herself. And her life had to continue. "It's so small, isn't it?" she mused. "So simply made. I suppose all of us had imagined something huge and ornate and extraordinary, but it's just a plain, serviceable chest. The kind that lasts." She took a deep breath. "Ready?"

With Margo and Kate beside her, she put a hand on the latch. It opened easily, soundlessly, the interior releasing a scent of lavender and cedar.

Inside were a young girl's treasures, and dreams. A rosary fashioned from lapis with a heavy silver crucifix. A brooch of garnets, rose petals drying to dust. Gold, yes, there was gold, glinting as it was poured out of a leather pouch.

But there were linens, meticulously embroidered and carefully folded. Handkerchiefs with lacy edges turning yellow. An amber necklace, a ring crafted to fit a small finger and studded with little ruby stones that glistened like new blood. Pretty pieces of jewelry that suited a young woman not yet married and a locket that held a curl of dark hair bound by gold thread.

Tucked in with them was a small book with a red leather cover. Inside was the careful convent-school writing of a well-bred woman: "We met on the cliffs today, early, when there was still dew on the grass and the sun was rising slowly from the sea. Felipe told me he loved me, and my heart was brighter than the dawn."

Laura rested her head against Margo's shoulder. "Her diary," she murmured. "She put her diary in with her treasures, locked away. Poor girl."

"I always thought I'd feel thrilled when we found it." Kate reached into the box, stroked a finger over the amber beads. "I just feel sad. She hid away everything that was important to her in this little box and left it behind."

"You shouldn't feel sad." Laura laid the open diary on her lap. "She wanted us to find it and to open it again. I like to think it had to wait until all three of us faced something we thought we couldn't face. But we did. We have."

She reached out, took each of their hands in hers. "And we should put these in the shop, in a special case."

"We couldn't sell any of it," Margo murmured. "We couldn't sell Seraphina's treasures."

"No, not to sell." Laura smiled at the simple box. "To let other people dream."

MICHAEL LEFT THE rubble of his living room just as it was. He was going to stand in the shower and drown out the aches and pains. After he'd had a drink. In fact, now that he thought of it, getting piss-faced drunk was probably a much happier way to drown out the pain.

He bypassed beer and took out a bottle of Jameson's. As he poured a tumbler half full, he ignored the insistent knocking on his door.

"Go the fuck away," he muttered and took one long swallow. It did little to improve his mood when Ann Sullivan pushed open his door.

"Well, I see you're already drowning your sorrows in the middle of this chaos." She set down a box on the counter and frowned at the destruction. "I wouldn't have thought there'd be this much damage. We lost only a few breakables at the main house."

"Laura did most of it." He lifted his glass again as Ann pursed her lips.

"Did she? It's rare for her to let her temper loose, but a wicked one it can be. Well, sit down, we'll tend to you before we clean up the mess."

•

"I don't want to clean it up, and I don't want to be tended to. Go away."

She merely reached into the box and took out a covered plate. "Mrs. Williamson sent you food. I asked her to let me come instead. She's worried about you."

"Nothing to worry about." He studied his hands. "I've had worse."

"I've no doubt, but you'll sit down and let me clean those cuts." She set a basin, bottles, bandages on the counter.

"I can take care of myself." He lifted the glass, peered at the level of whiskey. "I've already made a start."

In her no-nonsense style, Ann came around the counter and shoved him into a chair. "Sit when you're told."

"Shit." He rubbed his shoulder where she'd pushed. It burned like fire.

"And keep a civil tongue in your head." She busied herself filling the basin with hot water. "Got infection brewing already, I've no doubt. The sense of a bean is what you've got." She snatched one of his hands and got to work.

"If you're going to play Nurse Nancy, at least—goddamn, that hurts."

"I imagine. Don't you swear at me, Michael Fury." Her eyes stung when she saw just how badly he'd damaged his hands, but her movements remained brisk and not particularly sympathetic. "This'll bite some."

The burn of the antiseptic that she generously poured over open wounds made his eyes cross and filled the air with wild blue curses.

"You've a raw Irish tongue. Reminds me of my uncle Shamus. What part does your family come from?"

"Galway. Goddamn it, why don't you just use battery acid and be done with it?"

"Big, strong man like you, whining over a little peroxide and alcohol. Take another drink, then, as I haven't a bullet for you to bite on."

It scored his pride, as she'd meant it to. Michael tipped back the glass and scowled at her. He decided to brood while she wrapped gauze over his hands.

"Done?" he demanded.

"With those, for the time being. You'll want to keep the bandages dry and they'll need to be changed regular since I assume you'll be as stubborn as Miss Laura about a doctor."

"Don't need a doctor." He jerked his shoulder but regretted it when it throbbed. "She'll be fine, too. She's got enough people hovering over her."

"She inspires love and loyalty because she's generous with giving both." Rising, Ann emptied the basin, refilled it. "Take off what's left of your shirt."

He cocked a brow. "Well, Annie, I'm a little impaired, but if I'd known you had an urge to— Ow!" He gaped, shocked speechless as she gave his ear a hard twist.

"I'll twist more than your ear if you behave like a baboon. Take that shirt off, boy."

"Christ!" He sat for another moment, rubbing his stinging ear. "What's your problem?"

"Your hands aren't the only things you've cut to blazes. Now get the shirt off so I can see what you've done to yourself."

"What the hell do you care? I could bleed to damn death and you wouldn't bat an eye. You've always hated me."

"No. I've always been afraid of you, and that was foolish. You're just a pitiful man who hasn't a clue of his own worth. And I made mistakes I'm sorry for, and I hope I'm woman enough to admit it." Because he wasn't cooperating, she tugged off his tattered T-shirt herself. "I thought you had beaten your mother."

"What? My mother— I never—"

"I know that. Be still. Oh, Jesus, boy, you've done a job here. Oh, poor lad." She crooned now as she dabbed gently at the gashes on his back. "You'd have killed yourself for her, wouldn't you?"

Suddenly tired, unbearably tired, he laid his head on the counter, shut his eyes. "Go away. Leave me alone."

"I won't. Nor will anyone else. You'll have to be the one to do it. Hold on now, this is going to hurt."

He hissed between his teeth as the antiseptic bit. "I just wanna get drunk."

"You will if you must," she said easily. "But a man who would brave an earthquake to get to his woman should have enough nerve to face her sober. This bruising could use liniment. Well, we'll see to that after we've seen to the rest. Take off your pants."

"Oh, for Christ's sake, I'm not going to—Christ!" He yelped when she twisted his other ear. "All right, all right, you want me naked, you got it."

He rose, wrenched the button of his torn jeans, tugged them off. "I'd have gone to the hospital if I'd known what the alternative was going to be."

"That cut on your thigh could use stitches, but we'll do what we can."

He sat bad-temperedly but shoved the tumbler aside. He didn't feel like drinking any longer. "Is she all right?"

A smile ghosted around Ann's mouth, but she kept her head lowered. "She's hurting, in more ways than one. She needs you."

"No, she doesn't. The last thing. You know what I am."

Now she lifted her head, looked him dead in the eye. "Yes, I know what you are. But do you, Michael Fury? Do you know what you are?"

HE WORRIED OVER it like a man worrying over an aching tooth. How could he concentrate on what he needed to do when he kept seeing her the way she had been, white and still on that ledge? Or the way she had looked, eyes filled with hurt and temper, as she'd turned at the door and told him she loved him.

Distractions didn't help. He'd dealt with the mess of the apartment— because Ann had ordered him to get up off his butt and take out the trash. He'd calmed his horses, rehung his tack, then taken the tack down again and packed it.

He wasn't staying anyway.

In the end he'd given up and started across the lawn to Templeton House. It was reasonable, wasn't it? he argued with himself, to want to check on her. She probably should be in the hospital. Her family wouldn't push her. It was obvious to him that when Laura Templeton dug her heels in, no one could push her.

He would just check, then he'd make arrangements to stable his horses elsewhere until he could get the hell out of Dodge.

As he walked through the garden, Kayla and Ali popped up from their perch on the terrace where they'd been playing jacks. His first thought was that he hadn't known kids still played jacks. Then they launched themselves at him.

"You saved Mama from the earthquake." Kayla, all but climbing up into his arms, made his fresh bruises throb.

"Not exactly," he began. "I just—"

"You did." Solemn-eyed, Ali looked up into his face. "Everyone said so." He started to shrug, uncomfortable in the role of hero, but she took his hand and her eyes were clouded with worry. "They said she was going to be all right. Everyone said she was going to be all right. Is she?"

Why ask him? Damn it, how did he get to be the authority? But he crouched down, unable to resist that trembling lip. "Sure she is. She just got some bumps, that's all."

Ali's lips curved a little. "Okay."

"She fell off the cliff," Kayla continued. "And found Seraphina, and she got hurt, but you and Max came to pull her back up. Mrs. Williamson said Max should have a whole bushel of carrots."

He grinned, tousled her hair. "What do I get?"

"She said you already got your reward. What is it?"

"Search me."

"You got hurt too." Soberly, Kayla lifted his bandaged hands one at a time and kissed them. "Do they hurt? Does that make it better?"

Emotion swarmed through him, a stinging hive of bees that left behind a sweet ache. No one, in all his life, had ever kissed his hurts. "Yeah, much." He pressed his face into her hair for a moment. Wishing. Wanting.

"Is it all right if we go down and see Max?" Instinctively Ali stroked Michael's hair to soothe him. "To thank him."

"Yeah, he'd like that. Ah, your mom . . ."

"She's in the parlor. Everyone's supposed to be quiet so she can rest. But you can go in." Ali beamed at him. "She'd want to see you. And Kayla and I are going to get up every morning early before school and clean the stalls until your hands are better. You don't have to worry."

"I—" Coward, he thought. Tell them you won't be here. Tell them you're leaving. Couldn't. Just couldn't. "Thanks."

As they dashed off, he watched them, two pretty young girls racing away through fanciful gardens. He stepped over the scattered jacks, and after three tries managed to lift his hand and open the terrace door.

She wasn't lying on the couch as he'd expected, but standing at the window, her back to the room, looking out toward the cliffs.

She was so . . . small, he thought. Everything about her telegraphed fragility, and yet she was the strongest woman he'd ever known.

She should have seemed delicate just then, highly breakable, with her hair pulled back, the soft, fluid folds of a white robe wrapped around her. But when she turned, and those last gilded beams of the setting sun danced against the window at her back, she seemed simply indestructible.

"I was hoping you'd come." Her voice was calm, as was she. A close brush with death had shown her that she could indeed survive anything. Even Michael Fury. "I wasn't able to thank you coherently before, or to see how badly you were hurt."

"I'm fine. How's the head?"

She smiled. "It feels as though I smashed it on a rock. Would you like a brandy? I'm not allowed, myself. My many medical advisers tell me I can't have any alcohol for twenty-four hours."

"No, I'll pass." The whiskey he'd downed earlier wasn't sitting very well as it was.

"Please, sit down." Leading with manners, she gestured to a chair. "We've had quite a day, haven't we, Michael?"

"I won't forget it anytime soon. Your shoulder—"

"I've had enough fussing. It's sore." She sat, smoothing down her robe as she did. "I'm sore. My head aches, and occasionally I get this quick twist in my stomach when I let myself think about what might have happened. What would have happened if you hadn't found me."

Her brow lifted as she watched him prowl the room. Other than that first long stare when she'd turned to him, he'd barely looked at her. To keep her own hands still, she linked them in her lap.

"Is something else on your mind, Michael, other than my medical report?"

"I just wanted to see—" He stopped, hooked his thumbs in his pockets, and made himself look at her. "Listen, I don't see any point in leaving this business hanging between us."

"What business?"

"You're not in love with me."

Patiently attentive, she angled her head. "I'm not?"

"No, you've just got it all mixed up with sex, and now probably with gratitude, and that's just stupid."

"So now I'm stupid."

"Don't twist things around."

"I'm trying to untwist them." She leaned forward to touch the box, still open on the coffee table. "You haven't seen Seraphina's dowry. Aren't you curious?"

"It's nothing to do with me." But he looked down, saw the glint of gold, of silver, of glossy beads. "Not a hell of a lot, considering."

"You're wrong, it's quite a bit, considering." Her gaze lifted to his again. "Quite a bit. Why did you go back down for it?"

"I told you I would."

"A man of your word," she murmured. "I was fuzzy at the time, but things are clearer now. I remember lying there watching you climb up that rock wall. Clinging like a lizard. Your hands bleeding, slipping when the wall would give way. You could have been killed."

"I guess I should have just left you there."

"You couldn't have done that. You'd have gone down for anyone. That's who you are. And you went back, for this." She stroked the lid of the box. "Because I asked you."

"You're making it bigger than it was."

"You brought me something I've looked for my entire life." Her eyes, swimming with emotion, stayed on his. "I can't make that bigger than it is. How many times did you climb up, climb down, for me, Michael?" When he said nothing, only turned away to pace again, she sighed. "It makes you uncomfortable—gratitude, admiration, love."

"You're not in love with me."

"Don't tell me what I feel."

Because her voice had sharpened, he glanced back warily. If she started throwing things again, he doubted he had the energy to dodge.

"Don't you dare to tell me what I feel. You're entitled not to feel the same way, entitled not to want me to love you, but you're not entitled to tell me what I feel."

"Then you are stupid," he exploded. "You don't even know who I am. I killed for money."

She waited a beat, then rose and walked over to pour herself a glass of mineral water. "You're referring to when you were a mercenary."

"It doesn't matter what title you put on it. I killed, I got paid for it."

"I don't suppose you believed in the cause you were fighting for."

He opened his mouth, shut it. Wasn't she hearing him? "It doesn't matter what I believed or didn't. I killed for profit, I've spent the night in a cell, I've slept with women I didn't know."

Calmly, she sipped. "Are you apologizing, Michael, or bragging?"

"Christ Almighty, don't pull that snotty lady-of-the-house routine on me. I've done things you can't even imagine in this rarefied world you live in."

She drank. "Rarefied, is it?" she murmured. "As compared to the reality you live in. Michael Fury, you're a snob."

"Jesus Christ."

"You are. As you see it, I'm above desperation or needs or sins because I come from money and maintain a certain social status. I'm not supposed to understand a man like you, much less care for him. Is that right?"

"Yeah." He ached everywhere. "That about sums it up."

"Let me tell you what I see, Michael. I see someone who has done what he had to do to survive. And I understand that very well, even living in my pathetic, rarefied world."

"I didn't mean—"

"Someone who didn't give up, no matter what got in the way," she interrupted, staring him down. "I see someone who decided to take a new direction in his life and is making it work. He has ambition, decency, and courage. And I see a man who can still grieve over a child he never had a chance to know."

She was making him into something he wasn't, and she was scaring the life out of him. "I'm not what you're looking for."

"You're what I found. I have to live with that, and when you go, I will."

"I'm doing you a favor," he muttered. "You can't even see it. You'd have figured it out for yourself sooner or later. You've already got the seed in your head."

"Which means?"

"You know it isn't going anywhere with us. It can't, and you knew it."

"Did I? Why don't you explain how you've come to that conclusion?"

There were dozens of examples, but only one stuck out. "You're damn careful not to touch me when anyone's around."

"Is that so?" She set down her glass with a snap. "Stay right there." Incensed, she marched to the door and out, leaving him scowling after her.

Why the hell was he getting into all this? he asked himself. Why was he arguing with her? Why couldn't he just touch her one more time, just hold her one more time. Then he'd go.

Laura strode back in, dragging Thomas in her wake. "You're supposed to be resting," her father scolded. "Oh, hello, Michael. I was about to go down and—"

"Talk later," Laura ordered, then marched straight to Michael.

"Hey," was all he managed before she grabbed him by the hair, dragged his head down, and fixed her lips hotly on his. He lifted his hands, dropped them again, then gave up and crushed her against him. Her body was drum-tight, all but vibrating with fury, but her mouth was soft, sweet, and the kiss weakened his knees.

"There." She pulled away, spun toward a baffled and grinning Thomas. "Thanks, Dad. If you wouldn't mind leaving us alone again?"

"No, fine. Michael, I believe you and I will have a little talk later." Thomas closed the door discreetly behind him.

"Satisfied?" Laura demanded.

Not nearly. She'd just churned up all the urges he'd nearly managed to quell. Saying nothing, he yanked her against him again. "What the hell was that supposed to prove? It doesn't change—"

And then he broke, just broke. Shuddering, he buried his face in her hair, fought to find his breath. "I thought you were dead," he managed. "Oh, God, Laura, I thought you were dead."

"Oh, Michael." Every drop of temper drained out of her as she stroked his back. "It was horrible for you. I'm sorry, so sorry. We're fine now. You saved me."

Gently, she cupped his face and studied those dark, stormy eyes. "You saved my life," she murmured and touched her lips to his.

"No." He jerked back, shocked at how close she'd come to bringing him to his knees. "We're not going that route, we're not mixing this up again."

She stood where she was, watching all those violent emotions flit over his face. And slowly, her aching heart began to swell, and to heal. Her smile bloomed. "Why, you're afraid of me, aren't you? Afraid of us. I see I have been stupid after all, thinking it was only me. You're in love with me, Michael, and it scares you."

"Don't put words in my mouth," he began, then backed up a full step as she came toward him. "Don't."

"What'll happen if I touch you now?" The sense of power, of right, glowed inside her. "You might shatter. Tough guy, holding it all in. I could break you, just by doing this." And she laid her hand on his cheek.

"You're making a mistake." He clamped a hand on her wrist, and his fingers trembled. "You don't know what you're doing. I can't be what you need."

"Why don't you tell me what you think I need, then?"

"You figure I'll polish up and start playing tennis at the club? Go to the gallery openings and buy a tux? It's never going to happen. I'm not going to start drinking brandy and playing billiards or sit in a steam room with a bunch of overweight rich guys and talk about the latest stock reports."

She began to laugh, and the laughter made her head ache and spin so that she had to sit on the arm of the settee until she caught her breath. "That's telling me."

"You think this is a joke? So will all your fancy friends. There goes Laura Templeton with that mongrel she picked up."

She sobered quickly. "I could slap you. I could actually slap you for that." In fact, she had to grip her hands together to stop herself from doing just that. "That's insulting, to me and to those I consider my friends. You think I care about any of that? Do you really think so little of me?"

"I think everything of you," he said and stopped her tirade before it could begin.

"If that's true, then you should respect what it is I do need. With some alterations it's the same thing I've needed my whole life. I need my family and my work. My home. I need to feel that I put in as much as I take out. I need my children to be happy and safe. And I need someone I love, and who loves me, to share it all, to be there for me. I need someone who'll depend on me and whom I can depend on. I want someone who'll listen and understand, who'll touch me when I need to be touched. Who'll make my heart beat a little faster when he looks at me. The way you look at me, Michael. The way you're looking at me right now."

"You're not going to let me walk," he said quietly.

"Yes, yes, I will." She reached into the box, took out the locket. "If you need to go, to prove something, to escape from something, even if that something is what we feel for each other, I can't stop you."

She laid the locket down again, gently. "But I won't stop loving you, or needing you. I'll just live without you. I'll live without the life we could make, without seeing my children light up when you walk into the room, without the other children we could make together."

She narrowed her eyes when she saw the flicker in his eye. "Did you think I wouldn't want more children? That I haven't already dreamed what it would be like to hold a baby we made together?"

"No, I didn't think you'd want more children, with me." She was breaking him, bit by bit. "Laura . . ."

She rose, waited, but he only shook his head. "A family, Michael, that's all I've ever really dreamed of. You changed a great deal inside of me, but never that. You gave me all those firsts, and because I was so dazzled by you, so in love with you, I didn't see that I could give you something back. I'll give you a family, Michael."

He wondered if he could speak, how any man could when faced with the gift of everything he would ever need. Every treasure imagined and sought and despaired of.

"I'm wrong for you. I've got to be wrong for you, and it was never supposed to come to this between us. I took you because I could, because I wanted you more than I'd ever wanted anything."

"You're right for me," she corrected. "You have to be right for me. And what was it never supposed to come to between us, Michael?"

"To plans. To futures." His gaze was drawn to the open box again, and all those tiny, precious treasures. "I've barely started to get my business off the ground, hardly made a dent in getting my life into some kind of decent order. I've got nothing for you."

"Don't you? Don't you have dreams, Michael? And aren't some of them the same as mine?" She wanted to reach for him then, but this time he would have to reach first.

She would let him walk, he realized. If he turned and stepped back out the door, they would both go on.

She was waiting for him. She was willing to take him just as he was. And with her, he realized, he might find there was more in him, more for him, than he'd ever allowed himself to dream.

"I'm going to give you one more chance before I say what I have to say. What I wasn't going to say. What I didn't think you'd want to hear."

How many chances did a man get? he wondered. How many lives? How many offers of everything that mattered? He took a step toward her, stopped.

"Once I say it, the door closes. For both of us. Do you understand that?"

Her lips curved. "Do you?"

"I understood it the minute I saw you again." His eyes went dark, dangerous. "Stay or run, Laura."

She lifted her chin. This time she would say it. "Stay."

"Then you'll have to live with it. And me." He took her hand. Not gently, but possessively, his battered fingers clamping onto hers. "I've never loved another woman. That's a first you gave me."

She closed her eyes. "I feel as though I've waited my whole life to hear you say that."

"I haven't said it yet." He lifted his free hand to her face. "Look at me when I do. I love you, Laura," he said when her eyes opened. "Maybe I always did. I know I always will. I'll never lie to you or leave you to handle things alone. I'll be a father to your children. All of them. I'll love them, all of them. And they'll never have to wonder if I do."

"Michael." Overcome, she turned her lips into his palm, kissing his hurts much as Kayla had. "That's everything."

"No, it's not. So here's the rest." He waited until her eyes cleared and met his. "If you want to take a chance on this, I'll give you whatever I have, whatever I can make and whatever I can be."

The words were just there, he realized. Just there, waiting to be said. Absently he reached over, plucked a tulip from the vase on the table beside them. Held it out to her. "Marry me. Be my family."

Rather than take the flower, she closed her hand over his around the stem. "Yes." She touched her lips to his cheek, settled her head with a sigh on his shoulder. "Yes," she said again, feeling his heart thud against hers as she looked into the simple box filled with dreams.

"I've found you," she murmured, turning her mouth up to Michael's. "We've found each other. Finally."